D1736210

THE BEST OF LUCIUS SHEPARD

THE BEST OF LUCIUS SHEPARD

LUCIUS SHEPARD

Subterranean Press 2008

First Edition

ISBN
978-1-59606-133-0

Subterranean Press
PO Box 190106
Burton, MI 48519

www.subterraneanpress.com

TABLE OF CONTENTS

The Man Who Painted the Dragon Griaule

Other than the Sichi Collection, Cattanay's only surviving works are to be found in the Municipal Gallery at Regensburg, a group of eight oils-on-canvas, most notable among them being Woman With Oranges. *These paintings constitute his portion of a student exhibition hung some weeks after he had left the city of his birth and traveled south to Teocinte, there to present his proposal to the city fathers; it is unlikely he ever learned of the disposition of his work, and even more unlikely that he was aware of the general critical indifference with which it was received. Perhaps the most interesting of the group to modern scholars, the most indicative as to Cattanay's later preoccupations, is the* Self-Portrait, *painted at the age of twenty-eight, a year before his departure.*

The majority of the canvas is a richly varnished black in which the vague shapes of floorboards are presented, barely visible. Two irregular slashes of gold cross the blackness, and within these we can see a section of the artist's thin features and the shoulder panel of his shirt. The perspective given is that we are looking down at the artist, perhaps through a tear in the roof, and that he is looking up at us, squinting into the light, his mouth distorted by a grimace born of intense concentration. On first viewing the painting, I was struck by the atmosphere of tension that radiated from it. It seemed I was spying upon a man imprisoned within a shadow having two golden bars, tormented by the possibilities of light beyond the walls. And though this may be the reaction of the art historian, not the less knowledgeable and therefore more trustworthy response of the gallery-goer, it also seemed that this imprisonment was self-imposed, that he could have easily escaped his confine; but that he had realized a feeling of stricture was an essential fuel to his ambition, and so had chained himself to this arduous and thoroughly unreasonable chore of perception ....

—FROM *MERIC CATTANAY: THE POLITICS OF CONCEPTION*
BY READE HOLLAND, PH.D.

— I —

In 1853, in a country far to the south, in a world separated from this one by the thinnest margin of possibility, a dragon named Griaule dominated the region of the Carbonates Valley, a fertile area centering upon the town of Teocinte and renowned for its production of silver, mahogany, and indigo. There were other dragons in those days, most dwelling on the rocky islands west of Patagonia—tiny, irascible creatures, the largest of them no bigger than a swallow. But Griaule was one of the great Beasts who had ruled an age. Over the centuries he had grown to stand 750 feet high at the midback, and from the tip of his tail to his nose he was six thousand feet long. (It should be noted here that the growth of dragons was due not to caloric intake, but to the absorption of energy derived from the passage of time.) Had it not been for a miscast spell, Griaule would have died millennia before. The wizard entrusted with the task of slaying him—knowing his own life would be forfeited as a result of the magical backwash—had experienced a last-second twinge of fear, and, diminished by this ounce of courage, the spell had flown a mortal inch awry. Though the wizard's whereabouts were unknown, Griaule had remained alive. His heart had stopped, his breath stilled, but his mind continued to seethe, to send forth the gloomy vibrations that enslaved all who stayed for long within range of his influence.

This dominance of Griaule's was an elusive thing. The people of the valley attributed their dour character to years of living under his mental shadow, yet there were other regional populations who maintained a harsh face to the world and had no dragon on which to blame the condition; they also attributed their frequent raids against the neighboring states to Griaule's effect, claiming to be a peaceful folk at heart—but again, was this not human nature? Perhaps the most certifiable proof of Griaule's primacy was the fact that despite a standing offer of a fortune in silver to anyone who could kill him, no one had succeeded. Hundreds of plans had been put forward, and all had failed, either through inanition or impracticality. The archives of Teocinte were filled with schematics for enormous steam-powered swords and other such improbable devices, and the architects of these plans had every one stayed too long in the valley and become part of the disgruntled populace. And so they went on with their lives, coming and going, always returning, bound to the valley, until one spring day in 1853, Meric Cattanay arrived and proposed that the dragon be painted.

He was a lanky young man with a shock of black hair and a pinched look to his cheeks; he affected the loose trousers and shirt of a peasant, and waved his arms to make a point. His eyes grew wide when listening, as if his brain were bursting with illumination, and at times he talked incoherently about "the conceptual statement of death by art." And though the city fathers could not be sure, though they allowed for the possibility that he simply had an unfortunate manner, it seemed he was mocking them. All in all, he was not the sort they were inclined to trust. But, because he had come armed with such a wealth of diagrams and charts, they were forced to give him serious consideration.

"I don't believe Griaule will be able to perceive the menace in a process as subtle as art," Meric told them. "We'll proceed as if we were going to illustrate him, grace his side with a work of true vision, and all the while we'll be poisoning him with the paint."

The city fathers voiced their incredulity, and Meric waited impatiently until they quieted. He did not enjoy dealing with these worthies. Seated at their long table, sour-faced, a huge smudge of soot on the wall above their heads like an ugly thought they were sharing, they reminded him of the Wine Merchants Association in Regensburg, the time they had rejected his group portrait.

"Paint can be deadly stuff," he said after their muttering had died down. "Take Vert Veronese, for example. It's derived from oxide of chrome and barium. Just a whiff would make you keel over. But we have to go about it seriously, create a real piece of art. If we just slap paint on his side, he might see through us."

The first step in the process, he told them, would be to build a tower of scaffolding, complete with hoists and ladders, that would brace against the supraorbital plates above the dragon's eye; this would provide a direct route to a seven-hundred-foot-square loading platform and base station behind the eye. He estimated it would take eight-one-thousand board feet of lumber, and a crew of ninety men should be able to finish construction within five months. Ground crews accompanied by chemists and geologists would search out limestone deposits (useful in priming the scales) and sources of pigments, whether organic or minerals such as azurite and hematite. Other teams would be set to scraping the dragon's side clean of algae, peeled skin, any decayed material, and afterward would laminate the surface with resins.

"It would be easier to bleach him with quicklime," he said. "But that way we lose the discolorations and ridges generated by growth and age, and I think what we'll paint will be defined by those shapes. Anything else would look like a damn tattoo!"

There would be storage vats and mills: edge-runner mills to separate pigments from crude ores, ball mills to powder the pigments, pug mills to mix them with oil. There would be boiling vats and calciners—fifteen-foot-high furnaces used to produce caustic lime for sealant solutions.

"We'll build most of them atop the dragon's head for purposes of access," he said. "On the frontoparietal plate." He checked some figures. "By my reckoning, the plate's about 350 feet wide. Does that sound accurate?"

Most of the city fathers were stunned by the prospect, but one managed a nod, and another asked, "How long will it take for him to die?"

"Hard to say," came the answer. "Who knows how much poison he's capable of absorbing? It might just take a few years. But in the worst instance, within forty or fifty years, enough chemicals will have seeped through the scales to have weakened the skeleton and he'll fall in like an old barn."

"Forty years!" exclaimed someone. "Preposterous!"

"Or fifty." Meric smiled. "That way we'll have time to finish the painting." He turned and walked to the window and stood gazing out at the white stone houses of Teocinte. This was going to be the sticky part, but if he read them right, they would not believe in the plan if it seemed too easy. They needed to feel they were making a sacrifice, that they were nobly bound to a great labor. "If it does take forty or fifty years," he went on, "the project will drain your resources. Timber, animal life, minerals. Everything will be used up by the work. Your lives will be totally changed. But I guarantee you'll be rid of him."

The city fathers broke into an outraged babble.

"Do you really want to kill him?" cried Meric, stalking over to them and planting his fists on the table. "You've been waiting centuries for someone to come along and chop off his head or send him up in a puff of smoke. That's not going to happen! There is no easy solution. But there is a practical one, an elegant one. To use the stuff of the land he dominates to destroy him. It will *not* be easy, but you *will* be rid of him. And that's what you want, isn't it?"

They were silent, exchanging glances, and he saw that they now believed he could do what he proposed and were wondering if the cost was too high.

"I'll need five hundred ounces of silver to hire engineers and artisans," said Meric. "Think it over. I'll take a few days and go see this dragon of yours…inspect the scales and so forth. When I return, you can give me your answer."

The city fathers grumbled and scratched their heads, but at last they agreed to put the question before the body politic. They asked for a week in which to decide and appointed Jarcke, who was the mayoress of Hangtown, to guide Meric to Griaule.

▲▼▲

The valley extended seventy miles from north to south, and was enclosed by jungled hills whose folded sides and spiny backs gave rise to the idea that beasts were sleeping beneath them. The valley floor was cultivated into fields of bananas and cane and melons, and where it was not cultivated, there were stands of thistle palms and berry thickets and the occasional giant fig brooding sentinel over the rest. Jarcke and Meric tethered their horses a half-hour's ride from town and began to ascend a gentle incline that rose into the notch between two hills. Sweaty and short of breath, Meric stopped a third of the way up; but Jarcke kept plodding along, unaware he was no longer following. She was by nature as blunt as her name—a stump beer-keg of a woman with a brown weathered face. Though she appeared to be ten years older then Meric, she was nearly the same age. She wore a gray robe belted at the waist with a leather band that held four throwing knives, and a coil of rope was slung over her shoulder.

"How much farther?" called Meric.

She turned and frowned. "You're standin' on his tail. Rest of him's around back of the hill."

A pinprick of chill bloomed in Meric's abdomen, and he stared down at the grass, expecting it to dissolve and reveal a mass of glittering scales.

"Why don't we take the horses?" he asked.

"Horses don't like it up here." She grunted with amusement. "Neither do most people, for that matter." She trudged off.

Another twenty minutes brought them to the other side of the hill high above the valley floor. The land continued to slope upward, but more gently than before. Gnarled, stunted oaks pushed up from thickets of chokecherry, and insects sizzled in the weeds. They might have been walking on a natural shelf several hundred feet across; but ahead of them, where the ground rose abruptly, a number of thick greenish-black columns broke from the earth. Leathery folds hung between them, and these were encrusted with clumps of earth and brocaded with mold. They had the look of a collapsed palisade and the ghosted feel of ancient ruins.

"Them's the wings," said Jarcke. "Mostly they's covered, but you can catch sight of 'em off the edge, and up near Hangtown there's places where you can walk in under 'em...but I wouldn't advise it."

"I'd like to take a look off the edge," said Meric, unable to tear his eyes away from the wings; though the surfaces of the leaves gleamed in the strong sun, the wings seemed to absorb the light, as if their age and strangeness were proof against reflection.

Jarcke led him to a glade in which tree ferns and oaks crowded together and cast a green gloom, and where the earth sloped sharply downward. She lashed her rope to an oak and tied the other end around Meric's waist. "Give a yank when you want to stop, and another when you want to be hauled up," she said, and began paying out the rope, letting him walk backward against her pull.

Ferns tickled Meric's neck as he pushed through the brush, and the oak leaves pricked his cheeks. Suddenly he emerged into bright sunlight. On looking down, he found his feet were braced against a fold of the dragon's wing, and on looking up, he saw that the wing vanished beneath a mantle of earth and vegetation. He let Jarcke lower him a dozen feet more, yanked, and gazed off northward along the enormous swell of Griaule's side.

The scales were hexagonals thirty feet across and half that distance high; their basic color was a pale greenish gold, but some were whitish, draped with peels of dead skin, and others were overgrown by viridian moss, and the rest were scrolled with patterns of lichen and algae that resembled the characters of a serpentine alphabet. Birds had nested in the cracks, and ferns plumed from the interstices, thousands of them lifting in the breeze. It was a great hanging garden whose scope took Meric's breath away—like looking around the curve of a fossil moon. The sense of all the centuries accreted in the scales made him dizzy, and he found he could not turn his head, but could only stare at the panorama, his soul shriveling with a comprehension of the timelessness and bulk of this creature to which he clung like a fly. He lost perspective on the scene—Griaule's side was bigger than the sky, possessing its own potent gravity, and it seemed completely reasonable that he should be able to walk out along it and suffer no fall. He started to do so, and Jarcke, mistaking the strain on the rope for a signal, hauled him up, dragging him across the wing, through the dirt and ferns, and back into the glade. He lay speechless and gasping at her feet.

"Big 'un, ain't he," she said, and grinned.

After Meric had gotten his legs under him, they set off toward Hangtown; but they had not gone a hundred yards, following a trail that wound through the thickets, before Jarcke whipped out a knife and hurled it at a racoon-sized creature that leaped out in front of them.

"Skizzer," she said, kneeling beside it and pulling the knife from its neck. "Calls 'em that 'cause they hisses when they runs. They eats snakes, but they'll go after children what ain't careful."

Meric dropped down next to her. The skizzer's body was covered with short black fur, but its head was hairless, corpse-pale, the skin wrinkled as if it had been immersed too long in water. Its face was squinty-eyed, flat-nosed, with a disproportionately large jaw that hinged open to expose a nasty set of teeth.

"They's the dragon's critters," said Jarcke. "Used to live in his bunghole." She pressed one of its paws, and claws curved like hooks slid forth. "They'd hang around the lip and drop on other critters what wandered in. And if nothin' wandered in...." She pried out the tongue with her knife—its surface was studded with jagged points like the blade of a rasp. "Then they'd lick Griaule clean for their supper."

Back in Teocinte, the dragon had seemed to Meric a simple thing, a big lizard with a tick of life left inside, the residue of a dim sensibility; but he was beginning to suspect that this tick of life was more complex than any he had encountered.

"My gram used to say," Jarcke went on, "that the old dragons could fling themselves up to the sun in a blink and travel back to their own world, and when they come back, they'd bring the skizzers and all the rest with 'em. They was immortal, she said. Only the young ones came here 'cause later on they grew too big to fly on Earth." She made a sour face. "Don't know as I believe it."

"Then you're a fool," said Meric.

Jarcke glanced up at him, her hand twitching toward her belt.

"How can you live here and *not* believe it!" he said, surprised to hear himself so fervently defending a myth. "God! This...." He broke off, noticing the flicker of a smile on her face.

She clucked her tongue, apparently satisfied by something. "Come on," she said. "I want to be at the eye before sunset."

▲▼▲

The peaks of Griaule's folded wings, completely overgrown by grass and shrubs and dwarfish trees, formed two spiny hills that cast a shadow over Hangtown and the narrow lake around which it sprawled. Jarcke said the lake was a stream flowing off the hill behind the dragon, and that it drained away through the membranes of his wing and down onto his shoulder. It was beautiful beneath the wing, she told him. Ferns and waterfalls. But it was reckoned an evil place. From a distance the town looked picturesque—rustic cabins, smoking chimneys. As they approached, however, the cabins resolved into dilapidated shanties with missing boards and broken windows; suds and garbage and offal floated in the shallows of the lake. Aside from a few men idling on the stoops, who squinted at Meric and nodded glumly at Jarcke, no one was about. The grass-blades stirred in the breeze, spiders scuttled under the shanties, and there was an air of torpor and dissolution.

Jarcke seemed embarrassed by the town. She made no attempt at introductions, stopping only long enough to fetch another coil of rope from one of the shanties, and as they walked between the wings, down through the neck spines—a forest of greenish gold spikes burnished by the lowering sun—she explained how the townsfolk grubbed a livelihood from Griaule. Herbs gathered on his back were valued as medicine and charms, as were the peels of dead skin; the artifacts left by previous Hangtown generations were of some worth to various collectors.

"Then there's scale hunters," she said with disgust. "Henry Sichi from Port Chantay'll pay good money for pieces of scale, and though it's bad luck to do it, some'll have a go at chippin' off the loose 'uns." She walked a few paces in silence. "But there's others who've got better reasons for livin' here."

The frontal spike above Griaule's eyes was whorled at the base like a narwhal's horn and curved back toward the wings. Jarcke attached the ropes to eyebolts drilled into the spike, tied one about her waist, the other about Meric's; she cautioned him to wait, and rappelled off the side. In a moment she called for him to come down. Once again he grew dizzy as he descended; he glimpsed a clawed foot far below, mossy fangs jutting from an impossibly long jaw; and then he began to spin and bash against the scales. Jarcke gathered him in and helped him sit on the lip of the socket.

"Damn!" she said, stamping her foot.

A three-foot-long section of the adjoining scale shifted slowly away. Peering close, Meric saw that while in texture and hue it was indistinguishable from the scale, there was a hairline division between it and the surface. Jarcke, her face twisted in disgust, continued to harry the thing until it moved out of reach.

"Call 'em flakes," she said when he asked what it was. "Some kind of insect. Got a long tube that they pokes down between the scales and sucks the blood. See there?" She pointed off to where a flock of birds was wheeling close to Griaule's side; a chip of pale gold broke loose and went tumbling down to the valley. "Birds pry 'em off, let 'em bust open, and eats the innards." She hunkered down beside him and after a moment asked, "You really think you can do it?"

"What? You mean kill the dragon?"

She nodded.

"Certainly," he said, and then added, lying, "I've spent years devising the method."

"If all the paint's goin' to be atop his head, how're you goin' to get it to where the paintin's done?"

"That's no problem. We'll pipe it to wherever it's needed."

She nodded again. "You're a clever fellow," she said; and when Meric, pleased, made as if to thank her for the compliment, she cut in and said, "Don't mean nothin' by it. Bein' clever ain't an accomplishment. It's just somethin' you come by, like bein' tall." She turned away, ending the conversation.

Meric was weary of being awestruck, but even so he could not help marveling at the eye. By his estimate it was seventy feet long and fifty feet high, and it was shuttered by an opaque membrane that was unusually clear of algae and lichen, glistening, with vague glints of color visible behind it. As the westering sun reddened and sank between two distant hills, the membrane began to quiver and then split open down the center. With the ponderous slowness of a theater curtain opening, the halves slid apart to reveal the glowing humor. Terrified by the idea that Griaule could see him, Meric sprang to his feet, but Jarcke restrained him.

"Stay still and watch," she said.

He had no choice—the eye was mesmerizing. The pupil was slit and featureless black, but the humor...he had never seen such fiery blues and crimsons and golds. What had looked to be vague glints, odd refractions of the sunset, he now realized were photic reactions of some sort. Fairy rings of light developed deep within the eye, expanded into spoked shapes, flooded the humor, and faded—only to be replaced by another and another. He felt the pressure of Griaule's vision, his ancient mind, pouring through him, and as if in response to this pressure, memories bubbled up in his thoughts. Particularly sharp ones. The way a bowlful of brush water had looked after freezing over during a winter's night—a delicate, fractured flower of murky yellow. An archipelago of orange peels that his girl had left strewn across the floor of the studio. Sketching atop Jokenam Hill one sunrise, the snow-capped roofs of Regensburg below pitched at all angles like broken paving stones, and silver shafts of the sun striking down through a leaden overcast. It was as if these things were being drawn forth for his inspection. Then they were washed away by what also seemed a memory, though at the same time it was wholly unfamiliar. Essentially it was a landscape of light, and he was plunging through it, up and up. Prisms and lattices of iridescent fire bloomed around him, and everything was a roaring fall into brightness, and finally he was clear into its white furnace heart, his own heart swelling with the joy of his strength and dominion.

It was dusk before Meric realized the eye had closed. His mouth hung open, his eyes ached from straining to see, and his tongue was glued to his palate. Jarcke sat motionless, buried in shadow.

"Th...." He had to swallow to clear his throat of mucus. "This is the reason you live here, isn't it?"

"Part of the reason," she said. "I can see things comin' way up here. Things to watch out for, things to study on."

She stood and walked to the lip of the socket and spat off the edge; the valley stretched out gray and unreal behind her, the folds of the hills barely visible in the gathering dusk.

"I seen you comin' " she said.

▲▼▲

A week later, after much exploration, much talk, they went down into Teocinte. The town was a shambles—shattered windows, slogans painted on the walls, glass and torn banners and spoiled food littering the streets—as if there had been both a celebration and a battle. Which there had. The city fathers met with Meric in the town hall and informed him that his plan had been approved. They presented him a chest containing five hundred ounces of silver and said that the entire resources of the community were at his disposal. They offered a wagon and a team to transport him and the chest to Regensburg and asked if any of the preliminary work could be begun during his absence.

Meric hefted one of the silver bars. In its cold gleam he saw the object of his desire—two, perhaps three years of freedom, of doing the work he wanted and not having to accept commissions. But all that had been confused. He glanced at Jarcke; she was staring out the window, leaving it to him. He set the bar back in the chest and shut the lid.

"You'll have to send someone else," he said. And then, as the city fathers looked at each other askance, he laughed and laughed at how easily he had discarded all his dreams and expectations.

It had been eleven years since I had been to the valley, twelve since work had begun on the painting, and I was appalled by the changes that had taken place. Many of the hills were scraped brown and treeless, and there was a general dearth of wildlife. Griaule, of course, was most changed. Scaffolding hung from his back; artisans, suspended by webworks of ropes, crawled over his side; and all the scales to be worked had either been painted or primed. The tower rising to his eye was swarmed by laborers, and at night the calciners and vats atop his head belched flame into the sky, making it seem there was a mill town in the heavens. At his feet was a brawling shantytown populated by prostitutes, workers, gamblers, ne'er-do-wells of every sort, and soldiers: the burdensome cost of the project had encouraged the city fathers of Teocinte to form a regular militia, which regularly plundered the adjoining states and had posted occupation forces to some areas. Herds of frightened animals milled in the slaughtering pens, waiting to be rendered into oils and pigments. Wagons filled with ores and vegetable products rattled in the streets. I myself had brought a cargo of madder roots from which a rose tint would be derived.

It was not easy to arrange a meeting with Cattanay. While he did none of the actual painting, he was always busy in his office consulting with engineers and artisans, or involved in some other part of the logistical process. When at last I did meet with him, I found he had changed as drastically as Griaule. His hair had gone gray, deep lines scored his features, and his right shoulder had a peculiar bulge at its midpoint—the product of a fall. He was amused by the fact that I wanted to buy the painting, to collect the scales after Griaule's death, and I do not believe he took me at all seriously. But the woman Jarcke, his constant companion, informed him that I was a responsible businessman, that I had already bought the bones, the teeth, even the dirt beneath Griaule's belly (this I eventually sold as having magical properties).

"Well," said Cattanay, "I suppose someone has to own them."

He led me outside, and we stood looking at the painting.

"You'll keep them together?" he asked.

I said, "Yes."

"If you'll put that in writing," he said, "then they're yours."

Having expected to haggle long and hard over the price, I was flabbergasted; but I was even more flabbergasted by what he said next.

"Do you think it's any good?" he asked.

Cattanay did not consider the painting to be the work of his imagination; he felt he was simply illuminating the shapes that appeared on Griaule's side and was convinced that once the paint was applied, new shapes were produced beneath it, causing him to make constant changes. He saw himself as an artisan more than a creative artist. But to put his question into perspective, people were beginning to flock from all over the world and marvel at the painting. Some claimed they saw intimations of the future in its gleaming surface; others underwent transfiguring experiences; still others—artists themselves—attempted to capture something of the work on canvas, hopeful of establishing reputations merely by being competent copyists of Cattanay's art. The painting was nonrepresentational in character, essentially a wash of pale gold spread across the dragon's side; but buried beneath the laminated surface were a myriad tints of iridescent color that, as the sun passed through the heavens and the light bloomed and faded, solidified into innumerable forms and figures that seemed to flow back and forth. I will not try to categorize these forms, because there was no end to them; they were as varied as the conditions under which they were viewed. But I will say that on the morning I met with Cattanay, I—who was the soul of the practical man, without a visionary bone in my body—felt as though I were being whirled away into the painting, up through geometries of light, latticeworks of rainbow color that built the way the edges of a cloud build, past orbs, spirals, wheels of flame....

—FROM *THIS BUSINESS OF GRIAULE*
BY HENRY SICHI

— 2 —

There had been several women in Meric's life since he arrived in the valley; most had been attracted by his growing fame and his association with the mystery of the dragon, and most had left for the same reasons, feeling daunted and unappreciated. But Lise was different in two respects. First, because she loved Meric truly and well; and second, because she was married—albeit unhappily—to a man named Pardiel, the foreman of the calciner crew. She did not love him as she did Meric, yet she respected him and felt obliged to consider carefully before ending the relationship. Meric had never known such an introspective soul. She was twelve years younger than he, tall and lovely, with sun-streaked hair and brown eyes that went dark and seemed to turn inward whenever she was pensive. She was in the habit of analyzing everything that affected her, drawing back from her emotions and inspecting them as if they were a clutch of strange insects she had discovered crawling on her skirt. Though her penchant for self-examination kept her from him, Meric viewed it as a kind of baffling virtue. He had the classic malady and could find no fault with her. For almost a year they were as happy as could be expected; they talked long hours and walked together on those occasions when Pardiel worked double shifts and was forced to bed down by his furnaces, they spent the nights making love in the cavernous spaces beneath the dragon's wing.

It was still reckoned an evil place. Something far worse than skizzers or flakes was rumored to live there, and the ravages of this creature were blamed for every disappearance, even that of the most malcontented laborer. But Meric did not give credence to the rumors. He half believed Griaule had chosen him to be his executioner and that the dragon would never let him be harmed; and besides, it was the only place where they could be assured of privacy.

A crude stair led under the wing, handholds and steps hacked from the scales—doubtless the work of scale hunters. It was a treacherous passage, six hundred feet above the valley floor; but Lise and Meric were secured by ropes, and over the months, driven by the urgency of passion, they adapted to it. Their favorite spot lay fifty feet in (Lise would go no farther; she was afraid even if he was not), near a waterfall that trickled over the leathery folds, causing them to glisten with a mineral brilliance. It was eerily beautiful, a haunted gallery. Peels of dead skin hung down from the shadows like torn veils of ectoplasm; ferns sprouted from the vanes, which were thicker than cathedral columns; swallows curved through the black air. Sometimes, lying with her hidden by a tuck of the wing, Meric would think the beating of their hearts was what really animated the place, that the instant they left, the water ceased flowing and the swallows vanished. He had an unshakable faith in the transforming power of their affections, and one morning as they dressed, preparing to return to Hangtown, he asked her to leave with him.

"To another part of the valley?" She laughed sadly. "What good would that do? Pardiel would follow us."

"No," he said. "To another country. Anywhere far from here."

"We can't," she said, kicking at the wing. "Not until Griaule dies. Have you forgotten?"

"We haven't tried."

"Others have."

"But we'd be strong enough. I know it!"

"You're a romantic," she said gloomily, and stared out over the slope of Griaule's back at the valley. Sunrise had washed the hills to crimson, and even the tips of the wings were glowing a dull red.

"Of course I'm a romantic!" He stood, angry. "What the hell's wrong with that?"

She sighed with exasperation. "You wouldn't leave your work," she said. "And if we did leave, what work would you do? Would—"

"Why must everything be a problem in advance!" he shouted. "I'll tattoo elephants! I'll paint murals on the chests of giants, I'll illuminate whales! Who else is better qualified?"

She smiled, and his anger evaporated.

"I didn't mean it that way," she said. "I just wondered if you could be satisfied with anything else."

She reached out her hand to be pulled up, and he drew her into an embrace. As he held her, inhaling the scent of vanilla water from her hair, he saw a diminutive figure silhouetted against the backdrop of the valley. It did not seem real—a black homunculus—and even when it began to come forward, growing larger and larger, it looked less a man than a magical keyhole opening in a crimson-set hillside. But Meric knew from the man's rolling walk and the hulking set of his shoulders that it was Pardiel; he was carrying a long-handled hook, one of those used by artisans to maneuver along the scales.

Meric tensed, and Lise looked back to see what had alarmed him. "Oh, my God!" she said, moving out of the embrace.

Pardiel stopped a dozen feet away. He said nothing. His face was in shadow, and the hook swung lazily from his hand. Lise took a step toward him, then stepped back and stood in front of Meric as if to shield him. Seeing this, Pardiel let out an inarticulate yell and charged, slashing with the hook. Meric pushed Lise aside and ducked. He caught a brimstone whiff of the calciners as Pardiel rushed past and went sprawling, tripped by some irregularity in the scale. Deathly afraid, knowing he was no match for the foreman, Meric seized Lise's hand and ran deeper under the wing. He hoped Pardiel would be too frightened to follow, leery of the creature that was rumored to live there; but he was not. He came after them at a measured pace, tapping the hook against his leg.

Higher on Griaule's back, the wing was dimpled downward by hundreds of bulges, and this created a maze of small chambers and tunnels so low that they had to crouch to pass along them. The sound of their breathing and the scrape of their feet were amplified by the enclosed spaces, and Meric could no longer hear Pardiel. He had never been this deep before. He had thought it would be pitch-dark; but the lichen and algae adhering to the wing were luminescent and patterned every surface, even the scales beneath them, with whorls of blue and green fire that shed a sickly radiance. It was as if they were giants crawling through a universe whose starry matter had not yet congealed into galaxies and nebulas. In the wan light, Lise's face—turned back to him now and again—was teary and frantic; and then, as she straightened, passing into still another chamber, she drew in breath with a shriek.

At first Meric thought Pardiel had somehow managed to get ahead of them; but on entering he saw that the cause of her fright was a man propped in a sitting position against the far wall. He looked mummified. Wisps of brittle hair poked up from his scalp, the shapes of his bones were visible through his skin, and his eyes were empty holes. Between his legs was a scatter of dust where his genitals had been. Meric pushed Lise toward the next tunnel, but she resisted and pointed at the man.

"His eyes," she said, horror-struck.

Though the eyes were mostly a negative black, Meric now realized they were shot through by opalescent flickers. He felt compelled to kneel beside the man—it was a sudden, motiveless urge that gripped him, bent him to its will, and released him a second later. As he rested his hand on the scale, he brushed a massive ring that was lying beneath the shrunken fingers. Its stone was black, shot through by flickers identical to those within the eyes, and incised with the letter *S*. He found his gaze was deflected away from both the stone and the eyes, as if they contained charges repellent to the senses. He touched the man's withered arm; the flesh was rock-hard, petrified. But alive. From that brief touch he gained an impression of the man's life, of gazing for centuries at the same patch of unearthly fire, of a mind gone beyond mere madness into a perverse rapture, a meditation upon some foul principle. He snatched back his hand in revulsion.

There was a noise behind them, and Meric jumped up, pushing Lise into the next tunnel. "Go right," he whispered. "We'll circle back toward the stair." But Pardiel was too close to confuse with such tactics, and their flight became a wild chase, scrambling, falling, catching glimpses of Pardiel's smoke-stained face, until finally—as Meric came to a large chamber—he felt the hook bite into his thigh. He went down, clutching at the wound, pulling the hook loose. The next moment Pardiel was atop him; Lise appeared over his shoulder, but he knocked her away and locked his fingers in Meric's hair and smashed his head against the scale. Lise screamed, and white lights fired through Meric's skull. Again his head was smashed down. And again. Dimly, he saw Lise struggling with Pardiel, saw her shoved away, saw the hook raised high and the foreman's mouth distorted by a grimace. Then the grimace vanished. His jaw dropped open, and he reached behind him as if to scratch his shoulder blade. A line of dark blood eeled from his mouth and he collapsed, smothering Meric beneath his chest. Meric heard voices. He tried to dislodge the body, and the effects drained the last of his strength. He whirled down through a blackness that seemed as negative and inexhaustible as the petrified man's eyes.

▲▼▲

Someone had propped his head on their lap and was bathing his brow with a damp cloth. He assumed it was Lise, but when he asked what had happened, it was Jarcke who answered, saying, "Had to kill him." His head throbbed, his leg throbbed even worse, and his eyes would not focus. The peels of dead skin hanging overhead appeared to be writhing. He realized they were out near the edge of the wing.

"Where's Lise?"

"Don't worry," said Jarcke. "You'll see her again." She made it sound like an indictment.

"Where is she?"

"Sent her back to Hangtown. Won't do you two bein' seen hand in hand the same day Pardiel's missin'."

"She wouldn't have left...." He blinked, trying to see her face; the lines around her mouth were etched deep and reminded him of the patterns of lichen on the dragon's scale. "What did you do?"

"Convinced her it was best," said Jarcke. "Don't you know she's just foolin' with you?"

"I've got to talk to her." He was full of remorse, and it was unthinkable that Lise should be bearing her grief alone; but when he struggled to rise, pain lanced through his leg.

"You wouldn't get ten feet," she said. "Soon as your head's clear, I'll help you with the stairs."

He closed his eyes, resolving to find Lise the instant he got back to Hangtown—together they would decide what to do. The scale beneath him was cool, and that coolness was transmitted to his skin, his flesh, as if he were merging with it, becoming one of its ridges.

"What was the wizard's name?" he asked after a while, recalling the petrified man, the ring and its incised letter. "The one who tried to kill Griaule...."

"Don't know as I ever heard it," said Jarcke. "But I reckon it's him back there."

"You saw him?"

"I was chasin' a scale hunter once what stole some rope, and I found him instead. Pretty miserable sort, whoever he is."

Her fingers trailed over his shoulder—a gentle, treasuring touch. He did not understand what it signaled, being too concerned with Lise, with the terrifying potentials of all that had happened; but years later, after things had passed beyond remedy, he cursed himself for not having understood.

At length Jarcke helped him to his feet, and they climbed up to Hangtown, to bitter realizations and regrets, leaving Pardiel to the birds or the weather or worse.

> *It seems it is considered irreligious for a woman in love to hesitate or examine the situation, to do anything other than blindly follow the impulse of her emotions. I felt the brunt of such an attitude—people judged it my fault for not having acted quickly and decisively one way or another. Perhaps I was overcautious. I do not claim to be free of blame, only innocent of sacrilege. I believe I might have eventually left Pardiel—there was not enough in the relationship to sustain happiness for either of us. But I had good reason for cautious*

examination. My husband was not an evil man, and there were matters of loyalty between us.

I could not face Meric after Pardiel's death, and I moved to another part of the valley. He tried to see me on many occasions, but I always refused. Though I was greatly tempted, my guilt was greater. Four years later, after Jarcke died—crushed by a runaway wagon—one of her associates wrote and told me Jarcke had been in love with Meric, that it had been she who had informed Pardiel of the affair, and that she may well have staged the murder. The letter acted somewhat to expiate my guilt, and I weighed the possibility of seeing Meric again. But too much time had passed, and we had both assumed other lives. I decided against it. Six years later, when Griaule's influence had weakened sufficiently to allow emigration, I moved to Port Chantay. I did not hear from Meric for almost twenty years after that, and then one day I received a letter, which I will reproduce in part:

"...My old friend from Regensburg, Louis Dardano, has been living here for the past few years, engaged in writing my biography. The narrative has a breezy feel, like a tale being told in a tavern, which—if you recall my telling you how this all began—is quite appropriate. But on reading it, I am amazed my life has had such a simple shape. One task, one passion. God, Lise! Seventy years old, and I still dream of you. And I still think of what happened that morning under the wing. Strange, that it has taken me all this time to realize it was not Jarcke, not you or I who was culpable, but Griaule. How obvious it seems now. I was leaving, and he needed me to complete the expression on his side, his dream of flying, of escape, to grant him the death of his desire. I am certain you will think I have leaped to this assumption, but I remind you that it has been a leap of forty years' duration. I know Griaule, know his monstrous subtlety. I can see it at work in every action that has taken place in the valley since my arrival. I was a fool not to understand that his powers were at the heart of our sad conclusion.

"The army now runs everything here, as no doubt you are aware. It is rumored they are planning a winter campaign against Regensburg. Can you believe it! Their

fathers were ignorant, but this generation is brutally stupid. Otherwise, the work goes well and things are as usual with me. My shoulder aches, children stare at me on the street, and it is whispered I am mad...."

—FROM *UNDER GRIAULE'S WING*
BY LISE CLAVERIE

– 3 –

Acne-scarred, lean, arrogant, Major Hauk was a very young major with a limp. When Meric had entered, the major had been practicing his signature—it was a thing of elegant loops and flourishes, obviously intended to have a place in posterity.

As he strode back and forth during their conversation, he paused frequently to admire himself in the window glass, settling the hang of his red jacket or running his fingers along the crease of his white trousers. It was the new style of uniform, the first Meric had seen at close range, and he noted with amusement the dragons embossed on the epaulets. He wondered if Griaule was capable of such an irony, if his influence was sufficiently discreet to have planted the idea for this comic-opera apparel in the brain of some general's wife.

"...not a question of manpower," the major was saying, "but of...." He broke off, and after a moment cleared his throat.

Meric, who had been studying the blotches on the backs of his hands, glanced up; the cane that had been resting against his knee slipped and clattered to the floor.

"A question of materiel," said the major firmly. "The price of antimony, for example...."

"Hardly use it anymore," said Meric. "I'm almost done with the mineral reds."

A look of impatience crossed the major's face. "Very well," he said; he stooped to his desk and shuffled through some papers. "Ah! Here's a bill for a shipment of cuttlefish from which you derive...." He shuffled more papers.

"Syrian brown," said Meric gruffly. "I'm done with that, too. Golds and violets are all I need anymore. A little blue and rose." He wished the man would stop badgering him; he wanted to be at the eye befeore sunset.

As the major continued his accounting, Meric's gaze wandered out the window. The shantytown surrounding Griaule had swelled into a city and now sprawled across the hills. Most of the buildings were permanent, wood and stone, and the cant of the roofs, the smoke from the factories around the perimeter, put him in mind of Regensburg. All the natural beauty of the land had been drained into the painting. Blackish gray rain clouds were muscling up from the east, but the afternoon sun shone clear and shed a heavy gold radiance on Griaule's side. It looked as if the sunlight were an extension of the gleaming resins, as if the thickness of the paint were becoming infinite. He let the major's voice recede to a buzz and followed the scatter and dazzle of the images; and then, with a start, he realized the major was sounding him out about stopping the work.

The idea panicked him at first. He tried to interrupt, to raise objections; but the major talked through him, and as Meric thought it over, he grew less and less opposed. The painting would never be finished, and he was tired. Perhaps it was time to have done with it, to accept a university post somewhere and enjoy life for a while.

"We've been thinking about a temporary stoppage," said Major Hauk. "Then if the winter campaign goes well...." He smiled. "If we're not visited by plague and pestilence, we'll assume things are in hand. Of course we'd like your opinion."

Meric felt a surge of anger toward this smug little monster. "In my opinion, you people are idiots," he said. "You wear Griaule's image on your shoulders, weave him on your flags, and yet you don't have the least comprehension of what that means. You think it's just a useful symbol...."

"Excuse me," said the major stiffly.

"The hell I will!" Meric groped for his cane and heaved up to his feet. "You see yourselves as conquerors. Shapers of destiny. But all your rapes and slaughters are Griaule's expressions. His will. You're every bit as much his parasites as the skizzers."

The major sat, picked up a pen, and began to write.

"It astounds me," Meric went on, "that you can live next to a miracle, a source of mystery, and treat him as if he were an oddly shaped rock."

The major kept writing.

"What are you doing?" asked Meric.

"My recommendation," said the major without looking up.

"Which is?"

"That we initiate stoppage at once."

They exchanged hostile stares, and Meric turned to leave; but as he took hold of the doorknob, the major spoke again.

"We owe you so much," he said; he wore an expression of mingled pity and respect that further irritated Meric.

"How many men have you killed, Major?" he asked, opening the door.

"I'm not sure. I was in the artillery. We were never able to be sure."

"Well, I'm sure of my tally," said Meric. "It's taken me forty years to amass it. Fifteen hundred and ninety-three men and women. Poisoned, scalded, broken by falls, savaged by animals. Murdered. Why don't we—you and I—just call it even."

▲▼▲

Though it was a sultry afternoon, he felt cold as he walked toward the tower—an internal cold that left him light-headed and weak. He tried to think what he would do. The idea of a university post seemed less appealing away from the major's office; he would soon grow weary of worshipful students and in-depth dissections of his work by jealous academics. A man hailed him as he turned into the market. Meric waved but did not stop, and heard another man say, "That's *Cattanay*?" (That ragged old ruin?)

The colors of the market were too bright, the smells of charcoal cookery too cloying, the crowds too thick, and he made for the side streets, hobbling past one-room stucco houses and tiny stores where they sold cooking oil by the ounce and cut cigars in half if you could not afford a whole one. Garbage, tornadoes of dust and flies, drunks with bloody mouths. Somebody had tied wires around a pariah dog—a bitch with slack teats; the wires had sliced into her flesh, and she lay panting in an alley mouth, gaunt ribs flecked with pink lather, gazing into nowhere. She, thought Meric, and not Griaule, should be the symbol of their flag.

As he rode the hoist up the side of the tower, he fell into his old habit of jotting down notes for the next day. What's that cord of wood doing on level five? Slow leak of chrome yellow from pipes on level twelve. Only when he saw a man dismantling some scaffolding did he recall Major Hauk's recommendation and understand that the order must already have been given. The loss of his work struck home to him then, and he leaned against the railing, his chest constricted and his eyes brimming. He straightened, ashamed of himself. The sun hung in a haze of iron-colored light low above the western hills, looking red and bloated and vile as a vulture's ruff. That polluted sky was his creation as much as was the painting, and it would be good to leave it behind. Once away from the valley, from all the influences of the place, he would be able to consider the future.

A young girl was sitting on the twentieth level just beneath the eye. Years before, the ritual of viewing the eye had grown to cultish proportions; there had been group chanting and praying and discussions of the experience. But these were more practical times, and no doubt the young men and women who had congregated here were now manning administrative desks somewhere in the burgeoning empire. They were the ones about whom Dardano should write; they, and all the eccentric characters who had played roles in this slow pageant. The gypsy woman who had danced every night by the eye, hoping to charm Griaule into killing her faithless lover—she had gone away satisfied. The man who had tried to extract one of the fangs—nobody knew what had become of him. The scale hunters, the artisans. A history of Hangtown would be a volume in itself.

The walk had left Meric weak and breathless; he sat down clumsily beside the girl, who smiled. He could not remember her name, but she came often to the eye. Small and dark, with an inner reserve that reminded him of Lise. He laughed inwardly—most women reminded him of Lise in some way.

"Are you all right?" she asked, her brow wrinkled with concern.

"Oh, yes," he said; he felt a need for conversation to take his mind off things, but he could think of nothing more to say. She was so young! All freshness and gleam and nerves.

"This will be my last time," she said. "At least for a while. I'll miss it." And then, before he could ask why, she added, "I'm getting married tomorrow, and we're moving away."

He offered congratulations and asked her who was the lucky fellow.

"Just a boy." She tossed her hair, as if to dismiss the boy's importance; she gazed up at the shuttered membrane. "What's it like for you when the eye opens?" she asked.

"Like everyone else," he said. "I remember...memories of my life. Other lives, too." He did not tell her about Griaule's memory of flight; he had never told anyone except Lise about that.

"All those bits of souls trapped in there," she said, gesturing at the eye. "What do they mean to him? Why does he show them to us?"

"I imagine he has his purposes, but I can't explain them."

"Once I remembered being with you," said the girl, peeking at him shyly through a dark curl. "We were under the wing."

He glanced at her sharply. "Tell me."

"We were...together," she said, blushing. "Intimate, you know. I was very afraid of the place, of the sounds and shadows. But I loved you so much, it didn't matter. We made love all night, and I was surprised because I thought that kind of passion was just in stories, something people had invented to make up for how ordinary it really was. And in the morning even that dreadful place had become beautiful, with the wing tips glowing red and the waterfall echoing...." She lowered her eyes. "Ever since I had that memory, I've been a little in love with you."

"Lise," he said, feeling helpless before her.

"Was that her name?"

He nodded and put a hand to his brow, trying to pinch back the emotions that flooded him.

"I'm sorry." Her lips grazed his cheek, and just that slight touch seemed to weaken him further. "I wanted to tell you how she felt in case she hadn't told you herself. She was very troubled by something, and I wasn't sure she had."

She shifted away from him, made uncomfortable by the intensity of his reaction, and they sat without speaking. Meric became lost in watching how the sun glazed the scales to reddish gold, how the light was channeled along the ridges in molten streams that paled as the day wound down. He was startled when the girl jumped to her feet and backed toward the hoist.

"He's dead," she said wonderingly.

Meric looked at her, uncomprehending.

"See?" She pointed at the sun, which showed a crimson silver above the hill. "He's dead," she repeated, and the expression on her face flowed between fear and exultation.

The idea of Griaule's death was too large for Meric's mind to encompass, and he turned to the eye to find a counterproof—no glints of color flickered beneath the membrane. He heard the hoist creak as the girl headed down, but he continued to wait. Perhaps only the dragon's vision had failed. No. It was likely not a coincidence that work had been officially terminated today. Stunned, he sat staring at the lifeless membrane until the sun sank below the hills; then he stood and went over to the hoist. Before he could throw the switch, the cables thrummed—somebody heading up. Of course. The girl would have spread the news, and all the Major Hauks and their underlings would be hurrying to test Griaule's reflexes. He did not want to be there when they arrived, to watch them pose with their trophy like successful fishermen.

It was hard work climbing up to the frontoparietal plate. The ladder swayed, the wind buffeted him, and by the time he clambered onto the plate he was giddy, his chest full of twinges. He hobbled forward and leaned against the rust-caked side of a boiling vat. Shadowy in the twilight, the great furnaces and vats towered around him, and it seemed this system of fiery devices reeking of cooked flesh and minerals was the actual machinery of Griaule's thought materialized above his skull. Energyless, abandoned. They had been replaced by more efficient equipment down below, and it had been—what was it?—almost five years since they were last used. Cobwebs veiled a pyramid of firewood; the stairs leading to the rims of the vats were crumbling. The plate itself was scarred and coated with sludge.

"Cattanay!"

Someone shouted from below, and the top of the ladder trembled. God, they were coming after him! Bubbling over with congratulations and plans for testimonial dinners, memorial plaques, specially struck medals. They would have him draped in bunting and bronzed and covered with pigeon shit before they were done. All these years he had been among them, both their slave and their master, yet he had never felt at home. Leaning heavily on his cane, he made his way past the frontal spike—blackened by years of oily smoke—and down between the wings to Hangtown. It was a ghost town, now.

Weeds overgrowing the collapsed shanties; the lake a stinking pit, drained after some children had drowned in the summer of '91. Where Jarcke's home had stood was a huge pile of animal bones, taking a pale shine from the half-light. Wind keened through the tattered shrubs.

"Meric!" "Cattanay."

The voices were closer.

Well, there was one place where they would not follow.

The leaves of the thickets were speckled with mold and brittle, flaking away as he brushed them. He hesitated at the top of the scale hunters' stair. He had no rope. Though he had done the climb unaided many times, it had been quite a few years. The gusts of wind, the shouts, the sweep of the valley and the lights scattered across it like diamonds on gray velvet—it all seemed a single inconstant medium. He heard the brush crunch behind him, more voices. To hell with it! Gritting his teeth against a twinge of pain in his shoulder, hooking his cane over his belt, he inched onto the stair and locked his fingers in the handholds. The wind whipped his clothes and threatened to pry him loose and send him pinwheeling off. Once he slipped; once he froze, unable to move backward or forward. But at last he reached the bottom and edged upslope until he found a spot flat enough to stand.

The mystery of the place suddenly bore in upon him, and he was afraid. He half turned to the stair, thinking he would go back to Hangtown and accept the hurly-burly. But a moment later he realized how foolish a thought that was. Waves of weakness poured through him, his heart hammered, and white dazzles flared in his vision. His chest felt heavy as iron. Rattled, he went a few steps forward, the cane pocking the silence. It was too dark to see more than outlines, but up ahead was the fold of wing where he and Lise had sheltered. He walked toward it, intent on revisiting it; then he remembered the girl beneath the eye and understood that he had already said that goodbye. And it was goodbye—that he understood vividly. He kept walking. Blackness looked to be welling from the wing joint, from the entrances to the maze of luminous tunnels where they had stumbled onto the petrified man. Had it really been the old wizard, doomed by magical justice to molder and live on and on? It made sense. At least it accorded with what happened to wizards who slew their dragons.

"Griaule?" he whispered to the darkness, and cocked his head, half-expecting an answer. The sound of his voice pointed up the immensity of the great gallery under the wing, the emptiness, and he recalled how vital a habitat it had once been. Flakes shifting over the surface, skizzers, peculiar insects fuming in the thickets, the glum populace of Hangtown, waterfalls. He had never been able to picture Griaule fully alive—that kind of vitality was beyond the powers of the imagination. Yet he wondered if by some miracle the dragon were alive now, flying up through his golden night to the sun's core. Or had that merely been a dream, a bit of tissue glittering deep in the cold tons of his brain? He laughed. Ask the stars for their first names, and you'd be more likely to receive a reply.

He decided not to walk any farther—it was really no decision. Pain was spreading through his shoulder, so intense he imagined it must be glowing inside. Carefully, carefully, he lowered himself and lay propped on an elbow, hanging on to the cane. Good, magical wood. Cut from a hawthorn atop Griaule's haunch. A man had once offered him a small fortune for it. Who would claim it now? Probably old Henry Sichi would snatch it for his museum, stick it in a glass case next to his boots. What a joke! He decided to lie flat on his stomach, resting his chin on an arm—the stony coolness beneath acted to muffle the pain. Amusing, how the range of one's decision dwindled. You decided to paint a dragon, to send hundreds of men searching for malachite and cochineal beetles, to love a woman, to heighten an undertone here and there, and finally to position your body a certain way. He seemed to have reached the end of the process. What next? He tried to regulate his breathing, to ease the pressure on his chest. Then, as something rustled out near the wing joint, he turned on his side. He thought he detected movement, a gleaming blackness flowing toward him...or else it was only the haphazard firing of his nerves playing tricks with his vision. More surprised than afraid, wanting to see, he peered into the darkness and felt his heart beating erratically against the dragon's scale.

> *It's foolish to draw simple conclusions from complex events, but I suppose there must be both moral and truth to this life, these events. I'll leave that to the gadflies. The historians, the social scientists, the expert apologists for reality. All I know is that he had a fight with his girlfriend over money and walked out. He sent her a letter saying he had gone south and would be back in a few months with more money than she could ever spend. I had no idea what he'd done. The whole thing about Griaule had just been a bunch of us sitting around the Red Bear, drinking up my pay—I'd sold an article—and somebody said, "Wouldn't it be great if Dardano didn't have to write articles, if we didn't have to paint pictures that color-coordinated with people's furniture or slave at getting the gooey smiles of little nieces and nephews just right?" All sorts of improbable moneymaking schemes were put forward. Robberies, kidnappings. Then the idea of swindling the city fathers of Teocinte came up, and the entire plan was fleshed out in minutes. Scribbled on napkins, scrawled on sketchpads. A group effort. I keep trying to remember if anyone got a glassy look in their eye, if I felt a cold tendril of Griaule's thought stirring my brains. But I can't. It was a half-hour's sensation, nothing more. A drunken whimsy, an art-school metaphor. Shortly thereafter, we ran out of money and staggered into the streets. It was snowing—big wet flakes that melted down our collars. God, we were drunk! Laughing, balancing on the icy railing of the University Bridge. Making faces at the bundled-up burghers and their fat ladies who huffed and puffed past, spouting steam and never giving us a glance, and none of us—not even the burghers—knowing that we were living our happy ending in advance....*
>
> —FROM *THE MAN WHO PAINTED THE DRAGON GRIAULE*
> BY LOUIS DARDANO

Salvador

Three weeks before they wasted Tecolutla, Dantzler had his baptism of fire. The platoon was crossing a meadow at the foot of an emerald-green volcano, and being a dreamy sort, he was idling along, swatting tall grasses with his rifle barrel and thinking how it might have been a first-grader with crayons who had devised this elementary landscape of a perfect cone rising into a cloudless sky, when cap-pistol noises sounded on the slope. Someone screamed for the medic, and Dantzler dove into the grass, fumbling for his ampules. He slipped one from the dispenser and popped it under his nose, inhaling frantically; then, to be on the safe side, he popped another—"A double helpin' of martial arts," as DT would say—and lay with his head down until the drugs had worked their magic. There was dirt in his mouth, and he was very afraid.

Gradually his arms and legs lost their heaviness, and his heart rate slowed. His vision sharpened to the point that he could see not only the pinpricks of fire blooming on the slope, but also the figures behind them, half-obscured by brush. A bubble of grim anger welled up in his brain, hardened to a fierce resolve, and he started moving toward the volcano. By the time he reached the base of the cone, he was all rage and reflexes. He spent the next forty minutes spinning acrobatically through the thickets, spraying shadows with bursts of his M-18; yet part of his mind remained distant from the action, marveling at his efficiency, at the comic-strip enthusiasm he felt for the task of killing. He shouted at the men he shot, and he shot them many more times than was necessary, like a child playing soldier.

"Playin' my ass!" DT would say. "You just actin' natural."

DT was a firm believer in the ampules; though the official line was that they contained tailored RNA compounds and pseudoendorphins modified to an inhalant form, he held the opinion that they opened a man up to his inner nature. He was big, black, with heavily muscled arms and crudely stamped features, and he had come to the Special Forces direct from prison, where he had done a stretch for attempted murder; the palms of his hands were covered by jail tattoos—a pentagram and a horned monster. The words DIE HIGH were painted on his helmet. This was his second tour in Salvador, and Moody—who was Dantzler's buddy—said the drugs had addled DT's brains, that he was crazy and gone to hell.

"He collects trophies," Moody had said. "And not just ears like they done in 'Nam."

When Dantzler had finally gotten a glimpse of the trophies, he had been appalled. They were kept in a tin box in DT's pack and were nearly unrecognizable; they looked like withered brown orchids. But despite his revulsion, despite the fact that he was afraid of DT, he admired the man's capacity for survival and had taken to heart his advice to rely on the drugs.

On the way back down the slope they discovered a live casualty, an Indian kid about Dantzler's age, nineteen or twenty. Black hair, adobe skin, and heavy-lidded brown eyes. Dantzler, whose father was an anthropologist and had done fieldwork in Salvador, figured him for a Santa Ana tribesman; before leaving the States, Dantzler had pored over his father's notes, hoping this would give him an edge, and had learned to identify the various regional types. The kid had a minor leg wound and was wearing fatigue pants and a faded COKE ADDS LIFE T-shirt. This T-shirt irritated DT no end.

"What the hell you know 'bout Coke?" he asked the kid as they headed for the chopper that was to carry them deeper into Morazán Province. "You think it's funny or somethin'?" He whacked the kid in the back with his rifle butt, and when they reached the chopper, he slung him inside and had him sit by the door. He sat beside him, tapped out a joint from a pack of Kools, and asked, "Where's Infante?"

"Dead," said the medic.

"Shit!" DT licked the joint so it would burn evenly. "Goddamn beaner ain't no use 'cept somebody else know Spanish."

"I know a little," Dantzler volunteered.

Staring at Dantzler, DT's eyes went empty and unfocused. "Naw," he said. "You don't know no Spanish."

Dantzler ducked his head to avoid DT's stare and said nothing; he thought he understood what DT meant, but he ducked away from the understanding as well. The chopper bore them aloft, and DT lit the joint. He let the smoke out his nostrils and passed the joint to the kid, who accepted gratefully.

"Qué sabor!" he said, exhaling a billow; he smiled and nodded, wanting to be friends.

Dantzler turned his gaze to the open door. They were flying low between the hills, and looking as the deep bays of shadow in their folds acted to drain away the residue of the drugs, leaving him weary and frazzled. Sunlight poured in, dazzling the oil-smeared floor.

"Hey, Dantzler!" DT had to shout over the noise of the rotors. "Ask him whass his name!"

The kid's eyelids were drooping from the joint, but on hearing Spanish he perked up; he shook his head, though, refusing its answer. Dantzler smiled and told him not to be afraid.

"Ricardo Quu," said the kid.

"Kool!" said DT with false heartiness. "Thass my brand!"

He offered his pack to the kid.

"Gracias, no." The kid waved the joint and grinned.

"Dude's named for a goddamn cigarette," said DT disparagingly, as if this were the height of insanity.

Dantzler asked the kid if there were more soldiers nearby, and once again received no reply; but, apparently sensing in Dantzler a kindred soul, the kid leaned forward and spoke rapidly, saying that his village was Santander Jiménez, that his father was—he hesitated—a man of power. He asked where they were taking him. Dantzler returned a stony glare. He found it easy to reject the kid, and he realized later this was because he had already given up on him.

Latching his hands behind his head, DT began to sing—a wordless melody. His voice was discordant, barely audible above the rotors; but the tune had a familiar ring and Dantzler soon placed it. The theme from *Star Trek*. It brought back memories of watching TV with his sister, laughing at the low-budget aliens and Scotty's Actors' Equity accent. He gazed out the door again. The sun was behind the hills, and the hillsides were unfeatured blurs of dark green smoke. Oh, God, he wanted to be home, to be anywhere but Salvador! A couple of the guys joined in the singing at DT's urging, and as the volume swelled, Dantzler's emotion peaked. He was on the verge of tears, remembering tastes and sights, the way his girl Jeanine had smelled, so clean and fresh, not reeking of sweat and perfume like the whores around Ilopango—finding all this substance in the banal touchstone of his culture and the illusions of the hillsides rushing past. Then Moody tensed beside him, and he glanced up to learn the reason why.

In the gloom of the chopper's belly, DT was as unfeatured as the hills—a black presence ruling them, more the leader of a coven than a platoon. The other two guys were singing their lungs out, and even the kid was getting into the spirit of things. *"Música!"* he said at one point, smiling at everybody, trying to fan the flame of good feeling. He swayed to the rhythm and essayed a "la-la" now and again. But no one else was responding.

The singing stopped, and Dantzler saw that the whole platoon was staring at the kid, their expressions slack and dispirited.

"Space!" shouted DT, giving the kid a little shove. "The final frontier!"

The smile had not yet left the kid's face when he toppled out the door. DT peered after him; a few seconds later he smacked his hand against the floor and sat back, grinning. Dantzler felt like screaming, the stupid horror of the joke was so at odds with the languor of his homesickness. He looked to the others for reaction. They were sitting with their heads down, fiddling with trigger guards and pack straps, studying their bootlaces, and seeing this, he quickly imitated them.

▲▼▲

Morazán Province was spook country. Santa Ana spooks. Flights of birds had been reported to attack patrols; animals appeared at the perimeters of campsites and vanished when you shot at them; dreams afflicted everyone who ventured there. Dantzler could not testify to the birds and animals, but he did have a recurring dream. In it the kid DT had killed was pinwheeling down through a golden fog, his T-shirt visible against the roiling backdrop, and sometimes a voice would boom out of the fog, saying, "You are killing my son." No, no, Dantzler would reply, it wasn't me, and besides, he's already dead. Then he would wake covered with sweat, groping for his rifle, his heart racing.

But the dream was not an important terror, and he assigned it no significance. The land was far more terrifying. Pine-forested ridges that stood out against the sky like fringes of electrified hair; little trails winding off into thickets and petering out, as if what they led to had been magicked away; gray rock faces along which they were forced to walk, hopelessly exposed to ambush. There were innumerable booby traps set by the guerrillas, and they lost several men to rockfalls. It was the emptiest place of Dantzler's experience. No people, no animals, just a few hawks circling the solitudes between the ridges. Once in a while they found tunnels, and these they blew with the new gas grenades; the gas ignited the rich concentrations of hydrocarbons and sent flame sweeping through the entire system. DT would praise whoever had discovered the tunnel and would estimate in a loud voice how many beaners they had "refried." But Dantzler knew they were traversing pure emptiness and burning empty holes. Days, under debilitating heat, they humped the mountains, traveling seven, eight, even ten klicks up trails so steep that frequently the feet of the guy ahead of you would be on a level with your face; nights, it was cold, the darkness absolute, the silence so profound that Dantzler imagined he could hear the great humming vibration of the earth. They might have been anywhere or nowhere. Their fear was nourished by the isolation, and the only remedy was "martial arts."

Dantzler took to popping the pills without the excuse of combat. Moody cautioned him against abusing the drugs, citing rumors of bad side effects and DT's madness; but even he was using them more and more often. During basic training, Dantzler's D.I. had told the boots that the drugs were available only to the Special Forces, that their use was optional; but there had been too many instances of lackluster battlefield performance in the last war, and this was to prevent a reoccurrence.

"The chickenshit infantry should take 'em," the D.I. had said. "You bastards are brave already. You're born killers, right?"

"Right, sir!" they had shouted.

"What are you?"

"Born killers, sir!"

But Dantzler was not a born killer; he was not even clear as to how he had been drafted, less clear as to how he had been manipulated into the Special Forces, and he had learned that nothing was optional in Salvador, with the possible exception of life itself.

The platoon's mission was reconnaissance and mop-up. Along with other Special Forces platoons, they were to secure Morazán prior to the invasion of Nicaragua; specifically, they were to proceed to the village of Tecolutla, where a Sandinista patrol had recently been spotted, and following that they were to join up with the First Infantry and take part in the offensive against Leon, a provincial capital just across the Nicaraguan border. As Dantzler and Moody walked together, they frequently talked about the offensive, how it would be good to get down into flat country; occasionally they talked about the possibility of reporting DT, and once, after he had led them on a forced night march, they toyed with the idea of killing him. But most often they discussed the ways of the Indians and the land, since this was what had caused them to become buddies.

Moody was slightly built, freckled, and red-haired; his eyes had the "thousand-yard stare" that came from too much war. Dantzler had seen winos with such vacant, lusterless stares. Moody's father had been in 'Nam, and Moody said it had been worse than Salvador because there had been no real commitment to win; but he thought Nicaragua and Guatemala might be the worst of all, especially if the Cubans sent in troops as they had threatened. He was adept at locating tunnels and detecting booby traps, and it was for this reason Dantzler had cultivated his friendship. Essentially a loner, Moody had resisted all advances until learning of Dantzler's father; thereafter he had buddied up, eager to hear about the field notes, believing they might give him an edge.

"They think the land has animal traits," said Dantzler one day as they climbed along a ridgetop. "Just like some kinds of fish look like plants or sea bottom, parts of the land look like plain ground, jungle... whatever. But when you enter them, you find you've entered the spirit world, the world of *Sukias*."

"What's *Sukias*?" asked Moody.

"Magicians." A twig snapped behind Dantzler, and he spun around, twitching off the safety of his rifle. It was only Hodge—a lanky kid with the beginnings of a beer gut. He stared hollow-eyed at Dantzler and popped an ampule.

Moody made a noise of disbelief. "If they got magicians, why ain't they winnin'? Why ain't they zappin' us off the cliffs?"

"It's not their business," said Dantzler. "They don't believe in messing with worldly affairs unless it concerns them directly. Anyway, these places—the ones that look like normal land but aren't—they're called...." He drew a blank on the name. "*Aya*-something. I can't remember. But they have different laws. They're where your spirit goes to die after your body dies."

"Don't they got no Heaven?"

"Nope. It just takes longer for your spirit to die, and so it goes to one of these places that's between everything and nothing."

"Nothin'," said Moody disconsolately, as if all his hopes for an afterlife had been dashed. "Don't make no sense to have spirits and not have no Heaven."

"Hey," said Dantzler, tensing as wind rustled the pine boughs. "They're just a bunch of damn primitives. You know what their sacred drink is? Hot chocolate! My old man was a guest at one of their funerals, and he said they carried cups of hot chocolate balanced on these little red towers and acted like drinking it was going to wake them to the secrets of the universe." He laughed, and the laughter sounded tinny and psychotic to his own ears. "So you're going to worry about fools who think hot chocolate's holy water?"

"Maybe they just like it," said Moody. "Maybe somebody dyin' just give 'em an excuse to drink it."

But Dantzler was no longer listening. A moment before, as they emerged from pine cover onto the highest point of the ridge, a stony scarp open to the winds and providing a view of rumpled mountains and valleys extending to the horizon, he had popped an ampule. He felt so strong, so full of righteous purpose and controlled fury, it seemed only the sky was around him, that he was still ascending, preparing to do battle with the gods themselves.

▲▼▲

Tecolutla was a village of whitewashed stone tucked into a notch between two hills. From above, the houses—with their shadow-blackened windows and doorways—looked like an unlucky throw of dice. The streets ran uphill and down, diverging around boulders. Bougainvilleas and hibiscuses speckled the hillsides, and there were tilled fields on the gentler slopes. It was a sweet, peaceful place when they arrived, and after they had gone it was once again peaceful; but its sweetness had been permanently banished. The reports of Sandinistas had proved accurate, and though they were casualties left behind to recuperate, DT had decided their presence called for extreme measures. Fu gas, frag grenades, and such. He had fired an M-60 until the barrel melted down, and then had manned the flamethrower. Afterward, as they rested atop the next ridge, exhausted and begrimed, having radioed in a chopper for resupply, he could not get over how one of the houses he had torched had come to resemble a toasted marshmallow.

"Ain't that how it was, man?" he asked, striding up and down the line. He did not care if they agreed about the house; it was a deeper question he was asking, one concerning the ethics of their actions.

"Yeah," said Dantzler, forcing a smile. "Sure did."

DT grunted with laughter. "You *know* I'm right, don'tcha, man?"

The sun hung directly behind his head, a golden corona rimming a black oval, and Dantzler could not turn his eyes away. He felt weak and weakening, as if threads of himself were being spun loose and sucked into the blackness. He had popped three ampules prior to the firefight, and his experience of Tecolutla had been a kind of mad whirling dance through the streets, spraying erratic bursts that appeared to be writing weird names on the walls. The leader of the Sandinistas had worn a mask—a gray face with a surprised hole of a mouth and pink circles around the eyes. A ghost face. Dantzler had been afraid of the mask and had poured round after round into it. Then, leaving the village, he had seen a small girl standing beside the shell of the last house, watching them, her colorless rag of a dress tattering in the breeze. She had been a victim of that malnutrition disease, the one that paled your skin and whitened your hair and left you retarded. He could not recall the name of the disease—things like names were slipping away from him—nor could he believe anyone had survived, and for a moment he had thought the spirit of the village had come out to mark their trail.

That was all he could remember of Tecolutla, all he wanted to remember. But he knew he had been brave.

▲▼▲

Four days later, they headed up into a cloud forest. It was the dry season, but dry season or not, blackish gray clouds always shrouded these peaks. They were shot through by ugly glimmers of lightning, making it seem that malfunctioning neon signs were hidden beneath them, advertisements for evil. Everyone was jittery, and Jerry LeDoux—a slim dark-haired Cajun kid—flat-out refused to go.

"It ain't reasonable," he said. "Be easier to go through the passes."

"We're on recon, man! You think the beaners be waitin' in the passes, wavin' their white flags?" DT whipped his rifle into firing position and pointed it at LeDoux. "C'mon, Louisiana man. Pop a few, and you feel different."

As LeDoux popped the ampules, DT talked to him.

"Look at it this way, man. This is your big adventure. Up there it be like all them animal shows on the tube. The savage kingdom, the unknown. Could be like Mars or somethin'. Monsters and shit, with big red eyes and tentacles. You wanna miss that, man? You wanna miss bein' the first grunt on Mars?"

Soon LeDoux was raring to go, giggling at DT's rap.

Moody kept his mouth shut, but he fingered the safety of his rifle and glared at DT's back. When DT turned to him, however, he relaxed. Since Tecolutla he had grown taciturn, and there seemed to be a shifting of lights and darks in his eyes, as if something were scurrying back and forth behind them. He had taken to wearing banana leaves on his head, arranging them under his helmet so the frayed ends stuck out the sides like strange green hair. He said this was camouflage, but Dantzler was certain it bespoke some secretive irrational purpose. Of course DT had noticed Moody's spiritual erosion, and as they prepared to move out, he called Dantzler aside.

"He done found someplace inside his head that feel good to him," said DT. "He's tryin' to curl up into it, and once he do that he ain't gon' be responsible. Keep an eye on him."

Dantzler mumbled his assent, but was not enthused.

"I know he your fren', man, but that don't mean shit. Not the way things are. Now me, I don't give a damn 'bout you personally. But I'm your brother-in-arms, and thass somethin' you can count on...y'understand."

To Dantzler's shame, he did understand.

They had planned on negotiating the cloud forest by nightfall, but they had underestimated the difficulty. The vegetation beneath the clouds was lush—thick, juicy leaves that mashed underfoot, tangles of vines, trees with slick, pale bark and waxy leaves—and the visibility was only about fifteen feet. They were gray wraiths passing through grayness. The vague shapes of the foliage reminded Dantzler of fancifully engraved letters, and for a while he entertained himself with the notion that they were walking among the half-formed phrases of a constitution not yet manifest in the land. They barged off the trail, losing it completely, becoming veiled in spiderwebs and drenched by spills of water; their voices were oddly muffled, the tag ends of words swallowed up. After seven hours of this, DR reluctantly gave the order to pitch camp. They set electric lamps around the perimeter so they could see to string the jungle hammocks; the beam of light illuminated the moisture in the air, piercing the murk with jeweled blades. They talked in hushed tones, alarmed by the eerie atmosphere. When they had done with the hammocks, DT posted four sentries—Moody, LeDoux, Dantzler, and himself. Then they switched off the lamps.

It grew pitch-dark, and the darkness was picked out by plips and plops, the entire spectrum of dripping sounds. To Dantzler's ears they blended into a gabbling speech. He imagined tiny Santa Ana demons talking about him, and to stave off paranoia he popped two ampules. He continued to pop them, trying to limit himself to one every half hour; but he was uneasy, unsure where to train his rifle in the dark, and he exceeded his limit. Soon it began to grow light again, and he assumed that more time had passed than he had thought. That often happened with the ampules—it was easy to lose yourself in being alert, in the wealth of perceptual detail available to your sharpened senses. Yet on checking his watch, he saw it was only a few minutes after two o'clock. His system was too inundated with the drugs to allow panic, but he twitched his head from side to side in tight little arcs to determine the source of the brightness. There did not appear to be a single source; it was simply that filaments of the cloud were gleaming, casting a diffuse golden glow, as if they were elements of a nervous system coming to life. He started to call out, then held back. The others must have seen the light, and they had given no cry; they probably had a good reason for their silence. He scrunched down flat, pointing his rifle out from the campsite.

Bathed in the golden mist, the forest had acquired an alchemic beauty. Beads of water glittered with gemmy brilliance; the leaves and vines and bark were gilded. Every surface shimmered with light...everything except a fleck of blackness hovering between two of the trunks, its size gradually increasing. As it swelled in his vision, he saw it had the shape of a bird, its wings beating, flying toward him from an inconceivable distance—inconceivable, because the dense vegetation did not permit you to see very far in a straight line, and yet the bird was growing larger with such slowness that it must have been coming from a long way off. It was not really flying, he realized; rather, it was as if the forest were painted on a piece of paper, as if someone were holding a lit match behind it and burning a hole, a hole that maintained the shape of a bird as it spread. He was transfixed, unable to react. Even when it had blotted out half the light, when he lay before it no bigger than a mote in relation to its huge span, he could not move or squeeze the trigger. And then the blackness swept over him, He had the sensation of being borne along at incredible speed, and he could no longer hear the dripping of the forest.

"Moody!" he shouted. "DT!"

But the voice that answered belonged to neither of them. It was hoarse, issuing from every part of the surrounding blackness, and he recognized it as the voice of his recurring dream.

"You are killing my son," it said. "I have led you here, to this *ayahuamaco,* so he may judge you."

Dantzler knew to his bones the voice was that of the *Sukia* of the village of Santander Jiménez. He wanted to offer a denial, to explain his innocence, but all he could manage was, "No." He said it tearfully, hopelessly, his forehead resting on his rifle barrel. Then his mind gave a savage twist, and his soldiery self regained control. He ejected an ampule from his dispenser and popped it.

The voice laughed—malefic, damning laughter whose vibrations shuddered Dantzler. He opened up with the rifle, spraying fire in all directions. Filigrees of golden holes appeared in the blackness, tendrils of mist coiled through them. He kept on firing until the blackness shattered and fell in jagged sections toward him. Slowly. Like shards of black glass dropping through water. He emptied the rifle and flung himself flat, shielding his head with his arms, expecting to be sliced into bits; but nothing touched him. At last he peeked between his arms; then—amazed, because the forest was now a uniform lustrous yellow—he rose to his knees. He scraped his hand on one of the crushed leaves beneath him, and blood welled from the cut. The broken fibers of the leaf were as stiff as wires. He stood, a giddy trickle of hysteria leaking up from the bottom of his soul. It was no forest, but a building of solid gold worked to resemble a forest—the sort of conceit that might have been fabricated for the child of an emperor. Canopied by golden leaves, columned by slender golden trunks, carpeted by golden grasses. The water beads were diamonds. All the gleam and glitter soothed his apprehension; here was something out of a myth, a habitat for princesses and wizards and dragons. Almost gleeful, he turned to the campsite to see how the others were reacting.

Once, when he was nine years old, he had sneaked into the attic to rummage through the boxes and trunks, and he had run across an old morocco-bound copy of *Gulliver's Travels*. He had been taught to treasure old books, and so he had opened it eagerly to look at the illustrations, only to find that the centers of the pages had been eaten away, and there, right in the heart of the fiction, was a nest of larvae. Pulpy, horrid things. It had been an awful sight, but one unique in his experience, and he might have studied those crawling scraps of life for a very long time if his father had not interrupted. Such a sight was now before him, and he was numb with it.

They were all dead. He should have guessed they would be; he had given no thought to them while firing his rifle. They had been struggling out of their hammocks when the bullets hit, and as a result they were hanging half-in, half-out, their limbs dangling, blood pooled beneath them. The veils of golden mist made them look dark and mysterious and malformed, like monsters killed as they emerged from their cocoons. Dantzler could not stop staring, but he was shrinking inside himself. It was not his fault. That thought keep swooping in and out of a flock of less acceptable thoughts; he wanted it to stay put, to be true, to alleviate the sick horror he was beginning to feel.

"What's your name?" asked a girl's voice behind him.

She was sitting on a stone about twenty feet away. Her hair was a tawny shade of gold, her skin a half-tone lighter, and her dress was cunningly formed out of the mist. Only her eyes were real. Brown heavy-lidded eyes—they were at variance with the rest of her face, which had the fresh, unaffected beauty of an American teenager.

"Don't be afraid," she said, and patted the ground, inviting him to sit beside her.

He recognized the eyes, but it was no matter. He badly needed the consolation she could offer; he walked over and sat down. She let him lean his head against her thigh.

"What's your name?" she repeated.

"Dantzler," he said. "John Dantzler." And then he added, "I'm from Boston. My father's...." It would be too difficult to explain about anthropology. "He's a teacher."

"Are there many soldiers in Boston?" She stroked his cheek with a golden finger.

The caress made Dantzler happy. "Oh, no," he said. "They hardly know there's a war going on."

"This is true?" she said, incredulous.

"Well, they do know about it, but it's just news on the TV to them. They've got more pressing problems. Their jobs, families."

"Will you let them know about the war when you return home?" she asked. "Will you do that for me?"

Dantzler had given up hope of returning home, of surviving, and her assumption that he would do both acted to awaken his gratitude. "Yes," he said fervently. "I will."

"You must hurry," she said. "If you stay in the *ayahuamaco* too long, you will never leave. You must find the way out. It is a way not of directions or trails, but of events."

"Where is this place?" he asked, suddenly aware of much he had taken it for granted.

She shifted her leg away, and if he had not caught himself on the stone, he would have fallen. When he looked up, she had vanished. He was surprised that her disappearance did not alarm him; in reflex he slipped out a couple of ampules, but after a moment's reflection he decided not to use them. It was impossible to slip them back into the dispenser, so he tucked them into the interior webbing of his helmet for later. He doubted he would need them, though. He felt strong, competent, and unafraid.

▲▼▲

Dantzler stepped carefully between the hammocks, not wanting to brush against them; it might have been his imagination, but they seemed to be bulged down lower than before, as if death had weighed out heavier than life. That heaviness was in the air, pressuring him. Mist rose like golden steam from the corpses, but the sight no longer affected him—perhaps because the mist gave the illusion of being their souls. He picked up a rifle with a full magazine and headed off into the forest.

The tips of the golden leaves were sharp, and he had to ease past them to avoid being cut; but he was at the top of his form, moving gracefully, and the obstacles barely slowed his pace. He was not even anxious about the girl's warning to hurry; he was certain the way out would soon present itself. After a minute or so he heard voices, and after another few seconds he came to a clearing divided by a stream, one so perfectly reflecting that its banks appeared to enclose a wedge of golden mist. Moody was squatting to the left of the stream, staring at the blade of his survival knife and singing under his breath—a wordless melody that had the erratic rhythm of a trapped fly. Beside him lay Jerry LeDoux, his throat slashed from ear to ear. DT was sitting on the other side of the stream; he had been shot just above the knee, and though he had ripped up his shirt for bandages and tied off the leg with a tourniquet, he was not in good shape. He was sweating, and a gray chalky pallor infused his skin. The entire scene had the weird vitality of something that had materialized in a magic mirror, a bubble of reality enclosed within a gilt frame.

DT heard Dantzler's footfalls and glanced up. "Waste him!" he shouted, pointing to Moody.

Moody did not turn from contemplation of the knife. "No," he said, as if speaking to someone whose image was held in the blade.

"Waste him, man!" screamed DT. "He killed LeDoux!"

"Please," said Moody to the knife. "I don't want to."

There was blood clotted on his face, more blood on the banana leaves sticking out of his helmet.

"Did you kill Jerry?" asked Dantzler; while he addressed the question to Moody, he did not relate to him as an individual, only as part of a design whose message he had to unravel.

"Jesus Christ! Waste him!" DT smashed his fist against the ground in frustration.

"Okay," said Moody. With an apologetic look, he sprang to his feet and charged Dantzler, swinging the knife.

Emotionless, Dantzler stitched a line of fire across Moody's chest; he went sideways into the bushes and down.

"What the hell was you waitin' for!" DT tried to rise, but winced and fell back. "Damn! Don't know if I can walk."

"Pop a few," Dantzler suggested mildly.

"Yeah. Good thinkin', man." DT fumbled for his dispenser.

Dantzler peered into the bushes to see where Moody had fallen. He felt nothing, and this pleased him. He was weary of feeling.

DT popped an ampule with a flourish, as if making a toast, and inhaled. "Ain't you gon' to do some, man?"

"I don't need them," said Dantzler. "I'm fine."

The stream interested him; it did not reflect the mist, as he had supposed, but was itself a seam of the mist.

"How many you think they was?" asked DT.

"How many what?"

"Beaners, man! I wasted three or four after they hit us, but I couldn't tell how many they was."

Dantzler considered this in light of his own interpretation of events and Moody's conversation with the knife. It made sense. A Santa Ana kind of sense.

"Beats me," he said. "But I guess there's less than there used to be."

DT snorted. "You got *that* right!" He heaved to his feet and limped to the edge of the stream. "Gimme a hand across."

Dantzler reached out to him, but instead of taking his hand, he grabbed his wrist and pulled him off-balance. DT teetered on his good leg, then toppled and vanished beneath the mist. Dantzler had expected him to fall, but he surfaced instantly, mist clinging to his skin. Of course, thought Dantzler; his body would have to die before his spirit would fall.

"What you doin', man?" DT was more disbelieving than enraged.

Dantzler planted a foot in the middle of his back and pushed him down until his head was submerged. DT bucked and clawed at the foot and managed to come to his hands and knees. Mist slithered from his eyes, his nose, and he choked out the words "...kill you..." Dantzler pushed him down again; he got into pushing him down and letting him up, over and over. Not so as to torture him. Not really. It was because he had suddenly understood the nature of the *ayahuamaco*'s laws, that they were approximations of normal laws, and he further understood that his actions had to approximate those of someone jiggling a key in a lock. DT was the key to the way out, and Dantzler was jiggling him, making sure all the tumblers were engaged.

Some of the vessels in DT's eyes had burst, and the whites were occluded by films of blood. When he tried to speak, mist curled from his mouth. Gradually his struggles subsided; he clawed runnels in the gleaming yellow dirt of the bank and shuddered. His shoulders were knobs of black land foundering in a mystic sea.

For a long time after DT sank from view, Dantzler stood beside the stream, uncertain of what was left to do and unable to remember a lesson he had been taught. Finally he shouldered his rifle and walked away from the clearing. Morning had broken, the mist had thinned, and the forest had regained its usual coloration. But he scarcely noticed these changes, still troubled by his faulty memory. Eventually, he let it slide—it would all come clear sooner or later. He was just happy to be alive. After a while he began to kick the stones as he went, and to swing his rifle in a carefree fashion against the weeds.

▲▼▲

When the First Infantry poured across the Nicaraguan border and wasted Leon, Dantzler was having a quiet time at the VA hospital in Ann Arbor, Michigan; and at the precise moment the bulletin was flashed nationwide, he was sitting in the lounge, watching the American League playoffs between Detroit and Texas. Some of the patients ranted at the interruption, while others shouted them down, wanting to hear the details. Dantzler expressed no reaction whatsoever. He was solely concerned with being a model patient; however, noticing that one of the staff was giving him a clinical stare, he added his weight on the side of the baseball fans. He did not want to appear too controlled. The doctors were as suspicious of that sort of behavior as they were of its contrary. But the funny thing was—at least it was funny to Dantzler—that his feigned annoyance at the bulletin was an exemplary proof of his control, his expertise at moving through life the way he had moved through the golden leaves of the cloud forest. Cautiously, gracefully, efficiently. Touching nothing, and being touched by nothing. That was the lesson he had learned—to be as perfect a counterfeit of a man as the *ayahuamaco* had been of the land; to adopt the various stances of a man, and yet, by virtue of his distance from things human, to be all the more prepared for the onset of crisis or a call to action. He saw nothing aberrant in this; even the doctors would admit that men were little more than organized pretense. If he was different from other men, it was only that he had a deeper awareness of the principles on which his personality was founded.

When the battle of Managua was joined, Dantzler was living at home. His parents had urged him to go easy in readjusting to civilian life, but he had immediately gotten a job as a management trainee in a bank. Each morning he would drive to work and spend a controlled, quiet eight hours; each night he would watch TV with his mother, and before going to bed, he would climb to the attic and inspect the trunk containing his souvenirs of war—helmet, fatigues, knife, boots. The doctors had insisted he face his experiences, and this ritual was his way of following their instructions. All in all, he was quite pleased with his progress, but he still had problems. He had not been able to force himself to venture out at night, remembering all too well the darkness in the cloud forest, and he had rejected his friends, refusing to see them or answer their calls—he was not secure with the idea of friendship. Further, despite his methodical approach to life, he was prone to a nagging restlessness, the feeling of a chore left undone.

One night his mother came into his room and told him that an old friend, Phil Curry, was on the phone. "Please talk to him, Johnny," she said. "He's been drafted, and I think he's a little scared."

The word *drafted* struck a responsive chord in Dantzler's soul, and after brief deliberation he went downstairs and picked up the receiver.

"Hey," said Phil. "What's the story, man? Three months, and you don't even give me a call."

"I'm sorry," said Dantzler. "I haven't been feeling so hot."

"Yeah, I understand," Phil was silent a moment. "Listen, man. I'm leaving', y'know, and we're having a big send-off at Sparky's. It's goin' on right now. Why don't you come down?"

"I don't know."

"Jeanine's here, man. Y'know, she's still crazy 'bout you, talks 'bout you alla time. She don't go out with nobody."

Dantzler was unable to think of anything to say.

"Look," said Phil, "I'm pretty weirded out by this soldier shit. I hear it's pretty bad down there. If you got anything you can tell me 'bout what it's like, man, I'd 'preciate it."

Dantzler could relate to Phil's concern, his desire for an edge, and besides, it felt right to go. Very right. He would take some precautions against the darkness.

"I'll be there," he said.

It was a foul night, spitting snow, but Sparky's parking lot was jammed. Dantzler's mind was flurried like the snow, crowded like the lot—thoughts whirling in, jockeying for position, melting away. He hoped his mother would not wait up, he wondered if Jeanine still wore her hair long, he was worried because the palms of his hands were unnaturally warm. Even with the car windows rolled up, he could hear loud music coming from inside the club. Above the door the words SPARKY'S ROCK CITY were being spelled out a letter at a time in red neon, and when the spelling was complete, the letters flashed off and on and a golden neon explosion bloomed around them. After the explosion, the entire sign went dark for a split second, and the big ramshackle building seemed to grow large and merge with the black sky. He had an idea it was watching him, and he shuddered—one of those sudden lurches downward of the kind that take you just before you fall asleep. He knew the people inside did not intend him any harm, but he also knew that places have a way of changing people's intent, and he did not want to be caught off guard. Sparky's might be such a place, might be a huge black presence camouflaged by neon, its true substance one with the abyss of the sky, the phosphorescent snowflakes jittering in his headlights, the wind keening through the side vent. He would have liked very much to drive home and forget about his promise to Phil; however, he felt a responsibility to explain about the war. More than a responsibility, an evangelistic urge. He would tell them about the kid falling out of the chopper, the white-haired girl in Tecolutla, the emptiness. God, yes! How you went down chock-full of ordinary American thoughts and dreams, memories of smoking weed and chasing tail and hanging out and freeway flying with a case of something cold, and how you smuggled back a human-shaped container of pure Salvadorian emptiness. Primo grade. Smuggled it back to the land of silk and money, of mindfuck video games and topless tennis matches and fast-food solutions to the nutritional problem. Just a taste of Salvador would banish all those trivial obsessions. Just a taste. It would be easy to explain.

Of course, some things beggared explanation.

He bent down and adjusted the survival knife in his boot so the hilt would not rub against his calf. From his coat pocket he withdrew the two ampules he had secreted in his helmet that long-ago night in the cloud forest. As the neon explosion flashed once more, glimmers of gold coursed along their shiny surfaces. He did not think he would need them; his hand was steady, and his purpose was clear. But to be on the safe side, he popped them both. —

A Spanish Lesson

That winter of '64, when I was seventeen and prone to obey the impulses of my heart as if they were illuminations produced by years of contemplative study, I dropped out of college and sailed to Europe, landing in Belfast, hitchhiking across Britain, down through France and Spain, and winding up on the Costa del Sol—to be specific, in a village near Malaga by the name of Pedregalejo—where one night I was to learn something of importance. What had attracted me to the village was not its quaintness, its vista of the placid Mediterranean and neat white stucco houses and little bandy-legged fishermen mending nets; rather, it was the fact that the houses along the shore were occupied by a group of expatriates, mostly Americans, who posed for me a bohemian ideal.

The youngest of them was seven years older than I, the eldest three times my age, and among them they had amassed a wealth of experience that caused me envy and made me want to become like them: bearded, be-earringed, and travel-wise. There was, for example, Leonard Somstaad, a Swedish poet with the poetic malady of a weak heart and a fondness for *marjoun* (hashish candy); there was Art Shapiro, a wanderer who had for ten years migrated between Pedregalejo and Istanbul; there was Don Washington, a black ex-GI and blues singer, whose Danish girlfriend—much to the delight of the locals—was given to nude sunbathing; there was Robert Braehme, a New York actor who, in the best theatrical tradition, attempted halfheartedly to kill several of the others, suffered a nervous breakdown, and had to be returned to the States under restraint.

And then there was Richard Shockley, a tanned, hook-nosed man in his late twenties, who was the celebrity of the group. A part-time smuggler (mainly of marijuana) and a writer of some accomplishment. His first novel, *The Celebrant*, had created a minor critical stir. Being a fledgling writer myself, it was he whom I most envied. In appearance and manner he suited my notion of what a writer should be. For a while he took an interest in me, teaching me smuggling tricks and lecturing on the moral imperatives of art; but shortly thereafter he became preoccupied with his own affairs and our relationship deteriorated.

In retrospect I can see that these people were unremarkable; but at the time they seemed impossibly wise, and in order to align myself with them I rented a small beach house, bought a supply of notebooks, and began to fill them with page after page of attempted poetry.

Though I had insinuated myself into the group, I was not immediately accepted. My adolescence showed plainly against the backdrop of their experience. I had no store of anecdotes, no expertise with flute or guitar, and my conversation was lacking in hip savoir faire. In their eyes I was a kid, a baby, a clever puppy who had learned how to beg, and I was often the object of ridicule. Three factors saved me from worse ridicule: my size (six foot three, one-ninety), my erratic temper, and my ability to consume enormous quantities of drugs. This last was my great trick, my means of gaining respect. I would perform feats of ingestion that would leave Don Washington, a consummate doper, shaking his head in awe. Pills, powders, herbs—I was indiscriminate, and I initiated several dangerous dependencies in hopes of achieving equal status.

Six weeks after moving to the beach, I raised myself a notch in the general esteem by acquiring a girlfriend, a fey California blonde named Anne Fisher. It amuses me to recall the event that led Anne to my bed, because it smacked of the worst of cinema verité, an existential moment opening onto a bittersweet romance. We were walking on the beach, a rainy day, sea and sky blending in a slate fog toward Africa, both of us stoned near to the point of catatonia, when we happened upon a drowned kitten. Had I been unaccompanied, I might have inspected the corpse for bugs and passed on; but as it was, being under Anne's scrutiny, I babbled some nonsense about "this inconstant image of the world," half of which I was parroting from a Eugenio Montale poem, and proceeded to give the kitten decent burial beneath a flat rock.

After completing this nasty chore, I stood and discovered Anne staring at me wetly, her maidenly nature overborne by my unexpected sensitivity. No words were needed. We were alone on the beach, with Nina Simone's bluesy whisper issuing from a window of one of the houses, gray waves slopping at our feet. As if pressed together by the vast emptiness around us, we kissed. Anne clawed my back and ground herself against me: you might have thought she had been thirsting for me all her nineteen years, but I came to understand that her desperation was born of philosophical bias and not sexual compulsion. She was deep into sadness as a motif for passion, and she liked thinking of us as two worthless strangers united by a sudden perception of life's pathetic fragility. Fits of weeping and malaise alternating with furious bouts of lovemaking were her idea of romantic counterpoint.

By the time she left me some months later, I had grown thoroughly sick of her; but she had—I believed—served her purpose in establishing me as a full-fledged expatriate.

Wrong. I soon found that I was still the kid, the baby, and I realized that I would remain so until someone of even lesser status moved to the beach, thereby nudging me closer to the mainstream. This didn't seem likely, and in truth I no longer cared; I had lost respect for the group: had I not, at seventeen, become as hiply expatriated as they, and wouldn't I, when I reached their age, be off to brighter horizons? Then, as is often the case with reality, presenting us with what we desire at the moment desire begins to flag, two suitably substandard people rented the house next to mine.

Their names were Tom and Alise, and they were twins a couple of years older than I, uncannily alike in appearance, and hailing from—if you were to believe their story—Canada. Yet they had no knowledge of things Canadian, and their accent was definitely northern European. Not an auspicious entree into a society as picky as Pedregalejo's. Everyone was put off by them, especially Richard Shockley, who saw them as a threat. "Those kind of people make trouble for everyone else," he said to me at once. "They're just too damn weird." (It has always astounded me that those who pride themselves on eccentricity are so quick to deride this quality in strangers.) Others as well testified to the twins' weirdness: they were secretive, hostile; they had been seen making strange passes in the air on the beach, and that led some to believe they were religious nuts; they set lanterns in their windows at night and left them burning until dawn. Their most disturbing aspect, however, was their appearance. Both were scarcely five feet tall, emaciated, pale, with black hair and squinty dark eyes and an elfin cleverness of feature that Shockley described as "prettily ugly, like Munchkins." He suggested that this look might be a product of inbreeding, and I thought he might be right: the twins had the sort of dulled presence that one associates with the retarded or the severely tranquilized. The fishermen treated them as if they were the devil's spawn, crossing themselves and spitting at the sight of them, and the expatriates were concerned that the fishermen's enmity would focus the attention of the Guardia Civil upon the beach.

The Guardia—with their comic-opera uniforms, their machine guns, their funny patent-leather hats that from a distance looked like Mickey Mouse ears—were a legitimate menace. They had a long-standing reputation for murder and corruption, and were particularly fond of harassing foreigners. Therefore I was not surprised when a committee led by Shockley asked me to keep an eye on my new neighbors, the idea being that we should close ranks against them, even to the point of reporting any illegalities. Despite knowing that refusal would consolidate my status as a young nothing, I told Shockley and his pals to screw off. I'm not able to take pride in this—had they been friendlier to me in the past, I might have gone along with the scheme; but as it was, I was happy to reject them. And further, in the spirit of revenge, I went next door to warn Tom and Alise.

My knock roused a stirring inside the house, whispers, and at last the door was cracked and an eye peeped forth. "Yes?" said Alise.

"Uh," I said, taken aback by this suspicious response. "My name's Lucius. From next door. I've got something to tell you about the people around here." Silence. "They're afraid of you," I went on. "They're nervous because they've got dope and stuff, and they think you're going to bring the cops down on them."

Alise glanced behind her, more whispers, and then she said, "Why would we do that?"

"It's not that you'd do it on purpose," I said. "It's just that you're...different. You're attracting a lot of attention, and everyone's afraid that the cops will investigate you and then decide to bust the whole beach."

"Oh." Another conference, and finally she said, "Would you please come in?"

The door swung open, creaking like a coffin lid centuries closed, and I crossed the threshold. Tom was behind the door, and after shutting it, Alise ranged herself beside him. Her chest was so flat, their features so alike, it was only the length of her hair that allowed me to tell them apart. She gestured at a table-and-chairs set in the far corner, and, feeling a prickle of nervousness, I took a seat there. The room was similar to the living room of my house: whitewashed walls, unadorned and flaking; cheap production-line furniture (the signal difference being that they had two beds instead of one); a gas stove in a niche to the left of the door. Mounted just above the light switch was a plastic crucifix; a frayed cord ran up behind the cross to the fixture on the ceiling, giving the impression that Christ had some role to play in the transmission of the current.

They had kept the place scrupulously neat; the one sign of occupancy was a pile of notebooks and a sketchpad lying on the table. The pad was open to what appeared to be a rendering of complex circuitry. Before I could get a better look at it, Tom picked up the pad and tossed it onto the stove. Then they sat across from me, hands in their laps, as meek and quiet as two white mice. It was dark in the room, knife-edges of golden sunlight slanting through gaps in the shutter boards, and the twins' eyes were like dirty smudges on their pale skins.

"I don't know what more to tell you," I said. "And I don't have any idea what you should do. But I'd watch myself." They did not exchange glances or in any way visibly communicate, yet there was a peculiar tension to their silence, and I had the notion that they were again conferring: this increased my nervousness.

"We realize we're different," said Tom at length; his voice had the exact pitch and timbre of Alise's, soft and faintly blurred. "We don't want to cause harm, but there's something we have to do here. It's dangerous, but we have to do it. We can't leave until it's done."

"We think you're a good boy," chimed in Alise, rankling me with this characterization. "We wonder if you would help us?"

I was perplexed. "What can I do?"

"The problem is one of appearances," said Tom. "We can't change the way we look, but perhaps we can change the way others perceive us. If we were to become more a part of the community, we might not be so noticeable."

"They won't have anything to do with you," I told him. "They're too...."

"We have an idea," Alise cut in.

"Yes," said Tom. "We thought if there was the appearance of a romantic involvement between you and Alise, people might take us more for granted. We hoped you would be agreeable to having Alise move in with you."

"Now wait!" I said, startled. "I don't mind helping you, but I...."

"It would only be for appearance' sake," said Alise, deadpan. "There'd be no need for physical contact, and I would try not to be an imposition. I could clean for you and do the shopping."

Perhaps it was something in Alise's voice or a subtle shift in attitude, but for whatever reason, it was then that I sensed their desperation. They were very, very afraid...of what, I had no inkling. But fear was palpable, a thready pulse in the air. It was a symptom of my youth that I did not associate their fear with any potential threat to myself; I was merely made the more curious. "What sort of danger are you in?" I asked.

Once again there was that peculiar nervy silence, at the end of which Tom said, "We ask that you treat this as a confidence."

"Sure," I said casually. "Who am I gonna tell?"

The story Tom told was plausible; in fact, considering my own history—a repressive, intellectual father who considered me a major disappointment, who had characterized my dropping out as "the irresponsible actions of a glandular case"—it seemed programmed to enlist my sympathy. He said that they were not Canadian but German, and had been raised by a dictatorial stepfather after their mother's death. They had been beaten, locked in closets, and fed so poorly that their growth had been affected. Several months before, after almost twenty years of virtual confinement, they had managed to escape, and since then they had kept one step ahead of detectives hired by the stepfather. Now, penniless, they were trying to sell some antiquities that they had stolen from their home; and once they succeeded in this, they planned to travel east, perhaps to India, where they would be beyond detection. But they were afraid that they would be caught while waiting for the sale to go through; they had had too little practice with the world to be able to pass as ordinary citizens.

"Well," I said when he had finished. "If you want to move in"—I nodded at Alise—"I guess it's all right. I'll do what I can to help you. But first thing you should do is quit leaving lanterns in your window all night. That's what really weirds the fishermen out. They think you're doing some kind of magic or something:" I glanced back and forth between them. "What are you doing?"

"It's just a habit," said Alise. "Our stepfather made us sleep with the lights on."

"You'd better stop it," I said firmly; I suddenly saw myself playing Anne Sullivan to their Helen Keller, paving their way to a full and happy life, and this noble self-image caused me to wax enthusiastic. "Don't worry," I told them. "Before I'm through, you people are going to pass for genu-*wine* All-American freaks. I guarantee it!"

If I had expected thanks, I would have been disappointed. Alise stood, saying that she'd be right back, she was going to pack her things, and Tom stared at me with an expression that—had I not been so pleased with myself—I might have recognized for pained distaste.

▲▼▲

The beach at Pedregalejo inscribed a grayish white crescent for about a hundred yards along the Mediterranean, bounded on the west by a rocky point and on the east by a condominium under construction, among the first of many that were gradually to obliterate the beauty of the coast. Beyond the beachfront houses occupied by the expatriates were several dusty streets lined with similar houses, and beyond them rose a cliff of ocher rock surmounted by a number of villas, one of which had been rented by an English actor who was in the area shooting a bullfighting movie: I had been earning my living of late as an extra on the film, receiving the equivalent of five dollars a day and lunch (also an equivalent value, consisting of a greasy sandwich and soda pop).

My house was at the extreme eastern end of the beach and differed from the rest in that it had a stucco porch that extended into the water. Inside, as mentioned, it was almost identical to the twins' house; but despite this likeness, when Alise entered, clutching an airline bag to her chest, she acted as if she had walked into an alien spacecraft. At first, ignoring my invitation to sit, she stood stiffly in the corner, flinching every time I passed; then, keeping as close to the walls as a cat exploring new territory, she inspected my possessions, peeking into my backpack, touching the strings of my guitar, studying the crude watercolors with which I had covered up flaking spots in the whitewash. Finally she sat at the table, knees pressed tightly together and staring at her hands. I tried to draw her into a conversation but received mumbles in reply, and eventually, near sunset, I took a notebook and a bagful of dope, and went out onto the porch to write.

When I was even younger than I was in 1964, a boy, I'd assumed that all seas were wild storm-tossed enormities, rife with monsters and mysteries; and so, at first sight, the relatively tame waters of the Mediterranean had proved a disappointment. However, as time had passed, I'd come to appreciate the Mediterranean's subtle shifts in mood. On that particular afternoon the sea near to shore lay in a rippled sheet stained reddish orange by the dying light; farther out, a golden haze obscured the horizon and made the skeletal riggings of the returning fishing boats seem like the crawling of huge insects in a cloud of pollen. It was the kind of antique weather from which you might expect the glowing figure of Agamemnon, say, or of some martial Roman soul to emerge with ghostly news concerning the sack of Troy or Masada.

I smoked several pipefuls of dope—it was Moroccan kef, a fine grade of marijuana salted with flecks of white opium—and was busy recording the moment in overwrought poetry when Alise came up beside me and, again reminding me of a white mouse, sniffed the air. "What's that?" she asked, pointing at the pipe. I explained and offered a toke. "Oh, no," she said, but continued peering at the dope and after a second added, "My stepfather used to give us drugs. Pills that made us sleepy."

"This might do the same thing," I said airily, and went back to my scribbling.

"Well," she said a short while later. "Perhaps I'll try a little."

I doubt that she had ever smoked before. She coughed and hacked, and her eyes grew red-veined and weepy, but she denied that the kef was having any effect. Gradually, though, she lapsed into silence and sat staring at the water; then, perhaps five minutes after finishing her last pipe, she ran into the house and returned with a sketchpad. "This is wonderful," she said. "Wonderful! Usually it's so hard to see." And began sketching with a charcoal pencil.

I giggled, taking perverse delight in having gotten her high, and asked, "What's wonderful?" She merely shook her head, intent on her work. I would have pursued the question, but at that moment I noticed a group of expatriates strolling toward us along the beach. "Here's your chance to act normal," I said, too stoned to recognize the cruelty of my words.

She glanced up. "What do you mean?"

I nodded in the direction of the proto-hippies. They appeared to be as ripped as we were: one of the women was doing a clumsy skipping dance along the tidal margin, and the others were staggering, laughing, shouting encouragement. Silhouetted against the violent colors of sunset, with their floppy hats and jerky movements, they had the look of shadow actors in a medieval mystery play. "Kiss me," I suggested to Alise. "Or act affectionate. Reports of your normalcy will be all over the beach before dark."

Alise's eyes widened, but she set down her pad. She hesitated briefly, then edged her chair closer; she leaned forward, hesitated again, waiting until the group had come within good viewing range, and pressed her lips to mine.

Though I was not in the least attracted to Alise, kissing her was a powerful sexual experience. It was a chaste kiss. Her lips trembled but did not part, and it lasted only a matter of seconds; yet for its duration, as if her mouth had been coated with some psychochemical, my senses sharpened to embrace the moment in microscopic detail. Kissing had always struck me as a blurred pleasure, a smashing together of pulpy flesh accompanied by a flurry of groping. But with Alise I could feel the exact conformation of our lips, the minuscule changes in pressure as they settled into place, the rough material of her blouse grazing my arm, the erratic measures of her breath (which was surprisingly sweet). The delicacy of the act aroused me as no other kiss had before, and when I drew back I half expected her to have been transformed into a beautiful princess. Not so. She was as ever small and pale. Prettily ugly.

Stunned, I turned toward the beach. The expatriates were gawping at us, and their astonishment reoriented me. I gave them a cheery wave, put my arm around Alise, and inclining my head to hers in a pretense of young love, I led her into the house.

That night I went to sleep while she was off visiting Tom. I tried to station myself on the extreme edge of the bed, leaving her enough room to be comfortable; but by the time she returned I had rolled onto the center of the mattress, and when she slipped in beside me, turning on her side, her thin buttocks nipped spoon-style by my groin, I came drowsily awake and realized that my erection was butting between her legs. Once again physical contact with her caused a sharpening of my senses, and due to the intimacy of the contact my desire, too, was sharpened. I could no more have stopped myself than I could have stopped breathing. Gently, as gently as though she were the truest of trueloves—and, indeed, I felt that sort of tenderness toward her—I began moving against her, thrusting more and more forcefully until I had eased partway inside. All this time she had made no sound, no comment, but now she cocked her leg back over my hip, wriggled closer, and let me penetrate her fully.

It had been a month since Anne had left, and I was undeniably horny; but not even this could explain the fervor of my performance that night. I lost track of how many times we made love. And yet we never exchanged endearments, never spoke or in any way acknowledged one another as lovers. Though Alise's breath quickened, her face remained set in that characteristic deadpan, and I wasn't sure if she was deriving pleasure from the act or simply providing a service, paying rent. It didn't matter. I was having enough fun for both of us. The last thing I recall is that she had mounted me, female superior, her skin glowing ghost-pale in the dawn light, single-scoop breasts barely jiggling; her charcoal eyes were fixed on the wall, as if she saw there an important destination toward which she was galloping me posthaste.

▲▼▲

My romance with Alise—this, and the fact that she and Tom had taken to smoking vast amounts of kef and wandering the beach glassy-eyed, thus emulating the behavior of the other expatriates—had more or less the desired effect upon everyone...everyone except Richard Shockley. He accosted me on my way to work one morning and told me in no uncertain terms that if I knew what was good for me, I should break all ties with the twins. I had about three inches and thirty pounds on him, and—for reasons I will shortly explain—I was in an irascible mood; I gave him a push and asked him to keep out of my business or suffer the consequences.

"You stupid punk!" he said, but backed away.

"Punk?" I laughed—laughter has always been for me a spark to fuel rage—and followed him. "Come on, Rich. You can work up a better insult than that. A verbal guy like you. Come on! Give me a reason to get really crazy."

We were standing in one of the dusty streets back of the beach, not far from a bakery, a little shop with dozens of loaves of bread laid neatly in the window, and at that moment a member of the Guardia Civil poked his head out the door. He was munching a sweet roll, watching us with casual interest: a short, swarthy man, wearing an olive green uniform with fancy epaulets, an automatic rifle slung over his shoulder, and sporting one of those goofy patent-leather hats. Shockley blanched at the sight, wheeled around, and walked away. I was about to walk away myself, but the guardsman beckoned. With a sinking feeling in the pit of my stomach, I went over to him.

"Cobarde," he said, gesturing at Shockley.

My Spanish was poor, but I knew that word: *coward.* "Yeah," I said. "In *inglés, cobarde* means chickenshit."

"Cheek-sheet," he said; then, more forcefully: "Cheek-sheet!"

He asked me to teach him some more English; he wanted to know all the curse words. His name was Francisco, he had fierce bad breath, and he seemed genuinely friendly. But I knew damn well that he was most likely trying to recruit me as an informant. He talked about his family in Seville, his girlfriend, how beautiful it was in Spain. I smiled, kept repeating. *"Sí, sí,"* and was very relieved when he had to go off on his rounds.

Despite Shockley's attitude, the rest of the expatriates began to accept the twins, lumping us together as weirdos of the most perverted sort, yet explicable in our weirdness. From Don Washington I learned that Tom, Alise, and I were thought to be involved in a ménage à trois, and when I attempted to deny this, he said it was no big thing. He did ask, however, what I saw in Alise; I gave some high-school reply about it all being the same in the dark, but in truth I had no answer to his question. Since Alise had moved in, my life had assumed a distinct pattern. Each morning I would hurry off to Malaga to work on the movie set; each night I would return home and enter into brainless rut with Alise. I found this confusing. Separated from Alise, I felt only mild pity for her, yet her proximity would drive me into a lustful frenzy. I lost interest in writing, in Spain, in everything except Alise's undernourished body. I slept hardly at all, my temper worsened, and I began to wonder if she were a witch and had ensorcelled me. Often I would come home to discover her and Tom sitting stoned on my porch, the floor littered with sketches of those circuitlike designs (actually they less resembled circuits than a kind of mechanistic vegetation). I asked once what they were. "A game," replied Alise, and distracted me with a caress.

Two weeks after she moved in, I shouted at the assistant director of the movie (he had been instructing me on how to throw a wineskin with the proper degree of adulation as the English actor-matador paraded in triumph around the bullring) and was fired. After being hustled off the set, I vowed to get rid of Alise, whom I blamed for all my troubles. But when I arrived home, she was nowhere to be seen. I stumped over to Tom's house and pounded on the door. It swung open, and I peeked inside. Empty. Half a dozen notebooks were scattered on the floor. Curiosity overrode my anger. I stepped in and picked up a notebook.

The front cover was decorated with a hand-drawn swastika, and while it is not uncommon to find swastikas on notebook covers—they make for entertaining doodling—the sight of this one gave me a chill. I leafed through the pages, noticing that though the entries were in English, there were occasional words and phrases in German, these having question marks beside them; then I went back and read the first entry.

> *The Führer had been dead three days, and still no one had ventured into the office where he had been exposed to the poisoned blooms, although a servant had crawled along the ledge to the window and returned with the news that the corpse was stiffened in its leather tunic, its cheeks bristling with a dead man's growth, and strings of desiccated blood were hanging from its chin. But as we well remembered his habit of reviving the dead for a final bout of torture, we were afraid that he might have set an igniter in his cells to ensure rebirth, and so we waited while the wine in his goblet turned to vinegar and then to a murky gas that hid him from our view. Nothing had changed. The garden of hydrophobic roses fertilized with his blood continued to lash and slather, and the hieroglyphs of his shadow selves could be seen patrolling the streets....*

The entry went on in like fashion for several pages, depicting a magical-seeming Third Reich, ruled by a dead or moribund Hitler, policed by shadow men known collectively as The Disciples, and populated by a terrified citizenry. All the entries were similar in character, but in the margins were brief notations, most having to do with either Tom's or Alise's physical state, and one passage in particular caught my eye:

> *Alise's control of her endocrine system continues to outpace mine. Could this simply be a product of male*

and female differences? It seems likely, since we have all else in common.

Endocrine? Didn't that have something to do with glands and secretions? And if so, couldn't this be a clue to Alise's seductive powers? I wished that old Mrs. Adkins (General Science, fifth period) had been more persevering with me. I picked up another notebook. No swastika on the cover, but on the foreleaf was written: "Tom and Alise, 'born' 12 March 1944." The entire notebook contained a single entry, apparently autobiographical, and after checking out the window to see if the twins were in sight, I sat down to read it.

Five pages later I had become convinced that Tom was either seriously crazy or that he and Alise were the subjects of an insane Nazi experiment...or both. The word *clone* was not then in my vocabulary, but this was exactly what Tom claimed that he and Alise were. They, he said, along with eighteen others, had been grown from a single cell (donor unknown), part of an attempt to speed up development of a true Master Race. A successful attempt, according to him, for not only were the twenty possessed of supernormal physical and mental abilities, but they were stronger and more handsome than the run of humanity: this seemed to me wish fulfillment, pure and simple, and other elements of the story—for example, the continuation of an exotic Third Reich past 1945—seemed delusion. But upon reading further, learning that they had been sequestered in a cave for almost twenty years, being educated by scientific personnel, I realized that Tom and Alise could have been told these things and have assumed their truth. One could easily make a case for some portion of the Reich having survived the war.

I was about to put down the notebook when I noticed several loose sheets of paper stuck in the rear; I pulled them out and unfolded them. The first appeared to be a map of part of a city, with a large central square labeled "Citadel," and the rest were covered in a neat script that—after reading a paragraph or two—I deduced to be Alise's.

Tom says that since I'm the only one ever to leave the caves (before we all finally left them, that is), I should set down my experiences. He seems to think that having even a horrid past is preferable to having none, and insists that we should document it as well as we can. For myself, I would like to forget the past, but I'll write down what I remember to satisfy his compulsiveness.

When we were first experimenting with the tunnel, we knew nothing more about it than that it was a metaphysical construct of some sort. Our control of it was poor, and we had no idea how far it reached or through what medium it penetrated. Nor had we explored it to any great extent. It was terrifying. The only constant was that it was always dark, with fuzzy different-colored lights shining at what seemed tremendous distances away. Often you would feel disembodied, and sometimes your body was painfully real, subject to odd twinges and shocks. Sometimes it was hard to move—like walking through black glue, and other times it was as if the darkness were a frictionless substance that squeezed you along faster than you wanted to go. Horrible afterimages materialized and vanished on all sides—monsters, animals, things to which I couldn't put a name. We were almost as frightened of the tunnel as we were of our masters. Almost.

One night after the guards had taken some of the girls into their quarters, we opened the tunnel and three of us entered it. I was in the lead when our control slipped and the tunnel began to constrict. I started to turn back, and the next I knew I was standing under the sky, surrounded by window-less buildings. Warehouses, I think. The street was deserted, and I had no idea where I was. In a panic, I ran down the street and soon I heard the sounds of traffic. I turned a corner and stopped short. A broad avenue lined with gray buildings—all decorated with carved eagles—led away from where I stood and terminated in front of an enormous building of black stone. I recognized it at once from pictures we had been shown—Hitler's Citadel.

Though I was still very afraid, perhaps even more so, I realized that I had learned two things of importance. First, that no matter through what otherworldly medium it stretched, the tunnel also negotiated a worldly distance. Second, I understood that the portrait painted of the world by our masters was more or less accurate. We had never been sure of this, despite having been visited by Disciples and other of Hitler's creatures, their purpose being to frighten us into compliance.

I only stood a few minutes in that place, yet I'll never be able to forget it. No description could convey its air of menace, its oppressiveness. The avenue was thronged with people, all—like our guards—shorter and less attractive than I and my siblings, all standing stock-still, silent, and gazing at the Citadel. A procession of electric cars was passing through their midst, blowing horns, apparently to celebrate a triumph, because no one was obstructing their path. Several Disciples were prowling the fringes of the crowd, and overhead a huge winged shape was flying. It was no aircraft; its wings beat, and it swooped and soared like a live thing. Yet it must have been forty or fifty feet long. I couldn't make out what it was; it kept close to the sun, and therefore was always partly in silhouette. (I should mention that although the sun was at meridian, the sky was a deep blue such as I have come to associate with the late-afternoon skies of this world, and the sun itself was tinged with red, its globe well defined—I think it may have been farther along the path to dwarfism than the sun of this world.) All these elements contributed to the menace of the scene, but the dominant force was the Citadel. Unlike the other buildings, no carvings adorned it. No screaming eagles, no symbols of terror and war. It was a construct of simple curves and straight lines; but that simplicity implied an animal sleekness, communicated a sense of great power under restraint, and I had the feeling that at any moment the building might come alive and devour everyone within its reach. It seemed to give its darkness to the air.

I approached a man standing nearby and asked what was going on. He looked at me askance, then checked around to see if anyone was watching us. "Haven't you heard?" he said.

"I've been away," I told him.

This, I could see, struck him as peculiar, but he accepted the fact and said, "They thought he was coming back to life, but it was a false alarm. Now they're offering sacrifices."

The procession of cars had reached the steps of the Citadel, and from them emerged a number of people with

> *their hands bound behind their backs, and a lesser number of very large men, who began shoving them up the steps toward the main doors. Those doors swung open, and from the depths of the Citadel issued a kind of growling music overlaid with fanfares of trumpets. A reddish glow—feeble at first, then brightening to a blaze—shone from within. The light and the music set my heart racing. I backed away, and as I did, I thought I saw a face forming in the midst of that red glow. Hitler's face, I believe. But I didn't wait to validate this. I ran, ran as hard as I could back to the street behind the warehouses, and there, to my relief, I discovered that the tunnel had once again been opened.*

I leaned back, trying to compare what I had read with my knowledge of the twins. Those instances of silent communication. Telepathy? Alise's endocrinal control. Their habit of turning lamps on to burn away the night—could this be some residual behavior left over from cave life? Tom had mentioned that the lights had never been completely extinguished, merely dimmed. Was this all an elaborate fantasy he had concocted to obscure their pitiful reality? I was certain this was the case with Alise's testimony; but whatever, I found that I was no longer angry at the twins, that they had been elevated in my thoughts from nuisance to mystery. Looking back, I can see that my new attitude was every bit as discriminatory as my previous one. I felt for them an adolescent avidity such as I might have exhibited toward a strange pet. They were neat, weird, with the freakish appeal of Venus's-flytraps and sea monkeys. Nobody else had one like them, and having them to myself made me feel superior. I would discover what sort of tricks they could perform, takes notes on their peculiarities, and then, eventually growing bored, I'd move along to a more consuming interest. Though I was intelligent enough to understand that this attitude was—in its indulgence and lack of concern for others—typically ugly-American, I saw no harm in adopting it. Why, they might even benefit from my attention.

At that moment I heard voices outside. I skimmed the notebook toward the others on the floor and affected nonchalance. The door opened; they entered and froze upon seeing me. "Hi," I said. "Door was open, so I waited for you here. What you been up to?"

Tom's eyes flicked to the notebooks, and Alise said, "We've been walking."

"Yeah?" I said this with great good cheer, as if pleased that they had been taking exercise. "Too bad I didn't get back earlier. I could have gone with you."

"Why are you back?" asked Tom, gathering the notebooks. I didn't want to let on about the loss of my job, thinking that the subterfuge would give me a means of keeping track of them. "Some screw-up on the set," I told him. "They had to put off filming. What say we go into town?"

From that point on, no question I asked them was casual; I was always testing, probing, trying to ferret out some of their truth.

"Oh, I don't know," said Tom. "I thought I'd have a swim."

I took a mental note: why do subjects exhibit avoidance of town? For an instant I had an unpleasant vision of myself, a teenage monster gloating over his two gifted white mice, but this was overborne by my delight in the puzzle they presented. "Yeah," I said breezily. "A swim would be nice."

▲▼▲

That night making love with Alise was a whole new experience. I wasn't merely screwing; I was exploring the unknown, penetrating mystery. Watching her pale, passionless face, I imagined the brain behind it to be a strange glowing jewel, with facets instead of convolutions. *National Enquirer* headlines flashed through my head. NAZI MUTANTS ALIVE IN SPAIN. AMERICAN TEEN UNCOVERS HITLER'S SECRET PLOT. Of course there would be no such publicity. Even if Tom's story was true—and I was far from certain that it was—I had no intention of betraying them. I wasn't that big a jerk.

For the next month I maintained the illusion that I was still employed by the film company and left home each morning at dawn; but rather than catching the bus into Malaga, I would hide between the houses, and as soon as Tom and Alise went off on one of their walks (they always walked west along the beach, vanishing behind a rocky point), I would sneak into Tom's house and continue investigating the notebooks. The more I read, the more firmly I believed the story. There was a flatness to the narrative tone that reminded me of a man I had heard speaking about the concentration camps, dully recounting atrocities, staring into space, as if the things he said were putting him into a trance. For example:

> *...It was on July 2nd that they came for Urduja and Klaus. For the past few months they had been making*

us sleep together in a room lit by harsh fluorescents. There were no mattresses, no pillows, and they took our clothes so we could not use them as covering. It was like day under those trays of white light, and we lay curled around each other for warmth. They gassed us before they entered, but we had long since learned how to neutralize the gas, and so we were all awake, linked, pretending to be asleep. Three of them came into the room, and three more stood at the door with guns. At first it seemed that this would be just another instance of rape. The three men violated Urduja, one after the other. She kept up her pretense of unconsciousness, but she felt everything. We tried to comfort her; sending out our love and encouragement. But I could sense her hysteria, her pain. They were rough with her, and when they had finished, her thighs were bloody. She was very brave and gave no cry; she was determined not to give us away. Finally they picked her and Klaus up and carried them off. An hour later we felt them die. It was horrible, as if part of my mind had short-circuited, a corner of it left forever dim.

We were angry and confused. Why would they kill what they had worked so hard to create? Some of us, Uwe and Peter foremost among them, wanted to give up the tunnel and revenge ourselves as best we could; but the rest of us managed to calm things down. Was it revenge we wanted, we asked, or was it freedom? If freedom was to be our choice, then the tunnel was our best hope. Would I—I wonder—have lobbied so hard for the tunnel if I had known that only Alise and I would survive it?

The story ended shortly before the escape attempt was to be made; the remainder of the notebooks contained further depictions of that fantastic Third Reich—genetically-created giants who served as executioners, fountains of blood in the squares of Berlin, dogs that spoke with human voices and spied for the government—and also marginalia concerning the twins' abilities, among them being the control of certain forms of energy: these particular powers had apparently been used to create the tunnel. All this fanciful detail unsettled me, as did several elements of the story. Tom had stated that the usual avenues of escape had been closed to the twenty clones, but what was a tunnel if not a usual avenue of escape? Once he had mentioned that the tunnel was "unstable." What did that mean? And he seemed to imply that the escape had not yet been effected.

By the time I had digested the notebooks, I had begun to notice the regular pattern of the twins' walks; they would disappear around the point that bounded the western end of the beach, and then, a half hour later, they would return, looking worn-out. Perhaps, I thought, they were doing something there that would shed light on my confusion, and so one morning I decided to follow them.

The point was a spine of blackish rock shaped like a lizard's tail that extended about fifty feet out into the water. Tom and Alise would always wade around it. I, however, scrambled up the side and lay flat like a sniper atop it. From my vantage I overlooked a narrow stretch of gravelly shingle, a little trough scooped out between the point and low brown hills that rolled away inland. Tom and Alise were sitting ten or twelve feet below, passing a kef pipe, coughing, exhaling billows of smoke.

That puzzled me. Why would they come here just to get high? I scrunched into a more comfortable position. It was a bright, breezy day; the sea was heaving with a light chop, but the waves slopping onto the shingle were ripples. A few fishing boats were herding a freighter along the horizon. I turned my attention back to the twins. They were standing, making peculiar gestures that reminded me of T'ai Chi, though these were more labored. Then I noticed that the air above the tidal margin had become distorted as with a heat haze...yet it was not hot in the least. I stared at the patch of distorted air—it was growing larger and larger—and I began to see odd translucent shapes eddying within it: they were similar to the shapes that the twins were always sketching. There was a funny pressure in my ears; a drop of sweat slid down the hollow of my throat, leaving a cold track.

Suddenly the twins broke off gesturing and leaned against each other; the patch of distorted air misted away. Both were breathing heavily, obviously exhausted. They sat down a couple of feet from the water's edge, and after a long silence Tom said, "We should try again to be certain."

"Why don't we finish it now?" said Alise. "I'm so tired of this place."

"It's too dangerous in the daylight." Tom shied a pebble out over the water. "If they're waiting at the other end, we might have to run. We'll need the darkness for cover."

"What about tonight?"

"I'd rather wait until tomorrow night. There's supposed to be a storm front coming, and nobody will be outside."

Alise sighed.

"What's wrong?" Tom asked. "Is it Lucius?"

I listened with even more intent.

"No," she said. "I just want it to be over."

Tom nodded and gazed out to sea. The freighter appeared to have moved a couple of inches eastward; gulls were flying under the sun, becoming invisible as they passed across its glaring face, and then swooping away like bits of winged matter blown from its core. Tom picked up the kef pipe. "Let's try it again," he said.

At that instant someone shouted, "Hey!" Richard Shockley came striding down out of the hills behind the shingle. Tom and Alise got to their feet. "I can't believe you people are so fucking uncool," said Shockley, walking up to them; his face was dark with anger, and the breeze was lashing his hair as if it, too, were enraged. "What the hell are you trying to do? Get everyone busted?"

"We're not doing anything," said Alise.

"Naw!" sneered Shockley. "You're just breaking the law in plain view. Plain fucking view!" His fists clenched, and I thought for a moment he was going to hit them. They were so much smaller than he that they looked like children facing an irate parent.

"You won't have to be concerned with us much longer," said Tom. "We're leaving soon."

"Good," said Shockley. "That's real good. But lemme tell you something, man. I catch you smoking out here again, and you might be leaving quicker than you think."

"What do you mean?" asked Alise.

"Don't you worry about what I fucking mean," said Shockley. "You just watch your behavior. We had a good scene going here until you people showed up, and I'll be damned if I'm going to let you blow it." He snatched the pipe from Tom's hand and slung it out to sea. He shook his finger in Tom's face. "I swear, man! One more fuckup, and I'll be on you like white on rice!" Then he stalked off around the point.

As soon as he was out of sight, without a word exchanged between them, Tom and Alise waded into the water and began groping beneath the surface, searching for the pipe. To my amazement, because the shallows were murky and full of floating litter, they found it almost instantly.

▲▼▲

I was angry at Shockley, both for his treatment of the twins and for his invasion of what I considered my private preserve, and I headed toward his house to tell him to lay off. When I entered I was greeted by a skinny, sandy-haired guy—Skipper by name—who was sprawled on pillows in the front room; from the refuse of candy wrappers, crumpled cigarette packs, and empty pop bottles surrounding him, I judged him to have been in this position for quite some time. He was so opiated that he spoke in mumbles and could scarcely open his eyes, but from him I learned the reason for Shockley's outburst. "You don't wanna see him now, man," said Skipper, and flicked out his tongue to retrieve a runner of drool that had leaked from the corner of his mouth. "Dude's on a rampage, y'know?"

"Yeah," I said. "I know."

"Fucker's paranoid," said Skipper. "Be paranoid myself if I was holding a key of smack."

"Heroin?"

"King H," said Skipper with immense satisfaction, as if pronouncing the name of his favorite restaurant, remembering past culinary treats. "He's gonna run it up to Copenhagen soon as—"

"Shut the hell up!" It was Shockley, standing in the front door. "Get out," he said to me.

"Be a pleasure." I strolled over to him. "The twins are leaving tomorrow night. Stay off their case."

He squared his shoulders, trying to be taller. "Or what?"

"Gee, Rich," I said. "I'd hate to see anything get in the way of your mission to Denmark."

Though in most areas of experience I was a neophyte compared to Shockley, he was just a beginner compared to me as regarded fighting. I could tell a punch was coming from the slight widening of his eyes, the tensing of his shoulders. It was a silly school-girlish punch. I stepped inside it, forced him against the wall, and jammed my forearm under his chin. "Listen, Rich," I said mildly. "Nobody wants trouble with the Guardia, right?" My hold prevented him from speaking, but he nodded. Spit bubbled between his teeth. "Then there's no problem. You leave the twins alone, and I'll forget about the dope. Okay?" Again he nodded. I let him go, and he slumped to the floor, holding his throat. "See how easy things go when you just sit down and talk about them?" I said, and grinned. He glared at me. I gave him a cheerful wink and walked off along the beach.

▲▼▲

I see now that I credited Shockley with too much wisdom; I assumed that he was an expert smuggler and would maintain a professional calm. I underestimated his paranoia and gave no thought to his reasons for dealing with a substance as volatile as heroin: they must have involved a measure of desperation, because he was not a man prone to taking whimsical risks. But I wasn't thinking about the consequences of my actions. After what I had seen earlier beyond the point, I believed that I had figured out what Tom and Alise were up to. It seemed implausible, yet equally inescapable. And if I was right, this was my chance to witness something extraordinary. I wanted nothing to interfere.

Gray clouds blew in the next morning from the east, and a steady downpour hung a silver beaded curtain from the eaves of my porch. I spent the day pretending to write and watching Alise out of the corner of my eye. She went about her routines, washing the dishes, straightening up, sketching—the sketching was done with a bit more intensity than usual. Finally, late that afternoon, having concluded that she was not going to tell me she was leaving, I sat down beside her at the table and initiated a conversation. "You ever read science fiction?" I asked.

"No," she said, and continued sketching.

"Interesting staff. Lots of weird ideas. Time travel, aliens…" I jiggled the table, causing her to look up, and fixed her with a stare. "Alternate worlds."

She tensed but said nothing.

"I've read your notebooks," I told her.

"Tom thought you might have." She closed the sketchpad.

"And I saw you trying to open the tunnel yesterday. I know that you're leaving."

She fingered the edge of the pad. I couldn't tell if she was nervous or merely thinking.

I kept after her. "What I can't figure out is why you're leaving. No matter who's chasing you, this world can't be as bad as the one described in the notebooks. At least we don't have anything like The Disciples."

"You've got it wrong," she said after a silence. "The Disciples are of my world."

I had more or less deduced what she was admitting to, but I hadn't really been prepared to accept that it was true, and for a moment I retrenched, believing again that she was crazy, that she had tricked me into swallowing her craziness as fact. She must have seen this in my face or read my thoughts, because she said then, "It's the truth."

"I don't understand," I said. "Why are you going back?"

"We're not; we're going to collapse the tunnel, and to do that we have to activate it. It took all of us to manage it before; Tom and I wouldn't have been able to see the configurations clearly enough if it hadn't been for your drugs. We owe you a great deal." A worry line creased her brow. "You mustn't spy on us tonight. It could be dangerous."

"Because someone might be waiting," I said. "The Disciples?"

She nodded. "We think one followed us into the tunnel and was trapped. It apparently can't control the fields involved in the tunnel, but if it's nearby when we activate the opening...." She shrugged.

"What'll you do if it is?"

"Lead it away from the beach," she said.

She seemed assured in this, and I let the topic drop. "What are they, anyway?" I asked.

"Hitler once gave a speech in which he told us they were magical reproductions of his soul. Who knows? They're horrid enough for that to be true."

"If you collapse the tunnel, then you'll be safe from pursuit. Right?"

"Yes."

"Then why leave Pedregalejo?"

"We don't fit in," she said, and let the words hang in the air a few seconds. "Look at me. Can you believe that in my world I'm considered beautiful?"

An awkward silence ensued. Then she smiled. I'd never seen her smile before. I can't say it made her beautiful—her skin looked dead-pale in the dreary light, her features asexual—but in the smile I could detect the passive confidence with which beauty encounters the world. It was the first time I had perceived her as a person and not as a hobby, a project.

"But that's not the point," she went on. "There's somewhere we want to go."

"Where?"

She reached into her airline bag, which was beside the chair, and pulled out a dog-eared copy of *The Tibetan Book of the Dead*. "To find the people who understand this."

I scoffed. "You believe that crap?"

"What would you know?" she snapped. "It's chaos inside the tunnel. It's...." She waved her hand in disgust, as if it weren't worth explaining anything to such an idiot.

"Tell me about it," I said. Her anger had eroded some of my skepticism.

"If you've read the notebooks, you've seen my best attempt at telling about it. Ordinary referents don't often apply inside the tunnel. But it appears to pass by places described in this book. You catch glimpses of lights, and you're drawn to them. You seem to have an innate understanding that the lights are the entrances to worlds, and you sense that they're fearsome. But you're afraid that if you don't stop at one of them, you'll be killed. The others let themselves be drawn. Tom and I kept going. This light, this world, felt less fearsome than the rest." She gave a doleful laugh. "Now I'm not so sure."

"In one of the notebooks," I said, "Tom wrote that the others didn't survive."

"He doesn't really know," she said. "Perhaps he wrote that to make himself feel better about having wound up here. That would be like him."

We continued talking until dark. It was the longest time I had spent in her company without making love, and yet—because of this abstinence—we were more lovers then than we had ever been before. I listened to her not with an eye toward collecting data, but with genuine interest, and though everything she told me about her world smacked of insanity, I believed her. There were, she said, rivers that sprang from enormous crystals, birds with teeth, bats as large as eagles, cave cities, wizards, winged men who inhabited the thin Andean air. It was a place of evil grandeur, and at its heart, its ruler, was the dead Hitler, his body uncorrupting, his death a matter of conjecture, his terrible rule maintained by a myriad of servants in hopes of his rebirth.

At the time Alise's world seemed wholly alien to me, as distinct from our own as Jupiter or Venus. But now I wonder if—at least in the manner of its rule—it is not much the same: are we not also governed by the dead, by the uncorrupting laws they have made, laws whose outmoded concepts enforce a logical tyranny upon a populace that no longer meets their standards of morality? And I wonder further if each alternate world (Alise told me they were infinite in number) is but a distillation of the one adjoining, and if somewhere at the heart of this complex lies a compacted essence of a world, a blazing point of pure principle that plays cosmic Hitler to its shadow selves.

The storm that blew in just after dark was—like the Mediterranean—an age-worn elemental. Distant thunder, a few strokes of lightning, spreading glowing cracks down the sky, a blustery wind. Alise cautioned me again against following her and told me she'd be back to say goodbye. I told her I'd wait, but as soon as she and Tom had left, I set out toward the point. I would no more have missed their performance than I would have turned down, say, a free ticket to see the Rolling Stones. A few drops of rain were falling, but a foggy moon was visible through high clouds inland. Shadows were moving in the lighted windows of the houses; shards of atonal jazz alternated with mournful gusts of wind. Once Tom and Alise glanced back, and I dropped down on the mucky sand, lying flat until they had waded around the point. By the time I reached the top of the rocks, the rain had stopped. Directly below me were two shadows and the glowing coal of the kef pipe. I was exhilarated. I wished my father were there so I could say to him, "All your crap about 'slow and steady wins the race,' all your rationalist bullshit, it doesn't mean anything in the face of this. There's mystery in the world, and if I'd stayed in school, I'd never have known it."

I was so caught up in thinking about my father's reactions that I lost track of Tom and Alise. When I looked down again, I found that they had taken a stand by the shore and were performing those odd, graceful gestures. Just beyond them, its lowest edge level with the water, was a patch of darkness blacker than night, roughly circular, and approximately the size of a circus ring. Lightning was still striking down out to sea, but the moon had sailed clear of the clouds, staining silver the surrounding hilltops, bringing them close, and in that light I could see that the patch of darkness had depth…depth, and agitated motion. Staring into it was like staring into a fire while hallucinating, watching the flames adopt the forms of monsters; only in this case there were no flames but the vague impressions of monstrous faces melting up from the tunnel walls, showing a shinier black, then fading. I was at an angle to the tunnel, and while I could see inside it, I could also see that it had no exterior walls, that it was a hole hanging in midair, leading to an unearthly distance. Every muscle in my body was tensed, pressure was building in my ears, and I heard a static hiss overriding the grumble of thunder and the mash of the waves against the point.

My opinion of the twins had gone up another notch. Anyone who would enter that fuming nothingness was worthy of respect. They looked the image of courage: two pale children daring the darkness to swallow them. They kept on with their gestures until the depths of the tunnel began to pulse like a black gulping throat. The static hiss grew louder, oscillating in pitch, and the twins tipped their heads to the side, admiring their handiwork.

Then a shout in Spanish, a beam of light probing at the twins from the seaward reach of the point.

Seconds later Richard Shockley splashed through the shallows and onto shore; he was holding a flashlight, and the wind was whipping his hair. Behind him came a short dark-skinned man carrying an automatic rifle, wearing the hat and uniform of the Guardia Civil. As he drew near I recognized him to be Francisco, the guardsman who had tried to cozy up to me. He had a Band-Aid on his chin, which—despite his weapon and traditions—made him seem an innocent. The two men's attention was fixed on the twins, and they didn't notice the tunnel, though they passed close to its edge. Francisco began to harangue the twins in Spanish, menacing them with his gun. I crept nearer and heard the word *heroina.* Heroin. I managed to hear enough to realize what had happened. Shockley, either for the sake of vengeance or—more likely—panicked by what he considered a threat to his security, had planted heroin in Tom's house and informed on him, hoping perhaps to divert suspicion and ingratiate himself with the Guardia. Alise was denying the charges, but Francisco was shouting her down.

And then he caught sight of the tunnel. His mouth fell open, and he backed against the rocks directly beneath me. Shockley spotted it, too. He shined his flashlight into the tunnel, and the beam was sheared off where it entered the blackness, as if it had been bitten in half. For a moment they were frozen in a tableau. Only the moonlight seemed in motion, coursing along Francisco's patent-leather hat.

What got into me then was not bravery or any analogue thereof, but a sudden violent impulse such as had often landed me in trouble. I jumped feetfirst onto Francisco's back. I heard a grunt as we hit the ground, a snapping noise, and the next I knew I was scrambling off him, reaching for his gun, which had flown a couple of yards away. I had no clue of how to operate the safety or even of where it was located. But Shockley wasn't aware of that. His eyes were popped, and he sidled along the rocks toward the water, his head twitching from side to side, searching for a way out.

Hefting the cold, slick weight of the gun gave me a sense of power—a feeling tinged with hilarity—and as I came to my feet, aiming at Shockley's chest, I let out a purposefully demented laugh. "Tell me, Rich," I said. "Do you believe in God?"

He held out a hand palm-up and said, "Don't," in a choked voice.

"Remember that garbage you used to feed me about the moral force of poetry?" I said. "How you figure that jibes with setting up these two?" I waved the rifle barrel at the twins; they were staring into the tunnel, unmindful of me and Shockley.

"You don't understand," said Shockley.

"Sure I do, Rich." I essayed another deranged-teenage-killer laugh. "You're not a nice guy."

In the moonlight his face looked glossy with sweat. "Wait a minute," he said. "I'll...."

Then Alise screamed, and I never did learn what Shockley had in mind. I spun around and was so shocked that I nearly dropped the gun. The tunnel was still pulsing, its depths shrinking and expanding like the gullet of a black worm, and in front of it stood a...my first impulse is to say "a shadow," but that description would not do justice to the Disciple. To picture it you must imagine the mold of an androgynous human body constructed from a material of such translucency that you couldn't see it under any condition of light; then you must further imagine that the mold contains a black substance (negatively black) that shares the properties of both gas and fluid, which is slipping around inside, never filling the mold completely—at one moment presenting to you a knife-edge, the next a frontal silhouette, and at other times displaying all the other possible angles of attitude, shifting among them. Watching it made me dizzy. Tom and Alise cowered from it, and when it turned full face to me, I, too, cowered. Red glowing pinpricks appeared in the places where its eyes should have been; the pinpricks swelled, developing into real eyes. The pupils were black planets eclipsing bloody suns.

I wanted to run, but those eyes held me. Insanity was like a heat in them. They radiated fury, loathing, hatred, and I wonder now if anything human, even some perverted fraction of mad Hitler's soul, could have achieved such an alien resolve. My blood felt as thick as syrup, my scrotum tightened. Then something splashed behind me, and though I couldn't look away from the eyes, I knew that Shockley had run. The Disciple moved after him. And how it moved! It was as if it were turning sideways and vanishing, repeating the process over and over, and doing this so rapidly that it seemed to be strobing, winking in and out of existence, each wink transporting it several feet farther along. Shockley never had a chance. It was too dark out near the end of the point for me to tell what really happened, but I saw two shadows merge and heard a bubbling scream.

A moment later the Disciple came whirling back toward the shore. Instinctively I clawed the trigger of Francisco's gun—the safety had not been on. Bullets stitched across the Disciple's torso, throwing up geysers of blackness that almost instantly were reabsorbed into its body, as if by force of gravity. Otherwise they had no effect. The Disciple stopped just beyond arm's reach, nailing me with its burning gaze, flickering with the rhythm of a shadow cast by a fire. Only its eyes were constant, harrowing me.

Someone shouted—I think it was Tom, but I'm not sure; I had shrunk so far within myself that every element of the scene except the glowing red eyes had a dim value. Abruptly the Disciple moved away. Tom was standing at the mouth of the tunnel. When the Disciple had come half the distance toward him, he took a step forward and—like a man walking into a black mirror—disappeared. The Disciple sped into the tunnel after him. For a time I could see their shapes melting up and fading among the other, more monstrous shapes.

A couple of minutes after they had entered it, the tunnel collapsed. Accompanied by a keening hiss, the interior walls constricted utterly and flecks of ebony space flew up from the mouth. Night flowed in to take its place. Alise remained standing by the shore, staring at the spot where the tunnel had been. In a daze, I walked over and put an arm around her shoulder, wanting to comfort her. But she shook me off and went a few steps into the water, as if to say that she would rather drown than accept my consolation.

My thoughts were in chaos, and needing something to focus them, I knelt beside Francisco, who was still lying facedown. I rolled him onto his back, and his head turned with a horrid grating sound. Blood and sand crusted his mouth. He was dead, his neck broken. For a long while I sat there, noticing the particulars of death, absorbed by them: how the blood within him had begun to settle to one side, discoloring his cheek; how his eyes, though glazed, had maintained a bewildered look. The Band-Aid on his chin had come unstuck, revealing a shaving nick. I might have sat there forever, hypnotized by the sight; but then a bank of clouds overswept the moon, and the pitch-darkness shocked me, alerted me to the possible consequences of what I had done.

From that point on I was operating in a panic, inspired by fear to acts of survival. I dragged Francisco's body into the hills; I waded into the water and found Shockley's body floating in the shallows. Every inch of his skin was horribly charred, and as I hauled him to his resting place beside Francisco, black flakes came away on my fingers. After I had covered the bodies with brush, I led Alise—by then unresisting—back to the house, packed for us both, and hailed a taxi for the airport. There I had a moment of hysteria, realizing that she would not have a passport. But she did. A Canadian one, forged in Malaga. We boarded the midnight flight to Casablanca, and the next day—because I was still fearful of pursuit—we began hitchhiking east across the desert.

▲▼▲

Our travels were arduous. I had only three hundred dollars, and Alise had none. Tom's story about their having valuables to sell had been more or less true, but in our haste we had left them behind. In Cairo, partly due to our lack of funds and partly to medical expenses incurred by Alise's illness (amoebic dysentery), I was forced to take a job. I worked for a perfume merchant in the Khan el-Khalili Bazaar, steering tourists to his shop, where they could buy rare essences and drugs and change money at the black market rates. In order to save enough to pay our passage east, I began to cheat my employer, servicing some of his clients myself, and when he found me out I had to flee with Alise, who had not yet shaken her illness.

I felt responsible for her, guilty about my role in the proceedings. I'd come to terms with Francisco's death. Naturally I regretted it, and sometimes I would see that dark, surprised face in my dreams. But acts of violence did not trouble my heart then as they do now. I had grown up violent in a violent culture, and I was able to rationalize the death as an accident. And, too, it had been no saint I had killed. I could not, however, rationalize my guilt concerning Alise, and this confounded me. Hadn't I tried to save her and Tom? I realized that my actions had essentially been an expression of adolescent fury, yet they had been somewhat on the twins' behalf. And no one could have stood against the Disciple. What more could I have done? Nothing, I told myself. But this answer failed to satisfy me.

In Afghanistan, Alise suffered a severe recurrence of her dysentery. This time I had sufficient funds (money earned by smuggling, thanks to Shockley's lessons) to avoid having to work, and we rented a house on the outskirts of Kabul. We lived there three months until she had regained her health. I fed her yogurt, red meat, vegetables; I bought her books and a tape recorder and music to play on it; I brought people in whom I thought she might be interested to visit her. I wish I could report that we grew to be friends, but she had withdrawn into herself and thus remained a mystery to me, something curious and inexplicable. She would lie in her room—a cubicle of whitewashed stone—with the sunlight slanting in across her bed, paling her further, transforming her into a piece of ivory sculpture, and would gaze out the window for hours, seeing, I believe, not the exotic traffic on the street—robed horsemen from the north, ox-drawn carts, and Chinese-made trucks—but some otherworldly vista. Often I wanted to ask her more about her world, about the tunnel and Tom and a hundred other things. But while I could not institute a new relationship with her, I did not care to reinstitute our previous one. And so my questions went unasked. And so certain threads of this narrative must be left untied, reflecting the messiness of reality as opposed to the neatness of fiction.

Though this story is true, I do not ask that you believe it. To my mind it is true enough, and if you have read it to the end, then you have sufficiently extended your belief. In any case, it is a verity that the truth becomes a lie when it is written down, and it is the art of writing to wring as much truth as possible from its own dishonest fabric. I have but a single truth to offer, one that came home to me on the last day I saw Alise, one that stands outside both the story and the act of writing it.

We had reached the object of our months-long journey, the gates of a Tibetan nunnery on a hill beneath Dhaulagiri in Nepal, a high blue day with a chill wind blowing. It was here that Alise planned to stay. Why? She never told me more than she had in our conversation shortly before she and Tom set out to collapse the tunnel. The gates—huge wooden barriers carved with the faces of gods—swung open, and the female lamas began to applaud, their way of frightening off demons who might try to enter. They formed a crowd of yellow robes and tanned, smiling faces that seemed to me another kind of barrier, a deceptively plain facade masking some rarefied contentment. Alise and I had said a perfunctory goodbye, but as she walked inside, I thought—I hoped—that she would turn back and give vent to emotion.

She did not. The gates swung shut, and she was gone into the only haven that might accept her as commonplace.

Gone, and I had never really known her.

I sat down outside the gates, alone for the first time in many months, with no urgent destination or commanding purpose, and took stock. High above, the snowy fang of Dhaulagiri reared against a cloudless sky; its sheer faces deepened to gentler slopes seamed with the ice-blue tongues of glaciers, and those slopes eroded into barren brown hills such as the one upon which the nunnery was situated. That was half the world. The other half, the half I faced, was steep green hills terraced into barley fields, and winding through them a river, looking as unfeatured as a shiny aluminum ribbon. Hawks were circling the middle distance, and somewhere, perhaps from the monastery that I knew to be off among the hills, a horn sounded a great bass note like a distant dragon signaling its hunger or its rage.

I sat at the center of these events and things, at the dividing line of these half-worlds that seemed to me less in opposition than equally empty, and I felt that emptiness pouring into me. I was so empty, I thought that if the wind were to strike me at the correct angle, I might chime like a bell…and perhaps it did, perhaps the clarity of the Himalayan weather and this sudden increment of emptiness acted to produce a tone, an illumination, for I saw myself then as Tom and Alise must have seen me. Brawling, loutish, indulgent. The two most notable facts of my life were negatives: I had killed a man, and I had encountered the unknown and let it elude me. I tried once again to think what more I could have done, and this time, rather than arriving at the usual conclusion, I started to understand what lesson I had been taught on the beach at Pedregalejo.

Some years ago a friend of mine, a writer and a teacher of writing, told me that my stories had a tendency to run on past the climax, and that I frequently ended them with a moral, a technique he considered outmoded. He was, in the main, correct. But it occurs to me that sometimes a moral—whether or not clearly stated by the prose—is what provides us with the real climax, the good weight that makes the story resonate beyond the measure of the page. So, in this instance, I will go contrary to my friend's advice and tell you what I learned, because it strikes me as being particularly applicable to the American consciousness, which is insulated from much painful reality, and further because it relates to a process of indifference that puts us all at risk.

When the tragedies of others become for us diversions, sad stories with which to enthrall our friends, interesting bits of data to toss out at cocktail parties, a means of presenting a pose of political concern, or whatever...when this happens we commit the gravest of sins, condemn ourselves to ignominy, and consign the world to a dangerous course. We begin to justify our casual overview of pain and suffering by portraying ourselves as do-gooders incapacitated by the inexorable forces of poverty, famine, and war. "What can I do?" we say. "I'm only one person, and these things are beyond my control. I care about the world's trouble, but there are no solutions."

Yet no matter how accurate this assessment, most of us are relying on it to be true, using it to mask our indulgence, our deep-seated lack of concern, our pathological self-involvement. In adopting this attitude we delimit the possibilities for action by letting events progress to a point at which, indeed, action becomes impossible, at which we can righteously say that nothing can be done. And so we are born, we breed, we are happy, we are sad, we deal with consequential problems of our own, we have cancer or a car crash, and in the end our actions prove insignificant. Some will tell you that to feel guilt or remorse over the vast inaction of our society is utter foolishness; life, they insist, is patently unfair, and all anyone can do is to look out for his own interest. Perhaps they are right; perhaps we are so mired in our self-conceptions that we can change nothing. Perhaps this is the way of the world. But, for the sake of my soul and because I no longer wish to hide my sins behind a guise of mortal incapacity, I tell you it is not. —

The Jaguar Hunter

It was his wife's debt to Onofrio Esteves, the appliance dealer, that brought Esteban Caax to town for the first time in almost a year. By nature he was a man who enjoyed the sweetness of the countryside above all else; the placid measures of a farmer's day invigorated him, and he took great pleasure in nights spent joking and telling stories around a fire, or lying beside his wife, Encarnación. Puerto Morada, with its fruit company imperatives and sullen dogs and cantinas that blared American music, was a place he avoided like the plague: indeed, from his home atop the mountain whose slopes formed the northernmost enclosure of Bahía Onda, the rusted tin roofs ringing the bay resembled a dried crust of blood such as might appear upon the lips of a dying man.

On this particular morning, however, he had no choice but to visit the town. Encarnación had—without his knowledge—purchased a battery-operated television set on credit from Onofrio, and he was threatening to seize Esteban's three milk cows in lieu of the eight hundred *lempira* that was owed; he refused to accept the return of the television, but had sent word that he was willing to discuss an alternate method of payment. Should Esteban lose the cows, his income would drop below a subsistence level and he would be forced to take up his old occupation, an occupation far more onerous than farming.

As he walked down the mountain, past huts of thatch and brushwood poles identical to his own, following a trail that wound through sun-browned thickets lorded over by banana trees, he was not thinking of Onofrio but of Encarnación. It was in her nature to be frivolous, and he had known this when he had married her; yet the television was emblematic of the differences that had developed between them since their children had reached maturity. She had begun to put on sophisticated airs, to laugh at Esteban's country ways, and she had become the doyenne of a group of older women, mostly widows, all of whom aspired to sophistication. Each night they would huddle around the television and strive to outdo one another in making sagacious comments about the American detective shows they watched; and each night

Esteban would sit outside the hut and gloomily ponder the state of his marriage. He believed Encarnación's association with the widows was her manner of telling him that she looked forward to adopting the black skirt and shawl, that—having served his purpose as a father—he was now an impediment to her. Though she was only forty-one, younger by three years than Esteban, she was withdrawing from the life of the senses; they rarely made love anymore, and he was certain that this partially embodied her resentment to the fact that the years had been kind to him. He had the look of one of the Old Patuca—tall, with chiseled features and wide-set eyes; his coppery skin was relatively unlined and his hair jet black. Encarnación's hair was streaked with gray, and the clean beauty of her limbs had dissolved beneath layers of fat. He had not expected her to remain beautiful, and he had tried to assure her that he loved the woman she was and not merely the girl she had been. But that woman was dying, infected by the same disease that had infected Puerto Morada, and perhaps his love for her was dying, too.

The dusty street on which the appliance store was situated ran in back of the movie theater and the Hotel Circo del Mar, and from the inland side of the street Esteban could see the bell towers of Santa María del Onda rising above the hotel roof like the horns of a great stone snail. As a young man, obeying his mother's wish that he become a priest, he had spent three years cloistered beneath those towers, preparing for the seminary under the tutelage of old Father Gonsalvo. It was the part of his life he most regretted, because the academic disciplines he had mastered seemed to have stranded him between the world of the Indian and that of contemporary society; in his heart he held to his father's teachings—the principles of magic, the history of the tribe, the lore of nature—and yet he could never escape the feeling that such wisdom was either superstitious or simply unimportant. The shadows of the towers lay upon his soul as surely as they did upon the cobbled square in front of the church, and the sight of them caused him to pick up his pace and lower his eyes.

Farther along the street was the Cantina Atómica, a gathering place for the well-to-do youth of the town, and across from it was the appliance store, a one-story building of yellow stucco with corrugated metal doors that were lowered at night. Its facade was decorated by a mural that supposedly represented the merchandise within: sparkling refrigerators and televisions and washing machines, all given the impression of enormity by the tiny men and women painted below them, their hands upflung in awe. The actual merchandise was much less imposing, consisting mainly of radios and used kitchen equipment. Few people in Puerto Morada could afford more, and those who could generally bought elsewhere.

The majority of Onofrio's clientele were poor, hard-pressed to meet his schedule of payments, and to a large degree his wealth derived from selling repossessed appliances over and over.

Raimundo Esteves, a pale young man with puffy cheeks and heavily lidded eyes and a petulant mouth, was leaning against the counter when Esteban entered; Raimundo smirked and let out a piercing whistle, and a few seconds later his father emerged from the back room: a huge slug of a man, even paler than Raimundo. Filaments of gray hair were slicked down across his mottled scalp, and his belly stretched the front of a starched *guayabera.* He beamed and extended a hand.

"How good to see you;" he said. "Raimundo! Bring us coffee and two chairs."

Much as he disliked Onofrio, Esteban was in no position to be uncivil: he accepted the handshake. Raimundo spilled coffee in the saucers and clattered the chairs and glowered, angry at being forced to serve an Indian.

"Why will you not let me return the television?" asked Esteban after taking a seat; and then, unable to bite back the words, he added, "Is it no longer your policy to swindle my people?"

Onofrio sighed, as if it were exhausting to explain things to a fool such as Esteban. "I do not swindle your people. I go beyond the letter of the contracts in allowing them to make returns rather than pursuing matters through the courts. In your case, however, I have devised a way whereby you can keep the television without any further payments and yet settle the account. Is this a swindle?"

It was pointless to argue with a man whose logic was as facile and self-serving as Onofrio's. "Tell me what you want," said Esteban.

Onofrio wetted his lips, which were the color of raw sausage. "I want you to kill the jaguar of Barrio Carolina."

"I no longer hunt," said Esteban.

"The Indian is afraid," said Raimundo, moving up behind Onofrio's shoulder. "I told you."

Onofrio waved him away and said to Esteban, "That is unreasonable. If I take the cows, you will once again be hunting jaguars. But if you do this, you will have to hunt only one jaguar."

"One that has killed eight hunters," Esteban set down his coffee cup and stood. "It is no ordinary jaguar."

Raimundo laughed disparagingly, and Esteban skewered him with a stare.

"Ah!" said Onofrio, smiling a flatterer's smile. "But none of the eight used your method."

"Your pardon, Don Onofrio," said Esteban with mock formality. "I have other business to attend."

"I will pay you five hundred *lempira* in addition to erasing the debt," said Onofrio.

"Why?" asked Esteban. "Forgive me, but I cannot believe it is due to a concern for the public welfare."

Onofrio's fat throat pulsed, his face darkened.

"Never mind," said Esteban. "It is not enough."

"Very well. A thousand." Onofrio's casual manner could not conceal the anxiety in his voice.

Intrigued, curious to learn the extent of Onofrio's anxiety, Esteban plucked a figure from the air. "Ten thousand," he said. "And in advance."

"Ridiculous! I could hire ten hunters for this much! Twenty!"

Esteban shrugged. "But none with my method."

For a moment Onofrio sat with hands enlaced, twisting them, as if struggling with some pious conception. "All right," he said, the words squeezed out of him. "Ten thousand!"

The reason for Onofrio's interest in Barrio Carolina suddenly dawned on Esteban, and he understood that the profits involved would make his fee seem pitifully small. But he was possessed by the thought of what ten thousand *lempira* could mean: a herd of cows, a small truck to haul produce, or—and as he thought it, he realized this was the happiest possibility—the little stucco house in Barrio Clarín that Encarnación had set her heart on. Perhaps owning it would soften her toward him. He noticed Raimundo staring at him, his expression a knowing smirk; and even Onofrio, though still outraged by the fee, was beginning to show signs of satisfaction, adjusting the fit of his *guayabera*, slicking down his already-slicked-down hair. Esteban felt debased by their capacity to buy him, and to preserve a last shred of dignity, he turned and walked to the door.

"I will consider it," he tossed back over his shoulder. "And I will give you my answer in the morning."

▲▼▲

Murder Squad of New York, starring a bald American actor, was the featured attraction on Encarnación's television that night, and the widows sat cross-legged on the floor, filling the hut so completely that the charcoal stove and the sleeping hammock had been moved outside in order to provide good viewing angles for the latecomers. To

Esteban, standing in the doorway, it seemed his home had been invaded by a covey of large black birds with cowled heads, who were receiving evil instruction from the core of a flickering gray jewel. Reluctantly, he pushed between them and made his way to the shelves mounted on the wall behind the set; he reached up to the top shelf and pulled down a long bundle wrapped in oilstained newspapers. Out of the corner of his eye, he saw Encarnación watching him, her lips thinned, curved in a smile, and that cicatrix of a smile branded its mark on Esteban's heart. She knew what he was about, and she was delighted! Not in the least worried! Perhaps she had known of Onofrio's plan to kill the jaguar, perhaps she had schemed with Onofrio to entrap him. Infuriated, he barged through the widows, setting them to gabbling, and walked out into his banana grove and sat on a stone amidst it. The night was cloudy, and only a handful of stars showed between the tattered dark shapes of the leaves; the wind sent the leaves slithering together, and he heard one of his cows snorting and smelled the ripe odor of the corral. It was as if the solidity of his life had been reduced to this isolated perspective, and he bitterly felt the isolation. Though he would admit to fault in the marriage, he could think of nothing he had done that could have bred Encarnación's hateful smile.

After a while, he unwrapped the bundle of newspapers and drew out a thin-bladed machete of the sort used to chop banana stalks, but which he used to kill jaguars. Just holding it renewed his confidence and gave him a feeling of strength. It had been four years since he had hunted, yet he knew he had not lost the skill. Once he had been proclaimed the greatest hunter in the province of Nueva Esperanza, as had his father before him, and he had not retired from hunting because of age or infirmity, but because the jaguars were beautiful, and their beauty had begun to outweigh the reasons he had for killing them. He had no better reason to kill the jaguar of Barrio Carolina. It menaced no one other than those who hunted it, who sought to invade its territory, and its death would profit only a dishonorable man and a shrewish wife, and would spread the contamination of Puerto Morada. And besides, it was a black jaguar.

"Black jaguars," his father had told him, "are creatures of the moon. They have other forms and magical purposes with which we must not interfere. Never hunt them!"

His father had not said that the black jaguars lived on the moon, simply that they utilized its power; but as a child, Esteban had dreamed about a moon of ivory forests and silver meadows through which the jaguars flowed as swiftly as black water; and when he had told his father of the dreams, his father had said that such dreams were representations of a truth, and that sooner or later he would discover the truth underlying them. Esteban had never stopped believing in the dreams, not even in face of the rocky, airless place depicted by the science programs on Encarnación's television: that moon, its mystery explained, was merely a less enlightening kind of dream, a statement of fact that reduced reality to the knowable.

But as he thought this, Esteban suddenly realized that killing the jaguar might be the solution to his problems; that by going against his father's teaching, that by killing his dreams, his Indian conception of the world, he might be able to find accord with his wife's; he had been standing halfway between the two conceptions for too long, and it was time for him to choose. And there was no real choice. It was this world he inhabited, not that of the jaguars; if it took the death of a magical creature to permit him to embrace as joys the television and trips to the movies and a stucco house in Barrio Clarín, well, he had faith in this method. He swung the machete, slicing the dark air, and laughed. Encarnación's frivolousness, his skill at hunting, Onofrio's greed, the jaguar, the television...all these things were neatly woven together like the elements of a spell, one whose products would be a denial of magic and a furthering of the unmagical doctrines that had corrupted Puerto Morada. He laughed again, but a second later he chided himself: it was exactly this sort of thinking he was preparing to root out.

Esteban waked Encarnación early the next morning and forced her to accompany him to the appliance store. His machete swung by his side in a leather sheath, and he carried a burlap sack containing food and the herbs he would need for the hunt. Encarnación trotted along beside him, silent, her face hidden by a shawl. When they reached the store, Esteban had Onofrio stamp the bill PAID IN FULL, then he handed the bill and the money to Encarnación.

"If I kill the jaguar or if it kills me," he said harshly, "this will be yours. Should I fail to return within a week, you may assume that I will never return."

She retreated a step, her face registering alarm, as if she had seen him in a new light and understood the consequences of her actions; but she made no move to stop him as he walked out the door.

Across the street, Raimundo Esteves was leaning against the wall of the Cantina Atómica, talking to two girls wearing jeans and frilly blouses; the girls were fluttering their hands and dancing to the music that issued from the cantina, and to Esteban they seemed more alien than the creature he was to hunt. Raimundo spotted him and whispered to the girls; they peeked over their shoulders and laughed. Already angry at Encarnación, Esteban was washed over by a cold fury. He crossed the street to them, rested his hand on the hilt of the machete, and stared at Raimundo; he had never before noticed how soft he was, how empty of presence. A crop of pimples straggled along his jaw, the flesh beneath his eyes was pocked by tiny indentations like those made by a silver-smith's hammer, and, unequal to the stare, his eyes darted back and forth between the two girls.

Esteban's anger dissolved into revulsion. "I am Esteban Caax," he said. "I have built my own house, tilled my soil, and brought four children into the world. This day I am going to hunt the jaguar of Barrio Carolina in order to make you and your father even fatter than you are." He ran his gaze up and down Raimundo's body, and, letting his voice fill with disgust, he asked, "Who are you?"

Raimundo's puffy face cinched in a knot of hatred, but he offered no response. The girls tittered and skipped through the door of the cantina; Esteban could hear them describing the incident, laughter, and he continued to stare at Raimundo. Several other girls poked their heads out the door, giggling and whispering. After a moment Esteban spun on his heel and walked away. Behind him there was a chorus of unrestrained laughter, and a girl's voice called mockingly, "Raimundo! Who are you?" Other voices joined in, and it soon became a chant.

▲▼▲

Barrio Carolina was not truly a barrio of Puerto Morada; it lay beyond Punta Manabique, the southernmost enclosure of the bay, and was fronted by a palm hammock and the loveliest stretch of beach in all the province, a curving slice of white sand giving way to jade-green shallows. Forty years before, it had been the headquarters of the fruit company's experimental farm, a project of such vast scope that a small town had been built on the site: rows of white frame houses with shingle roofs and screen porches, the kind you might see in a magazine illustration of rural America. The company had touted the project as being the keystone of the country's future and had promised to develop high-yield crops that would banish starvation; but in 1947 a cholera epidemic had ravaged the coast and the town had been abandoned. By the time the cholera scare had died down, the company had become well entrenched in national politics and no longer needed to maintain a benevolent image; the project had been dropped and the property abandoned until—in the same year that Esteban had retired from hunting—developers had bought it, planning to build a major resort. It was then the jaguar had appeared. Though it had not killed any of the workmen, it had terrorized them to the point that they had refused to begin the job. Hunters had been sent, and these the jaguar had killed. The last party of hunters had been equipped with automatic rifles, all manner of technological aids; but the jaguar had picked them off one by one, and this project, too, had been abandoned. Rumor had it that the land had recently been resold (now Esteban knew to whom), and that the idea of a resort was once more under consideration.

The walk from Puerto Morada was hot and tiring, and upon arrival Esteban sat beneath a palm and ate a lunch of cold banana fritters. Combers as white as toothpaste broke on the shore, and there was no human litter, just dead fronds and driftwood and coconuts. All but four of the houses had been swallowed by the jungle, and only sections of those four remained visible, embedded like moldering gates in a blackish green wall of vegetation. Even under the bright sunlight, they were haunted-looking: their screens ripped, boards weathered gray, vines cascading over their facades. A mango tree had sprouted from one of the porches, and wild parrots were eating its fruit. He had not visited the barrio since childhood: the ruins had frightened him then, but now he found them appealing, testifying to the dominion of natural law. It distressed him that he would help transform it all into a place where the parrots would be chained to perches and the jaguars would be designs on tablecloths, a place of swimming pools and tourists sipping from coconut shells. Nonetheless, after he had finished lunch, he set out to explore the jungle and soon discovered a trail used by the jaguar: a narrow path that wound between the vine-matted shells of the houses for about a half mile and ended at the Rio Dulce. The river was a murkier green than the sea, curving away through the jungle walls; the jaguar's tracks were everywhere along the bank, especially thick upon a tussocky rise some five or six feet above the water. This baffled Esteban. The jaguar could not drink from the rise, and it certainly would not sleep there. He puzzled over it awhile, but eventually shrugged it off, returned to the beach, and, because he planned to keep watch that night, took a nap beneath the palms.

Some hours later, around midafternoon, he was started from his nap by a voice hailing him. A tall, slim, copper-skinned woman was walking toward him, wearing a dress of dark green—almost the exact color of the jungle walls—that exposed the swell of her breasts. As she drew near, he saw that though her features had a Patucan cast, they were of a lapidary fineness uncommon to the tribe; it was as if they had been refined into a lovely mask: cheeks planed into subtle hollows, lips sculpted full, stylized feathers of ebony inlaid for eyebrows, eyes of jet and white onyx, and all this given a human gloss. A sheen of sweat covered her breasts, and a single curl of black hair lay over her collarbone, so artful-seeming it appeared to have been placed there by design. She knelt beside him, gazing at him impassively, and Esteban was flustered by her heated air of sensuality. The sea breeze bore her scent to him, a sweet musk that reminded him of mangoes left ripening in the sun.

"My name is Esteban Caax," he said, painfully aware of his own sweaty odor.

"I have heard of you," she said. "The jaguar hunter. Have you come to kill the jaguar of the barrio?"

"Yes," he said, and felt shame at admitting it.

She picked up a handful of sand and watched it sift through her fingers.

"What is your name?" he asked.

"If we become friends, I will tell you my name," she said. "Why must you kill the jaguar?"

He told her about the television set, and then, to his surprise, he found himself describing his problems with Encarnación, explaining how he intended to adapt to her ways. These were not proper subjects to discuss with a stranger, yet he was lured to intimacy; he thought he sensed an affinity between them, and that prompted him to portray his marriage as more dismal than it was, for though he had never once been unfaithful to Encarnación, he would have welcomed the chance to do so now.

"This is a black jaguar," she said. "Surely you know they are not ordinary animals, that they have purposes with which we must not interfere?"

Esteban was startled to hear his father's words from her mouth, but he dismissed it as coincidence and replied, "Perhaps. But they are not mine."

"Truly, they are," she said. "You have simply chosen to ignore them." She scooped up another handful of sand. "How will you do it? You have no gun. Only a machete."

"I have this as well," he said, and from his sack he pulled out a small parcel of herbs and handed it to her.

She opened it and sniffed the contents. "Herbs? Ah! You plan to drug the jaguar."

"Not the jaguar. Myself." He took back the parcel. "The herbs slow the heart and give the body a semblance of death. They induce a trance, but one that can be thrown off at a moment's notice. After I chew them, I will lie down in a place that the jaguar must pass on its nightly hunt. It will think I am dead, but it will not feed unless it is sure that the spirit has left the flesh, and to determine this, it will sit on the body so it can feel the spirit rise up. As soon as it starts to settle, I will throw off the trance and stab it between the ribs. If my hand is steady, it will die instantly."

"And if your hand is unsteady?"

"I have killed nearly fifty jaguars,' he said. "I no longer fear unsteadiness. The method comes down through my family from the Old Patuca, and it has never failed, to my knowledge."

"But a black jaguar—"

"Black or spotted, it makes no difference. Jaguars are creatures of instinct, and one is like another when it comes to feeding."

"Well," she said, "I cannot wish you luck, but neither do I wish you ill." She came to her feet, brushing the sand from her dress.

He wanted to ask her to stay, but pride prevented him, and she laughed as if she knew his mind.

"Perhaps we will talk again, Esteban," she said. "It would be a pity if we did not, for more lies between us than we have spoken of this day."

She walked swiftly down the beach, becoming a diminutive black figure that was rippled away by the heat haze.

▲▼▲

That evening, needing a place from which to keep watch, Esteban pried open the screen door of one of the houses facing the beach and went onto the porch. Chameleons skittered into the corners, and an iguana slithered off a rusted lawn chair sheathed in spiderweb and vanished through a gap in the floor. The interior of the house was dark and forbidding, except for the bathroom, the roof of which was missing, webbed over by vines that admitted a gray-green infusion of twilight. The cracked toilet was full of rainwater and dead insects. Uneasy, Esteban returned to the porch, cleaned the lawn chair, and sat.

Out on the horizon the sea and sky were blending in a haze of silver and gray; the wind had died, and the palms were as still as sculpture; a string of pelicans flying low above the waves seemed to be spelling a sentence of cryptic black syllables. But the eerie beauty of the scene was lost on him. He could not stop thinking of the woman. The memory of her hips rolling beneath the fabric of her dress as she walked away was repeated over and over in his thoughts, and whenever he tried to turn his attention to the matter at hand, the memory became more compelling. He imagined her naked, the play of muscles rippling her haunches, and this so enflamed him that he started to pace, unmindful of the fact that the creaking boards were signaling his presence. He could not understand her effect upon him. Perhaps, he thought, it was her defense of the jaguar, her calling to mind of all he was putting behind him...and then a realization settled over him like an icy shroud.

It was commonly held among the Patuca that a man about to suffer a solitary and unexpected death would be visited by an envoy of death, who—standing in for family and friends—would prepare him to face the event; and Esteban was now very sure that the woman had been such an envoy, that her allure had been specifically designed to attract his soul to its imminent fate. He sat back down in the lawn chair, numb with the realization. Her knowledge of his father's words, the odd flavor of her conversation, her intimation that more lay between them: it all accorded perfectly with the traditional wisdom. The moon rose three-quarters full, silvering the sands of the barrio, and still he sat there, rooted to the spot by his fear of death.

He had been watching the jaguar for several seconds before he registered its presence. It seemed at first that a scrap of night sky had fallen onto the sand and was being blown by a fitful breeze; but soon he saw that it was the jaguar, that it was inching along as if stalking some prey. Then it leaped high into the air, twisting and turning, and began to race up and down the beach: a ribbon of black water flowing across the silver sands. He had never before seen a jaguar at play, and this alone was cause for wonder; but most of all, he wondered at the fact that here were his childhood dreams come to life. He might have been peering out onto a silvery meadow of the moon, spying on one of its magical creatures. His fear was eroded by the sight, and like a child he pressed his nose to the screen, trying not to blink, anxious that he might miss a single moment.

At length the jaguar left off its play and came prowling up the beach toward the jungle. By the set of its ears and the purposeful sway of its walk, Esteban recognized that it was hunting. It stopped beneath a palm about twenty feet from the house, lifted its head, and tested the air. Moonlight frayed down through the fronds, applying liquid gleams to its haunches; its eyes, glinting yellow-green, were like peepholes into a lurid dimension of fire. The jaguar's beauty was heartstopping—the embodiment of a flawless principle—and Esteban, contrasting this beauty with the pallid ugliness of his employer, with the ugly principle that had led to his hiring, doubted that he could ever bring himself to kill it.

All the following day he debated the question. He had hoped the woman would return, because he had rejected the idea that she was death's envoy—that perception, he thought, must have been induced by the mysterious atmosphere of the barrio—and he felt that if she was to argue the jaguar's cause again, he would let himself be persuaded. But she did not put in an appearance, and as he sat upon the beach, watching the evening sun decline through strata of dusky orange and lavender clouds, casting wild glitters over the sea, he understood once more that he had no choice. Whether or not the jaguar was beautiful, whether or not the woman had been on a supernatural errand, he must treat these things as if they had no substance. The point of the hunt had been to deny mysteries of this sort, and he had lost sight of it under the influence of old dreams.

He waited until moonrise to take the herbs, and then lay down beneath the palm tree where the jaguar had paused the previous night. Lizards whispered past in the grasses, sand fleas hopped onto his face: he hardly felt them, sinking deeper into the languor of the herbs. The fronds overhead showed an ashen green in the moonlight, lifting, rustling; and the stars between their feathered edges flickered crazily as if the breeze were fanning their flames. He became immersed in the landscape, savoring the smells of brine and rotting foliage that were blowing across the beach, drifting with them; but when he heard the pad of the jaguar's step, he came alert. Through narrowed eyes he saw it sitting a dozen feet away, a bulky shadow craning its neck toward him, investigating his scent. After a moment it began to circle him, each circle a bit tighter than the one before, and whenever it passed out of view he had to repress a trickle of fear. Then, as it passed close on the seaward side, he caught a whiff of its odor.

A sweet, musky odor that reminded him of mangoes left ripening in the sun.

Fear welled up in him, and he tried to banish it, to tell himself that the odor could not possibly be what he thought. The jaguar snarled, a razor stroke of sound that slit the peaceful mesh of wind and surf, and realizing it had scented his fear, he sprang to his feet, waving his machete. In a whirl of vision he saw the jaguar leap back, then he shouted at it, waved the machete again, and sprinted for the house where he had kept watch. He slipped through the door and went staggering into the front room. There was a crash behind him, and turning, he had a glimpse of a huge black shape struggling to extricate itself from a moonlit tangle of vines and ripped screen. He darted into the bathroom, sat with his back against the toilet bowl, and braced the door shut with his feet.

The sound of the jaguar's struggles subsided, and for a moment he thought it had given up. Sweat left cold trails down his sides, his heart pounded. He held his breath, listening, and it seemed the whole world was holding its breath as well. The noises of wind and surf and insects were a faint seething; moonlight shed a sickly white radiance through the enlaced vines overhead, and a chameleon was frozen among peels of wallpaper beside the door. He let out a sigh and wiped the sweat from his eyes. He swallowed.

Then the top panel of the door exploded, shattered by a black paw. Splinters of rotten wood flew into his face, and he screamed. The sleek wedge of the jaguar's head thrust through the hole, roaring. A gateway of gleaming fangs guarding a plush red throat. Half-paralyzed, Esteban jabbed weakly with the machete. The jaguar withdrew, reached in with its paw, and clawed at his leg. More by accident than design, he managed to slice the jaguar, and the paw, too, was withdrawn. He heard it rumbling in the front room, and then, seconds later, a heavy thump against the wall behind him. The jaguar's head appeared above the edge of the wall; it was hanging by its forepaws, trying to gain a perch from which to leap down into the room. Esteban scrambled to his feet and slashed wildly, severing vines. The jaguar fell back, yowling. For a while it prowled along the wall, fuming to itself. Finally there was silence.

When sunlight began to filter through the vines, Esteban walked out of the house and headed down the beach to Puerto Morada. He went with his head lowered, desolate, thinking of the grim future that awaited him after he returned the money to Onofrio: a life of trying to please an increasingly shrewish Encarnación, of killing lesser jaguars for much less money. He was so mired in depression that he did not notice the woman until she called to him. She was leaning against a palm about thirty feet away, wearing a filmy white dress through which he could see the dark jut of her nipples. He drew his machete and backed off a pace.

"Why do you fear me, Esteban?" she called, walking toward him.

"You tricked me into revealing my method and tried to kill me," he said. "Is that not reason for fear?"

"I did not know you or your method in that form. I knew only that you were hunting me. But now the hunt has ended, and we can be as man and woman."

He kept his machete at point. "What are you?" he asked.

She smiled. "My name is Miranda. I am Patuca."

"Patucas do not have black fur and fangs."

"I am of the Old Patuca," she said. "We have this power."

"Keep away!" He lifted the machete as if to strike, and she stopped just beyond his reach.

"You can kill me if that is your wish, Esteban." She spread her arms, and her breasts thrust forward against the fabric of her dress. "You are stronger than I, now. But listen to me first."

He did not lower the machete, but his fear and anger were being overridden by a sweeter emotion.

"Long ago," she said, "there was a great healer who foresaw that one day the Patuca would lose their place in the world, and so, with the help of the gods, he opened a door into another world where the tribe could flourish. But many of the tribe were afraid and would not follow him. Since then, the door has been left open for those who would come after." She waved at the ruined houses. "Barrio Carolina is the site of the door, and the jaguar is its guardian. But soon the fevers of this world will sweep over the barrio, and the door will close forever. For though our hunt has ended, there is no end to hunters or to greed." She came a step nearer. "If you listen to the sounding of your heart, you will know this is the truth."

He half believed her, yet he also believed her words masked a more poignant truth, one that fitted inside the other the way his machete fitted into its sheath.

"What is it?" she asked. "What troubles you?"

"I think you have come to prepare me for death," he said, "and that your door leads only to death."

"Then why do you not run from me?" She pointed toward Puerto Morada. "That is death, Esteban. The cries of the gulls are death, and when the hearts of lovers stop at the moment of greatest pleasure, that, too, is death. This world is no more than a thin covering of life drawn over a foundation of death, like a scum of algae upon a rock. Perhaps you are right, perhaps my world lies beyond death. The two ideas are not opposed. But if I am death to you, Esteban, then it is death you love."

He turned his eyes to the sea, not wanting her to see his face. "I do not love you," he said.

"Love awaits us," she said. "And someday you will join me in my world."

He looked back to her, ready with a denial, but was shocked to silence. Her dress had fallen to the sand, and she was smiling. The litheness and purity of the jaguar were reflected in every line of her body; her secret hair was so absolute a black that it seemed an absence in her flesh. She moved close, pushing aside the machete. The tips of her breasts brushed against him, warm through the coarse cloth of his shirt; her hands cupped his face, and he was drowning in her heated scent, weakened by both fear and desire.

"We are of one soul, you and I," she said. "One blood and one truth. You cannot reject me."

▲▼▲

Days passed, though Esteban was unclear as to how many. Night and day were unimportant incidences of his relationship with Miranda, serving only to color their lovemaking with a spectral or a sunny mood; and each time they made love, it was as if a thousand new colors were being added to his senses. He had never been so content. Sometimes, gazing at the haunted facades of the barrio, he believed that they might well conceal shadowy avenues leading to another world; however, whenever Miranda tried to convince him to leave with her, he refused: he could not overcome his fear and would never admit—even to himself—that he loved her. He attempted to fix his thoughts on Encarnación, hoping this would undermine his fixation with Miranda and free him to return to Puerto Morada; but he found that he could not picture his wife except as a black bird hunched before a flickering gray jewel. Miranda, however, seemed equally unreal at times. Once as they sat on the bank of the Rio Dulce, watching the reflection of the moon—almost full—floating upon the water, she pointed to it and said, "My world is that near, Esteban. That touchable. You may think the moon above is real and this is only a reflection, but the thing most real, that most illustrates the real, is the surface that permits the illusion of reflection. Passing through this surface is what you fear, and yet it is so insubstantial, you would scarcely notice the passage."

"You sound like the old priest who taught me philosophy," said Esteban. "His world—his heaven—was also philosophy. Is that what your world is? The idea of a place? Or are there birds and jungles and rivers?"

Her expression was in partial eclipse, half-moonlit, half-shadowed, and her voice revealed nothing of her mood. "No more than there are here," she said.

"What does that mean?" he said angrily. "Why will you not give me a clear answer?"

"If I were to describe my world, you would simply think me a clever liar." She rested her head on his shoulder. "Sooner or later you will understand. We did not find each other merely to have the pain of being parted."

In that moment her beauty—like her words—seemed a kind of evasion, obscuring a dark and frightening beauty beneath; and yet he knew that she was right, that no proof of hers could persuade him contrary to his fear.

One afternoon, an afternoon of such brightness that it was impossible to look at the sea without squinting, they swam out to a sandbar that showed as a thin curving island of white against the green water. Esteban floundered and splashed, but Miranda swam as if born to the element; she darted beneath him, tickling him, pulling at his feet, eeling away before he could catch her. They walked along the sand, turning over starfish with their toes, collecting whelks to boil for their dinner, and then Esteban spotted a dark stain hundreds of yards wide that was moving below the water beyond the bar: a great school of king mackerel.

"It is too bad we have no boat," he said. "Mackerel would taste better than whelks."

"We need no boat," she said. "I will show you an old way of catching fish."

She traced a complicated design in the sand, and when she had done, she led him into the shallows and had him stand facing her a few feet away.

"Look down at the water between us," she said. "Do not look up, and keep perfectly still until I tell you."

She began to sing with a faltering rhythm, a rhythm that put him in mind of the ragged breezes of the season. Most of the words were unfamiliar, but others he recognized as Patuca. After a minute he experienced a wave of dizziness, as if his legs had grown long and spindly, and he was now looking down from a great height, breathing rarefied air. Then a tiny dark stain materialized below the expanse of water between him and Miranda. He remembered his grandfather's stories of the Old Patuca, how—with the help of the gods—they had been able to shrink the world, to bring enemies close and cross vast distances in a matter of moments. But the gods were dead, their powers gone from the world. He wanted to glance back to shore and see if he and Miranda had become coppery giants taller than the palms.

"Now," she said, breaking off her song, "you must put your hand into the water on the seaward side of the school and gently wiggle your fingers. Very gently! Be sure not to disturb the surface."

But when Esteban made to do as he was told, he slipped and caused a splash. Miranda cried out. Looking up, he saw a wall of jade-green water bearing down on them, its face thickly studded with the fleeting dark shapes of the mackerel. Before he could move, the wave swept over the sandbar and carried him under, dragging him along the bottom and finally casting him onto shore. The beach was littered with flopping mackerel; Miranda lay in the shallows, laughing at him. Esteban laughed, too, but only to cover up his rekindled fear of this woman who drew upon the powers of dead gods. He had no wish to hear her explanation; he was certain she would tell him that the gods lived on in her world, and this would only confuse him further.

Later that day as Esteban was cleaning the fish, while Miranda was off picking bananas to cook with them—the sweet little ones that grew along the riverbank—a Land-Rover came jouncing up the beach from Puerto Morada, an orange fire of the setting sun dancing on its windshield. It pulled up beside him, and Onofrio climbed out the passenger side. A hectic flush dappled his cheeks, and he was dabbing his sweaty brow with a handkerchief. Raimundo climbed out the driver's side and leaned against the door, staring hatefully at Esteban.

"Nine days and not a word," said Onofrio gruffly. "We thought you were dead. How goes the hunt?"

Esteban set down the fish he had been scaling and stood. "I have failed," he said. "I will give you back the money."

Raimundo chuckled—a dull, cluttered sound—and Onofrio grunted with amusement. "Impossible," he said. "Encarnación has spent the money on a house in Barrio Clarín. You must kill the jaguar."

"I cannot," said Esteban. "I will repay you somehow."

"The Indian has lost his nerve, Father." Raimundo spat in the sand. "Let me and my friends hunt the jaguar."

The idea of Raimundo and his loutish friends thrashing through the jungle was so ludicrous that Esteban could not restrain a laugh.

"Be careful, Indian!" Raimundo banged the flat of his hand on the roof of the car.

"It is you who should be careful," said Esteban. "Most likely the jaguar will be hunting you." Esteban picked up his machete. "And whoever hunts this jaguar will answer to me as well."

Raimundo reached for something in the driver's seat and walked around in front of the hood. In his hand was a silvered automatic. "I await your answer," he said.

"Put that away!" Onofrio's tone was that of a man addressing a child whose menace was inconsequential, but the intent surfacing in Raimundo's face was not childish. A tic marred the plump curve of his cheek, the ligature of his neck was cabled, and his lips were drawn back in a joyless grin. It was, thought Esteban—strangely fascinated by the transformation—like watching a demon dissolve its false shape: the true lean features melting up from the illusion of the soft.

"This son of a whore insulted me in front of Julia!" Raimundo's gun hand was shaking.

"Your personal differences can wait," said Onofrio. "This is a business matter." He held out his hand. "Give me the gun."

"If he is not going to kill the jaguar, what use is he?" said Raimundo.

"Perhaps we can convince him to change his mind." Onofrio beamed at Esteban. "What do you say? Shall I let my son collect his debt of honor, or will you fulfill our contract?"

"Father!" complained Raimundo; his eyes flicked sideways. "He—"

Esteban broke for the jungle. The gun roared, a white-hot claw swiped at his side, and he went flying. For an instant he did not know where he was; but then, one by one, his impressions began to sort themselves. He was lying on his injured side, and it was throbbing fiercely. Sand crusted his mouth and eyelids. He was curled up around his machete, which was still clutched in his hand. Voices above him, sand fleas hopping on his face. He resisted the urge to brush them off and lay without moving. The throb of his wound and his hatred had the same red force behind them.

"...carry him to the river," Raimundo was saying, his voice atremble with excitement. "Everyone will think the jaguar killed him!"

"Fool!" said Onofrio. "He might have killed the jaguar, and you could have had a sweeter revenge. His wife—"

"This was sweet enough," said Raimundo.

A shadow fell over Esteban, and he held his breath. He needed no herbs to deceive this pale, flabby jaguar who was bending to him, turning him onto his back.

"Watch out!" cried Onofrio.

Esteban let himself be turned and lashed out with the machete. His contempt for Onofrio and Encarnación, as well as his hatred of Raimundo, was involved in the blow, and the blade lodged deep in Raimundo's side, grating on bone. Raimundo shrieked and would have fallen, but the blade helped to keep him upright; his hands fluttered around the machete as if he wanted to adjust it to a more comfortable position, and his eyes were wide with disbelief. A shudder vibrated the hilt of the machete—it seemed sensual, the spasm of a spent passion—and Raimundo sank to his knees. Blood spilled from his mouth, adding tragic lines to the corners of his lips. He pitched forward, not falling flat but remaining kneeling, his face pressed into the sand: the attitude of an Arab at prayer.

Esteban wrenched the machete free, fearful of an attack by Onofrio, but the appliance dealer was squirming into the Land-Rover. The engine caught, the wheels spun, and the car lurched off, turning through the edge of the surf and heading for Puerto Morada. An orange dazzle flared on the rear window, as if the spirit who had lured it to the barrio was now harrying it away.

Unsteadily, Esteban got to his feet. He peeled his shirt back from the bullet wound. There was a lot of blood, but it was only a crease. He avoided looking at Raimundo and walked down to the water and stood gazing out at the waves; his thoughts rolled in with them, less thoughts than tidal sweeps of emotion.

It was twilight by the time Miranda returned, her arms full of bananas and wild figs. She had not heard the shot. He told her what had happened as she dressed his wounds with a poultice of herbs and banana leaves. "It will mend," she said of the wound. "But this"—she gestured at Raimundo—" this will not. You must come with me, Esteban. The soldiers will kill you."

"No," he said. "They will come, but they are Patuca...except for the captain, who is a drunkard, a shell of a man. I doubt he will even be notified. They will listen to my story, and we will reach an accommodation. No matter what lies Onofrio tells, his word will not stand against theirs."

"And then?"

"I may have to go to jail for a while, or I may have to leave the province. But I will not be killed."

She sat for a minute without speaking, the whites of her eyes glowing in the half-light. Finally she stood and walked off along the beach.

"Where are you going?" he called.

She turned back. "You speak so casually of losing me...." she began.

"It is not casual!"

"No!" She laughed bitterly. "I suppose not. You are so afraid of life, you call it death and would prefer jail or exile to living it. That is hardly casual." She stared at him, her expression a cypher at that distance. "I will not lose you, Esteban," she said. She walked away again, and this time when he called she did not turn.

▲▼▲

Twilight deepened to dusk, a slow fill of shadow graying the world into negative, and Esteban felt himself graying along with it, his thougths reduced to echoing the dull wash of the receding tide. The dusk lingered, and he had the idea that night would never fall, that the act of violence had driven a nail through the substance of his irresolute life, pinned him forever to this ashen moment and deserted shore. As a child he had been terrified by the possibility of such magical isolations, but now the prospect seemed a consolation for Miranda's absence, a remembrance of her magic. Despite her parting words, he did not think she would be back—there had been sadness and finality in her voice—and this roused in him feelings of both relief and desolation, feelings that set him to pacing up and down the tidal margin of the shore.

The full moon rose, the sands of the barrio burned silver, and shortly thereafter four soldiers came in a jeep from Puerto Morada. They were gnomish copper-skinned men, and their uniforms were the dark blue of the night sky, bearing no device or decoration. Though they were not close friends, he knew them each by name: Sebastian, Amador, Carlito, and Ramón. In their headlights Raimundo's corpse—startlingly pale, the blood on his face dried into intricate whorls—looked like an exotic creature cast up by the sea, and their inspection of it smacked more of curiosity than of a search for evidence. Amador unearthed Raimundo's gun, sighted along it toward the jungle, and asked Ramón how much he thought it was worth.

"Perhaps Onofrio will give you a good price," said Ramón, and the others laughed.

They built a fire of driftwood and coconut shells, and sat around it while Esteban told his story; he did not mention either Miranda or her relation to the jaguar, because these men—estranged from the tribe by their government service—had grown conservative in their judgments, and he did not want them to consider him irrational. They listened without comment; the firelight burnished their skins to reddish gold and glinted on their rifle barrels.

"Onofrio will take his charge to the capital if we do nothing," said Amador after Esteban had finished.

"He may in any case," said Carlito. "And then it will go hard with Esteban."

"And," said Sebastian, "if an agent is sent to Puerto Morada and sees how things are with Captain Portales, they will surely replace him and it will go hard with us."

They stared into the flames, mulling over the problem, and Esteban chose the moment to ask Amador, who lived near him on the mountain, if he had seen Encarnación.

"She will be amazed to learn you are alive," said Amador. "I saw her yesterday in the dressmaker's shop. She was admiring the fit of a new black skirt in the mirror."

It was as if a black swath of Encarnación's skirt had folded around Esteban's thoughts. He lowered his head and carved lines in the sand with the point of his machete.

"I have it," said Ramón. "A boycott!"

The others expressed confusion.

"If we do not buy from Onofrio, who will?" said Ramón. "He will lose his business. Threatened with this, he will not dare involve the government. He will allow Esteban to plead self-defense."

"But Raimundo was his only son," said Amador. "It may be that grief will count more than greed in this instance."

Again they fell silent. It mattered little to Esteban what was decided. He was coming to understand that without Miranda, his future held nothing but uninteresting choices; he turned his gaze to the sky and noticed that the stars and the fire were flickering with the same rhythm, and he imagined each of them ringed by a group of gnomish copper-skinned men, debating the question of his fate.

"Aha!" said Carlito. "I know what to do. We will occupy Barrio Carolina—the entire company—and *we* will kill the jaguar. Onofrio's greed cannot withstand this temptation."

"That you must not do," said Esteban.

"But why?" asked Amador. "We may not kill the jaguar, but with so many men we will certainly drive it away."

Before Esteban could answer, the jaguar roared. It was prowling down the beach toward the fire, like a black flame itself shifting over the glowing sand. Its ears were laid back, and silver drops of moonlight gleamed in its eyes. Amador grabbed his rifle, came to one knee, and fired: the bullet sprayed sand a dozen feet to the left of the jaguar.

"Wait!" cried Esteban, pushing him down.

But the rest had begun to fire, and the jaguar was hit. It leaped high as it had that first night while playing, but this time it landed in a heap, snarling, snapping at its shoulder; it regained its feet and limped toward the jungle, favoring its right foreleg. Excited by their success, the soldiers ran a few paces after it and stopped to fire again. Carlito dropped to one knee, taking careful aim.

"No!" shouted Esteban, and as he hurled his machete at Carlito, desperate to prevent further harm to Miranda, he recognized the trap that had been sprung and the consequences he would face.

The blade sliced across Carlito's thigh, knocking him onto his side. He screamed, and Amador, seeing what had happened, fired wildly at Esteban and called to the others. Esteban ran toward the jungle, making for the jaguar's path. A fusillade of shots rang out behind him, bullets whipped past his ears. Each time his feet slipped in the soft sand, the moonstruck facades of the barrio appeared to lurch sideways as if trying to block his way. And then, as he reached the verge of the jungle, he was hit.

The bullet seemed to throw him forward, to increase his speed, but somehow he managed to keep his feet. He careened along the path, arms waving, breath shrieking in his throat. Palmetto fronds swatted his face, vines tangled his legs. He felt no pain, only a peculiar numbness that pulsed low in his back; he pictured the wound opening and closing like the mouth of an anemone. The soldiers were shouting his name. They would follow, but cautiously, afraid of the jaguar, and he thought he might be able to cross the river before they could catch up. But when he came to the river, he found the jaguar waiting.

It was crouched on the tussocky rise, its neck craned over the water, and below, half a dozen feet from the bank, floated the reflection of the full moon, huge and silvery, an unblemished circle of light. Blood glistened scarlet on the jaguar's shoulder, like a fresh rose pinned in place, and this made it look even more an embodiment of principle: the shape a god might choose, that some universal constant might assume. It gazed calmly at Esteban, growled low in its throat, and dove into the river, cleaving and shattering the moon's reflection, vanishing beneath the surface. The ripples subsided, the image of the moon re-formed. And there, silhouetted against it, Esteban saw the figure of a woman swimming, each stroke causing her to grow smaller and smaller until she seemed no more than a character incised upon a silver plate. It was not only Miranda he saw, but all mystery and beauty receding from him, and he realized how blind he had been not to perceive the truth sheathed inside the truth of death that had been sheathed inside her truth of another world. It was clear to him now. It sang to him from his wound, every syllable a heartbeat. It was written by the dying ripples, it swayed in the banana leaves, it sighed on the wind. It was everywhere, and he had always known it: if you deny mystery—even in the guise of death—then you deny life and you will walk like a ghost through your days, never knowing the secrets of the extremes. The deep sorrows, the absolute joys.

He drew a breath of the rank jungle air, and with it drew a breath of a world no longer his, of the girl Encarnación, of friends and children and country nights...all his lost sweetness. His chest tightened as with the onset of tears, but the sensation quickly abated, and he understood that the sweetness of the past had been subsumed by a scent of mangoes, that nine magical days—a magical number of days, the number it takes to sing the soul to rest—lay between him and tears. Freed of those associations, he felt as if he were undergoing a subtle refinement of form, a winnowing, and he remembered having felt much the same on the day when he had run out the door of Santa María del Onda, putting behind him its dark geometries and cobwebbed catechisms and generations of swallows that had never flown beyond the walls, casting off his acolyte's robe and racing across the square toward the mountain and Encarnación: it had been she who had lured him then, just as his mother had lured him to the church and as Miranda was luring him now, and he laughed at seeing how easily these three women had diverted the flow of his life, how like other men he was in this.

The strange bloom of painlessness in his back was sending out tendrils into his arms and legs, and the cries of the soldiers had grown louder. Miranda was a tiny speck shrinking against a silver immensity. For a moment he hesitated, experiencing a resurgence of fear; then Miranda's face materialized in his mind's eye, and all the emotion he had suppressed for nine days poured through him, washing away the fear. It was a silvery, flawless emotion, and he was giddy with it, light with it; it was like thunder and fire fused into one element and boiling up inside him, and he was overwhelmed by a need to express it, to mold it into a form that would reflect its power and purity. But he was no singer, no poet. There was but a single mode of expression open to him. Hoping he was not too late, that Miranda's door had not shut forever, Esteban dove into the river, cleaving the image of the full moon; and—his eyes still closed from the shock of the splash—with the last of his mortal strength, he swam hard down after her.

R&R

— 1 —

One of the new Sikorsky gunships, an element of the First Air Cavalry with the words *Whispering Death* painted on its side, gave Mingolla and Gilbey and Baylor a lift from the Ant Farm to San Francisco de Juticlan, a small town located inside the green zone, which on the latest maps was designated Free Occupied Guatemala. To the east of this green zone lay an undesignated band of yellow that crossed the country from the Mexican border to the Caribbean. The Ant Farm was a firebase on the eastern edge of the yellow band, and it was from there that Mingolla—an artillery specialist not yet twenty-one years old—lobbed shells into an area that the maps depicted in black-and-white terrain markings. And thus it was that he often thought of himself as engaged in a struggle to keep the world safe for primary colors.

Mingolla and his buddies could have taken their R&R in Rio or Caracas, but they had noticed that the men who visited these cities had a tendency to grow careless upon their return; they understood from this that the more exuberant your R&R, the more likely you were to wind up a casualty, and so they always opted for the lesser distractions of the Guatemalan towns. They were not really friends: they had little in common, and under different circumstances they might well have been enemies. But taking their R&R together had come to be a ritual of survival, and once they had reached the town of their choice, they would go their separate ways and perform further rituals. Because the three had survived so much already, they believed that if they continued to perform these same rituals they would complete their tours unscathed. They had never acknowledged their belief to one another, speaking of it only obliquely—that, too, was part of the ritual—and had this belief been challenged they would have admitted its irrationality; yet they would also have pointed out that the strange character of the war acted to enforce it.

The gunship set down at an airbase a mile west of town, a concrete strip penned in on three sides by barracks and offices, with the jungle rising behind them. At the center of the strip another Sikorsky was practicing takeoffs and landings—a drunken, camouflage-colored dragonfly—and two others were hovering overhead like anxious parents. As Mingolla jumped out, a hot breeze fluttered his shirt. He was wearing civvies for the first time in weeks, and they felt flimsy compared to his combat gear; he glanced around nervously, half-expecting an unseen enemy to take advantage of his exposure. Some mechanics were lounging in the shade of a chopper whose cockpit had been destroyed, leaving fanglike shards of plastic curving from the charred metal. Dusty jeeps trundled back and forth between the buildings; a brace of crisply starched lieutenants were making a brisk beeline toward a forklift stacked high with aluminum coffins. Afternoon sunlight fired dazzles on the seams and handles of the coffins, and through the heat haze the distant line of barracks shifted like waves in a troubled olive-drab sea. The incongruity of the scene—its What's-Wrong-With-This-Picture mix of the horrid and the commonplace—wrenched at Mingolla. His left hand trembled, and the light seemed to grow brighter, making him weak and vague. He leaned against the Sikorsky's rocket pod to steady himself. Far above, contrails were fraying in the deep blue range of the sky: XL-16s off to blow holes in Nicaragua. He stared after them with something akin to longing, listening for their engines, but heard only the spacy whisper of the Sikorskys.

Gilbey hopped down from the hatch that led to the computer deck behind the cockpit; he brushed imaginary dirt from his jeans, sauntered over to Mingolla, and stood with hands on hips: a short muscular kid whose blond crewcut and petulant mouth gave him the look of a grumpy child. Baylor stuck his head out of the hatch and worriedly scanned the horizon. Then he, too, hopped down. He was tall and rawboned, a couple of years older than Mingolla, with lank black hair and pimply olive skin and features so sharp that they appeared to have been hatcheted into shape. He rested a hand on the side of the Sikorsky, but almost instantly, noticing that he was touching the flaming letter *W* in *Whispering Death,* he jerked the hand away as if he'd been scorched. Three days before there had been an all-out assault on the Ant Farm, and Baylor had not recovered from it. Neither had Mingolla. It was hard to tell whether or not Gilbey had been affected.

One of the Sikorskys pilots cracked the cockpit door. "Y'all can catch a ride into 'Frisco at the PX," he said, his voice muffled by the black bubble of his visor. The sun shined a white blaze on the visor, making it seem that the helmet contained night and a single star.

"Where's the PX?" asked Gilbey.

The pilot said something too muffled to be understood.

"What?" said Gilbey.

Again the pilot's response was muffled, and Gilbey became angry. "Take that damn thing off?" he said.

"This?" The pilot pointed to his visor. "What for?"

"So I can hear what the hell you sayin'."

"You can hear now, can'tcha?"

"Okay," said Gilbey, his voice tight. "Where's the goddamn PX?"

The pilot's reply was unintelligible; his faceless mask regarded Gilbey with inscrutable intent.

Gilbey balled up his fists. "Take that son of a bitch off?"

"Can't do it, soldier," said the second pilot, leaning over so that the two black bubbles were nearly side by side. "These here doobies"—he tapped his visor—"they got microcircuits that beams shit into our eyes. 'Fects the optic nerve. Makes it so we can see the beaners even when they undercover. Longer we wear 'em, the better we see."

Baylor laughed edgily, and Gilbey said, "Bullshit!" Mingolla naturally assumed that the pilots were putting Gilbey on, or else their reluctance to remove the helmets stemmed from a superstition, perhaps from a deluded belief, that the visors actually did bestow special powers. But given a war in which combat drugs were issued and psychics predicted enemy movements, anything was possible, even microcircuits that enhanced vision.

"You don't wanna see us, nohow," said the first pilot. "The beams fuck up our faces. We're deformed-lookin' mothers."

"Course you might not notice the changes," said the second pilot. "Lotsa people don't. But if you did, it'd mess you up."

Imagining the pilots' deformities sent a sick chill mounting from Mingolla's stomach. Gilbey, however, wasn't buying it. "You think I'm stupid?" he shouted, his neck reddening.

"Naw," said the first pilot. "We can *see* you ain't stupid. We can see lotsa shit other people can't, 'cause of the beams."

"All kindsa weird stuff," chipped in the second pilot. "Like souls."

"Ghosts."

"Even the future."

"The future's our best thing," said the first pilot. "You guys wanna know what's ahead, we'll tell you."

They nodded in unison, the blaze of sunlight sliding across both visors: two evil robots responding to the same program.

Gilbey lunged for the cockpit door. The first pilot slammed it shut, and Gilbey pounded on the plastic, screaming curses. The second pilot flipped a switch on the control console, and a moment later his amplified voice boomed out: "Make straight past that forklift 'til you hit the barracks. You'll run right into the PX."

It took both Mingolla and Baylor to drag Gilbey away from the Sikorsky, and he didn't stop shouting until they drew near the forklift with its load of coffins: a giant's treasure of enormous silver ingots. Then he grew silent and lowered his eyes. They wangled a ride with an MP corporal outside the PX, and as the jeep hummed across the concrete, Mingolla glanced over at the Sikorsky that had transported them. The two pilots had spread a canvas on the ground, had stripped to shorts and were sunning themselves. But they had not removed their helmets. The weird juxtaposition of tanned bodies and shiny black heads disturbed Mingolla, reminding him of an old movie in which a guy had gone through a matter transmitter along with a fly and had ended up with the fly's head on his shoulders. Maybe, he thought, the helmets were like that, impossible to remove. Maybe the war had gotten that strange.

The MP corporal noticed him watching the pilots and let out a barking laugh. "Those guys," he said, with the flat emphatic tone of a man who knew whereof he spoke, "are fuckin' nuts!"

▲▼▲

Six years before, San Francisco de Juticlan had been a scatter of thatched huts and concrete block structures deployed among palms and banana leaves on the east bank of the Rio Dulce, at the junction of the river and a gravel road that connected with the Pan American Highway; but it had since grown to occupy substantial sections of both banks, increased by dozens of bars and brothels: stucco cubes painted all the colors of the rainbow, with a fantastic bestiary of neon signs mounted atop their tin roofs. Dragons; unicorns; fiery birds; centaurs. The MP corporal told Mingolla that the signs were not advertisements but coded symbols of pride; for example, from the representation of a winged red tiger crouched amidst green lilies and blue crosses, you could deduce that the owner was wealthy, a member of a Catholic secret society, and ambivalent toward government policies. Old signs were constantly being dismantled, and larger, more ornate ones erected in their stead as testament to improved profits, and this warfare of light and image was appropriate to the time and place because San Francisco de Juticlan was less a town than a symptom of war. Though by night the sky above it was radiant, at ground level it was mean and squalid. Pariah dogs foraged in piles of garbage, hard-bitten whores spat from the windows, and according to the corporal, it was not unusual to stumble across a corpse, likely a victim of the gangs of abandoned children who lived in the fringes of the jungle. Narrow streets of tawny dirt cut between the bars, carpeted with a litter of flattened cans and feces and broken glass; refugees begged at every corner, displaying burns and bullet wounds. Many of the buildings had been thrown up with such haste that their walls were tilted, their roofs canted, and this made the shadows they cast appear exaggerated in their jaggedness, like shadows in the work of a psychotic artist, giving visual expression to a pervasive undercurrent of tension. Yet as Mingolla moved along, he felt at ease, almost happy. His mood was due in part to his hunch that it was going to be one hell of an R&R (he had learned to trust his hunches); but it mainly spoke to the fact that towns like this had become for him a kind of afterlife, a reward for having endured a harsh term of existence.

The corporal dropped them off at a drugstore, where Mingolla bought a box of stationery, and then they stopped for a drink at the Club Demonio: a tiny place whose whitewashed walls were shined to faint phosphorescence by the glare of purple light bulbs dangling from the ceiling like radioactive fruit. The club was packed with soldiers and whores, most sitting at tables around a dance floor not much bigger than a king-size mattress. Two couples were swaying to a ballad that welled from a jukebox encaged in chicken wire and two-by-fours; veils of cigarette smoke drifted with underwater slowness above their heads. Some of the soldiers were mauling their whores, and one whore was trying to steal the wallet of a soldier who was on the verge of passing out; her hand worked between his legs, encouraging him to thrust his hips forward, and when he did this, she pried with her other hand at the wallet stuck in the back pocket of his tight-fitting jeans. But all the action seemed listless, halfhearted, as if the dimness and syrupy music had thickened the air and were hampering movement. Mingolla took a seat at the bar. The bartender glanced at him inquiringly, his pupils becoming cored with purple reflections, and Mingolla said, "Beer."

"Hey, check that out!" Gilbey slid onto an adjoining stool and jerked his thumb toward a whore at the end of the bar. Her skirt was hiked to midthigh, and her breasts, judging by their fullness and lack of sag, were likely the product of elective surgery.

"Nice," said Mingolla, disinterested. The bartender set a bottle of beer in front of him, and he had a swig; it tasted sour, watery, like a distillation of the stale air.

Baylor slumped onto the stool next to Gilbey and buried his face in his hands. Gilbey said something to him that Mingolla didn't catch, and Baylor lifted his head. "I ain't goin' back," he said.

"Aw, Jesus!" said Gilbey. "Don't start that crap."

In the half-dark Baylor's eye sockets were clotted with shadows. His stare locked onto Mingolla. "They'll get us next time," he said. "We should head downriver. They got boats in Livingston that'll take you to Panama."

"Panama!" sneered Gilbey. "Nothin' there 'cept more beaners."

"We'll be okay at the Farm," offered Mingolla. "Things get too heavy, they'll pull us back."

"'Too heavy'?" A vein throbbed in Baylor's temple. "What the fuck you call 'too heavy'?"

"Screw this!" Gilbey heaved up from his stool. "You deal with him, man," he said to Mingolla; he gestured at the big-breasted whore. "I'm gonna climb Mount Silicon."

"Nine o'clock," said Mingolla. "The PX. Okay?"

Gilbey said, "Yeah," and moved off. Baylor took over his stool and leaned close to Mingolla. "You *know* I'm right," he said in an urgent whisper. "They almost got us this time."

"Air Cav'll handle 'em," said Mingolla, affecting nonchalance. He opened the box of stationery and unclipped a pen from his shirt pocket.

"You *know* I'm right," Baylor repeated.

Mingolla tapped the pen against his lips, pretending to be distracted.

"Air Cav!" said Baylor with a despairing laugh. "Air Cav ain't gonna do squat!"

"Why don't you put on some decent tunes?" Mingolla suggested. "See if they got any Prowler on the box."

"Dammit!" Baylor grabbed his wrist. "Don't you understand, man? This shit ain't workin' no more!"

Mingolla shook him off. "Maybe you need some change," he said coldly; he dug out a handful of coins and tossed them on the counter. "There! There's some change."

"I'm tellin' you…."

"I don't wanna hear it!" snapped Mingolla.

"You don't wanna hear it?" said Baylor, incredulous. He was on the verge of losing control. His dark face slick with sweat, one eyelid fluttering. He pounded the countertop for emphasis. "Man, you better hear it! Cause we don't pull somethin' together soon, *real* soon, we're gonna fuckin' die! You hear that, don'tcha?"

Mingolla caught him by the shirtfront. "Shut up!"

"I ain't shuttin' up!" Baylor shrilled. "You and Gilbey, man, you think you can save your ass by stickin' your head in the sand. But I'm gonna make you listen." He threw back his head, his voice rose to a shout. "We're gonna die!"

The way he shouted it—almost gleefully, like a kid yelling a dirty word to spite his parents—pissed Mingolla off. He was sick of Baylor's scenes. Without planning it, he hit him, pulling the punch at the last instant. Kept a hold of his shirt and clipped him on the jaw, just enough to rock back his head. Baylor blinked at him, stunned, his mouth open. Blood seeped from his gums. At the opposite end of the counter, the bartender was leaning beside a choirlike arrangement of liquor bottles, watching Mingolla and Baylor, and some of the soldiers were watching, too: they looked pleased, as if they had been hoping for a spot of violence to liven things up. Mingolla felt debased by their attentiveness, ashamed of his bullying. "Hey, I'm sorry, man," he said. "I—"

"I don't give a shit 'bout you're sorry," said Baylor, rubbing his mouth. "Don't give a shit 'bout nothin' 'cept gettin' the hell outta here."

"Leave it alone, all right?"

But Baylor wouldn't leave it alone. He continued to argue, adopting the long-suffering tone of someone carrying on bravely in the face of great injustice. Mingolla tried to ignore him by studying the label on his beer bottle: a red and black graphic portraying a Guatemalan soldier, his rifle upheld in victory. It was an attractive design, putting him in mind of the poster work he had done before being drafted; but considering the unreliability of Guatemalan troops, he perceived the heroic pose as a bad joke. Mingolla gouged a trench through the center of the label with his thumbnail.

At last Baylor gave it up and sat staring down at the warped veneer of the counter. Mingolla let him sit a minute; then, without shifting his gaze from the bottle, he said, "Why don't you put on some decent tunes?"

Baylor tucked his chin onto his chest, maintaining a stubborn silence.

"It's your only option, man," Mingolla went on. "What else you gonna do?"

"You're crazy," said Baylor; he flicked his eyes toward Mingolla and hissed it like a curse. "Crazy!"

"You gonna take off for Panama by yourself? Un-unh. You know the three of us got something going. We come this far together, and if you just hang tough, we'll go home together."

"I don't know," said Baylor. "I don't know anymore."

"Look at it this way," said Mingolla. "Maybe we're all three of us right. Maybe Panama is the answer, but the time just isn't ripe. If that's true, me and Gilbey will see it sooner or later."

With a heavy sigh, Baylor got to his feet. "You ain't never gonna see it, man," he said dejectedly.

Mingolla had a swallow of beer. "Check if they got any Prowler on the box. I could relate to some Prowler."

Baylor stood for a moment, indecisive. He started for the jukebox, then veered toward the door. Mingolla tensed, preparing to run after him. But Baylor stopped and walked back over to the bar. Lines of strain were etched deep in his forehead. "Okay," he said, a catch in his voice. "Okay. What time tomorrow? Nine o'clock?"

"Right," said Mingolla, turning away. "The PX."

Out of the corner of his eye he saw Baylor cross the room and bend over the jukebox to inspect the selections. He felt relieved. This was the way all their R&Rs had begun, with Gilbey chasing a whore and Baylor feeding the jukebox while he wrote a letter home. On their first R&R he had written his parents about the war and its bizarre forms of attrition; then, realizing that the letter would alarm his mother, he had torn it up and written another, saying merely that he was fine. He would tear this letter up as well, but he wondered how his father would react if he were to read it. Most likely with anger. His father was a firm believer in God and country, and though Mingolla understood the futility of adhering to any moral code in light of the insanity around him, he had found that something of his father's tenets had been ingrained in him: he would never be able to desert as Baylor kept insisting. He knew it wasn't that simple, that other factors, too, were responsible for his devotion to duty; but since his father would have been happy to accept the responsibility, Mingolla tended to blame it on him. He tried to picture what his parents were doing at that moment—father watching the Mets on TV, mother puttering in the garden—and then, holding those images in mind, he began to write.

> *Dear Mom and Dad,*
>
> *In your last letter you asked if I thought we were winning the war. Down here you'd get a lot of blank stares in response to that question, because most people have a perspective on the war to which the overall result isn't relevant. Like there's a guy I know who has this rap about how the war is a magical operation of immense proportions, how the movements of the planes and troops are inscribing a mystical sign on the surface of reality, and to survive you have to figure out your location within the design and move accordingly. I'm sure that sounds crazy to you, but down here everyone's crazy the same way (some shrink's actually done a study on the incidence of*

> *superstition among the occupation forces). They're looking for a magic that will ensure their survival. You may find it hard to believe that I subscribe to this sort of thing, but I do. I carve my initials on the shell casings, wear parrot feathers inside my helmet...and a lot more.*
>
> *To get back to your question, I'll try to do better than a blank stare, but I can't give you a simple Yes or No. The matter can't be summed up that neatly. But I can illustrate the situation by telling you a story and let you draw your own conclusions. There are hundreds of stories that would do, but the one that comes to mind now concerns the Lost Patrol....*

A Prowler tune blasted from the jukebox, and Mingolla broke off writing to listen: it was a furious, jittery music, fueled—it seemed—by the same aggressive paranoia that had generated the war. People shoved back chairs, overturned tables, and began dancing in the vacated spaces; they were crammed together, able to do no more than shuffle in rhythm, but their tread set the light bulbs jiggling at the end of their cords, the purple glare slopping over the walls. A slim acne-scarred whore came to dance in front of Mingolla, shaking her breasts, holding out her arms to him. Her face was corpse-pale in the unsteady light, her smile a dead leer. Trickling from one eye like some exquisite secretion of death, was a black tear of sweat and mascara. Mingolla couldn't be sure he was seeing her right. His left hand started trembling, and for a couple of seconds the entire scene lost its cohesiveness. Everything looked scattered, unrecognizable, embedded in a separate context from everything else: a welter of meaningless objects bobbing up and down on a tide of deranged music. Then somebody opened the door, admitting a wedge of sunlight, and the room settled back to normal. Scowling, the whore danced away. Mingolla breathed easier. The tremors in his hand subsided. He spotted Baylor near the door talking to a scruffy Guatemalan guy...probably a coke connection. Coke was Baylor's panacea, his remedy for fear and desperation. He always returned from R&R bleary-eyed and prone to nosebleeds, boasting about the great dope he'd scored. Pleased that he was following routine, Mingolla went back to his letter.

> *...Remember me telling you that the Green Berets took drugs to make them better fighters? Most everyone calls the drugs "Sammy," which is short for "samurai." They come in ampule form, and when you pop them*

under your nose, for the next thirty minutes or so you feel like a cross between a Medal of Honor winner and Superman. The trouble is that a lot of Berets overdo them and flip out. They sell them on the black market, too, and some guys use them for sport. They take the ampules and fight each other in pits...like human cockfights.

Anyway, about two years ago a patrol of Berets went on patrol up in Fire Zone Emerald, not far from my base, and they didn't come back. They were listed MIA. A month or so after they'd disappeared, somebody started ripping off ampules from various dispensaries. At first the crimes were chalked up to guerrillas, but then a doctor caught sight of the robbers and said they were Americans. They were wearing rotted fatigues, acting nuts. An artist did a sketch of their leader according to the doctor's description, and it turned out to be a dead ringer for the sergeant of that missing patrol. After that they were sighted all over the place. Some of the sightings were obviously false, but others sounded like the real thing. They were said to have shot down a couple of our choppers and to have knocked over a supply column near Zacapa.

I'd never put much stock in the story, to tell you the truth, but about four months ago this infantryman came walking out of the jungle and reported to the firebase. He claimed he'd been captured by the Lost Patrol, and when I heard his story, I believed him. He said they had told him that they weren't Americans anymore but citizens of the jungle. They lived like animals, sleeping under palm fronds, popping the ampules night and day. They were crazy, but they'd become geniuses at survival. They knew everything about the jungle. When the weather was going to change, what animals were near. And they had this weird religion based on the beams of light that would shine down through the canopy. Theyd sit under those beams, like saints being blessed by God, and rave about the purity of the light, the joys of killing, and the new world they were going to build.

So that's what occurs to me when you ask your question, Mom and Dad. The Lost Patrol. I'm not attempting to be circumspect in order to make a point about the horrors of war. Not at all. When I think about the Lost

Patrol I'm not thinking about how sad and crazy they are. I'm wondering what it is they see in that light, wondering if it might be of help to me. And maybe therein lies your answer....

It was nearly sunset by the time Mingolla left the bar to begin the second part of his ritual, to wander innocent as a tourist through the native quarter, partaking of whatever fell to hand, maybe having dinner with a Guatemalan family, or buddying up with a soldier from another outfit and going to church, or hanging out with some young guys who'd ask him about America. He had done each of these things on previous R&Rs, and his pretense of innocence always amused him. If he were to follow his inner directives, he would burn out the horrors of the firebase with whores and drugs; but on that first R&R—stunned by the experience of combat and needing solitude—a protracted walk had been his course of action, and he was committed not only to repeating it but also to recapturing his dazed mental set: it would not do to half-ass the ritual. In this instance, given recent events at the Ant Farm, he did not have to work very hard to achieve confusion.

The Rio Dulce was a wide blue river, heaving with a light chop. Thick jungle hedged its banks, and yellowish reed beds grew out from both shores. At the spot where the gravel road ended was a concrete pier, and moored to it a barge that served as a ferry; it was already loaded with its full complement of vehicles—two trucks—and carried about thirty pedestrians. Mingolla boarded and stood in the stern beside three infantrymen who were still wearing their combat suits and helmets, holding double-barreled rifles that were connected by flexible tubing to backpack computers; through their smoked faceplates he could see green reflections from the readouts on their visor displays. They made him uneasy, reminding him of the two pilots, and he felt better after they had removed their helmets and proved to have normal human faces. Spanning a third of the way across the river was a sweeping curve of white concrete supported by slender columns, like a piece fallen out of a Dali landscape: a bridge upon which construction had been halted. Mingolla had noticed it from the air just before landing and hadn't thought much about it; but now the sight took him by storm. It seemed less an unfinished bridge than a monument to some exalted ideal, more beautiful than any finished bridge could be. And as he stood rapt, with the ferry's oily smoke farting out around him, he sensed there was an analogue of that beautiful curving shape inside him; that he, too, was a road ending in midair. It gave him confidence to associate himself with such loftiness and purity, and for a moment he let himself believe that he also might have—as the upward-angled terminus of the bridge implied—a point of completion lying far beyond the one anticipated by the architects of his fate.

On the west bank past the town the gravel road was lined with stalls: skeletal frameworks of brushwood poles roofed with palm thatch. Children chased in and out among them, pretending to aim and fire at each other with stalks of sugarcane. But hardly any soldiers were in evidence. The crowds that moved along the road were composed mostly of Indians: young couples too shy to hold hands; old men who looked lost and poked litter with their canes; dumpy matrons who made outraged faces at the high prices; shoeless farmers who kept their backs ramrod-straight and wore grave expressions and carried their money knotted in handkerchiefs. At one of the stalls Mingolla bought a fish sandwich and a Coca-Cola. He sat on a stool and ate contentedly, relishing the hot bread and the spicy meat cooked inside it, watching the passing parade. Gray clouds were bulking up and moving in from the south, from the Caribbean; now and then a flight of XL-16s would arrow northward toward the oil fields beyond Lake Izabal, where the fighting was very bad. Twilight fell. The lights of town began to be picked out sharply against the empurpling air. Guitars were plucked, hoarse voices sang, the crowds thinned. Mingolla ordered another sandwich and Coke. He leaned back, sipped and chewed, steeping himself in the good magic of the land, the sweetness of the moment. Beside the sandwich stall, four old women were squatting by a cooking fire, preparing chicken stew and corn fritters; scraps of black ash drifted up from the flames, and as twilight deepened, it seemed these scraps were the pieces of a jigsaw puzzle that were fitting together overhead into the image of a starless night.

Darkness closed in, the crowds thickened again, and Mingolla continued his walk, strolling past stalls with necklaces of light bulbs strung along their frames, wires leading off them to generators whose rattle drowned out the chirring of frogs and crickets. Stalls selling plastic rosaries, Chinese switchblades, tin lanterns; others selling embroidered Indian shirts, flour-sack trousers, wooden masks; others yet where old men in shabby suit coats sat cross-legged behind pyramids of tomatoes and melons and green peppers, each with a candle cemented in melted wax atop them, like primitive altars. Laughter, shrieks, vendors shouting. Mingolla breathed in perfume, charcoal smoke, the scents of rotting fruit. He began to idle from stall to stall, buying a few souvenirs for friends back in New York, feeling part of the hustle, the noise, the shining black air, and eventually he came to a stall around which forty or fifty people had gathered, blocking all but its thatched roof from view. A woman's amplified voice cried out, *"LA MARIPOSA!"* Excited squeals from the crowd. Again the woman cried out, *"EL CUCHILLO!"* The two words she had called—the butterfly and the knife—intrigued Mingolla, and he peered over heads.

Framed by the thatch and rickety poles, a dusky-skinned young woman was turning a handle that spun a wire cage: it was filled with white plastic cubes, bolted to a plank counter. Her black hair was pulled back from her face, tied behind her neck, and she wore a red sundress that left her shoulders bare. She stopped cranking, reached into the cage, and without looking plucked one of the cubes; she examined it, picked up a microphone and cried, *"LA LUNA!"* A bearded man pushed forward and handed her a card. She checked the card, comparing it with some cubes that were lined up on the counter; then she gave the man a few bills in Guatemalan currency.

The composition of the game appealed to Mingolla. The dark woman; her red dress and cryptic words; the runelike shadow of the wire cage—all this seemed magical, an image out of an occult dream. Part of the crowd moved off, accompanying the winner, and Mingolla let himself be forced closer by new arrivals pressing in from behind. He secured a position at the corner of the stall, fought to maintain it against the eddying of the crowd, and on glancing up, he saw the woman smiling at him from a couple of feet away, holding out a card and a pencil stub. "Only ten cents Guatemalan," she said in American-sounding English.

The people flanking Mingolla urged him to play, grinning and clapping him on the back. But he didn't need urging. He knew he was going to win: it was the clearest premonition he had ever had, and it was signaled mostly by the woman herself. He felt a powerful attraction to her. It was as if she were a source of heat...not of heat alone but also of vitality, sensuality, and now that he was within range, that heat was washing over him, making him aware of a sexual tension developing between them, bringing with it the knowledge that he would win. The strength of the attraction surprised him, because his first impression had been that she was exotic-looking but not beautiful. Though slim, she was a little wide-hipped, and her breasts, mounded high and served up in separate scoops by her tight bodice, were quite small. Her face, like her coloring, had an East Indian cast, its features too large and voluptuous to suit the delicate bone structure; yet they were so expressive, so finely cut, that their disproportion came to seem a virtue. Except that it was thinner, her face resembled one of those handmaidens featured on Hindu religious posters, kneeling beneath Krishna's throne. Very sexy, very serene. That serenity, Mingolla decided, wasn't just a veneer. It ran deep. But at the moment he was more interested in her breasts. They looked nice pushed up like that, gleaming with a sheen of sweat. Two helpings of shaky pudding.

The woman waggled the card, and he took it: a simplified Bingo card with symbols instead of letters and numbers. "Good luck," she said, and laughed, as if in reaction to some private irony. Then she began to spin the cage.

Mingolla didn't recognize many of the words she called, but an old man cozied up to him and pointed to the appropriate square whenever he got a match. Soon several rows were almost complete. "LA MANZANA!" cried the woman, and the old man tugged at Mingolla's sleeve, shouting, *"Se ganó!"*

As the woman checked his card, Mingolla thought about the mystery she presented. Her calmness, her unaccented English and the upper class background it implied, made her seem out of place here. Could be she was a student, her education interrupted by the war...though she might be a bit too old for that. He figured her to be twenty-two or twenty-three. Graduate school, maybe. But there was an air of worldliness about her that didn't support that theory. He watched her eyes dart back and forth between the card and the plastic cubes. Large heavy-lidded eyes. The whites stood in such sharp contrast to her dusky skin that they looked fake: milky stones with black centers.

"You see?" she said, handing him his winnings—about three dollars—and another card.

"See what?" Mingolla asked, perplexed.

But she had already begun to spin the cage again.

He won three of the next seven cards. People congratulated him, shaking their heads in amazement; the old man cozied up further, suggesting in sign language that he was the agency responsible for Mingolla's good fortune. Mingolla, however, was nervous. His ritual was founded on a principle of small miracles, and though he was certain the woman was cheating on his behalf (that, he assumed, had been the meaning of her laughter, her "You see?"), though his luck was not really luck, its excessiveness menaced that principle. He lost three cards in a row, but thereafter won two of four and grew even more nervous. He considered leaving. But what if it was luck? Leaving might run him afoul of a higher principle, interfere with some cosmic process and draw down misfortune. It was a ridiculous idea, but he couldn't bring himself to risk the faint chance that it might be true.

He continued to win. The people who had congratulated him became disgruntled and drifted off, and when there were only a handful of players left, the woman closed down the game. A grimy street kid materialized from the shadows and began dismantling the equipment. Unbolting the wire cage, unplugging the microphone, boxing up the plastic cubes, stuffing it all into a burlap sack. The woman moved out from behind the stall and leaned against one of the roofpoles. Half-smiling, she cocked her head, appraising Mingolla, and then—just as the silence between them began to get prickly—she said, "My name's Debora."

"David." Mingolla felt as awkward as a fourteen-year-old; he had to resist the urge to jam his hands into his pockets and look away. "Why'd you cheat?" he asked; in trying to cover his nervousness, he said it too loudly and it sounded like an accusation.

"I wanted to get your attention," she said. "I'm...interested in you. Didn't you notice?"

"I didn't want to take it for granted."

She laughed. "I approve! It's always best to be cautious."

He liked her laughter; it had an easiness that made him think she would celebrate the least good thing.

Three men passed by arm in arm, singing drunkenly. One yelled at Debora, and she responded with an angry burst of Spanish. Mingolla could guess what had been said, that she had been insulted for associating with an American. "Maybe we should go somewhere," he said. "Get off the streets."

"After he's finished." She gestured at the boy, who was now taking down the string of light bulbs. "It's funny," she said. "I have the gift myself, and I'm usually uncomfortable around anyone else who has it. But not with you."

"The gift?" Mingolla thought he knew what she was referring to, but was leery about admitting to it.

"What do you call it? ESP?"

He gave up the idea of denying it. "I never put a name on it," he said.

"It's strong in you. I'm surprised you're not with Psicorp."

He wanted to impress her, to cloak himself in a mystery equal to hers. "How do you know I'm not?"

"I could tell." She pulled a black purse from behind the counter. "After drug therapy there's a change in the gift, in the way it comes across. It doesn't feel as hot, for one thing." She glanced up from the purse. "Or don't you perceive it that way? As heat."

"I've been around people who felt hot to me," he said. "But I didn't know what it meant."

"That's what it means...sometimes." She stuffed some bills into the purse. "So, why aren't you with Psicorp?"

Mingolla thought back to his first interview with a Psicorp agent: a pale, balding man with the innocent look around the eyes that some blind people have. While Mingolla had talked, the agent had fondled the ring Mingolla had given him to hold, paying no mind to what was being said, and had gazed off distractedly, as if listening for echoes. "They tried hard to recruit me," Mingolla said. "But I was scared of the drugs. I heard they had bad side-effects."

"You're lucky it was voluntary," she said. "Here they just snap you up."

The boy said something to her; he swung the burlap sack over his shoulder, and after a rapid-fire exchange of Spanish he ran off toward the river. The crowds were still thick, but more than half the stalls had shut down; those that remained open looked—with their thatched roofs and strung lights and beshawled women—like crude nativity scenes ranging the darkness. Beyond the stalls, neon signs winked on and off a chaotic menagerie of silver eagles and crimson spiders and indigo dragons. Watching them burn and vanish, Mingolla experienced a wave of dizziness. Things were starting to appear disconnected as they had at the Club Demonio.

"Don't you feel well?" she asked.

"I'm just tired."

She turned him to face her, put her hands on his shoulders. "No," she said. "It's something else."

The weight of her hands, the smell of her perfume, helped to steady him. "There was an assault on the firebase a few days ago," he said. "It's still with me a little, y'know."

She gave his shoulders a squeeze and stepped back. "Maybe I can do something." She said this with such gravity, he thought she must have something specific in mind. "How's that?" he asked.

"I'll tell you at dinner...that is, if you're buying." She took his arm, jollying him. "You owe me that much, don't you think, after all your good luck?"

▲▼▲

"Why aren't *you* with Psicorp?" he asked as they walked.

She didn't answer immediately, keeping her head down, nudging a scrap of cellophane with her toe. They were moving along an uncrowded street, bordered on the left by the river—a channel of sluggish black lacquer—and on the right by the windowless rear walls of some bars. Overhead, behind a latticework of supports, a neon lion shed a baleful green nimbus. "I was in school in Miami when they started testing here," she said at last. "And after I came home, my family got on the wrong side of Department Six. You know Department Six?"

"I've heard some stuff."

"Sadists don't make efficient bureaucrats," she said. "They were more interested in torturing us than in determining our value."

Their footsteps crunched in the dirt; husky jukebox voices cried out for love from the next street over. "What happened?" Mingolla asked.

"To my family?" She shrugged. "Dead. No one ever bothered to confirm it, but it wasn't necessary. Confirmation, I mean." She went a few steps in silence. "As for me...." A muscle bunched at the corner of her mouth. "I did what I had to."

He was tempted to ask for specifics, but thought better of it. "I'm sorry," he said, and then kicked himself for having made such a banal comment.

They passed a bar lorded over by a grinning red-and-purple neon ape. Mingolla wondered if these glowing figures had meaning for guerrillas with binoculars in the hills: gone-dead tubes signaling times of attack or troop movements. He cocked an eye toward Debora. She didn't look despondent as she had a second before, and that accorded with his impression that her calmness was a product of self-control, that her emotions were strong but held in tight check and only let out for exercise. From the river came a solitary splash, some cold fleck of life surfacing briefly, then returning to its long ignorant glide through the darkness... and his life no different really, though maybe less graceful. How strange it was to be walking beside this woman who gave off heat like a candle flame, with earth and sky blended into a black gas, and neon totems standing guard overhead.

"Shit," said Debora under her breath.

It surprised him to hear her curse. "What is it?"

"Nothing," she said wearily. "Just 'shit.'" She pointed ahead and quickened her pace. "Here we are."

The restaurant was a working-class place that occupied the ground floor of a hotel: a two-story building of yellow concrete block with a buzzing Fanta sign hung above the entrance. Hundreds of moths swarmed about the sign, flickering whitely against the darkness, and in front of the steps stood a group of teenage boys who were throwing knives at an iguana. The iguana was tied by its hind legs to the step railing. It had amber eyes, a hide the color of boiled cabbage, and it strained at the end of its cord, digging its claws into the dirt and arching its neck like a pint-size dragon about to take flight. As Mingolla and Debora walked up, one of the boys scored a hit in the iguana's tail and it flipped high into the air, shaking loose the knife. The boys passed around a bottle of rum to celebrate.

Except for the waiter—a pudgy young man leaning beside a door that opened onto a smoke-filled kitchen—the place was empty. Glaring overhead lights shined up the grease spots on the plastic tablecloths and made the uneven thicknesses of yellow paint appear to be dripping. The concrete floor was freckled with dark stains that Mingolla discovered to be the remains of insects. The food turned out to be decent, however, and Mingolla shoveled down a plateful of chicken and rice before Debora had half finished hers. She ate deliberately, chewing each bite a long time, and he had to carry the conversation. He told her about New York, his painting, how a couple of galleries had showed interest even though he was just a student. He compared his work to Rauschenberg, to Silvestre. Not as good, of course. Not yet. He had the notion that everything he told her—no matter its irrelevance to the moment—was securing the relationship, establishing subtle ties: he pictured the two of them enwebbed in a network of luminous threads that acted as conduits for their attraction. He could feel her heat more strongly than ever, and he wondered what it would be like to make love to her, to be swallowed by that perception of heat. The instant he wondered this, she glanced up and smiled, as if sharing the thought. He wanted to ratify his sense of intimacy, to tell her something he had told no one else, and so having only one important secret—he told her about the ritual.

She laid down her fork and gave him a penetrating look. "You can't really believe that," she said.

"I know it sounds—"

"Ridiculous," she broke in. "That's how it sounds."

"It's the truth," he said defiantly.

She picked up her fork again, pushed around some grains of rice. "How is it for you," she said, "when you have a premonition? I mean, what happens? Do you have dreams, hear voices?"

"Sometimes I just know things," he said, taken aback by her abrupt change of subject. "And sometimes I see pictures. It's like with a TV that's not working right. Fuzziness at first, then a sharp image."

"With me, it's dreams. And hallucinations. I don't know what else to call them." Her lips thinned; she sighed, appearing to have reached some decision. "When I first saw you, just for a second, you were wearing battle gear. There were inputs on the gauntlets, cables attached to the helmet. The faceplate was shattered; and your face...it was pale, bloody." She put her hand out to cover his. "What I saw was very clear, David. You can't go back."

He hadn't described artilleryman's gear to her, and no way could she have seen it. Shaken, he said, "Where am I gonna go?"

"Panama," she said. "I can help you get there."

She suddenly snapped into focus. You find her, dozens like her, in any of the R&R towns. Preaching pacifism, encouraging desertion. Do-gooders, most with guerrilla connections. And that, he realized, must be how she had known about his gear. She had probably gathered information on the different types of units in order to lend authenticity to her dire pronouncements. His opinion of her wasn't diminished; on the contrary, it went up a notch. She was risking her life by talking to him. But her mystery had been dimmed.

"I can't do that," he said.

"Why not? Don't you believe me?"

"It wouldn't make any difference if I did."

"Look," he said. "This friend of mine, he's always trying to convince me to desert, and there've been times I wanted to. But it's just not in me. My feet won't move that way. Maybe you don't understand, but that's how it is."

"This childish thing you do with your two friends," she said after a pause. "That's what's holding you here, isn't it?"

"It isn't childish."

"That's exactly what it is. Like a child walking home in the dark and thinking that if he doesn't look at the shadows, nothing will jump out at him."

"You don't understand," he said.

"No, I suppose I don't." Angry, she threw her napkin down on the table and stared intently at her plate as if reading some oracle from the chicken bones.

"Let's talk about something else," said Mingolla.

"I have to go," she said coldly.

"Because I won't desert?"

"Because of what'll happen if you don't." She leaned toward him, her voice burred with emotion. "Because knowing what I do about your future, I don't want to wind up in bed with you."

Her intensity frightened him. Maybe she *had* been telling the truth. But he dismissed the possibility. "Stay," he said. "We'll talk some more about it."

"You wouldn't listen." She picked up her purse and got to her feet.

The waiter ambled over and laid the check beside Mingolla's plate; he pulled a plastic bag filled with marijuana from his apron pocket and dangled it in front of Mingolla. "Gotta get her in the mood, man," he said. Debora railed at him in Spanish. He shrugged and moved off, his slow-footed walk an advertisement for his goods.

"Meet me tomorrow then," said Mingolla. "We can talk more about it tomorrow."

"No."

"Why don't you gimme a break?" he said. "This is all coming down pretty fast, y'know. I get here this afternoon, meet you, and an hour later you're saying, 'Death is in the cards, and Panama's your only hope.' I need some time to think. Maybe by tomorrow I'll have a different attitude."

Her expression softened, but she shook her head, *No*.

"Don't you think it's worth it?"

She lowered her eyes, fussed with the zipper of her purse a second, and let out a rueful hiss. "Where do you want to meet?"

"How 'bout the pier on this side? 'Round noon."

She hesitated. "All right." She came around to his side of the table, bent down and brushed her lips across his cheek. He tried to pull her close and deepen the kiss, but she slipped away. He felt giddy, overheated. "You really gonna be there?" he asked.

She nodded but seemed troubled, and she didn't look back before vanishing down the steps.

Mingolla sat awhile, thinking about the kiss, its promise. He might have stayed even longer, but three drunken soldiers staggered in and began knocking over chairs, giving the waiter a hard time. Annoyed, Mingolla went to the door and stood taking in hits of the humid air. Moths were loosely constellated on the curved plastic of the Fanta sign, trying to get next to the bright heat inside it, and he had a sense of relation, of sharing their yearning for the impossible. He started down the steps but was brought up short. The teenage boys had gone; however, their captive iguana lay on the bottom step, bloody and unmoving. Bluish-gray strings spilled from a gash in its throat. It was such a clear sign of bad luck, Mingolla went back inside and checked into the hotel upstairs.

▲▼▲

The hotel corridors stank of urine and disinfectant. A drunken Indian with his fly unzipped and a bloody mouth was pounding on one of the doors. As Mingolla passed him, he bowed and made a sweeping gesture, a parody of welcome. Then he went back to his pounding. Mingolla's room was a windowless cell five feet wide and coffin-length, furnished with a sink and a cot and a chair. Cobwebs and dust clotted the glass of the transom, reducing the hallway light to a cold bluish-white glow. The walls were filmy with more cobwebs, and the sheets were so dirty that they appeared to have a pattern. He lay down and closed his eyes, thinking about Debora. About ripping off that red dress and giving her a vicious screwing. How she'd cry out. That both made him ashamed and gave him a hard-on. He tried to think about making love to her tenderly. But tenderness, it seemed, was beyond him. He went flaccid. Jerking off wasn't worth the effort, he decided. He started to unbutton his shirt, remembered the sheets and figured he'd be better off with his clothes on.

In the blackness behind his lids he began to see explosive flashes, and within those flashes were images of the assault on the Ant Farm. The mist, the tunnels. He blotted them out with the image of Debora's face, but they kept coming back. Finally he opened his eyes. Two...no, three fuzzy-looking black stars were silhouetted against the transom. It was only when they began to crawl that he recognized them to be spiders. Big ones. He wasn't usually afraid of spiders, but these particular spiders terrified him. If he hit them with his shoe, he'd break the glass and they'd eject him from the hotel. He didn't want to kill them with his hands. After a while he sat up, switched on the overhead, and searched under the cot. There weren't any more spiders. He lay back down, feeling shaky and short of breath. Wishing he could talk to someone, hear a familiar voice. "It's okay," he said to the dark air. But that didn't help. And for a long time, until he felt secure enough to sleep, he watched the three black stars crawling across the transom, moving toward the center, touching each other, moving apart, never making any real progress, never straying from their area of bright confinement, their universe of curdled, frozen light.

— 2 —

In the morning Mingolla crossed to the west bank and walked toward the airbase. It was already hot, but the air still held a trace of freshness and the sweat that beaded on his forehead felt clean and healthy. White dust was settling along the gravel road, testifying to the recent passage of traffic; past the town and the cutoff that led to the uncompleted bridge, high walls of vegetation crowded close to the road, and from within them he heard monkeys and insects and birds: sharp sounds that enlivened him, making him conscious of the play of his muscles.

About halfway to the base he spotted six Guatemalan soldiers coming out of the jungle, dragging a couple of bodies; they tossed them onto the hood of their jeep, where two other bodies were lying. Drawing near, Mingolla saw that the dead were naked children, each with a neat hole in his back. He had intended to walk on past, but one of the soldiers—a gnomish copper-skinned man in dark blue fatigues—blocked his path and demanded to check his papers. All the soldiers gathered around to study the papers, whispering, turning them sideways, scratching their heads. Used to such hassles, Mingolla paid them no attention and looked at the dead children.

They were scrawny, sun-darkened, lying facedown with their ragged hair hanging a fringe off the hood; their skins were pocked by infected mosquito bites, and the flesh around the bullet holes was ridged up and bruised. Judging by their size, Mingolla guessed them to be about ten years old; but then he noticed that one was a girl with a teenage fullness to her buttocks, her breasts squashed against the metal. That made him indignant. They were only wild children who survived by robbing and killing, and the Guatemalan soldiers were only doing their duty: they performed a function comparable to that of the birds that hunted ticks on the hide of a rhinoceros, keeping their American beast pest-free and happy. But it wasn't right for the children to be laid out like game.

The soldier gave back Mingolla's papers. He was now all smiles, and—perhaps in the interest of solidifying Guatemalan-American relations, perhaps because he was proud of his work—he went over to the jeep and lifted the girl's head by the hair so Mingolla could see her face. "*Bandida!*" he said, arranging his features into a comical frown. The girl's face was not unlike the soldier's, with the same blade of a nose and prominent cheekbones. Fresh blood glistened on her lips, and the faded tattoo of a coiled serpent centered her forehead. Her eyes were open, and staring into them—despite their cloudiness—Mingolla felt that he had made a connection, that she was regarding him sadly from somewhere behind those eyes, continuing to die past the point of clinical death. Then an ant crawled out of her nostril, perching on the crimson curve of her lip, and the eyes looked merely vacant. The soldier let her head fall and wrapped his hand in the hair of a second corpse; but before he could lift it, Mingolla turned away and headed down the road toward the airbase.

There was a row of helicopters lined up at the edge of the landing strip, and walking between them, Mingolla saw the two pilots who had given him a ride from the Ant Farm. They were stripped to shorts and helmets, wearing baseball gloves, and they were playing catch, lofting high flies to one another. Behind them, atop their Sikorsky, a mechanic was fussing with the main rotor housing. The sight of the pilots didn't disturb Mingolla as it had the previous day; in fact, he found their weirdness somehow comforting. Just then, the ball eluded one of them and bounced Mingolla's way. He snagged it and flipped it back to the nearer of the pilots, who came loping over and stood pounding the ball into the pocket of his glove. With his black reflecting face and sweaty, muscular torso, he looked like an eager young mutant.

"How's she goin?" he asked. "Seem like you a little tore down this mornin'."

"I feel okay," said Mingolla defensively. "'Course"—he smiled, making light of his defensiveness—"maybe you see something I don't."

The pilot shrugged; the sprightliness of the gesture seemed to convey good humor.

Mingolla pointed to the mechanic. "You guys broke down, huh?"

"Just overhaul. We're goin' back up early tomorrow. Need a lift?"

"Naw, I'm here for a week."

An eerie current flowed through Mingolla's left hand, setting up a palsied shaking. It was bad this time, and he jammed the hand into his hip pocket. The olive-drab line of barracks appeared to twitch, to suffer a dislocation and shift farther away; the choppers and jeeps and uniformed men on the strip looked toylike: pieces in a really neat GI Joe Airbase kit. Mingolla's hand beat against the fabric of his trousers like a sick heart.

"I gotta get going," he said.

"Hang in there," said the pilot. "You be awright."

The words had a flavor of diagnostic assurance that almost convinced Mingolla of the pilot's ability to know his fate, that things such as fate could be known. "You honestly believe what you were saying yesterday, man?" he asked. "'Bout your helmets? 'Bout knowing the future?"

The pilot bounced the ball on the concrete, snatched it at the peak of its rebound, and stared down at it. Mingolla could see the seams and brand name reflected in the visor, but nothing of the face behind it, no evidence either of normalcy or deformity. "I get asked that a lot," said the pilot. "People raggin' me, y'know. But you ain't raggin' me, are you, man?"

"No," said Mingolla. "I'm not."

"Well," said the pilot, "it's this way. We buzz 'round up in the nothin', and we see shit down on the ground, shit nobody else sees. Then we blow that shit away. Been doin' it like that for ten months, and we're still alive. Fuckin' A, I believe it!"

Mingolla was disappointed. “Yeah, okay,” he said.

“You hear what I’m sayin’?” asked the pilot. “I mean we’re livin’ goddamn proof.”

“Uh-huh.” Mingolla scratched his neck, trying to think of a diplomatic response, but thought of none. “Guess I’ll see you.”

He started toward the PX.

“Hang in there, man!” the pilot called after him. “Take it from me! Things gonna be lookin’ up for you real soon!”

▲▼▲

The canteen in the PX was a big barnlike room of unpainted boards; it was of such recent construction that Mingolla could still smell sawdust and resin. Thirty or forty tables; a jukebox; bare walls. Behind the bar at the rear of the room, a sour-faced corporal with a clipboard was doing a liquor inventory, and Gilbey—the only customer—was sitting by one of the east windows, stirring a cup of coffee. His brow was furrowed, and a ray of sunlight shone down around him, making it look that he was being divinely inspired to do some soul-searching.

“Where’s Baylor?” asked Mingolla, sitting opposite him.

“Fuck, I dunno,” said Gilbey, not taking his eyes from the coffee cup. “He’ll be here.”

Mingolla kept his left hand in his pocket. The tremors were diminishing, but not quickly enough to suit him; he was worried that the shaking would spread as it had after the assault. He let out a sigh, and in letting it out he could feel all his nervous flutters. The ray of sunlight seemed to be humming a wavery golden note, and that, too, worried him. Hallucinations. Then he noticed a fly buzzing against the windowpane. “How was it last night?” he asked.

Gilbey glanced up sharply. “Oh, you mean Big Tits. She lemme check her for lumps.” He forced a grin, then went back to stirring his coffee.

Mingolla was hurt that Gilbey hadn’t asked about his night; he wanted to tell him about Debora. But that was typical of Gilbey’s self-involvement. His narrow eyes and sulky mouth were the imprints of a mean-spiritedness that permitted few concerns aside from his own well-being. Yet despite his insensitivity, his stupid rages and limited conversation, Mingolla believed that he was smarter than he appeared, that disguising one’s intelligence must have been a survival tactic in Detroit, where he had grown up. It was his craftiness that gave him away: his insights into the personalities of adversary lieutenants; his slickness at avoiding unpleasant duty; his ability to manipulate his peers. He wore stupidity like a cloak, and perhaps he had worn it for so long that it could not be removed. Still, Mingolla envied him its virtues, especially the way it had numbed him to the assault.

"He's never been late before," said Mingolla after a while.

"So what, he's fuckin' late!" snapped Gilbey, glowering. "He'll be here!"

Behind the bar, the corporal switched on a radio and spun the dial past Latin music, past Top Forty, then past an American voice reporting the baseball scores. "Hey!" called Gilbey. "Let's hear that, man! I wanna see what happened to the Tigers." With a shrug, the corporal complied.

"...White Sox six, A's three," said the announcer. "That's eight in a row for the Sox...."

"White Sox are kickin' some ass," said the corporal, pleased.

"The White Sox!" Gilbey sneered. "What the White Sox got 'cept a buncha beaners hittin' two hunnerd and some coke-sniffin' niggers? Shit! Every fuckin' spring the White Sox are flyin', man. But then 'long comes summer and the good drugs hit the street and they fuckin' die!"

"Yeah," said the corporal, "but this year—"

"Take that son of a bitch Caldwell," said Gilbey, ignoring him. "I seen him coupla years back when he had a trial with the Tigers. Man, that nigger could hit! Now he shuffles up there like he's just feelin' the breeze."

"They ain't takin' drugs, man," said the corporal testily. "They can't take 'em 'cause there's these tests that show if they's on somethin'."

Gilbey barreled ahead. "White Sox ain't gotta chance, man! Know what the guy on TV calls 'em sometimes? The Pale Hose! The fuckin' Pale Hose! How you gonna win with a name like that? The Tigers, now, they got the right kinda name. The Yankees, the Braves, the—"

"Bullshit, man!" The corporal was becoming upset; he set down his clipboard and walked to the end of the bar. "What 'bout the Dodgers? They gotta wimpy name and they're a good team. Your name don't mean shit!"

"The Reds," suggested Mingolla; he was enjoying Gilbey's rap, its stubbornness and irrationality. Yet at the same time he was concerned by its undertone of desperation: appearances to the contrary, Gilbey was not himself this morning.

"Oh, yeah!" Gilbey smacked the table with the flat of his hand.

"The Reds! Lookit the Reds, man! Lookit how good they been doin since the Cubans come into the war. You think that don't mean nothin'? You think their name ain't helpin' 'em? Even if they get in the Series, the Pale fuckin' Hose don't gotta prayer against the Reds." He laughed—a hoarse grunt. "I'm a Tiger fan, man, but I gotta feelin' this ain't their year, y'know. The Reds are tearin' up the NL East, and the Yankees is comin' on, and when they get together in October, man, then we gonna find out alla 'bout everything. Alla 'bout fuckin' everything!" His voice grew tight and tremulous. "So don't gimme no trouble 'bout the candyass Pale Hose, man! They ain't shit and they never was and they ain't gonna be shit 'til they change their fuckin' name!"

Sensing danger, the corporal backed away from confrontation, and Gilbey lapsed into a moody silence. For a while there were only the sounds of chopper blades and the radio blatting out cocktail jazz. Two mechanics wandered in for an early morning beer, and not long after that three fatherly-looking sergeants with potbellies and thinning hair and quartermaster insignia on their shoulders sat at a nearby table and started up a game of rummy. The corporal brought them a pot of coffee and a bottle of whiskey, which they mixed and drank as they played. Their game had an air of custom, of something done at this time every day, and watching them, taking note of their fat, pampered ease, their old-buddy familiarity, Mingolla felt proud of his palsied hand. It was an honorable affliction, a sign that he had participated in the heart of the war as these men had not. Yet he bore them no resentment. None whatsoever. Rather it gave him a sense of security to know that three such fatherly men were here to provide him with food and liquor and new boots. He basked in the doll, happy clutter of their talk, in the haze of cigar smoke that seemed the exhaust of their contentment. He believed that he could go to them, tell them his problems, and receive folksy advice. They were here to assure him of the rightness of his purpose, to remind him of simple American values, to lend an illusion of fraternal involvement to the war, to make clear that it was merely an exercise in good fellowship and tough-mindedness, an initiation rite that these three men had long ago passed through, and after the war they would all get rings and medals and pal around together and talk about bloodshed and terror with head-shaking wonderment and nostalgia, as if bloodshed and terror were old lost friends whose natures they had not fully appreciated at the time.... Mingolla realized then that a smile had stretched his facial muscles taut, and that his train of thought had been leading him into spooky mental territory. The tremors in his hand were worse than ever. He checked his watch. It was almost ten o'clock. *Ten o'clock!* In a panic he scraped back his chair and stood.

"Let's look for him," he said to Gilbey.

Gilbey started to say something but kept it to himself. He tapped his spoon hard against the edge of the table. Then he, too, scraped back his chair and stood.

▲▼▲

Baylor was not to be found at the Club Demonio or any of the bars on the west bank. Gilbey and Mingolla described him to everyone they met, but no one remembered him. The longer the search went on, the more insecure Mingolla became. Baylor was necessary, an essential underpinning of the platform of habits and routines that supported him, that let him live beyond the range of war's weapons and the laws of chance, and should that underpinning be destroyed.... In his mind's eye he saw the platform tipping, he and Gilbey toppling over the edge, cartwheeling down into an abyss filled with black flames. Once Gilbey said, "Panama! The son of a bitch run off to Panama." But Mingolla didn't think this was the case. He was certain that Baylor was close at hand. His certainty had such a valence of clarity that he became even more insecure, knowing that this sort of clarity often heralded a bad conclusion.

The sun climbed higher, its heat an enormous weight pressing down, its light leaching color from the stucco walls, and Mingolla's sweat began to smell rancid. Only a few soldiers were on the streets, mixed in with the usual run of kids and beggars, and the bars were empty except for a smattering of drunks still on a binge from the night before. Gilbey stumped along, grabbing people by the shirt and asking his questions. Mingolla however, terribly conscious of his trembling hand, nervous to the point of stammering, was forced to work out a stock approach whereby he could get through these brief interviews. He would amble up, keeping his right side forward, and say, "I'm looking for a friend of mine. Maybe you seen him? Tall guy. Olive skin, black hair, thin. Name's Baylor." He learned to let this slide off his tongue in a casual unreeling.

Finally Gilbey had had enough. "I'm gonna hang out with Big Tits," he said. "Meet'cha at the PX tomorrow." He started to walk off, but turned and added, "You wanna get in touch 'fore tomorrow, I'll be at the Club Demonio." He had an odd expression on his face. It was as if he were trying to smile reassuringly, but—due to his lack of practice with smiles—it looked forced and foolish and not in the least reassuring.

Around eleven o'clock Mingolla wound up leaning against a pink stucco wall, watching out for Baylor in the thickening crowds. Beside him, the sun-browned fronds of a banana tree were feathering in the wind, making a crispy sound whenever a gust blew them back into the wall. The roof of the bar across the street was being repaired; sheets of new tin alternating with narrow patches of rust that looked like enormous strips of bacon laid there to fry. Now and then he would let his gaze drift up to the unfinished bridge, a great sweep of magical whiteness curving into the blue, rising above the town and the jungle and the war. Not even the heat haze rippling from the tin roof could warp its smoothness. It seemed to be orchestrating the stench, the mutter of the crowds, and the jukebox music into a tranquil unity, absorbing those energies and returning them purified, enriched. He thought that if he stared at it long enough, it would speak to him, pronounce a white word that would grant his wishes.

Two flat cracks—pistol shots—sent him stumbling away from the wall, his heart racing, Inside his head the shots had spoken the two syllables of Baylor's name. All the kids and beggars had vanished. All the soldiers had stopped and turned to face the direction from which the shots had come: zombies who had heard their master's voice.

Another shot.

Some soldiers milled out of a side street, talking excitedly "…fuckin' nuts!" one was saying, and his buddy said, "It was Sammy, man! You see his eyes?"

Mingolla pushed his way through them and sprinted down the side street. At the end of the block a cordon of MPs had sealed off access to the right-hand turn, and when Mingolla ran up, one of them told him to stay back.

"What is it?" Mingolla asked. "Some guy playing Sammy?"

"Fuck off," the MP said mildly.

"Listen," said Mingolla. "It might be this friend of mine. Tall, skinny guy. Black hair. Maybe I can talk to him."

The MP exchanged glances with his buddies, who shrugged and acted otherwise unconcerned. "Okay," he said. He pulled Mingolla to him and pointed out a bar with turquoise walls on the next corner down. "Go on in there and talk to the captain."

Two more shots, then a third.

"Better hurry," said the MP. "Ol' Captain Haynesworth there, he don't put much stock in negotiations."

It was cool and dark inside the bar; two shadowy figures were flattened against the wall beside a window that opened onto the cross street. Mingolla could make out the glint of automatic pistols in their hands. Then, through the window, he saw Baylor pop up from behind a retaining wall: a three-foot-high structure of mud bricks running between a herbal drugstore and another bar. Baylor was shirtless, his chest painted with reddish-brown smears of dried blood, and he was standing in a nonchalant pose, with his thumbs hooked in his trouser pockets. One of the men by the window fired at him. The report was deafening, causing Mingolla to flinch and close his eyes. When he looked out the window again, Baylor was nowhere in sight.

"Fucker's just tryin' to draw fire," said the man who had shot at Baylor. "Sammy's fast today."

"Yeah, but he's slowin' some," said a lazy voice from the darkness at the rear of the bar. "I do believe he's outta dope,"

"Hey," said Mingolla. "Don't kill him! I know the guy. I can talk to him."

"Talk?" said the lazy voice. "You kin talk 'til yo' ass turns green, boy, and Sammy ain't gon' listen."

Mingolla peered into the shadows. A big sloppy-looking man was leaning on the counter; brass insignia gleamed on his beret. "You the captain?" he asked. "They told me outside to talk to the captain."

"Yes, indeed," said the man. "And I'd be purely delighted to talk with you, boy. What you wanna talk 'bout?"

The other men laughed.

"Why are you trying to kill him?" asked Mingolla, hearing the pitch of desperation in his voice. "You don't have to kill him. You could use a trank gun."

"Got one comin'," said the captain, "Thing is, though, yo' buddy got hisself a coupla hostages back of that wall, and we get a chance at him 'fore the trank gun 'rives, we bound to take it."

"But—" Mingolla began.

"Lemme finish, boy." The captain hitched up his gunbelt, strolled over, and draped an arm around Mingolla's shoulder, enveloping him in an aura of body odor and whiskey breath. "See," he went on, "we had everything under control. Sammy there—"

"Baylor!" said Mingolla angrily. "His name's Baylor."

The captain lifted his arm from Mingolla's shoulder and looked at him with amusement. Even in the gloom Mingolla could see the network of broken capillaries on his cheeks, the bloated alcoholic features. "Right," said the captain, "Like I's sayin', yo' good buddy Mister Baylor there wasn't doin' no harm. Just sorta ravin' and runnin' round. But then 'long comes a coupla our Marine brothers. Seems like they'd been givin' our beaner friends a demonstration of the latest combat gear, and they was headin' back from said demonstration when they seen our little problem and took it 'pon themselves to play hero. Well sir, puttin' it in a nutshell, Mister Baylor flat kicked their ass. Stomped all over their *esprit de corps.* Then he drags 'em back of that wall and starts messin' with one of their guns. And—"

Two more shots.

"Shit!" said one of the men by the window.

"And there he sits," said the captain. "Fuckin' with us. Now either the gun's outta ammo or else he ain't figgered out how it works. If it's the latter case, and he does figger it out...." The captain shook his head dolefully, as if picturing dire consequences "See my predicament?"

"I could try talking to him," said Mingolla. "What harm would it do?"

"You get yourself killed, it's your life, boy. But it's my ass that's gonna get hauled up on charges." The captain steered Mingolla to the door and gave him a gentle shove toward the cordon of MPs, "'Preciate you volunteerin', boy."

Later Mingolla was to reflect that what he had done had made no sense, because—whether or not Baylor had survived—he would never have been returned to the Ant Farm. But at the time, desperate to preserve the ritual, none of this occurred to him. He walked around the corner and toward the retaining wall. His mouth was dry, his heart pounded. But the shaking in his hand had stopped, and he had the presence of mind to walk in such a way that he blocked the MPs' line of fire. About twenty feet from the wall he called out, "Hey, Baylor! It's Mingolla, man!" And as if propelled by a spring, Baylor jumped up, staring at him. It was an awful stare. His eyes were like bull's-eyes, white showing all around the irises; trickles of blood ran from his nostrils, and nerves were twitching in his cheeks with the regularity of watchworks. The dried blood on his chest came from three long gouges; they were partially scabbed over but were oozing a clear fluid. For a moment he remained motionless. Then he reached down behind the wall, picked up a double-barreled rifle from whose stock trailed a length of flexible tubing, and brought it to bear on Mingolla.

He squeezed the trigger.

No flame, no explosion. Not even a click. But Mingolla felt that he'd been dipped in ice water. "Christ!" he said. "Baylor! It's me!" Baylor squeezed the trigger again, with the same result. An expression of intense frustration washed over his face, then lapsed into that dead man's stare. He looked directly up into the sun, and after a few seconds he smiled: he might have been receiving terrific news from on high.

Mingolla's senses had become wonderfully acute. Somewhere far away a radio was playing a country-and-western tune, and with its plaintiveness, its intermittent bursts of static, it seemed to him the whining of a nervous system on the blink. He could hear the MPs talking in the bar, could smell the sour acids of Baylor's madness, and he thought he could feel the pulse of Baylor's rage, an inconstant flow of heat eddying around him, intensifying his fear, rooting him to the spot. Baylor laid the gun down, laid it down with the tenderness he might have shown toward a sick child, and stepped over the retaining wall. The animal fluidity of the movement made Mingolla's skin crawl. He managed to shuffle backward a pace and held up his hands to ward Baylor off. "C'mon, man," he said weakly. Baylor let out a fuming noise—part hiss, part whimper—and a runner of saliva slid between his lips. The sun was a golden bath drenching the street, kindling glints and shimmers from every bright surface, as if it were bringing reality to a boil. Somebody yelled, "Get down, boy!"

Then Baylor flew at him, and they fell together, rolling on the hard-packed dirt. Fingers dug in behind his Adam's apple. He twisted away, saw Baylor grinning down, all staring eyes and yellowed teeth. Strings of drool flapping from his chin. A Halloween face. Knees pinned Mingolla's shoulders, hands gripped his hair and bashed his head against the ground. Again, and again. A keening sound switched on inside his ears. He wrenched an arm free and tried to gouge Baylor's eyes; but Baylor bit his thumb, gnawing at the joint. Mingolla's vision dimmed, and he couldn't hear anything anymore. The back of his head felt mushy. It seemed to be rebounding very slowly from the dirt, higher and slower after each impact. Framed by blue sky, Baylor's face looked to be receding, spiraling off. And then, just as Mingolla began to fade, Baylor disappeared.

Dust was in Mingolla's mouth, his nostrils. He heard shouts, grunts. Still dazed, he propped himself onto an elbow. A short ways off, khaki arms and legs and butts were thrashing around in a cloud of dust. Like a comic-strip fight. You expected asterisks and exclamation points overhead to signify profanity. Somebody grabbed his arm, hauled him upright. The MP captain, his beefy face flushed. He frowned reprovingly as he brushed dirt from Mingolla's clothes, "Real gutsy, boy," he said. "And real, real stupid. He hadn't been at the end of his run, you'd be drawin' flies 'bout now." He turned to a sergeant standing nearby. "How stupid you reckon that was, Phil?"

The sergeant said that it beat him.

"Well," the captain said, "I figger if the boy here was in combat that'd be 'bout Bronze-Star stupid."

That, allowed the sergeant, was pretty goddamn stupid.

"'Course here in 'Frisco"—the captain gave Mingolla a final dusting—"it don't get you diddley-shit."

The MPs were piling off Baylor, who lay on his side, bleeding from his nose and mouth. Blood thick as gravy filmed over his cheeks.

"Panama," said Mingolla dully. Maybe it was an option. He saw how it would be...a night beach, palm shadows a lacework on the white sand.

"What say?" asked the captain.

"He wanted to go to Panama," said Mingolla.

"Don't we all," said the captain.

One of the MPs rolled Baylor onto his stomach and handcuffed him; another manacled his feet. Then they rolled him back over. Yellow dirt had mired with the blood on his cheeks and forehead, fitting him with a blotchy mask. His eyes snapped open in the middle of that mask, widening when he felt the restraints. He started to hump up and down, trying to bounce his way to freedom. He kept on humping for almost a minute; then he went rigid and—his gone eyes fixed on the molten disc of the sun—he let out a roar. That was the only word for it. It wasn't a scream or a shout, but a devil's exultant roar, so loud and full of fury, it seemed to be generating all the blazing light and heat dance. Listening to it had a seductive effect, and Mingolla began to get behind it, to feel it in his body like a good rock 'n' roll tune, to sympathize with its life-hating exuberance.

"Whoo-ee!" said the captain, marveling. "They gon' have to build a whole new zoo for that boy."

▲▼▲

After giving his statement, letting a Corpsman check his head, Mingolla caught the ferry to meet Debora on the east bank. He sat in the stern, gazing out at the unfinished bridge, this time unable to derive from it any sense of hope or magic. Panama kept cropping up in his thoughts. Now that Baylor was gone, was it really an option? He knew he should try to figure things out, plan what to do, but he couldn't stop seeing Baylor's bloody, demented face. He'd seen worse, Christ yes, a whole lot worse. Guys reduced to spare parts, so little of them left that they didn't need a shiny silver coffin, just a black metal can the size of a cookie jar. Guys scorched and one-eyed and bloody, clawing blindly at the air like creatures out of a monster movie. But the idea of Baylor trapped forever in some raw, red place inside his brain, in the heart of that raw, red noise he'd made, maybe that idea was worse than anything Mingolla had seen. He didn't want to die; he rejected the prospect with the impassioned stubbornness a child displays when confronted with a hard truth. Yet he would rather die than endure madness. Compared to what Baylor had in store, death and Panama seemed to offer the same peaceful sweetness.

Someone sat down beside Mingolla: a kid who couldn't have been older than eighteen. A new kid with a new haircut, new boots, new fatigues. Even his face looked new, freshly broken from the mold. Shiny, pudgy cheeks; clear skin; bright, unused blue eyes. He was eager to talk. He asked Mingolla about his home, his family, and said, Oh, wow, it must be great living in New York, wow. But he appeared to have some other reason for initiating the conversation, something he was leading up to, and finally he spat it out.

"You know the Sammy that went animal back there?" he said. "I seen him pitted last night. Little place in the jungle west of the base. Guy name Chaco owns it. Man, it was fuckin' incredible!"

Mingolla had only heard of the pits third- and fourth-hand, but what he had heard was bad, and it was hard to believe that this kid with his air of home-boy innocence could be an aficionado of something so vile. And, despite what he had just witnessed, it was even harder to believe that Baylor could have been a participant.

The kid didn't need prompting. "It was pretty early on," he said. "There'd been a coupla bouts, nothin' special, and then this guy walks in lookin' real twitchy. I knew he was Sammy by the way he's starin' at the pit, y'know, like it's somethin' he's been wishin' for. And this guy with me, friend of mine, he gives me a poke and says, 'Holy shit! That's the Black Knight, man! I seen him fight over in Reunión a while back. Put your money on him,' he says. 'The fucker's an ace!' "

Their last R&R had been in Reunión. Mingolla tried to frame a question but couldn't think of one whose answer would have any meaning.

"Well," said the kid, "I ain't been down long, but I'd even heard 'bout the Knight. So I went over and kinda hung out near him, thinkin' maybe I can get a line on how he's feelin', y'know, 'cause you don't wanna just bet the guy's rep. Pretty soon Chaco comes over and asks the Knight if he wants some action. The Knight says, 'Yeah, but I wanna fight an animal. Somethin' fierce, man. I wanna fight somethin' fierce.' Chaco says he's got some monkeys and shit, and the Knight says he hears Chaco's got a jaguar, Chaco he hems and haws, says, 'Maybe so, maybe not, but it don't matter 'cause a jaguar's too strong for Sammy.' And then the Knight tells Chaco who he is. Lemme tell ya, Chaco's whole fuckin' attitude changed. He could see how the bettin' was gonna go for somethin' like the Black Knight versus a jaguar. And he says, 'Yes sir, Mister Black Knight, sir! Anything you want!' And he makes the announcement. Man, the place goes nuts. People wavin' money, screamin' odds, drinkin' fast so's they can get ripped in time for the main event, and the Knight's just standin' there, smilin', like he's feedin' off the confusion. Then Chaco lets the jaguar in through the tunnel and into the pit. It ain't a full-growed jaguar, half-growed maybe, but that's all you figure even the Knight can handle."

The kid paused for breath; his eyes seemed to have grown brighter. "Anyway, the jaguar's sneakin' 'round and 'round, keepin' close to the pit wall, snarlin' and spittin', and the Knight's watchin' him from up above, checkin' his moves, y'know. And everybody starts chantin', 'Sam-mee, Sam-mee, Sam-mee,' and after the chant builds up loud the Knight pulls three ampules outta his pocket. I mean, shit, man! Three! I ain't never been 'round Sammy when he's done more'n two. Three gets you clear into the fuckin' sky! So when the Knight holds up these three ampules, the crowd's tuned to burn, howlin' like they's playin' Sammy themselves. But the Knight, man, he keeps his cool. He is *so* cool! He just holds up the ampules and lets 'em take the shine, soakin' up the noise and energy, gettin' strong off the crowd's juice. Chaco waves everybody quiet and gives the speech, y'know, 'bout how in the heart of every man there's a warrior-soul waitin' to be loosed and shit. I tell ya, man, I always thought that speech was crap before, but the Knight's makin' me buy it a hunnerd percent. He is so goddamn cool! He takes off his shirt and shoes, and he ties this piece of black silk 'round his arm. Then he pops the ampules, one after another, real quick, and breathes it all in. I can see it hittin', catchin' fire in his eyes. Pumpin' him up. And soon as he's popped the last one, he jumps into the pit. He don't use the tunnel, man! He jumps! Twenty-five feet down to the sand, and lands in a crouch."

Three other soldiers were leaning in, listening, and the kid was now addressing all of them, playing to his audience. He was so excited that he could barely keep his speech coherent, and Mingolla realized with disgust that he, too, was excited by the image of Baylor crouched on the sand. Baylor, who had cried after the assault. Baylor, who had been so afraid of snipers that he had once pissed in his pants rather than walk from his gun to the latrine.

Baylor, the Black Knight.

"The jaguar's screechin' and snarlin' and slashin' at the air," the kid went on. "Tryin' to put fear into the Knight. 'Cause the jaguar knows in his mind the Knight's big trouble. This ain't some jerk like Chaco, this is Sammy. The Knight moves to the center of the pit, still in a crouch." Here the kid pitched his voice low and dramatic. "Nothin' happens for a coupla minutes, 'cept it's tense. Nobody's hardly breathin'. The jaguar springs a coupla times, but the Knight dances off to the side and makes him miss, and there ain't no damage either way. Whenever the jaguar springs, the crowd sighs and squeals, not just 'cause they's scared of seein' the Knight tore up, but also 'cause they can see how fast he is. Silky fast, man! Unreal. He looks 'bout as fast as the jaguar. He keeps on dancin' away, and no matter how the jaguar twists and turns, no matter if he comes at him along the sand, he can't get his claws into the Knight. And then, man...oh, it was so smooth! Then the jaguar springs again, and this time 'stead of dancin' away, the Knight drops onto his back, does this half-roll onto his shoulders, and when the jaguar passes over him, he kicks up with both feet. Kicks up hard! And smashes his heels into the jaguar's side. The jaguar slams into the pit wall and comes down screamin', snappin' at his ribs. They was busted, man. Pokin' out the skin like tent posts."

The kid wiped his mouth with the back of his hand and flicked his eyes toward Mingolla and the other soldiers to see if they were into the story. "We was shoutin', man," he said. "Poundin' the top of the pit wall. It was so loud, the guy I'm with is yellin' in my ear and I can't hear nothin'. Now maybe it's the noise, maybe it's his ribs, whatever...the jaguar goes berserk. Makin' these scuttlin' lunges at the Knight, tryin' to get close 'fore he springs so the Knight can't pull that same trick. He's snarlin' like a goddamn chain saw! The Knight keeps leapin' and spinnin' away. But then he slips, man, grabs the air for balance, and the jaguar's on him, clawin' at his chest. For a second they're like waltzin' together. Then the Knight pries loose the paw that's hooked him, pushes the jaguar's head back, and smashes his fist into the jaguar's eye. The jaguar flops onto the sand, and the Knight scoots to the other side of the pit. He's checkin' the scratches on his chest, which is bleedin' wicked. Meantime, the jaguar gets to his feet, and he's fucked up worse than ever. His one eye's fulla blood, and his hindquarters is all loosey-goosey. Like if this was boxin', they'd call in the doctor. The jaguar figures he's had enough of this crap, and he starts tryin' to jump outta the pit. This one time he jumps right up to where I'm leanin' over the edge. Comes so close I can smell his breath, I can see myself reflected in his good eye. He's clawin' for a grip, wantin' to haul hisself up into the crowd. People are freakin', thinkin' he might be gonna make it. But 'fore he gets the chance, the Knight catches him by the tail and slings him against the wall. Just like you'd beat a goddamn rug, that's how he's dealin' with the jaguar. And the jaguar's a real mess, now. He's quiverin'. Blood's pourin' outta his mouth, his fangs is all red. The Knight starts makin' these little feints, wavin' his arms, growlin'. He's toyin' with the jaguar. People don't believe what they're seein', man. Sammy's kickin' a jaguar's ass so bad he's got room to toy with it. If the place was nuts before, now, it's a fuckin' zoo. Fights in the crowd, guys singin' the Marine Hymn. Some beaner squint's takin' off her clothes. The jaguar tries to scuttle up close to the Knight again, but he's too fucked up. He can't keep it together. And the Knight, he's still growlin' and feintin'. A guy behind me is booin', claimin' the Knight's defamin' the purity of the sport by playin' with the jaguar. But hell, man, I can see he's just timin' the jaguar, waitin' for the right moment, the right move."

Staring off downriver, the kid wore a wistful expression: he might have been thinking about his girlfriend. "We all knew it was comin'," he said. "Everybody got real quiet. So quiet you could hear the Knight's feet scrapin' on the sand. You could feel it in the air, and you knew the jaguar was savin' up for one big effort. Then the Knight slips again, 'cept he's fakin'. I could see that, but the jaguar couldn't. When the Knight reels sideways, the jaguar springs. I thought the Knight was gonna drop down like he did the first time but he springs, too. Feet first. And he catches the jaguar under the jaw. You could hear bone splinterin', and the jaguar falls in a heap. He struggles to get up, but no way! He's whinin', and he craps all over the sand. The Knight walks up behind him, takes his head in both hands, and gives it a twist. Crack!"

As if identifying with the jaguar's fate, the kid closed his eyes and sighed. "Everybody'd been quiet 'til they heard that crack, then all hell broke loose. People chantin', 'Sam-mee, Sam-mee,' and people shovin', tryin' to get close to the pit wall so they can watch the Knight take the heart. He reaches into the jaguar's mouth and snaps off one of the fangs and tosses it to somebody. Then Chaco comes in through the tunnel and hands him the knife. Right when he's 'bout to cut, somebody knocks me over and by the time I'm back on my feet, he's already took the heart and tasted it. He's just standin' there with the jaguar's blood on his mouth and his own blood runnin' down his chest. He looks kinda confused, y'know. Like now the fight's over and he don't know what to do. But then he starts roarin'. He sounds the same as the jaguar did 'fore it got hurt. Crazy fierce. Ready to get it on with the whole goddamn world. Man, I lost it! I was right with that roar. Maybe I was roarin' with him, maybe everybody was. That's what it felt like, man. Like bein' in the middle of this roar that's comin' outta every throat in the universe." The kid engaged Mingolla with a sober look. "Lotsa people go 'round sayin' the pits are evil, and maybe they are. I don't know. How you s'posed to tell 'bout what's evil and what's not down here? They say you can go to the pits a thousand times and not see nothin' like the jaguar and the Black Knight. I don't know 'bout that, either. But I'm goin' back just in case I get lucky. 'Cause what I saw last night, if it was evil, man, it was so fuckin' evil it was beautiful, too."

— 3 —

Debora was waiting at the pier, carrying a picnic basket and wearing a blue dress with a high neckline and a full skirt: a schoolgirl dress. Mingolla homed in on her. The way she had her hair, falling about her shoulders in thick dark curls, made him think of smoke turned solid, and her face seemed the map of a beautiful country with black lakes and dusky plains, a country in which he could hide. They walked along the river past the town and came to a spot where ceiba trees with massy crowns of slick green leaves and whitish bark and roots like alligator tails grew close to the shore, and there they ate and talked and listened to the water gulping against the clay bank, to the birds, to the faint noises from the airbase that at this distance sounded part of nature. Sunlight dazzled the water, and whenever wind riffled the surface, it seemed to be spreading the dazzles into a crawling crust of diamonds. Mingolla imagined that they had taken a secret path, rounded a corner on the world and reached some eternally peaceful land. The illusion of peace was so profound that he began to see hope in it. Perhaps, he thought, something was being offered here. Some new magic. Maybe there would be a sign. Signs were everywhere if you knew how to read them. He glanced around. Thick white trunks rising into greenery, dark leafy avenues leading off between them... nothing there, but what about those weeds growing at the edge of the bank? They cast precise fleur-de-lis shadows on the clay, shadows that didn't have much in common with the ragged configurations of the weeds themselves. Possibly a sign, though not a clear one. He lifted his gaze to the reeds growing in the shallows. Yellow reeds with jointed stalks bent akimbo, some with clumps of insect eggs like seed pearls hanging from loose fibers, and others dappled by patches of algae. That's how they looked one moment. Then Mingolla's vision rippled, as if the whole of reality had shivered, and the reeds were transformed into rudimentary shapes: yellow sticks poking up from flat blue. On the far side of the river, the jungle was a simple smear of Crayola green; a speedboat passing was a red slash unzippering the blue. It seemed that the rippling had jostled all the elements of the landscape a fraction out of kilter, revealing every object as characterless as a building block. Mingolla gave his head a shake. Nothing changed. He rubbed his brow. No effect. Terrified, he squeezed his eyes shut. He felt like the only meaningful piece in a nonsensical puzzle, vulnerable by virtue of his uniqueness. His breath came rapidly, his left hand fluttered.

"David? Don't you want to hear it?" Debora sounded peeved.

"Hear what?" He kept his eyes closed.

"About my dream. Weren't you listening?"

He peeked at her. Everything was back to normal. She was sitting with her knees tucked under her, all her features in sharp focus. "I'm sorry," he said. "I was thinking."

"You looked frightened."

"Frightened?" He put on a bewildered face. "Naw, just had a thought, is all."

"It couldn't have been pleasant."

He shrugged off the comment and sat up smartly to prove his attentiveness. "So tell me 'bout the dream."

"All right," she said doubtfully. The breeze drifted fine strands of hair across her face and she brushed them back. "You were in a room the color of blood, with red chairs and a red table. Even the paintings on the wall were done in shades of red, and...." She broke off, peering at him. "Do you want to hear this? You have that look again."

"Sure," he said. But he was afraid. How could she have known about the red room? She must have had a vision of it, and.... Then he realized that she might not have been talking about the room itself. He'd told her about the assault, hadn't he? And if she had guerrilla contacts, she would know that the emergency lights were switched on during an assault. That had to be it! She was trying to frighten him into deserting again, psyching him the way Christians played upon the fears of sinners with images of fiery rivers and torture. It infuriated him. Who the hell was she to tell him what was right or wise? Whatever he did, it was going to be his decision.

"There were three doors in the room," she went on. "You wanted to leave the room, but you couldn't tell which of the doors was safe to use. You tried the first door, and it turned out to be a façade. The knob of the second door turned easily, but the door itself was stuck. Rather than forcing it, you went to the third door. The knob of this door was made of glass and cut your hand. After that you just walked back and forth, unsure what to do." She waited for a reaction, and when he gave none, she said, "Do you understand?"

He kept silent, biting back anger.

"I'll interpret it for you," she said.

"Don't bother."

"The red room is war, and the false door is the way of your childish...."

"Stop!" He grabbed her wrist, squeezing it hard.

She glared at him until he released her. "Your childish magic," she finished.

"What is it with you?" he asked. "You have some kinda quota to fill? Five deserters a month, and you get a medal?"

She tucked her skirt down to cover her knees, fiddled with a loose thread. From the way she was acting, Mingolla wondered whether he had asked an intimate question and she was framing an answer that wouldn't be indelicate. Finally she said, "Is that who you believe I am to you?"

"Isn't that right? Why else would you be handing me this bullshit?"

"What's the matter with you, David?" She leaned forward, cupping his face in her hands. "Why—"

He pushed her hands away. "What's the matter with me? This"—his gesture included the sky, the river, the trees—"that's what's the matter. You remind me of my parents. They ask the same sorta ignorant questions." Suddenly he wanted to injure her with answers, to find an answer like acid to throw in her face and watch it eat away her tranquility. "Know what I do for my parents?" he said. "When they ask dumb-ass questions like 'What's the matter?' I tell 'em a story. A war story. You wanna hear a war story? Something happened a few days back that'll do for an answer just fine."

"You don't have to tell me anything," she said, discouraged.

"No problem," he said. "Be my pleasure."

▲▼▲

The Ant Farm was a large sugarloaf hill overlooking dense jungle on the eastern border of Fire Zone Emerald; jutting out from its summit were rocket and gun emplacements that at a distance resembled a crown of thorns jammed down over a green scalp. For several hundred yards around, the land had been cleared of all vegetation. The big guns had been lowered to maximum declension and in a mad moment had obliterated huge swaths of jungle, snapping off regiments of massive tree trunks a couple of feet above the ground, leaving a moat of blackened stumps and scorched red dirt seamed with fissures. Tangles of razor wire had replaced the trees and bushes, forming surreal blue-steel hedges, and buried beneath the wire was a variety of mines and detection devices. These did little good, however, because the Cubans possessed technology that would neutralize most of them. On clear nights there was scant likelihood of trouble, but on misty nights trouble could be expected. Under cover of the mist, Cuban and guerrilla troops would come through the wire and attempt to infiltrate the tunnels that honeycombed the interior of the hill. Occasionally one of the mines would be triggered, and a ghostly fireball would bloom in the swirling whiteness, tiny black figures being flung outward from its center. Lately some of these casualties had been found to be wearing red berets and scorpion-shaped brass pins, and from this it was known that the Cubans had sent in the Alacrán Division, which had been instrumental in routing the American forces in Miskitia.

There were nine levels of tunnels inside the hill, most lined with little round rooms that served as living quarters (the only exception being the bottom level, which was given over to the computer center and offices); all the rooms and tunnels were coated with a bubbled white plastic that looked like hardened sea-foam and was proof against antipersonnel explosives. In Mingolla's room, where he and Baylor and Gilbey bunked, a scarlet paper lantern had been hung on the overhead light fixture, making it seem that they were inhabiting a blood cell: Baylor had insisted on the lantern, saying that the overhead was too bright and hurt his eyes. Three cots were arranged against the walls, as far apart as space allowed. The floor around Baylor's cot was littered with cigarette butts and used Kleenex; under his pillow he kept a tin box containing a stash of pills and marijuana. Whenever he lit a joint he would always offer Mingolla a hit, and Mingolla always refused, feeling that the experience of the firebase would not be enhanced by drugs. Taped to the wall above Gilbey's cot was a collage of beaver shots, and each day after duty, whether or not Mingolla and Baylor were in the room, he would lie beneath them and masturbate. His lack of shame caused Mingolla to be embarrassed by his own secretiveness in the act, and he was also embarrassed by the pimply-youth quality of the objects taped above his cot: a Yankee pennant; a photograph of his old girlfriend and another of his senior-year high school basketball team; several sketches he had made of the surrounding jungle. Gilbey teased him constantly about this display, calling him "the boy next door," which struck Mingolla as odd, because back home he had been considered something of an eccentric.

It was toward this room that Mingolla was heading when the assault began. Large cargo elevators capable of carrying sixty men ran up and down just inside the east and west slopes of the hill; but to provide quick access between adjoining levels, and also as a safeguard in case of power failures, an auxiliary tunnel corkscrewed down through the center of the hill like a huge coil of white intestine. It was slightly more than twice as wide as the electric carts that traveled it, carrying officers and VIPs on tours. Mingolla was in the habit of using the tunnel for his exercise. Each night he would put on sweat clothes and jog up and down the entire nine levels, doing this out of a conviction that exhaustion prevented bad dreams. That night, as he passed Level Four on his final leg up, he heard a rumbling: an explosion, and not far off. Alarms sounded, the big guns atop the hill began to thunder. From directly above came shouts and the stutter of automatic fire. The tunnel lights flickered, went dark, and the emergency lights winked on.

Mingolla flattened against the wall. The dim red lighting caused the bubbled surfaces of the tunnel to appear as smooth as a chamber in a gigantic nautilus, and this resemblance intensified his sense of helplessness, making him feel like a child trapped within an evil undersea palace. He couldn't think clearly, picturing the chaos around him. Muzzle flashes, armies of ant-men seething through the tunnels, screams spraying blood, and the big guns bucking, every shell burst kindling miles of sky. He would have preferred to keep going up, to get out into the open where he might have a chance to hide in the jungle. But down was his only hope. Pushing away from the wall, he ran full-tilt, arms waving, skidding around corners, almost falling, past Level Four, Level Five. Then, halfway between Levels Five and Six, he nearly tripped over a dead man: an American lying curled up around a belly wound, a slick of blood spreading beneath him and a machete by his hand. As Mingolla stooped for the machete, he thought nothing about the man, only about how weird it was for an American to be defending himself against Cubans with such a weapon. There was no use, he decided, in going any farther. Whoever had killed the man would be somewhere below, and the safest course would be to hide out in one of the rooms on Level Five. Holding the machete before him, he moved cautiously back up the tunnel.

Levels Five, Six, and Seven were officer country, and though the tunnels were the same as the ones above—gently curving tubes eight feet high and ten feet wide—the rooms were larger and contained only two cots. The rooms Mingolla peered into were empty, and this, despite the sounds of battle, gave him a secure feeling. But as he passed beyond the tunnel curve, he heard shouts in Spanish from his rear. He peeked back around the curve. A skinny black soldier wearing a red beret and gray fatigues was inching toward the first doorway; then, rifle at the ready, he ducked inside. Two other Cubans—slim bearded men; their skins sallow-looking in the bloody light—were standing by the arched entranceway to the auxiliary tunnel; when they saw the black soldier emerge from the room, they walked off in the opposite direction, probably to check the rooms at the far end of the level.

Mingolla began to operate in a kind of luminous panic. He realized that he would have to kill the black soldier. Kill him without any fuss, take his rifle, and hope that he could catch the other two off-guard when they came back for him. He slipped into the nearest room and stationed himself against the wall to the right of the door. The Cuban, he had noticed, had turned left on entering the room; he would have been vulnerable to someone positioned like Mingolla. Vulnerable for a split second. Less than a count of one. The pulse in Mingolla's temple throbbed, and he gripped the machete tightly in his left hand. He rehearsed mentally what he would have to do. Stab; clamp a hand over the Cuban's mouth; bring his knee up to jar loose the rifle. And he would have to perform these actions simultaneously, execute them perfectly.

Perfect execution.

He almost laughed out loud, remembering his paunchy old basketball coach saying, "Perfect execution, boys. That's what beats a zone. Forget the fancy crap. Just set your screens, run your patterns, and get your shots down."

Hoops ain't nothin' but life in short pants, huh, Coach?

Mingolla drew a deep breath and let it sigh out to rough his nostrils. He couldn't believe he was going to die. He had spent the past nine months worrying about death, but now when circumstances had arisen that made death likely, he had trouble taking that likelihood seriously. It didn't seem reasonable that a skinny black guy should be his nemesis. His death should involve massive detonations of light, special Mingolla-killing rays, astronomical portents. Not some scrawny little fuck with a rifle. He drew another breath and for the first time registered the contents of the room. Two cots; clothes strewn everywhere; taped-up Polaroids and pornography. Officer country or not, it was your basic Ant Farm decor; under the red light it looked squalid, long-abandoned. He was amazed by how calm he felt. Oh, he was afraid all right! But fear was tucked into the dark folds of his personality like a murderer's knife hidden inside an old coat on a closet shelf. Glowing in secret, waiting its chance to shine. Sooner or later it would skewer him, but for now it was an ally, acting to sharpen his senses. He could see every bubbled pucker on the white walls, could hear the scrape of the Cuban's boots as he darted into the room next door, could feel how the Cuban swung the rifle left to right, paused, turned....

He could!

He could feel the Cuban, feel his heat, his heated shape, the exact position of his body. It was as if a thermal imager had been switched on inside his head, one that worked through walls.

The Cuban eased toward Mingolla's door, his progress tangible, like a burning match moving behind a sheet of paper. Mingolla's calm was shattered. The man's heat, his fleshy temperature, was what disturbed him. He had imagined himself killing with a cinematic swiftness and lack of mess; now he thought of hogs being butchered and pile drivers smashing the skulls of cows. And could he trust this freakish form of perception? What if he couldn't? What if he stabbed too late? Too soon? Then the hot, alive thing was almost at the door, and having no choice, Mingolla timed his attack to its movements, stabbing just as the Cuban entered.

He executed perfectly.

The blade slid home beneath the Cuban's ribs, and Mingolla clamped a hand over his mouth, muffling his outcry. His knee nailed the rifle stock, sending it clattering to the floor. The Cuban thrashed wildly. He stank of rotten jungle air and cigarettes. His eyes rolled back, trying to see Mingolla. Crazy animal eyes, with liverish whites and expanded pupils. Sweat beads glittered redly on his brow. Mingolla twisted the machete, and the Cuban's eyelids fluttered down. But a second later they snapped open, and he lunged. They went staggering deeper into the room and teetered beside one of the cots. Mingolla wrangled the Cuban sideways and rammed him against the wall, pinning him there. Writhing, the Cuban nearly broke free. He seemed to be getting stronger, his squeals leaking out from Mingolla's hand. He reached behind him, clawing at Mingolla's face; he grabbed a clump of hair, yanked it. Desperate, Mingolla sawed with the machete. That tuned the Cuban's squeals higher, louder. He squirmed and clawed at the wall. Mingolla's clamped hand was slick with the Cuban's saliva, his nostrils full of the man's rank scent. He felt queasy, weak, and he wasn't sure how much longer he could hang on. The son of a bitch was never going to die, he was deriving strength from the steel in his guts, he was changing into some deathless force. But just then the Cuban stiffened. Then he relaxed, and Mingolla caught a whiff of feces.

He let the Cuban slump to the floor, but before he could turn loose of the machete, a shudder passed through the body, flowed up the hilt, and vibrated his left hand. It continued to shudder inside his hand, feeling dirty, sexy, like a postcoital tremor. Something, some animal essence, some oily scrap of bad life, was slithering around in there, squirting toward his wrist. He stared at the hand, horrified. It was gloved in the Cuban's blood, trembling. He smashed it against his hip, and that seemed to stun whatever was inside it. But within seconds it had revived and was wriggling in and out of his fingers with the mad celerity of a tadpole.

"Teo!" someone called. *"Vamos!"*

Electrified by the shout, Mingolla hustled to the door. His foot nudged the Cuban's rifle. He picked it up, and the shaking of his hand lessened—he had the idea it had been soothed by a familiar texture and weight.

"Teo! Dónde estás?"

Mingolla had no good choices, but he realized it would be far more dangerous to hang back than to take the initiative. He grunted *"Aqui!"* and walked out into the tunnel, making lots of noise with his heels.

"Date prisa, hombre!"

Mingolla opened fire as he rounded the curve. The two Cubans were standing by the entrance to the auxiliary tunnel. Their rifles chattered briefly, sending a harmless spray of bullets off the walls; they whirled, flung out their arms, and fell. Mingolla was too shocked by how easy it had been to feel relief: He kept watching, expecting them to do something. Moan, or twitch.

After the echoes of the shots had died, though he could hear the big guns jolting and the crackle of firefights, a heavy silence seemed to fill in through the tunnel, as if his bullets had pierced something that had dammed silence up. The silence made him aware of his isolation. No telling where the battle lines were drawn...if, indeed, they existed. It was conceivable that small units had infiltrated every level, that the battle for the Ant Farm was in microcosm the battle for Guatemala: a conflict having no patterns, no real borders, no orderly confrontations, but which, like a plague, could pop up anywhere at any time and kill. That being the case, his best bet would be to head for the computer center, where friendly forces were sure to be concentrated.

He walked to the entrance and stared at the two dead Cubans. They had fallen, blocking his way, and he was hesitant about stepping over them, half-believing they were playing possum, that they would reach up and grab him. The awkward attitudes of their limbs made him think they were holding a difficult pose, waiting for him to try. Their blood looked purple in the red glow of the emergencies, thicker and shinier than ordinary blood. He noted their moles and scars and sores, the crude stitching of their fatigues, gold fillings glinting from their open mouths. It was funny, he could have met these guys while they were alive and they might have made only a vague impression; but seeing them dead, he had cataloged their physical worth in a single glance. Maybe, he thought, death revealed your essentials as life could not. He studied the dead men, wanting to read them. Couple of slim, wiry guys. Nice guys, into rum and the ladies and sports. He'd bet they were baseball players, infielders, a double-play combo. Maybe he should have called to them,

Hey, I'm a Yankee fan. Be cool! Meet'cha after the war for a game of flies and grounders. Fuck this killing shit. Let's play some ball.

He laughed, and the high, cracking sound of his laughter startled him. Christ! Standing around here was just asking for it. As if to second that opinion, the thing inside his hand exploded into life, eeling and frisking about. Swallowing back his fear, Mingolla stepped over the two dead men, and this time, when nothing clutched at his trouser legs, he felt very, very relieved.

▲▼▲

Below Level Six there was a good deal of mist in the auxiliary tunnel, and from this Mingolla understood that the Cubans had penetrated the hillside, probably with a borer mine. Chances were the hole they had made was somewhere close, and he decided that if he could find it, he would use it to get the hell out of the Farm and hide in the jungle. On Level Seven the mist was extremely thick; the emergency lights stained it pale red, giving it the look of surgical cotton packing a huge artery. Scorch marks from grenade bursts showed on the walls like primitive graphics, and quite a few bodies were visible beside the doorways. Most of them Americans, badly mutilated. Uneasy, Mingolla picked his way among them, and when a man spoke behind him, saying, "Don't move," he let out a hoarse cry and dropped his rifle and spun around, his heart pounding,

A giant of a man—he had to go six-seven, six-eight, with the arms and torso of a weight lifter—was standing in a doorway, training a forty-five at Mingolla's chest. He wore khakis with lieutenant's bars, and his babyish face, though cinched into a frown, gave an impression of gentleness and stolidity: he conjured for Mingolla the image of Ferdinand the Bull weighing a knotty problem. "I told you not to move," he said peevishly.

"It's okay," said Mingolla. "I'm on your side."

The lieutenant ran a hand through his thick shock of brown hair; he seemed to be blinking more than was normal. "I'd better check," he said. "Let's go down to the storeroom."

"What's to check?" said Mingolla, his paranoia increasing.

"Please!" said the lieutenant, a genuine wealth of entreaty in his voice. "There's been too much violence already."

The storeroom was a long, narrow L-shaped room at the end of the level; it was ranged by packing crates, and through the gauzy mist the emergency lights looked like a string of dying red suns. The lieutenant marched Mingolla to the corner of the L, and turning it, Mingolla saw that the rear wall of the room was missing. A tunnel had been blown into the hillside, opening onto blackness. Forked roots with balls of dirt attached hung from its roof, giving it the witchy appearance of a tunnel into some world of dark magic; rubble and clods of earth were piled at its lip. Mingolla could smell the jungle, and he realized that the big guns had stopped firing. Which meant that whoever had won the battle of the summit would soon be sending down mop-up squads. "We can't stay here," he told the lieutenant. "The Cubans'll he back."

"We're perfectly safe," said the lieutenant. "Take my word." He motioned with the gun, indicating that Mingolla should sit on the floor.

Mingolla did as ordered and was frozen by the sight of a corpse, a Cuban corpse, lying between two packing crates opposite him, its head propped against the wall. "Jesus!" he said, coming back up to his knees.

"He won't bite," said the lieutenant. With the lack of self-consciousness of someone squeezing into a subway seat, he settled beside the corpse; the two of them neatly filled the space between the crates, touching elbow to shoulder.

"Hey," said Mingolla, feeling giddy and scattered. "I'm not sitting here with this fucking dead guy, man!"

The lieutenant flourished his gun. "You'll get used to him."

Mingolla eased back to a sitting position, unable to look away from the corpse. Actually, compared to the bodies he had just been stepping over, it was quite presentable. The only signs of damage were blood on its mouth and bushy black beard, and a mire of blood and shredded cloth at the center of its chest. Its beret had slid down at a rakish angle to cover one eyebrow; the brass scorpion pin was scarred and tarnished. Its eyes were open, reflecting glowing red chips of the emergency lights, and this gave it a baleful semblance of life. But the reflections made it appear less real, easier to bear.

"Listen to me," said the lieutenant.

Mingolla rubbed at the blood on his shaking hand, hoping that cleaning it would have some good effect.

"Are you listening?" the lieutenant asked.

Mingolla had a peculiar perception of the lieutenant and the corpse as dummy and ventriloquist. Despite its glowing eyes, the corpse had too much reality for any trick of the light to gloss over for long. Precise crescents showed on its fingernails, and because its head was tipped to one side, blood had settled into that side, darkening its cheek and temple, leaving the rest of the face pallid. It was the lieutenant, with his neat khakis and polished shoes and nice haircut, who now looked less than real.

"Listen!" said the lieutenant vehemently. "I want you to understand that I have to do what's right for me!" The biceps of his gun arm bunched to the size of a cannonball.

"I understand," said Mingolla, thoroughly unnerved.

"Do you? Do you really?" The lieutenant seemed aggravated by Mingolla's claim to understanding. "I doubt it. I doubt you could possibly understand."

"Maybe I can't," said Mingolla, "Whatever you say, man. I'm just trying to get along, y'know."

The lieutenant sat silent, blinking. Then he smiled. "My name's Jay," he said. "And you are...?"

"David." Mingolla tried to bring his concentration to bear on the gun, wondering if he could kick it away, but the sliver of life in his hand distracted him.

"Where are your quarters, David?"

"Level Three."

"I live here," said Jay. "But I'm going to move. I couldn't bear to stay in a place where...." He broke off and leaned forward, adopting a conspiratorial stance. "Did you know it takes a long time for someone to die, even after their heart has stopped?"

"No, I didn't." The thing in Mingolla's hand squirmed toward his wrist, and he squeezed the wrist, trying to block it.

"It's true," said Jay with vast assurance. "None of these people"—he gave the corpse a gentle nudge with his elbow, a gesture that conveyed to Mingolla a creepy sort of familiarity—"have finished dying. Life doesn't just switch off. It fades. And these people are still alive, though it's only a half-life." He grinned. "The half-life of life, you might say."

Mingolla kept the pressure on his wrist and smiled, as if in appreciation of the play on words. Pale red tendrils of mist curled between them.

"Of course you aren't attuned," said Jay. "So you wouldn't understand. But I'd be lost without Eligio."

"Who's Eligio?"

Jay nodded toward the corpse. "We're attuned, Eligio and I. That's how I know we're safe. Eligio's perceptions aren't limited to the here and now any longer. He's with his men at this very moment, and he tells me they're all dead or dying."

"Uh-huh," said Mingolla, tensing. He had managed to squeeze the thing in his hand back into his fingers, and he thought he might be able to reach the gun. But Jay disrupted his plan by shifting the gun to his other hand. His eyes seemed to be growing more reflective, acquiring a ruby glaze, and Mingolla realized this was because he had opened them wide and angled his stare toward the emergency lights.

"It makes you wonder," said Jay. "It really does."

"What?" said Mingolla, easing sideways, shortening the range for a kick.

"Half-lives," said Jay. "If the mind has a half-life, maybe our separate emotions do, too. The half-life of love, of hate. Maybe they still exist somewhere." He drew up his knees, shielding the gun. "Anyway, I can't stay here. I think I'll go back to Oakland." His tone became whispery. "Where are you from, David?"

"New York."

"Not my cup of tea," said Jay. "But I love the Bay Area. I own an antique shop there. It's beautiful in the mornings. Peaceful. The sun comes through the window, creeping across the floor, y'know, like a tide, inching up over the furniture. It's as if the original varnishes are being reborn, the whole shop shining with ancient lights."

"Sounds nice," said Mingolla, taken aback by Jay's lyricism.

"You seem like a good person." Jay straightened up a bit. "But I'm sorry. Eligio tells me your mind's too cloudy for him to read. He says I can't risk keeping you alive. I'm going to have to shoot."

Mingolla set himself to kick, but then listlessness washed over him. What the hell did it matter? Even if he knocked the gun away, Jay could probably break him in half. "Why?" he said. "Why do you have to?"

"You might inform on me." Jay's soft features sagged into a sorrowful expression. "Tell them I was hiding."

"Nobody gives a shit you were hiding," said Mingolla. "That's what I was doing. I bet there's fifty other guys doing the same damn thing."

"I don't know," Jay's brow furrowed. "I'll ask again. Maybe your mind's less cloudy now." He turned his gaze to the dead man.

Mingolla noticed that the Cuban's irises were angled upward and to the left—exactly the same angle to which Jay's eyes had drifted earlier—and reflected an identical ruby glaze.

"Sorry," said Jay, leveling the gun. "I have to." He licked his lips. "Would you please turn your head? I'd rather you weren't looking at me when it happens. That's how Eligio and I became attuned."

Looking into the aperture of the gun's muzzle was like peering over a cliff, feeling the chill allure of falling. It was more out of contrariness than a will to survive that Mingolla popped his eyes at Jay and said, "Go ahead."

Jay blinked, but he held the gun steady. "Your hand's shaking," he said after a pause.

"No shit," said Mingolla.

"How come it's shaking?"

"Because I killed someone with it." said Mingolla, "Because I'm as fucking crazy as you are."

Jay mulled this over. "I was supposed to be assigned to a gay unit," he said finally. "But all the slots were filled, and when I had to be assigned here they gave me a drug. Now I...I...." He blinked rapidly, his lips parted, and Mingolla found that he was straining toward Jay, wanting to apply Body English, to do something to push him over this agonizing hump. "I can't...be with men anymore," Jay finished, and once again blinked rapidly; then his words came easier. "Did they give you a drug too? I mean I'm not trying to imply you're gay. It's just they have drugs for everything these days, and I thought that might be the problem."

Mingolla was suddenly, inutterably sad. He felt that his emotions had been twisted into a thin black wire, that the wire was frayed and spraying black sparks of sadness. That was all that energized him, all his life. Those little black sparks.

"I always fought before," said Jay. "And I was fighting this time. But when I shot Eligio...I just couldn't keep going,"

"I really don't give a shit," said Mingolla, "I really don't."

"Maybe I can trust you." Jay sighed. "I just wish you were attuned. Eligio's a good soul. You'd appreciate him."

Jay kept on talking, enumerating Eligio's virtues, and Mingolla tuned him out, not wanting to hear about the Cuban's love for his family, his posthumous concerns for them. Staring at his bloody hand, he had a magical overview of the situation. Sitting in the root cellar of this evil mountain, bathed in an eerie red glow, a scrap of a dead man's life trapped in his flesh, listening to a deranged giant who took his orders from a corpse, waiting for scorpion soldiers to pour through a tunnel that appeared to lead into a dimension of mist and blackness. It was insane to look at it that way. But there it was. You couldn't reason it away; it had a brutal glamour that surpassed reason, that made reason unnecessary.

"...and once you're attuned," Jay was saying, "you can't ever be separated. Not even by death. So Eligio's always going to be alive inside me. Of course I can't let them find out. I mean"—he chuckled, a sound like dice rattling in a cup—"talk about giving aid and comfort to the enemy!"

Mingolla lowered his head, closed his eyes. Maybe Jay would shoot. But he doubted that. Jay only wanted company in his madness.

"You swear you won't tell them?" Jay asked.

"Yeah," said Mingolla. "I swear."

"All right," said Jay. "But remember, my future's in your hands. You have a responsibility to me."

"Don't worry."

Gunfire crackled in the distance.

"I'm glad we could talk," said Jay. "I feel much better."

Mingolla said that he felt better, too.

They sat without speaking. It wasn't the most secure way to pass the night, but Mingolla no longer put any store in the concept of security. He was too weary to be afraid. Jay seemed entranced, staring at a point above Mingolla's head, but Mingolla made no move for the gun. He was content to sit and wait and let fate take its course. His thoughts uncoiled with vegetable sluggishness.

They must have been sitting a couple of hours when Mingolla heard the whisper of helicopters and noticed that the mist had thinned, that the darkness at the end of the tunnel had gone gray. "Hey," he said to Jay. "I think we're okay now." Jay offered no reply, and Mingolla saw that his eyes were angled upward and to the left just like the Cuban's eyes, glazed over with ruby reflection. Tentatively, he reached out and touched the gun. Jay's hand flopped to the floor, but his fingers remained clenched around the butt. Mingolla recoiled, disbelieving. It couldn't be! Again he reached out, feeling for a pulse. Jay's wrist was cool, still, and his lips had a bluish cast. Mingolla had a flutter of hysteria, thinking that Jay had gotten it wrong about being attuned: instead of Eligio's becoming part of his life, he had become part of Eligio's death. There was a tightness in Mingolla's chest, and he thought he was going to cry. He would have welcomed tears, and when they failed to materialize he grew both annoyed at himself and defensive. Why should he cry? The guy had meant nothing to him...though the fact that he could be so devoid of compassion was reason enough for tears. Still, if you were going to cry over something as commonplace as a single guy dying, you'd be crying every minute of the day, and what was the future in that? He glanced at Jay. At the Cuban. Despite the smoothness of Jay's skin, the Cuban's bushy heard, Mingolla could have sworn they were starting to resemble each other the way old married couples did. And, yep, all four eyes were fixed on exactly the same point of forever. It was either a hell of a coincidence or else Jay's craziness had been of such magnitude that he had willed himself to die in this fashion just to lend credence to his theory of half-lives. And maybe he was still alive. Half alive. Maybe he and Mingolla were now attuned, and if that were true, maybe.... Alarmed by the prospect of joining Jay and the Cuban in their deathwatch, Mingolla scrambled to his feet and ran into the tunnel. He might have kept running, but on coming out into the dawn light he was brought up short by the view from the tunnel entrance.

At his back, the green dome of the hill swelled high, its sides brocaded with shrubs and vines; an infinity of pattern as eye-catching as the intricately carved facade of a Hindu temple; atop it, one of the gun emplacements had taken a hit: splinters of charred metal curved up like peels of black rind. Before him lay the moat of red dirt with its hedgerows of razor wire, and beyond that loomed the blackish-green snarl of the jungle. Caught on the wire were hundreds of baggy shapes wearing bloodstained fatigues; frays of smoke twisted up from the fresh craters beside them. Overhead, half-hidden by the lifting gray mist, three Sikorskys were hovering. Their pilots were invisible behind layers of mist and reflection, and the choppers themselves looked like enormous carrion flies with bulging eyes and whirling wings. Like devils. Like gods. They seemed to be whispering to one another in anticipation of the feast they were soon to share.

The scene was horrid, yet it had the purity of a stanza from a ballad come to life, a ballad composed about tragic events in some border hell. You could never paint it, or if you could the canvas would have to be as large as the scene itself, and you would have to incorporate the slow boil of the mist, the whirling of the chopper blades, the drifting smoke. No detail could be omitted. It was the perfect illustration of the war, of its secret magical splendor, and Mingolla, too, was an element of the design, the figure of the artist painted in for a joke or to lend scale and perspective to its vastness, its importance. He knew that he should report to his station, but he couldn't turn away from the glimpse into the heart of the war. He sat down on the hillside, cradling his sick hand in his lap, and watched as—with the ponderous aplomb of idols floating to earth, fighting the cross-draft, the wind of their descent whipping up furies of red dust—the Sikorskys made skillful landings among the dead.

— 4 —

Halfway through the telling of his story, Mingolla had realized that he was not really trying to offend or shock Debora, but rather was unburdening himself; and he further realized that by telling it he had to an extent cut loose from the past, weakened its hold on him. For the first time he felt able to give serious consideration to the idea of desertion. He did not rush to it, embrace it, but he did acknowledge its logic and understand the terrible illogic of returning to more assaults, more death, without any magic to protect him. He made a pact with himself: he would pretend to go along as if desertion were his intent and see what signs were offered.

When he had finished, Debora asked whether or not he was over his anger. He was pleased that she hadn't tried to offer sympathy. "I'm sorry," he said. "I wasn't really angry at you...at least that was only part of it."

"It's all right." She pushed back the dark mass of her hair so that it fell to one side and looked down at the grass beside her knees. With her head inclined, eyes half-lidded, the graceful line of her neck and chin like a character in some exotic script, she seemed a good sign herself. "I don't know what to talk to you about," she said. "The things I feel I have to tell you make you mad, and I can't muster any small talk."

"I don't want to be pushed," he said. "But believe me, I'm thinking about what you've told me."

"I won't push. But I still don't know what to talk about." She plucked a grass-blade, chewed on the tip. He watched her lips purse, wondered how she'd taste. Mouth sweet in the way of a jar that had once held spices. And down below, she'd taste sweet there, too: honey gone a little sour in the comb. She tossed the grass-blade aside. "I know," she said brightly. "Would you like to see where I live?"

"I'd just as soon not go back to 'Frisco yet." Where you live, he thought; I want to touch where you live.

"It's not in town," she said. "It's a village downriver."

"Sounds good." He came to his feet, took her arm, and helped her up. For an instant they were close together, her breasts grazing his shirt. Her heat coursed around him, and he thought if anyone were to see them, they would see two figures wavering as in a mirage. He had an urge to tell her he loved her. Though most of what he felt was for the salvation she might provide, part of his feelings seemed real and that puzzled him, because all she had been to him was a few hours out of the war, dinner in a cheap restaurant and a walk along the river. There was no basis for consequential emotion. Before he could say anything, do anything, she turned and picked up her basket.

"It's not far," she said, walking away. Her blue skirt swayed like a rung bell.

They followed a track of brown clay overgrown by ferns, overspread by saplings with pale translucent leaves, and soon came to a grouping of thatched huts at the mouth of a stream that flowed into the river. Naked children were wading in the stream, laughing and splashing each other.

Their skins were the color of amber and their eyes were as wet-looking and purplish-dark as plums. Palms and acacias loomed above the huts, which were constructed of sapling trunks lashed together by nylon cord; their thatch had been trimmed to resemble bowl-cut hair. Flies crawled over strips of meat hung on a clothesline stretched between two of the huts. Fish heads and chicken droppings littered the ocher ground. But Mingolla scarcely noticed these signs of poverty, seeing instead a sign of the peace that might await him in Panama. And another sign was soon forthcoming. Debora bought a bottle of rum at a tiny store, then led him to the hut nearest the mouth of the stream and introduced him to a lean white-haired old man who was sitting on a bench outside it. Tío Moisés. After three drinks Tío Moisés began to tell stories.

The first story concerned the personal pilot of an ex-president of Panama. The president had made billions from smuggling cocaine into the States with the help of the CIA, whom he had assisted on numerous occasions, and was himself an addict in the last stages of mental deterioration. It had become his sole pleasure to be flown from city to city in his country, to sit on the landing strips, gaze out the window, and do cocaine. At any hour of night or day, he was likely to call the pilot and order him to prepare a flight plan to Colón or Bocas del Toro or Penonomé. As the president's condition worsened, the pilot realized that soon the CIA would see he was no longer useful and would kill him. And the most obvious manner of killing him would be by means of an airplane crash. The pilot did not want to die alongside him. He tried to resign, but the president would not permit it. He gave thought to mutilating himself, but being a good Catholic, he could not flout God's law. If he were to flee, his family would suffer. His life became a nightmare. Prior to each flight, he would spend hours searching the plane for evidence of sabotage, and upon each landing he would remain in the cockpit, shaking from nervous exhaustion. The president's condition grew even worse. He had to be carried aboard the plane and have the cocaine administered by an aide, while a second aide stood by with cotton swabs to attend his nosebleeds. Knowing his life could be measured in weeks, the pilot asked his priest for guidance. "Pray," the priest advised. The pilot had been praying all along, so this was no help. Next he went to the commandant of his military college, and the commandant told him he must do his duty. This, too, was something the pilot had been doing all along. Finally he went to the chief of the San Blas Indians, who were his mother's people. The chief told him he must accept his fate, which—while not something he had been doing all along—was hardly encouraging. Nonetheless, he saw it was the only available path and he did as the chief had counseled.

Rather than spending hours in a preflight check, he would arrive minutes before takeoff and taxi away without even inspecting the fuel gauge. His recklessness came to be the talk of the capitol. Obeying the president's every whim, he flew in gales and in fogs, while drunk and drugged, and during those hours in the air, suspended between the laws of gravity and fate, he gained a new appreciation of life. Once back on the ground, he engaged in living with a fierce avidity, making passionate love to his wife, carousing with friends, and staying out until dawn. Then one day as he was preparing to leave for the airport, an American man came to his house and told him he had been replaced. "If we let the president fly with so negligent a pilot, we'll be blamed for anything that happens," said the American. The pilot did not have to ask whom he had meant by "we." Six weeks later the president's plane crashed in the Darien Mountains. The pilot was overjoyed. Panama had been ridded of a villain, and his own life had not been forfeited. But a week after the crash, after the new president—another smuggler with CIA connections—had been appointed, the commandant of the air force summoned the pilot, told him that the crash would never have occurred had he been on the job, and assigned him to fly the new president's plane.

All through the afternoon Mingolla listened and drank, and drunkenness fitted a lens to his eyes that let him see how these stories applied to him. They were all fables of irresolution, cautioning him to act, and they detailed the core problems of the Central American people who—as he was now—were trapped between the poles of magic and reason, their lives governed by the politics of the ultrareal, their spirits ruled by myths and legends, with the rectangular computerized bulk of North America above and the conch-shell-shaped continental mystery of South America below. He assumed that Debora had orchestrated the types of stories Tío Moisés told, but that did not detract from their potency as signs: they had the ring of truth, not of something tailored to his needs. Nor did it matter that his hand was shaking, his vision playing tricks. Those things would pass when he reached Panama.

Shadows blurred, insects droned like tambouras, and twilight washed down the sky, making the air look grainy, the chop on the river appear slower and heavier. Tío Moisés's granddaughter served plates of roast corn and fish, and Mingolla stuffed himself. Afterward, when the old man signaled his weariness, Mingolla and Debora strolled off along the stream. Between two of the huts, mounted on a pole, was a warped backboard with a netless hoop, and some young men were shooting baskets. Mingolla joined them. It was hard dribbling on the bumpy dirt, but he had never played better. The residue of drunkenness fueled his game, and his jump shots followed perfect arcs down through the hoop. Even at improbable angles, his shots fell true. He lost himself in flicking out his hands to make a steal, in feinting and leaping high to snag a rebound, becoming—as dusk faded—the most adroit of ten arm-waving, jitter-stepping shadows.

The game ended and the stars came out, looking like holes punched into fire through a billow of black silk overhanging the palms. Flickering chutes of lamplight illuminated the ground in front of the huts, and as Debora and Mingolla walked among them, he heard a radio tuned to the Armed Forces network giving a play-by-play of a baseball game. There was a crack of the bat, the crowd roared, the announcer cried, "He got it all!" Mingolla imagined the ball vanishing into the darkness above the stadium, bouncing out into parking-lot America, lodging under a tire where some kid would find it and think it a miracle, or rolling across the street to rest under a used car, shimmering there, secretly white and fuming with home-run energies. The score was three-to-one, top of the second. Mingolla didn't know who was playing and didn't care. Home runs were happening for him, mystical jump shots curved along predestined tracks. He was at the center of incalculable forces.

One of the huts was unlit, with two wooden chairs out front, and as they approached, the sight of it soured Mingolla's mood. Something about it bothered him: its air of preparedness, of being a little stage-set. He was just paranoid, he thought. The signs had been good so far, hadn't they? When they reached the hut, Debora sat in the chair nearer the door and looked up at him. Starlight pointed her eyes with brilliance. Behind her, through the doorway, he made out the shadowy cocoon of a strung hammock, and beneath it, a sack from which part of a wire cage protruded. "What about your game?" he asked.

"I thought it was more important to be with you," she said.

That, too, bothered him. It was all starting to bother him, and he couldn't understand why. The thing in his hand wiggled. He balled the hand into a fist and sat next to Debora. "What's going on between you and me?" he asked, nervous. "Is anything gonna happen? I keep thinking it will, but...." He wiped sweat from his forehead and forgot what he had been driving at.

"I'm not sure what you mean," she said.

A shadow moved across the yellow glare, spilling from the hut next door. Rippling, undulating, Mingolla squeezed his eyes shut.

"If you mean...romantically," she said, "I'm confused about that myself. Whether you return to your base or go to Panama, we don't seem to have much of a future. And we certainly don't have much of a past."

It boosted his confidence in her, in the situation, that she didn't have an assured answer. But he felt shaky. Very shaky. He gave his head a twitch, fighting off more ripples. "What's it like in Panama?"

"I've never been there. Probably a lot like Guatemala, except without the fighting."

Maybe he should get up, walk around. Maybe that would help. Or maybe he should just sit and talk. Talking seemed to steady him. "I bet," he said, "I bet it's beautiful, y'know. Panama. Green mountains, jungle waterfalls. I bet there's lots of birds. Macaws and parrots. Millions of 'em."

"I suppose so."

"And hummingbirds. This friend of mine was down there once on a hummingbird expedition, said there was a million kinds. I thought he was sort of a creep, y'know, for being into collecting hummingbirds." He opened his eyes and had to close them again. "I guess I thought hummingbird collecting wasn't very relevant to the big issues."

"David?" Concern in her voice.

"I'm okay." The smell of her perfume was more cloying than he remembered. "You get there by boat, right? Must be a pretty big boat. I've never been on a real boat, just this rowboat my uncle had. He used to take me fishing off Coney Island, we'd tie up to a buoy and catch all these poison fish. You shoulda seen some of 'em. Like mutants. Rainbow-colored eyes, weird growths all over. Scared the hell outta me to think about eating fish."

"I had an uncle who—"

"I used to think about all the ones that must be down there too deep for us to catch. Giant blowfish, genius sharks, whales with hands. I'd see 'em swallowing the boat, I'd—"

"Calm down, David." She kneaded the back of his neck, sending a shiver down his spine.

"I'm okay, I'm okay." He pushed her hand away; he did not need shivers along with everything else. "Lemme hear some more 'bout Panama."

"I told you, I've never been there."

"Oh, yeah. Well, how 'bout Costa Rica? You been to Costa Rica." Sweat was popping out all over his body. Maybe he should go for a swim. He'd heard there were manatees in the Rio Dulce. "Ever seen a manatee?" he asked.

"David!"

She must have leaned close, because he could feel her heat spreading all through him, and he thought maybe that would help, smothering in her heat, heavy motion, get rid of this shakiness. He'd take her into that hammock and see just how hot she got. *How* hot *she got, how* hot *she got.* The words did a train rhythm in his head. Afraid to open his eyes, he reached out blindly and pulled her to him. Bumped faces, searched for her mouth. Kissed her. She kissed back. His hand slipped up to cup a breast. Jesus, she felt good! She felt like salvation, like Panama, like what you fall into when you sleep.

But then it changed, changed slowly, so slowly that he didn't notice until it was almost complete, and her tongue was squirming in his mouth, as thick and stupid as a snail's foot, and her breast, oh shit, her breast was jiggling, trembling with the same wormy juices that were in his left hand. He pushed her off, opened his eyes. Saw crude-stitch eyelashes sewn to her cheeks. Lips parted, mouth full of bones. Blank face of meat. He got to his feet, pawing the air, wanting to rip down the film of ugliness that had settled over him.

"David?" She warped his name, gulping the syllables as if she were trying to swallow and talk at once. Frog voice, devil voice.

He spun around, caught an eyeful of black sky and spiky trees and a pitted bone-knob moon trapped in a weave of branches. Dark warty shapes of the huts, doors into yellow flame with crooked shadow men inside. He blinked, shook his head. It wasn't going away, it was real. What was this place? Not a village in Guatemala, naw, un-unh. He heard a strangled wild-man grunt come from his throat, and he backed away, backed away from everything. She walked after him, croaking his name. Wig of black straw, dabs of shining jelly for eyes. Some of the shadow men were herky-jerking out of their doors, gathering behind her, talking about him in devil language. Faceless nothings from the dimension of sickness, demons in *péon* drag. He backed another few steps.

"I can see you," he said. "I know what you are."

"It's all right, David," she said, and smiled.

Sure! She thought he was going to buy the smile, but he wasn't fooled. He saw how it broke over her face the way something rotten melts through the bottom of a wet grocery sack after it's been in the garbage for a week. Gloating smile of the Queen Devil Bitch. She had done this to him, had teamed up with the bad life in his hand and done witchy things to his head. Made him see down to the layer of shit-magic she lived in.

"I see you," he said.

He tripped, went backward flailing, stumbling, and came out of it running toward the town.

Ferns whipped his legs, branches cut at his face. Webs of shadow and moonlight fettered the trail, and the shrilling insects had the sound of a metal edge being honed. Up ahead, he spotted a big moonstruck tree standing by itself on a rise overlooking the water, a grandfather tree, a white-magic tree. It called to him. He stopped beside it, sucking air. The moonlight cooled him off, drenched him with silver, and he understood the purpose of the tree. Fountain of whiteness in the dark wood, shining for him alone. He made a fist of his left hand. The thing inside the hand eeled frantically as if it knew what was coming; he studied the deeply grooved, mystic patterns of the bark and found the point of confluence. He steeled himself. Then he drove his fist into the trunk. Brilliant pain lanced up his arm, and he cried out. But he hit the tree again, hit it a third time. He held the hand tight against his body, muffling the pain. It was already swelling, becoming a knuckleless cartoon hand; but nothing moved inside it. The riverbank, with its rustlings and shadows, no longer menaced him; it had been transformed into a place of ordinary lights, ordinary darks, and even the whiteness of the tree looked unmagically bright.

"David!" Debora's voice, and not far off.

Part of him wanted to wait, to see whether or not she had changed for the innocent, for the ordinary. But he couldn't trust her, couldn't trust himself, and he set out running once again.

▲▼▲

Mingolla caught the ferry to the west bank, thinking that he would find Gilbey, that a dose of Gilbey's belligerence would ground him in reality. He sat in the bow next to a group of five other soldiers, one of whom was puking over the side, and to avoid a conversation he turned away and looked down into the black water slipping past. Moonlight edged the wavelets with silver, and among those gleams it seemed he could see reflected the broken curve of his life: a kid living for Christmas, drawing pictures, receiving praise, growing up mindless to high school, sex, and drugs; growing beyond that, beginning to draw pictures again, and then, right where you might expect the curve to assume a more meaningful shape, it was sheared off, left hanging, its process demystified and explicable. He realized how foolish the idea of the ritual had been. Like a dying man clutching a vial of holy water, he had clutched at magic when the logic of existence had proved untenable. Now the frail linkages of that magic had been dissolved, and nothing supported him: he was falling through the dark zones of the war, waiting to be snatched by one of its monsters. He lifted his head and gazed at the west bank. The shore toward which he was heading was as black as a bat's wing and inscribed with arcana of violent light. Rooftops and palms were cast in silhouette against a rainbow haze of neon; gassy arcs of bloodred and lime green and indigo were visible between them: fragments of glowing beasts. The wind bore screams and wild music. The soldiers beside him laughed and cursed, and the one guy kept on puking. Mingolla rested his forehead on the wooden rail, just to feel something solid.

At the Club Demonio, Gilbey's big-breasted whore was lounging by the bar, staring into her drink. Mingolla pushed through the dancers, through heat and noise and veils of lavender smoke; when he walked up to the whore, she put on a professional smile and made a grab for his crotch. He fended her off. "Where's Gilbey?" he shouted. She gave him a befuddled look; then the light dawned. "Meen-golla?" she said. He nodded. She fumbled in her purse and pulled out a folded paper. "Ees frawm Geel-bee," she said. "Forr me, five dol-larrs."

He handed her the money and took the paper. It proved to be a Christian pamphlet with a pen-and-ink sketch of a rail-thin, aggrieved-looking Jesus on the front, and beneath the sketch, a tract whose first line read, "The last days are in season." He turned it over and found a handwritten note on the back. The note was pure Gilbey. No explanation, no sentiment. Just the basics.

> *I'm gone to Panama. You want to make that trip, check out a guy named Ray Barros in Livingston. He'll fix you up. Maybe I'll see you.*
>
> *G.*

Mingolla had believed that his confusion had peaked, but the fact of Gilbey's desertion wouldn't fit inside his head, and when he tried to make it fit he was left more confused than ever. It wasn't that he couldn't understand what had happened. He understood it perfectly; he might have predicted it. Like a crafty rat who had seen his favorite hole blocked by a trap, Gilbey had simply chewed a new hole and vanished through it. The thing that confused Mingolla was his total lack of referents. He and Gilbey and Baylor had seemed to triangulate reality, to locate each other within a coherent map of duties and places and events; and now that they were both gone, Mingolla felt utterly bewildered. Outside the club, he let the crowds push him along and gazed up at the neon animals atop the bars. Giant blue rooster, green bull, golden turtle with fiery red eyes. An advertising man's hellish pantheon. Bleeds of color washed from the signs, staining the air to a garish paleness, giving everyone a mealy complexion. Amazing, Mingolla thought, that you could breathe such grainy discolored stuff, that it didn't start you choking. It was all amazing, all nonsensical. Everything he saw struck him as unique and unfathomable, even the most commonplace of sights. He found himself staring at people—at whores, at street kids, at an MP who was talking to another MP, patting the fender of his jeep as if it were his big olive-drab pet—and trying to figure out what they were really doing, what special significance their actions held for him, what clues they presented that might help him unravel the snarl of his own existence. At last, realizing that he needed peace and quiet, he set out toward the airbase, thinking he would find an empty bunk and sleep off his confusion; but when he came to the cutoff that led to the unfinished bridge, he turned down it, deciding that he wasn't ready to deal with gate sentries and duty officers. Dense thickets buzzing with insects narrowed the cutoff to a path, and at its end stood a line of sawhorses. He climbed over them and soon was mounting a sharply inclined curve that appeared to lead to a point not far below the lumpish silver moon.

Despite a litter of rubble and cardboard sheeting, the concrete looked pure under the moon, blazing bright, like a fragment of snowy light not quite hardened to the material; and as he ascended he thought he could feel the bridge trembling to his footsteps with the sensitivity of a white nerve. He seemed to be walking into darkness and stars, a solitude the size of creation. It felt good and damn lonely, maybe a little too much so, with the wind lapping pieces of cardboard and the sounds of the insects left behind. After a few minutes he glimpsed the ragged terminus ahead. When he reached it, he sat down carefully, letting his legs dangle. Wind keened through the exposed girders, tugging at his ankles; his hand throbbed and was fever-hot. Below, multi-colored brilliance clung to the black margin of the east bank like a colony of bioluminescent algae. He wondered how high he was. Not high enough, he thought. Faint music was fraying on the wind—the inexhaustible delirium of San Francisco de Juticlan—and he imagined that the flickering of the stars was caused by this thin smoke of music drifting across them.

He tried to think what to do. Not much occurred to him. He pictured Gilbey in Panama. Whoring, drinking, fighting. Doing just as he had in Guatemala. That was where the idea of desertion failed Mingolla. In Panama he would be afraid; in Panama, though his hand might not shake, some other malignant twitch would develop; in Panama he would resort to magical cures for his afflictions because he would be too imperiled by the real to derive strength from it. And eventually the war would come to Panama. Desertion would have gained him nothing. He stared out across the moon-silvered jungle, and it seemed that some essential part of him was pouring from his eyes, entering the flow of the wind and rushing away past the Ant Farm and its smoking craters, past guerrilla territory, past the seamless join of sky and horizon, being irresistibly pulled toward a point into which the world's vitality was emptying. He felt himself emptying as well, growing cold and vacant and slow. His brain became incapable of thought, capable only of recording perceptions. The wind brought green scents that made his nostrils flare. The sky's blackness folded around him, and the stars were golden pinpricks of sensation. He didn't sleep, but something in him slept.

▲▼▲

A whisper drew him back from the edge of the world. At first he thought it had been his imagination, and he continued staring at the sky, which had lightened to the vivid blue of predawn. Then he heard it again and glanced behind him. Strung out across the bridge, about twenty feet away, were a dozen or so children. Some standing, some crouched. Most were clad in rags, a few wore coverings of vines and leaves, and others were naked. Watchful; silent. Knives glinted in their hands. They were all emaciated, their hair long and matted, and Mingolla, recalling the dead children he had seen that morning, was for a moment afraid. But only for a moment. Fear flared in him like a coal puffed to life by a breeze and then died an instant later, suppressed not by any rational accommodation but by a perception of those ragged figures as an opportunity for surrender. He wasn't eager to die, yet neither did he want to put forth more effort in the cause of survival. Survival, he had learned, was not the soul's ultimate priority. He kept staring at the children. The way they were posed reminded him of a Neanderthal grouping in the Museum of Natural History. The moon was still up, and they cast vaguely defined shadows like smudges of graphite. Finally Mingolla turned away; the horizon was showing a distinct line of green darkness.

He had expected to be stabbed or pushed, to pinwheel down and break against the Río Dulce, its waters gone a steely color beneath the brightening sky. But instead a voice spoke in his ear: "Hey, gringo." Squatting beside him was a boy of fourteen or fifteen, with a swarthy monkeylike face framed by tangles of shoulder-length dark hair. Wearing tattered shorts. Coiled serpent tattooed on his brow. He tipped his head to one side, then the other. Perplexed. He might have been trying to see the true Mingolla through layers of false appearance. He made a growly noise in his throat and held up a knife, twisting it this way and that, letting Mingolla observe its keen edge, how it channeled the moonlight along its blade. An army-issue survival knife with a brass-knuckle grip. Mingolla gave an amused sniff.

The boy seemed alarmed by this reaction, he lowered the knife and shifted away. "What you doing here, gringo?" he asked.

A number of answers occurred to Mingolla, most demanding too much energy to voice; he chose the simplest. "I like it here. I like the bridge."

The boy squinted at Mingolla. "The bridge is magic," he said. "You know this?"

"There was a time I might have believed you," said Mingolla.

"You got to talk slow, man." The boy frowned. "Too fast, I can't understan'."

Mingolla repeated his comment, and the boy said, "You believe it, gringo. Why else you here?" With a planing motion of his arm he described an imaginary continuance of the bridge's upward course. "That's where the bridge travels now. Don't have not'ing to do wit' crossing the river. It's a piece of white stone. Don't mean the same t'ing a bridge means."

Mingolla was surprised to hear his thoughts echoed by someone who so resembled a hominid.

"I come here," the boy went on. "I listen to the wind, hear it in the iron. And I know t'ings from it. I can see the future." He grinned, exposing blackened teeth, and pointed south toward the Caribbean. "Future's that way, man."

Mingolla liked the joke; he felt an affinity for the boy, for anyone who could manage jokes from the boy's perspective, but he couldn't think of a way to express his good feeling. Finally he said, "You speak English well."

"Shit! What you think? 'Cause we live in the jungle, we talk like animals? Shit!" The boyjabbed the point of his knife into the concrete. "I talk English all my life. Gringos, they too stupid to learn Spanish."

▲▼▲

A girl's voice sounded behind them, harsh and peremptory. The other children had closed to within ten feet, their savage faces intent upon Mingolla, and the girl was standing a bit forward of them. She had sunken checks and deep-set eyes; ratty cables of hair hung down over her single-scoop breasts. Her hip bones tented up a rag of a skirt, which the wind pushed back between her legs. The boy let her finish, then gave a prolonged response, punctuating his words by smashing the brass-knuckle grip of his knife against the concrete, striking sparks with every blow.

"Gracela," he said to Mingolla, "she wants to kill you. But I say, some men they got one foot in the worl' of death, and if you kill them, death will take you, too. And you know what?"

"What?" said Mingolla.

"It's true. You and death"—the boy clasped his hands—"like this."

"Maybe," Mingolla said.

"No 'maybe.' The bridge tol' me. Tol' me I be tankful if I let you live. So you be t'ankful to the bridge. That magic you don' believe, it save your ass." The boy lowered out of his squat and sat cross-legged. "Gracela, she don' care 'bout you live or die. She jus' go 'gainst me 'cause when I leave here, she going to be chief. She's, you know, impatient."

Mingolla looked at the girl. She met his gaze coldly: a witchchild with slitted eyes, bramble hair, and ribs poking out.

"Where are you going?" he asked the boy.

"I have a dream I will live in the south; I dream I own a warehouse full of gold and cocaine."

The girl began to harangue him again, and he shot back a string of angry syllables.

"What did you say?" Mingolla asked.

"I say, 'Gracela, you give me shit, I going to fuck you and t'row you in the river."' He winked at Mingolla. "Gracela she a virgin so she worry 'bout that firs' t'ing."

The sky was graying, pink streaks fading in from the east; birds wheeled up from the jungle below, forming into flocks above the river. In the half-light Mingolla saw that the boy's chest was crosshatched with ridged scars: knife wounds that hadn't received proper treatment. Bits of vegetation were trapped in his hair, like primitive adornments.

"Tell me, gringo," said the boy. "I hear in America there is a machine wit' the soul of a man. This is true?"

"More or less," said Mingolla.

The boy nodded gravely, his suspicions confirmed, "I hear also America has builded a metal worl' in the sky."

"They're building it now."

"In the house of your president, is there a stone that holds the mind of a dead magician?"

Mingolla gave this due consideration. "I doubt it," he said. "But it's possible."

Wind thudded against the bridge, startling him. He felt its freshness on his face and relished the sensation. That—the fact that he could still take simple pleasure from life—startled him more than had the sudden noise.

The pink streaks in the east were deepening to crimson and fanning wider; shafts of light pierced upward to stain the bellies of some low-lying clouds to mauve. Several of the children began to mutter in unison. A chant. They were speaking in Spanish, but the way their voices jumbled the words, it sounded guttural and malevolent, a language for trolls. Listening to them, Mingolla imagined them crouched around fires in bamboo thickets. Bloody knives lifted sunward over their fallen prey. Making love in the green nights among fleshy Rousseau-like vegetation, while pythons with ember eyes coiled in the branches above their heads.

"Truly, gringo," said the boy, apparently still contemplating Mingolla's answers. "These are evil times." He stared gloomily down at the river; the wind shifted the heavy snarls of his hair.

Watching him, Mingolla grew envious. Despite the bleakness of his existence, this little monkey king was content with his place in the world, assured of its nature. Perhaps he was deluded, but Mingolla envied his delusion, and he especially envied his dream of gold and cocaine. His own dreams had been dispersed by the war. The idea of sitting and daubing colors onto canvas no longer held any real attraction for him. Nor did the thought of returning to New York. Though survival had been his priority all these months, he had never stopped to consider what survival portended, and now he did not believe he could return. He had, he realized, become acclimated to the war, able to breathe its toxins; he would gag on the air of peace and home. The war was his new home, his newly rightful place.

Then the truth of this struck him with the force of an illumination, and he understood what he had to do.

Baylor and Gilbey had acted according to their natures, and he would have to act according to his, which imposed upon him the path of acceptance. He remembered Tío Moisés's story about the pilot and laughed inwardly. In a sense his friend—the guy he had mentioned in his unsent letter—had been right about the war, about the world. It was full of designs, patterns, coincidences, and cycles that appeared to indicate the workings of some magical power. But these things were the result of a subtle natural process. The longer you lived, the wider your experience, the more complicated your life became, and eventually you were bound in the midst of so many interactions, a web of circumstance and emotion and event, that nothing was simple anymore and everything was subject to interpretation. Interpretation, however, was a waste of time. Even the most logical of interpretations was merely an attempt to herd mystery into a cage and lock the door on it. It made life no less mysterious. And it was equally pointless to seize upon patterns, to rely on them, to obey the mystical regulations they seemed to imply. Your one effective course had to be entrenchment. You had to admit to mystery, to the incomprehensibility of your situation, and protect yourself against it. Shore up your web, clear it of blind corners, set alarms. You had to plan aggressively. You had to become the monster in your own maze, as brutal and devious as the fate you sought to escape. It was the kind of militant acceptance that Tío Moisés's pilot had not the opportunity to display, that Mingolla himself—though the opportunity had been his—had failed to display. He saw that now. He had merely reacted to danger and had not challenged or used forethought against it, But he thought he would be able to do that now.

He turned to the boy, thinking he might appreciate this insight into "magic," and caught a flicker of movement out of the corner of his eye. Gracela. Coming up behind the boy, her knife held low, ready to stab. In reflex, Mingolla flung out his injured hand to block her. The knife nicked the edge of his hand, deflected upward, and sliced the top of the boy's shoulder.

The pain in Mingolla's hand was excruciating, blinding him momentarily; and then as he grabbed Gracela's forearm to prevent her from stabbing again, he felt another sensation, one almost covered by the pain. He had thought the thing inside his hand was dead, but now he could feel it fluttering at the edges of the wound, leaking out in the rich trickle of blood that flowed over his wrist. It was trying to worm back inside, wriggling against the flow, but the pumping of his heart was too strong, and soon it was gone, dripping on the white stone of the bridge.

Before he could feel relief or surprise or in any way absorb what had happened, Gracela tried to pull free. Mingolla got to his knees, dragged her down, and dallied her knife-hand against the bridge. The knife skittered away. Gracela struggled wildly, clawing at his face, and the other children edged forward. Mingolla levered his left arm under Gracela's chin, choking her; with his right hand, he picked up the knife and pressed the point into her breast. The children stopped their advance, and Gracela went limp. He could feel her trembling. Tears streaked the grime in her cheeks. She looked like a scared little girl, not a witch.

"Puta!" said the boy. He had come to his feet, holding his shoulder, and was staring daggers at Gracela.

"Is it bad?" Mingolla asked. "The shoulder?"

The boy inspected the bright blood on his fingertips. "It hurts," he said. He stepped over to stand in front of Gracela and smiled down at her; he unbuttoned the top of his shorts. Gracela tensed.

"What are you doing?" Mingolla suddenly felt responsible for the girl.

"I going to do what I tol' her, man." The boy undid the rest of the buttons and shimmied out of his shorts; he was already half erect, as if the violence had aroused him.

"No," said Mingolla, realizing as he spoke that this was not at all wise.

"Take your life," said the boy sternly. "Walk away."

A long powerful gust of wind struck the bridge; it seemed to Mingolla that the vibration of the bridge, the beating of his heart, and Gracela's trembling were driven by the same shimmering. He felt an almost visceral commitment to the moment, one that had nothing to do with his concern for the girl. Maybe, he thought, it was an implementation of his new convictions.

The boy lost patience. He shouted at the other children, herding them away with slashing gestures. Sullenly, they moved off the curve of the bridge, positioning themselves along the miling, leaving an open avenue. Beyond them, beneath a lavender sky, the jungle stretched to the horizon, broken only by the rectangular hollow made by the airbase. The boy hunkered at Gracela's feet. "Tonight," he said to Mingolla, "the bridge have set us together. Tonight we sit, we talk. Now, that's over. My heart say to kill you. But 'cause you stop Gracela from cutting deep, I give you a chance. She mus' make a judgmen'. If she say she go wit' you, we"—he waved toward the other children—"will kill you. If she wan' to stay, then you mus' go. No more talk, no bullshit. You jus' go, Understan'?"

Mingolla wasn't afraid, and his lack of fear was not born of an indifference to life, but of clarity and confidence. It was time to stop reacting away from challenges, time to meet them. He came up with a plan. There was no doubt that Gracela would choose him, choose a chance at life, no matter how slim. But before she could decide, he would kill the boy. Then he would run straight at the others; without their leader, they might not hang together. It wasn't much of a plan, and he didn't like the idea of hurting the boy; but he thought he might be able to pull it off.

"I understand," he said.

The boy spoke to Gracela; he told Mingolla to release her. She sat up, rubbing the spot where Mingolla had pricked her with the knife. She glanced coyly at him, then at the boy; she pushed her hair back behind her neck and thrust out her breasts as if preening for two suitors. Mingolla was astonished by her behavior. Maybe, he thought, she was playing for time. He stood and pretended to be shaking out his kinks, edging closer to the boy, who remained crouched beside Gracela. In the east a red fireball had cleared the horizon; its sanguine light inspired Mingolla, fueled his resolve. He yawned and edged closer yet, firming his grip on the knife. He would yank the boy's head back by the hair, cut his throat. Nerves jumped in his chest. A pressure was building inside him, demanding that he act, that he move now. He restrained himself. Another step should do it, another step to be absolutely sure. But as he was about to take that step, Gracela reached out and tapped the boy on the shoulder.

Surprise must have showed on Mingolla's face, because the boy looked at him and grunted laughter, "You t'ink she pick you?" he said. "Shit! You don' know Gracela, man. Gringos burn village. She lick the devil's ass 'fore she even shake hands wit' you." He grinned, stroked her hair. "'Sides, she t'ink if she fuck me good, maybe I say, 'Oh, Gracela, I got to have some more of that!' And who knows? Maybe she right."

Gracela lay back and wriggled out of her skirt. Between her legs, she was nearly hairless. A smile touched the corners of her mouth. Mingolla stared at her, dumbfounded.

"I not going to kill you, gringo," said the boy without looking up; he was running his hand across Gracela's stomach. "I tol' you I won' kill a man so close wit' death." Again he laughed. "You look pretty funny trying to sneak up. I like watching that."

Mingolla was stunned. All the while he had been gearing himself up to kill, shunting aside anxiety and revulsion, he had merely been providing an entertainment for the boy. The heft of the knife seemed to be drawing his anger into a compact shape, and he wanted to carry out his attack, to cut down this little animal who had ridiculed him; but humiliation mixed with the anger, neutralizing it. The poisons of rage shook him; he could feel every incidence of pain and fatigue in his body. His hand was throbbing, bloated and discolored like the hand of a corpse. Weakness pervaded him. And relief.

"Go," said the boy: He lay down beside Gracela, propped on an elbow, and began to tease one of her nipples erect.

Mingolla took a few hesitant steps away. Behind him, Gracela made a mewling noise and the boy whispered something. Mingolla's anger was rekindled—they had already forgotten him!—but he kept going. As he passed the other children, one spat at him and another shied a pebble. He fixed his eyes on the white concrete slipping beneath his feet.

When he reached the midpoint of the curve, he turned back. The children had hemmed in Gracela and the boy against the terminus, blocking them from view. The sky had gone bluish-gray behind them, and the wind carried their voices. They were singing a ragged, chirpy song that sounded celebratory. Mingolla's anger subsided, his humiliation ebbed. He had nothing to be ashamed of; though he had acted unwisely, he had done so from a posture of strength and no amount of ridicule could diminish that. Things were going to work out. Yes, they were! He would make them work out.

For a while he watched the children. At this remove their singing had an appealing savagery, and he felt a trace of wistfulness leaving them behind. He wondered what would happen after the boy had done with Gracela. He was not concerned, only curious. The way you feel when you think you may have to leave a movie before the big finish. Will our heroine survive? Will justice prevail? Will survival and justice bring happiness in their wake? Soon the end of the bridge came to be bathed in the golden rays of the sunburst; the children seemed to be blackening and dissolving in heavenly fire. That was a sufficient resolution for Mingolla. He tossed Gracela's knife into the river and went down from the bridge in whose magic he no longer believed, walking toward the war whose mystery he had accepted as his own.

— 5 —

At the airbase Mingolla took a stand beside the Sikorsky that had brought him to San Francisco de Juticlan; he had recognized it by the painted flaming letters of the words *Whispering Death*. He rested his head against the letter *g* and recalled how Baylor had recoiled from the letters, worried that they might transmit some deadly essence. Mingolla didn't mind the contact. The painted flames seemed to be warming the inside of his head, stirring up thoughts as slow and indefinite as smoke. Comforting thoughts that embodied no images or ideas. Just a gentle buzz of mental activity, like the idling of an engine. The base was coming to life around him. Jeeps pulling away from barracks; a couple of officers inspecting the belly of a cargo plane; some guy repairing a forklift. Peaceful, homey. Mingolla closed his eyes, lulled into half-sleep, letting the sun and the painted flames bracket him with heat, real and imagined.

Sometime later—how much later, he could not be sure—a voice said, "Fucked up your hand pretty good, didn'tcha?"

The two pilots were standing by the cockpit door. In their black flight suits and helmets they looked neither weird nor whimsical, but creatures of functional menace. Masters of the Machine. "Yeah," said Mingolla. "Fucked it up."

"How'd ya do it?" asked the pilot on the left.

"Hit a tree."

"Musta been goddamn crocked to hit a tree," said the pilot on the right. "Tree ain't goin' nowhere if you hit it."

Mingolla made a noncommittal noise. "You guys going up to the Farm?"

"You bet! What's the matter, man? Had enough of them wild women?" Pilot on the right.

"Guess so. Wanna gimme a ride?"

"Sure thing," said the pilot on the left. "Whyn't you climb on to front. You can sit back of us."

"Where your buddies?" asked the pilot on the right.

"Gone," said Mingolla as he climbed into the cockpit.

One of the pilots said, "Didn't think we'd be seein' them boys again."

Mingolla strapped into the observer's seat behind the copilot's position. He had assumed there would be a lengthy instrument check, but as soon as the engines had been warmed, the Sikorsky lurched up and veered northward. With the exception of the weapons systems, none of the defenses had been activated. The radar, the thermal imager and terrain display, all showed blank screens. A nervous thrill ran across the muscles of Mingolla's stomach as he considered the varieties of danger to which the pilots' reliance upon their miraculous helmets had laid them open; but his nervousness was subsumed by the whispery rhythms of the rotors and his sense of the Sikorsky's power. He recalled having a similar feeling of secure potency while sitting at the controls of his gun. He had never let that feeling grow, never let it empower him. He had been a fool.

They followed the northeasterly course of the river, which coiled like a length of blue-steel razor wire between jungled hills. The pilots laughed and joked, and the flight came to have the air of a ride with a couple of good of boys going nowhere fast and full of free beer. At one point the copilot piped his voice through the on-board speakers and launched into a dolorous country song.

"Whenever we kiss, dear, our two lips meet,
And whenever you're not with me, we're apart.
When you sawed my dog in half, that was depressin',
But when you shot me in the chest, you broke my heart."

As the copilot sang, the pilot rocked the Sikorsky back and forth in a drunken accompaniment, and after the song ended, he called back to Mingolla, "You believe this here son of a bitch wrote that? He did! Picks a guitar, too! Boy's a genius!"

"It's a great song," said Mingolla, and he meant it. The song made him happy, and that was no small thing.

They went rocking through the skies, singing the first verse over and over. But then, as they left the river behind, still mainlining a northeasterly course, the copilot pointed to a section of jungle ahead and shouted, "Beaners! Quadrant Four! You got 'em?"

"Got 'em!" said the pilot. The Sikorsky swerved down toward the jungle, shuddered, and flame veered from beneath them. An instant later, a huge swath of jungle erupted into a gout of marbled smoke and fire. "Whee-oo!" the copilot sang out jubilant, "*Whisperin' Death* strikes again!" With guns blazing they went swooping through blowing veils of dark smoke. Acres of trees were burning, and still they kept up the attack. Mingolla gritted his teeth against the noise, and when at last the firing stopped, dismayed by this insanity, he sat slumped, his head down. He suddenly doubted his ability to cope with the insanity of the Ant Farm and remembered all his reasons for fear.

The copilot turned back to him. "You ain't got no call to look so gloomy, man," he said. "You're a lucky son of a bitch, y'know that?"

The pilot began a bank toward the east, toward the Ant Farm. "How you figure that?" Mingolla asked.

"I gotta clear sight of you, man," said the copilot. "I can tell you for true you ain't gonna be at the Farm much longer. It ain't clear why or nothin'. But I 'spect you gonna be wounded. Not bad, though. Just a goin'-home wound."

As the pilot completed the bank, a ray of sun slanted into the cockpit, illuminating the copilot's visor, and for a split second Mingolla could make out the vague shadow of the face beneath. It seemed lumpy and malformed. His imagination added details. Bizarre growths, cracked cheeks, an eye webbed shut. Like a face out of a movie about nuclear mutants. He was tempted to believe that he had really seen this; the copilot's deformities would validate his prediction of a secure future. But Mingolla rejected the temptation. He was afraid of dying, afraid of the terrors held by life at the Ant Farm, yet he wanted no more to do with magic...unless there was magic involved in being a good soldier. In obeying the disciplines, in the practice of fierceness.

"Could be his hand'll get him home," said the pilot. "That hand looks pretty fucked up to me. Looks like a million-dollar wound, that hand."

"Naw, I don't get it's his hand," said the copilot. "Somethin' else. Whatever, it's gonna do the trick."

Mingolla could see his own face floating in the black plastic of the copilot's visor; he looked warped and pale, so thoroughly unfamiliar that for a moment he thought the face might be a bad dream the copilot was having.

"What the hell's with you, man?" the copilot asked. "You don't believe me?"

Mingolla wanted to explain that his attitude had nothing to do with belief or disbelief, that it signaled his intent to obtain a safe future by means of securing his present; but he couldn't think how to put it into words the copilot would accept. The copilot would merely refer again to his visor as testimony to a magical reality or perhaps would point up ahead where—because the cockpit plastic had gone opaque under the impact of direct sunlight—the sun now appeared to hover in a smoky darkness: a distinct fiery sphere with a streaming corona, like one of those cabalistic emblems embossed on ancient seals. It was an evil, fearsome-looking thing, and though Mingolla was unmoved by it, he knew the pilot would see in it a powerful sign.

"You think I'm lyin'?" said the copilot angrily. "You think I'd be bullshittin' you 'bout somethin' like this? Man, I ain't lyin'! I'm givin' you the good goddamn word!"

They flew east into the sun, whispering death, into a world disguised as a strange bloody enchantment, over the dark green wild where war had taken root, where men in combat armor fought for no good reason against men wearing brass scorpions on their berets, where crazy lost men wandered the mystic light of Fire Zone Emerald and mental wizards brooded upon things not yet seen. The copilot kept the black bubble of his visor angled back toward Mingolla, waiting for a response. But Mingolla just stared, and before too long the copilot turned away. —

The Arcevoalo

One morning nearly five hundred years after the September War, whose effects had transformed the Amazon into a region of supernal mystery, a young man with olive skin and delicate features and short black hair awoke to find himself lying amid a bed of ferns not far from the ruined city of Manaus. It seemed to him that some great darkness had just been lifted away, but he could recall nothing more concrete of his past, neither his name nor those of his parents or place of birth. Indeed, he was so lacking in human referents that he remained untroubled by this state of affairs and gazed calmly around at the high green canopy and the dust-hung shafts of sun and the tapestry of golden radiance and shadow overlying the jungle floor. Everywhere he turned he saw marvelous creatures: butterflies with translucent wings; birds with hinged, needle-thin beaks; snakes with faceted eyes that glowed more brightly than live coals. Yet the object that commanded his attention was a common orchid, its bloom a dusky lavender, that depended from the lowermost branch of a guanacaste tree. The sight mesmerized him, and intuitions about the orchid flowed into his thoughts: how soft its petals were, how subtle its fragrance, and, lastly, that it was not what it appeared to be. At that moment, as if realizing that he had penetrated its disguise, the bloom flew apart, revealing itself to have been composed of glittering insects, all of which now whirled off toward the canopy, shifting in color like particles of an exploded rainbow; and the young man understood—a further intuition—that he, too, was not what he appeared.

Puzzled, and somewhat afraid, he glanced down at the ferns and saw scattered among them pieces of a fibrous black husk. Upon examining them, he discovered that the insides of the pieces were figured by smooth indentations that conformed exactly to the shapes of his face and limbs. There could be no doubt that prior to his awakening, he had been enclosed within the husk, like a seed in its casing. His anxiety increased when—on setting down one of the pieces—his fingers brushed the clay beneath the ferns and he saw before his mind's eye the pitching deck of a vast wooden ship, with wild seas bursting over the railings. Men wearing steel helmets and carrying pikes were huddled in the bow, and standing in the door that led to the gun decks (how had he known that?) was a gray-haired man who beckoned to him. To him? No, to someone he had partly been. João Merín Nascimento. That name—like his vision of the ship—surfaced in his thoughts following contact with the clay. And with the name came a thousand fragments of memory, sufficient to make the young man realize that Nascimento, a Portuguese soldier of centuries past, lay buried beneath the spot where he was sitting, and that he was in essence the reincarnation of the old soldier: for just as the toxins and radiations of the September War had transformed the jungle, so the changed jungle had worked a process of alchemy on those ancient bones and produced a new creature, human to a degree, yet—to a greater degree—quite inhuman. Understanding this eased the young man's anxiety, because he now knew that he was safe in the dominion of the jungle, whose creature he truly was. But he understood, too, that his manlike form embodied a cunning purpose, and in hopes of discerning that purpose, he set out to explore the jungle, walking along a trail that led (though he was not aware of it) to the ruins of Manaus.

Nine days he walked; and during those days he learned much about the jungle's character and—consequently—about his own. From a creature with a dozen bodies, each identical, yet only one of which contained its vital spark, he learned an ultimate caution; from the malgatón, a fierce jaguarlike beast whose strange eyes could make a man dream of pleasure while he died, he learned the need for circumspection in the cause of violence; from the deadly jicaparee vine with its exquisite flowers, he learned the importance of setting a lure and gained an appreciation of the feral principles underlying all beauty.

From each of these creatures and more, he learned that no living thing is without its parasites and symbiotes, and that in the moment they are born their death is also born. But not until he came in sight of the ruined city, when he saw its crumbling, vine-draped towers tilting above the canopy like grotesque vegetable chessmen whose board was in process of being overthrown, not until then did he at last fathom his purpose: that he was to be the jungle's weapon against mankind, its mortal enemy who time and again had sought to destroy it.

The young man could not conceive how—fangless and clawless—he would prove a threat to an enemy with weapons that had poisoned a world. Perplexed, hoping some further illumination would strike him, took to wandering the city streets, over cracked flagstones between which he could see the tunnels of guerilla ants, past ornate wrought-iron streetlamps in whose fractured globes white phosphorescent spiders the size of skull crabs had spun their webs (by night their soft glow conveyed a semblance of the city's fabulous heyday into this, its rotting decline), and through the cavernous mansions of the wealthy dead. Everywhere he wandered he encountered danger, for Manaus had been heavily dusted during the September War and thus was home to the most perverse of the jungle's mutations: flying lizards that spit streams of venom; albino peacocks whose shrill cries could make a man bleed from the ears; the sortilene, a mysterious creature never glimpsed by human eyes, known only by the horrid malignancies that sprouted from the flesh of its victims; herds of peccaries, superficially unchanged but possessing vocal chords that could duplicate the cries of despairing women. At night an enormous shadow obscured the stars, testifying to an even more dire presence. Yet none of these creatures troubled the young man—they seemed to know him for an ally. And, indeed, often as he explored the gloomy interiors of the ruined houses, he would see hundreds of eyes gazing at him, slit pupils and round, showing all colors like a spectrum of stars ranging the dusky green shade, and then he would have the idea that they were watching over him.

At length he entered the lobby of a hotel that—judging by the sumptuous rags of its drapes, the silver-cloth stripe visible in the moss-furred wallpaper, the immensity of the reception desk—must once have been a palace among hotels. Thousands of slitherings stilled when he entered. The dark green shadows seemed the visual expression of a cloying mustiness, one redolent of a thousand insignificant deaths. His footsteps shaking loose falls of plaster dust, he walked along the main hallway, past elevator shafts choked with vines and epithytes, and came eventually to a foyer whose roof was holed in such a fashion that sharply defined sunbeams hung down from it, dappling the scummy surface of an ornamental pond with coins of golden light. There, sitting naked and cross-legged on a large lily pad—the sort that once hampered navigation on the Rio Negro due to the toughness of its fiber—was an old Indian man, so wizened that he appeared to be a homunculus. His eyes were closed, his white hair filthy and matted, and his coppery skin bore a greenish tinge (whether this was natural coloration or a product of the shadows, the young man could not determine). The young man expected intuitions about the Indian to flow into his thoughts; but when this did not occur, he realized that though the Indians, too, had been changed by the September War, though they were partially the jungle's creatures, they were still men, and the jungle had no knowledge of men other than that it derived from the bones of the dead. How then, he wondered, could he defeat an enemy about whom he was ignorant? He stretched out a hand to the Indian, thinking a touch might transmit some bit of information. But the Indian's eyes blinked open, and with a furious splashing he paddled the lily pad beyond the young man's reach. "The arcevoalo must be cautious with his touch," he said in a creaky voice that seemed to stir the atoms of the dust within the sunbeams. "Haven't you learned that?"

Though the young man—the arcevoalo—had not heard his name before, he recognized it immediately. With its Latinate echoes of wings and arcs, it spoke to him of the life he would lead, how he would soar briefly through the world of men and then return to give his knowledge of them to the jungle. Knowing his name opened him to his full strength—he felt it flooding him like a golden heat—and served to align his character more precisely with that of the jungle. He stared down at the Indian, who now struck him as being wholly alien, and asked how he had known the name.

"This truth I have eaten has told it to me," said the Indian, holding up a pouch containing a quantity of white powder. Grains of it adhered to his fingers. "I was called here to speak the truth to someone...doubtless to you. But now I must leave." He slipped off the lily pad and waded toward the edge of the pond.

Moving so quickly that he caused the merest flutter of shadow upon the surface of the water, the arcevoalo leaped to the far side of the pond, blocking the Indian's path. "What is this 'truth?' " he asked. "And who called you here?"

"The powder derives from the asuero flower," said the Indian. "A plant fertilized with the blood of honest men. As to who called me, if I had known that I might not have come." He made as if to haul himself from the pond, but the arcevoalo stayed him.

"How must I go about conquering my enemy?" he asked.

"To do battle one must first understand the foe."

"Then I will keep you with me and learn your ways," countered the arcevoalo.

The Indian hissed impatiently. "I am as different from those you must understand as you are from me. You must go to the city of Sangue do Lume. It is a new city, inhabited by Brazilians who fled the September War. Until recently they dwelled in metal worlds that circle the darkness behind the sky. Now they have returned to claim their ancient holdings, to reap the fruits of the jungle and to kill its animals for profit. It is they with whom you will contend."

"How will I contend? I have no weapons."

"You have speed and strength," said the Indian. "But your greatest weapon is a mere touch."

He instructed the arcevoalo to press the pads of his fingers hard, and when he did droplets of clear fluid welled from beneath the nails.

"A single drop will enslave any man's heart for a time," said the Indian. "But you must use this power sparingly, for your body can produce the fluid only in a limited quantity."

He flicked his eyes nervously from side to side, obviously afraid, eager to be gone. The arcevoalo continued to ask questions, but the effects of the "truth" drug were wearing off, and the Indian began to whine and to lie, saying that his cousin, whom he had not seen since the Year of Fabulous Sorrows, was coming to visit and he would be remiss if he were not home to greet him. With a wave of his hand, the arcevoalo dismissed him, and the Indian went scuttling away toward the lobby.

For a long time the arcevoalo stood beside the pond, thinking about what the Indian had said, watching the sunlight fade; in its stead a gray-green dusk filtered down from the holes in the roof. Soon he felt himself dimming, his thoughts growing slow, his blood sluggish, his muscles draining of strength: it was as if the dusk were also taking place inside his soul and body, and a gray-green fluid seeping into him and making him terribly weak and vague, incapable of movement. He saw that from every crack and cranny, jeweled eyes and scaly snouts and tendriled mouths were peering and thrusting and gaping. And in this manifold scrutiny, he sensed the infinitude of lives for whom he was to be the standard-bearer: those creatures in the ruined foyer were but the innermost ring of an audience focused upon him from every corner of the jungle. He apprehended them singly and as one, and from the combined intelligence of their regard he understood that dusk for him was an hour during which he must be solitary, both to hide from men the weakness brought on by the transition from light to dark, and to commune with the source of his imperatives. Dusk thickened to night, shafts of silvery moonlight shone down to replace those of the sun, which now burned over Africa, and with the darkness a new moon of power rose inside the arcevoalo, a silver strength equal yet distinct from the golden strength he possessed by day, geared more to elusiveness than to acts of domination. Freed of his intangible bonds, he walked from the hotel and set forth to find Sangue do Lume.

▲▼▲

During the twenty-seven days it took the arcevoalo to reach Sangue do Lume—which means "Blood of Light" in Portuguese, which is the language of sanguinary pleasures and heartbreak—he tested himself against the jungle. He outran the malgatón, outclimbed the tarzanal, and successfully spied upon the mysterious sortilene. He tested himself joyfully, and perhaps he never came to be happier than he was in those days, living in a harmony of green light and birds by day, and by night gazing into the ruby eyes of a malgatón, into those curious pupils that flickered and changed shape and brought the comfort of dreams. One evening he scaled a peak, hoping to lure down the huge shadow that each night obscured the stars, and when it flew near he saw that it was almost literally a shadow, being millimeters thick and having neither eyes nor mouth nor any feature that he could discern. There was something familiar about it, and he sensed that it was interested in him, that it—like him—was the sole member of its species. But otherwise it remained a puzzle: a rippling field of opaque darkness as incomprehensible as a flat black thought.

Sangue do Lume lay in a hilly valley between three mountains and was modeled after the old colonial towns, with cobbled streets and white stucco houses that had ironwork balconies and tiled roofs and gardens in their courtyards. Surrounding it—also after the style of the old colonial towns—was a slum where lived the laborers who had built the city. And surrounding the slum was a high wall of gray metal from which energy weapons were aimed at the jungle (no such weapons, however, were permitted within the wall). Despite the aesthetic incompatibility of its defenses, the city was beautiful, beautiful even to the eyes of the arcevoalo as he studied it from afar. He could not understand why it seemed so, being the home of his enemy; but he was later to learn that the walls of the houses contained machines that refined the images of the real, causing the visual aspect of every object to tend toward the ideal. Thus it was that the precise indigo shadows were in actuality blurred and dead-black; thus it was that women who went beyond the walls veiled themselves to prevent their husbands from taking note of their coarsened appearance; thus it was that the flies and rats and other pests of Sangue do Lume possessed a certain eyecatching appeal.

Each morning dozens of ships shaped like flat arrowpoints would lift from the city and fly off across the jungle; each afternoon they would return, their holds filled with dead plants and bloody carcasses, which would be unloaded into slots in the metal wall, presumably for testing. Seeing this, the arcevoalo grew enraged. Still, he bided his time and studied the city's ways, and it was not until a week after his arrival that he finally went down to the gate. The gatekeepers were amazed to see a naked man walk out of the jungle and were at first suspicious, but he told them a convincing tale of childhood abandonment (a childhood of which, he said, he could recall only his name—João Merín Nascimento), of endless wandering and narrow escapes, and soon the gatekeepers, their eyes moist with pity, admitted him and brought him before the governor, Caudez do Tuscanduva: a burly, middle-aged man with fierce black eyes and a piratical black beard and skin the color of sandalwood. The audience was brief, for the governor was a busy and a practical man, and when he discovered the arcevoalo's knowledge of the jungle, he assigned him to work on the flying ships and gave orders that every measure should be taken to ensure his comfort.

Such was the arcevoalo's novelty that all the best families clamored to provide him with food and shelter, and thus it was deemed strange that Caudez do Tuscanduva chose to quarter him in the Valverde house. The Valverdes were involved in a long-standing blood feud with the governor, one initiated years before upon the worlds behind the sky. The governor had been constrained by his vows of office from settling the matter violently, and it was assumed that this conferring of an honored guest must be his way of making peace. But the Valverdes themselves were not wholly persuaded by the idea, and therefore—with the exception of Orlando, the eldest son—they maintained an aloof stance toward the arcevoalo. Orlando piloted one of the ships that plundered the jungle, and it was to his ship that the arcevoalo had been assigned. He realized that by assisting in this work he would better understand his enemy, and so he did the work well, using his knowledge to track down the malgatón and the sortilene and creatures even more elusive. Yet it dismayed him, nonetheless. And what most dismayed him was the fact that as the weeks went by, he began to derive a human satisfaction from a job well done and to cherish his growing friendship with Orlando, who, by virtue of his delicate features and olive skin, might have been the arcevoalo's close relation.

Orlando was typical of the citizenry in his attitude of divine right concerning the land, in his arrogance toward the poor ("They are eternal," he once said. "You'll sooner find a cure for death than for poverty.") and in his single-minded pursuit of pleasure; yet there was about him a courage and soulfulness that gained the arcevoalo's respect. On most nights he and Orlando would dress in black trousers and blousy silk shirts, and would join similarly dressed young men by the fountain in the main square. There they would practice at dueling with the knife and the cintral (a jungle weed with sharp-edged tendrils and a rudimentary nervous system that could be employed as a living cat-o'-nine-tails), while the young women would promenade around them and cast shy glances at their favorites. The arcevoalo pretended clumsiness with the weapons, not wanting to display his speed and strength, and he was therefore often the subject of ridicule. This was just as well, for occasionally these play-duels would escalate, and then—since even death was beautiful in Sangue do Lume—blood would eel across the cobblestones, assuming lovely serpentine forms, and the palms ringing the square would rustle their fronds, and sad music would issue from the fountain, mingling with the splash of the waters.

Many of these duels stemmed from disputes over the affections of the governor's daughter, Sylvana, the sole child of his dead wife, his pride and joy. The bond between father and daughter was of such intimacy, it was said that should one's heart stop, the other would not long survive. Sylvana was pale, slim, blonde, and angelic of countenance, but was afflicted by a brittleness of expression that bespoke coldness and insensitivity. Observing this, the arcevoalo was led to ask Orlando why the young men would risk themselves for so heartless a prize. Orlando laughed and said, "How can you understand when you have no experience of women?" And he invited the arcevoalo to gain this experience by coming with him to the Favelin, which was the name of the slum surrounding the city.

The next night, Orlando and the arcevoalo entered the cluttered, smelly streets of the Favelin. The hovels there were made of rotting boards, pitched like wreckage at every angle; and were populated by a malnourished, shrunken folk who looked to be of a different species from Orlando. Twists of oily smoke fumed from the chimneys; feathered lizards slept in the dirt next to grimy children; hags in black shawls sacrificed pigs beneath glass bells full of luminescent fungus and scrawled bloody words in the dust to cure the sick. How ugly all this might have been beyond the range of the city's machines, the arcevoalo could not conceive. They came to a street whereon the doors were hung with red curtains, and Orlando ushered him through one of these and into a room furnished with a pallet and a chair. Mounted on the wall was the holograph of a bearded man who—though the cross to which he was nailed had burst into emerald flames—had maintained a beatific expression. The flames shed a ghastly light over a skinny girl lying on a pallet. She was hollowcheeked, with large, empty-looking eyes and jaundiced skin and ragged dark hair. Orlando whispered to her, gave her a coin, and—grinning as he prepared to leave—said, "Her name is Ana."

Without altering her glum expression, Ana stood and removed her shift. Her breasts had the convexity of upturned saucers, her ribs showed, and her genitals were almost hairless. Nevertheless, the arcevoalo became aroused, and when he sank down onto the pallet and entered her, he felt a rush of dominance and joy that roared through him like a whirlwind. He clutched at Ana's hips with all his strength, building toward completion. And staring into her hopeless eyes, he sensed the profound alienness of women, their mystical endurance, the eerie valences of their moods, and how even their common thoughts turn hidden corners into bizarre mental worlds. Knowing his dominance over this peculiar segment of humanity acted to heighten his desire, and with a hoarse cry he fell spent beside Ana and into a deep sleep.

He awoke to find her gazing at him with a look of such rapt contemplation that when she turned her eyes away, the image of his face remained reflected in her pupils. Timorously, shyly, she asked if he planned to return to the Favelin, to her. He recalled then the force with which he had clutched her, and he inspected the tips of his fingers. Droplets glistened beneath the nails, and there were damp bruises on Ana's hips. He realized that his touch, his secret chemistry, had manifested as love, an emotion whose power he apprehended but whose nature he did not understand.

"Will you return?" she asked again.

"Yes," he said, feeling pity for her. "Tomorrow."

And he did return, many times, for in his loveless domination of that wretched girl he had taken a step closer to adopting the ways of man. He had come to see that there was little difference between the city and the jungle, that "civilization" was merely a name given to comfort, and that the process of life in Sangue do Lume obeyed the same uncivilized laws as did the excesses of the sortilene. What point was there in warring against man? And, in any case, how could he win such a war? His touch was a useless power against an enemy who could summon countless allies from its worlds behind the sky.

Over the ensuing weeks the arcevoalo grew ever more despondent, and in the throes of despondency the human elements of his soul grew more and more predominant. At dusk his reverie was troubled by images of lust and conquest stirred from the memories of João Merín Nascimento. And his work aboard Orlando's ship became so proficient that Caudez do Tuscanduva held a fete in his honor, a night of delirium and pleasure during which a constellation of his profile appeared in the sky, and the swaying of the palms was choreographed by artificial winds, and the machines within the walls were turned high, beautifying everyone to such an extent that everyone's heart was broken...broken, and then healed by the consumption of tiny, soft-boned animals that induced a narcissistic ecstasy when eaten alive. Despite his revulsion for this practice, the arcevoalo indulged in it, and, his teeth stained with blood, he spent the remainder of the night wandering the incomparably beautiful streets and gazing longingly at himself in mirrors.

Thereafter Caudez do Tuscanduva took Orlando and the arcevoalo under his wing, telling them they were to be his protégés, that he had great plans for them. Further, he urged them to pay court to Sylvana, saying that, yes, she was an icy sort, but the right man would be able to thaw her. In this Orlando needed no urging. He plied her with gifts and composed lyrics to her charms. But Sylvana was disdainful of his efforts, and though for the most part she was equally disdainful of the arcevoalo, now and then she would favor him with a chilly smile, which—while scarcely encouraging—made Orlando quite jealous.

"You'd do better to set your sights elsewhere," the arcevoalo once told Orlando. "Even if you win her, you'll regret it. She's the kind of woman who uses marriage like a vise, and before you know it she'll have you squealing like a stuck pig." He had no idea whether or not this was true—it was something he had overheard another disappointed suitor say—but it accorded with his own impressions of her. He believed that Orlando was leaving himself open to the possibility of grievous hurt, and he told him as much. No matter how forcefully he argued, though, Orlando refused to listen.

"I know you're only trying to protect me, friend," he said. "And perhaps you're right. But this is an affair of the heart, and the heart is ruled by its own counsel."

And so the arcevoalo could do nothing more than to step aside and let Orlando have a clear field with Sylvana.

On one occasion Caudez invited them to dine at the governor's mansion. They sat at a long mahogany table graced by golden candelabra through whose branches the arcevoalo watched Sylvana daintily picking at her food, ignoring the heated glances that Orlando sent her way. After the meal, Caudez led them into his study, its windows open onto the orchid-spangled courtyard where Sylvana could be seen strolling—as elegant as an orchid herself—and held forth on his scheme to milk the resources of the Amazon: how he would reopen the gold mines at Serra Pelada, reinstitute the extensive-farming procedures that once had brought an unparalleled harvest, and thus feed and finance hundreds of new orbital colonies. Orlando's attention was fixed upon Sylvana, but the arcevoalo listened closely. Caudez, with his piratical air and his dream of transforming the Amazon into a tame backyard, struck him as being a force equal to the jungle. Pacing up and down, declaiming about the glorious future, Caudez seemed to walk with the pride of a continent. Late in the evening he turned his fierce black stare upon the arcevoalo and questioned him about his past. The questions were complex, fraught with opportunities for the arcevoalo to compromise the secret of his birth; he had to summon all his wits to avoid these pitfalls, and he wondered if Caudez were suspicious of him. But then Caudez laughed and clapped him on the shoulder, saying what a marvel he was, and that allayed his fears.

▲▼▲

Whereas in the jungle, time passed in a dark green flow, a single fluid moment infinitely prolonged, within the walls of Sangue do Lume it passed in sharply delineated segments so that occasionally one would become alerted to the fact that a certain period had elapsed—this due to the minuscule interruptions in the flow of time caused by the instruments men have for measuring it. And thus it was that one morning the arcevoalo awoke to the realization that he had lived in the city for a year. A year! And what progress had he made? His life, which had once had the form of purpose, of a quest, had resolved into a passive shape defined by his associations: his friendship with Orlando (whose wooing of Sylvana had reached fever pitch), his sexual encounters with Ana, his apprenticeship to Caudez. Each night he was reminded of his deeper associations with the jungle by the huge shadow that obscured the stars; yet he felt trapped between the two worlds, at home in neither, incapable of effecting any change. He might have continued at this impasse had not Ana announced to him one evening that she was with child. It would be, according to the old woman who had listened to her belly, a son. Standing in the garish light of her burning Christ, displaying her new roundness, flushed with a love no longer dependent on his touch, she presented him with a choice he could not avoid making. If he did nothing, his son would be born into the world of men; he had to be certain this was right.

But how could he decide such a complex issue, one that had baffled him for an entire year?

At the point of desperation, he remembered the old Indian man and his "truth," and that same night, after the machines in the walls had been switched off, leaving the flaking whitewash of the buildings exposed, he sneaked into the warehouse where the plant samples were kept and pilfered a quantity of asuero flowers. He returned to the Valverde house, ground the petals into a fine powder, and ate the entire amount. Soon pearls of sweat beaded on his forehead, his limbs trembled, and the moonlight flooding his room appeared to grow brighter than day.

Truth came to him in the clarity of his vision. Between the floorboards he saw microscopic insects and plants, and darting through the air were even tinier incidences of life. From these sights he understood anew that the city and the jungle were interpenetrating. Just as the ruins of Manaus lay beneath the foliage, so did the jungle's skeins infiltrate the living city. One was not good, the other evil. They were two halves of a whole, and the war between them was not truly a war but an everlasting pattern, a game in which he was a powerful pawn moved from the grotesque chessboard of Manaus to the neat squares of Sangue do Lume, a move that had set in motion a pawn of perhaps even greater power: his son. He realized now that no matter with which side he cast his lot, his son would make the opposite choice, for it was an immutable truth that fathers and sons go contrary to the other's will. Thus he had to make his own choice according to the dictates of his soul. A soul in confusion. And to dissolve that confusion, to know his options fully, he had to complete his knowledge of man by understanding the nature of love. He thought first of going to Ana, of infecting himself with the chemicals of his touch and falling under her spell; but then he recognized that the kind of love he sought to understand—the all-consuming love that motivates and destroys—had to embody the quality of the unattainable. With this in mind, still trembling from the fevers of the asuero powder, he went out again into the night and headed toward the governor's mansion, toward the unattainable Sylvana.

Since the concept of security in Sangue do Lume was chiefly geared to keeping the jungle out, the systems protecting the mansion were minimal, easily penetrated by a creature of the arcevoalo's stealth. He crept up the stairs, along the hall, cracked Sylvana's door, and eased inside. As was the custom with high-born women of the city, she was sleeping nude beneath a skylight through which the rays of the moon shone down in a silvery fan. A diamond pulsed coldly in the hollow of her throat, a tourmaline winked between her breasts, and in the tuft of her secret hair—trimmed to the shape of an orchid—an emerald shimmered wetly. These gems were bound in place by silken threads and were no ordinary stones but crystalline machines that focused the moonlight downward to produce a salubrious effect upon the organs, and also served as telltales of those organs' health. The unclouded states of the emerald, the tourmaline, and the diamond testified that Sylvana was virginal and of sound heart and respiration. But she was so lovely that the arcevoalo would not have cared if the stones had been black, signaling wantonness and infection. Rivulets of blonde hair streamed over her porcelain shoulders, and the soft brush of sleep had smoothed away her brittleness of expression, giving her the look of an angel under an enchantment.

Fixing his gaze upon her, the arcevoalo gripped his left forearm with the fingers of his right hand and pressed down hard. He maintained the grip for some time, uncertain how much of the chemical would be needed to affect him—indeed, he was uncertain whether or not he could be affected. But soon he felt a languorous sensation that made his eyelids droop and stilled the trembling caused by the asuero powder. When he opened his eyes, the sight of the naked Sylvana pierced him: it was as if an essential color had all along been missing from his portrait of her. Staring at her through the doubled lens of truth and love, he knew her coldness, her cunning and duplicity; yet he perceived these flaws in the way he might have perceived the fracture planes inside a crystal, how they channeled the light to create a lovely illusion of depth and complexity. Faint with desire, he walked over to the bed. A branching of bluish veins spread from the tops of her breasts, twined together and vanished beneath the diamond in the hollow of her throat, as if deriving sustenance from the stone; a tiny mole lay like a drop of obsidian by the corner of her lips. Carefully, knowing she could never truly love him, yet willing to risk his life to have her love this one and false time, he stretched out a hand and clamped it over Sylvana's mouth, while with the other hand he gripped her shoulder hard. Her eyes shot open, she squealed and kicked and clawed. He held her firmly, waiting for the chemistry of love to take effect. But it did not. Astounded, he examined his fingertips. They were dry, and he realized that in his urgency to know love he had exhausted the potency of his touch. He was full of despair, knowing he would have to flee the city...but then Sylvana's struggles ceased. The panic in her eyes softened, and she drew him into an embrace, whispering that her fearful reaction was due to the shock of being awakened so roughly, that she had been hoping for this moment ever since they had met. And with the power of truth which—though diminished by the truth of love—still allowed him a modicum of clear sight; the arcevoalo saw that, indeed, she had been hoping for this moment. She seemed charged with desire, overwhelmed by a passion no less ardent than his. But when he entered her, sinking into her plush warmth, he felt a nugget of chill against his belly; he knew it was the diamond bound by its silken thread, yet he could not help thinking of it as a node of her quintessential self that not even love could dissolve.

Some hours later, after the power of truth had been drained from the arcevoalo, Sylvana spoke to him. "Leave me," she said. "I have no more use for you." She was standing by the open door, smiling at him; the threads of her telltale jewels dangled from her right hand.

"What do you mean?" he asked. "What use have you made of me?" He was shocked by the wealth of cruelty in her smile, by her transformation from the voluptuous, the soft, into this glacial creature with glittering eyes.

She laughed—a thin, hard laugh that seemed to chart the jagged edge of such a vengeful thought. "I've never known such a fool," she said. "It's hard to believe you're even a man. I wondered if I'd have to drag you into my bed."

Again she laughed, and, suddenly afraid, the arcevoalo pulled on his clothes and ran, her derisive laughter chasing him down the hall and out into the dove-gray dawn of Sangue do Lume, whose machines were already beginning to restore a fraudulent perfection to its flaking walls.

▲▼▲

All that day the arcevoalo kept to his room in the Valverde house. He knew he should leave the city before Sylvana called down judgment upon him, but he found that he could not leave her, no matter how little affection she had for him. He understood now the nature of love, its blurred, irrational compulsions, its torments and its joys, and he doubted it would ever loosen its grip on him. But understanding it had made his choice no easier, and so perhaps he did not entirely understand, perhaps he did not see that love enforces its own continuum of choices, even upon an inhuman celebrant. There was no end to his confusion. One moment he would feel drawn back to the jungle, the next he would wonder how he could have considered such a reckless course. At dusk his reverie alternated between a perception of formless urges and a sequence of memories in which João Merín Nascimento staggered through a green hell, his brain afire and death a poisoned sugar clotting his veins. Night fell, and having some frail hope that Sylvana would do nothing, that things might go on as before, the arcevoalo left the house and walked toward the main square.

Though it was no holiday, though no fete had been scheduled, of all the beautiful nights in Sangue do Lume, this night came the closest to perfection, marred only by the whining of the machines functioning at peak levels. In the square the palm crowns flickered like green torches beneath an unequaled array of stars, and beams of light from the window shone like benedictions upon the fountain, whose spouts cast up sprays of silver droplets that fell to the ear as a cascade of guitar notes. Against the backdrop of gray stones and white stucco, the graceful attitudes of the young men and women, strolling and dueling, lost in a haze of mutual admiration, seemed a tapestry come to life. Even the arcevoalo's grim mood was brightened by the scene, but on drawing near the group of young men gathered about Orlando, on hearing Orlando's boastful voice, his mood darkened once again.

"...his blessing to Sylvana and I," Orlando was saying. "We'll be wed during the Festival of Erzulie."

The arcevoalo pushed through the group of listeners and confronted Orlando, too enraged to speak. Orlando put a hand on his shoulder. "My friend!" he said. "Great news!" But the arcevoalo struck his hand aside and said, "Your news is a lie! You will never marry her!"

It may have been that Orlando thought his friend was still trying to protect him from a loveless marriage, for he said, "Don't worry—"

"It's I who made love to her last night," the arcevoalo cut in. "And it's I who'll marry her."

Orlando reached for his cintral, whose green tendrils were dangling over the edge of the fountain; but he hesitated. Perhaps it was friendship that stayed his hand, or perhaps he believed that arcevoalo's friendship was so great that he would lie and risk a duel to prevent the marriage.

Then a woman laughed—a thin derisive laugh.

The arcevoalo turned and saw Sylvana and Caudez standing a dozen feet away. Hanging from a gold chain about Sylvana's neck was her telltale emerald, its blackness expressing the malefic use she had made of her body the previous night. Caudez was smiling, a crescent of white teeth showing forth from this thicket of a beard.

▲▼▲

Finally convinced that his friend had told the truth, Orlando's face twisted into an aggrieved knot, displaying his humiliation and pain. He picked up the cintral and lashed out at the arcevoalo. The sharp tendrils slithered through the air like liquid green swords; but at the last second—recognizing their ally—they veered aside, spasmed, and drooped lifelessly from Orlando's hand. His mind a boil of rage, unable by logic to direct his anger toward his true enemy, the arcevoalo plucked a knife from a bystander's sash and plunged it deep into Orlando's chest. As Orlando toppled onto his back, a hush fell over the assemblage, for never had they witnessed a death more beautiful than that of the Valverde's eldest son. The palms inclined their spiky heads, the fountain wept tears of crystalline music. Orlando's features acquired a noble rectitude they had not had in life; his blood shone with a saintly radiance and appeared to be spelling out a new language of poetry over the cobblestones.

"Now!" cried Caudez do Tuscanduva, his black eyes throwing off glints that were no reflections but sparks of an inner fire banked high. "Now has the great wrong done my father by the House of Valverde been avenged! And not by my hand!"

Murmurs of admiration for the sublety of his vengeance spread through the crowd. But the arcevoalo—gone cold with the horror of his act, full of self-loathing at having allowed himself to be manipulated—advanced upon Caudez and Sylvana, his knife at the ready.

"Kill him!" shouted Caudez, exhorting the young men. "I have no quarrel with his choice of victims, but he has struck down a man whose weapon failed him. Such cowardice must not go unpunished!"

And the young men, who had always suspected the arcevoalo of being lowborn and thus had no love for him, ranged themselves in front of Caudez and Sylvana, posing a barrier of grim faces and shining knives.

When men refer to the arcevoalo, they speak not only of the one who stood then beside the fountain, but also of his incarnations, and they will tell you that none of these ever fought so bravely in victory as did their original in defeat that night in Sangue do Lume. Fueled by the potentials of hatred and love (though that love had been mingled with bitterness), he spun and leaped, living in a chaos of agonized faces and flowers of blood blooming on silk blouses; and while the sad music of the fountain evolved into a skirling tantara, he left more than twenty dead in his wake, cutting a path toward Caudez and Sylvana. He received wounds that would have killed a man yet merely served to goad him on, and utilizing all his moon-given elusiveness, he avoided the most consequential of the young men's thrusts. In the end, however, there were too many young men, too many knives, and, weakening, he knew he would not be able to reach the governor and his daughter.

There came a moment of calm in the storm of battle, a moment when nine of the young men had hemmed the arcevoalo in against the fountain. Others waited their chance behind them. They were wary of him now, yet confident, and they all wore one expression: the dogged, stuporous expression that comes with the anticipation of a slaughter. Their unanimity weakened the arcevoalo further, and he thought it might be best to lay his weapon down and accept his fate. The young men sidled nearer, shifting their knives from hand to hand; the music of the fountain built to a glorious crescendo of trumpets and guitars, and the pale, beautiful bodies of the dead enmeshed in a lacework of blood seemed to be entreating the arcevoalo, tempting him to join them in their eternal poise. But in the next moment he spotted Caudez smiling at him between the shoulders of his adversaries, and Sylvana laughing at his side. That sight rekindled the arcevoalo's rage. With an open-throated scream, choosing his target in a flash of poignant bitterness, he hurled his knife. The blade whirled end over end, accumulating silver fire, growing brighter and brighter until its hilt sprouted from Sylvana's breast. Before anyone could take note of the artful character of her death, she sank beneath the feet of the milling defenders, leaving Caudez to stare in horror at the droplets of her blood stippling his chest. And then, seizing the opportunity provided by the young men's consternation, the arcevoalo ran from the square, through the flawless streets and into the Favelin, past the hovel where Ana and his unborn son awaited an unguessable future in the light of her dying god. He clambered over the gray metal wall and sprinted into the jungle.

Such was the efficacy of the city's machines that even the natural beauty of the moonlit jungle had been enhanced. It seemed to the arcevoalo that he was passing through an intricate design of silver and black, figured by the glowing eyes of those creatures who had come forth from hiding to honor his return. Despite his wounds, his panic, he had a sense of homecoming, of peacefulness and dominion. He came at length to a mountaintop east of Sangue do Lume and paused there to catch his breath. His muscles urged him onward, but his thoughts—heavy with the poisons of murder and betrayal—were a sickly ballast holding him in place. At any second, ships would arrow up from the city to track him, and he thought now that he would welcome them.

But as he stood there, grieving and empty of hope, a shadow obscured the stars: a great rippling field of shadow that swooped down and wrapped him in its filmy, almost weightless folds. He felt himself lifted and borne eastward and—after what could have been no more than a matter of seconds—gently lowered to earth. Through the dim opacity of the folds, he made out a high canopy of leaves and branches, silvery shafts of moonlight, and a bed of ferns. He could feel the creature merging with him, its folds becoming fibrous, gradually thickening to a husk, and—recalling the darkness that had passed from him at birth—he realized that this incomprehensible shadow was the death that had been born with him, had haunted all his nights, and had come at last to define the shape of his life.

The world dwindled to a dark green vibration, and with half his soul he yearned toward the pleasures of the city, toward love, toward all the sweet futilities of the human condition. But with the other half he exulted in the knowledge that his purpose had been achieved, that he had understood the nature of man. And (a final intuition) he knew that someday, long after he had decayed into a clay of old memories, just as it had with the bones of João Merín Nascimento, the jungle would breed from his bones a new creature, who—guided by his understanding—would make of love a weapon and of war a passion, and would bring inspired tactics to the eternal game. This knowledge gave him a measure of happiness, but that was soon eroded by his fear of what lay—or did not lie—ahead.

Something nudged the outside of the thickening husk. The arcevoalo peered out, straining to see, and spied the ruby eyes of a malgatón peering in at him, come to give him the comfort of dreams. Grateful, not wanting to feel the snip of death's black scissors, he concentrated on those strange pupils, watching them shift and dissolve and grow spidery, and then it was as if he were running again, running in the joyful way he had before he had reached Sangue do Lume, running in a harmony of green light and birds, in a wind that sang like a harp on fire, in a moment that seemed to last forever and lead beyond to other lives.

Shades

This little gook cadre with a pitted complexion drove me through the heart of Saigon—I couldn't relate to it as Ho Chi Minh City—and checked me into the Hotel Heroes of Tet, a place that must have been quietly elegant and very French back in the days when philosophy was discussed over Cointreau rather than practiced in the streets, but now was filled with cheap production-line furniture and tinted photographs of Uncle Ho. Glaring at me, the cadre suggested I would be advised to keep to my room until I left for Cam Le; to annoy him I strolled into the bar, where a couple of Americans—reporters, their table laden with notebooks and tape cassettes—were drinking shots from a bottle of George Dickel. "How's it goin'?" I said, ambling over. "Name's Tom Puleo. I'm doin' a piece on Stoner for *Esquire*."

The bigger of them—chubby, red-faced guy about my age, maybe thirty-five, thirty-six—returned a fishy stare; but the younger one, who was thin and tanned and weaselly handsome, perked up and said, "Hey, you're the guy was in Stoner's outfit, right?" I admitted it, and the chubby guy changed his attitude. He put on a welcome-to-the-lodge smile, stuck out a hand, and introduced himself as Ed Fierman, *Chicago Sun-Times*. His pal, he said, was Ken Witcover, CNN.

They tried to draw me out about Stoner, but I told them maybe later, that I wanted to unwind from the airplane ride, and we proceeded to do damage to the whiskey. By the time we'd sucked down three drinks, Fierman and I were into some heavy reminiscence. Turned out he had covered the war during my tour and knew my old top. Witcover was cherry in Vietnam, so he just tried to look wise and to laugh in the right spots. It got pretty drunk at that table. A security cadre—fortyish, cadaverous gook in yellow fatigues—sat nearby, cocking an ear toward us, and we pretended to be engaged in subversive activity, whispering and drawing maps on napkins. But it was Stoner who was really on all our minds, and Fierman—the drunkest of us—finally broached the subject, saying, "A machine that traps ghosts! It's just like the gooks to come up with something that goddamn worthless!"

Witcover shushed him, glancing nervously at the security cadre, but Fierman was beyond caution. "They coulda done humanity a service," he said, chuckling. "Turned alla Russians into women or something. But, nah! The gooks get behind worthlessness. They may claim to be Marxists, but at heart they still wanna be inscrutable."

"So," said Witcover to me, ignoring Fierman, "when you gonna fill us in on Stoner?"

I didn't care much for Witcover. It wasn't anything personal; I simply wasn't fond of his breed: compulsively neat (pencils lined up, name inscribed on every possession), edgy, on the make. I disliked him the way some people dislike yappy little dogs. But I couldn't argue with his desire to change the subject. "He was a good soldier," I said.

Fierman let out a mulish guffaw. "Now that," he said, "that's what I call in-depth analysis."

Witcover snickered.

"Tell you the truth"—I scowled at him, freighting my words with malice—"I hated the son of a bitch. He had this young-professor air, this way of lookin' at you as if you were an interestin' specimen. And he came across pure phony. Y'know, the kind who's always talkin' like a black dude, sayin' 'right on' and shit, and sayin' it all wrong."

"Doesn't seem much reason for hating him," said Witcover, and by his injured tone, I judged I had touched a nerve. Most likely he had once entertained soul-brother pretensions.

"Maybe not. Maybe if I'd met him back home, I'd have passed him off as a creep and gone about my business. But in combat situations, you don't have the energy to maintain that sort of neutrality. It's easier to hate. And anyway, Stoner could be a genuine pain in the ass."

"How's that?" Fierman asked, getting interested.

"It was never anything unforgivable; he just never let up with it. Like one time a bunch of us were in this guy Gurney's hooch, and he was tellin' 'bout this badass he'd known in Detroit. The cops had been chasin' this guy across the rooftops, and he'd missed a jump. Fell seven floors and emptied his gun at the cops on the way down. Reaction was typical. Guys sayin' 'Wow' and tryin' to think of a story to top it. But Stoner he nods sagely and says, 'Yeah, there's a lot of that goin' around.' As if this was a syndrome to which he's devoted years of study. But you knew he didn't have a clue, that he was too upscale to have met anybody like Gurney's badass." I had a slug of whiskey. "'There's a lot of that goin' around' was a totally inept comment. All it did was to bring everyone down from a nice buzz and make us aware of the shithole where we lived."

Witcover looked puzzled, but Fierman made a noise that seemed to imply comprehension. "How'd he die?" he asked. "The handout says he was KIA, but it doesn't say what kind of action."

"The fuckup kind," I said. I didn't want to tell them. The closer I came to seeing Stoner, the leerier I got about the topic. Until this business had begun, I thought I'd buried all the death-tripping weirdness of Vietnam; now Stoner had unearthed it and I was having dreams again and I hated him for that worse than I ever had in life. What was I supposed to do? Feel sorry for him? Maybe ghosts didn't have bad dreams. Maybe it was terrific being a ghost, like with Casper.... Anyway, I did tell them. How we had entered Cam Le, what was left of the patrol. How we had lined up the villagers, interrogated them, hit them, and God knows we might have killed them—we were freaked, bone-weary, an atrocity waiting to happen—if Stoner hadn't distracted us. He'd been wandering around, poking at stuff with his rifle, and then, with this ferocious expression on his face, he'd fired into one of the huts. The hut had been empty, but there must have been explosives hidden inside, because after a few rounds the whole damn thing had blown and taken Stoner with it.

Talking about him soured me on company, and shortly afterward I broke it off with Fierman and Witcover, and walked out into the city. The security cadre tagged along, his hand resting on the butt of his sidearm. I had a real load on and barely noticed my surroundings. The only salient points of difference between Saigon today and fifteen years before were the ubiquitous representations of Uncle Ho that covered the façades of many of the buildings, and the absence of motor scooters: the traffic consisted mainly of bicycles. I went a dozen blocks or so and stopped at a sidewalk café beneath sun-browned tamarinds, where I paid two dong for food tickets, my first experience with what the Communists called "goods exchange"—a system they hoped would undermine the concept of monetary trade; I handed the tickets to the waitress, and she gave me a bottle of beer and a dish of fried peanuts. The security cadre, who had taken a table opposite mine, seemed no more impressed with the system than was I; he chided the waitress for her slowness and acted perturbed by the complexity accruing to his order of tea and cakes.

I sat and sipped and stared, thoughtless and unfocused. The bicyclists zipping past were bright blurs with jingling bells, and the light was that heavy leaded-gold light that occurs when a tropical sun has broken free of an overcast. Smells of charcoal, fish sauce, grease. The heat squeezed sweat from my every pore. I was brought back to alertness by angry voices. The security cadre was arguing with the waitress, insisting that the recorded music be turned on, and she was explaining that there weren't enough customers to warrant turning it on. He began to offer formal "constructive criticism," making clear that he considered her refusal both a breach of party ethics and the code of honorable service. About then, I realized I had begun to cry. Not sobs, just tears leaking. The tears had nothing to do with the argument or the depersonalized ugliness it signaled. I believe that the heat and the light and the smells had seeped into me, triggering a recognition of an awful familiarity that my mind had thus far rejected. I wiped my face and tried to suck it up before anyone could notice my emotionality; but a teenage boy on a bicycle slowed and gazed at me with an amused expression. To show my contempt, I spat on the sidewalk. Almost instantly, I felt much better.

▲▼▲

Early the next day, thirty of us—all journalists—were bussed north to Cam Le. Mist still wreathed the paddies, the light had a yellowish green cast, and along the road women in black dresses were waiting for a southbound bus, with rumpled sacks of produce like sleepy brown animals at their feet. I sat beside Fierman, who, being as hung over as I was, made no effort at conversation; however, Witcover—sitting across the aisle—peppered me with inane questions until I told him to leave me alone. Just before we turned onto the dirt road that led to Cam Le, an information cadre boarded the bus and for the duration proceeded to fill us in on everything we already knew. Stuff about the machine, how its fields were generated, and so forth. Technical jargon gives me a pain, and I tried hard not to listen. But then he got off onto a tack that caught my interest. "Since the machine has been in operation," he said, "the apparition seems to have grown more vital."

"What's that mean?" I asked, waving my hand to attract his attention. "Is he coming back to life?"

My colleagues laughed.

The cadre pondered this. "It simply means that his effect has become more observable," he said at last. And beyond that he would not specify.

Cam Le had been evacuated, its population shifted to temporary housing three miles east. The village itself was nothing like the place I had entered fifteen years before. Gone were the thatched huts, and in their stead were about two dozen small houses of concrete block painted a quarantine yellow, with banana trees set between them. All this encircled by thick jungle. Standing on the far side of the road from the group of houses was the long tin-roofed building that contained the machine.

Two soldiers were lounging in front of it, and as the bus pulled up, they snapped to attention; a clutch of officers came out the door, followed by a portly white-haired gook: Phan Thnah Tuu, the machine's inventor. I disembarked and studied him while he shook hands with the other journalists; it wasn't every day that I met someone who claimed to be both Marxist and mystic, and had gone more than the required mile in establishing the validity of each. His hair was as fine as corn silk, a fat black mole punctuated one cheek, and his benign smile was unflagging, seeming a fixture of some deeply held good opinion attaching to everything he saw. Maybe, I thought, Fierman was right. In-fucking-scrutable.

"Ah," he said, coming up, enveloping me in a cloud of perfumy cologne. "Mr. Puleo. I hope this won't be painful for you."

"Really," I said. "You hope that, do you?"

"I beg your pardon," he said, taken aback.

"It's okay." I grinned. "You're forgiven."

An unsmiling major led him away to press more flesh, and he glanced back at me, perplexed. I was mildly ashamed of having fucked with him, but unlike Cassius Clay, I had plenty against them Viet Congs. Besides, my wiseass front was helping to stave off the yips.

After a brief welcome-to-the-wonderful-wacky-world-of-the-Commie-techno-paradise speech given by the major, Tuu delivered an oration upon the nature of ghosts, worthy of mention only in that it rehashed every crackpot notion I'd ever heard: apparently Stoner hadn't yielded much in the way of hard data. He then warned us to keep our distance from the village. The fields would not harm us; they were currently in operation, undetectable to our senses and needing but a slight manipulation to "focus" Stoner. But if we were to pass inside the fields, it was possible that Stoner himself might be able to cause us injury. With that, Tim bowed and reentered the building.

We stood facing the village, which—with its red dirt and yellow houses and green banana leaves—looked elementary and innocent under the leaden sky. Some of my colleagues whispered together, others checked their cameras. I felt numb and shaky, prepared to turn away quickly, much the way I once had felt when forced to identify the body of a chance acquaintance at a police morgue. Several minutes after Tuu had left us, there was a disturbance in the air at the center of the village. Similar to heat haze, but the ripples were slower. And then, with the suddenness of a slide shunted into a projector, Stoner appeared.

I think I had been expecting something bloody and ghoulish, or perhaps a gauzy insubstantial form; but he looked no different than he had on the day he died. Haggard; wearing sweat-stained fatigues; his face half-obscured by a week's growth of stubble. On his helmet were painted the words *Didi Mao* ("Fuck Off" in Vietnamese), and I could make out the yellowing photograph of his girl that he'd taped to his rifle stock. He didn't act startled by our presence; on the contrary, his attitude was nonchalant. He shouldered his rifle, tipped back his helmet, and sauntered toward us. He seemed to be recessed into the backdrop: it was as if reality were two-dimensional and he was a cutout held behind it to give the illusion of depth. At least that's how it was one moment. The next, he would appear to be set forward of the backdrop like a pop-up figure in a fancy greeting card. Watching him shift between these modes was unsettling...more than unsettling. My heart hammered, my mouth was cottony. I bumped into someone and realized that I had been backing away, that I was making a scratchy noise deep in my throat. Stoner's eyes, those eyes that had looked dead even in life, pupils about .45 caliber and hardly any iris showing, they were locked onto mine and the pressure of his stare was like two black bolts punching through into my skull.

"Puleo," he said.

I couldn't hear him, but I saw his lips shape the name. With a mixture of longing and hopelessness harrowing his features, he kept on repeating it. And then I noticed something else. The closer he drew to me, the more in focus he became. It wasn't just a matter of the shortening distance; his stubble and sweat stains, the frays in his fatigues, his worry lines—all these were sharpening the way details become fixed in a developing photograph. But none of that disturbed me half as much as did the fact of a dead man calling my name. I couldn't handle that. I began to hyperventilate, to get dizzy, and I believe I might have blacked out; but before that could happen, Stoner reached the edge of the fields, the barrier beyond which he could not pass.

Had I had more mental distance from the event, I might have enjoyed the sound-and-light that ensued: it was spectacular. The instant Stoner hit the end of his tether, there was an earsplitting shriek of the kind metal emits under immense stress; it seemed to issue from the air, the trees, the earth, as if some ironclad physical constant had been breached. Stoner was frozen midstep, his mouth open, and opaque lightnings were forking away from him, taking on a violet tinge as they vanished, their passage illuminating the curvature of the fields. I heard a scream and assumed it must be Stoner. But somebody grabbed me, shook me, and I understood that I was the one screaming, screaming with throat-tearing abandon because his eyes were boring into me and I could have sworn that his thoughts, his sensations, were flowing to me along the track of his vision. I knew what he was feeling: not pain, not desperation, but emptiness. An emptiness made unbearable by his proximity to life, to fullness. It was the worst thing I'd ever felt, worse than grief and bullet wounds, and it had to be worse than dying—dying, you see, had an end, whereas this went on and on, and every time you thought you had adapted to it, it grew worse yet. I wanted it to stop. That was all I wanted. Ever. Just for it to stop.

Then, with the same abruptness that he had appeared, Stoner winked out of existence and the feeling of emptiness faded.

People pressed in, asking questions. I shouldered them aside and walked off a few paces. My hands were shaking, my eyes weepy. I stared at the ground. It looked blurred, an undifferentiated smear of green with a brown clot in the middle: this gradually resolved into grass and my left shoe. Ants were crawling over the laces, poking their heads into the eyelets. The sight was strengthening, a reassurance of the ordinary.

"Hey, man." Witcover hove up beside me. "You okay?" He rested a hand on my shoulder. I kept my eyes on the ants, saying nothing. If it had been anyone else, I might have responded to his solicitude; but I knew he was only sucking up to me, hoping to score some human interest for his satellite report. I glanced at him. He was wearing a pair of mirrored sunglasses, and that consolidated my anger. Why is it, I ask you, that every measly little wimp in the universe thinks he can put on a pair of mirrored sunglasses and instantly acquire magical hipness and cool, rather than—as is the case—looking like an asshole with reflecting eyes?

"Fuck off," I told him in a tone that implied dire consequences were I not humored. He started to talk back, but thought better of it and stalked off. I returned to watching the ants; they were caravanning up inside my trousers and onto my calf. I would become a legend among them: The Human Who Stood Still for Biting.

From behind me came the sound of peremptory gook voices, angry American voices. I paid them no heed, content with my insect pals and the comforting state of thoughtlessness that watching them induced. A minute or so later, someone else moved up beside me and stood without speaking. I recognized Tuu's cologne and looked up. "Mr. Puleo," he said. "I'd like to offer you an exclusive on this story." Over his shoulder, I saw my colleagues staring at us through the windows of the bus, as wistful and forlorn as kids who have been denied Disneyland: they, like me, knew that big bucks were to be had from exploiting Stoner's plight.

"Why?" I asked.

"We want your help in conducting an experiment."

I waited for him to continue.

"Did you notice," he said, "that after Stoner identified you, his image grew sharper?"

I nodded.

"We're interested in observing the two of you in close proximity. His reaction to you was unique."

"You mean go in there?" I pointed to the village. "You said it was dangerous."

"Other subjects have entered the fields and shown no ill effects. But Stoner was not as intrigued by them as he was with you." Tuu brushed a lock of hair back from his forehead. "We have no idea of Stoner's capabilities, Mr. Puleo. It *is* a risk. But since you served in the Army, I assume you are accustomed to risk."

I let him try to persuade me—the longer I held out, the stronger my bargaining position—but I had already decided to accept the offer. Though I wasn't eager to feel that emptiness again, I had convinced myself that it had been a product of nerves and an overactive imagination; now that I had confronted Stoner, I believed I would be able to control my reactions. Tim said that he would have the others driven back to Saigon, but I balked at that. I was not sufficiently secure to savor the prospect of being alone among the gooks, and I told Tuu I wanted Fierman and Witcover to stay. Why Witcover? At the time I might have said it was because he and Fierman were the only two of my colleagues whom I knew; but in retrospect, I think I may have anticipated the need for a whipping boy.

▲▼▲

We were quartered in a house at the eastern edge of the village, one that the fields did not enclose. Three cots were set up inside, along with a table and chairs; the yellow walls were brocaded with mildew, and weeds grew sideways from chinks in the concrete blocks. Light was provided by an oil lamp that—as darkness fell—sent an inconstant glow lapping over the walls, making it appear that the room was filled with dirty orange water.

After dinner Fierman produced a bottle of whiskey—his briefcase contained three more—and a deck of cards, and we sat down to while away the evening. The one game we all knew was Hearts, and we each played according to the dictates of our personalities. Fierman became quickly drunk and attempted to Shoot the Moon on every hand, no matter how bad his cards; he seemed to be asking fate to pity a fool.

I paid little attention to the game, my ears tuned to the night sounds, half expecting to hear the sputter of small-arms fire, the rumor of some ghostly engagement; it was by dint of luck alone that I maintained second place. Witcover played conservatively, building his score through our mistakes, and though we were only betting a nickel a point, to watch him sweat out every trick you would have thought a fortune hung in the balance; he chortled over our pitiful fuckups, rolling his eyes and shaking his head in delight, and whistled as he totaled up his winnings. The self-importance he derived from winning fouled the atmosphere, and the room acquired the staleness of a cell where we had been incarcerated for years. Finally, after a particularly childish display of glee, I pushed back my chair and stood.

"Where you going?" asked Witcover. "Let's play."

"No, thanks," I said.

"Christ!" He picked up the discards and muttered something about sore losers.

"It's not that," I told him. "I'm worried if you win another hand, you're gonna come all over the fuckin' table. I don't wanna watch."

Fierman snorted laughter.

Witcover shot me an aggrieved look. "What's with you, man? You been on my case ever since the hotel."

I shrugged and headed for the door.

"Asshole," he said half under his breath.

"What?" An angry flush numbed my face as I turned back.

He tried to project an expression of manly belligerence, but his eyes darted from side to side.

"Asshole?" I said. "Is that right?" I took a step toward him.

Fierman scrambled up, knocking over his chair, and began pushing me away. "C'mon," he said. "It's not worth it. Chill out." His boozy sincerity acted to diminish my anger, and I let him urge me out the door.

The night was moonless, with a few stars showing low on the horizon; the spiky crowns of the palms ringing the village were silhouettes pinned onto a lesser blackness. It was so humid, it felt like you could spoon in the air. I crossed the dirt road, found a patch of grass near the tin-roofed building, and sat down. The door to the building was cracked, spilling a diagonal of white radiance onto the ground, and I had the notion that there was no machine inside, only a mystic boil of whiteness emanating from Tuu's silky hair. A couple of soldiers walked past and nodded to me; they paused a few feet farther along to light cigarettes, which proceeded to brighten and fade with the regularity of tiny beacons.

Crickets sawed, frogs chirred, and listening to them, smelling the odor of sweet rot from the jungle, I thought about a similar night when I'd been stationed at Phnoc Vinh, about a party we'd had with a company of artillery. There had been a barbecue pit and iced beer and our CO had given special permission for whores to come on the base. It had been a great party; in fact, those days at Phnoc Vinh had been the best time of the war for me. The artillery company had had this terrific cook, and on movie nights he'd make doughnuts. Jesus, I'd loved those doughnuts! They'd tasted like home, like peace. I'd kick back and munch a doughnut and watch the bullshit movie, and it was almost like being in my own living room, watching the tube. Trouble was, Phnoc Vinh had softened me up, and after three weeks, when we'd been airlifted to Quan Loi, which was constantly under mortar and rocket fire, I'd nearly gotten my ass blown off.

Footsteps behind me. Startled, I turned and saw what looked to be a disembodied white shirt floating toward me. I came to one knee, convinced for the moment that some other ghost had been lured to the machine; but a second later a complete figure emerged from the dark: Tuu. Without a word, he sat cross-legged beside me. He was smoking a cigarette...or so I thought until I caught a whiff of marijuana. He took a deep drag, the coal illuminating his placid features, and offered me the joint. I hesitated, not wanting to be pals; but tempted by the smell, I accepted it, biting back a smartass remark about Marxist permissiveness. It was good shit. I could feel the smoke twisting through me, finding out all my hollow places. I handed it back, but he made a gesture of warding it off, and after a brief silence he said, "What do you think about all this, Mr. Puleo?"

"About Stoner?"

"Yes."

"I think"—I jetted smoke from my nostrils—"it's crap that you've got him penned up in that astral tiger cage."

"Had this discovery been made in the United States," he said, "the circumstances would be no different. Humane considerations—if, indeed, they apply—would have low priority."

"Maybe," I said. "It's still crap."

"Why? Do you believe Stoner is unhappy?"

"Don't you?" I had another hit. It was very good shit. The ground seemed to have a pulse. "Ghosts are by nature unhappy."

"Then you know what a ghost is?"

"Not hardly. But I figure unhappy's part of it." The roach was getting too hot; I took a final hit and flipped it away. "How 'bout you? You believe that garbage you preached this mornin'?"

His laugh was soft and cultivated. "That was a press release. However, my actual opinion is neither less absurd-sounding nor more verifiable."

"And what's that?"

He plucked a blade of grass, twiddled it. "I believe a ghost is a quality that dies in a man long before he experiences physical death. Something that has grown acclimated to death and thus survives the body. It might be love or an ambition. An element of character.... Anything." He regarded me with his lips pursed. "I have such a ghost within me. As do you, Mr. Puleo. My ghost senses yours."

The theory was as harebrained as his others, but I wasn't able to deny it. I knew he was partly right, that a moral filament had snapped inside me during the war and since that time I had lacked the ingredient necessary to the development of a generous soul. Now it seemed that I could feel that lack as a restless presence straining against my flesh. The sawing of the crickets intensified, and I had a rush of paranoia, wondering if Tuu was fucking with my head. Then, moods shifting at the chemical mercies of the dope, my paranoia eroded and Tuu snapped into focus for me...or at least his ghost did. He had, I recalled, written poetry prior to the war, and I thought I saw the features of that lost poet melting up from his face: a dreamy fellow given to watching petals fall and contemplating the moon's reflection. I closed my eyes, trying to get a grip. This was the best dope I'd ever smoked. Commie Pink, pure buds of the revolution.

"Are you worried about tomorrow?" Tuu asked.

"Should I be?"

"I can only tell you what I did before—no one has been harmed."

"What happened during those other experiments?" I asked.

"Very little, really. Stoner approached each subject, spoke to them. Then he lost interest and wandered off."

"Spoke to them? Could they hear him?"

"Faintly. However, considering his reaction to you, I wouldn't be surprised if you could hear him quite well."

I wasn't thrilled by that prospect. Having to look at Stoner was bad enough. I thought about the eerie shit he might say: admonitory pronouncements, sad questions, windy vowels gusting from his strange depths. Tuu said something and had to repeat it to snap me out of my reverie. He asked how it felt to be back in Vietnam, and without forethought, I said it wasn't a problem.

"And the first time you were here," he said, an edge to his voice. "Was that a problem?"

"What are you gettin' at?"

"I noticed in your records that you were awarded a Silver Star."

"Yeah?"

"You must have been a good soldier. I wondered if you might not have found a calling in war."

"If you're askin' what I think about the war," I said, getting pissed, "I don't make judgments about it. It was a torment for me, nothing more. Its geopolitical consequences, cultural effects, they're irrelevant to me... maybe they're ultimately irrelevant. Though I doubt you'd agree."

"We may agree more than you suspect." He sighed pensively. "For both of us, apparently, the war was a passion. In your case, an agonizing one. In mine, while there was also agony, it was essentially a love affair with revolution, with the idea of revolution. And as with all great passions, what was most alluring was not the object of passion but the new depth of my own feelings. Thus I was blind to the realities underlying it. Now"—he waved at the sky, the trees—"now I inhabit those realities and I am not as much in love as once I was. Yet no matter how extreme my disillusionment, the passion continues. I want it to continue. I need the significance with which it imbues my past actions." He studied me. "Isn't that how it is for you? You say war was a torment, but don't you find those days empowering?"

Just as when he had offered me the joint, I realized that I didn't want this sort of peaceful intimacy with him; I preferred him to be my inscrutable enemy. Maybe he was right, maybe—like him—I needed this passion to continue in order to give significance to my past. Whatever, I felt vulnerable to him, to my perception of his humanity. "Good night," I said, getting to my feet. My ass was numb from sitting and soaked with dew.

He gazed up at me, unreadable, and fingered something from his shirt pocket. Another joint. He lit up, exhaling a billow of smoke. "Good night," he said coldly.

▲▼▲

The next morning—sunny, cloudless—I staked myself out on the red dirt of Cam Le to wait for Stoner. Nervous, I paced back and forth until the air began to ripple and he materialized less than thirty feet away. He walked slowly toward me, his rifle dangling; a drop of sweat carved a cold groove across my rib cage. "Puleo," he said, and this time I heard him. His voice was faint, but it shook me.

Looking into his blown-out pupils, I was reminded of a day not long before he had died. We had been hunkered down together after a firefight, and our eyes had met, had locked as if sealed by a vacuum:

like two senile old men, incapable of any communication aside from a recognition of the other's vacancy. As I remembered this, it hit home to me that though he hadn't been a friend, he was my brother-in-arms, and that as such, I owed him more than journalistic interest.

"Stoner!" I hadn't intended to shout, but in that outcry was a wealth of repressed emotion, of regret and guilt and anguish at not being able to help him elude the fate by which he had been overtaken.

He stopped short; for an instant the hopelessness drained from his face. His image was undergoing that uncanny sharpening of focus: sweat beads popping from his brow, a scab appearing on his chin. The lines of strain around his mouth and eyes were etched deep, filled in with grime, like cracks in his tan.

Tides of emotion were washing over me, and irrational though it seemed, I knew that some of these emotions—the fierce hunger for life in particular—were Stoner's. I believe we had made some sort of connection, and all our thoughts were in flux between us. He moved toward me again. My hands trembled, my knees buckled, and I had to sit down, overwhelmed not by fear but by the combination of his familiarity and utter strangeness. "Jesus, Stoner," I said. "Jesus."

He stood gazing dully down at me. "My sending," he said, his voice louder and with a pronounced resonance. "Did you get it?"

A chill articulated my spine, but I forced myself to ignore it. "Sending?" I said.

"Yesterday," he said, "I sent you what I was feeling. What it's like for me here."

"How?" I asked, recalling the feeling of emptiness. "How'd you do that?"

"It's easy, Puleo," he said. "All you have to do is die, and thoughts... dreams, they'll flake off you like old paint. But believe me, it's hardly adequate compensation." He sat beside me, resting the rifle across his knees. This was no ordinary sequence of movements. His outline wavered, and his limbs appeared to drift apart: I might have been watching the collapse of a lifelike statue through a volume of disturbed water. It took all my self-control to keep from flinging myself away. His image steadied, and he stared at me. "Last person I was this close to ran like hell," he said. "You always were a tough motherfucker, Puleo. I used to envy you that."

If I hadn't believed before that he was Stoner, the way he spoke the word *motherfucker* would have cinched it for me: it had the stiffness of a practiced vernacular, a mode of expression that he hadn't mastered. This and his pathetic manner made him seem less menacing. "You were tough, too," I said glibly.

"I tried to be," he said. "I tried to copy you guys. But it was an act, a veneer. And when we hit Cam Le, the veneer cracked."

"You remember...." I broke off because it didn't feel right, my asking him questions; the idea of translating his blood and bones into a best-seller was no longer acceptable.

"Dying?" His lips thinned. "Oh, yeah. Every detail. You guys were hassling the villagers, and I thought, Christ, they're going to kill them. I didn't want to be involved, and...I was so tired, you know, so tired in my head, and I figured if I walked off a little ways, I wouldn't be part of it. I'd be innocent. So I did. I moved a ways off, and the wails, the shouts, they weren't real anymore. Then I came to this hut. I'd lost track of what was happening by that time. In my mind I was sure you'd already started shooting, and I said to myself, I'll show them I'm doing my bit, put a few rounds into this hut. Maybe"—his Adam's apple worked—"maybe they'll think I killed somebody. Maybe that'll satisfy them."

I looked down at the dirt, troubled by what I now understood to be my complicity in his death, and troubled also by a new understanding of the events surrounding the death. I realized that if anyone else had gotten himself blown up, the rest of us would have flipped out and likely have wasted the villagers. But since it had been Stoner, the explosion had had almost a calming effect: Cam Le had rid us of a nuisance.

Stoner reached out his hand to me. I was too mesmerized by the gesture, which left afterimages in the air, to recoil from it, and I watched horrified as his fingers gripped my upper arm, pressing wrinkles in my shirtsleeve. His touch was light and transmitted a dry coolness, and with it came a sensation of weakness. By all appearances, it was a normal hand, yet I kept expecting it to become translucent and merge with my flesh.

"It's going to be okay," said Stoner.

His tone, though bemused, was confident, and I thought I detected a change in his face, but I couldn't put my finger on what the change was. "Why's it gonna be okay?" I asked, my voice more frail and ghostly-sounding than his. "It doesn't seem okay to me."

"Because you're part of my process, my circuitry. Understand?"

"No," I said. I had identified what had changed about him. Whereas a few moments before he had looked real, now he looked more than real, ultrareal; his features had acquired the kind of gloss found in air-brushed photographs, and for a split second his eyes were cored with points of glitter as if reflecting a camera flash...except these points were bluish white, not red. There was a coarseness to his face that hadn't been previously evident, and in contrast to my earlier perception of him, he now struck me as dangerous, malevolent.

He squinted and cocked his head. "What's wrong, man? You scared of me?" He gave an amused sniff. "Hang in there, Puleo. Tough guy like you, you'll make an adjustment." My feeling of weakness had intensified: it was as if blood or some even more vital essence were trickling out of me. "Come on, Puleo," he said mockingly. "Ask me some questions? That's what you're here for, isn't it? I mean this must be the goddamn scoop of the century. Good News From Beyond the Grave! Of course"—he pitched his voice low and sepulchral—"the news isn't all that good."

Those glittering cores resurfaced in his pupils, and I wanted to wrench free; but I felt helpless, wholly in his thrall.

"You see," he went on, "when I appeared in the village, when I walked around and"—he chuckled—"haunted the place, those times were like sleepwalking. I barely knew what was happening. But the rest of the time, I was somewhere else. Somewhere really fucking weird."

My weakness was bordering on vertigo, but I mustered my strength and croaked, "Where?"

"The Land of Shades," he said. "That's what I call it, anyway. You wouldn't like it, Puleo. It wouldn't fit your idea of order."

The lights burned in his eyes, winking bright, and—as if in correspondence to their brightness—my dizziness increased. "Tell me about it," I said, trying to take my mind off the discomfort.

"I'd be delighted!" He grinned nastily. "But not now. It's too complicated. Tonight, man. I'll send you a dream tonight. A bad dream. That'll satisfy your curiosity."

My head was spinning, my stomach abubble with nausea. "Lemme go, Stoner," I said.

"Isn't this good for you, man? It's very good for me." With a flick of his hand, he released my wrist.

I braced myself to keep from falling over, drew a deep breath, and gradually my strength returned. Stoner's eyes continued to burn, and his features maintained their coarsened appearance. The difference between the way he looked now and the lost soul I had first seen was like that between night and day, and I began to wonder whether or not his touching me and my resultant weakness had anything to do with the transformation. "Part of your process," I said. "Does that...."

He looked me straight in the eyes, and I had the impression he was cautioning me to silence. It was more than a caution: a wordless command, a sending. "Let me explain something," he said. "A ghost is merely a stage of growth. He walks because he grows strong by walking. The more he walks, the less he's bound to the world. When he's strong enough"—he made a planing gesture with his hand—"he goes away."

He seemed to be expecting a response. "Where's he go?" I asked.

"Where he belongs," he said. "And if he's prevented from walking, from growing strong, he's doomed."

"You mean he'll die?"

"Or worse."

"And there's no other way out for him?"

"No."

He was lying—I was sure of it. Somehow I posed for him a way out of Cam Le. "Well...so," I said, flustered, uncertain of what to do and at the same time pleased with the prospect of conspiring against Tuu.

"Just sit with me awhile," he said, easing his left foot forward to touch my right ankle.

Once again I experienced weakness, and over the next seven or eight hours, he would alternately move his foot away, allowing me to recover, and then bring it back into contact with me. I'm not certain what was happening. One logic dictates that since I had been peripherally involved in his death—"part of his process"—he was therefore able to draw strength from me. Likely as not, this was the case. Yet I've never been convinced that ordinary logic applied to our circumstance: it may be that we were governed by an arcane rationality to which we both were blind. Though his outward aspect did not appear to undergo further changes, his strength became tangible, a cold radiation that pulsed with the steadiness of an icy heart. I came to feel that the image I was seeing was the tip of an iceberg, the perceptible extremity of a huge power cell that existed mainly in dimensions beyond the range of mortal vision. I tried to give the impression of an interview to our observers by continuing to ask questions; but Stoner sat with his head down, his face hidden, and gave terse, disinterested replies.

The sun declined to the tops of the palms, the yellow paint of the houses took on a tawny hue, and—drained by the day-long alternation of weakness and recovery—I told Stoner I needed to rest. "Tomorrow," he said without looking up. "Come back tomorrow."

"All right." I had no doubt that Tuu would be eager to go on with the experiment. I stood and turned to leave; but then another question, a pertinent one, occurred to me. "If a ghost is a stage of growth," I said, "what's he grow into?"

He lifted his head, and I staggered back, terrified. His eyes were ablaze, even the whites winking with cold fire, as if nuggets of phosphorus were embedded in his skull.

"Tomorrow," he said again.

▲▼▲

During the debriefing that followed, I developed a bad case of the shakes and experienced a number of other, equally unpleasant, reactions; the places where Stoner had touched me seemed to have retained a chill, and the thought of that dead hand leeching me of energy was in retrospect thoroughly repellent. A good many of Tuu's subordinates, alarmed by Stoner's transformation, lobbied to break off the experiment. I did my best to soothe them, but I wasn't at all sure I wanted to return to the village. I couldn't tell whether Tuu noticed either my trepidation or the fact that I was being less than candid; he was too busy bringing his subordinates in line to question me in depth.

That night, when Fierman broke out his whiskey, I swilled it down as if it were an antidote to poison. To put it bluntly, I got shit-faced. Both Fierman and Witcover seemed warm human beings, old buddies, and our filthy yellow room with its flickering lamp took on the coziness of a cottage and hearth. The first stage of my drunk was maudlin, filled with self-recriminations over my past treatment of Stoner: I vowed not to shrink from helping him. The second stage.... Well, once I caught Fierman gazing at me askance and registered that my behavior was verging on the manic. Laughing hysterically, talking like a speed freak. We talked about everything except Stoner, and I suppose it was inevitable that the conversation work itself around to the war and its aftermath. Dimly, I heard myself pontificating on a variety of related subjects. At one point Fierman asked what I thought of the Vietnam Memorial, and I told him I had mixed emotions.

"Why?" he asked.

"I go to the Memorial, man," I said, standing up from the table where we had all been sitting. "And I cry. You can't help but cryin', 'cause that"—I hunted for an appropriate image—"that black dividin' line between nowheres, that says it just right 'bout the war. It feels good to cry, to go public with grief and take your place with all the vets of the truly outstandin' wars." I swayed, righted myself. "But the Memorial, the Unknown, the parades...basically they're bullshit." I started to wander around the room, realized that I had forgotten why I had stood and leaned against the wall.

"How you mean?" asked Witcover, who was nearly as drunk as I was.

"Man," I said, "it's a shuck! I mean ten goddamn years go by, and alla sudden there's this blast of media warmth and government-sponsored emotion. 'Welcome home, guys,' ever'body's sayin'. 'We're sorry we treated you so bad. Next time it's gonna be different. You wait and see.' " I went back to the table and braced myself on it with both hands, staring blearily at Witcover: his tan looked blotchy. "Hear that, man? 'Next time.' That's all it is. Nobody really gives a shit 'bout the vets. They're just pavin' the way for the next time."

"I don't know," said Witcover. "Seems to—"

"Right!" I spanked the table with the flat of my hand. "You don't know. You don't know shit 'bout it, so shut the fuck up!"

"Be cool," advised Fierman. "Man's entitled to his 'pinion."

I looked at him, saw a flushed, fat face with bloodshot eyes and a stupid reproving frown. "Fuck you," I said. "And fuck his 'pinion." I turned back to Witcover. "Whaddya think, man? That there's this genuine breath of conscience sweepin' the land? Open your goddamn eyes! You been to the movies lately? Jesus Christ! Courageous grunts strikin' fear into the heart of the Red Menace! Miraculous one-man missions to save our honor. Huh! Honor!" I took a long pull from the bottle. "Those movies, they make war seem like a mystical opportunity. Well, man, when I was here it wasn't quite that way, y'know. It was leeches, fungus, the shits. It was searchin' in the weeds for your buddy's arm. It was lookin' into the snaky eyes of some whore you were bangin' and feelin' weird shit crawl along your spine and expectin' her head to do a Linda Blair three-sixty spin." I slumped into a chair and leaned close to Witcover. "It was Mordor, man. Stephen King-land. Horror. And now, now I look around at all these movies and monuments and crap, and it makes me wanna fuckin' puke to see what a noble hell it's turnin' out to be!"

I felt pleased with myself, having said this, and I leaned back, basking in a righteous glow. But Witcover was unimpressed. His face cinched into a scowl, and he said in a tight voice, "You're startin' to really piss me off, y'know."

"Yeah?" I said, and grinned. "How 'bout that?"

"Yeah, all you war-torn creeps, you think you got papers sayin' you can make an ass outta yourself and everybody else gotta say, 'Oh, you poor fucker! Give us more of your tortured wisdom!' "

Fierman muffled a laugh, and—rankled—I said, "That so?"

Witcover hunched his shoulders as if preparing for an off-tackle plunge. "I been listenin' to you guys for years, and you're alla goddamn same. You think you're owed something 'cause you got ground around in the political mill. Shit! I been in Salvador, Nicaragua, Afghanistan. Compared to those people, you didn't go through diddley. But you use what happened as an excuse for fuckin' up your lives...or for being assholes. Like you, man." He affected a macho-sounding bass voice. " 'I been in a war. I am an expert on reality.' You don't know how ridiculous you are."

"Am I?" I was shaking again, but with adrenaline not fear, and I knew I was going to hit Witcover. He didn't know it—he was smirking, his eyes flicking toward Fierman, seeking approval—and that in itself was a sufficient reason to hit him, purely for educational purposes: I had, you see, reached the level of drunkenness at which an amoral man such as myself understands his whimsies to be moral imperatives. But the real reason, the one that had begun to rumble inside me, was Stoner. All my fear, all my reactions thus far, had merely been tremors signaling an imminent explosion, and now, thinking about him nearby, old horrors were stirred up, and I saw myself walking in a napalmed ville rife with dead VC, crispy critters, and beside me this weird little guy named Fellowes who claimed he could read the future from their scorched remains and would point at a hexagramlike structure of charred bone and gristle and say, "That there means a bad moon on Wednesday," and claimed, too, that he could read the past from the blood of head wounds, and then I was leaning over this Canadian nurse, beautiful blonde girl, disemboweled by a mine and somehow still alive, her organs dark and wet and pulsing, and somebody giggling, whispering about what he'd like to do, and then another scene that was whirled away so quickly, I could only make out the color of blood, and Witcover said something else, and a dead man was stretching out his hand to me and....

I nailed Witcover, and he flew sideways off the chair and rolled on the floor. I got to my feet, and Fierman grabbed me, trying to wrestle me away; but that was unnecessary, because all my craziness had been dissipated. "I'm okay now," I said, slurring the words, pushing him aside. He threw a looping punch that glanced off my neck, not even staggering me. Then Witcover yelled. He had pulled himself erect and was weaving toward me; an egg-shaped lump was swelling on his cheekbone. I laughed—he looked so puffed up with rage—and started for the door. As I went through it, he hit me on the back of the head. The blow stunned me a bit, but I was more amused than hurt; his fist had made a funny bonk sound on my skull, and that set me to laughing harder.

I stumbled between the houses, bouncing off walls, reeling out of control, and heard shouts...Vietnamese shouts. By the time I had regained my balance, I had reached the center of the village. The moon was almost full, pale yellow, its craters showing: a pitted eye in the black air. It kept shrinking and expanding, and—as it seemed to lurch farther off—I realized I had fallen and was lying flat on my back. More shouts. They sounded distant, a world away, and the moon had begun to spiral, to dwindle, like water being sucked down a drain. Jesus, I remember thinking just before I passed out, Jesus, how'd I get so drunk?

▲▼▲

I'd forgotten Stoner's promise to tell me about the Land of Shades, but apparently he had not, for that night I had a dream in which I was Stoner. It was not that I thought I was him: I was him, prone to all his twitches, all his moods. I was walking in a pitch-dark void, possessed by a great hunger. Once this hunger might have been characterized as a yearning for the life I had lost, but it had been transformed into a lust for the life I might someday attain if I proved equal to the tests with which I was presented. That was all I knew of the land of Shades—that it was a testing ground, less a place than a sequence of events. It was up to me to gain strength from the tests, to ease my hunger as best I could. I was ruled by this hunger, and it was my only wish to ease it.

Soon I spotted an island of brightness floating in the dark, and as I drew near, the brightness resolved into an old French plantation house fronted by tamarinds and rubber trees; sections of white stucco wall and a verandah and a red tile roof were visible between the trunks. Patterns of soft radiance overlaid the grounds, yet there were neither stars nor moon nor any source of light I could discern. I was not alarmed by this—such discrepancies were typical of the Land of Shades.

When I reached the trees I paused, steeling myself for whatever lay ahead. Breezes sprang up to stir the leaves, and a sizzling chorus of crickets faded in from nowhere as if a recording of sensory detail had been switched on. Alert to every shift of shadow, I moved cautiously through the trees and up the verandah steps. Broken roof tiles crunched beneath my feet. Beside the door stood a bottomed-out cane chair; the rooms, however, were devoid of furnishings, the floors dusty, the whitewash flaking from the walls. The house appeared to be deserted, but I knew I was not alone. There was a hush in the air, the sort that arises from a secretive presence. Even had I failed to notice this, I could scarcely have missed the scent of perfume. I had never tested against a woman before, and, excited by the prospect, I was tempted to run through the house and ferret her out. But this would have been foolhardy, and I continued at a measured pace.

At the center of the house lay a courtyard, a rectangular space choked with waist-high growths of jungle plants, dominated by a stone fountain in the shape of a stylized orchid. The woman was leaning against the fountain, and despite the grayish-green half-light—a light that seemed to arise from the plants—I could see she was beautiful. Slim and honey-colored, with falls of black hair spilling over the shoulders of her *ao dai.* She did not move or speak, but the casualness of her pose was an invitation. I felt drawn to her, and as I pushed through the foliage, the fleshy leaves clung to my thighs and groin, touches that seemed designed to provoke arousal. I stopped an arm's length away and studied her. Her features were of a feline delicacy, and in the fullness of her lower lip, the petulant set of her mouth, I detected a trace of French breeding. She stared at me with palpable sexual interest. It had not occurred to me that the confrontation might take place on a sexual level, yet now I was certain this would be the case. I had to restrain myself from initiating the contact: there are rigorous formalities that must be observed prior to each test. And besides, I wanted to savor the experience.

"I am Tuyet," she said in a voice that seemed to combine the qualities of smoke and music.

"Stoner," I said.

The names hung in the air like the echoes of two gongs.

She lifted her hand as if to touch me, but lowered it: she, too, was practicing restraint. "I was a prostitute," she said. "My home was Lai Khe, but I was an outcast. I worked the water points along Highway Thirteen."

It was conceivable, I thought, that I may have known her. While I had been laid up in An Loc, I'd frequented those water points: bomb craters that had been turned into miniature lakes by the rains and served as filling stations for the water trucks attached to the First Infantry. Every morning the whores and their mama sans would drive out to the water points in three-wheeled motorcycle trucks; with them would be vendors selling combs and pushbutton knives and rubbers that came wrapped in gold foil, making them look like those disks of chocolate you can buy in the States. Most of these girls were more friendly than the city girls, and knowing that Tuyet had been one of them caused me to feel an affinity with her.

She went on to tell me that she had gone into the jungle with an American soldier and had been killed by a sniper. I told her my story in brief and then asked what she had learned of the Land of Shades. This is the most rigorous formality: I had never met anyone with whom I had failed to exchange information.

"Once," Tuyet said, "I met an old man, a Cao Dai medium from Black Virgin Mountain, who told me he had been to a place where a pillar of whirling light and dust joined earth to sky. Voices spoke from the pillar, sometimes many at once, and from them he understood that all wars are merely reflections of a deeper struggle, of a demon breaking free. The demon freed by our war, he said, was very strong, very dangerous. We the dead had been recruited to wage war against him."

I had been told a similar story by an NLF captain, and once, while crawling through a tunnel system, I myself had heard voices speaking from a skull half buried in the earth. But I had been too frightened to stay and listen. I related all this to Tuyet, and her response was to trail her fingers across my arm. My restraint, too, had frayed. I dragged her down into the thick foliage. It was as if we had been submerged in a sea of green light and fleshy stalks, as if the plantation house had vanished and we were adrift in an infinite vegetable depth where gravity had been replaced by some buoyant principle. I tore at her clothes, she at mine. Her *ao dai* shredded like crepe, and my fatigues came away in ribbons that dangled from her hooked fingers. Greedy for her, I pressed my mouth to her breasts. Her nipples looked black in contrast to her skin, and it seemed I could taste their blackness, tart and sour. Our breathing was hoarse, urgent, and the only other sound was the soft mulching of the leaves. With surprising strength, she pushed me onto my back and straddled my hips, guiding me inside her, sinking down until her buttocks were grinding against my thighs.

Her head flung back, she lifted and lowered herself. The leaves and stalks churned and intertwined around us as if they, too, were copulating. For a few moments my hunger was assuaged, but soon I noticed that the harder I thrust, the more fiercely she plunged, the less intense the sensations became. Though she gripped me tightly, the friction seemed to have been reduced. Frustrated, I dug my fingers into her plump hips and battered at her, trying to drive myself deeper. Then I squeezed one of her breasts and felt a searing pain to my palm. I snatched back my hand and saw that her nipple, both nipples, were twisting, elongating; I realized that they had been transformed into the heads of two black centipedes, and the artful movements of her internal muscles...they were too artful, too disconnectedly in motion. An instant later I felt that same searing pain in my cock and knew I was screwing myself into a nest of creatures like those protruding from her breasts. All her skin was rippling, reflecting the humping of thousands of centipedes beneath.

The pain was enormous, so much so that I thought my entire body must be glowing with it. But I did not dare fail this test, and I continued pumping into her, thrusting harder than ever. The leaves thrashed, the stalks thrashed as in a gale, and the green light grew livid. Tuyet began to scream—God knows what manner of pain I was causing her—and her screams completed a perverse circuit within me. I found I could channel my own pain into those shrill sounds. Still joined to her, I rolled atop her, clamped her wrists together, and pinned them above her head. Her screams rang louder, inspiring me to greater efforts yet. Despite the centipedes tipping her breasts, or perhaps because of them, because of the grotesque juxtaposition of the sensual and the horrid, her beauty seemed to have been enhanced, and my mastery over her actually provided me a modicum of pleasure.

The light began to whiten, and looking off, I saw that we were being borne by an invisible current through—as I had imagined—an infinite depth of stalks and leaves. The stalks that lashed around us thickened far below into huge pale trunks with circular ribbing. I could not make out where they met the earth—if, indeed, they did—and they appeared to rise an equal height above. The light brightened further, casting the distant stalks in silhouette, and I realized we were drifting toward the source of the whiteness, beyond which would lie another test, another confrontation. I glanced at Tuyet. Her skin no longer displayed that obscene rippling, her nipples had reverted to normal. Pain was evolving into pleasure, but I knew it would be shortlived, and I tried to resist the current, to hold on to pain, because even pain was preferable to the hunger I would soon experience. Tuyet clawed my back, and I felt the first dissolute rush of my orgasm. The current was irresistible. It flowed through my blood, my cells. It was part of me, or rather I was part of it. I let it move me, bringing me to completion.

Gradually the whipping of the stalks subsided to a pliant swaying motion. They parted for us, and we drifted through their interstices as serenely as a barge carved to resemble a coupling of two naked figures. I found I could not disengage from Tuyet, that the current enforced our union, and resigned to this, I gazed around, marveling at the vastness of this vegetable labyrinth and the strangeness of our fates. Beams of white light shined through the stalks, the brightness growing so profound that I thought I heard in it a roaring; and as my consciousness frayed, I saw myself reflected in Tuyet's eyes—a ragged dark creature wholly unlike my own self-image—and wondered for the thousandth time who had placed us in this world, who had placed these worlds in us.

▲▼▲

Other dreams followed, but they were ordinary, the dreams of an ordinarily anxious, ordinarily drunken man, and it was the memory of this first dream that dominated my waking moments. I didn't want to wake because—along with a headache and other symptoms of hangover

—I felt incredibly weak, incapable of standing and facing the world. Muzzy-headed, I ignored the reddish light prying under my eyelids and tried to remember more of the dream. Despite Stoner's attempts to appear streetwise, despite the changes I had observed in him, he had been at heart an innocent and it was difficult to accept that the oddly formal, brutally sexual protagonist of the dream had been in any way akin to him. Maybe, I thought, recalling Tuu's theory of ghosts, maybe that was the quality that had died in Stoner: his innocence. I began once again to suffer guilt feelings over my hatred of him, and, preferring a hangover to that, I propped myself on one elbow and opened my eyes.

I doubt more than a second or two passed before I sprang to my feet, hangover forgotten, electrified with fear; but in that brief span the reason for my weakness was made plain. Stoner was sitting close to where I had been lying, his hand outstretched to touch me, head down...exactly as he had sat the previous day. Aside from his pose, however, very little about him was the same.

The scene was of such complexity that now, thinking back on it, it strikes me as implausible that I could have noticed its every detail; yet I suppose that its power was equal to its complexity and thus I did not so much see it as it was imprinted on my eyes. Dawn was a crimson smear fanning across the lower sky, and the palms stood out blackly against it, their fronds twitching in the breeze like spiders impaled on pins. The ruddy light gave the rutted dirt of the street the look of a trough full of congealed blood. Stoner was motionless—that is to say, he didn't move his limbs, his head, or shift his position; but his image was pulsing, swelling to half again its normal size and then deflating, all with the rhythm of steady breathing. As he expanded, the cold white fire blazing from his eyes would spread in cracks that veined his entire form; as he contracted, the cracks would disappear and for a moment he would be—except for his eyes—the familiar figure I had known. It seemed that his outward appearance—his fatigues and helmet, his skin—was a shell from which some glowing inner man was attempting to break free. Grains of dust were whirling up from the ground beside him, more and more all the time: a miniature cyclone wherein he sat calm and ultimately distracted, the likeness of a warrior monk whose meditations had borne fruit.

Shouts behind me. I turned and saw Fierman, Tuu, Witcover, and various of the gooks standing at the edge of the village. Tuu beckoned to me, and I wanted to comply, to run, but I wasn't sure I had the strength. And, too, I didn't think Stoner would let me. His power surged around me, a cold windy voltage that whipped my clothes and set static charges crackling in my hair. "Turn it off!" I shouted, pointing at the tin-roofed building. They shook their heads, shouting in return. "...can't," I heard, and something about "...feedback."

Then Stoner spoke. "Puleo," he said. His voice wasn't loud, but it was all-encompassing. I seemed to be inside it, balanced on a tongue of red dirt, within a throat of sky and jungle and yellow stone. I turned back to him. Looked into his eyes...fell into them, into a world of cold brilliance where a thousand fiery forms were materialized and dispersed every second, forms both of such beauty and hideousness that their effect on me, their beholder, was identical, a confusion of terror and exaltation. Whatever they were, the forms of Stoner's spirit, his potentials, or even of his thoughts, they were in their momentary life more vital and consequential than I could ever hope to be. Compelled by them, I walked over to him. I must have been afraid—I could feel wetness on my thighs and realized that my bladder had emptied—but he so dominated me that I knew only the need to obey. He did not stand, yet with each expansion his image would loom up before my eyes and I would stare into that dead face seamed by rivulets of molten diamond, its expression losing coherence, features splitting apart. Then he would shrink, leaving me gazing dumbly down at the top of his helmet. Dust stung my eyelids, my cheeks.

"What—" I began, intending to ask what he wanted; but before I could finish, he seized my wrist. Ice flowed up my arm, shocking my heart, and I heard myself...not screaming. No, this was the sound life makes leaving the body, like the squealing of gas released from a balloon that's half pinched shut.

Within seconds, drained of strength, I slumped to the ground, my vision reduced to a darkening fog. If he had maintained his hold much longer, I'm sure I would have died...and I was resigned to the idea. I had no weapon with which to fight him. But then I realized that the cold had receded from my limbs. Dazed, I looked around, and when I spotted him, I tried to stand, to run. Neither my arms nor legs would support me, and—desperate—I flopped on the red dirt, trying to crawl to safety; but after that initial burst of panic, the gland that governed my reactions must have overloaded, because I stopped crawling, rolled onto my back and stayed put, feeling stunned, weak, transfixed by what I saw. Yet not in the least afraid.

Stoner's inner man, now twice human-size, had broken free and was standing at the center of the village, some twenty feet off a bipedal silhouette through which it seemed you could look forever into a dimension of fire and crystal, like a hole burned in the fabric of the world. His movements were slow, tentative, as if he hadn't quite adapted to his new form, and penetrating him, arcing through the air from the tin-roofed building, their substance flowing toward him, were what appeared to be thousands of translucent wires, the structures of the fields. As I watched, they began to glow with Stoner's blue-white-diamond color, their substance to reverse its flow and pour back toward the building, and to emit a bass hum. Dents popped in the tin roof, the walls bulged inward, and with a grinding noise, a narrow fissure forked open in the earth beside it. The glowing wires grew brighter and brighter, and the building started to crumple, never collapsing, but—as if giant hands were pushing at it from every direction—compacting with terrible slowness until it had been squashed to perhaps a quarter of its original height. The hum died away. A fire broke out in the wreckage, pale flames leaping high and winnowing into black smoke.

Somebody clutched my shoulder, hands hauled me to my feet. It was Tuu and one of his soldiers. Their faces were knitted by lines of concern, and that concern rekindled my fear. I clawed at them, full of gratitude, and let them hustle me away. We took our places among the other observers, the smoking building at our backs, all gazing at the yellow houses and the burning giant in their midst.

The air around Stoner had become murky, turbulent, and this turbulence spread to obscure the center of the village. He stood unmoving, while small dust devils kicked up at his heels and went zipping about like a god's zany pets. One of the houses caved in with a *whump*, and pieces of yellow concrete began to lift from the ruins, to float toward Stoner; drawing near him, they acquired some of his brightness, glowing in their own right, and then vanished into the turbulence. Another house imploded, and the same process was initiated. The fact that all this was happening in dead silence—except for the caving in of the houses—made it seem even more eerie and menacing than if there had been sound.

The turbulence eddied faster and faster, thickening, and at last a strange vista faded in from the dark air, taking its place the way the picture melts up from the screen of an old television set. Four or five minutes must have passed before it became completely clear, and then it seemed sharper and more in focus than did the jungle and the houses, more even than the blazing figure who had summoned it: an acre-sized patch of hell or heaven or something in between, shining through the dilapidated structures and shabby colors of the ordinary, paling them. Beyond Stoner lay a vast forested plain dotted with fires...or maybe they weren't fires but some less chaotic form of energy, for though they gave off smoke, the flames maintained rigorous stylized shapes, showing like red fountains and poinsettias and other shapes yet against the poisonous green of the trees. Smoke hung like a gray pall over the plain and now and again beams of radiance—all so complexly figured, they appeared to be pillars of crystal—would shoot up from the forest into the grayness and resolve into a burst of light; and at the far limit of the plain, beyond a string of ragged hills, the dark sky would intermittently flash reddish orange as if great batteries of artillery were homing in upon some target there.

I had thought that Stoner would set forth at once into this other world, but instead he backed a step away and I felt despair for him, fear that he wouldn't seize his opportunity to escape. It may seem odd that I still thought of him as Stoner, and it may be that prior to that moment I had forgotten his human past; but now, sensing his trepidation, I understood that what enlivened this awesome figure was some scrap of soul belonging to the man-child I once had known. Silently, I urged him on. Yet he continued to hesitate.

It wasn't until someone tried to pull me back that I realized I was moving toward Stoner. I shook off whoever it was, walked to the edge of the village, and called Stoner's name. I didn't really expect him to acknowledge me, and I'm not clear as to what my motivations were: maybe it was just that since I had come this far with him I didn't want my efforts wasted. But I think it was something more, some old loyalty resurrected, one I had denied while he was alive.

"Get outta here!" I shouted. "Go on! Get out!"

He turned that blind, fiery face toward me and despite its featurelessness, I could read therein the record of his solitude, his fears concerning its resolution. It was, I knew, a final sending. I sensed again his emptiness, but it wasn't so harrowing and hopeless as before; in it there was a measure of determination, of purpose, and, too, a kind of...I'm tempted to say gratitude, but in truth it was more a simple acknowledgment, like the wave of a hand given by one workman to another after the completion of a difficult task.

"Go." I said it softly, the way you'd speak when urging a child to take his first step, and Stoner walked away.

For a few moments, though his legs moved, he didn't appear to be making any headway; his figure remained undiminished by distance. There was a tension in the air, an almost impalpable disturbance that quickly evolved into a heated pulse. One of the banana trees burst into flames, its leaves shriveling; a second tree ignited, a third, and soon all those trees close to the demarcation of that other world were burning like green ceremonial candles. The heat intensified, and the veils of dust that blew toward me carried a stinging residue of that heat; the sky for hundreds of feet above rippled as with the effects of an immense conflagration.

I stumbled back, tripped, and fell heavily. When I recovered I saw that Stoner was receding, that the world into which he was traveling was receding with him, or rather seeming to fold, to bisect and collapse around him: it looked as if that plain dotted with fires were painted on a curtain, and as he pushed forward, the fabric was drawn with him, its painted distances becoming foreshortened, its perspectives exaggerated and surreal, molding into a tunnel that conformed to his shape. His figure shrank to half its previous size, and then—some limit reached, some barrier penetrated—the heat died away, its dissipation accompanied by a seething hiss, and Stoner's white fire began to shine brighter and brighter, his form eroding in brightness. I had to shield my eyes, then shut them; but even so, I could see the soundless explosion that followed through my lids, and for several minutes I could make out its vague afterimage. A blast of wind pressed me flat, hot at first, but blowing colder and colder, setting my teeth to chattering. At last this subsided, and on opening my eyes I found that Stoner had vanished, and where the plain had been now lay a wreckage of yellow stone and seared banana trees, ringed by a few undamaged houses on the perimeter.

The only sound was the crackle of flames from the tin-roofed building. Moments later, however, I heard a patter of applause. I looked behind me: the gooks were all applauding Tuu, who was smiling and bowing like the author of a successful play. I was shocked at their reaction. How could they be concerned with accolades? Hadn't they been dazzled, as I had, their humanity diminished by the mystery and power of Stoner's metamorphosis? I went over to them, and drawing near, I overheard an officer congratulate Tuu on "another triumph." It took me a while to register the significance of those words, and when I did I pushed through the group and confronted Tuu.

"'Another triumph'?" I said.

He met my eyes, imperturbable. "I wasn't aware you spoke our language, Mr. Puleo."

"You've done this before," I said, getting angry. "Haven't you?"

"Twice before." He tapped a cigarette from a pack of Marlboros; an officer rushed to light it. "But never with an American spirit."

"You coulda killed me!" I shouted, lunging for him. Two soldiers came between us, menacing me with their rifles.

Tuu blew out a plume of smoke that seemed to give visible evidence of his self-satisfaction. "I told you it was a risk," he said. "Does it matter that I knew the extent of the risk and you did not? You were in no greater danger because of that. We were prepared to take steps if the situation warranted."

"Don't bullshit me! You couldn't have done nothin' with Stoner!"

He let a smile nick the corners of his mouth.

"You had no right," I said. "You—"

Tuu's face hardened. "We had no right to mislead you? Please, Mr. Puleo. Between our peoples, deception is a tradition."

I fumed, wanting to get at him. Frustrated, I slugged my thigh with my fist, spun on my heel, and walked off. The two soldiers caught up with me and blocked my path. Furious, I swatted at their rifles; they disengaged their safeties and aimed at my stomach.

"If you wish to be alone," Tuu called, "I have no objection to you taking a walk. We have tests to complete. But please keep to the road. A car will come for you."

Before the soldiers could step aside, I pushed past them.

"Keep to the road, Mr. Puleo!" In Tuu's voice was more than a touch of amusement. "If you recall, we're quite adept at tracking."

▲▼▲

Anger was good for me; it kept my mind off what I had seen. I wasn't ready to deal with Stoner's evolution. I wanted to consider things in simple terms: a man I had hated had died to the world a second time and I had played a part in his release, a part in which I had no reason to take pride or bear shame, because I had been manipulated every step of the way. I was so full of anger, I must have done the first mile in under fifteen minutes, the next in not much more. By then the sun had risen above the treeline and I had worked up a sweat. Insects buzzed; monkeys screamed. I slowed my pace and turned my head from side to side as I went, as if I were walking point again. I had the idea my own ghost was walking with me, shifting around inside and burning to get out on its own.

After an hour or so I came to the temporary housing that had been erected for the populace of Cam Le: thatched huts; scrawny dogs slinking and chickens pecking; orange peels, palm litter, and piles of shit in the streets. Some old men smoking pipes by a cookfire blinked at me. Three girls carrying plastic jugs giggled, ran off behind a hut, and peeked back around the corner.

Vietnam.

I thought about the way I'd used to sneer the word. 'Nam, I'd say. Viet-fucking-nam! Now it was spoken proudly, printed in Twentieth

Century-Fox monolithic capitals, brazen with hype. Perhaps between those two extremes was a mode of expression that captured the ordinary reality of the place, the poverty and peacefulness of this village; but if so, it wasn't accessible to me.

Some of the villagers were coming out of their doors to have a look at the stranger. I wondered if any of them recognized me. Maybe, I thought, chuckling madly, maybe if I bashed a couple on the head and screamed "Number Ten VC!" maybe then they'd remember. I suddenly felt tired and empty, and I sat down by the road to wait. I was so distracted, I didn't notice at first that a number of flies had mistaken me for a new and bigger piece of shit and were orbiting me, crawling over my knuckles. I flicked them away, watched them spiral off and land on other parts of my body. I got into controlling their patterns of flight, seeing if I could make them all congregate on my left hand, which I kept still. Weird shudders began passing through my chest, and the vacuum inside my head filled with memories of Stoner, his bizarre dream, his terrible Valhalla. I tried to banish them, but they stuck there, replaying themselves over and over. I couldn't order them, couldn't derive any satisfaction from them. Like the passage of a comet, Stoner's escape from Cam Le had been a trivial cosmic event, causing momentary awe and providing a few more worthless clues to the nature of the absolute, but offering no human solutions. Nothing consequential had changed for me: I was as fucked up as ever, as hard-core disoriented. The buzzing sunlight grew hotter and hotter; the flies' dance quickened in the rippling air.

At long last a dusty car with a gook corporal at the wheel pulled up beside me. Fierman and Witcover were in back, and Witcover's eye was discolored, swollen shut. I went around to the passenger side, opened the front door, and heard behind me a spit-filled explosive sound. Turning, I saw that a kid of about eight or nine had jumped out of hiding to ambush me. He had a dirt-smeared belly that popped from the waist of his ragged shorts, and he was aiming a toy rifle made of sticks. He shot me again, jiggling the gun to simulate automatic fire. Little monster with slit black eyes. Staring daggers at me, thinking I'd killed his daddy. He probably would have loved it if I had keeled over, clutching my chest; but I wasn't in the mood. I pointed my finger, cocked the thumb, and shot him down like a dog.

He stared meanly and fired a third time: this was serious business, and he wanted me to die. "Row-nal Ray-gun," he said, and pretended to spit.

I just laughed and climbed into the car. The gook corporal engaged the gears, and we sped off into a boil of dust and light, as if—like Stoner—we were passing through a metaphysical barrier between worlds. My head bounced against the back of the seat, and with each impact I felt that my thoughts were clearing, that a poisonous sediment was being jolted loose and flushed from my bloodstream. Thick silence welled from the rear of the car, and not wanting to ride with hostiles all the way to Saigon, I turned to Witcover and apologized for having hit him. Pressure had done it to me, I told him. That, and bad memories of a bad time. His features tightened into a sour knot and he looked out the window, wholly unforgiving. But I refused to allow his response to disturb me—let him have his petty hate, his grudge, for whatever good it would do him—and I turned away to face the violent green sweep of the jungle, the great troubled rush of the world ahead, with a heart that seemed lighter by an ounce of anger, by one bitterness removed. To the end of that passion, at least, I had become reconciled. —

Delta Sly Honey

There was this guy I knew at Noc Linh, worked the corpse detail, guy name of Randall J. Willingham, a skinny red-haired Southern boy with a plague of freckles and eyes blue as poker chips, and sometimes when he got high, he'd wander up to the operations bunker and start spouting all kinds of shit over the radio, telling about his hometown and his dog, his opinion of the war (he was against it), and what it was like making love to his girlfriend, talking real pretty and wistful about her ways, the things she'd whisper and how she'd draw her knees up tight to her chest to let him go in deep. There was something pure and peaceful in his voice, his phrasing, and listening to him, you could feel the war draining out of you, and soon you'd be remembering your own girl, your own dog and hometown, not with heartsick longing but with joy in knowing you'd had at least that much sweetness of life. For many of us, his voice came to be the oracle of our luck, our survival, and even the brass who tried to stop his broadcasts finally realized he was doing a damn sight more good than any morale officer, and it got to where anytime the war was going slow and there was some free air, they'd call Randall up and ask if he felt in the mood to do a little talking.

The funny thing was that except for when he had a mike in his hand, you could hardly drag a word out of Randall. He had been a loner from day one of his tour, limiting his conversation to "Hey" and "How you?" and such, and his celebrity status caused him to become even less talkative. This was best explained by what he told us once over the air: "You meet ol' Randall J. on the street, and you gonna say, 'Why, that can't be Randall J.! That dumb-lookin' hillbilly couldn't recite the swearin'-in-oath, let alone be the hottest damn radio personality in South Vietnam!' And you'd be right on the money, 'cause Randall J. don't go more'n double figures for IQ, and he ain't got the imagination of a stump, and if you stopped him to say 'Howdy,' chances are he'd be stuck for a response. But lemme tell ya, when he puts his voice into a mike, ol' Randall J. becomes one with the airwaves, and the light that's been dark inside him goes bright, and his spirit streams out along Thunder

Road and past the Napalm Coast, mixin' with the ozone and changin' into Randall J. Willingham, the High Priest of the Soulful Truth and the Holy Ghost of the Sixty-Cycle Hum."

The base was situated on a gently inclined hill set among other hills, all of which had once been part of the Michelin rubber plantation, but now were almost completely defoliated, transformed into dusty brown lumps. Nearly seven thousand men were stationed there, living in bunkers and tents dotting the slopes, and the only building with any degree of permanence was an outsized Quonset but that housed the PX; it stood just inside the wire at the base of the hill. I was part of the MP contingent, and I guess I was the closest thing Randall had to a friend. We weren't really tight, but being from a small Southern town myself, the son of gentry, I was familiar with his type—fey, quiet farmboys whose vulnerabilities run deep—and I felt both sympathy and responsibility for him. My sympathy wasn't misplaced: nobody could have had a worse job, especially when you took into account the fact that his top sergeant, a beady-eyed, brush-cut, tackle-sized Army lifer named Andrew Moon, had chosen him for his whipping boy. Every morning I'd pass the tin-roofed shed where the corpses were off-loaded (it, too, was just inside the wire, but on the opposite side of the hill from the PX), and there Randall would be, laboring among body bags that were piled around like huge black fruit, with Moon hovering in the background and scowling. I always made it a point to stop and talk to Randall in order to give him a break from Moon's tyranny, and though he never expressed his gratitude or said very much about anything, soon he began to call me by my Christian name, Curt, instead of by my rank. Each time I made to leave, I would see the strain come back into his face, and before I had gone beyond earshot I would hear Moon reviling him. I believe it was those days of staring into stomach cavities, into charred hearts and brains, and Moon all the while screaming at him...I believe that was what had squeezed the poetry out of Randall and birthed his radio soul.

I tried to get Moon to lighten up. One afternoon I bearded him in his tent and asked why he was mistreating Randall. Of course I knew the answer. Men like Moon, men who have secured a little power and grown bloated from its use, they don't need an excuse for brutality; there's so much meanness inside them, it's bound to slop over onto somebody. But—thinking I could handle him better than Randall—I planned to divert his meanness, set myself up as his target, and this seemed a good way to open.

He didn't bite, however; he just lay on his cot, squinting up at me and nodding sagely, as if he saw through my charade. His jowls were speckled with a few days' growth of stubble, hairs sparse and black as pig bristles. "Y'know," he said, "I couldn't figure why you were buddyin' up to that fool, so I had a look at your records." He grunted laughter. "Now I got it."

"Oh?" I said, maintaining my cool.

"You got quite a heritage, son! All that noble Southern blood, all them dead generals and senators. When I seen that, I said to myself, 'Don't get on this boy's case too heavy, Andy. He's just tryin' to be like his great-grandaddy, doin' a kindness now and then for the darkies and the poor white trash.' Ain't that right?"

I couldn't deny that a shadow of the truth attached to what he had said, but I refused to let him rankle me. "My motives aren't in question here," I told him.

"Well, neither are mine...'least not by anyone who counts." He swung his legs off the cot and sat up, glowering at me. "You got some nice duty here, son. But you go fuckin' with me, I'll have your ass walkin' point in Quanh Tri 'fore you can blink. Understand?"

I felt as if I had been dipped in ice water. I knew he could do as he threatened—any man who's made top sergeant has also made some powerful friends—and I wanted no part of Quanh Tri.

He saw my fear and laughed. "Go on, get out!" he said, and as I stepped through the door, he added, "Come 'round the shed anytime, son. I ain't got nothin' against *noblesse oblige*. Fact is, I love to watch."

And I walked away, knowing that Randall was lost.

▲▼▲

In retrospect, it's clear that Randall had broken under Moon's whip early on, that his drifty radio spiels were symptomatic of his dissolution. In another time and place, someone might have noticed his condition; but in Vietnam everything he did seemed a normal reaction to the craziness of the war, perhaps even a bit more restrained than normal, and we would have thought him really nuts if he hadn't acted weird. As it was, we considered him a flake, but not wrapped so tight that you couldn't poke fun at him, and I believe it was this misconception that brought matters to a head....

Yet I'm not absolutely certain of that.

Several nights after my talk with Moon, I was on duty in the operations bunker when Randall did his broadcast. He always signed off in the same distinctive fashion, trying to contact the patrols of ghosts he claimed were haunting the free-fire zones. Instead of using ordinary call signs like Charlie Baker Able, he would invent others that suited the country lyricism of his style, names such as Lobo Angel Silver and Prairie Dawn Omega.

"Delta Sly Honey," he said that night. "Do you read? Over."

He sat a moment, listening to static filling in from nowhere.

"I know you're out there, Delta Sly Honey," he went on. "I can see you clear, walkin' the high country near Black Virgin Mountain, movin' through twists of fog like battle smoke and feelin' a little afraid, 'cause though you gone from the world, there's a world of fear 'tween here and the hereafter. Come back at me, Delta Sly Honey, and tell me how it's goin'." He stopped sending for a bit, and when he received no reply, he spoke again. "Maybe you don't think I'd understand your troubles, brothers. But I truly do. I know your hopes and fears, and how the spell of too much poison and fire and flyin' steel warped the chemistry of fate and made you wander off into the wars of the spirit 'stead of findin' rest beyond the grave. My soul's trackin' you as you move higher and higher toward the peace at the end of everything, passin' through mortar bursts throwin' up thick gouts of silence, with angels like tracers leadin' you on, listenin' to the cold white song of incoming stars.... Come on back at me, Delta Sly Honey. This here's your good buddy Randall J., earth-bound at Noc Linh. Do you read?"

There was a wild burst of static, and then a voice answered, saying, "Randall J., Randall J.! This is Delta Sly Honey. Readin' you loud and clear."

I let out a laugh, and the officers sitting at the far end of the bunker turned their heads, grinning. But Randall stared in horror at the radio, as if it were leaking blood, not static. He thumbed the switch and said shakily, "What's your position, Delta Sly Honey? I repeat. What's your position?"

"Guess you might say our position's kinda relative," came the reply. "But far as you concerned, man, we just down the road. There's a place for you with us, Randall J. We waitin' for you."

Randall's Adam's apple worked, and he wetted his lips. Under the hot bunker lights, his freckles stood out sharply.

"Y'know how it is when you're pinned down by fire?" the voice continued. "Lyin' flat with the flow of bullets passin' inches over your head? And you start thinkin' how easy it'd be just to raise up and get it over with.... You ever feel like that, Randall J.? Most times you keep flat, 'cause things ain't bad enough to make you go that route. But the way things been goin' for you, man, what with stickin' your hands into dead meat night and day—"

"Shut up," said Randall, his voice tight and small.

"—and that asshole Moon fuckin' with your mind, maybe it's time to consider your options."

"Shut up!" Randall screamed it, and I grabbed him by the shoulders. "Take it easy," I told him. "It's just some jerkoff puttin' you on." He shook me off; the vein in his temple was throbbing.

"I ain't tryin' to mess with you, man," said the voice. "I'm just layin' it out, showin' you there ain't no real options here. I know all them crazy thoughts that been flappin' 'round in your head, and I know how hard you been tryin' to control 'em. Ain't no point in controllin' 'em anymore, Randall J. You belong to us now. All you gotta do is to take a little walk down the road, and we be waitin'. We got some serious humpin' ahead of us, man. Out past the Napalm Coast, up beyond the high country...."

Randall bolted for the door, but I caught him and spun him around. He was breathing rapidly through his mouth, and his eyes seemed to be shining too brightly—like the way an old light bulb will flare up right before it goes dark for good. "Lemme go!" he said. "I gotta find 'em! I gotta tell 'em it ain't my time!"

"It's just someone playin' a goddamn joke," I said, and then it dawned on me. "It's Moon, Randall! You know it's him puttin' somebody up to this."

"I gotta find 'em!" he repeated, and with more strength than I would have given him credit for, he pushed me away and ran off into the dark.

▲▼▲

He didn't return, not that night, not the next morning, and we reported him AWOL. We searched the base and the nearby villes to no avail, and since the countryside was rife with NLF patrols and VC, it was logical to assume he had been killed or captured. Over the next couple of days, Moon made frequent public denials of his complicity in the joke, but no one bought it. He took to walking around with his holster unlatched, a wary expression on his face. Though Randall hadn't had any real friends, many of us had been devoted to his broadcasts, and among those devotees were a number of men who...well, a civilian psychiatrist might have called them unstable, but in truth they were men who had chosen to exalt instability, to ritualize insanity as a means of maintaining their equilibrium in an unstable medium: it was likely some of them would attempt reprisals. Moon's best hope was that something would divert their attention, but three days after Randall's disappearance, a peculiar transmission came into operations; like all

Randall's broadcasts, it was piped over the PA, and thus Moon's fate was sealed.

"Howdy, Noc Linh," said Randall or someone who sounded identical to him. "This here's Randall J. Willingham on patrol with Delta Sly Honey, speakin' to you from beyond the Napalm Coast. We been humpin' through rain and fog most of the day, with no sign of the enemy, just a few demons twistin' up from the gray and fadin' when we come near, and now we all hunkered down by the radio, restin' for tomorrow. Y'know, brothers, I used to be scared shitless of wakin' up here in the big nothin', but now it's gone and happened, I'm findin' it ain't so bad. 'Least I got the feelin' I'm headed someplace, whereas back at Noc Linh I was just spinnin' round and round, and close to losin' my mind. I hated ol' Sergeant Moon, and I hated him worse after he put someone up to hasslin' me on the radio. But now, though I reckon he's still pretty hateful, I can see he was actin' under the influence of a higher agency, one who was tryin' to help me get clear of Noc Linh...which was somethin' that had to be, no matter if I had to die to do it. Seems to me that's the nature of war, that all the violence has the effect of lettin' a little magic seep into the world by way of compensation...."

To most of us, this broadcast signaled that Randall was alive, but we also knew what it portended for Moon. And therefore I wasn't terribly surprised when he summoned me to his tent the next morning. At first he tried to play sergeant, ordering me to ally myself with him; but seeing that this didn't work, he begged for my help. He was a mess: red-eyed, unshaven, an eyelid twitching.

"I can't do a thing," I told him.

"You're his friend!" he said. "If you tell 'em I didn't have nothin' to do with it, they'll believe you."

"The hell they will! They'll think I helped you." I studied him a second, enjoying his anxiety. "Who did help you?"

"I didn't do it, goddammit!" His voice had risen to a shout, and he had to struggle to keep calm. "I swear! It wasn't me!"

It was strange, my mental set at that moment. I found I believed him—I didn't think him capable of manufacturing sincerity—and yet I suddenly believed everything: that Randall was somehow both dead and alive, that Delta Sly Honey both did and did not exist, that whatever was happening was an event in which all possibility was manifest, in which truth and falsity had the same valence, in which the real and the illusory were undifferentiated. And at the center of this complex circumstance—a bulky, sweating monster—stood Moon. Innocent, perhaps. But guilty of a seminal crime.

"I can make it good for you," he said. "Hawaii...you want duty in Hawaii, I can arrange it. Hell, I can get you shipped Stateside."

He struck me then as a hideous genie offering three wishes, and the fact that he had the power to make this offer infuriated me. "If you can do all that," I said, "you ain't got a worry in the world." And I strode off, feeling righteous in my judgment.

Two nights later while returning to my hooch, I spotted a couple of men wearing tiger shorts dragging a large and apparently unconscious someone toward the barrier of concertina wire beside the PX—I knew it had to be Moon. I drew my pistol, sneaked along the back wall of the PX, and when they came abreast I stepped out and told them to put their burden down. They stopped but didn't turn loose of Moon. Both had blackened their faces with greasepaint, and to this had added fanciful designs in crimson, blue, and yellow that gave them the look of savages. They carried combat knives, and their eyes were pointed with the reflected brilliance of the perimeter lights. It was a hot night, but it seemed hotter there beside them, as if their craziness had a radiant value. "This ain't none of your affair, Curt," said the taller of the two; despite his bad grammar, he had a soft, well-modulated voice, and I thought I heard a trace of amusement in it.

I peered at him, but was unable to recognize him beneath the paint. Again I told them to put Moon down.

"Sorry," said the tall guy. "Man's gotta pay for his crimes."

"He didn't do anything," I said. "You know damn well Randall's just AWOL."

The tall guy chuckled, and the other guy said, "Naw, we don't know that a-tall."

Moon groaned, tried to lift his head, then slumped back.

"No matter what he did or didn't do," said the tall guy, "the man deserves what's comin'."

"Yeah," said his pal. "And if it ain't us what does it, it'll be somebody else."

I knew he was right, and the idea of killing two men to save a third who was doomed in any event just didn't stack up. But though my sense of duty was weak where Moon was concerned, it hadn't entirely dissipated. "Let him go," I said.

The tall guy grinned, and the other one shook his head as if dismayed by my stubbornness. They appeared wholly untroubled by the pistol, possessed of an irrational confidence. "Be reasonable, Curt," said the tall guy. "This ain't gettin' you nowhere."

I couldn't believe his foolhardiness. "You see this?" I said, flourishing the pistol. "Gun, y'know? I'm gonna fuckin' shoot you with it, you don't let him go."

Moon let out another groan, and the tall guy rapped him hard on the back of the head with the hilt of his knife.

"Hey!" I said, training the pistol on his chest.

"Look here, Curt—" he began.

"Who the hell are you?" I stepped closer, but was still unable to identify him. "I don't know you."

"Randall told us 'bout you, Curt. He's a buddy of ours, ol' Randall is. We're with Delta Sly Honey."

I believed him for that first split second. My mouth grew cottony, and my hand trembled. But then I essayed a laugh. "Sure you are! Now put his ass down!"

"That's what you really want, huh?"

"Damn right!" I said. "Now!"

"Okay," he said. "You got it." And with a fluid stroke, he cut Moon's throat.

Moon's eyes popped open as the knife sliced through his tissues, and that—not the blood spilling onto the dust—was the thing that froze me: those bugged eyes in which an awful realization dawned and faded. They let him fall facedownward. His legs spasmed, his right hand jittered. For a long moment, stunned, I stared at him, at the blood puddling beneath his head, and when I looked up I found that the two men were sprinting away, about to round the curve of the hill. I couldn't bring myself to fire. Mixed in my thoughts were the knowledge that killing them served no purpose and the fear that my bullets would have no effect. I glanced left and right, behind me, making sure that no one was watching, and then ran up the slope to my hooch.

Under my cot was a bottle of sour mash. I pulled it out and had a couple of drinks to steady myself; but steadiness was beyond me. I switched on a battery lamp and sat cross-legged, listening to the snores of my bunkmate. Lying on my duffel bag was an unfinished letter home, one I had begun nearly two weeks before; I doubted now I'd ever finish it. What would I tell my folks? That I had more or less sanctioned an execution? That I was losing my fucking mind? Usually I told them everything was fine, but after the scene I had just witnessed, I felt I was forever past that sort of blithe invention. I switched off the lamp and lay in the dark, the bottle resting on my chest. I had a third drink, a fourth, and gradually lost both count and consciousness.

▲▼▲

I had a week's R & R coming and I took it, hoping debauch would shore me up. But I spent much of that week attempting to justify my inaction in terms of the inevitable and the supernatural, and failing in that attempt. You see, now as then, if pressed for an opinion, I would tell you that what happened at Noc Linh was the sad consequence of a joke gone sour, of a war twisted into a demonic exercise. Everything was explicable in that wise. And yet it's conceivable that the supernatural was involved, that—as Randall had suggested—a little magic had seeped into the world. In Vietnam, with all its horror and strangeness, it was difficult to distinguish between the magical and the mundane, and it's possible that thousands of supernatural events went unnoticed as such, obscured by the poignancies of death and fear, becoming quirky memories that years later might pass through your mind while you were washing the dishes or walking the dog, and give you a moment's pause, an eerie feeling that would almost instantly be ground away by the mills of the ordinary. But I'm certain that my qualification is due to the fact that I want there to have been some magic involved, anything to lessen my culpability, to shed a less damning light on the perversity and viciousness of my brothers-in-arms.

On returning to Noc Linh, I found that Randall had also returned. He claimed to be suffering from amnesia and would not admit to having made the broadcast that had triggered Moon's murder. The shrinks had decided that he was bucking for a Section Eight, had ordered him put back on the corpse detail, and as before, Randall could be seen laboring beneath the tin-roofed shed, transferring the contents of body bags into aluminum coffins. On the surface, little appeared to have changed. But Randall had become a pariah. He was insulted and whispered about and shunned. Whenever he came near, necks would stiffen and conversations die. If he had offed Moon himself, he would have been cheered; but the notion that he had used his influence to have his dirty work jobbed out didn't accord with the prevailing concept of honorable vengeance. Though I tried not to, I couldn't help feeling badly toward him myself. It was weird. I would approach with the best of intentions, but by the time I reached him, my hackles would have risen and I would walk on in hostile silence, as if he were exuding a chemical that had evoked my contempt. I did get close enough to him, however, to see that the mad brightness was missing from his eyes; I had the feeling that all his brightness was missing, that whatever quality had enabled him to do his broadcasts had been sucked dry.

One morning as I was passing the PX, whose shiny surfaces reflected a dynamited white glare of sun, I noticed a crowd of men pressing through the front door, apparently trying to catch sight of something inside. I pushed through them and found one of the canteen clerks—a lean kid with black hair and a wolfish face—engaged in beating Randall to a pulp. I pulled him off, threw him into a table, and kneeled beside Randall, who had collapsed to the floor. His cheekbones were lumped and discolored; blood poured from his nose, trickled from his mouth. His eyes met mine, and I felt nothing from him: he seemed muffled, vibeless, as if heavily sedated.

"They out to get me, Curt," he mumbled.

All my sympathy for him was suddenly resurrected. "It's okay, man," I said. "Sooner or later, it'll blow over." I handed him my bandanna, and he dabbed ineffectually at the flow from his nose. Watching him, I recalled Moon's categorization of my motives for befriending him, and I understood now that my true motives had less to do with our relative social status than with my belief that he could be saved, that—after months of standing by helplessly while the unsalvageable marched to their fates—I thought I might be able to effect some small good work. This may seem altruistic to the point of naïveté, and perhaps it was, perhaps the brimstone oppressiveness of the war had from the residue of old sermons heard and disregarded provoked some vain Christian reflex; but the need was strong in me, nonetheless, and I realized that I had fixed on it as a prerequisite to my own salvation.

Randall handed back the bandanna. "Ain't gonna blow over," he said. "Not with these guys."

I grabbed his elbow and hauled him to his feet. "What guys?"

He looked around as if afraid of eavesdroppers. "Delta Sly Honey!"

"Christ, Randall! Come on." I tried to guide him toward the door, but he wrenched free.

"They out to get me! They say I crossed over and they took care of Moon for me...and then I got away from 'em." He dug his fingers into my arm. "But I can't remember, Curt! I can't remember nothin'!"

My first impulse was to tell him to drop the amnesia act, but then I thought about the painted men who had scragged Moon: if they were after Randall, he was in big trouble. "Let's get you patched up," I said. "We'll talk about this later."

He gazed at me, dull and uncomprehending. "You gonna help me?" he asked in a tone of disbelief.

I doubted anyone could help him now, and maybe, I thought, that was also part of my motivation—the desire to know the good sin of honest failure. "Sure," I told him. "We'll figure out somethin'."

We started for the door, but on seeing the men gathered there, Randall balked. "What you want from me?" he shouted, giving a flailing, awkward wave with his left arm as if to make them vanish. "What the fuck you want?"

They stared coldly at him, and those stares were like bad answers. He hung his head and kept it hung all the way to the infirmary.

▲▼▲

That night I set out to visit Randall, intending to advise him to confess, a tactic I perceived as his one hope of survival. I'd planned to see him early in the evening, but was called back on duty and didn't get clear until well after midnight. The base was quiet and deserted-feeling. Only a few lights picked out the darkened slopes, and had it not been for the heat and stench, it would have been easy to believe that the hill with its illuminated caves was a place of mild enchantment, inhabited by elves and not frightened men. The moon was almost full, and beneath it the PX shone like an immense silver lozenge. Though it had closed an hour before, its windows were lit, and—MP instincts engaged—I peered inside. Randall was backed against the bar, holding a knife to the neck of the wolfish clerk who had beaten him, and ranged in a loose circle around him, standing among the tables, were five men wearing tiger shorts, their faces painted with savage designs. I drew my pistol, eased around to the front, and—wanting my entrance to have shock value—kicked the door open.

The five men turned their heads to me, but appeared not at all disconcerted. "How's she goin', Curt?" said one, and by his soft voice I recognized the tall guy who had slit Moon's throat.

"Tell 'em to leave me be!" Randall shrilled.

I fixed my gaze on the tall guy and with gunslinger menace said, "I'm not messin' with you tonight. Get out now or I'll take you down."

"You can't hurt me, Curt," he said.

"Don't gimme that ghost shit! Fuck with me, and you'll be humpin' with Delta Sly Honey for real."

"Even if you were right 'bout me, Curt, I wouldn't be scared of dyin'. I was dead where it counts halfway through my tour."

A scuffling at the bar, and I saw that Randall had wrestled the clerk to the floor. He wrapped his legs around the clerk's waist in a scissors and yanked his head back by the hair to expose his throat. "Leave me be," he said. Every nerve in his face was jumping.

"Let him go, Randall," said the tall guy. "We ain't after no innocent blood. We just want you to take a little walk...to cross back over."

"Get out!" I told him.

"You're workin' yourself in real deep, man," he said.

"This ain't no bullshit!" I said. "I will shoot."

"Look here, Curt," he said. "S'pose we're just plain ol' ordinary grunts. You gonna shoot us all? And if you do, don't you think we'd have friends who'd take it hard? Any way you slice it, you bookin' yourself a silver box and air freight home."

He came a step toward me, and I said, "Watch it, man!" He came another step, his devil mask split by a fierce grin. My heart felt hot and solid in my chest, no beats, and I thought, He's a ghost, his flesh is smoke, the paint a color in my eye. "Keep back!" I warned.

"Gonna kill me?" Again he grinned. "Go ahead." He lunged, a feint only, and I squeezed the trigger.

The gun jammed.

When I think now how this astounded me, I wonder at my idiocy. The gun jammed frequently. It was an absolute piece of shit, that weapon. But at the time its failure seemed a magical coincidence, a denial of the laws of chance. And adding to my astonishment was the reaction of the other men: they made no move toward Randall, as if no opportunity had been provided, no danger passed. Yet the tall guy looked somewhat shaken to me.

Randall let out a mewling noise, and that sound enlisted my competence. I edged between the tables and took a stand next to him. "Let me get the knife from him," I said. "No point in both of 'em dyin'."

The tall guy drew a deep breath as if to settle himself. "You reckon you can do that, Curt?"

"Maybe. If you guys wait outside, he won't be as scared and maybe I can get it."

They stared at me, unreadable.

"Gimme a chance."

"We ain't after no innocent blood." The tall guy's tone was firm, as if this were policy. "But—"

"Just a coupla minutes," I said. "That's all I'm askin'."

I could almost hear the tick of the tall guy's judgment. "Okay," he said at last. "But don't you go tryin' nothin' hinkey, Curt." Then, to Randall. "We be waitin', Randall J."

As soon as they were out the door, I kneeled beside Randall. Spittle flecked the clerk's lips, and when Randall shifted the knife a tad, his eyes rolled up into heaven. "Leave me be," said Randall. He might have been talking to the air, the walls, the world.

"Give it up," I said.

He just blinked.

"Let him go and I'll help you," I said. "But if you cut him, you on your own. That how you want it?"

"Un-unh."

"Well, turn him loose."

"I can't," he said, a catch in his voice. "I'm all froze up. If I move, I'll cut him." Sweat dripped into his eyes, and he blinked some more.

"How 'bout I take it from you? If you keep real still, if you lemme ease it outta your hand, maybe we can work it that way."

"I don't know.... I might mess up."

The clerk gave a long shuddery sigh and squeezed his eyes shut.

"You gonna be fine," I said to Randall. "Just keep your eyes on me, and you gonna be fine."

I stretched out my hand. The clerk was trembling, Randall was trembling, and when I touched the blade it was so full of vibration, it felt alive, as if all the energy in the room had been concentrated there. I tried pulling it away from the clerk's neck, but it wouldn't budge.

"You gotta loosen up, Randall," I said.

I tried again and, gripping the blade between my forefinger and thumb, managed to pry it an inch or so away from the line of blood it had drawn. My fingers were sweaty, the metal slick, and the blade felt like it was connected to a spring, that any second it would snap back and bite deep.

"My fingers are slippin'," I said, and the clerk whimpered.

"Ain't my fault if they do." Randall said this pleadingly, as if testing the waters, the potentials of his guilt and innocence, and I realized he was setting me up the way he had Moon's killers. It was a childlike attempt compared to the other, but I knew to his mind it would work out the same.

"The hell it ain't!" I said. "Don't do it, man!"

"It ain't my fault!" he insisted.

"Randall!"

I could feel his intent in the quiver of the blade. With my free hand, I grabbed the clerk's upper arm, and as the knife slipped, I jerked him to the side. The blade sliced his jaw, and he screeched; but the wound wasn't mortal.

I plucked the knife from Randall's hand, wanting to kill him myself. But I had invested too much in his salvation. I hauled him erect and over to the window; I smashed out the glass with a chair and pushed him through. Then I jumped after him. As I came to my feet, I saw the painted men closing in from the front of the PX and—still towing Randall along—I sprinted around the corner of the building and up the slope, calling for help. Lights flicked on, and heads popped from tent flaps. But when they spotted Randall, they ducked back inside.

I was afraid, but Randall's abject helplessness—his eyes rolling like a freaked calf's, his hands clawing at me for support—helped to steady me. The painted men seemed to be everywhere. They would materialize from behind tents, out of bunker mouths, grinning madly and waving moonstruck knives, and send us veering off in another direction, back and forth across the hill. Time and again, I thought they had us, and on several occasions, it was only by a hairsbreadth that I eluded the slash of a blade that looked to be bearing a charge of winking silver energy on its tip. I was wearing down, stumbling, gasping, and I was certain we couldn't last much longer. But we continued to evade them, and I began to sense that they were in no hurry to conclude the hunt; their pursuit had less an air of frenzy than of a ritual harassment, and eventually, as we staggered up to the mouth of the operations bunker and—I believed—safety, I realized that they had been herding us. I pushed Randall inside and glanced back from the sandbagged entrance. The five men stood motionless a second, perhaps fifty feet away, then melted into the darkness.

▲▼▲

I explained what had happened to the MP on duty in the bunker—a heavyset guy named Cousins—and though he had no love for Randall, he was a dutiful sort and gave us permission to wait out the night inside. Randall slumped down against the wall, resting his head on his knees, the picture of despair. But I believed that his survival was assured. With the testimony of the clerk, I thought the shrinks would have no choice but to send him elsewhere for examination and possible institutionalization. I felt good, accomplished, and passed the night chain-smoking, bullshitting with Cousins.

Then, toward dawn, a voice issued from the radio. It was greatly distorted, but it sounded very much like Randall's.

"Randall J.," it said. "This here's Delta Sly Honey. Do you read? Over."

Randall looked up, hearkening to the spit and fizzle of the static.

"I know you out there, Randall J.," the voice went on. "I can see you clear, sitting with the shadows of the bars upon your soul and blood on your hands. Ain't no virtuous blood, that's true. But it stains you alla same. Come back at me, Randall J. We gotta talk, you and me."

Randall let his head fall; with a finger, he traced a line in the dust.

"What's the point in keepin' this up, Randall J.?" said the voice. "You left the best part of you over here, the soulful part, and you can't go on much longer without it. Time to take that little walk for real, man. Time to get clear of what you done and pass on to what must be. We waitin' for you just north of base, Randall J. Don't make us come for you."

It was in my mind to say something to Randall, to break the disconsolate spell the voice appeared to be casting over him; but I found I had nothing left to give him, that I had spent my fund of altruism and was mostly weary of the whole business...as he must have been.

"Ain't nothin' to be 'fraid of out here," said the voice. "Only the wind and the gray whispers of phantom Charlie and the trail leadin' away from the world. There's good company for you, Randall J. Gotta man here used to be a poet, and he'll tell you stories 'bout the Wild North King and the Woman of Crystal. Got another fella, guy used to live in Indonesia, and he's fulla tales 'bout watchin' tigers come out on the highways to shit and cities of men dressed like women and islands where dragons still live. Then there's this kid from Opelika, claims to know some of your people down that way, and when he talks, you can just see that ol' farmboy moon heavin' up big and yellow over the barns, shinin' the blacktop so it looks like polished jet, and you can hear crazy music leakin' from the Dixieland Café and smell the perfumed heat steamin' off the young girls' breasts. Don't make us wait no more, Randall J. We got work to do. Maybe it ain't much, just breakin' trail and walkin' point and keepin' a sharp eye out for demons...but it sure as hell beats shepherdin' the dead, now, don't it?" A long pause. "You come on and take that walk, Randall J. We'll make you welcome, I promise. This here's Delta Sly Honey. Over and out."

Randall pulled himself to his feet and took a faltering few steps toward the mouth of the bunker. I blocked his path and he said, "Lemme go, Curt."

"Look here, Randall," I said. "I might can get you home if you just hang on."

"Home." The concept seemed to amuse him, as if it were something with the dubious reality of heaven or hell. "Lemme go."

In his eyes, then, I thought I could see all his broken parts, a disjointed shifting of lights and darks, and when I spoke I felt I was giving tongue to a vast consensus, one arrived at without either ballots or reasonable discourse. "If I let you go," I said, "be best you don't come back this time."

He stared at me, his face gone slack, and nodded.

Hardly anybody was outside, yet I had the idea everyone was watching us as we walked down the hill; under a leaden overcast, the base had a tense, muted atmosphere such as must have attended rainy dawns beneath the guillotine. The sentries at the main gate passed Randall through without question. He went a few paces along the road, then turned back, his face pale as a star in the half-light, and I wondered if he thought we were driving him off or if he believed he was being called to a better world. In my heart I knew which was the case. At last he set out again, quickly becoming a shadow, then the rumor of a shadow, then gone.

Walking back up the hill, I tried to sort out my thoughts, to determine what I was feeling, and it may be a testament to how crazy I was, how crazy we all were, that I felt less regret for a man lost than satisfaction in knowing that some perverted justice had been served, that the world of the war—tipped off-center by this unmilitary engagement and our focus upon it—could now go back to spinning true.

That night there was fried chicken in the mess, and vanilla ice cream, and afterward a movie about a more reasonable war, full of villainous Germans with Dracula accents and heroic grunts who took nothing but flesh wounds. When it was done, I walked back to my hooch and stood out front and had a smoke. In the northern sky was a flickering orange glow, one accompanied by the rumble of artillery. It was, I realized, just about this time of night that Randall had customarily begun his broadcasts. Somebody else must have realized this, because at that moment the PA was switched on. I half expected to hear Randall giving the news of Delta Sly Honey, but there was only static, sounding like the crackling of enormous flames. Listening to it, I felt disoriented, completely vulnerable, as if some huge black presence were on the verge of swallowing me up. And then a voice did speak. It wasn't Randall's, yet it had a similar countrified accent, and though the words weren't quite as fluent, they were redolent of his old raps, lending a folksy comprehensibility to the vastness of the cosmos, the strangeness of the war. I had no idea whether or not it was the voice that had summoned Randall to take his walk, no longer affecting an imitation, yet I thought I recognized its soft well-modulated tones. But none of that mattered. I was so grateful, so relieved by this end to silence, that I went into my hooch and—armed with lies—sat down to finish my interrupted letter home. —

Life of Buddha

Whenever the cops scheduled a raid on the shooting gallery to collect their protection money, old cotton-headed Pete Mason, who ran the place, would give Buddha the day off. Buddha rarely said a word to anyone, and Pete had learned that cops were offended by silence. If you didn't scream and run when they busted in, if like Buddha you just sat there and stared at them, they figured you were concealing a superior attitude, and they then tended to get inside your head.

They had beaten Buddha half to death a couple of times for this very reason, and while Buddha hadn't complained (he never complained about anything), Pete did not want to risk losing such a faithful employee. So on the night prior to the September raid, Pete went downstairs to where Buddha was nodding on a stained mattress by the front door and said, "Why don't you hang out over at Taboo's place tomorrow? Police is comin' 'round to do they thang."

Buddha shook himself out of his nod and said, "Talked to him already. Johnny Wardell's gon' be over sometime makin' a buy, but he say to come ahead anyway." He was a squat black man in his late thirties, his head stone bald, with sleepy heavy-lidded eyes and the beginning of jowls; he was wearing chinos stippled with blood from his last fix, and a too-small T-shirt that showed every tuck and billow of his round belly and womanly breasts. Sitting there, he looked like a Buddha carved from ebony that somebody had outfitted with Salvation Army clothes, and that was why Pete had given him the name. His real name was Richard Damon, but he wouldn't respond to it anymore. Buddha suited him just fine.

"Beats me why Taboo wanna do business with Johnny Wardell," Pete said, hitching his pants up over his ample stomach. "Sooner or later Wardell he be gettin' crazy all over a faggot like Taboo...y'know?"

Buddha grunted, scratched the tracks on his wrist, and gazed out the window beside the front door. He knew Pete was trying to draw him into a conversation, and he had no intention of letting himself be drawn. It wasn't that he disliked Pete; he liked him as much as anyone. He simply had no opinions he wanted to share; he had cultivated this lack of opinion, and he had found that the more he talked, the more opinions came to mind.

"You tell Taboo from me," Pete went on, "I been livin' in Detroit more'n sixty years, and I done business wit' a lotta bad dogs, but I ain't never met one meaner than Wardell. You tell him he better watch his behavior, y'understan'?"

"Awright."

"Well...." Pete turned and with a laborious gait, dragging his bad leg, mounted the stairs. "You come on up 'round two and get your good-nighter. I'll cut ya out a spoon of China White."

"'Preciate it," said Buddha.

As soon as Pete was out of sight, Buddha lay down and stared at the flaking grayish-white paint of the ceiling. He picked a sliver of paint from the wall and crumbled it between his fingers. Then he ran the back of his hand along the worn nap of the runner that covered the hallway floor. All as if to reassure himself of the familiar surroundings. He had spent the best part of fifteen years as Pete's watchdog, lying on the same mattress, staring at that same dried-up paint, caressing that same runner. Before taking up residence on the mattress, he had been a young man with a fixture. Everybody had said, "That Richard Damon, he's gon' be headlines, he's gon' be *Live at Five*, he's gon' be *People* magazine." Not that he had started out different from his peers. He'd been into a little dealing, a little numbers, a little of whatever would pay him for doing nothing. But he'd been smarter than most and had kept his record clean, and when he told people he had his eye on the political arena, nobody laughed. They could see he had the stuff to make it. The trouble was, though, he had been so full of himself, so taken with his smarts and his fine clothes and his way with the ladies, he had destroyed the only two people who had cared about him. Destroyed them without noticing. Worried his mama into an early grave, driven his wife to suicide. For a while after they had died, he'd gone on as always, but then he'd come up against guilt.

He hadn't known then what that word *guilt* meant; but he had since learned its meaning to the bone. Guilt started out as a minor irritation no worse than a case of heartburn and grew into a pain with claws that tore out your guts and hollowed your heart. Guilt made you sweat for no reason, jump at the least noise, look behind you in every dark place. Guilt kept you from sleeping, and when you did manage to drop off, it sent you dreams about your dead, dreams so strong they began to invade your waking moments. Guilt was a monster against which the only defense was oblivion.... Once he had discovered that truth, he had sought oblivion with the fervor of a converted sinner.

He had tried to kill himself but had not been able to muster the necessary courage and instead had turned to drugs. To heroin and the mattress in the shooting gallery. And there he had discovered another truth: that this life was in itself a kind of oblivion, that it was carving him slow and simple, emptying him of dreams and memories. And of guilt.

The porch steps creaked under someone's weight. Buddha peered out the window just as a knock sounded at the door. It was Marlene, one of the hookers who worked out of Dally's Show Bar down the block: a pretty cocoa-skinned girl carrying an overnight bag, her breasts hushed up by a tight bra.

Her pimp—a long-haired white kid—was standing on a lower step. Buddha opened the door, and they brushed past him. "Pete 'round?" Marlene asked.

Buddha pointed up the stairs and shut the door. The white kid grinned, whispered to Marlene, and she laughed. "John think you look like you could use some lovin'," she said. "What say you come on up, and I'll give you a sweet ride for free?" She chucked him under the chin. "How that sound, Buddha?"

He remained silent, denying desire and humiliation, practicing being the nothing she perceived. He had become perfect at ignoring ridicule, but desire was still a problem: the plump upper slopes of her breasts gleamed with sweat and looked full of juice. She turned away, apparently ashamed of having teased him.

"Take it easy now, Buddha," she said with studied indifference, and hand-led the white kid up the stairs.

Buddha plucked at a frayed thread on the mattress. He knew the history of its every stain, its every rip. Knew them so thoroughly that the knowledge was no longer something he could say: it was part of him, and he was part of it. He and the mattress had become a unity of place and purpose. He wished he could risk going to sleep, but it was Friday night, and there would be too many customers, too many interruptions. He fixed his gaze on the tarnished brass doorknob, let it blur until it became a greenish-gold sun spinning within a misty corona. Watched it whirl around and around, growing brighter and brighter. Correspondingly his thoughts spun and brightened, becoming less thoughts than reflections of the inconstant light. And thus did Buddha pass the middle hours of the night.

▲▼▲

At two o'clock Buddha double-bolted the door and went upstairs for his goodnighter. He walked slowly along the corridor, scuffing the threadbare carpet, its pattern eroded into grimy darkness and worm trails of murky gold. Laughter and tinny music came from behind closed doors, seeming to share the staleness of the cooking odors that pervaded the house. A group of customers had gathered by Pete's door, and Buddha stopped beside them. Somebody else wandered up, asked what was happening, and was told that Pete was having trouble getting a vein. Marlene was going to hit him up in the neck. Pete's raspy voice issued from the room, saying, "Damn it! Hurry up, woman!"

Getting a vein was a frequent problem for Pete; the big veins in his arms were burned-out, and the rest weren't much better. Buddha peered over shoulders into the room. Pete was lying in bed, on sheets so dirty they appeared to have a design of dark clouds. His freckly brown skin was suffused by a chalky pallor. Three young men—one of them Marlene's pimp—were gathered around him, murmuring comforts. On the night table a lamp with a ruffled shade cast a buttery yellow light, giving shadows to the strips of linoleum peeling up from the floor.

Marlene came out of the bathroom, wearing an emerald-green robe. When she leaned over Pete, the halves of the robe fell apart, and her breasts hung free, catching a shine from the lamp. The needle in her hand showed a sparkle on its tip. She swabbed Pete's neck with a clump of cotton and held the needle poised an inch or two away.

The heaviness of the light, the tableau of figures around the bed, Marlene's gleaming skin, the wrong-looking shadows on the floor, too sharp to be real: taken all together, these things had the same richness and artful composition, the same important stillness, as an old painting that Buddha had once seen in the Museum of Art. He liked the idea that such beauty could exist in this ruinous house, that the sad souls therein could become even this much of a unity. But he rejected his pleasure in the sight, as was his habit with almost every pleasure.

Pete groaned and twisted about. "Stop that shit!" Marlene snapped. "Want me to bleed you dry?"

Other people closed in around the bed, blocking Buddha's view. Pete's voice dropped to a whisper, instructing Marlene. Then people began moving away from the bed, revealing Pete lying on his back, holding a bloody Kleenex to the side of his neck. Buddha spotted his goodnighter on the dresser: a needle resting on a mirror beside a tiny heap of white powder.

"How you doin'?" Pete asked weakly as Buddha walked in.

He returned a diffident wave, went over to the dresser, and inspected the powder: it looked like a nice dose. He lifted the mirror and headed off downstairs to cook up.

"Goddamn!" said Pete. "Fifteen years I been takin' care of you. Feedin' your Jones, buyin' your supper. Think we'd have a relationship by now." His tone grew even more irascible. "I should never have give you that damn name! Got you thinkin' you inscrutable, when all you is is ignorant!"

▲▼▲

Nodding on his mattress in the moonlit dark, feeling the rosy glow of the fix in his heart, the pure flotation of China White in his flesh, Buddha experienced little flash dreams: bizarre images that materialized and faded so quickly, he was unable to categorize them. After these had passed he lay down, covered himself with a blanket, and concentrated upon his dream of Africa, the one pleasure he allowed himself to nourish. His conception of Africa bore no relation to the ethnic revival of the sixties, to Afros and dashikis, except that otherwise he might have had no cognizance of the Dark Continent. Buddha's African kingdom was a fantasy derived from images in old movies, color layouts in National Geographic, from drugs and drugged visions of Nirvana as a theme park. He was not always able to summon the dream, but that night he felt disconnected from all his crimes and passionate failures, stainless and empty, and thus worthy of this guardian bliss. He closed his eyes, then squeezed his eyelids tight until golden pinpricks flowered in the blackness. Those pinpricks expanded and opened into Africa.

He was flowing like wind across a tawny plain, a plain familiar from many such crossings. Tall grasses swayed with his passage, antelope started up, and the gamy smell of lions was in the air. The grasslands evolved into a veld dotted with scum-coated ponds and crooked trees with scant pale foliage. Black stick figures leaped from cover and menaced him with spears, guarding a collage peopled by storytellers and long-legged women who wore one-eyed white masks and whose shadows danced when they walked. Smoke plumed from wart-shaped thatched huts and turned into music; voices spoke from cooking fires. Beyond the village stood green mountains that rose into the clouds, and there among the orchids and ferns were the secret kingdoms of the gorillas. And beyond the mountains lay a vast blue lake, its far reaches fringed by shifting veils of mist in whose folds miragelike images materialized and faded.

Buddha had never penetrated the mists: there was something ominous about their unstable borders and the ghostly whiteness they enclosed. At the center of the lake a fish floated halfway between the surface and the bottom, like the single thought of a liquid brain. Knowing that he must soon face the stresses of the outside world, Buddha needed the solace offered by the fish; he sank beneath the waters until he came face-to-face with it, floating a few inches away.

The fish resembled a carp and measured three feet from its head to its tail; its overlapping scales were a muddy brown, and its face was the mask of a lugubrious god, with huge golden eyes and a fleshy downturned mouth. It seemed to be regarding Buddha sadly, registering him as another of life's disappointments, a subject with which it was quite familiar, for its swollen belly encaged all the evil and heartache to the world, both in principle and reality. Buddha gazed into its eyes, and the pupils expanded into black funnels that connected with his own pupils, opening channels along which torrents of grief and fear began to flow. The deaths of his wife and mother were nothing compared with the hallucinatory terrors that now confronted him: demons with mouths large enough to swallow planets; gales composed of a trillion dying breaths; armies of dead men and women and children. Their bodies maimed by an infinity of malefic usage. Had he witnessed these visions while awake, he would have been overwhelmed; but protected by the conditions of the dream, he withstood them and was made strong.

And before long he fell asleep in the midst of this infinite torment contained within the belly of the fish in his dream, contained in turn within his skull, within the ramshackle frame house, within the gunshot-riddled spiritual realm of the Detroit ghetto, whose agonies became a fleeting instance of distress—the fluttering of an eyelid, the twitching of a nerve—within the dreamed-of peace of Buddha's sleep.

▲▼▲

The shooting gallery was located in the Jefferson-Chalmers district, the section of the ghetto most affected by the '67 riots. Hundreds of gutted houses still stood as memorials to that event, and between them—where once had stood other houses—lay vacant lots overgrown with weeds and stunted trees of heaven. The following afternoon, as he walked past the lot adjoining the shooting gallery, Buddha was struck by the sight of a charred sofa set among weeds at the center of the lot, and obeying an impulse, he walked over to it and sat down. It was the first day of fall weather. The air was crisp, the full moon pinned like a disfigured cameo of bone to a cloudless blue sky. In front of the sofa was a pile of ashes over which somebody had placed a grill; half a dozen scorched cans were scattered around it. Buddha studied the ashes, the grill, the cans, mesmerized by the pattern they formed. Sirens squealed in the distance, a metallic clanging seemed to be issuing from beyond the sky, and Buddha felt himself enthroned, the desireless king of a ruined world in which all desire had faltered.

He had been sitting for perhaps an hour when a teenage boy with a freckly complexion like Pete's came running along the sidewalk. Dressed in jeans and a sweatshirt and lugging an immense ghetto blaster. The boy looked behind him, then sprinted across the lot toward Buddha and flung himself down behind the sofa. "You tell 'em I'm here," he said breathlessly, "I'll cut ya!" He waggled a switchblade in front of Buddha's face. Buddha just kept staring at the toppled brick chimneys and vacated premises. A dragonfly wobbled up from the leaves and vanished into the sun dazzle of a piece of broken mirror canted against the ash heap.

Less than a minute later two black men ran past the lot. Spotting Buddha, one shouted, "See a kid come this way?" Buddha made no reply.

"Tell 'em I headed toward Cass," the kid whispered urgently, but Buddha maintained his silence, his lack of concern.

"Y'hear me?" the man shouted.

"Tell 'em!" the boy whispered.

Buddha said nothing.

The two men conferred and after a second ran back in the direction from which they had come. "Damn, blood! You take some chances!" said the boy, and when Buddha gave no response, he added, "They come back, you just sit there like you done. Maybe they think you a dummy." He switched on the ghetto blaster, and rap music leaked out, the volume too low for the words to be audible.

Buddha looked at the boy, and the boy grinned, his nervousness evident despite the mask of confidence.

"Ain't this a fine box?" he said. "Fools leave it settin' on the stoop, they deserve to get it took. " He squinted as if trying to scry out Buddha's hidden meaning. "Can't you talk, man?"

"Nothin' to say," Buddha answered.

"That's cool.... Too much bullshit in the air, anyhow."

The boy reminded Buddha of his younger self, and this disquieted him: he had the urge to offer advice, and he knew advice would be useless. The boy's fate was spelled out by the anger lying dormant in the set of his mouth. Buddha pitied him, but pity—like love, like hate—was a violation of his policy of noninvolvement, an impediment of the emptiness to which he aspired. He got to his feet and headed for the sidewalk.

"Hey!" yelled the boy. "You tell them mothafuckas where I'm at, I'll kill yo' ass!"

Buddha kept walking.

"I mean it, man!" And as if in defiance, as if he needed some help to verbalize it, the boy turned up the ghetto blaster, and a gassed voice blared, "Don't listen to the shuck and jive from Chairman Channel Twenty-Five...."

Buddha picked up his pace, and soon the voice mixed in with the faint sounds of traffic, distant shouts, other musics, absorbed into the troubled sea from which it had surfaced.

▲▼▲

From the shooting gallery to Taboo's apartment should have been about a twenty-minute walk, but that day—still troubled by his encounter with the boy—Buddha cut the time in half. He had learned that it was impossible to avoid involvement on his day off, impossible not to confront his past, and in Taboo he had found a means of making the experience tolerable, letting it be the exception that proved the rule. When he had first met Taboo seven years before, Taboo's name had been Yancey; he had been eighteen, married to a pretty girl, and holding down a steady job at Pontiac Motors.

Three years later, when he had next run into him, Taboo had come out of the closet, was working as a psychic healer, curing neighborhood ladies of various minor complaints, and through hormone treatments had developed a small yet shapely pair of breasts, whose existence he hid from the world beneath loose-fitting clothes.

Buddha had caught a glimpse of Taboo's breasts by accident, having once entered his bathroom while he was washing up, and after this chance revelation, Taboo had fixed upon him as a confidant, a circumstance that Buddha had welcomed—though he did not welcome Taboo's sexual advances. He derived several benefits from the relationship. For one thing, Taboo's specialty was curing warts, and Buddha had a problem with warts on his hands (one such had given him an excuse to visit that day); for another, Taboo—who dealt on the side—always had drugs on hand. But the most important benefit was that Taboo provided Buddha with an opportunity to show kindness to someone who brought to mind his dead wife. In their solitary moments together, Taboo would don a wig and a dress, transforming himself into the semblance of a beautiful young woman, and Buddha would try to persuade him to follow his inner directives and proceed with the final stage of his sex change. He would argue long and hard, claiming that Taboo's magical powers would mature once he completed the transformation, telling Taboo stories of how wonderful his new life would be. But Taboo was deathly afraid of the surgeon's knife, and no matter how forcefully Buddha argued, he refused to pay heed. Buddha knew there had to be an answer to Taboo's problem, and sometimes he felt that answer was staring him in the face. But it never would come clear. He had the notion, though, that sooner or later the time would be right for answers.

It was a beautiful spring day in Taboo's living room. The walls were painted to resemble a blue sky dappled with fluffy white clouds, and the floor was carpeted with artificial grass. In Taboo's bedroom where he did his healing, it was a mystical night. The walls were figured with cabalistic signs and stars and a crescent moon, and the corner table was ebony, and the chairs upholstered in black velour. Black drapes hid the windows; a black satin quilt covered the bed. Muted radiance shone from the ceiling onto the corner table, and after he had fixed, it was there that Buddha sat soaking his wart in a crystal bowl filled with herb-steeped water, while Taboo sat beside him and muttered charms.

Taboo was not in drag because he was waiting for Johnny Wardell to show; but even so he exhibited a feminine beauty. The soft lighting applied sensual gleams to his chocolate skin and enhanced the delicacy of his high cheekbones and generous mouth and almond-shaped eyes. When he leaned forward to inspect Buddha's wart, the tips of his breasts dimpled the fabric of his blousy shirt. Buddha could make out his magic: a disturbance like heat haze in the air around him.

"There, darlin'," said Taboo. "All gone. Your hand back the way it s'posed to be."

Buddha peered into the bowl. At the bottom rested a wrinkled black thing like a raisin. Taboo lifted his hand from the water and dried it with a towel. Where the wart had been was now only smooth skin. Buddha touched the place; it felt hot and smelled bitter from the herbs.

"Wish Johnny'd hurry up," said Taboo. "I bought a new dress I wanna try on for ya...."

"Whyn't you try it on now? If the buzzer goes, you can pretend you ain't at home."

" 'Cause I just have to deal wit' him later, and no tellin' what kinda mood Johnny be in then."

Buddha had no need to ask Taboo why he had to deal with Johnny Wardell at all. Taboo's reason for risking himself among the bad dogs was similar to Buddha's reason for retreating from life: he felt guilty for the way he was, and this risk was his self-inflicted punishment.

Taboo pulled out a packet of white powder and a drinking straw and told Buddha to toot a few lines, to put a shine on his high. Buddha did as he suggested. A luxuriant warmth spread through his head and chest, and little sparkles danced in the air, vanishing like snowflakes. He started getting drowsy. Taboo steered him to the bed, then curled up beside him, his arm around Buddha's waist.

"I love you so much, Buddha," he said. "Don't know what I'd do without you to talk to...I swear I don't." His soft breasts nudged against Buddha's arm, his fingers toyed with Buddha's belt buckle, and despite himself, Buddha experienced the beginnings of arousal. But he felt no love coming from Taboo, only a flux of lust and anxiety. Love was unmistakable—a warm pressure as steady as a beam from a flashlight—and Taboo was too unformed, too confused, to be its source.

"Naw, man," Buddha said, pushing Taboo's hand away.

"I just wanna love you!"

In Taboo's eyes Buddha could read the sweet fucked-up sadness of a woman born wrong; but though he was sympathetic, he forced himself to be stern. "Don't mess wit' me!"

The buzzer sounded.

"Damn!" Taboo sat up, tucked in his shirt. He walked over to the table, picked up the white powder and the drinking straw, and brought them over to Buddha. "You do a little bit more of this here bad boy. But don't you be runnin' it. I don't want you fallin' out on me." He went out into the living room, closing the door behind him.

There seemed to be a curious weight inside Buddha's head, less an ache than a sense of something askew, and to rid himself of it he did most of the remaining heroin. It was enough to set him dreaming, though not of Africa. These dreams were ugly, featuring shrieks and thuds and nasty smears of laughter, and once somebody said, "The man got tits! Dig it! The man's a fuckin' woman!"

Gradually he arrived at the realization that the dreams were real, that something bad was happening, and he struggled back to full consciousness. He got to his feet, swayed, staggered forward, and threw open the door to the living room.

Taboo was naked and spread-eagled facedown over some pillow, his rump in the air, and Johnny Wardell—a young leather-clad blood with a hawkish face—was holding his arms. Another man, darker and heavier than Wardell, was kneeling between Taboo's legs and was just zipping up his trousers.

For a split second nobody moved. Framed by the vivid green grass and blue sky and innocent clouds, the scene had a surreal biblical quality, like a hideous act perpetrated in some unspoiled corner of the Garden of Eden, and Buddha was transfixed by it. What he saw was vile, but he saw, too, that it was an accurate statement of the world's worth, of its grotesque beauty, and he felt distanced, as if he were watching through a peephole whose far end was a thousand miles away.

"Lookit here," said Wardell, a mean grin slicing across his face. "The ho already done got herself a man. C'mon, bro'! We saved ya a piece."

Long-buried emotions were kindled in Buddha's heart. Rage, love, fear. Their onset too swift and powerful for him to reject. "Get your hand off him," he said, pitching his voice deep and full of menace.

Wardell's lean face went slack, and his grin seemed to deepen, as if the lustful expression engraved on his skull were showing through the skin, as if he perceived in Buddha an object of desire infinitely more gratifying than Taboo.

Wardell nodded at the man kneeling between Taboo's legs, and the man flung himself at Buddha, pulling a knife and swinging it in a vicious arc. Buddha caught the man's wrist, and the man's violence was transmitted through his flesh, seeding fury in his heart. He squeezed the man's wristbones until they ground together, and the knife fell to the floor. Then he pinned the man against the wall and began smashing his head against it, avoiding the fingers that clawed at his eyes. He heard himself yelling, heard bone splinter.

The man's eyes went unfocused, and he grew heavy in Buddha's grasp; he slumped down, the back of his head leaving a glistening red track across a puffy cloud. Buddha knew he was dead, but before he could absorb the fact, something struck him in the back, a liver punch that landed with the stunning impact of a bullet, and he dropped like a stone.

The pain was luminous. He imagined it lighting him up inside with the precise articulation of an X-ray. Other blows rained in upon him, but he felt only the effects of that first one. He made out Wardell looming over him, a slim leathery giant delivering kick after kick. Blackness frittered at the edges of his vision. Then a scream—a sound like a silver splinter driven into Buddha's brain—and there was Taboo, something bright in his hand, something that flashed downward into Wardell's chest as he turned, lifted, flashed down again. Wardell stumbled back, looking puzzled, touching a red stain on the shirtfront, and then appeared to slide away into the blackness at the corner of Buddha's left eye. Buddha lay gasping for breath: the last kick had landed in the pit of his stomach. After a second his vision began to clear, and he saw Taboo standing above Wardell's body, the other man's knife in his hand.

With his sleek breasts and male genitalia and the bloody knife, he seemed a creature out of a myth. He kneeled beside Buddha. "You awright?" he asked. "Buddha? You awright?"

Buddha managed a nod. Taboo's eyes reminded him of the eyes of the fish in his dream—aswarm with terrors—and his magic was heavy wash in the air, stronger than Buddha had ever seen it.

"I never wanted to kill nobody," said Taboo tremulously. "That's the *last* thing I wanted to do." He glanced at the two corpses, and his lips quivered. Buddha looked at them, too.

Sprawled in oddly graceful attitudes on the green grass amid a calligraphy of blood, they appeared to be spelling out some kind of cryptic message. Buddha thought if he kept staring at them, their meaning would come clear.

"Oh, God!" said Taboo. "They gon' be comin' for me, they gon' put me in jail! I can't live in jail. What am I gon' do?"

And to his astonishment, looking back and forth between the corpses and Taboo's magical aura, Buddha found he could answer that question.

▲▼▲

The answer was, he realized, also the solution to the problem of his life; it was a means of redemption, one he could have arrived at by no other process than that of his fifteen-year retreat.

Its conception had demanded an empty womb in which to breed and had demanded as well an apprehension of magical principle: that had been supplied by his dream of Africa. And having apprehended the full measure of this principle, he further realized he had misunderstood the nature of Taboo's powers. He had assumed that they had been weakened by the wrongness of his birth and would mature once he went under the knife; but he now saw that they were in themselves a way of effecting the transformation with a superior result, that they had needed this moment of violence and desperation to attain sufficient strength. Buddha felt himself filling with calm, as if the knowledge had breached an internal reservoir that had dammed calmness up.

"You need a disguise," he said. "And you got the perfect disguise right at your fingertips." He proceeded to explain.

"You crazy, Buddha!" said Taboo. "No way I can do that."

"You ain't got no choice."

"You crazy!" Taboo repeated, backing away. "Crazy!"

"C'mon back here!"

"Naw, man! I gotta get away, I gotta...." Taboo backed into the door, felt for the knob, and—eyes wide, panic-stricken—wrenched it open. His mouth opened as if he were going to say something else, but instead he turned and bolted down the hall.

The pain in Buddha's back was throbbing, spreading a sick weakness all through his flesh, and he passed out for a few seconds.

When he regained consciousness, he saw Taboo standing in the doorway, looking insubstantial due to the heavy wash of magic around him; in fact, the whole room had an underwater lucidity, everything wavering, like a dream fading in from the immaterial. "See?" said Buddha. "Where you gon' go, man? You barely able to make it here!"

"I don't know, I'll...maybe I'll...." Taboo's voice, too, had the qualities of something out of a dream; distant and having a faint echo.

"Sheeit!" Buddha reached out to Taboo. "Gimme a hand up."

Taboo helped him to his feet and into the bedroom and lowered him onto the bed. Buddha felt as if he might sink forever into the black satin coverlet.

"Show me that new dress you bought," he said. Taboo went to the closet, pulled out a hanger, and held the dress against his body to display its effect. It was white silk, low-cut, with a scattering of sequins all over.

"Aw, man," said Buddha. "Yeah, that's your dress. You be knockin' the boys' eyes out wearin' that...if they could ever see it. If you'd just do what's right. You'd be too beautiful for Detroit. You'd need to get someplace south, place where the moon shines bright as the sun. 'Cause that's what kinda beautiful you gon' be. Moon beautiful. Miami, maybe. That'd suit ya. Get you a big white car, drive down by them fancy hotels, and let all them fancy people have a look at ya. And they gon' lay down and beg to get next to you, man...."

As Buddha talked, conjuring the feminine future with greater seductiveness and invention than ever before, the heat haze of Taboo's magic grew still more visible, taking on the eerie miragelike aspect of the mists beyond the lake in Buddha's Africa; and after Buddha had finished, Taboo sat on the edge of the bed, holding the dress across his lap. "I'm scared," he said. "What if it don't work?"

"You always been scared," said Buddha. "You bein' scared's what got them two men dead out there. Time for that to stop. You know you got the power. So go on!"

"I can't!"

"You ain't got no choice." Buddha pulled Taboo's head down gently and kissed him openmouthed, breathing into him a calming breath. "Do it," he said. "Do it now."

Hesitantly Taboo came to his feet. "Don't you go nowhere now. You wait for me."

"You know I will."

"Awright." Taboo took a few steps toward the bathroom, then stopped. "Buddha, I don't...."

"Go on!"

Taboo lowered his head, walked slowly into the bathroom, and closed the door.

Buddha heard the tub filling, heard the splashing as Taboo climbed into it. Then heard him begin to mutter his charms. He needed to sleep, to fix, but he kept awake as long as he could, trying to help Taboo with the effort of his will. He could feel the vibrations of the magic working through the bathroom door. Finally he gave in to the pressures of exhaustion and the throbbing in his back and drifted off to sleep; the pain followed him into the blackness of sleep, glowing like the core of his being. He woke sometime later to hear Taboo calling his name and spotted him in the darkest corner of the room—a shadow outlined by painted stars.

"Taboo?"

"It don't feel right, Buddha." Taboo's voice had acquired a husky timbre.

"C'mere, man."

Taboo came a step closer, and though Buddha was still unable to see him, he could smell the heat and bitterness of the herbs.

"It worked, didn't it?" Buddha asked. "It musta worked."

"I think.... But I feel so peculiar."

"You just ain't used to it is all.... Now c'mere!"

Taboo moved still closer, and Buddha made out a naked young woman standing a few feet away. Slim and sexy, with shoulder-length black hair and high, small breasts and a pubic triangle that showed no sign of ever having been male.

The air around Taboo was still and dark. No ripples, no heat haze. The magic had all been used.

"I told ya," said Buddha. "You beautiful."

"I ain't...I just ordinary." But Taboo sounded pleased.

"Ordinary as angels," Buddha said. "That's how ordinary you are."

Taboo smiled. It was faltering at first, that smile, but it grew wider when Buddha repeated the compliment: the smile of a woman gradually becoming confident of her feminine powers. She lay down beside Buddha and fingered his belt buckle. "I love you, Buddha," she said. "Make me feel right."

Love was a steady flow from her, as tangible as a perfume, and Buddha felt it seeping into him, coloring his calm emptiness. On instinct he started to reject the emotion, but then he realized he had one more duty to fulfill, the most taxing and compromising duty of all. He reached down and touched the place between Taboo's legs. Taboo stiffened and pushed her hips against his finger.

"Make me feel right," she said again.

Buddha tried to turn onto his side, but the pain in his back flared. He winced and lay motionless. "Don't know if I can. I'm hurtin' pretty bad."

"I'll help you," she said, her fingers working at his buckle, his zipper. "You won't have to do nothin', Buddha. You just let it happen now."

But Buddha knew he couldn't just let it happen, knew he had to return Taboo's love in order to persuade her of her rightness, her desirability. As she mounted him, a shadow woman lifting and writhing against the false night of the ceiling stars, strangely weightless, he pinned his dead wife's features to her darkened face, remembered *her* ways, *her* secrets. All the love and lust he had fought so long to deny came boiling up from nowhere, annihilating his calm. He dug his fingers into the plump flesh of her hips, wedging himself deep; he plunged and grunted, ignoring the pain in his back, immersed again in the suety richness of desire, in the animal turbulence of this most alluring of human involvements. And when she cried out, a mournful note that planed away to a whisper, like the sound a spirit makes falling through eternity, he felt the profound satisfaction of a musician who by his dominance and skill has brought forth a perfect tone from chaos. But afterward as she snuggled close to him, telling him of her pleasure, her excitement, he felt only despair, fearing that the empty product of his years of ascetic employment had been wasted in a single night.

"Come with me, Buddha," she said. "Come with me to Miami. We can get us a house on the beach and...."

"Lemme be," he said, his despair increasing because he wanted to go with her, to live high in Miami and share her self-discovery, her elation. Only the pain in his back—intensifying with every passing minute—dissuaded him, and it took all his willpower to convince her of his resolve, to insist that she leave without him, for Taboo and his dead wife had fused into a single entity in his mind, and the thought of losing her again was a pain equal to the one inflicted by Johnny Wardell.

At last, suitcase in hand, she stood in the doorway, the temptation of the world in a white silk dress, and said, "Buddha, please won'tcha...."

"Damn it!" he said. "You got what you want. Now get on outta here!"

"Don't be so harsh wit' me, Buddha. You know I love you."

Buddha let his labored breathing be the answer.

"I'll come see ya after a while," she said. "I'll bring you a piece of Miami."

"Don't bother."

"Buddha?"

"Yeah."

"In the bathtub, Buddha...I just couldn't touch it."

"I'll take care of it."

She half-turned, glanced back. "I'll always love you, Buddha." The door swung shut behind her, but the radiance of her love kept beaming through the wood, strong and contaminating.

"Go on," he murmured. "Get you a big white car."

He waited until he heard the front door close then struggled up from the bed, clamping his hand over his liver to muffle the pain. He swayed, on the verge of passing out; but after a moment he felt steadier, although he remained disoriented by unaccustomed emotion. However, the sight of the pitiful human fragment lying in the herb-steeped water of the bathtub served to diminish even that. He scooped it up in a drinking glass and flushed it down the toilet. Then he lay back on the bed again. Closed his eyes for a minute...at least he thought it was just a minute. But he couldn't shake the notion that he'd been asleep for a long, long time.

▲▼▲

Buddha had to stop and rest half a dozen times on the way back to the shooting gallery, overcome by pain, by emotions...mostly by emotions. They were all around him as well as inside.

The shadows of the ruined houses were the ghosts of his loves and hates; the rustlings in the weeds were long-dead memories with red eyes and claws just waiting for a chance to leap out and snatch him; the moon—lopsided and orange and bloated—was the emblem of his forsaken ambitions shining on him anew. By loving Taboo he had wasted fifteen years of effort and opened himself to all the indulgent errors of his past, and he wished to God now he'd never done it. Then, remembering how dreamlike everything had seemed, he had the thought that maybe it hadn't happened, that it had been a hallucination brought on by the liver punch. But recalling how it had felt to make love, the womanly fervor of Taboo's moves, he decided it had to have been real. And real or not, he had lived it, he was suffering for it.

When he reached the shooting gallery he sat cross-legged on his mattress, heavy with despair. His back ached something fierce. Pete was angry with him for being late, but on seeing his discomfort he limped upstairs and brought down a needle and helped him fix. "What happened to ya?" he asked, and Buddha said it wasn't nothin', just a muscle spasm.

"Don't gimme that shit," said Pete. "You get hit by a goddamn car, and you be tellin' me it ain't 'bout nothin'." He shook his head ruefully. "Well, to hell wit' ya! I'm sick of worryin' 'bout ya!"

Buddha began to feel drowsy and secure there on his mattress, and he thought if he could rid himself of the love that Taboo had imparted to him, things might be better than before. Clearer, emptier. But he couldn't think how to manage it. Then he saw the opportunity that the old man presented, the need for affection he embodied, his hollow heart.

Pete turned to go back up the stairs, and Buddha said, "Hey, Pete!"

"Yeah, what?"

"I love you, man," said Buddha, and sent his love in a focused beam of such strength that he shivered as it went out of him.

Pete looked at him, perplexed. His expression changed to one of pleasure, then to annoyance. "You *love* me? Huh? Man, you been hangin' out with that faggot too much, that's what you been doin'!"

He clumped a couple of steps higher and stopped. "Don't bother comin' upstairs for your goodnighter," he said in gentler tones. "I'll send it down wit' somebody."

" 'Preciate it," said Buddha.

He watched Pete round the corner of the stairwell, then lay down on the mattress. He was so free of desire and human connections that the instant he closed his eyes, golden pinpricks bloomed behind his lids, opened into Africa, and he was flying across the grasslands faster than ever, flying on the wings of the pain that beat like a sick heart in his back. The antelope did not run away but stared at him with wet, dark eyes, and the stick figures of those who guarded the village saluted him with their spears. The shadows of the masked women danced with the abandon of black flames, and in one of the huts a bearded old man was relating the story of a beautiful young woman who had driven a white car south to Miami and had lived wild for a time, had inspired a thousand men to greater wildness, had married and....Buddha flew onward, not wanting to hear the end of the story, knowing that the quality of the beginning was what counted, because all stories ended the same. He was satisfied that Taboo's beginning had been worthwhile. He soared low above the green mountains, low enough to hear the peaceful chants of the gorillas booming through the hidden valleys, and soon was speeding above the lake wherein the solitary fish swam a slow and celebratory circle, arrowing toward the mists on its far side, toward those hallucinatory borders that he previously had neither the necessary courage nor clarity to cross.

From behind him sounded a distant pounding that he recognized to be someone knocking on the door of the shooting gallery, summoning him to his duty. For an instant he had an urge to turn back, to reinhabit the world of the senses, of bluesy-souled hookers and wired white kids and punks who came around looking to trade a night's muscle work for a fix. And that urge intensified when he heard Pete shouting, "Hey, Buddha! Ain't you gon' answer the goddamn door?" But before he could act upon his impulse, he penetrated the mists and felt himself irresistibly drawn by their mysterious central whiteness, and he knew that when old Pete came downstairs, still shouting his angry question, the only answer he would receive would be an almost impalpable pulse in the air like the vibration of a gong whose clangor had just faded beneath the threshold of hearing, the pure signal struck from oblivion, the fanfare announcing Buddha's dominion over the final country of the mind.

White Trains

Concerning the strange events
outside the Castle Monosodium Glutamate Works.

White trains with no tracks
have been appearing on the outskirts
of small anonymous towns,
picket fence towns in Ohio, say,
or Iowa, places rife with solid American values,
populated by men with ruddy faces and weak hearts,
and women whose thoughts slide
like swaths of gingham through their minds.
They materialize from vapor or a cloud,
glide soundlessly to a halt in some proximate meadow,
old-fashioned white trains with pot-bellied smokestacks,
their coaches adorned with filigrees of palest ivory,
packed with men in ice cream suits and bowlers,
and lovely dark-haired women in lace gowns.
The passengers disembark, form into rows,
facing one another as if preparing for a cotillion.
and the men undo their trouser buttons,
their erections springing forth like lean white twigs,
and they enter the embrace of the women,
who lift their skirts to enfold them,
hiding them completely, making it appear
that strange lacy cocoons have dropped from the sky
to tremble and whisper on the bright green grass.
And when at last the women let fall their skirts,
each of them bears a single speck of blood
at the corner of their perfect mouths.
As for the men, they have vanished
like snow on a summer's day.

I myself was witness to one such apparition
on the outskirts of Parma, New York,
home to the Castle Monosodium Glutamate Works,
a town whose more prominent sophisticates
often drive to Buffalo for the weekend.
I had just completed a thirty-day sentence
for sullying the bail bondsman's beautiful daughter
(They all said she was a good girl
but you could find her name on every bathroom wall
between Nisack and Mitswego),
and having no wish to extend my stay
I headed for the city limits.
It was early morning, the eastern sky
still streaked with pink, mist threading
the hedgerows, and upon a meadow bordering
three convenience stores and a laundromat,
I found a number of worthies gathered,
watching the arrival of a white train.
There was Ernest Cardwell, the minister
of the Church of the Absolute Solstice,
whose congregation alone of all the Empire State
has written guarantee of salvation,
and there were a couple of cops big as bears
in blue suits, carrying standard issue golden guns,
and there was a group of scientists huddled
around the machines with which they were
attempting to measure the phenomenon,
and the mayor, too, was there, passing out
his card and declaring that he had no hand
in this unnatural business, and the scientists
were murmuring, and Cardwell was shouting
"Abomination," at the handsome men
and lovely women filing out of the coaches,
and as for me, well, thirty days and the memory
of the bail bondsman's beautiful daughter
had left me with a more pragmatic attitude,
and ignoring the scientists' cries of warning and
Cardwell's predictions of eternal hellfire,
the mayor's threats, and the cops' growling,
I went toward the nearest of the women
and gave her male partner a shove and was amazed

to see him vanish in a haze of sparkles
as if he had been made of something insubstantial
like Perrier or truth.

The woman's smile was cool and enigmatic
and as I unzipped, her gown enfolded me
in an aura of perfume and calm,
and through the lacework the sun acquired
a dim red value, and every sound was faraway,
and I could not feel the ground beneath my feet,
only the bright sensation of slipping inside her.
Her mouth was such a simple curve, so pure
a crimson, it looked to be a statement of principle,
and her dark brown eyes had no pupils.
Looking into them, I heard a sonorous music;
heavy German stuff, with lots of trumpet fanfares
and skirling crescendos, and the heaviness
of the music transfigured my thoughts,
so that it seemed what followed was a white act,
that I had become a magical beast with golden eyes,
coupling with an ephemera, a butterfly woman,
a creature of lace and heat and silky muscle...
though in retrospect I can say with assurance
that I've had better in my time.

I think I expected to vanish, to travel
on a white train through some egoless dimension,
taking the place of the poor soul I'd pushed aside,
(although it may be he never existed, that only
the women were real, or that from those blood drops
dark and solid as rubies at the corners of their mouths,
they bred new ranks of insubstantial partners),
but I only stood there jelly-kneed watching
the women board the train, still smiling.
The scientists surrounded me, asking questions,
offering great sums if I would allow them to do tests
and follow-ups to determine whether or not
I had contracted some sort of astral social disease,
and Cardwell was supplicating God to strike me down,
and the mayor was bawling at the cops to take me
in for questioning, but I was beyond the city limits

and they had no rights in the matter, and I walked
away from Parma, bearing signed contracts
from the scientists, and another presented me
by a publisher who, disguised as a tree stump,
had watched the entire proceeding, and now
owned the rights to the lie of my life story.
My future, it seemed, was assured.

White trains, with no tracks
continue to appear on the outskirts
of small anonymous towns, places
whose reasons have dried up, towns
upon which dusk settles
like a statement of intrinsic greyness,
and some will tell you these trains
signal an Apocalyptic doom, and
others will say they are symptomatic
of mass hysteria, the reduction of culture
to a fearful and obscure whimsey, and
others yet will claim that the vanishing men
are emblematic of the realities of sexual politics
in this muddled, weak-muscled age.
But I believe they are expressions of a season
that occurs once every millennium or so,
a cosmic leap year, that they are merely
a kind of weather, as unimportant and unique
as a sun shower or a spell of warmth in mid-winter,
a brief white interruption of the ordinary
into which we may walk and emerge somewhat
refreshed, but nothing more.
I lecture frequently upon this subject
in towns such as Parma, towns whose lights
can be seen glittering in the dark folds of lost America
like formless scatters of stars, ruined constellations
whose mythic figure has abdicated to a better sky,
and my purpose is neither to illuminate nor confound,
but is rather to engage the interest of those women
whose touch is generally accompanied by
thirty days durance on cornbread and cold beans,
a sentence against which I have been immunized
by my elevated status, and perhaps my usage

of the experience is a measure of its truth,
or perhaps it is a measure of mine.

Whatever the case, white trains move silent as thought
through the empty fields, voyaging from nowhere to nowhere,
taking on no passengers, violating
no regulation other than the idea of order,
and once they have passed we shake our heads,
returning to the mild seasons of our lives,
and perhaps for a while we cling more avidly
to love and loves, realizing we inhabit a medium
of small magical transformations that like overcoats
can insulate us against the onset of heartbreak weather,
hoping at best to end in a thunder of agony
and prayer that will move us down through
archipelagoes of silver light to a morbid fairy tale
wherein we will labor like dwarves at the question
of forever, and listen to a grumbling static from above
that may or may not explain in some mystic tongue
the passage of white trains.

Jack's Decline

At first they strapped him to the bed and let him howl, let him try to vomit out the red, raw thing inside his hate. He would scream until his voice became a hoarse, scratchy chord, and then he would lapse into a fugue, his mind gone as blank as the gray stone walls. Often during these quiet times, the man who washed and fed him would bring strangers into the room, charging them a fee to have a peek at the greatest villain of the age, and they would stand beside the bed, shadows in the half light, and say, "*That's* the Ripper? Why, that poor sod couldn't butter his own toast, let alone do murder. I want me money back!" And their disbelief would rankle the demon within him, and he would scream louder than ever, shaking the bed and delighting in his visitors' fearful attitudes.

Later, after dozens of therapies—torments, really—and doctors whose manner was unanimously neutral, years and years later when he began to suffer guilt and wanted to atone, he realized there was no possibility of atonement, that his demon was not accessible to moral remedies. For a while he tried to deny the horrors of his past, to steep himself in the genteel associations of his childhood, in memories of gracious estates and garden parties. But he found that more vivid memories possessed him. Those five slatternly faces going slack when they saw the blade, their scent of sweat and cheap perfume, and the hot true perfume of their blood bubbling over his fingers. He yearned to engage once again in those terrible *amours*; yet he was also repelled by that yearning, and these contrary pressures drove him to consider suicide. But it did not seem a sufficient punishment: death for him would be surcease, and he could think of no means of extinction vile enough to earn him absolution. And so, despairing, dulled by despair, he wandered the corridors of his family's keep, becoming—as the years passed and the century turned—a numb meat of a man with graying hair and a gray pallor, whose fingers would sometimes clench spasmodically, and whose eyes would sometimes appear to grow dark and lose their animation, like pools in which the fish had long since ceased to spawn.

In 1903 there was a reawakening of interest in the murders, new clues and rumors that struck close to the bone, and his family—none of whom he had seen since the beginning of his confinement—gave orders that he be moved from England, fearing that their awful secret would be brought to light. He was issued a German passport under the name of Gerhard Steigler, and one night in the autumn of that year, along with his warders, his doctor of the moment, and a trunkful of the drugs that kept his demon tame, he crossed the English Channel to Calais, and there entrained for Krakow in Poland. From Krakow he was transported by coach to a hunting lodge in the northeast of the country, a rambling structure of whitewashed walls and pitch-coated beams, set among rumpled hills thicketed with chokecherry, forested with chestnuts and stunted water oaks. Travel had rekindled his spirits somewhat, and during his first year at the lodge, he came again to derive a mild pleasure from life. He liked the isolation of the place, and he would walk for hours through the woods, often winding up atop a hill from which he could look westward over a checkerboard of cultivated fields, of wheat and barley and sorghum. Here he would sit and watch cloud shadows rushing across the land, great shafts of light piercing down and fading, the golden fields dappling with an alternation of bright and dark, and it seemed to him that this constant shifting display was an airy machinery, immaterial clockwork that registered the inner processes of time. He realized that but for a brief, bloody season, his life had evinced this same insubstantiality, this same lack of true configuration, and as the years slipped away, he returned each afternoon to commune with that vast, complicated emblem of light and shade, believing that therein he could perceive the winnowing of his days.

If he were to look eastward from the hilltop—something he rarely permitted himself to do—his eye would encounter a smallish town of thatch and whitewash and curling chimney smokes, its church steeple poking up like a rifle sight. There, he knew, would be women of the sort he fancied. The thought of their bellies gleaming pale, the neatly packaged meats of their sex awaited a knife to reveal their mysteries, that would start him trembling, and for days thereafter he would be overborne by his demon's urges and have to be restrained.

During that first winter, in order to perfect his role as a member of the German aristocracy, he immersed himself in the study of the language. He had always been adept at learning, and by the time the spring thaw had arrived, he had become fluent in the spoken tongue and was capable of reading even the most difficult of texts. He enjoyed the works of Schiller and Nietzsche, but when he came to *Faustus* and its humanistic depiction of evil, he was so nettled by the author's dearth of understanding that he hurled the book out the window. Demons were not nearly as personable as Goethe had described them. They were parasites, less creatures unto themselves than the seepage of a dark force that underlay all creation, that—presented with an opening—would pour inside you, seducing not your soul but your blood, your cells, feeding upon you and growing to assume hideous shapes. He had seen the nesting places of such demons in the bodies of the women he had slain, had caught brief glimpses of them as they scurried for cover deeper into their bloody caves.

Turning from literature, he developed an interest in gardening, and would work from dawn until dusk in his plot, exerting himself so strenuously that his sleep was free of nightmares. But in the end this, too, failed him. Things grew to obscenely feminine proportions in that rich soil. Beneath heart-shaped leaves, the snap beans dangled like a bawd's earrings, and he would unearth strange hairy roots that with their puckered surfaces bore an uncanny resemblance to the female genitalia. Once again he despaired, considered suicide, and sank into a torpor.

In December of 1915, when he was fifty-six years old, a new doctor came to the lodge: a dapper little man in his forties, brimming with energy and good humor and talk of subconscious drives, neuroses, and the libido. The doctor treated him as if he were a man and not an aberration, and through hypnosis, several childhood traumas were revealed, notable among them a humiliating evening spent at a brothel when he was twelve, brought there by the family coachman and left alone in the common room, a target for the taunts of the whores. The doctor believed these incidents were seeds that had grown to fruition and inspired his murderous acts; but he rejected this theory.

"You claim, Doctor," he said, "that once I accept the connection between my childhood pain and the murders, a cure will be forthcoming. But those experiences only weakened me, made me susceptible to the demon and allowed him to enter and take possession of my body. There were supernatural forces in play. Witness the arrangements I made of the viscera...like some sort of cabalistic sign. I was driven to create that arrangement by my demon. It was the mark of his triumph over the demons encysted within the women."

The doctor sighed. "It seems to me you have invented this demon in order to shift blame to its shoulders."

"You think I am denying guilt?"

"Not entirely, but..."

"Believe me, Doctor," he said, "despite my inability to exorcise the demon, I am expert at guilt."

He enjoyed these exchanges not for their intellectual content, but because he felt the doctor liked him. He had been self-absorbed for so long that he had forgotten even the concept of friendship, and the hope that he could actually have a friend caused him no end of excitement. He had become a decent chef over the years, and he would prepare the doctor special dinners accompanied by fine wines and venerable brandies. He honed his chess game so as to provide worthy opposition for the doctor, who had been a schoolboy champion; he took renewed interest in worldly affairs in order to make better conversation. Things, he believed, were going swimmingly. But one afternoon as they walked along the crest of a wooded hill, in a companionable moment he threw his arm about the doctor's shoulder and felt the man stiffen and shrink away from his touch. He withdrew his arm, looked into the doctor's eyes, and saw there fear and revulsion. What he had taken for friendship, he realized, had merely been a superior form of bedside manner.

"I...." The doctor came a step toward him, contempt, and pity vying for control of his expression. "I'm sorry. It's just...."

The eviscerated flesh, the severed organs, the blood.

"I understand, Doctor," he said. "It's quite all right." He spun on his heel and walked back to the lodge alone, back to despair. It was, he knew, no less than he deserved. But he could not help feeling betrayed.

▲▼▲

His seventieth birthday passed, his seventy-fifth, and with the decline of his flesh, it seemed his menace also declined, for his family stopped sending doctors and he came to believe the men who cared for him were no longer warders but merely servants. This slackening of concern unsettled him, and like a good madman he continued to take his drugs and sleep in a bed with leather restraints. He had hoped senility would erode his memories, but he retained an uncommon clarity of mind and his body remained hale, albeit prone to aches and pains. It was, he thought, his demon that kept him strong, that refused to permit a collapse into peaceful decay. He still felt the violent urges that had destroyed his life and others, and to quell them he would spend hours each day maintaining a surgical sharpness to the edges of the kitchen knives, thinking that this pretense would convince the demon that its bloodlust would soon be sated.

Not long after his eightieth birthday, he received a visitor from the town: a doddering priest older than himself, who had come to warn him of imminent danger. The Nazis were massing on the border, and rumor had it an invasion was near. He invited the priest into the main hall, a high-ceilinged room centered by a long table and lorded over by a chandelier of iron and crystal, and he asked who these Nazis were, explaining that it had been years since he had paid any attention to politics.

"Evil men," the priest told him. "An army of monsters ruled by a madman."

Intrigued, he asked to hear more and listened intently to tales of outrage and excess, of Hitler and his bloody friends. He thought it would be interesting to meet these men, to learn if their demons were akin to his.

"I sense in you a troubled soul," said the priest as he made to leave. "If you wish I will hear your confession."

"Thank you, Father," he said. "But I have spent these past fifty years in confession and it has served no good purpose."

"Is there anything else I might do?"

He considered asking for the rite of exorcism, but the notion of this frail old man contending with the fierce horror inhabiting his flesh was ludicrous in the extreme. "No, Father," he said. "I fear my sins are beyond your precinct. I'm more likely to receive comfort from the Nazis."

One morning a month or so after the priest's visit, he waked to find himself alone. He went through the house, calling the names of his servants, to no avail; then, more puzzled than alarmed, he walked to his hilltop vantage and looked east. Dozens and dozens of tanks were cutting dusty swaths across the fields, rumbling, clanking, at that distance resembling toys run wild on a golden game board. Black smoke billowed from the little town, and the church steeple was no longer in evidence. When dusk began to gather, he returned to the lodge, half expecting to find it reduced to rubble. But it was intact, and though he waited up most of the night to greet them, no soldiers came to disrupt the peace and quiet.

The next afternoon, however, a touring car pulled up to the lodge and disgorged seven young men, all wearing shiny boots and black uniforms with silver emblems on the collars shaped like twin lightning bolts. They were suspicious of him at first, but on seeing his proof of German citizenship, they treated him as if he were a fine old gentleman, addressing him as "Herr Steigler" and asking permission to billet in the lodge. "My home is yours," he told them, and he set before them his finest wines, which they proceeded to swill down with not the least appreciation for their nose or bouquet.

They propped their feet on the table, scarring its varnish, and they told crude jokes, hooting and slapping their thighs, spilling the wines and breaking glasses, offering profane toasts to their venerable host. Watching them, he found it difficult to believe that these louts were creatures of evil; if they were possessed, it must be by demons of the lowest order, ones that would quail before his own. Still, he withheld final judgment, partly because their captain, who remained aloof from the carousing, was of a different cut. He was a thin, black-haired man with pale, pocked skin and a slit of a mouth.... Indeed, all his features seemed products of a minimalist creator, being barely raised upon his face, lending it an aspect both cruel and disinterested. His behavior, too, was governed by this minimalism. He sipped his wine, conversed in a monotone, and displayed an economy of gesture that—to his host's mind—appeared to signal a pathological measure of self-discipline.

"What do you do here, Herr Steigler?" he asked at one point. "I assume, of course, that you are retired, but I have seen no evidence of previous occupation."

"Poor health," said the old man, "has precluded my taking up a profession. I read, I walk in the woods and meditate."

"And what do you meditate upon?"

"The past, mostly. That, and the nature of evil."

The rigor of the captain's expression was disordered by a tick of a smile. "Evil," he said, savoring the word. "And have you arrived at any conclusions?"

The old man gave thought to bringing up the subject of demons, but instead said, "No, only that it exists."

"Perhaps," said the captain, with a superior smile, "you believe we are evil."

"Are you?"

"If I were, I would hardly admit to it."

"Why not? Even were I disposed against evil, I am old and feeble. I could do nothing to menace you."

"True," said the captain, running his finger around the mouth of his glass. "Then I will tell you that I may well be evil. Evil is a judgment made by history, and history may judge us as such."

"That is a fool's definition," said the old man. "To think that evil is not self-aware is foolish to the point of being evil. But you are not evil, Captain. You merely wish to be."

The captain dismissed this comment with a haughty laugh. "I am a soldier, Herr Steigler. A good one, I believe. This may call for a repression of one's conscience at times, but I would scarcely deem that evil. And as for my wishing to be so, my only wish is to win the war. Nothing more."

The old man made a gesture that directed the captain's attention toward his uniform. "Black cloth and patent leather and silver arcana. These are not the lineaments of a good soldier, Captain. They are designed to inspire dread. But apart from being psychological weapons, they are ritual expressions. Invocations of evil. You had best beware. Your invocations may prove effective and allow evil to possess you. Should that occur, you will have no joy in it. Take my word."

For an instant the captain's neutral mask dissolved, as if the old man's words had disconcerted him, and the old man could see the symptoms of insecurity: parted lips and twitching nerves and flicking tongue. But then the mask re-formed, and the captain said coldly, "I fear your long solitude has deluded you, Herr Steigler. You speak with the confidence of expertise, yet by your own admission you have little knowledge of the world beyond these hills. How can you be expert upon anything other than, say, regional wildlife?"

The old man was weary of the conversation and merely said that being widely traveled was no prerequisite to wisdom.

Later that afternoon a second touring car containing five women under guard arrived at the lodge. They were all young and lovely, with dusky complexions and doe eyes, and seeing them, the old man felt a dissolute warmth in his groin, a joyous rage in his heart.

"Jews," said the captain by way of explanation, and the old man nodded sagely as if he understood.

That night the house echoed with the women's screams, and the old man sat in his room ablaze with arousal, fevered with anger, his knees jittering, hands clenching and unclenching. He was barely able to restrain himself from taking a knife and hunting through the dark corridors of the lodge. Though wantonness had been imposed upon the women, it was in their nature to be wanton, alluring, and oh how he wanted to fall prey to their allure! Perhaps, he thought, he would ask the soldiers to give him one. No, no! He would *demand* one. As payment in lieu of rent. It was only fair.

The following morning, after the soldiers had locked the women in the basement and gone about their business, the old man crept down the stairs and peered through the barred window of the basement door. When they saw him, the women pressed themselves against the bars, pleading for his help. They were bruised, their dresses ripped, and they stank of sex. The sight of their breasts and nipples and ripely curved bellies made him faint. He would have liked to batter down the door and flash among them, drawing secret designs of blood across their soiled flesh.

"I cannot help you," he said. "They have taken the key."

They intensified their pleading, reaching through the bars, and he jumped back from their touch, fearing that it would further inflame him. "Perhaps there is a way," he said, his voice thick with urgency. "I will think on it."

He went back up the stairs and returned with wine, bread, and cheese. As they ate, he asked them about their lives; he felt a childlike curiosity about them, just as he had with the five women in Whitechapel. Three were farm wives, the fourth a butcher's daughter. The fifth, whom he thought the most beautiful—tall, with high cheekbones and full breasts—was the local schoolteacher. Her eyes were penetrating, and it was those eyes, their look of stern accusation, as if she knew his guilty soul, that made him aware of the magical opportunity with which he had been presented.

There were *five!*

Just as in Whitechapel, there were five, and one would be handy with a knife.

Here was the perfect resolution, the arc that would complete his mad journey and release him from his demon's grasp.

"I have a plan," he said. "But should it succeed, you must do something for me."

There was a chorus of eager assent from four of the women, but the schoolteacher stared at him with distaste and said, "If you wish to sleep with us, why not take your turn with the Germans?"

"It's not that, not that at all," he said, trying to inject a wealth of sincerity into his voice. "I promise you, you will not be harmed."

Again a chorus of assent, and again the schoolteacher favored him with a disdainful stare.

"You must swear you will do as I ask," he said to her. "No matter how repellent the task."

"Tell me what you want," she said.

"I will tell you afterward," he said. "Now swear!"

"Very well," she said, following a lengthy pause. "I swear."

Excited beyond measure, he hurried up the stairs, went to his desk, and wrote page after page of explicit instructions. Then he busied himself in the kitchen, preparing a feast for the soldiers. There would be veal and chicken, artichokes and asparagus, home-baked bread, and a delicate soup. And wine! Oh, yes. The wine would be the soul of the meal. As he went about these preparations, he whistled and sang, gleeful to the point of hysteria. His limbs trembled with anticipation, his heart pounded. Glasses and cutlery and china seemed to shine with unnatural brilliance as if they were registering and, indeed, sharing in his joy. Once the pots had been set to simmer, he returned to his room, stripped off his clothes, and, with his best pen, traced the mystic designs upon his groin and abdomen. He set half a dozen candelabra about the bed, and—satisfied with these arrangements—he opened his medicine chest and emptied his vials of the drugs with which he would treat the wine.

The soldiers had told him they would return by dusk, and six of them were true to their word—the captain, they said, had been held up in town. The old man could see that they were eager to be at the women again, but he begged and cajoled, and on beholding the sumptuous table he had laid, they could not reject his hospitality. Loosening their belts, they set to with hearty appetites, washing down every mouthful with liberal drafts of wine.

Oh, the old man was happy, he was sad, he was beset by storms of emotion, knowing that peace was soon to be his. Just as had happened in the kitchen, it was as if everything were in sympathy with his poignant moods. The room was giddy with light. The glaze on the veal shimmered, the varnished wood rippled like a grainy dark river, the chandelier glittered, and the silver lightning bolts twinkled on the collars of the doomed men as if accumulating the runoff of their vital charge. Three of the men keeled over almost immediately; two others managed to stagger to their feet, groping for their sidearms as they fell. The sixth actually succeeded in drawing his weapon. He fired twice, but the bullets ricocheted off the floor and he toppled facedown at the feet of the old man, who finished him with a knife stroke across the throat, switched off the lights, and went to wait for the captain.

Waiting grew long, and several times he nearly decided to go ahead with his plan; but at last he heard a motor, followed by footsteps in the foyer. "Uwe!" called the captain. "Horst!" The old man flattened against the wall, saw a shadow moving past, and swung his knife. Some sound must have given his presence away, for the shadow turned and the knife penetrated the captain's shoulder, not—as he had intended—the back. There was a shriek, and then the scrabbling of the captain trying to drag himself away. The old man eased along the wall, unable to locate the captain, not daring to switch on the lights for fear of posing a target. But darkness had always been his friend, and he was unconcerned. He held still and heard the captain's whistling breath and felt a joy so rich that it seemed to tinge the darkness with a shade of crimson.

"Herr Steigler?" said the captain. "Is that you?"

Ah! The old man spotted a lump of shadow huddled by a chair.

The captain fired at random—three distinct spearpoints of flame. "Why are you doing this?" Voice atremble with desperation. "Who *are* you?"

I am Red Jack, the old man said to himself. I am fear made flesh.

"Who are you?" the captain repeated, and fired again.

The old man inched closer; he could make out the shape of the gun in the captain's hand.

"For God's sake!" said the captain.

Moving a step closer, the old man kicked the gun. Heard it skitter across the floor. He kneeled beside the captain, who had slumped onto his back, and pricked his throat with the knife.

"Please," said the captain.

With his free hand, the old man felt for the pulse in the captain's neck. It was strong and rapid, and he kept his finger there, liking the heady sense of potency it transmitted. "Evil, Captain," he said. "Do you remember?"

"Herr Steigler! Please! What are you doing?"

"Killing you."

"But why? What have we done to you?" The captain tensed, and the old man pressed harder with the knife.

"You have a stringy neck, Captain," he said. "Necks should be soft and smooth. I may have to saw with the edge a little to do the job right." He prolonged the moment, exulting in the quiver transmitted along the blade by the man's straining muscles.

"Please, Herr Steigler!"

"I am not Herr Steigler," said Red Jack. "I am mystery." Then he nicked the carotid artery and jerked his hand away before the first jet could escape the wound. Male blood did not excite him.

▲▼▲

The women rushed forward when he opened the basement door, but on seeing the bloody knife, they shrank back, their faces going slack in a most familiar way. He had waited upstairs for an hour after killing the captain, letting the hungers of his demon subside; but despite that, they looked so vulnerable with their rags and bruises, it took all his self-control to keep from attacking them. "I have freed you," he said at last. "Now you must free me."

He led them to his room, lit the candelabra, and explained what must be done. To the butcher's daughter he handed his written instructions, detailing the depth of each incision and the precise order in which they should be made. Then he removed his clothing to display the bizarre template he had sketched on his body. The women were horror-struck, and the butcher's daughter flung down the papers as if they were vile to the touch. "I cannot do this," she said.

"You swore," he said to the schoolteacher.

She said nothing, fixing him with her black stare.

"Do you know who I am?" he asked them. "I am the Ripper! Red Jack!"

The name was lost on them.

"I have killed women!" He pointed to the papers. "Killed them exactly in the manner I have described. You must give me justice." They edged away. "You swore!" he said, hearing the petulance in his voice.

They turned to leave, and he clutched at the schoolteacher's arm. "You must help me!" he cried. Then he realized he was still holding the knife. He gripped it more tightly. In his mind's eye he saw her belly sliced open, its red fruit spilling into his hands. But before he could strike, she reached out and took the knife. Took it! Like a mother forbidding her child a dangerous toy. His fingers uncurled from the hilt as if she had worked magic to calm him.

He fell to his knees, eyes brimming with tears. "Please don't abandon me," he said. "Help me, please!"

The schoolteacher regarded him soberly, then looked to the butcher's daughter. "Can you manage it?" she said.

"No." The butcher's daughter lowered her eyes.

"Look at him." The schoolteacher forced the butcher's daughter to face the old man. "This is what he most desires. What he needs. We owe him our lives, and if you can find the strength, you must do as he asks...no matter what toll it takes."

"I can't!" cried the butcher's daughter, turning away; but the schoolteacher grabbed her by the shoulders, shook her, and said, "Do you see his pain? He is an old, mad creature torn by some cancer, one you must excise. If we deny him release, we condemn him to far worse than the knife."

The butcher's daughter stared at him for long seconds, and her face hardened as if she had seen therein some blameful thing that would make the chore endurable. "I will try," she said.

Babbling his thanks, he lay down upon the bed and told them to fasten the straps about his wrists and ankles. As they cinched them tight, he felt a trickle of fear, but when they had done, he knew a vast sense of relief. "Stand at the foot of the bed," he said to the schoolteacher. "And you"—he nodded at one of the farm wives—"stand beside her"—he nodded at the butchers daughter—"and hold the instructions in a good light." He positioned the two remaining women on the other side of the bed.

"Do you wish to pray?" asked the schoolteacher.

"No god would hear me," he said; then, to the butcher's daughter, "I will scream, but you must not heed the screams. They will be merely reflex and no signal of a desire for you to stop." He gazed up at the women ringing the bed. In the flickering light, with their widened eyes and parted lips, their secret flesh gleaming through rents in their dresses, they looked like the souls of his victims beatified by death, yet still sensual and sullied after years of phantom life. Eerie wings of shadow played across their faces. He drew a deep breath and said, "I am ready."

He had steeled himself against the pain of the first incision, but even so he was astonished by its enormity. His body arched, his tendons corded, and hearing himself scream, he was further astonished by how shrill and feminine was the voice of his agony. Pain became a medium in which he floated, too large to understand, and he knew only that it contained him, that he had gone forever inside it. Biting her lower lip, the butcher's daughter wielded the knife with marvelous deftness, and he could tell by the thin, hot trickles down his thighs that she was cutting neither too deeply nor too haphazardly, that he would survive the completion of the design. Once his eyes filmed over with redness and he nearly lost consciousness, but the schoolteacher's unswerving gaze centered him and pulled him back from oblivion. Reflected in her eyes, he saw the crimson light of his dying, and—growing numb to pain, able again to conjure whole thoughts—he reckoned her stern beauty a gift, a beacon set to guide him through the act.

Finally the butcher's daughter straightened and let fall the knife; on beholding the full extent of her work, she covered her face with her stained hands. Two of the farm wives had averted their eyes, and the other stood agape, her hand outstretched as if in a gesture of gentle restraint. Only the schoolteacher was unmoved. She engaged his stare unflinchingly, her voluptuous mouth firmed into cruel lines: the image of judgment.

"Lift my head!" he gasped as their lovely faces began to waver and recede, like angels passing ahead of him into the accumulating dark. It seemed he could feel an evacuation taking place, a lightening, a lessening of perverse cravings and violent urges, and he wanted to learn what manner of demon, what beast or wraith, was crawling from his guts. He needed sight of it to validate the fullness of his atonement, to assure himself that he would have a niche not in heaven, but in some less terrifying corner of hell, where he might from time to time secure a few moments' grace from the process of damnation. But his demon—if it existed—must have been invisible or otherwise proof against the eye, for when he looked down into the great cavity of the wound, he felt only the sick despair with which his every attempt to seek salvation had been met, and saw there nothing more demonic than his red, wrong life pulsing quick to the last. —

Beast of the Heartland

Mears has a dream the night after he fought the Alligator Man. The dream begins with words: "In the beginning was a dark little god with glowing red eyes..." And then, there it stands, hovering in the blackness of Mears' hotel room, a twisted mandrake root of a god, evil and African, with ember eyes and limbs like twists of leaf tobacco. Even after it vanishes, waking Mears, he can feel those eyes burning inside his head, merged into a single red pain that seems as if it will go on throbbing forever. He wonders if he should tell Leon about the pain—maybe he could give Mears something to ease it—but he figures this might be a bad idea. Leon might cut and run, not wanting to be held responsible should Mears keel over, and there Mears would be: without a trainer, without anyone to coach him for the eye exams, without an accomplice in his blindness. It's not a priority, he decides.

To distract himself, he lies back and thinks about the fight. He'd been doing pretty well until the ninth. Staying right on the Cuban's chest, mauling him in the corners, working the body. The Cuban didn't like it to the body. He was a honey-colored kid a couple of shades lighter than Mears and he punched like a kid, punches that stung but that didn't take your heart like the punches of a man. Fast, though. Jesus, he was fast! As the fight passed into the middle rounds, as Mears tired, the Cuban began to slip away, to circle out of the haze of ring light and vanish into the darkness at the corners of Mears' eyes, so that Mears saw the punches coming only at the last second, the wet-looking red blobs of the gloves looping in over his guard. Then, in the ninth, a left he never saw drove him into the turnbuckle, a flurry of shots under the ribs popped his mouthpiece halfway out and another left to the temple made him clinch, pinning the Cuban's gloves against his sides.

In the clinch, that's when he caught sight of the Alligator Man. The Cuban pulled back his head, trying to wrench his right glove free, and the blurred oval of his face sharpened, resolved into features: blazing yellow eyes and pebbly skin, and slit nostrils at the end of a long snout. Although used to such visions, hallucinations, whatever this was, Mears reacted in terror. He jolted the Alligator Man with an uppercut, he spun him, landed a clubbing right high on the head, another right, and as if those punches were magic, as if their force and number were removing a curse, breaking a spell, the Alligator Man's face melted away, becoming a blurred brown oval once again. Mears' terror also grew blurred, his attack less furious, and the Cuban came back at him, throwing shots from every angle. Mears tried to slide off along the ropes but his legs were gone, so he ducked his head and put his gloves up to block the shots. But they got through, anyway.

Somebody's arms went around him, hemming him in against the ropes, and he smelled flowery cologne and heard a smooth baritone saying, "Take it easy, man! It's over." Mears wanted to tell the ref he could have stood up through ten, the Cuban couldn't punch for shit. But he was too weak to say anything and he just rested his head on the ref's shoulder, strings of drool hanging off his mouthpiece, cooling on his chin. And for the first time in a long while, he heard the crowd screaming for the Cuban, the women's voices bright and crazy, piercing up from the male roar. Then Leon was there, Leon's astringent smell of Avitene and Vaseline and Gelfoam, and somebody shoved Mears down onto a stool and Leon pressed the ice-cold bar of the Enswell against the lump over his eye, and the Cuban elbowed his way through the commission officials and nobodies in the corner and said, "Man, you one tough motherfucker. You almos' kill me with them right hands." And Mears had the urge to tell him, "You think I'm tough, wait'll you see what's coming," but instead, moved by the sudden, heady love that possesses you after you have pounded on a man for nine rounds and he has not fallen, Mears told him that one day soon he would be champion of the world.

Mears wonders if the bestial faces that materialize in the midst of his fights are related to the pain in his head. In his heart he believes they are something else. It could be that he has been granted the magical power to see beneath the surface of things. Or they may be something his mind has created to compensate for his blindness, a kind of spiritual adrenaline that inspires him to fiercer effort, often to victory. Since his retinas became detached, he has slipped from the status of fringe contender to trial horse for young fighters on the way up, and his style has changed from one of grace and elusiveness to that of a brawler, of someone who must keep in constant physical contact with his opponent. Nevertheless, he has won twelve of seventeen fights with his handicap, and he owes much of his success to this symptom or gift or delusion.

He knows most people would consider him a fool for continuing to fight, and he accepts this. But he does not consider himself a greater fool than most people; his is only a more dramatic kind of foolishness than the foolishness of loving a bad woman or stealing a car or speculating on gold futures or smoking cigarettes or taking steroids or eating wrong or involving yourself with the trillion other things that lead to damage and death.

As he lies in that darkened room, in the pall of his own darkness, he imagines attending a benefit held to raise his medical expenses after his secret has been disclosed. All the legends are there. Ali, Frazier and Foreman are there, men who walk with the pride of a nation. Duran is there, Duran of the demonic fury, who TKO'd him in 1979, back when Mears was a welterweight. The Hit Man is there, Thomas Hearns, sinister and rangy, with a cobra-like jab that had once cut him so badly the flesh hung down into his eyes. Sugar Ray Leonard is there, talking about his own detached retina and how he could have gone the same way as Mears. And Hagler, who knocked Mears out in his only title shot, Hagler the tigerish southpaw, he is there, too. Mears ascends to the podium to offer thanks, and a reporter catches his arm and asks him "What the hell went wrong Bobby? What happened to you?" He thinks of all the things he could say in response. Bad managers, crooked promoters. Alimony. I forgot to duck. The classic answers. But there is one answer they've never heard, one that he's nourished for almost two years.

"I traveled into the heartland," he tells the reporter, "and when I got done fighting the animals there, I came out blind."

The reporter looks puzzled, but Ali and Foreman, Frazier and Hagler, Duran and Hearns, they nod sagely, they understand. They realize Mears' answer is partly a pride thing, partly intuitive, a summation of punches absorbed, hands lifted in victory, months of painful healing, hours of punishment in the gym. But mainly it is the recasting into a vow of a decision made years before. They would not argue that their sport is brutally stupid, run by uncaring bastards to whom it is a business of dollars and blood, and that tragedies occur, that fighters are swindled and outright robbed. Yet there is something about it they have needed, something they have chosen, and so in the end, unlike the asbestos worker who bitterly decries the management that has lied to him and led him down a fatal path, the fighter feels no core bitterness, not even at himself for being a fool, for making such a choice in the folly of youth, because he has forsworn the illusion of wisdom.

Mears is not without regrets. Sometimes, indeed, he regrets almost everything. He regrets his blindness, his taste in women, his rotten luck at having been a middleweight during the age of Marvin Hagler. But he has never regretted boxing. He loves what he does, loves the gym rats, the old dozers with their half-remembered tales of Beau Jack and Henry Armstrong, the crafty trainers, the quiet cut men with their satchels full of swabs and chemicals. He loves how he has been in the ring, honorable and determined and brave. And now, nodding off in a cheap hotel room, he feels love from the legends of the game returned in applause that has the sound of rushing water, a pure stream of affirmation that bears him away into the company of heroes and a restless sleep.

▲▼▲

Three mornings later, as Mears waits for Leon in the gym, he listens happily to the slapping of jump ropes, the grunt and thud of someone working the heavy bag, the jabber and pop of speed, bags, fighters shouting encouragement, the sandpapery whisk of shoes on canvas, the meaty thump of fourteen-ounce sparring gloves. Pale winter light chutes through the high windows like a Bethlehem star to Mears' eyes. The smell is a harsh perfume of antiseptic, resin and sweat. Now and then somebody passes by, says, "Yo, Bobby, what's happenin'?" or "Look good the other night, man!" and he will hold out his hand to be slapped without glancing up, pretending that his diffidence is an expression of cool, not a pose designed to disguise his impaired vision. His body still aches from the Cuban's fast hands, but in a few weeks, a few days if necessary, he'll be ready to fight again.

He hears Leon rasping at someone, smells his cigar, then spots a dark interruption in the light. Not having to see Leon, he thinks, is one of the few virtues of being legally blind. He is unsightly, a chocolate-coloured blob of a man with jowls and yellow teeth and a belly that hangs over his belt. The waist of Mears' boxing trunks would not fit over one of Leon's thighs. He is especially unsightly when he lies, which is often—weakness comes into his face, his popped eyes dart, the pink tip of the tongue slimes the gristly upper lip. He looks much better as a blur in an onion-colored shirt and dark trousers.

"Got a fight for us, my man." Leon drops onto a folding chair beside him, and the chair yields a metallic creak. "Mexican name Nazario. We gon' kick his fuckin' ass!"

This is the same thing Leon said about the Cuban, the same thing he said about every opponent. But this time he may actually be sincere. "Guy's made for us," he continues. "Comes straight ahead. Good hook, but a nothin' right. No fancy bullshit." He claps Bobby on the leg. "We need a W bad, man. We whup this guy in style, I can get us a main event on ESPN next month in Wichita."

Mears is dubious. "Fighting who?"

"Vederotta," says Leon, hurrying past the name to say the Nazario fight is in two weeks. "We can be ready by then, can't we, sure, we be ready, we gon' kill that motherfucker."

"That guy calls himself the Heat? Guy everybody's been duckin'?"

"Wasn't for everybody duckin' him, I couldn't get us the fight. He's tough, I ain't gon' tell you no lie. He busts people up. But check it out, man. Our end's twenty grand. Like that, Bobby? Tuh-wenty thousand dollars."

"You shittin' me?"

"They fuckin' desperate. They can't get nobody to fight the son of a bitch. They need a tune-up for a title shot." Leon sucks on his cigar, trying to puff it alight. "It's your ass out there, man. I'll do what you tell me. But we get past Nazario, we show good against Vederotta—I mean give him a few strong rounds, don't just fold in one—guy swears he'll book us three more fights on ESPN cards. Maybe not the main event, but TV bouts. That'd make our year, man. Your end could work out to forty, forty-five."

"You get that in writin' 'bout the three more fights?"

"Pretty sure. Man's so damn desperate for somebody with a decent chin, he'll throw in a weekend with his wife."

"I don't want his damn wife, I want it in writin' 'bout the fights."

"You ain't seen his wife! That bitch got a wiggle take the kinks outta a couch spring." Delighted by his wit, Leon laughs; the laugh turns into a wet, racking cough.

"I'm gon' need you on this one," says Mears after the coughing has subsided. "None of this bullshit 'bout you runnin' round all over after dope and pussy while I'm bustin' my balls in the gym, and then showin' up when the bell rings. I'm gon' need you really working. You hear that, Leon?"

Leon's breath comes hard. "I hear you."

"Square business, man. You gotta write me a book on that Vederotta dude."

"I'll do my thing," says Leon, wheezing. "You just take care of old Señor Nazario."

The deal concluded, Mears feels exposed, as if a vast, luminous eye—God's, perhaps—is shining on him, revealing all his frailties. He sits up straight, holds his head very still, rubs his palms along the tops of his thighs, certain that everyone is watching. Leon's breathing is hoarse and labored, like last breaths. The light is beginning to tighten up around that sound, to congeal into something cold and gray, like a piece of dirty ice in which they are all embedded.

Mears thinks of Vederotta, the things he's heard. The one-round knockouts, the vicious beatings. He knows he's just booked himself a world of hurt. As if in resonance with that thought, his vision ripples and there is a twinge inside his head, a little flash of red. He grips the seat of the chair, prepares for worse. But worse does not come, and after a minute or so, he begins to relax, thinking about the money, slipping back into the peace of morning in the gym, with the starred light shining from on high and the enthusiastic shouts of the young fighters and the slap of leather making a rhythm like a river slapping against a bank and the fat man who is not his friend beginning to breathe easier now beside him.

▲▼▲

When Mears phones his ex-wife, Amandla, the next night, he sits on the edge of the bed and closes his eyes so he can see her clearly. She's wearing her blue robe; slim-hipped and lightskinned, almost like a Latin girl, but her features are fine and eloquently African and her hair is kept short in the way of a girl from Brazzaville or Conakry. He remembers how good she looks in big gold hoop earrings. He remembers so much sweetness, so much consolation and love. She simply had not been able to bear his pain, coming home with butterfly patches over his stitched eyes, pissing blood at midnight, having to heave himself up from a chair like an old man. It was a weakness in her, he thinks, yet he knows it was an equivalent weakness in him, that fighting is his crack, his heroin—he would not give it up for her.

She picks up on the fourth ring, and he says, "How you been, baby?"

She hesitates a moment before saying, "Aw, Bobby, what you want?" But she says it softly, plaintively, so he'll know that though it's not a good thing to call, she's glad to hear his voice, anyway.

"Nothin', baby," he says. "I don't want nothin'. I just called to tell you I'll be sendin' money soon. Few weeks, maybe."

"You don't have to. I'm makin' it all right."

"Don't tell me you can't use a little extra. You got responsibilities."

A faded laugh. "I hear that."

There is silence for a few beats, then Mears says, "How's your mama holdin' up?"

"Not so good. Half the time I don't think she knows who I am. She goes to wanderin' off sometimes, and I got to—" She breaks off, lets air hiss out between her teeth. "I'm sorry, Bobby. This ain't your trouble."

That stings him, but he does not respond directly to it. "Well, maybe I send you a little somethin', you can ease back from it."

"I don't want to short you."

"You ain't gon' be shortin' me, baby." He tells her about Nazario, the twenty thousand dollars, but not about Vederotta.

"Twenty thousand!" she says. "They givin' you twenty thousand for fightin' a man you say's easy? That don't make any sense."

"Ain't like I'm just off the farm. I still got a name."

"Yeah, but you—"

"Don't worry about it," he says angrily, knowing that she's about to remind him he's on the downside. "I got it under control."

Another silence. He imagines that he can hear her irritation in the static on the line.

"But I do worry," she says. "God help me, I still worry about you after all this time."

"Ain't been that long. Three years."

She does not seem to have heard. "I still think about you under them lights gettin' pounded on. And now you offerin' me money you gon' earn for gettin' pounded on some more."

"Look here—" he begins.

"Blood money. That's what it is. It's blood money."

"Stop it," he says. "You stop that shit. It ain't no more blood money than any other wage. Money gets paid out, somebody always gettin' fucked over at the end of it. That's just what money is. But this here money, it ain't comin' 'cause of nothin' like that, not even 'cause some damn judge said I got to give it. It's comin' from me to you 'cause you need it and I got it."

He steers the conversation away from the topic of fighting, gets her talking about some of their old friends, even manages to get her laughing when he tells her how the cops caught Sidney Bodden and some woman doing the creature in Sidney's car in the parking lot of the A&P. The way she laughs, she tips her head and tucks her chin down onto her shoulder and never opens her mouth, just makes these pleased, musical noises like a shy little girl, and when she lifts her head, she looks so innocent and pretty he wants to kiss her, grazes the receiver with his lips, wishes it would open and let him pour through to her end of the line. The power behind the wish hits his heart like a mainlined drug, and he knows she still loves him, he still loves her, this is all wrong, this long-distance shit, and he can't stop himself from saying, "Baby, I want to see you again."

"No," she says.

It is such a terminal, door-slamming no, he can't come back with anything. His face is hot and numb, his arms and chest heavy as concrete, he feels the same bewildered, mule-stupid helplessness as he did when she told him she was leaving. He wonders if she's seeing somebody, but he promises himself he won't ask.

"I just can't, Bobby," she says.

"It's all right, baby," he says, his voice reduced to a whisper. "It's all right. I got to be goin'."

"I'm sorry, I really am sorry. But I just can't."

"I'll be sending you somethin' real soon. You take care now."

"Bobby?"

He hangs up, an effort, and sits there turning to stone. Brooding thoughts glide through his head like slow black sails. After a while he lifts his arms as if in an embrace. He feels Amandla begin to take on shape and solidity within the circle of his arms. He puts his left hand between her shoulder blades and smooths the other along her flanks, following the arch of her back, the tight rounds of her ass, the columned thighs, and he presses his face against her belly, smelling her warmth, letting all the trouble and ache of the fight with the Cuban go out of him. All the weight of loss and sadness. His chest seems to fill with something clear and buoyant. Peace, he thinks, we are at peace. But then some sly, peripheral sense alerts him to the fact that he is a fool to rely on this sentimental illusion, and he drops his arms, feeling her fading away like steam. He sits straight, hands on knees, and turns his head to the side, his expression rigid and contemptuous as it might be during a staredown at the center of a boxing ring. Since the onset of his blindness, he has never been able to escape the fear that people are spying on him, but lately he has begun to worry that they are not.

▲▼▲

For once Leon has not lied. The fight with Nazario is a simple contest of wills and left hooks, and though the two men's hooks are comparable, Mears' will is by far the stronger. Only in the fourth round does he feel his control slipping, and then the face of a hooded serpent materializes where Nazario's face should be, and he pounds the serpent image with right leads until it vanishes. Early in the fifth round, he bulls Nazario into a corner and following a sequence of twelve unanswered punches, the ref steps in and stops it.

Two hours after the fight, Mears is sitting in the dimly lit bar on the bottom floor of his hotel, having a draft beer and a shot of Gentleman

Jack, listening to Mariah Carey on the jukebox. The mirror is a black, rippling distance flocked by points of actinic light, a mysterious lake full of stars and no sign of his reflection. The hooker beside him is wearing a dark something sewn all over with spangles that move over breasts and hips and thighs like the scattering of moonlight on choppy water. The bartender, when he's visible at all, is a cryptic shadow. Mears is banged up some, a small but nasty cut at his hairline from a head butt and a knot on his left cheekbone, which the hooker is making much of, touching it, saying, "That's terrible-lookin', honey. Just terrible. You inna accident or somepin'?" Mears tells her to mind her own damn business, and she says, "Who you think you is, you ain't my business? You better quit yo' dissin' 'cause I ain't takin' that kinda shit from nobody!"

He buys her another drink to mollify her and goes back to his interior concerns. Although the pain from the fight is minimal, his eyes are acting up and there is a feeling of dread imminence inside his head, an apprehension of a slight wrongness that can bloom into a fiery red presence. He is trying, by maintaining a certain poise, to resist it.

The hooker leans against him. Her breasts are big and sloppy soft and her perfume smells cheap like flowered Listerine, but her waist is slender and firm, and despite her apparent toughness, he senses that she is very young, new to the life. This barely hardened innocence makes him think of Amandla.

"Don't you wan' go upstairs, baby?" she says as her hand traces loops and circles along the inside of his thigh.

"We be there soon enough," he says gruffly. "We got all night."

"Whoo!" She pulls back from him. "I never seen a young man act so stern! 'Mind me of my daddy!" From her stagey tone, he realizes she is playing to the other patrons of the place, whom he cannot see, invisible as gods on their bar stools. Then she is rubbing against him again, saying, "You gon' treat me like my daddy, honey? You gon' be hard on me?"

"Listen up," he says quietly, putting a hand on her arm. "Don't you be playin' these games. I'm payin' you good, so you just sit still and we'll have a couple drinks and talk a little bit. When the time comes, we"ll go upstairs. Can you deal with that?"

He feels resentment in the tension of her arm. "OK, baby," she says with casual falsity. "What you wan' talk about?"

Mariah Carey is having a vision of love, her sinewy falsetto going high into a gospel frequency, and Mears asks the hooker if she likes the song.

She shrugs. "It's all right."

"You know the words?"

"Uh-huh."

"Sing it with me?"

"Say what?"

He starts to sing, and after a couple of seconds the hooker joins in. Her voice is slight and sugary but blends well with Mears' tenor. As they sing, her enthusiasm grows and Mears feels a frail connection forming between them. When the record ends, she giggles, embarrassed, and says, "That was def, baby. You sing real good. You a musician?"

"Naw, just church stuff, you know."

"Bobby Mears!" A man's voice brays out behind him, a hand falls heavily onto his shoulder. "Goddamn, it is you! My fren', he saying, 'Ain't that Bobby Mears over there?' and I said, 'Shit, what he be doin' in here?' "

The man is huge, dark as a coal sack against the lesser darkness, and Mears has no clue to his identity.

"Yes, sir! Bobby 'the Magician' Mears! I'm your biggest fan, no shit! I seen you fight a dozen times. And I ain't talkin' TV. I mean in person. Man, this is great! Can I get you a drink? Lemme buy you one. Hey, buddy! Give us another round over here, OK?"

" 'Nother draft, 'nother shot of the Gentleman," says the bartender in a singsong delivery as he pours. He picks up the hooker's glass and says with less flair, "Vodka and coke."

"Sister," the man says to the hooker, "I don't know what Bobby's been tellin' you, but you settin' next to one of the greatest fighters ever lived."

The hooker says, "You a fighter, baby?" and Mears, who has been seething at this interruption, starts to say it's time to leave, but the man talks through him.

"The boy was slick! I'm tellin' you. Slickest thing you ever seen with that jab of his. Like to kill Marvin Hagler. That old baldhead was one lucky nigger that night. Ain't it the truth, man?"

"Bullshit," Mears says.

"Man's jus' bein' modest."

"I ain't bein' modest. Hagler was hurtin' me from round one, and all I's doin' was tryin' to survive." Mears digs a roll of bills from his pocket, peels a twenty from the top—the twenties are always on top; then the tens, then the fives. "Anybody saw that fight and thinks Hagler was lucky don't know jack shit. Hagler was the best, and it don't make me feel no better 'bout not bein' the best, you comin' round and bullshittin' me."

"Be cool, Bobby! All right, man? Be cool."

The hooker caresses Mears' shoulders, his neck, and he feels the knots of muscle, like hard tumors. It would take a thousand left hooks to work out that tension, a thousand solid impacts to drain off the poisons of fear lodged there, and he experiences a powerful welling up of despair that seems connected to no memory or incident, no stimulus whatsoever, a kind of bottom emotion, one you would never notice unless the light and the temperature and the noise level, all the conditions, were just right. But it's there all the time, the tarry stuff that floors your soul. He tells the man he's sorry for having lashed out at him. He's tired, he says, got shit on his mind.

"Hey," says the man, "hey, it's not a problem, OK?"

There follows a prickly silence that ends when Aaron Neville comes on the jukebox. Mears goes away with the tune, with the singer's liquid shifts and drops, like the voice of a saxophone, and is annoyed once again when the man says, "Who you fightin' next, Bobby? You got somethin' lined up?"

"Vederotta," Mears says.

"The Heat, man? You fightin' the Heat? No shit! Hey, you better watch your ass with that white boy! I seen him fight Reggie Williams couple months back. Hit that man so hard, two his teeth come away stuck in the mouthpiece."

Mears slides the twenty across the bar and says, "Keep it" to the bartender.

"That's right," says the man with apparent relish. "That white boy ain't normal, you ax me. He jus' be livin' to fuck you up, know what I mean? He got somethin' wrong in his head."

"Thanks for the drink," Mears says, standing.

"Any time, Bobby, any time," the man says as Mears lets the hooker lead him toward the stairs. "You take my advice, man. Watch yourself with that Vederotta. That boy he gon' come hard, and you ain't no way slick as you used to be."

▲▼▲

Cold blue neon winks on and off in the window of Mears" room, a vague nebular shine that might be radiating from a polar beacon or a ghostly police car, and as the hooker undresses, he lies on the bed in his shorts and watches the light. It's the only thing he sees, just that chilly blue in a black field, spreading across the surface of the glass like some undersea thing, shrinking and expanding like the contractions of an icy blue heart. He has always been afraid before a fight, yet now he's afraid in a different way. Or maybe it's not the fear that's different, maybe it's his resistance to it that has changed. Maybe he's weaker, wearier. He is so accustomed to suppressing fear, however, that when he tries to examine it, it slithers away into the cracks of his soul and hides there, lurking, eyes aglow, waiting for its time. Vederotta. The man's name even sounds strong, like a foreign sin, an age-old curse.

"Ain't you wan the lights on, honey?" asks the hooker. "I wan' you be able see what you doin'."

"I see you just fine," he says. "You come on lie down."

A siren curls into the distance; two car horns start to blow in an impatient rhythm like brass animals angry at each other; smells of barbecue and gasoline drift in to overwhelm the odor of industrial cleaner.

Training, he thinks. Once he starts to train, he'll handle the fear. He'll pave it over with thousands of sit-ups, miles of running, countless combinations, and by fight night there'll be just enough left to motivate him.

The hooker settles onto the bed, lies on her side, leaning over him, her breasts spilling onto his chest and arm. He lifts one in his palm, squeezing its heft, and she makes a soft, pleased noise.

"Why you didn't tell me you famous?" she asks.

"I ain't famous."

"Yeah, but you was."

"What difference it make? Bein' famous ain't about nothin'."

She moves her shoulders, making her breasts roll against him, and her hot, sweet scent seems to thicken. "Jus' nice to know is all." She runs a hand along his chest, his corded belly. "Ain't you somepin'," she says, and then, "How old're you, baby?"

"Thirty-two."

He expects her to say, "Thirty-two! Damn, baby. I thought you was twenty-five, you lookin' good." But all she does is give a little *mmm* sound as if she's filing the fact away and goes on caressing him. By this he knows that the connection they were starting to make in the bar has held and she's going to be herself with him, which is what he wants, not some play-acting bitch who will let him turn her into Amandla, because he is sick and tired of having that happen.

She helps him off with his shorts and brings him all the way hard with her hand, then touches his cock to her breasts, lets it butt and slide against her cheek, takes it in her mouth for just seconds, like into warm syrup, her tongue swirling, getting his hips to bridge up from the mattress, wise and playful in her moves, and finally she comes astride him and says, "I believe I'm ready for some of this, baby," her voice burred, and she reaches for him, puts him where she needs it, and then her whole dark, sweet weight swings down slick and hot around him, and his neck arches, his mouth strains open and his head pushes back into the pillow, feeling as if he's dipped the back of his brain into a dark green pool, this ancient place with mossy-stone temples beneath the water and strange carvings and spirits gliding in and out the columns. When that moment passes, he finds she's riding him slow and deep and easy, not talking hooker trash, but fucking him like a young girl, her breath shaky and musical, hands braced on the pillow by his head, and he slides his hands around to cup her ass, to her back, pressing down so that her breasts graze and nudge his chest, and it's all going so right he forgets to think how good it is and gives himself over to the arc of his feelings and the steady, sinuous beat of her heart-filled body.

Afterward there is something shy and delicate between them, something he knows won't survive for long, maybe not even until morning, and maybe it's all false, maybe they have only played a deeper game, but if so, it's deep enough that the truth doesn't matter, and they are for now in that small room somewhere dark and green, the edge of that pool he dipped into for a second, a wood, sacred, with the calls of those strange metal beasts sounding in the distance from the desolate town. A shadow is circling beneath the surface of the pool, it's old, wrinkled, hard with evil, like a pale crocodile that's never been up into the light, but it's not an animal, not even a thought, it's just a name: Vederotta. He holds her tight, keeps two fingers pushed between her legs touching the heated damp of her, feeling her pulse there, still rapid and trilling, and he wants to know a little more about her, anything, just one thing, and when he whispers the only question he can think to ask, she wriggles around, holding his two fingers in place, turns her face to his chest and says her name is Arlene.

▲▼▲

Training is like religion to Mears, the litanies of sparring, the penances of one-arm push-ups, the long retreats of his morning runs, the monastic breakfasts at four a.m., the vigils in the steam room during which he visualizes with the intensity of prayer what will happen in the ring, and as with a religion, he feels it simplifying him, paring him down, reducing his focus to a single consuming pursuit. On this occasion, however, he allows himself to be distracted and twice sleeps with Arlene. At first she tries to act flighty and brittle as she did in the bar, but when they go upstairs, that mask falls away and it is good for them again. The next night she displays no pretence whatsoever. They fuck wildly like lovers who have been long separated, and just before dawn they wind up lying on their sides, still joined, hips still moving sporadically. Mears' head is jangled and full of anxious incoherencies. He's worried about how he will suffer for this later in the gym and concerned by what is happening with Arlene. It seems he is being given a last sweetness, a young girl not yet hardened beyond repair, a girl who has some honest affection for him, who perhaps sees him as a means of salvation. This makes him think he is being prepared for something bad by God or whomever. Although he's been prepared for the worst for quite a while, now he wonders if the Vederotta fight will somehow prove to be worse than the worst, and frightened by this, he tells Arlene he can't see her again until after the fight. Being with her, he says, saps his strength and he needs all his strength for Vederotta. If she is the kind of woman who has hurt him in the past, he knows she will react badly, she will accuse him of trying to dump her, she will rave and screech and demand his attentions. And she does become angry, but when he explains that he is risking serious injury by losing his focus, her defensiveness—that's what has provoked her anger—subsides, and she pulls him atop her, draws up her knees and takes him deep, gluing him to her sticky thighs, and as the sky turns the color of tin and delivery traffic grumbles in the streets, and a great clanking and screech of metal comes from the docks, and garbage trucks groan and whine as they tip Dumpsters into their maws like iron gods draining their goblets, she and Mears rock and thrust and grind, tightening their hold on each other as the city seems to tighten around them, winching up its loose ends, notch by notch, in order to withstand the fierce pressures of the waking world.

That afternoon at the gym, Leon takes Mears into the locker room and sits him on a bench. He paces back and forth, emitting an exhaust of cigar smoke, and tells Mears that the boxing commission will be no problem, the physical exam—like most commission physicals—is going to be a joke, no eye charts, nothing, just blood pressure and heart and basic shit like that. He paces some more, then says he's finished watching films of Vederotta's last four fights.

"Ain't but one way to fight him," he says. "Smother his punches, grab him, hold him, frustrate the son of a bitch. Then when he get wild and come bullin' in, we start to throw uppercuts. Uppercuts all night long. That's our only shot. Understand?"

"I hear you."

"Man's strong." Leon sighs as he takes a seat on the bench opposite Mears. "Heavyweight strong. He gon' come at us from the bell and try to hurt us. He use his head, his elbows, whatever he gots. We can't let him back us up. We back up on this motherfucker, we goin' to sleep."

There is more, Mears can feel it, and he waits patiently, picking at the wrappings on his hands while he listens to the slap and babble from the gym.

"'Member that kid Tony Ayala?" Leon asks. "Junior middleweight 'bout ten years ago. Mean fuckin' kid, wound up rapin' some schoolteacher in Jersey. Big puncher. This Vederotta 'mind me of him. He knock Jeff Toney down and then he kick him. He hold up Reggie Williams 'gainst the ropes when the man out on his feet so he kin hit him five, six times more." Leon pauses. "Maybe he's too strong. Maybe we should pull out of this deal. What you think?"

Mears realizes that Leon is mainly afraid Vederotta will knock him into retirement, that his cut of the twenty thousand dollars will not compensate for a permanent loss of income. But the fact that Leon has asked what he thinks, that's new, that's a real surprise. He suspects that deep within that gross bulk, the pilot light of Leon's moral self, long extinguished, has been relit and he is experiencing a flicker of concern for Mears' well-being. Recognizing this, Mears is, for reasons he cannot fathom, less afraid.

"Ain't you listenin', man? I axed what you think."

"Got to have that money," Mears says.

Leon sucks on his cigar, spits. "I don't know 'bout this," he says, real doubt in his voice, real worry. "I just don't know."

Mears thinks about Leon, all the years, the lies, the petty betrayals and pragmatic loyalty, the confusion that Leon must be experiencing to be troubled by emotion at this stage of the relationship. He tries to picture who Leon is and conjures the image of something bloated and mottled washed up on a beach—something that would have been content to float and dream in the deep blue-green light, chewing on kelp, but would now have to heave itself erect and lumber unsightly through the bright, terrible days without solace or satisfaction. He puts a hand on the man's soft, sweaty back, feels the sick throb of his heart. "I know you don't," he says. "But it's all right."

▲▼▲

The first time he meets Vederotta, it's the morning of the fight, at the weigh-in. Just as he's stepping off the scale, he is startled to spot him standing a few feet away, a pale, vaguely human shape cut in the middle by a wide band of black, the trunks. And a face. That's the startling thing, the thing that causes Mears to shift quickly away. It's the sort of face that appears when a fight is going badly, when he needs more fear in order to keep going, but it's never happened so early, before the fight even begins. And this one is different from the rest. Not a comic-book image slapped onto a human mold, it seems fitted just below the surface of the skin, below the false human face, rippling like something seen through a thin film of water. It's coal black, with sculpted cheeks and a flattened bump of a nose and a slit mouth and hooded eyes, an inner mask of black lustreless metal. From its eyes and mouth leaks a crumbling red glow so radiant it blurs the definition of the features. Mears recognizes it for the face of his secret pain, and he can only stare at it. Then Vederotta smiles, the slit opening wider to show the furnace glow within, and says in a dull, stuporous voice, a voice like ashes, "You don't look so hot, man. Try and stay alive till tonight, will ya?" His handlers laugh and Leon curses them, but Mears, suddenly spiked with terror, can find no words, no solidity within himself on which to base a casual response. He lashes out at that evil, glowing face with a right hand, which Vederotta slips, and then everyone—handlers, officials, the press—is surging back and forth, pulling the two fighters apart, and as Leon hustles Mears away, saying, "Fuck's wrong with you, man? You crazy?" he hears Vederotta shouting at him, more bellowing than shouting, no words, nothing intelligible, just the raving of the black beast.

▲▼▲

Half an hour before the fight is scheduled to start, Mears is lying on a training table in the dressing room, alone, his wrapped hands folded on his belly. From the arena come intermittent announcements over the PA, the crowd booing one of the preliminary bouts, and some men are talking loudly outside his door. Mears scarcely registers any of this. He's trying to purge himself of fear but is not having much success. He believes his peculiar visual trick has revealed one of God's great killers, and that tonight the red seed of pain in his head will bloom and he will die, and nothing—no determined avowal, no life-affirming hope—will diminish that belief. He could back out of the fight, he could fake an injury of some sort, and he considers this possibility, but something—and it's not just pride—is pulling him onward. No matter whether or not that face he saw is real, there's something inhuman about Vederotta. Something evil and implacable. And stupid. Some slowness natural to sharks and demons. Maybe he's not a fate, a supernatural creature; maybe he's only malformed, twisted in spirit. Whatever, Mears senses his wrongness the way he would a change in the weather, not merely because of the mask but from a wealth of subtle yet undeniable clues. All these months of imagining beasts in the ring and now he's finally come up against a real one. Maybe the only real one there is. The one he always knew was waiting. Could be, he thinks, it's just his time. It's his time and he has to confront it. Then it strikes him that there may be another reason. It's as if he's been in training, sparring with the lesser beasts, Alligator Man, the Fang, Snakeman and the rest, in order to prepare for this bout. And what if there's some purpose to his sacrifice? What if he's supposed to do something out there tonight aside from dying?

Lying there, he realizes he's already positioned for the coffin, posed for eternity, and that recognition makes him roll up to his feet and begin his shadowboxing, working up a sweat. His sweat stinks of anxiety, but the effort tempers the morbidity of his thoughts.

A tremendous billow of applause issues from the arena, and not long thereafter, Leon pops in the door and says, "Quick knockout, man. We on in five." Then it goes very fast. The shuffling, bobbing walk along the aisle through the Wichita crowd, hearing shouted curses, focusing on that vast, dim tent of white light that hangs down over the ring. Climbing through the ropes, stepping into the resin box, getting his gloves checked a final time. It's all happening too quickly. He's being torn away from important details. Strands of tactics, sustaining memories, are being burned off him. He does not feel prepared. His belly knots and he wants to puke. He needs to see where he is, exactly where, not just this stretch of blue canvas that ripples like shallow water and the warped circles of lights suspended in blackness like an oddly geometric grouping of suns seen from outer space. The heat of those lights, along with the violent, murmurous heat of the crowd, it's sapping—it should be as bright as day in the ring, like noon on a tropic beach, and not this murky twilight reeking of Vaseline and concession food and fear. He keeps working, shaking his shoulders, testing the canvas with gliding footwork, jabbing and hooking. Yet all the while he's hoping the ring will collapse or Vederotta will sprain something, a power failure, anything to spare him. But when the announcer brays his weight, his record and name over the mike, he grows calm as if by reflex and submits to fate and listens to the boos and desultory clapping that follows.

"His opponent," the announcer continues, "in the black trunks with a red stripe, weighs in tonight at a lean and mean one hundred fifty-nine and one half pounds. He's undefeated and is currently ranked number one by both the WBC and WBA, with twenty-four wins, twenty-three by knockout! Let's have a great big prairie welcome for Wichita's favourite son, Toneee! The Heat! Ve-de-rot-taaaaa! Vederotta!"

Vederotta dances forward into the roar that celebrates him, arms lifted above his head, his back to Mears; then he turns, and as Leon and the cut man escort Mears to the center of the ring for the instructions, Mears sees that menacing face again. Those glowing eyes.

"When I say 'break'," the ref is saying, "I want you to break clean. Case of a knockdown, go to a neutral corner and stay there till I tell ya to come out. Any questions?"

One of Vederotta's handlers puts in his mouthpiece, a piece of opaque plastic that mutes the fiery glow, makes it look liquid and obscene; gassy red light steams from beneath the black metal hulls that shade his eyes.

"OK," says the ref. "Let's get it on."

Vederotta holds out his gloves and says something through his mouthpiece. Mears won't touch gloves with him, frightened of what this acquiescence might imply. Instead, he shoves him hard, and once again the handlers have to intervene. Screams from the crowd lacerate the air, and the ref admonishes him, saying, "Gimme a clean fight, Bobby, or I'll disqualify ya." But Mears is listening to Vederotta shouting fierce, garbled noises such as a lion might make with its mouth full of meat.

Leon hustles him back to the corner, puts in his mouthpiece and slips out through the ropes, saying, "Uppercuts, man! Keep throwin' them uppercuts!" Then he's alone, that strangely attenuated moment between the instructions and the bell, longer than usual tonight because the TV cameraman standing on the ring apron is having problems. Mears rolls his head, working out the kinks, shaking his arms to get them loose, and pictures himself as he must look from the cheap seats, a tiny dark figure buried inside a white pyramid. The image of Amandla comes into his head. She, too, is tiny. A doll in a blue robe, like a Madonna, she has that kind of power, a sweet, gentle idea, nothing more. And there's Arlene, whom he has never seen, of whom he knows next to nothing, African and voluptuous and mysterious like those big-breasted ebony statues they sell in the import stores. And Leon hunkered down at the corner of the ring, sweaty already, breath thick and quavery, peering with his pop eyes. Mears feels steadier and less afraid, triangulated by them: the only three people who have any force in his life. When he glances across the ring and finds that black death's head glaring at him, he is struck by something—he can see Vederotta. Since his eyes went bad, he's been unable to see his opponent until the man closes on him, and for that reason he circles tentatively at the beginning of each round, waiting for the figure to materialize from the murk, backing, letting his opponent come to him. Vederotta must know this, must have seen that tendency on film, and Mears thinks it may be possible to trick him, to start out circling and then surprise him with a quick attack. He turns, wanting to consult Leon, not sure this would be wise, but the bell sounds, clear and shocking, sending him forward as inexorably as a toy set in motion by a spark.

Less than ten seconds into the fight, goaded in equal measure by fear and hope, Mears feints a sidestep, plants his back foot and lunges forward behind a right that catches Vederotta solidly above the left eye, driving him into the ropes. Mears follows with a jab and two more rights before Vederotta backs him up with a wild flurry, and he sees that Vederotta has been cut. The cut is on the top of the eyelid, not big but in a bad place, difficult to treat. It shows as a fuming red slit in that black mask, like molten lava cracking open the side of a scorched hill. Vederotta rubs at the eye, holds up his glove to check for blood, then hurls himself at Mears, taking another right on the way in but managing to land two stunning shots under the ribs that nearly cave him in. From then on it's all downhill for Mears. Nobody, not Hagler or Hearns or Duran, has ever hit him with such terrible punches. His face is numb from Vederotta's battering jab and he thinks one of his back teeth may have been cracked. But the body shots are the worst. Their impact is the sort you receive in a car crash when the steering wheel or the dash slams into you. They sound like football tackles, they dredge up harsh groans as they sink deep into his sides, and he thinks he can feel Vederotta's fingers, his talons, groping inside the gloves, probing for his organs. With less than a minute to go in the round, a right hand to the heart drops him onto one knee. It takes him until the count of five to regain his breath, and he's up at seven, wobbly, dazed by the ache spreading across his chest. As Vederotta comes in, Mears wraps his arms about his waist and they go lurching about the ring, faces inches apart, Vederotta's arm barred under his throat, trying to push him off. Vederotta spews words in a goblin language, wet, gnashing sounds. He sprays fiery brimstone breath into Mears' face, acid spittle, the crack on his eyelid leaking a thin track of red phosphorus down a black cheek. When the ref finally manages to separate them, he tells Mears he's going to deduct a point if he keeps holding. Mears nods, grateful for the extra few seconds' rest, more grateful when he hears the bell.

Leon squirts water into Mears' mouth, tells him to rinse and spit. "You cut him," he says excitedly. "You cut the motherfucker!"

"I know," Mears says. "I can see him."

Leon, busy with the Enswell, refrains from comment, restrained by the presence of the cut man. "Left eye," he says, ignoring what Mears has told him. "Throw that right. Rights and uppercuts. All night long. That's a bad cut, huh, Eddie?"

"Could be a winner," the cut man says, "we keep chippin' on it."

Leon smears Vaseline on Mears' face. "How you holdin' up?"

"He's hurtin'' me. Everything he throws, he's hurtin' me."

Leon tells him to go ahead and grab, let the ref deduct the fucking points, just hang in there and work the right. The crowd is buzzing, rumorous, and from this, Mears suspects that he may really have Vederotta in some trouble, but he's still afraid, more afraid than ever now that he has felt Vederotta's power. And as the second round begins, he realizes he's the one in trouble. The cut has turned Vederotta cautious. Instead of brawling, he circles Mears, keeping his distance, popping his jab, throwing an occasional combination, wearing down his opponent inch by inch, a pale, indefinite monster, his face sheathed in black metal, eyes burning like red suns at midnight. Each time Mears gets inside to throw his shots or grab, the price is high—hooks to the liver and heart, rights to the side of the neck, the hinge of the jaw. His face is lumping up. Near the end of the round, a ferocious straight right to the temple blinds him utterly in the left eye for several seconds. When the bell rings, he sinks onto the stool, legs trembling, heartbeat ragged. Exotic eye trash floats in front of him. His head's full of hot poison, aching and unclear. But oddly enough, that little special pain of his has dissipated, chased away by the same straight right that caused his temporary blackout.

The doctor pokes his head into the desperate bustle of the corner and asked him where he is, how he's doing. Mears says, "Wichita" and "OK." When the ref asks him if he wants to continue, he's surprised to hear himself say, "Yeah," because he's been doing little other than wondering if it would be all right to quit. Must be some good reason, he thinks, or else you're one dumb son of a bitch. That makes him laugh.

"Fuck you doin' laughin'?" Leon says. "We ain't havin' that much fun out there. Work on that cut! You ain't done diddly to that cut!"

Mears just shakes his head, too drained to respond.

The first minute of the third round is one of the most agonizing times of Mears' life. Vederotta continues his cautious approach, but he's throwing heavier shots now, head-hunting, and Mears can do nothing other than walk forward and absorb them. He is rocked a dozen times, sent reeling. An uppercut jams the mouthpiece edge-on into his gums and his mouth fills with blood. A hook to the ear leaves him rubber-legged. Two rights send spears of white light into his left eye and the tissue around the eye swells, reducing his vision to a slit. A low blow smashes the edge of his cup, drives it sideways against his testicles, causing a pain that brings bile into his throat. But Vederotta does not follow up. After each assault he steps back to admire his work. It's clear he's prolonging things, trying to inflict maximum damage before the finish. Mears peers between his gloves at the beast stalking him and wonders when that other little red-eyed beast inside his head will start to twitch and burn. He's surprised it hasn't already, he's taken so many shots.

When the ref steps in after a series of jabs, Mears thinks he's stopping the fight, but it's only a matter of tape unravelling from his left glove. The ref leads him into the corner to let Leon retape it. He's so unsteady, he has to grip the ropes for balance, and glancing over his shoulder, he sees Vederotta spit his mouthpiece into his glove, which he holds up like a huge red paw. He expects Vederotta to say something, but all Vederotta does is let out a maniacal shout. Then he reinserts the mouthpiece into that glowing red maw and stares at Mears, shaking his black and crimson head the way a bear does before it charges, telling him—Mears realizes—that this is it, there's not going to be a fourth round. But Mears is too wasted to be further intimidated, his fear has bottomed out, and as Leon fumbles with the tape, giving him a little more rest, his pride is called forth, and he senses again just how stupid Vederotta is, bone stupid, dog stupid, maybe just stupid and overconfident enough to fall into the simplest of traps. No matter what happens to him, Mears thinks, maybe he can do something to make Vederotta remember this night.

The ref waves them together, and Mears sucks it up, banishes his pain into a place where he can forget about it for a while and shuffles forward, presenting a picture of reluctance and tentativeness. When Vederotta connects with a jab, then a right that Mears halfway picks off with his glove, Mears pretends to be sorely afflicted and staggers back against the ropes. Vederotta's in no hurry. He ambles toward him, dipping his left shoulder, so sure of himself he's not even trying to disguise his punches, he's going to come with the left hook under, he's going to hurt Mears some more before he whacks him out. Mears peeks between his gloves, elbows tight to his sides, knowing he's got this one moment, waiting, the crowd's roar like a jet engine around him, the vicious, smirking beast planting himself, his shoulder dipping lower yet, his head dropping down and forward as he cocks the left, and it's then, right at that precise instant, when Vederotta is completely exposed, that Mears explodes from his defensive posture and throws the uppercut, aiming not at the chin or the nose, but at that red slit on the black eyelid. He lands the shot clean, feels the impact, and above the crowd noise he hears Vederotta shriek like a woman, sees him stumble into the corner, his head lowered, glove held to the damaged eye. Mears follows, spins him about and throws another shot that knocks Vederotta's glove aside, rips at the eye. The slit, it's torn open now, has become an inch-long gash, and that steaming, luminous red shit is flowing into the eye, over the dull black cheek and jaw, dripping onto his belly and trunks. Mears pops a jab, a right, then another jab, not hard punches—they don't have to be hard, just accurate—splitting Vederotta's guard, each landing on the gash, slicing the eyelid almost its entire length. Then the ref's arms wrap around him from behind and haul him back, throwing him into ring center, where he stands, confused by this sudden cessation of violence, by this solitude imposed on him after all that brutal intimacy, as the doctor is called in to look at Vederotta's eye. He feels light and unreal, as if he's been shunted into a place where gravity is weaker and thought has no emotional value. The crowd has gone quiet and he hears the voice of Vederotta's manager above the babbling in the corner. Then a second voice shouting the manager down, saying, "I can see the bone, Mick! I can see the goddamn bone!" And then—this is the most confusing thing of all—the ref is lifting his arm and the announcer is declaring, without enthusiasm, to a response of mostly silence and some scattered boos, that "the referee stops the contest at a minute fifty-six seconds of the third round. Your winner by TKO: Bobby! The Magician! Mears!"

Mears' pain has returned, the TV people want to drag him off for an interview, Leon is there hugging him, saying, "We kicked his ass, man! We fuckin' kicked his ass!" and there are others, the promoter, the nobodies, trying to congratulate him, but he pushes them aside, shoulders his way to Vederotta's corner. He has to see him, because this is not how things were supposed to play. Vederotta is sitting on his stool, someone smearing his cut with Avitene. His face is still visible, still that of the beast. Those glowing red eyes stare up at Mears, connect with the eye of pain in his head, and he wants there to be a transfer of knowledge, to learn that one day soon that pain will open wide and he will fall the way a fighter falls after one punch too many, disjointed, graceless, gone from the body. But no such transfer occurs, and he begins to suspect that something is not wrong, or rather that what's wrong is not what he suspected.

There's one thing he thinks he knows, however, looking at Vederotta, and while the handlers stand respectfully by, acknowledging his place in this ritual, Mears says, "I was lucky, man. You a hell of a fighter. But that eye's never gon' be the same. Every fight they gon' be whacking at it, splittin' it open. You ain't gon' be fuckin' over nobody no more. You might as well hang 'em up now."

As he walks away, as the TV people surround him, saying, "Here's the winner, Bobby Mears"—and he wonders what exactly it is he's won—it's at that instant he hears a sound behind him, a gush of raw noise in which frustration and rage are commingled, both dirge and challenge, denial and lament, the final roar of the beast.

▲▼▲

Two weeks after the fight he's sitting in the hotel bar with Arlene, staring into that infinite dark mirror, feeling lost, undefined, sickly, like there's a cloud between him and the light that shines him into being, because he's not sure when he's going to fight again, maybe never, he's so busted up from Vederotta. His eyes especially seem worse, prone to dazzling white spots and blackouts, though the pain deep in his head has subsided, and he thinks that the pain may have had something to do only with his eyes, and now that they're fading, it's fading, too, and what will he do if that's the case? Leon has been working with this new lightweight, a real prospect, and he hasn't been returning Mears' calls, and when the bartender switches on the TV and a rapper's voice begins blurting out his simple, aggressive rhymes, Mears gets angry, thoughts like gnats swarming around that old reeking nightmare shape in his head, that thing that may never have existed, and he pictures a talking skull on the TV shelf, with a stuffed raven and a coiled snake beside it. He drops a twenty on the counter and tells Arlene he wants to take a walk, a disruption of their usual routine of a few drinks, then upstairs. It bewilders her, but she says, "OK, baby," and off they go into the streets, where the Christmas lights are gleaming against the black velour illusion of night like green and red galaxies, as if he's just stepped into an incredible distance hung here and there with plastic angels filled with radiance. And people, lots of people brushing past, dark and shiny as beetles, scuttling along in this holy immensity, chattering their bright gibberish, all hustling toward mysterious crossroads where they stop and freeze into silhouettes against the streams of light, and Mears, who is walking very fast because walking is dragging something out of him, some old weight of emotion, is dismayed by their stopping, it goes contrary to the flow he wants to become part of, and he bursts through a group of shadows assembled like pilgrims by a burning river, and steps out, out and down—he's forgotten the curb—and staggers forward into the traffic, into squealing brakes and shouts, where he waits for a collision he envisions as swift and ultimately stunning, luscious in its finality, like the fatal punch Vederotta should have known. Yet it never comes. Then Arlene, who has clattered up, unsteady in her high heels, hauls him back onto the sidewalk, saying, "You tryin' to kill yo'self, fool?" And Mears, truly lost now, truly bereft of understanding, either of what he has done or why he's done it, stands mute and tries to find her face, wishes he could put a face on her, not a mask, just a face that would be her, but she's nowhere to be found, she's only perfume, a sense of presence. He knows she's looking at him, though.

"You sick, Bobby?" she asks. "Ain't you gon' tell me what's wrong?"

How can he tell her that what's wrong is he's afraid he's not dying, that he'll live and go blind? How can that make sense?

And what does it say about how great a fool he's been? He's clear on nothing apart from that, the size of his folly.

"C'mon," Arlene says with exasperation, taking his arm. "I'm gon' cook you some dinner. Then you can tell me what's been bitin' yo' ass."

He lets her steer him along. He's too dazed to make decisions. Too worried. It's funny, he thinks, or maybe funny's not the word, maybe it's sad that what's beginning to worry him is exactly the opposite of what was troubling him a few seconds before. What if she proves to be someone who'll stand by him no matter how bad things get, what if the pain in his head hasn't gone away, it's just dormant, and instead of viewing death as a solution, one he feared but came to rely on, he now comes to view it as something miserable and dread? The darkness ahead will be tricky to negotiate, and the simple trials of what he's already starting to characterize as his old life seem, despite blood and attrition, unattainably desirable. But no good thing can arise from such futile longing, he realizes. Loving Amandla has taught him that.

Between two department stores, two great, diffuse masses of white light, there's an alley, a doorway, a dark interval of some sort, and as they pass, Mears draws Arlene into it and pulls her tightly to him, needing a moment to get his bearings. The blackness of street and sky is so uniform, it looks as if you could walk a black curve up among the blinking red and green lights, and as Arlene's breasts flatten against him, he feels like he is going high, like it feels when the man in the tuxedo tells you that you've won and the pain is washed away by perfect exhilaration and sweet relief. Then, as if jolted forward by the sound of a bell, he steps out into the crowds, becoming part of them, just another fool with short money and bad health and God knows what kind of woman trouble, who in another time might have been champion of the world. —

Radiant Green Star

Several months before my thirteenth birthday, my mother visited me in a dream and explained why she had sent me to live with the circus seven years before. The dream was a Mitsubishi, I believe, its style that of the Moonflower series of biochips, which set the standard for pornography in those days; it had been programmed to activate once my testosterone production reached a certain level, and it featured a voluptuous Asian woman to whose body my mother had apparently grafted the image of her own face. I imagined she must have been in a desperate hurry and thus forced to use whatever materials fell to hand; yet, taking into account the Machiavellian intricacies of the family history, I later came to think that her decision to alter a pornographic chip might be intentional, designed to provoke Oedipal conflicts that would imbue her message with a heightened urgency.

In the dream, my mother told me that when I was eighteen I would come into the trust created by my maternal grandfather, a fortune that would make me the wealthiest man in Viet Nam. Were I to remain in her care, she feared my father would eventually coerce me into assigning control of the trust to him, whereupon he would have me killed. Sending me to live with her old friend Vang Ky was the one means she had of guaranteeing my safety. If all went as planned, I would have several years to consider whether it was in my best interests to claim the trust or to forswear it and continue my life in secure anonymity. She had faith that Vang would educate me in a fashion that would prepare me to arrive at the proper decision.

Needless to say, I woke from the dream in tears. Vang had informed me not long after my arrival at his door that my mother was dead, and that my father was likely responsible for her death; but this fresh evidence of his perfidy, and of her courage and sweetness, mingled though it was with the confusions of intense eroticism, renewed my bitterness and sharpened my sense of loss. I sat the rest of the night with only the eerie music of tree frogs to distract me from despair, which roiled about in my brain as if it were a species of sluggish life both separate from and inimical to my own.

The next morning, I sought out Vang and told him of the dream and asked what I should do. He was sitting at the desk in the tiny cluttered trailer that served as his home and office, going over the accounts: a frail man in his late sixties with close-cropped gray hair, dressed in a white open-collared shirt and green cotton trousers. He had a long face—especially long from cheekbones to jaw—and an almost feminine delicacy of feature, a combination of characteristics that lent him a sly, witchy look; but though he was capable of slyness, and though at times I suspected him of possessing supernatural powers, at least as regards his ability to ferret out my misdeeds, I perceived him at the time to be an inwardly directed soul who felt misused by the world and whose only interests, apart from the circus, were a love of books and calligraphy. He would occasionally take a pipe of opium, but was otherwise devoid of vices, and it strikes me now that while he had told me of his family and his career in government (he said he still maintained those connections), of a life replete with joys and passionate errors, he was now in the process of putting all that behind him and withdrawing from the world of the senses.

"You must study the situation," he said, shifting in his chair, a movement that shook the wall behind him, disturbing the leaflets stacked in the cabinet above his head and causing one to sail down toward the desk; he batted it away, and for an instant it floated in the air before me, as if held by the hand of a spirit, a detailed pastel rendering of a magnificent tent—a thousand times more magnificent than the one in which we performed—and a hand-lettered legend proclaiming the imminent arrival of the Radiant Green Star Circus.

"You must learn everything possible about your father and his associates," he went on. "Thus you will uncover his weaknesses and define his strengths. But first and foremost, you must continue to live. The man you become will determine how best to use the knowledge you have gained, and you mustn't allow the pursuit of your studies to rise to the level of obsession, or else his judgment will be clouded. Of course, this is easier to do in theory than in practice. But if you set about it in a measured way, you will succeed."

I asked how I should go about seeking the necessary information, and he gestured with his pen at another cabinet, one with a glass front containing scrapbooks and bundles of computer paper; beneath it, a marmalade cat was asleep atop a broken radio, which—along with framed photographs of his wife, daughter, and grandson, all killed, he'd told me, in an airline accident years before—rested on a chest of drawers.

"Start there," he said. "When you are done with those, my friends in the government will provide us with your father's financial records and other materials."

I took a cautious step toward the cabinet—stacks of magazines and newspapers and file boxes made the floor of the trailer difficult to negotiate—but Vang held up a hand to restrain me. "First," he said, "you must live. We will put aside a few hours each day for you to study, but before all else you are a member of my troupe. Do your chores. Afterward we will sit down together and make a schedule."

On the desk, in addition to his computer, were a cup of coffee topped with a mixture of sugar and egg, and a plastic dish bearing several slices of melon. He offered me a slice and sat with his hands steepled on his stomach, watching me eat. "Would you like time alone to honor your mother?" he asked. "I suppose we can manage without you for a morning."

"Not now," I told him. "Later, though...."

I finished the melon, laid the rind on his plate, and turned to the door, but he called me back.

"Philip," he said, "I cannot remedy the past, but I can assure you to a degree as to the future. I have made you my heir. One day the circus will be yours. Everything I own will be yours."

I peered at him, not quite certain that he meant what he said, even though his words had been plain.

"It may not seem a grand gift," he said. "But perhaps you will discover that it is more than it appears."

I thanked him effusively, but he grimaced and waved me to silence—he was not comfortable with displays of affection. Once again he told me to see to my chores.

"Attend to the major as soon as you're able," he said. "He had a difficult night. I know he would be grateful for your company."

▲▼▲

Radiant Green Star was not a circus in the tradition of the spectacular traveling shows of the previous century. During my tenure, we never had more than eight performers and only a handful of exhibits, exotics that had been genetically altered in some fashion: a pair of miniature tigers with hands instead of paws, a monkey with a vocabulary of thirty-seven words, and the like. The entertainments we presented were unsophisticated; we could not compete with those available in Hanoi or Hue or Saigon, or, for that matter, those accessible in the villages. But the villagers perceived us as a link to a past they revered, and found in the crude charm of our performances a sop to their nostalgia—it was as if we carried the past with us, and we played to that illusion, keeping mainly to rural places that appeared on the surface to be part of another century. Even when the opportunity arose, Vang refused to play anywhere near large population centers because—he said—of the exorbitant bribes and licensing fees demanded by officials in such areas. Thus for the first eighteen years of my life, I did not venture into a city, and I came to know my country much as a tourist might, driving ceaselessly through it, isolated within the troupe. We traversed the north and central portions of Viet Nam in three battered methane-powered trucks, one of which towed Vang's trailer, and erected our tents in pastures and school yards and soccer fields, rarely staying anywhere longer than a few nights. On occasion, to accommodate a private celebration sponsored by a wealthy family, we would join forces with another troupe; but Vang was reluctant to participate in such events, because being surrounded by so many people caused our featured attraction to become agitated, thus imperiling his fragile health.

Even today the major remains a mystery to me. I have no idea if he was who he claimed to be; nor, I think, did he know—his statements concerning identity were usually vague and muddled, and the only point about which he was firm was that he had been orphaned as a young boy, raised by an uncle and aunt, and, being unmarried, was the last of his line. Further, it's unclear whether his claims were the product of actual memory, delusion, or implantation. For the benefit of our audiences, we let them stand as truth, and billed him as Major Martin Boyette, the last surviving POW of the American War, now well over a hundred years old and horribly disfigured, both conditions the result of experiments in genetic manipulation by means of viruses—this the opinion of a Hanoi physician who treated the major during a bout of illness. Since such unregulated experiments were performed with immoderate frequency throughout Southeast Asia after the turn of the century, it was not an unreasonable conclusion. Major Boyette himself had no recollection of the process that had rendered him so monstrous and—if one were to believe him—so long-lived.

We were camped that day near the village of Cam Lo, and the tent where the major was quartered had been set up at the edge of the jungle. He liked the jungle, liked its noise and shadow, the sense of enclosure it provided—he dreaded the prospect of being out in the open, so much so that whenever we escorted him to the main tent, we would walk with him, holding umbrellas to prevent him from seeing the sky and to shield him from the sight of god and man. But once inside the main tent, as if the formal structure of a performance neutralized his aversion to space and scrutiny, he showed himself pridefully, walking close to the bleachers, causing children to shy away and women to cover their eyes. His skin hung from his flesh in voluminous black folds (he was African-American), and when he raised his arms, the folds beneath them spread like the wings of a bat; his face, half-hidden by a layering of what appeared to be leather shawls, was the sort of uncanny face one might see emerging from a whorled pattern of bark, roughly human in form, yet animated by a force that seems hotter than the human soul, less self-aware. Bits of phosphorescence drifted in the darks of his eyes. His only clothing was a ragged gray shift, and he hobbled along with the aid of a staff cut from a sapling papaya—he might have been a prophet escaped after a term in hell, charred and magical and full of doom. But when he began to speak, relating stories from the American War, stories of ill-fated Viet Cong heroes and the supernatural forces whose aid they enlisted, all told in a deep rasping voice, his air of suffering and menace evaporated, and his ugliness became an intrinsic article of his power, as though he were a poet who had sacrificed superficial glamour for the ability to express more eloquently the beauty within. The audiences were won over, their alarm transformed to delight, and they saluted him with enthusiastic applause...but they never saw him as I did that morning: a decrepit hulk given to senile maundering and moments of bright terror when startled by a sound from outside the tent. Sitting in his own filth, too weak or too uncaring to move.

When I entered the tent, screwing up my face against the stench, he tucked his head into his shoulder and tried to shroud himself in the fetid folds of his skin. I talked softly, gentling him as I might a frightened animal, in order to persuade him to stand. Once he had heaved up to his feet, I bathed him, sloshing buckets of water over his convulsed surfaces; when at length I was satisfied that I'd done my best, I hauled in freshly cut boughs and made him a clean place to sit. Unsteadily, he lowered himself onto the boughs and started to eat from the bowl of rice and vegetables I had brought for his breakfast, using his fingers to mold bits of food into a ball and inserting it deep into his mouth—he often had difficulty swallowing.

"Is it good?" I asked. He made a growly noise of affirmation. In the half-dark, I could see the odd points of brilliance in his eyes.

I hated taking care of the major (this may have been the reason Vang put me in charge of him). His physical state repelled me, and though the American War had long since ceased to be a burning issue, I resented his purported historical reality—being half American, half Vietnamese, I felt doubly afflicted by the era he represented. But that morning, perhaps because my mother's message had inoculated me against the usual prejudices, he fascinated me. It was like watching a mythological creature feed, a chimera or a manticore, and I thought I perceived in him the soul of the inspired storyteller, the luminous half-inch of being that still burned behind the corroded ruin of his face.

"Do you know who I am?" I asked.

He swallowed and gazed at me with those haunted foxfire eyes. I repeated the question.

"Philip," he said tonelessly, giving equal value to both syllables, as if the name were a word he'd been taught but did not understand.

I wondered if he was—as Vang surmised—an ordinary man transformed into a monster, pumped full of glorious tales and false memories, all as a punishment for some unguessable crime or merely on a cruel whim. Or might he actually be who he claimed? A freak of history, a messenger from another time whose stories contained some core truth, just as the biochip had contained my mother's truth? All I knew for certain was that Vang had bought him from another circus, and that his previous owner had found him living in the jungle in the province of Quan Tri, kept alive by the charity of people from a nearby village who considered him the manifestation of a spirit.

Once he had finished his rice, I asked him to tell me about the war, and he launched into one of his mystical tales; but I stopped him, saying, "Tell me about the real war. The war you fought in."

He fell silent, and when at last he spoke, it was not in the resonant tones with which he entertained our audiences, but in an effortful whisper.

"We came to the firebase in...company strength. Tenth of May. Nineteen sixty-seven. The engineers had just finished construction and...and...there was still...." He paused to catch his breath. "The base was near the Laotian border. Overlooking a defoliated rubber plantation. Nothing but bare red earth in front of us...and wire. But at our rear...the jungle...it was too close. They brought in artillery to clear it. Lowered the batteries to full declension. The trees all toppled in the same direction... as if they'd been pushed down by the sweep...of an invisible hand."

His delivery, though still labored, grew less halting, and he made feeble gestures to illustrate the tale, movements that produced a faint slithering as folds of his skin rubbed together; the flickerings in his pupils grew more and more pronounced, and I half-believed his eyes were openings onto a battlefield at night, a place removed from us by miles and time.

"Because of the red dirt, the base was designated Firebase Ruby. But the dirt wasn't the color of rubies, it was the red of drying blood. For months we held the position with only token resistance. We'd expected serious opposition, and it was strange to sit there day after day with nothing to do except send out routine patrols. I tried to maintain discipline, but it was an impossible task. Everyone malingered. Drug use was rampant. If I'd gone by the book I could have brought charges against every man on the base. But what was the point? War was not truly being waged. We were engaged in a holding action. Policy was either directionless or misguided. And so I satisfied myself by maintaining a semblance of discipline as the summer heat and the monsoon melted away the men's resolve.

"October came, the rains slackened. There was no hint of increased enemy activity, but I had a feeling something big was on the horizon. I spoke to my battalion commander. He felt the same way. I was told we had intelligence suggesting that the enemy planned a fall and winter campaign building up to Tet. But no one took it seriously. I don't think I took it seriously myself. I was a professional soldier who'd been sitting idle for six months, and I was spoiling for a fight. I was so eager for engagement I failed to exercise good judgment. I ignored the signs, I...I refused...I...."

He broke off and pawed at something above him in the air—an apparition, perhaps; then he let out an anguished cry, covered his face with his hands, and began to shake like a man wracked by fever.

I sat with him until, exhausted, he lapsed into a fugue, staring dully at the ground. He was so perfectly still, if I had come across him in the jungle, I might have mistaken him for a root system that had assumed a hideous anthropomorphic shape. Only the glutinous surge of his breath opposed this impression. I didn't know what to think of his story. The plain style of its narration had been markedly different from that of his usual stories, and this lent it credibility; yet I recalled that whenever questioned about his identity, he would respond in a similar fashion. However, the ambiguous character of his personal tragedy did not diminish my new fascination with his mystery. It was as if I had been dusting a vase that rested on my mantelpiece, and, for the first time, I'd turned it over to inspect the bottom and found incised there a labyrinthine design, one that drew my eye inward along its black circuit, promising that should I be able to decipher the hidden character at its center, I would be granted a glimpse of something ultimately bleak and at the same time ultimately alluring. Not a secret, but rather the source of secrets. Not truth, but the ground upon which truth and its opposite were raised. I was a mere child—half a child, at any rate—thus I have no real understanding of how I arrived at this recognition, illusory though it may have been. But I can state with absolute surety why it seemed important at the time: I had a powerful sense of connection with the major, and, accompanying this, the presentiment that his mystery was somehow resonant with my own.

Except for my new program of study, researching my father's activities, and the enlarged parameters of my relationship with Major Boyette, whom I visited whenever I had the opportunity, over the next several years my days were much the same as ever, occupied by touring, performing (I functioned as a clown and an apprentice knife thrower), by all the tediums and pleasures that arose from life in Radiant Green Star. There were, of course, other changes. Vang grew increasingly frail and withdrawn, the major's psychological state deteriorated, and four members of the troupe left and were replaced. We gained two new acrobats, Kim and Kai, pretty Korean sisters aged seven and ten respectively—orphans trained by another circus—and Tranh, a middle-aged, moon-faced man whose potbelly did not hamper in the slightest his energetic tumbling and pratfalls. But to my mind, the most notable of the replacements was Vang's niece, Tan, a slim, quiet girl from Hue with whom I immediately fell in love.

Tan was nearly seventeen when she joined us, a year older than I, an age difference that seemed unbridgeable to my teenage sensibilities. Her shining black hair hung to her waist, her skin was the color of sandalwood dusted with gold, and her face was a perfect cameo in which the demure and the sensual commingled. Her father had been in failing health, and both he and his wife had been uploaded into a virtual community hosted by the Sony AI—Tan had then become her uncle's ward. She had no actual performing skills, but dressed in glittery revealing costumes, she danced and took part in comic skits and served as one of the targets for our knife thrower, a taciturn young man named Dat who was billed as James Bond Cochise. Dat's other target, Mei, a chunky girl of Taiwanese extraction who also served as the troupe's physician, having some knowledge of herbal medicine, would come prancing out and stand at the board, and Dat would plant his knives within a centimeter of her flesh; but when Tan took her place, he would exercise extreme caution and set the knives no closer than seven or eight inches away, a contrast that amused our audiences no end.

For months after her arrival, I hardly spoke to Tan, and then only for some utilitarian purpose; I was too shy to manage a normal conversation. I wished with all my heart that I was eighteen and a man, with the manly confidence that, I assumed, naturally flowed from having attained the age. As things stood I was condemned by my utter lack of self-confidence to admire her from afar, to imagine conversations and other intimacies, to burn with all the frustration of unrequited lust. But then, one afternoon, while I sat in the grass outside Vang's trailer, poring over some papers dealing with my father's investments, she approached, wearing loose black trousers and a white blouse, and asked what I was doing.

"I see you reading every day," she said. "You are so dedicated to your studies. Are you preparing for the university?"

We had set up our tents outside Bien Pho, a village some sixty miles south of Hanoi, on the grassy bank of a wide, meandering river whose water showed black beneath a pewter sky. Dark green conical hills with rocky outcroppings hemmed in the spot, and it was shaded here and there by smallish trees with crooked trunks and puffs of foliage at the ends of their corkscrew branches. The main tent had been erected at the base of the nearest hill and displayed atop it a pennant bearing the starry emblem of our troupe. Everyone else was inside, getting ready for the night's performance. It was a brooding yet tranquil scene, like a painting on an ancient Chinese scroll, but I noticed none of it—the world had shrunk to the bubble of grass and air that enclosed the two of us.

Tan sat beside me, crossed her legs in a half-lotus, and I caught her scent. Not perfume, but the natural musky yield of her flesh. I did my best to explain the purpose of my studies, the words rushing out as if I were unburdening myself of an awful secret. Which was more-or-less the case. No one apart from Vang knew what I was doing, and because his position relative to the task was tutelary, not that of a confidante, I felt oppressed, isolated by the responsibility I bore. Now it seemed that by disclosing the sad facts bracketing my life, I was acting to reduce their power over me. And so, hoping to exorcise them completely, I told her about my father.

"His name is William Ferrance," I said, hastening to add that I'd taken Ky for my own surname. "His father emigrated to Asia in the Nineties, during the onset of doi moi (this the Vietnamese equivalent of perestroika), and made a fortune in Saigon, adapting fleets of taxis to methane power. His son—my father—expanded the family interests. He invested in a number of construction projects, all of which lost money. He was in trouble financially when he married my mother, and he used her money to fund a casino in Danang. That allowed him to recoup most of his losses. Since then, he's established connections with the triads, Malaysian gambling syndicates, and the Bamboo Union in Taiwan. He's become an influential man, but his money's tied up. He has no room to maneuver. Should he gain control of my grandfather's estate, he'll be a very dangerous man."

"But this is so impersonal," Tan said. "Have you no memories of him?"

"Hazy ones," I said. "From all I can gather, he never took much interest in me...except as a potential tool. The truth is, I can scarcely remember my mother. Just the occasional moment. How she looked standing at a window. The sound of her voice when she sang. And I have a general impression of the person she was. Nothing more."

Tan looked off toward the river; some of the village children were chasing each other along the bank, and a cargo boat with a yellow sail was coming into view around the bend. "I wonder," she said. "Is it worse to remember those who've gone, or not to remember them?"

I guessed she was thinking about her parents, and I wanted to say something helpful, but the concept of uploading an intelligence, a personality, was so foreign to me I was afraid of appearing foolish. "I can see my mother and father whenever I want," Tan said, lowering her gaze to the grass. "I can go to a Sony office anywhere in the world and summon them with a code. When they appear they look like themselves, they sound like themselves, but I know it's not them. The things they say are always...appropriate. But something is missing. Some energy, some quality." She glanced up at me, and, looking into her beautiful dark eyes, I felt giddy, almost weightless. "Something dies," she went on. "I know it! We're not just electrical impulses, we can't be sucked up into a machine and live. Something dies, something important. What goes into the machine is nothing. It's only a colored shadow of what we are."

"I don't have much experience with computers," I said.

"But you've experienced life!" She touched the back of my hand. "Can't you feel it within you? I don't know what to call it...a soul? I don't know...."

It seemed then I could feel the presence of the thing she spoke of moving in my chest, my blood, going all through me, attached to my mind, my flesh, by an unfathomable connection, existing inside me the way breath exists inside a flute, breeding the brief, pretty life of a note, a unique tone, and then passing on into the ocean of the air. Whenever I think of Tan, how she looked that morning, I'm able to feel that delicate, tremulous thing, both temporary and eternal, hovering in the same space I occupy.

"This is too serious," she said. "I'm sorry. I've been thinking about my parents more than I should." She shook back the fall of her hair, put on a smile. "Do you play chess?"

"No," I admitted.

"You must learn! A knowledge of the game will help if you intend to wage war against your father." A regretful expression crossed her face, as if she thought she'd spoken out of turn. "Even if you don't...I mean..." Flustered, she waved her hands to dispel the awkwardness of the moment. "It's fun," she said. "I'll teach you."

I did not make a good chess player, I was far too distracted by the presence of my teacher to heed her lessons. But I'm grateful to the game, for through the movements of knights and queens, through my clumsiness and her patience, through hours of sitting with our heads bent close together, our hearts grew close. We were never merely friends—from that initial conversation on, it was apparent that we would someday take the next step in exploring our relationship, and I rarely felt any anxiety in this regard; I knew that when Tan was ready, she would tell me. For the time being, we enjoyed a kind of amplified friendship, spending our leisure moments together, our physical contact limited to hand-holding and kisses on the cheek. This is not to say that I always succeeded in conforming to those limits. Once as we lay atop Vang's trailer, watching the stars, I was overcome by her scent, the warmth of her shoulder against mine, and I propped myself up on an elbow and kissed her on the mouth. She responded, and I stealthily unbuttoned her blouse, exposing her breasts. Before I could proceed further, she sat bolt upright, holding her blouse closed, and gave me a injured look; then she slid down from the trailer and walked off into the dark, leaving me in a state of dismay and painful arousal. I slept little that night, worried that I had done permanent damage to the relationship; but the next day she acted as if nothing had happened, and we went on as before, except that I now wanted her more than ever.

Vang, however, was not so forgiving. How he knew I had taken liberties with his niece, I'm not sure—it may have been simply an incidence of his intuitive abilities; I cannot imagine that Tan told him. Whatever his sources, after our performance the next night he came into the main tent where I was practicing with my knives, hurling them into a sheet of plywood upon which the red outline of a human figure had been painted, and asked if my respect for him had dwindled to the point that I would dishonor his sister's daughter.

He was sitting in the first row of the bleachers, leaning back, resting his elbows on the row behind him, gazing at me with distaste. I was infuriated by this casual indictment, and rather than answer immediately I threw another knife, placing it between the outline's arm and its waist. I walked to the board, yanked the blade free, and said without turning to him, "I haven't dishonored her."

"But surely that is your intent," he said.

Unable to contain my anger, I spun about to face him. "Were you never young? Have you never been in love?"

"Love." He let out a dry chuckle. "If you are in love, perhaps you would care to enlighten me as to its nature."

I would have liked to tell him how I felt about Tan, to explain the sense of security I found with her, the varieties of tenderness, the niceties of my concern for her, the thousand nuances of longing, the intricate complicity of our two hearts and the complex specificity of my desire, for though I wanted to lose myself in the turns of her body, I also wanted to celebrate her, enliven her, to draw out of her the sadness that sometimes weighed her down, and to have her leach my sadness from me as well—I knew this was possible for us. But I was too young and too angry to articulate these things.

"Do you love your mother?" Vang asked, and before I could respond, he said, "You have admitted that you have but a few disjointed memories of her. And, of course, a dream. Yet you have chosen to devote yourself to pursuing the dictates of that dream, to making a life that honors your mother's wishes. That is love. How can you compare this to your infatuation with Tan?"

Frustrated, I cast my eyes up to the billow of patched gray canvas overhead, to the metal rings at the peak from which Kai and Kim were nightly suspended. When I looked back to Vang, I saw that he had gotten to his feet.

"Think on it," he said. "If the time comes when you can regard Tan with the same devotion, well...." He made a subtle dismissive gesture with his fingers that suggested this was an unlikely prospect.

I turned to the board and hefted another knife. The target suddenly appeared evil in its anonymity, a dangerous creature with a wood-grain face and blood-red skin, and as I drew back my arm, my anger at Vang merged with the greater anger I felt at the anonymous forces that had shaped my life, and I buried the knife dead center of the head—it took all my strength to work the blade free. Glancing up, I was surprised to see Vang watching from the entrance. I had assumed that, having spoken his piece, he had returned to his trailer. He stood there for a few seconds, giving no overt sign of his mood, but I had the impression he was pleased.

When she had no other duties, Tan would assist me with my chores: feeding the exotics, cleaning out their cages, and, though she did not relish his company, helping me care for the major. I must confess I was coming to enjoy my visits with him less and less; I still felt a connection to him, and I remained curious as to the particulars of his past, but his mental slippage had grown so pronounced, it was difficult to be around him. Frequently he insisted on trying to relate the story of Firebase Ruby, but he always lapsed into terror and grief at the same point he had previously broken off the narrative. It seemed that this was a tale that he was making up, not one he had been taught or programmed to tell, and that his mind was no longer capable of other than fragmentary invention. But one afternoon, as we were finishing up in his tent, he began to tell the story again, this time starting at the place where he had previously faltered, speaking without hesitancy in the deep, raspy voice he used while performing.

"It came to be October," he said. "The rains slackened, the snakes kept to their holes during the day, and the spiderwebs were not so thick with victims as they'd been during the monsoon. I began to have a feeling that something ominous was on the horizon, and when I communicated this sense of things to my superiors, I was told that according to intelligence, an intensification of enemy activity was expected, leading up to what was presumed to be a major offensive during the celebration of Tet. But I gave no real weight to either my feeling or to the intelligence reports. I was a professional soldier, and for six months I'd been engaged in nothing more than sitting in a bunker and surveying a wasteland of red dirt and razor wire. I was spoiling for a fight."

He was sitting on a nest of palm fronds, drenched in a spill of buttery light—we had partially unzipped the roof of the tent in order to increase ventilation—and it looked as if the fronds were an island adrift in a dark void and he a spiritual being who had been scorched and twisted by some cosmic fire, marooned in eternal emptiness.

"The evening of the fourteenth, I sent out the usual patrols and retired to my bunker. I sat at my desk reading a paperback novel and drinking whiskey. After a time, I put down the book and began a letter to my wife. I was tipsy, and instead of the usual sentimental lines designed to make her feel secure, I let my feelings pour onto the paper, writing about the lack of discipline, my fears concerning the enemy, my disgust at the way the war was being prosecuted. I told her how much I hated Viet Nam. The ubiquitous corruption, the stupidity of the South Vietnamese government. The smell of fish sauce, the poisonous greens of the jungle. Everything. The goddamn place had been a battlefield so long, it was good for nothing else. I kept drinking, and the liquor eroded my remaining inhibitions. I told her about the treachery and ineptitude of the ARVN forces, about the fuck-ups on our side who called themselves generals.

"I was still writing when, around 2100, something distracted me. I'm not sure what it was. A noise...or maybe a vibration. But I knew something had happened. I stepped out into the corridor and heard a cry. Then the crackling of small arms fire. I grabbed my rifle and ran outside. The VC were inside the wire. In the perimeter lights I saw dozens of diminutive men and women in black pajamas scurrying about, white stars sputtering from the muzzles of their weapons. I cut down several of them. I couldn't think how they had gotten through the wire and the minefields without alerting the sentries, but then, as I continued to fire, I spotted a man's head pop up out of the ground and realized that they had tunneled in. All that slow uneventful summer, they'd been busy beneath the surface of the earth, secretive as termites."

At this juncture the major fell prey once again to emotional collapse, and I prepared myself for the arduous process of helping him recover; but Tan kneeled beside him, took his hand, and said, "Martin? Martin, listen to me."

No one ever used the major's Christian name, except to introduce him to an audience, and I didn't doubt that it had been a long time since a woman had addressed him with tenderness. He abruptly stopped his shaking, as if the nerves that had betrayed him had been severed, and stared wonderingly at Tan. White pinprick suns flickered and died in the deep places behind his eyes.

"Where are you from, Martin?" she asked, and the major, in a dazed tone, replied, "Oakland...Oakland, California. But I was born up in Santa Cruz."

"Santa Cruz." Tan gave the name a bell-like reading. "Is it beautiful in Santa Cruz? It sounds like a beautiful place."

"Yeah...it's kinda pretty. There's old-growth redwoods not far from town. And there's the ocean. It's real pretty along the ocean."

To my amazement, Tan and the major began to carry on a coherent—albeit simplistic—conversation, and I realized that he had never spoken in this fashion before. His syntax had an uncustomary informality, and his voice held the trace of an accent. I thought that Tan's gentle approach must have penetrated his tormented psyche, either reaching the submerged individual, the real Martin Boyette, or else encountering a fresh layer of delusion. It was curious to hear him talk about such commonplace subjects as foggy weather and jazz music and Mexican food, all of which he claimed could be found in good supply in Santa Cruz. Though his usual nervous tics were in evidence, a new placidity showed in his face. But, of course this state of affairs didn't last.

"I can't," he said, taking a sudden turn from the subject at hand; he shook his head, dragging folds of skin across his neck and shoulders, "I can't go back anymore. I can't go back there."

"Don't be upset, Martin," Tan said. "There's no reason for you to worry. We'll stay with you, we'll...."

"I don't want you to stay." He tucked his head into his shoulder so his face was hidden by a bulge of skin. "I got to get back doin' what I was doin'."

"What's that?" I asked him. "What were you doing?"

A muffled rhythmic grunting issued from his throat—laughter that went on too long to be an expression of simple mirth. It swelled in volume, trebled in pitch, becoming a signature of instability.

"I'm figurin' it all out," he said. "That's what I'm doin'. Jus' you go away now."

"Figuring out what?" I asked, intrigued by the possibility—however unlikely—that the major might have a mental life other than the chaotic, that his apparent incoherence was merely an incidental byproduct of concentration, like the smoke that rises from a leaf upon which a beam of sunlight has been focused.

He made no reply, and Tan touched my hand, signaling that we should leave. As I ducked through the tent flap, behind me the major said, "I can't go back there, and I can't be here. So jus' where's that leave me, y'know?"

▲▼▲

Exactly what the major meant by this cryptic statement was unclear, but his words stirred something in me, reawakened me to internal conflicts that had been pushed aside by my studies and my involvement with Tan. When I had arrived to take up residence at Green Star, I was in a state of emotional upheaval, frightened, confused, longing for my mother. Yet even after I calmed down, I was troubled by the feeling that I had lost my place in the world, and it seemed this was not just a consequence of having been uprooted from my family, but that I had always felt this way, that the turbulence of my emotions had been a cloud obscuring what was a constant strain in my life. This was due in part to my mixed heritage. Though the taint associated with the children of Vietnamese mothers and American fathers (dust children, they had once been called) had dissipated since the end of the war, it had not done so entirely, and wherever the circus traveled, I would encounter people who, upon noticing the lightness of my skin and the shape of my eyes, expressed scorn and kept their distance. Further fueling this apprehension was the paucity of my memories deriving from the years before I had come to live with Vang. Whenever Tan spoke about her childhood, she brought up friends, birthdays, uncles and cousins, trips to Saigon, dances, hundreds of details and incidents that caused my own memory to appear grossly underpopulated by comparison. Trauma was to blame, I reckoned. The shock of my mother's abandonment, however well-intended, had ripped open my mental storehouse and scattered the contents. That and the fact that I had been six when I left home and thus hadn't had time to accumulate the sort of cohesive memories that lent color to Tan's stories of Hue. But explaining it away did not lessen my discomfort, and I became fixated on the belief that no matter the nature of the freakish lightning that had sheared away my past, I would never find a cure for the sense of dislocation it had provoked, only medicines that would suppress the symptoms and mask the disease—and, that being so masked, it would grow stronger, immune to treatment, until eventually I would be possessed by it, incapable of feeling at home anywhere.

I had no remedy for these anxieties other than to throw myself with greater intensity into my studies, and with this increase in intensity came a concomitant increase in anger. I would sit at Vang's computer, gazing at photographs of my father, imagining violent resolutions to our story. I doubted that he would recognize me; I favored my mother and bore little resemblance to him, a genetic blessing for which I was grateful: he was not particularly handsome, though he was imposing, standing nearly six and a half feet tall and weighing—according to a recent medical report—two hundred and sixty-four pounds, giving the impression not of a fat man, but a massive one. His large squarish head was kept shaved, and on his left cheek was the dark blue and green tattoo of his corporate emblem—a flying fish—ringed by three smaller tattoos denoting various of his business associations. At the base of his skull was an oblong silver plate beneath which lay a number of ports allowing him direct access to a computer. Whenever he posed for a picture, he affected what I assumed he would consider a look of hauteur, but the smallness of his eyes (grayish blue) and nose and mouth in contrast to the largeness of his face caused them to be limited in their capacity to convey character and emotional temperature, rather like the features on a distant planet seen through a telescope, and as a result this particular expression came across as prim. In less formal photographs, taken in the company of one or another of his sexual partners, predominately women, he was quite obviously intoxicated.

He owned an old French Colonial in Saigon, but spent the bulk of his time at his house in Binh Khoi, one of the flower towns—communities built at the turn of the century, intended to provide privacy and comfort for well-to-do Vietnamese whose sexual preferences did not conform to communist morality. Now that communism—if not the concept of sexual morality itself—had become quaint, a colorful patch of history dressed up with theme-park neatness to amuse the tourists, it would seem that these communities no longer had any reason to exist; yet exist they did. Their citizenry had come to comprise a kind of gay aristocracy that defined styles, set trends, and wielded significant political power. Though they maintained a rigid exclusivity, and though my father's bisexuality was motivated to a great degree—I believe—by concerns of business and status, he had managed to cajole and bribe his way into Binh Khoi, and as best I could determine, he was sincere in his attachment to the place.

The pictures taken at Binh Khoi rankled me the most—I hated to see him laughing and smiling. I would stare at those photographs, my emotions overheating, until it seemed I could focus rage into a beam and destroy any object upon which I turned my gaze. My eventual decision, I thought, would be easy to make. Anger and history, the history of his violence and greed, were making it for me, building a spiritual momentum impossible to stop. When the time came, I would avenge my mother and claim my inheritance. I knew exactly how to go about the task. My father feared no one less powerful than himself—if such a person moved against him, they would be the target of terrible reprisals—and he recognized the futility of trying to fend off an assassination attempt by anyone more powerful; thus his security was good, yet not impenetrable. The uniqueness of my situation lay in the fact that if I were able to kill him, I would as a consequence become more powerful than he or any of his connections; and so, without the least hesitancy, I began to plan his murder both in Binh Khoi and Saigon—I had schematics detailing the security systems of both homes. But in the midst of crafting the means of his death, I lost track of events that were in the process of altering the conditions attendant upon my decision.

One night long after my seventeenth birthday, I was working at the computer in the trailer, when Vang entered and lowered himself carefully in the chair opposite me, first shooing away the marmalade cat who had been sleeping there. He wore a threadbare gray cardigan and the striped trousers from an old suit, and carried a thin folder bound in plastic. I was preoccupied with tracking my father's movements via his banking records and I acknowledged Vang's presence with a nod. He sat without speaking awhile and finally said, "Forgive my intrusion, but would you be so kind as to allow me a minute of your time."

I realized he was angry, but my own anger took precedence. It was not just that I was furious with my father; I had grown weary of Vang's distant manner, his goading, his incessant demands for respect in face of his lack of respect for me. "What do you want?" I asked without looking away from the screen.

He tossed the folder onto the desk. "Your task has become more problematic."

The folder contained the personnel file of an attractive woman named Phuong Anh Nguyen, whom my father had hired as a bodyguard. Much of the data concerned her considerable expertise with weapons and her reaction times, which were remarkable—it was apparent that she had been bred for her occupation, genetically enhanced. According to the file her senses were so acute, she could detect shifts in the heat patterns of the brain, subtle changes in blood pressure, heart rate, pupillary dilation, speech, all the telltales that would betray the presence of a potential assassin. The information concerning her personal life was skimpy. Though Vietnamese, she had been born in China, and had spent her life until the age of sixteen behind the walls of a private security agency, where she had received her training. Serving a variety of employers, she had killed sixteen men and women over the next five years. Several months before, she had bought out her contract from the security agency and signed on long-term with my father. Like him, she was bisexual, and, also like him, the majority of her partners were women.

I glanced up from the file to find Vang studying me with an expectant air. "Well," he said, "what do you think?"

"She's not bad-looking," I said.

He folded his arms, made a disgusted noise.

"All right." I turned the pages of the file. "My father's upgrading of his security implies that he's looking ahead to bigger things. Preparing for the day when he can claim my trust."

"Is that all you're able to extract from the document?"

From outside came voices, laughter. They passed, faded. Mei, I thought, and Tranh. It was a cool night, the air heavy with the scent of rain. The door was cracked open, and I could see darkness and thin streamers of fog. "What else is there?" I asked.

"Use your mind, won't you?" Vang let his head top forward and closed his eyes—a formal notice of his exasperation. "Phuong would require a vast sum in order to pay off her contract. Several million, at least. Her wage is a good one, but even if she lived in poverty, which she does not, it would take her a decade or more to save sufficient funds. Where might she obtain such a sum?"

I had no idea.

"From her new employer, of course," Vang said.

"My father doesn't have that kind of money lying around."

"It seems that he does. Only a very wealthy man could afford such a servant as Phuong Anh Nguyen."

I took mental stock of my father's finances, but was unable to recall an excess of cash.

"It's safe to say the money did not come from your father's business enterprises," said Vang. "We have good information on them. So we may assume he either stole it or coerced someone else into stealing it." The cat jumped up into his lap, began kneading his abdomen. "Rather than taxing your brain further," he went on, "I'll tell you what I believe has happened. He's tapped into your trust. It's much too large to be managed by one individual, and it's quite possible he's succeeded in corrupting one of the officers in charge."

"You can't be sure of that."

"No, but I intend to contact my government friends and suggest an investigation into the trust. If your father has done what I suspect, it will prevent him from doing more damage." The cat had settled on his lap; he stroked its head. "But the trust is not the problem. Even if your father has stolen from it, he can't have taken much more than was necessary to secure this woman's services. Otherwise the man who gave me this"—he gestured at the folder—"would have detected evidence of other expenditures. There'll be more than enough left to make you a powerful man. Phuong Anh Nguyen is the problem. You'll have to kill her first."

The loopy cry of a night bird cut the silence. Someone with a flashlight was crossing the pasture where the trailer rested, the beam of light slicing through layers of fog, sweeping over shrubs and patches of grass. I suggested that one woman shouldn't pose that much of a problem, no matter how efficient she was at violence.

Vang closed his eyes again. "You have not witnessed this kind of professional in action. They're fearless, totally dedicated to their work. They develop a sixth sense concerning their clients; they bond with them. You'll need to be circumspect in dealing with her."

"Perhaps she's beyond my capacity to deal with," I said after a pause. "Perhaps I'm simply too thickheaded. I should probably let it all go and devote myself to Green Star."

"Do as you see fit."

Vang's expression did not shift from its stoic cast, but it appeared to harden, and I could tell that he was startled. I instructed the computer to sleep and leaned back, bracing one foot against the side of the desk. "There's no need for pretense," I said. "I know you want me to kill him. I just don't understand why."

I waited for him to respond, and when he did not, I said, "You were my mother's friend—that's reason enough to wish him dead, I suppose. But I've never felt that you were my friend. You've given me...everything. Life. A place to live. A purpose. Yet whenever I try to thank you, you dismiss it out of hand. I used to think this was because you were shy, because you were embarrassed by displays of emotion. Now, I'm not sure. Sometimes it seems you find my gratitude repugnant...or embarrassing in a way that has nothing to do with shyness. It's as if"—I struggled to collect my thoughts—"as if you have some reason for hating my father that you haven't told me. One you're ashamed to admit. Or maybe it's something else, some piece of information you have that gives you a different perspective on the situation."

Being honest with him was both exhilarating and frightening—I felt as though I were violating a taboo—and after this speech I was left breathless and disoriented, unsure of everything I'd said, though I'd been thoroughly convinced of its truth when I said it. "I'm sorry," I told him. "I've no right to doubt you."

He started to make a gesture of dismissal such as was his habit when uncomfortable with a conversation, but caught himself and petted the cat instead. "Despite the differences in our stations, I was very close to your mother," he said. "And to your grandfather. No longer having a family of my own, I made them into a surrogate. When they died, one after the other...you see, your grandfather's presence, his wealth, protected your mother, and once he was gone, your father had no qualms against misusing her." He blew out a breath, like a horse, through his lips. "When they died, I lost my heart. I'd lost so much already. I was unable to bear the sorrow I felt. I retreated from he world, I rejected my emotions. In effect, I shut myself down." He put a hand to his forehead, covering his eyes. I could see he was upset, and I felt badly that I had caused these old griefs to wound him again. "I know you have suffered as a result," he went on. "You've grown up without the affection of a parent, and that is a cruel condition. I wish I could change that. I wish I could change the way I am, but the idea of risking myself, of having everything ripped away from me a third time...it's unbearable." His hand began to tremble; he clenched it into a fist, pressed it against the bridge of his nose. "It is I who should apologize to you. Please, forgive me."

I assured him that he need not ask for forgiveness, I honored and respected him. I had the urge to tell him I loved him, and at that moment I did—I believed now that in loving my family, in carrying out my mother's wishes, he had established his love for me. Hoping to distract him from his grief, I asked him to tell me about my grandfather, a man concerning whom I knew next to nothing, only that he had been remarkably successful in business.

Vang seemed startled by the question, but after taking a second to compose himself, he said, "I'm not sure you would have approved of him. He was a strong man, and strong men often sacrifice much that ordinary men hold dear in order to achieve their ends. But he loved your mother, and he loved you."

This was not the sort of detail I'd been seeking, but it was plain that Vang was still gripped by emotion, and I decided it would be best to leave him alone. As I passed behind him, I laid a hand on his shoulder. He twitched, as if burned by the touch, and I thought he might respond by covering my hand with his own. But he only nodded and made a humming noise deep in his throat. I stood there for a few beats, wishing I could think of something else to say; then I bid him good night and went off into darkness to look for Tan.

▲▼▲

One morning about a month after this conversation, in the little seaside town of Vung Tao, Dat quit the circus following an argument with Vang, and I was forced that same evening to assume the role of James Bond Cochise. The prospect of performing the entire act in public—I had previously made token appearances along with Dat—gave rise to some anxiety, but I was confident in my skill. Tan took in Dat's tuxedo jacket a bit, so it would hang nicely, and helped me paint my face with Native American designs, and when Vang announced me, standing at the center of our single ring and extolling my legendary virtues into a microphone, I strode into the rich yellow glow of the tent, the warmth smelling of sawdust and cowshit (a small herd had been foraging on the spot before we arrived), with my arms overhead, flourishing the belt that held my hatchets and knives, and enjoying the applause. All seven rows of the bleachers were full, the audience consisting of resort workers, fishermen and their families, with a smattering of tourists, mainly backpackers, but also a group of immensely fat Russian women who had been transported from a hotel farther along the beach in cyclos pedaled by diminutive Vietnamese men. They were in a good mood, thanks to a comic skit in which Tan played a farm girl and Tranh a village buffoon hopelessly in love with her, his lust manifested by a telescoping rod that could spring outward to a length of fourteen inches and was belted to his hips beneath a pair of baggy trousers.

Mei, dressed in a red sequined costume that pushed up her breasts and squeezed the tops of her chubby thighs like sausage ends, assumed a spread-eagled position in front of the board, and the crowd fell silent. Sitting in a wooden chair at ring center, Vang switched on the music, the theme from a venerable James Bond film. I displayed a knife to the bleachers, took my mark, and sent the blade hurtling toward Mei, planting it solidly in the wood an inch above her head. The first four or five throws were perfect, outlining Mei's head and shoulders. The crowd oohed and ahhed each time the blade sank into the board. Supremely confident now, I flung the knives as I whirled and ducked, pretending to dodge the gunshots embedded in the theme music, throwing from a crouch, on my stomach, leaping—but then I made the slightest of missteps, and the knife I hurled flashed so close to Mei, it nicked the fleshy portion of her upper arm. She shrieked and staggered away from the board, holding the injury. She remained stock-still for an instant, fixing me with a look of anguish, then bolted for the entrance. The crowd was stunned. Vang jumped up, the microphone dangling from his hand. For a second or two, I was rooted to the spot, not certain what to do. The bombastic music isolated me as surely as if it were a fence, and when Tranh shut it off, the fence collapsed, and I felt the pressure of a thousand eyes upon me. Unable to withstand it, I followed Mei out into the night.

The main tent had been erected atop a dune overlooking a bay and a stretch of sandy beach. It was a warm, windy night, and as I emerged from the tent the tall grasses cresting the dune were blown flat by a gust. From behind me, Vang's amplified voice sounded above the rush of the wind and the heavier beat of the surf, urging the audience to stay seated, the show would continue momentarily. The moon was almost full, but it hung behind the clouds, edging an alp of cumulus with silver, and I couldn't find Mei at first. Then the moon sailed clear, paving a glittering avenue across the black water, touching the plumes of combers with phosphorous, brightening the sand, and I spotted Mei—recognizable by her red costume—and two other figures on the beach some thirty feet below; they appeared to be ministering to her.

I started down the face of the dune, slipped in the loose sand and fell. As I scrambled to my feet, I saw Tan struggling up the slope toward me. She caught at the lapels of my tuxedo for balance, nearly causing me to fall again, and we swayed together, holding each other upright.

She wore a nylon jacket over her costume, which was like Mei's in every respect but one—it was a shade of peacock blue spangled with silver stars. Her shining hair was gathered at the nape of her neck, crystal earrings sparkled in the lobes of her ears, her dark eyes brimmed with light. She looked made of light, an illusion that would fade once the clouds regrouped about the moon. But the thing that most affected me was not her beauty. Moment to moment, that was something of which I was always aware, how she flowed between states of beauty, shifting from schoolgirl to seductress to serious young woman, and now this starry incarnation materialized before me, the devi of a world that existed only for this precise second.... No, it was her calmness that affected me most. It poured over me, coursing around and through me, and even before she spoke, not mentioning what had happened to Mei, as if it were not a potentially fatal accident, a confidence-destroyer that would cause me to falter whenever I picked up a knife—even before that I was convinced by her unruffled manner that everything was as usual, there had been a slight disruption of routine, and now we should go back into the tent because Vang was running out of jokes to tell.

"Mei...." I said as we clambered over the crest of the dune, and Tan said, "It's not even a scratch." She took my arm and guided me toward the entrance, walking briskly yet unhurriedly.

I felt I'd been hypnotized—not by a sonorous voice or the pendulum swing of a shiny object, but by a heightened awareness of the ordinary, the steady pulse of time, all the background rhythms of the universe. I was filled with an immaculate calm, distant from the crowd and the booming music. It seemed that I wasn't throwing the knives so much as I was fitting them into slots and letting the turning of the earth whisk them away to thud and quiver in the board, creating a figure of steel slightly larger than the figure of soft brown flesh and peacock blue silk it contained. Dat had never received such applause—I think the crowd believed Mei's injury had been a trick designed to heighten suspense, and they showed their enthusiasm by standing as Tan and I took our bows and walked together through the entranceway. Once outside, she pressed herself against me, kissed my cheek, and said she would see me later. Then she went off toward the rear of the tent to change for the finale.

Under normal circumstances, I would have gone to help with the major, but on this occasion, feeling disconnected and now, bereft of Tan's soothing influence, upset at having injured Mei, I wandered along the top of the dune until I came to a gully choked with grasses that afforded protection from the wind, which was still gusting hard, filling the air with grit. I sat down amidst the grass and looked off along the curve of the beach. About fifteen meters to the north, the sand gave out into a narrow shingle and the land planed upward into low hills thick with vegetation. Half-hidden by the foliage was a row of small houses with sloping tiled roofs and open porches; they stood close to the sea, and chutes of yellow light spilled from their windows to illuminate the wavelets beneath. The moon was high, no longer silvery, resembling instead a piece of bloated bone china mottled with dark splotches, and appearing to lie directly beneath it among a hammock of coconut palms, was a pink stucco castle that guarded the point of the bay: the hotel where the tourists who had attended our performances were staying. I could make out antlike shapes scurrying back and forth on the brightly lit crescent of sand in front of it, and I heard a faint music shredded by the wind. The water beyond the break was black as opium.

My thoughts turned not to the accident with Mei, but to how I had performed with Tan. The act had passed quickly, a flurry of knives and light, yet now I recalled details: the coolness of the metal between my fingers; Vang watching anxiously off to the side; a fiery glint on a hatchet blade tumbling toward a spot between Tan's legs. My most significant memory, however, was of her eyes. How they had seemed to beam instructions, orchestrating my movements, so forceful that I'd imagined she was capable of deflecting a blade if my aim proved errant. Given my emotional investment in her, my absolute faith—though we'd never discussed it—in our future together, it was easy to believe she had that kind of power over me. Easy to believe, and somewhat troublesome, for it struck me that we were not equals, we couldn't be as long as she controlled every facet of the relationship. And having concluded this, as if the conclusion were the end of all possible logics concerning the subject, my mind slowed and became mired in despondency.

I'm not certain how long I had been sitting when Tan came walking down the beach, brushing windblown hair from her eyes. She had on a man's short-sleeved shirt and a pair of loose-fitting shorts, and was carrying a blanket. I was hidden from her by the grass, and I was at such a remove from things, not comfortable with but accepting of my solitude, I was half-inclined to let her pass; but then she stopped and called my name, and I, by reflex, responded. She spotted me and picked up her pace. When she reached my side she said without a hint of reproval, merely as if stating a fact, "You went so far. I wasn't sure I'd find you." She spread the blanket on the sand and encouraged me to join her on it. I felt guilty at having had clinical thoughts about her and our relationship—to put this sort of practical construction on what I tended to view as a magical union, a thing of fate and dharma, seemed unworthy, and as a consequence I was at a loss for words. The wind began to blow in a long unbroken stream off the water, and she shivered. I asked if she would like to put on my tuxedo jacket. She said, "No." The line of her mouth tightened, and with a sudden movement, she looked away from me, half-turning her upper body. I thought I must have done something to annoy her, and this so unnerved me, I didn't immediately notice that she was unbuttoning her shirt. She shrugged out of it, held it balled against her chest for a moment, then set it aside; she glanced at me over her shoulder, engaging my eyes. I could tell her usual calm was returning—I could almost see her filling with it—and I realized then that this calmness of hers was not hers alone, it was ours, a byproduct of our trust in one another, and what had happened in the main tent had not been a case of her controlling me, saving me from panic, but had been the two of us channeling each other's strength, converting nervousness and fear to certainty and precision. Just as we were doing now.

I kissed her mouth, her small breasts, exulting in their salty aftertaste of brine and dried sweat. Then I drew her down onto the blanket, and what followed, despite clumsiness and flashes of insecurity, was somehow both fierce and chaste, the natural culmination of two years of longing, of unspoken treaties and accommodations. Afterward, pressed together, wrapped in the silk and warmth of spent splendor, whispering the old yet never-less-than-astonishing secrets and promises, saying things that had long gone unsaid, I remember thinking that I would do anything for her. This was not an abstract thought, not simply the atavistic reaction of a man new to a feeling of mastery, though I can't deny that was in me—the sexual and the violent break from the same spring—but was an understanding founded on a considered appreciation of the trials I might have to overcome and the blood I might have to shed in order to keep her safe in a world where wife-murder was a crime for profit and patricide an act of self-defense. It's strange to recall with what a profound sense of reverence I accepted the idea that I was now willing to engage in every sort of human behavior, ranging from the self-sacrificial to the self-gratifying to the perpetration of acts so abhorrent that, once committed, they would harrow me until the end of my days.

▲▼▲

At dawn, the clouds closed in, the wind died, and the sea lay flat. Now and again, a weak sun penetrated the overcast, causing the water to glisten like an expanse of freshly applied gray paint. We climbed to the top of the dune and sat with our arms around each other, not wanting to return to the circus, to break the elastic of the long moment stretching backward into night. The unstirring grass, the energyless water and dead sky, made it appear that time itself had been becalmed. The beach in front of the pink hotel was littered with debris, deserted. You might have thought that our love-making had succeeded in emptying the world. But soon we caught sight of Tranh and Mei walking toward us across the dune, Kim and Kai skipping along behind. All were dressed in shorts and shirts, and Tranh carried a net shopping bag that—I saw as he lurched up, stumbling in the sand—contained mineral water and sandwiches.

"What have you kids been up to," he asked, displaying an exaggerated degree of concern.

Mei punched him on the arm, and, after glancing back and forth between us, as if he suddenly understood the situation, Tranh put on a shocked face and covered his mouth with a hand. Giggling, Kai and Kim went scampering down onto the beach. Mei tugged at Tranh's shirt, but he ignored her and sank onto his knees beside me. "I bet you're hungry," he said, and his round face was split by a gaptoothed grin. He thrust a sandwich wrapped in a paper napkin at me. "Better eat! You're probably going to need your strength."

With an apologetic look in Tan's direction, Mei kneeled beside him; she unwrapped sandwiches and opened two bottles of water. She caught my eye, frowned, pointed to her arm, and shook her forefinger as she might have done with a mischievous child. "Next time don't dance around so much," she said, and pretended to sprinkle something on one of the sandwiches. "Or else one night I'll put special herbs in your dinner." Tranh kept peering at Tan, then at me, grinning, nodding, and finally, with a laugh, Tan pushed him onto his back. Down by the water Kai and Kim were tossing pebbles into the sea with girlish ineptitude. Mei called to them and they came running, their braids bouncing; they threw themselves belly first onto the sand, squirmed up to sitting positions, and began gobbling sandwiches.

▲▼▲

"Don't eat so fast!" Mei cautioned. "You'll get sick."

Kim, the younger of the sisters, squinched her face at Mei and shoved half the sandwich into her mouth. Tranh contorted his features so his lips nearly touched his nose, and Kim laughed so hard she sprayed bits of bread and fried fish. Tan told her that this was not ladylike. Both girls sat up straight, nibbled their sandwiches—they took it to heart whenever Tan spoke to them about being ladies.

"Didn't you bring anything beside fish?" I asked, inspecting the filling of my sandwich.

"I guess we should have brought oysters," said Tranh. "Maybe some rhinoceros horn, some—"

"That stuff's for old guys like you," I told him. "Me, I just need peanut butter."

After we had done eating, Tranh lay back with his head in Mei's lap and told a story about a talking lizard that had convinced a farmer it was the Buddha. Kim and Kai cuddled together, sleepy from their feast. Tan leaned into the notch of my shoulder, and I put my arm around her. It came to me then, not suddenly, but gradually, as if I were being immersed in the knowledge like a man lowering his body into a warm bath, that for the first time in my life—all the life I could remember—I was at home. These people were my family, and the sense of dislocation that had burdened me all those years had evaporated. I closed my eyes and buried my face in Tan's hair, trying to hold onto the feeling, to seal it inside my head so I would never forget it.

Two men in T-shirts and bathing suits came walking along the water's edge in our direction. When they reached the dune they climbed up to where we were sitting. Both were not much older than I, and judging by their fleshiness and soft features, I presumed them to be Americans, a judgment confirmed when the taller of the two, a fellow with a heavy jaw and hundreds of white beads threaded on the strings of his long black hair, lending him a savage appearance, said, "You guys are with that tent show right?"

Mei, who did not care for Americans, stared meanly at him, but Tranh, who habitually viewed them as potential sources of income, told him that we were, indeed, performers with the circus. Kai and Kim whispered and giggled, and Tranh asked the American what his friend—skinnier, beadless, dull-eyed and open-mouthed, with a complicated headset covering his scalp—was studying.

"Parasailing. We're going parasailing...if there's ever any wind and the program doesn't screw up. I woulda left him at the house, but the program's fucked. Didn't want his ass convulsing." He extracted a sectioned strip of plastic from his shirt pocket; each square of plastic held a gelatin capsule shaped like a cut gem and filled with blue fluid. "Wanna brighten your day?" He dangled the strip as if tempting us with a treat. When no one accepted his offer, he shrugged, returned the strip to his pocket; he glanced down at me. "Hey, that shit with the knives... that was part of the fucking plan! Especially when you went benihana on Little Plum Blossom." He jerked his thumb at Mei and then stood nodding, gazing at the sea, as if receiving a transmission from that quarter. "Okay," he said. "Okay. It could be the drugs, but the trusty inner voice is telling me my foreign ways seem ludicrous...perhaps even offensive. It well may be that I am somewhat ludicrous. And I'm pretty torched, so I have to assume I've been offensive."

Tranh made to deny this, Mei grunted, Kim and Kai looked puzzled, and Tan asked the American if he was on vacation.

"Thank you," he said to Tan. "Beautiful lady. I am always grateful for the gift of courtesy. No, my friend and I—and two others—are playing at the hotel. We're musicians." He took out his wallet, which had been hinged over the waist of his trunks, and removed from it a thin gold square the size of a postage stamp; he handed it to Tan. "Have you seen these? They're new...souvenir things, like. They just play once, but it'll give you a taste, caress your finger on it until it you hear the sound. Then don't touch it again—they get extremely hot."

Tan started to do as he instructed but he said, "No, wait till we're gone. I want to imagine you enjoyed hearing it. If you do, come on down to the hotel after you're finished tonight. You'll be my guests."

"Is it one of your songs?" I asked, curious about him now that he had turned out to be more complicated than he first appeared.

He said, yes, it was an original composition.

"What's it called," Tranh asked.

"We haven't named it yet," said the American; then, after a pause: "What's the name of your circus?"

Almost as one we said, "Radiant Green Star."

"Perfect," said the American.

Once the two men were out of earshot, Tan pressed her fingertip to the gold square, and soon a throbbing music issued forth simply structured yet intricately layered by synthesizers, horns, guitars, densely figured by theme and subtle counter-theme, both insinuating and urgent. Kai and Kim stood and danced with one another. Tranh bobbed his head, tapped his foot, and even Mei was charmed, swaying, her eyes closed. Tan kissed me, and we watched a thin white smoke trickle upward from the square, which itself began to shrink, and I thought how amazing it was that things were often not what they seemed, and what a strange confluence of possibilities it had taken to bring all the troupe together—and the six of us were the entire troupe, for Vang was never really part of us even when he was there, and though the major was rarely with us, he was always there, a shadow in the corners of our minds.... How magical and ineluctable a thing it was for us all to be together at the precise place and time when a man—a rather unprepossessing man at that—walked up from a deserted beach and presented us with a golden square imprinted with a song that he named for our circus, a song that so accurately evoked the mixture of the commonplace and the exotic that characterized life in Radiant Green Star, music that was like smoke, rising up for a few perfect moments, and then vanishing with the wind.

▲▼▲

Had Vang asked me at any point during the months that followed to tell him about love, I might have spoken for hours, answering him not with definitions, principles, or homilies, but specific instances, moments, and anecdotes. I was happy. Despite the gloomy nature of my soul, I could think of no word that better described how I felt. Though I continued to study my father, to follow his comings and goings, his business maneuvers and social interactions, I now believed that I would never seek to confront him, never try to claim my inheritance. I had all I needed to live, and I only wanted to keep those I loved safe and free from worry.

Tan and I did not bother to hide our relationship, and I expected Vang to rail at me for my transgression. I half-expected him to drive me away from the circus—indeed, I prepared for that eventuality. But he never said a word. I did notice a certain cooling of the atmosphere. He snapped at me more often and on occasion refused to speak; yet that was the extent of his anger. I didn't know how to take this. Either, I thought, he had overstated his concern for Tan or else he had simply accepted the inevitable. That explanation didn't satisfy me, however. I suspected that he might have something more important on his mind, something so weighty that my involvement with his niece seemed a triviality by comparison, and one day, some seven months after Tan and I became lovers, my suspicions were proved correct.

I went to the trailer at mid-afternoon, thinking Vang would be in town. We were camped at the edge of a hardwood forest on a cleared acre of red dirt near Buon Ma Thuot in the Central Highlands, not far from the Cambodian border. Vang usually spent the day before a performance putting up posters, and I had intended to work on the computer; but when I entered, I saw him standing by his desk, folding a shirt, a suitcase open on the chair beside him. I asked what he was doing and he handed me a thick envelope; inside were the licenses and deeds of ownership relating to the circus and its property. "I've signed everything over," he said. "If you have any problems, contact my lawyer."

"I don't understand," I said, dumfounded. "You're leaving?"

He bent to the suitcase and laid the folded shirt inside it. "You can move into the trailer tonight. You and Tan. She'll be able to put it in order. I suppose you've noticed that she's almost morbidly neat." He straightened, pressed his hand against his lower back as if stricken by a pain. "The accounts, the bookings for next year...it's all in the computer. Everything else...." He gestured at the cabinets on the walls. "You remember where things are."

I couldn't get a grasp on the situation, overwhelmed by the thought that I was now responsible for Green Star, by the fact that the man who for years had been the only consistent presence in my life was about to walk out the door forever. "Why are you leaving?"

He turned to me, frowning. "If you must know, I'm ill."

"But why would you want to leave. We'll just...."

"I'm not going to recover," he said flatly.

I peered at him, trying to detect the signs of his mortality, but he looked no thinner, no grayer, than he had for some time. I felt the stirrings of a reaction that I knew he would not want to see, and I tamped down my emotions. "We can care for you here," I said.

He began to fold another shirt. "I plan to join my sister and her husband in what they insist upon calling"—he clicked his tongue against his teeth—"Heaven."'

I recalled the talks I'd had with Tan in which she had decried the process of uploading the intelligence, the personality. If the old man was dying, there was no real risk involved. Still, the concept of such a mechanical transmogrification did not sit well with me.

"Have you nothing to say on the subject?" he asked. "Tan was quite voluble."

"You've told her, then?"

"Of course." He inspected the tail of the shirt he'd been folding, and finding a hole, cast it aside. "We've said our goodbyes."

He continued to putter about, and as I watched him shuffling among the stacks of magazines and newspapers, kicking file boxes and books aside, dust rising wherever he set his hand, a tightness in my chest began to loosen, to work its way up into my throat. I went to the door and stood looking out, seeing nothing, letting the strong sunlight harden the glaze of my feelings. When I turned back, he was standing close to me, suitcase in hand. He held out a folded piece of paper and said, "This is the code by which you can contact me once I've been...." He laughed dryly. "Processed, I imagine, would be the appropriate verb. At any rate, I hope you will let me know what you decide concerning your father."

It was in my mind to tell him that I had no intention of contending with my father, but I thought that this would disappoint him, and I merely said that I would do as he asked. We stood facing one another, the air thick with unspoken feelings, with vibrations that communicated an entire history comprised of such mute, awkward moments. "If I'm to have a last walk in the sun," he said at length, "you'll have to let me pass."

That at the end of his days he viewed me only as a minor impediment—it angered me. But I reminded myself that this was all the sentiment of which he was capable. Without asking permission, I embraced him. He patted me lightly on the back and said, "I know you'll take care of things." And with that, he pushed past me and walked off in the direction of the town, vanishing behind one of the parked trucks.

I went into the rear of the trailer, into the partitioned cubicle where Vang slept, and sat down on his bunk. His pillowcase bore a silk-screened image of a beautiful Vietnamese woman and the words HONEY LADY KEEP YOU COMFORT EVERY NIGHT. In the cabinet beside his bed were a broken clock, a small plaster bust of Ho Chi Minh, a few books, several pieces of hard candy, and a plastic key chain in the shape of a butterfly. The meagerness of the life these items described caught at my emotions, and I thought I might weep, but it was as if by assuming Vang's position as the owner of Green Star, I had undergone a corresponding reduction in my natural responses, and I remained dry-eyed. I felt strangely aloof from myself, connected to the life of my mind and body by a tube along which impressions of the world around me were now and then transmitted. Looking back on my years with Vang, I could make no sense of them. He had nurtured and educated me, yet the sum of all that effort—not given cohesion by the glue of affection—came to scraps of memories no more illustrative of a comprehensible whole than were the memories of my mother. They had substance, yet no flavor... none, that is, except for a dusty gray aftertaste that I associated with disappointment and loss.

I didn't feel like talking to anyone, and for want of anything else to do, I went to the desk and started inspecting the accounts, working through dusk and into the night. When I had satisfied myself that all was in order, I turned to the bookings. Nothing out of the ordinary. The usual villages, the occasional festival. But when I accessed the bookings for the month of March, I saw that during the week of the 17th through the 23rd—the latter date just ten days from my birthday—we were scheduled to perform in Binh Khoi.

I thought this must be a mistake—Vang had probably been thinking of Binh Khoi and my father while recording a new booking and had inadvertently put down the wrong name. But when I called up the contract, I found that no mistake had been made. We were to be paid a great deal of money, sufficient to guarantee a profitable year, but I doubted that Vang's actions had been motivated by our financial needs. He must, I thought, have seen the way things were going with Tan and me, and he must have realized that I would never risk her in order to avenge a crime committed nearly two decades before—thus, he had decided to force a confrontation between me and my father. I was furious, and my first impulse was to break the contract; but after I had calmed down, I realized that doing so would put us all at risk—the citizens of Binh Khoi were not known for their generosity or flexibility, and if I were to renege on Vang's agreement, they would surely pursue the matter in the courts. I would have no chance of winning a judgment. The only thing to do was to play the festival and steel myself to ignore the presence of my father. Perhaps he would be elsewhere, or, even if he was in residence, perhaps he would not attend our little show. Whatever the circumstances, I swore I would not be caught in this trap, and when my eighteenth birthday arrived I would go to the nearest Sony office and take great pleasure in telling Vang—whatever was left of him—that his scheme had failed.

I was still sitting there, trying to comprehend whether or not by contracting the engagement, Vang hoped to provide me with a basis for an informed decision, or if his interests were purely self-serving, when Tan stepped into the trailer. She had on a sleeveless plaid smock, the garment she wore whenever she was cleaning, and it was evident that she'd been crying—the skin beneath her eyes was puffy and red. But she had regained her composure, and she listened patiently, perched on the edge of the desk, while I told her all I'd been thinking about Vang and what he had done to us.

"Maybe it's for the best," she said after I had run down. "This way you'll be sure you've done what you had to do."

I was startled by her reaction. "Are you saying that you think I should kill my father...that I should even entertain the possibility?"

She shrugged. "That's for you to decide."

"I've decided already," I said.

"Then there's not a problem."

The studied neutrality of her attitude puzzled me. "You don't think I'll stand by my decision, do you?"

She put a hand to her brow, hiding her face—a gesture that reminded me of Vang. "I don't think you have decided, and I don't think you should...not until you see your father." She pinched a fold of skin above the bridge of her nose, then looked up at me. "Let's not talk about this now."

We sat silently for half a minute or thereabouts, each following the path of our own thoughts; then she wrinkled up her nose and said, "It smells bad in here. Do you want to get some air?"

We climbed onto the roof of the trailer and sat gazing at the shadowy line of the forest to the west, the main tent bulking up above it, and a sky so thick with stars that the familiar constellations were assimilated into new and busier cosmic designs: a Buddha face with a diamond on its brow, a tiger's head, a palm tree—constructions of sparkling pinlights against a midnight blue canvas stretched from horizon to horizon. The wind brought the scent of sweet rot and the less pervasive odor of someone's cooking. Somebody switched on a radio in the main tent; a Chinese orchestra whined and jangled. I felt I was sixteen again, that Tan and I had just met, and I thought perhaps we had chosen to occupy this place where we spent so many hours before we were lovers, because here we could banish the daunting pressures of the present, the threat of the future, and be children again. But although those days were scarcely two years removed, we had forever shattered the comforting illusions and frustrating limitations of childhood. I lay back on the aluminum roof which still held a faint warmth of the day, and Tan hitched up her smock about her waist and mounted me, bracing her hands on my chest as I slipped inside her. Framed by the crowded stars, features made mysterious by the cowl of her hair, she seemed as distant and unreal as the imagined creatures of my zodiac; but this illusion, too, was shattered as she began to rock her hips with an accomplished passion and lifted her face to the sky, transfigured by a look of exalted, almost agonized yearning, like one of those Renaissance angels marooned on a scrap of painted cloud who has just witnessed something amazing pass overhead, a miracle of glowing promise too perfect to hold in the mind. She shook her head wildly when she came, her hair flying all to one side so that it resembled in shape the pennant flying on the main tent, a dark signal of release, and then collapsed against my chest. I held onto her hips, continuing to thrust until the knot of heat in my groin shuddered out of me, leaving a residue of black peace into which the last shreds of my thought were subsumed.

The sweat dried on our skin, and still we lay there, both—I believed—aware that once we went down from the roof, the world would close around us, restore us to its troubled spin. Someone changed stations on the radio, bringing in a Cambodian program—a cooler, wispier music played. A cough sounded close by the trailer, and I raised myself to an elbow, wanting to see who it was. The major was making his way with painful slowness across the cleared ground, leaning on his staff. In the starlight, his grotesque shape was lent a certain anonymity—he might have been a figure in a fantasy game, an old down-at-heels magician shrouded in a heavy, ragged cloak, or a beggar on a quest. He shuffled a few steps more, and then, shaking with effort, sank to his knees. For several seconds he remained motionless, then he scooped a handful of the red dirt and held it up to his face. And I recalled that Buon Ma Thuot was near the location of his fictive—or if not fictive, ill-remembered—firebase. Firebase Ruby. Built upon the red dirt of a defoliated plantation.

Tan sat up beside me and whispered, "What's he doing?"

I put a finger to my lips, urging her to silence; I was convinced that the major would not expose himself to the terror of the open sky unless moved by some equally terrifying inner force, and I hoped he might do something that would illuminate the underpinnings of his mystery.

He let the dirt sift through his fingers and struggled to stand.

Failed and sagged onto his haunches. His head fell back, and he held a spread-fingered hand up to it as if trying to shield himself from the starlight. His quavery voice ran out of him like a shredded battle flag. "Turn back!" he said. "Oh, God! God! Turn back!"

▲▼▲

During the next four months, I had little opportunity to brood over the prospect of meeting my father. Dealing with the minutiae of Green Star's daily operation took most of my energy and hours, and whenever I had a few minutes respite, Tan was there to fill them. So it was that by the time we arrived in Binh Khoi, I had made scarcely any progress in adjusting to the possibility that I might soon come face-to-face with the man who had killed my mother.

In one aspect, Binh Khoi was the perfect venue for us, since the town affected the same conceit as the circus, being designed to resemble a fragment of another time. It was situated near the Pass of the Ocean Clouds in the Truong Son Mountains some forty kilometers north of Danang, and many of the homes there were afforded a view of green hills declining toward the Coastal Plain. On the morning we arrived, those same hills were half-submerged in thick white fog, the plain was totally obscured, and a pale mist had infiltrated the narrow streets, casting an air of ominous enchantment over the place. The oldest of the houses had been built no more than fifty years before, yet they were all similar to nineteenth-century houses that still existed in certain sections of Hanoi: two and three stories tall and fashioned of stone, painted dull yellow and gray and various other sober hues, with sharply sloping roofs of dark green tile, and compounds hidden by high walls and shaded by bougainvillea, papaya, and banana trees. Except for street lights in the main square and pedestrians in bright eccentric clothing, we might have been driving through a hill station during the 1800s; but I knew that hidden behind this antiquated facade were state-of-the-art security systems that could have vaporized us had we not been cleared to enter.

The most unusual thing about Binh Khoi was its silence. I'd never been in a place where people lived in any considerable quantity that was so hushed, devoid of the stew of sounds natural to a human environment. No hens squabbling or dogs yipping, no whining motor scooters or humming cars, no children at play. In only one area was there anything approximating normal activity and noise: the marketplace, which occupied an unpaved street leading off the square. Here men and women in coolie hats hunkered beside baskets of jackfruit, chilies, garlic, custard apples, durians, geckos, and dried fish; meat and caged puppies and monkeys and innumerable other foodstuffs were sold in canvas-roofed stalls; and the shoppers, mostly male couples, haggled with the vendors, occasionally venting their dismay at the prices...this despite the fact that any one of them could have bought everything in the market without blinking. Though the troupe shared their immersion in a contrived past, I found the depth of their pretense alarming and somewhat perverse. As I maneuvered the truck cautiously through the press, they peered incuriously at me through the windows—faces rendered exotic and nearly unreadable by tattoos and implants and caps of silver wire and winking light that appeared to be woven into their hair—and I thought I could feel their amusement at the shabby counterfeit we offered of their more elegantly realized illusion. I believe I might have hated them for the fashionable play they made of arguing over minuscule sums with the poor vendors, for the triviality of spirit this mockery implied, if I had not already hated them so completely for being my father's friends and colleagues.

At the end of the street, beyond the last building, lay a grassy field bordered by a low whitewashed wall. Strings of light bulbs linked the banana trees and palms that grew close to the wall on three sides, and I noticed several paths leading off into the jungle that were lit in the same fashion. On the fourth side, beyond the wall, the land dropped off into a notch, now choked with fog, and on the far side of the notch, perhaps fifty yards away, a massive hill with a sheer rock face and the ruins of an old temple atop it lifted from the fog, looming above the field—it was such a dramatic sight and so completely free of mist, every palm frond articulated, every vine-enlaced crevice and knob of dark, discolored stone showing clear, that I wondered if it might be a clever projection, another element of Binh Khoi's decor.

We spent the morning and early afternoon setting up, and once I was satisfied that everything was in readiness, I sought out Tan, thinking we might go for a walk; but she was engaged in altering Kai's costume. I wandered into the main tent and busied myself by making sure the sawdust had been spread evenly. Kai was swinging high above on a rope suspended from the metal ring at the top of the tent, and one of our miniature tigers had climbed a second rope and was clinging to it by its furry hands, batting at her playfully whenever she swooped near. Tranh and Mei were playing cards in the bleachers, and Kim was walking hand-in-hand with our talking monkey, chattering away as if the creature could understand her—now and then it would turn its white face to her and squeak in response, saying "I love you" and "I'm hungry" and other equally non-responsive phrases. I stood by the entranceway, feeling rather paternal toward my little family gathered under the lights, and I was just considering whether or not I should return to the trailer and see if Tan had finished, when a baritone voice sounded behind me, saying, "Where can I find Vang Ky?"

My father was standing with hands in pockets a few feet away, wearing black trousers and a gray shirt of some shiny material. He looked softer and heavier than he did in his photographs, and the flying fish tattoo on his cheek was now surrounded by more than half-a-dozen tiny emblems denoting his business connections. With his immense head, his shaved skull gleaming in the hot lights, he himself seemed the emblem of some monumental and soulless concern. At his shoulder, over a foot shorter than he, was a striking Vietnamese woman with long straight hair, dressed in tight black slacks and a matching tunic: Phuong Alin Nguyen. She was staring at me intently.

Stunned, I managed to get out that Vang was no longer with the circus, and my father said, "How can that be? He's the owner, isn't he?"

Shock was giving way to anger, anger so fulminant I could barely contain it. My hands trembled. If I'd had one of my knives to hand, I would have plunged it without a thought into his chest. I did the best I could to conceal my mood, and told him what had become of Vang; but it seemed that as I catalogued each new detail of his face and body—a frown line, a reddened ear lobe, a crease in his fleshy neck—a vial of some furious chemical was tipped over and added to the mix of my blood.

"Goddamn it!" he said, casting his eyes up to the canvas; he appeared distraught. "Shit!" He glanced down at me. "Have you got his access code? It's never the same once they go to Heaven. I'm not sure they really know what's going on. But I guess it's my only option."

"I doubt he'd approve of my giving the code to a stranger," I told him.

"We're not strangers," he said. "Vang was my father-in-law. We had a falling-out after my wife died. I hoped having the circus here for a week, I'd be able to persuade him to sit down and talk. There's no reason for us to be at odds."

I suppose the most astonishing thing he said was that Vang was his father-in-law, and thus my grandfather. I didn't know what to make of that; I could think of no reason he might have for lying, yet it raised a number of troubling questions. But his last statement, his implicit denial of responsibility for my mother's death…it had come so easily to his lips! Hatred flowered in me like a cold star, acting to calm me, allowing me to exert a measure of control over my anger.

Phoung stepped forward and put a hand on my chest; my heart pounded against the pressure of her palm. "Is anything wrong?" she asked.

"I'm…surprised," I said. "That's all. I didn't realize Vang had a son-in-law."

Her make-up was severe, her lips painted a dark mauve, her eyes shaded by the same color, but in the fineness of her features and the long oval shape of her face, she bore a slight resemblance to Tan.

"Why are you angry?" she asked.

My father eased her aside. "It's all right. I came on pretty strong—he's got every right to be angry. Why don't the two of us…what's your name, kid?"

"Dat," I said, though I was tempted to tell him the truth.

"Dat and I will have a talk," he said to Phuong. "I'll meet you back at the house."

We went outside, and Phuong, displaying more than a little reluctance, headed off in the general direction of the trailer. It was going on dusk, and the fog was closing in. The many-colored bulbs strung in the trees close to the wall and lining the paths had been turned on; each bulb was englobed by a fuzzy halo, and altogether they imbued the encroaching jungle with an eerily festive air, as if the spirits lost in the dark green tangles were planning a party. We stood beside the wall, beneath the great hill rising from the shifting fogbank, and my father tried to convince me to hand over the code. When I refused, he offered money, and when I refused his money, he glared at me and said, "Maybe you don't get it. I really need the code. What's it going to take for you to give it to me?"

"Perhaps it's you who doesn't get it," I said. "If Vang wanted you to have the code he would have given it to you. But he gave it to me, and to no one else. I consider that a trust, and I won't break it unless he signifies that I should."

He looked off into the jungle, ran a hand across his scalp, and made a frustrated noise. I doubted he was experienced at rejection, and though it didn't satisfy my anger, it pleased me to have rejected him. Finally he laughed. "Either you're a hell of a businessman or an honorable man. Or maybe you're both. That's a scary notion." He shook his head in what I took for amiable acceptance. "Why not call Vang? Ask him if he'd mind having a talk with me."

I didn't understand how this was possible.

"What sort of computer do you own?" he asked.

I told him and he said, "That won't do it. Tell you what. Come over to my house tonight after your show. You can use my computer to contact him. I'll pay for your time."

I was suddenly suspicious. He seemed to be offering himself to me, making himself vulnerable, and I did not believe that was in his nature. His desire to contact Vang might be a charade. What if he had discovered my identity and was luring me into a trap?

"I don't know if I can get away," I said. "It may have to be in the morning."

He looked displeased, but said, "Very well." He fingered a business card from his pocket, gave it to me. "My address." Then he pressed what appeared to be a crystal button into my hand. "Don't lose it. Carry it with you whenever you come. If you don't, you'll be picked up on the street and taken somewhere quite unpleasant."

As soon as he was out of sight, I hurried over to the trailer, intending to sort things out with Tan. She was outside, sitting on a folding chair, framed by a spill of hazy yellow light from the door. Her head was down, and her blouse was torn, the top two buttons missing. I asked what was wrong; she shook her head and would not meet my eyes. But when I persisted she said, "That woman…the one who works for your father…."

"Phuong? Did she hurt you?"

She kept her head down, but I could see her chin quivering. "I was coming to find you, and I ran into her. She started talking to me. I thought she was just being friendly, but then she tried to kiss me. And when I resisted"—she displayed the tear in her blouse—"she did this."

She gathered herself. "She wants me to be with her tonight. If I refuse, she says she'll make trouble for us."

It would have been impossible for me to hate my father more, but this new insult, this threat to Tan, perfected it, added a finishing color, like the last brush stroke applied to a masterpiece. I stood a moment gazing off toward the hill—it seemed I had inside me an analogue to that forbidding shape, something equally stony and vast. I led Tan into the trailer, sat her down at the desk, and made her tea; then I repeated all my father had said. "Is it possible," I asked, "that Vang is my grandfather?"

She held the teacup in both hands, blew on the steaming liquid and took a sip. "I don't know. My family has always been secretive. All my parents told me was that Vang was once a wealthy man with a loving family, and that he had lost everything."

"If he is my grandfather," I said, "then we're cousins."

She set down the cup and stared dolefully into it as if she saw in its depths an inescapable resolution. "I don't care. If we were brother and sister, I wouldn't care."

I pulled her up, put my arms around her, and she pressed herself against me. I felt that I was at the center of an enormously complicated knot, too diminutive to be able to see all its loops and twists. If Vang was my grandfather, why had he treated me with such coldness? Perhaps my mother's death had deadened his heart, perhaps that explained it. But knowing that Tan and I were cousins, wouldn't he have told us the truth when he saw how close we were becoming? Or was he so old-fashioned that the idea of an intimate union between cousins didn't bother him? The most reasonable explanation was that my father had lied. I saw that now, saw it with absolute clarity. It was the only possibility that made sense. And if he had lied, it followed that he knew who I was. And if he knew who I was....

"I have to kill him," I said. "Tonight...it has to be tonight."

I was prepared to justify the decision, to explain why a course of inaction would be a greater risk, to lay out all the potentials of the situation for Tan to analyze, but she pushed me away, just enough so that she could see my face, and said, "You can't do it alone. That woman's a professional assassin." She rested her forehead against mine. "I'll help you."

"That's ridiculous! If I—"

"Listen to me, Philip! She can read physical signs, she can tell if someone's angry. If they're anxious. Well, she'll expect me to be angry. And anxious. She'll think it's just resentment...nerves. I'll be able to get close to her."

"And kill her? Will you be able to kill her?"

Tan broke from the embrace and went to stand at the doorway, gazing out at the fog. Her hair had come unbound, spilling down over her shoulders and back, the ribbon that had tied it dangling like a bright blue river winding across a ground of black silk.

"I'll ask Mei to give me something. She has herbs that will induce sleep." She glanced back at me. "There are things you can do to insure our safety once your father's dead. We should discuss them now."

I was amazed by her coolness, how easily she had made the transition from being distraught. "I can't ask you to do this," I said.

"You're not asking—I'm volunteering." I detected a note of sad distraction in her voice. "You'd do as much for me."

"Of course. But if it weren't for me, you wouldn't be involved in this."

"If it weren't for you," she said, the sadness even more evident in her tone, "I'd have no involvements at all."

▲▼▲

The first part of the show that evening, the entrance of the troupe to march music, Mei leading the way, wearing a red and white majorette's uniform, twirling—and frequently dropping—a baton, the tigers gamboling at her heels; then two comic skits; then Kai and Kim whirling and spinning aloft in their gold and sequined costumes, tumbling through the air happy as birds; then another skit and Tranh's clownish juggling, pretending to be drunk and making improbable catches as he tumbled, rolled, and staggered about...all this was received by the predominately male audience with a degree of ironic detachment. They laughed at Mei, they whispered and smirked during the skits, they stared dispassionately at Kim and Kai, and they jeered Tranh. It was plain that they had come to belittle us, that doing so validated their sense of superiority. I registered their reactions, but was so absorbed in thinking about what was to happen later, they seemed unreal, unimportant, and it took all my discipline to focus on my own act, a performance punctuated by a knife hurled from behind me that struck home between Tan's legs. There was a burst of enthusiastic cheers, and I turned to see Phuong some thirty feet away, taking a bow in the bleacher—it was she who had thrown the knife. She looked at me and shrugged, with that gesture dismissing my poor skills, and lifted her arms to receive the building applause. I searched the area around her for my father, but he was nowhere to be seen.

The audience remained abuzz, pleased that one of their own had achieved this victory, but when the major entered, led in by Mei and

Tranh, they fell silent at the sight of his dark, convulsed figure. Leaning on his staff, he hobbled along the edge of the bleachers, looking into this and that face as if hoping to find a familiar one, and then, moving to the center of the ring, he began to tell the story of Firebase Ruby. I was alarmed at first, but his delivery was eloquent, lyrical, not the plainspoken style in which he had originally couched the tale, and the audience was enthralled. When he came to tell of the letter he had written his wife detailing his hatred of all things Vietnamese, a uneasy muttering arose from the bleachers and rapt expressions turned to scowls; but then he was past that point, and as he described the Viet Cong assault, his listeners settled back and seemed once again riveted by his words.

"In the phosphor light of the hanging flares," he said, "I saw the blood-red ground spread out before me. Beyond the head-high hedgerows of coiled steel wire, black-clad men and women coursed from the jungle, myriad and quick as ants, and, inside the wire, emerging from their secret warrens, more sprouted from the earth like the demon yield of some infernal rain. All around me, my men were dying, and even in the midst of fear, I felt myself the object of a great calm observance, as if the tiny necklace-strung images of the Buddha the enemy held in their mouths when they attacked had been empowered to summon their ribbed original, and somewhere up above the flares, an enormous face had been conjured from the dark matter of the sky and was gazing down with serene approval.

"We could not hold the position long—that was clear. But I had no intention of surrendering. Drunk on whiskey and adrenaline, I was consumed by the thought of death, my own and others' and though I was afraid, I acted less out of fear than from the madness of battle and a kind of communion with death, a desire to make death grow and flourish and triumph. I retreated into the communications bunker and ordered the corporal in charge to call for an air strike on the coordinates of Firebase Ruby. When he balked I put a pistol to his head until he had obeyed. Then I emptied a clip into the radio so no one could countermand me."

The major bowed his head and spread his arms, as though preparing for a supreme display of magic; then his resonant voice sounded forth again, like the voice of a beast speaking from a cave, rough from the bones that have torn its throat. His eyes were chunks of phosphorous burning in the bark of a rotting log.

"When the explosions began, I was firing from a sandbagged position atop the communications bunker. The VC pouring from the jungle slowed their advance, milled about, and those inside the wire looked up in terror to see the jets screaming overhead, so low I could make out the stars on their wings. Victory was stitched across the sky in rocket trails. Gouts of flame gouged the red dirt, opening the tunnels to the air. The detonations began to blend one into the other, and the ground shook like a sheet of plywood under the pounding of a hammer. Clouds of marbled fire and smoke boiled across the earth, rising to form a dreadful second sky of orange and black, and I came to my feet, fearful yet delighted, astonished by the enormity of the destruction I had called down. Then I was knocked flat. Sandbags fell across my legs, a body flung from God knows where landed on my back, driving the breath from me, and in the instant before consciousness fled, I caught the rich stink of napalm.

"In the morning, I awoke and saw a bloody, jawless face with staring blue eyes pressed close to mine, looking as if it were still trying to convey a last desperate message. I clawed my way from beneath the corpse and staggered upright to find myself the lord of a killed land, of a raw, red scar littered with corpses in the midst of a charcoaled forest. I went down from the bunker and wandered among the dead. From every quarter issued the droning of flies. Everywhere lay arms, legs, and grisly relics I could not identify. I was numb, I had no feeling apart from a pale satisfaction at having survived. But as I wandered among the dead, taking notice of the awful intimacies death had imposed: a dozen child-sized bodies huddled in a crater, anonymous as a nest of scorched beetles; a horribly burned woman with buttocks exposed reaching out a clawed hand to touch the lips of a disembodied head—these and a hundred other such scenes brought home the truth that I was their author. It wasn't guilt I felt then. Guilt was irrelevant. We were all guilty, the dead and the living, the good and those who had abandoned God. Guilt is our inevitable portion of the world's great trouble. No, it was the recognition that at the moment when I knew the war was lost—my share of it, at least—I chose not to cut my losses but to align myself with a force so base and negative that we refuse to admit its place in human nature and dress it in mystical clothing and call it Satan or Shiva so as to separate it from ourselves. Perhaps this sort of choice is a soldier's virtue, but I can no longer view it in that light." He tapped his chest with the tip of his staff. "Though I will never say that my enemies were just, there is justice in what I have endured since that day. All men sin, all men do evil. And evil shows itself in our faces." Here he aimed the staff at the audience and tracked it from face-to-face, as if highlighting the misdeeds imprinted on each. "What you see of me now is not the man I was, but the thing I became at the instant I made my choice. Take from my story what you will, but understand this: I am unique only in that the judgment of my days is inscribed not merely on my face, but upon every inch of my body. We are all of us monsters waiting to be summoned forth by a moment of madness and pride."

As Tranh and I led him from the tent, across the damp grass, the major was excited, almost incoherently so, not by the acclaim he had received, but because he had managed to complete his story. He plucked at my sleeve, babbling, bobbing his head, but I paid him no mind, concerned about Tan, whom I had seen talking to Phuong in the bleachers. And when she came running from the main tent, a windbreaker thrown over her costume; I forgot him entirely.

"We're not going directly back to the house," she said. "She wants to take me to a club on the square. I don't know when we'll get to your father's."

"Maybe this isn't such a good idea. I think we should wait until morning."

"It's all right," she said. "Go to the house and as soon as you've dealt with your father, do exactly what I told you. When you hear us enter the house, stay out of sight. Don't do a thing until I come and get you. Understand?"

"I don't know," I said, perplexed at the way she had taken charge.

"Please!" She grabbed me by the lapels. "Promise you'll do as I say! Please!"

I promised, but as I watched her run off into the dark I had a resurgence of my old sense of dislocation, and though I had not truly listened to the major's story, having been occupied with my own troubles, the sound of him sputtering and chortling behind me, gloating over the treasure of his recovered memory, his invention, whatever it was, caused me to wonder then about the nature of my own choice, and the story that I might someday tell.

▲▼▲

My father's house was on Yen Phu Street—two stories of pocked gray stone with green vented shutters and a green door with a knocker carved in the shape of a water buffalo's head. I arrived shortly after midnight and stood in the lee of the high whitewashed wall that enclosed his compound. The fog had been cut by a steady drizzle, and no pedestrians were about. Light slanted from the vents of a shuttered upstairs window, and beneath it was parked a bicycle in whose basket rested a dozen white lilies, their stems wrapped in butcher paper. I imagined that my father had ridden the bicycle to market and had forgotten to retrieve the flowers after carrying his other purchases inside. They seemed omenical in their glossy pallor, a sterile emblem of the bloody work ahead.

The idea of killing my father held no terrors for me—I had performed the act in my mind hundreds of times, I'd conceived its every element—and as I stood there I felt the past accumulating at my back like the cars of a train stretching for eighteen years, building from my mother's death to the shuddering engine of the moment I was soon to inhabit. All the misgivings that earlier had nagged at me melted away, like fog before rain. I was secure in my hatred and in the knowledge that I had no choice, that my father was a menace who would never fade.

I crossed the street, knocked, and after a few seconds he admitted me into a brightly lit alcove with a darkened room opening off to the right. He was dressed in a voluminous robe of green silk, and as he proceeded me up the stairway to the left of the alcove, the sight of his bell-like shape and bald head with the silver plate collaring the base of his skull...these things along with the odor of jasmine incense led me to imagine that I was being escorted to an audience with some mysterious religious figure by one of his eunuch priests. At the head of the stair was a narrow white room furnished with two padded chrome chairs, a wallscreen, and, at the far end, a desk bearing papers, an ornamental vase, an old-fashioned letter opener, and a foot-high gilt and bronze Buddha. My father sat down in one of the chairs, triggered the wall screen's computer mode with a penlight, and set about accessing the Sony AI, working through various menus, all the while chatting away, saying he was sorry he'd missed our show, he hoped to attend the following night, and how was I enjoying my stay in Binh Khoi, it often seemed an unfriendly place to newcomers, but by week's end I'd feel right at home. I had brought no weapon, assuming that his security would detect it. The letter opener, I thought, would do the job. But my hand fell instead to the Buddha. It would be cleaner, I decided. A single blow. I picked it up, hefted it. I had anticipated that when the moment arrived, I would want to make myself known to my father, to relish his shock and dismay; but I understood that was no longer important, and I only wanted him to die. In any case, since he likely knew the truth about me, the dramatic scene I'd envisioned would be greatly diminished.

"That's Thai. Fifteenth century," he said, nodding at the statue, then returned his attention to the screen. "Beautiful, isn't it?"

"Very," I said.

Then, without a thought, all thinking necessary having already been done, and the deed itself merely an automatic function, the final surge of an eighteen-year-long momentum, I stepped behind him and swung the statue at the back of his head. I expected to hear a crack but the sound of impact was plush, muffled, such as might be caused by the flat of one's hand striking a pillow. He let out an explosive grunt, toppled with a twisting motion against the wall, ending up on his side, facing outward. There was so much blood, I assumed he must be dead. But then he groaned, his eyes blinked open, and he struggled to his knees. I saw that I'd hit the silver plate at the base of his skull. Blood was flowing out around the plate, but it had protected him from mortal damage. His robe had fallen open, and with his pale mottled belly bulging from the green silk and the blood streaking his neck, his smallish features knitted in pain and perplexity, he looked gross and clownishly pitiable. He held up an unsteady hand to block a second blow. His mouth worked, and he said, "Wait..." or "What...." Which, I can't be sure. But I was in no mood either to wait or to explain myself. A clean death might not have affected me so deeply, but that I had made of a whole healthy life this repellent half-dead thing wobbling at my feet—it assaulted my moral foundation, it washed the romantic tint of revenge from the simple, terrible act of slaughter, and when I struck at him again, this time smashing the statue down two-handed onto the top of his skull, I was charged with the kind of fear that afflicts a child when he more-or-less by accident wounds a bird with a stone and seeks to hide the act from God by tossing his victim onto an ash heap. My father sagged onto his back, blood gushing from his nose and mouth. I caught a whiff of feces and staggered away, dropping the Buddha. Now that my purpose had been accomplished, like a bee dying from having stung its enemy, I felt drained of poison, full of dull surprise that there had been no more rewarding result.

The penlight had rolled beneath the second chair. I picked it up, and, following Tan's instructions, I used the computer to contact a security agency in Danang. A blond woman with a brittle manner appeared on the screen and asked my business. I explained my circumstances, not bothering to characterize the murder as anything other than it was—the size of my trust would guarantee my legal immunity—and also provided her with the number of Vang's lawyer, as well as some particulars concerning the trust, thereby establishing my bona fides. The woman vanished, her image replaced by a shifting pattern of pastel colors, and, after several minutes, this in turn was replaced by a contract form with a glowing blue patch at the bottom to which I pressed the ball of my thumb. The woman reappeared, much more solicitous now, and cautioned me to remain where I was. She assured me that an armed force would be at the house within the hour. As an afterthought, she advised me to wipe the blood from my face.

The presence of the body—its meat reality—made me uncomfortable. I picked up the letter opener and went down the stairs and groped my way across the unlit room off the alcove and found a chair in a corner from which I could see the door. Sitting alone in the darkness amplified the torpor that had pervaded me, and though I sensed certain unsettling dissonances surrounding what had just taken place, I was not sufficiently alert to consider them as other than aggravations. I had been sitting there for perhaps ten minutes when the door opened and Phoung, laughing, stepped into the alcove with Tan behind her, wearing a blue skirt and checkered blouse. She kicked the door shut, pushed Tan against the wall, and began to kiss her, running a hand up under her skirt. Then her head snapped around, and although I didn't believe she could see in the dark, she stared directly at me.

Before I could react, before I could be sure that Phuong had detected me, Tan struck her beneath the jaw with the heel of her left hand, driving her against the opposite wall, and followed this with a kick to the stomach. Phuong rolled away and up into a crouch. She cried out my father's name: "William!" Whether in warning or—recognizing what had happened—in grief, I cannot say. Then the two women began to fight. It lasted no more than half-a-minute, but their speed and eerie grace were incredible to see: like watching two long-fingered witches dancing in a bright patch of weakened gravity and casting violent spells. Dazed by Tan's initial blows, Phoung went on the defensive, but soon she recovered and started to hold her own. I remembered the letter opener in my hand. The thing was poorly balanced and Phuong's quickness made the timing hard to judge, but then she paused, preparing to launch an attack and I flung the opener, lodging it squarely between her shoulderblades. Not a mortal wound—the blade was too dull to bite deep—but a distracting one. She shrieked, tried to reach the opener, and, as she reeled to the side, Tan came up behind her and broke her neck with a savage twist. She let the body fall and walked toward me, a shadow in the darkened room. It seemed impossible that she was the same woman I had known on the beach at Vung Tau, and I felt a spark of fear.

"Are you all right?" she asked, stopping a few feet away.

"All right?" I laughed. "What's going on here?"

She gave no reply, and I said, "Apparently you decided against using Mei's herbs."

"If you had done as I asked, if you'd stayed clear, it might not have been necessary to kill her." She came another step forward. "Have you called for security?"

I nodded. "Did you learn to fight like that in Hue?"

"In China," she said.

"At a private security company. Like Phuong."

"Yes."

"Then it would follow that you're not Vang's niece."

"But I am," she said. "He used the last of his fortune to have me trained so I could protect you. He was a bitter man...to have used his family so."

"And I suppose sleeping with me falls under the umbrella of protection."

She kneeled beside the chair, put a hand on my neck, and gazed at me entreatingly. "I love you, Philip. I would do anything for you. How can you doubt it?"

I was moved by her sincerity, but I could not help but to treat her coldly. It was as if a valve had been twisted shut to block the flow of my emotions. "That's right," I said. "Vang told me that your kind were conditioned to bond with their clients."

I watched the words hit home, a wounded expression washing across her features, then fading, like a ripple caused by a pebble dropped into a still pond. "Is that so important?" she asked. "Does it alter the fact that you fell in love with me?"

I ignored this, yet I was tempted to tell her, No, it did not. "If you were trained to protect me, why did Vang discourage our relationship?"

She got to her feet, her face unreadable, and went a few paces toward the alcove; she appeared to be staring at Phuong's body, lying crumpled in the light. "There was a time when I think he wanted me for himself. That may explain it."

"Did Phoung really accost you?" I asked. "Or was that—"

"I've never lied to you. I've deceived you by not revealing everything I knew about Vang," she said. "But I was bound to obey him in that. As you said, I've been conditioned."

I had other questions, but I could not frame one of them. The silence of the house seemed to breed a faint humming, and I became oppressed by the idea that Tan and I were living analogues of the two corpses, that the wealth I was soon to receive as a consequence of our actions would lead us to a pass wherein we would someday lie dead in separate rooms of a silent house, while two creatures like ourselves but younger would stand apart from one another in fretful isolation, pondering their future. I wanted to dispossess myself of this notion, to contrive a more potent reality, and I crossed the room to Tan and turned her to face me. She refused to meet my eyes, but I tipped up her chin and kissed her. A lover's kiss. I touched her breasts—a treasuring touch. But despite the sweet affirmation and openness of the kiss, I think it also served a formal purpose, the sealing of a bargain whose terms we did not fully understand.

▲▼▲

Six months and a bit after my eighteenth birthday, I was sitting in a room in the Sony offices in Saigon, a windowless space with black walls and carpet and silver-framed photographs of scenes along the Perfume River and in the South China Sea, when Vang flickered into being against the far wall. I thought I must seem to him, as he seemed to me, like a visitation, a figure from another time manifested in a dream. He appeared no different than he had on the day he left the circus—thin and gray-haired, dressed in careworn clothing—and his attitude toward me was, as ever, distant. I told him what had happened in Binh Khoi, and he said, "I presumed you would have more trouble with William. Of course, he thought he had leverage over me—he thought he had Tan in his clutches. So he let his guard down. He believed he had nothing to fear."

His logic was overly simplistic, but rather than pursue this, I asked the question foremost on my mind: why had he not told me that he was my grandfather? I had uncovered quite a lot about my past in the process of familiarizing myself with Vang's affairs, but I wanted to hear it all.

"Because I'm not your grandfather," he said. "I was William's father-in-law, but…." He shot me an amused look. "I should have thought you would have understood all this by now."

I saw no humor in the situation. "Explain it to me."

"As you wish." He paced away from me, stopped to inspect one of the framed photographs. "William engineered the death of my wife, my daughter, and my grandson in a plane crash. Once he had isolated me, he challenged my mental competency, intending to take over my business concerns. To thwart him, I faked my suicide. It was a very convincing fake. I used a body I'd had cloned to supply me with organs. I kept enough money to support Green Star and to pay for Tan's training. The rest you know."

"Not so," I said. "You haven't told me who I am."

"Ah, yes." He turned from the photograph and smiled pleasantly at me. "I suppose that would interest you. Your mother's name was Tuyet. Tuyet Su Vanh. She was an actress in various pornographic media. The woman you saw in your dream—that was she. We had a relationship for several years, then we drifted apart. Not long before I lost my family, she came to me and told me she was dying. One of the mutated HIVs. She said she'd borne a child by me. A son. She begged me to take care of you. I didn't believe her, of course. But she had given me pleasure, so I set up a trust for you. A small one."

"And then you decided to use me."

"William had undermined my authority to the extent that I could not confront him directly. I needed an arrow to aim at his heart. I told your mother that if she cooperated with me I'd adopt you, place my fortune in the trust, and make you my heir. She gave permission to have your memory wiped. I wanted you empty so I could fill you with my purpose. After you were re-educated, she helped construct some fragmentary memories that were implanted by means of a biochip. Nonetheless, you were a difficult child to mold. I couldn't be certain that you would seek William out, and so, since I was old and tired and likely not far from Heaven, I decided to feign an illness and withdraw. This allowed me to arrange a confrontation without risk to myself."

I should have hated Vang, but after six months of running his businesses, of viewing the world from a position of governance and control, I understood him far too well to hate—though at that moment, understanding the dispassionate requisites and protocols of such a position seemed as harsh a form of judgment as the most bitter of hatreds. "What happened to my mother?" I asked.

"I arranged for her to receive terminal care in an Australian hospital."

"And her claim that I was your biological son....did you investigate it?"

"Why should I? It didn't matter. A man in my position could not acknowledge an illegitimate child, and once I had made my decision to abdicate my old life, it mattered even less. If it has any meaning for you, there are medical records you can access."

"I think I'd prefer it to remain a mystery," I told him.

"You've no reason to be angry at me," he said. "I've made you wealthy. And what did it cost? A few memories."

I shifted in my chair, steepled my hands on my stomach. "Are you convinced that my...that William had your family killed? He seemed to think there had been a misunderstanding."

"That was a charade! If you're asking whether or not I had proof—of course I didn't. William knew how to disguise his hand."

"So everything you did was based solely on the grounds of your suspicions."

"No! It was based on my knowledge of the man!" His tone softened.

"What does it matter? Only William and I knew the truth, and he is dead. If you doubt me, if you pursue this further, you'll never be able to satisfy yourself."

"I suppose you're right," I said, getting to my feet.

"Are you leaving already? " He wore an aggrieved expression. "I was hoping you'd tell me about Tan...and Green Star. What has happened with my little circus?"

"Tan is well. As for Green Star, I gave it to Mei and Tranh." I opened the door, and Vang made a gesture of restraint. "Stay awhile longer, Philip. Please. You and Tan are the only people with whom I have an emotional connection. It heartens me to spend time with you."

Hearing him describe our relationship in these terms gave me pause. I recalled the conversation in which Tan had asserted that something central to the idea of life died when one was uploaded into Heaven—Vang's uncharacteristic claim to an emotional debt caused me to think that he might well be, as she'd described her parents, a colored shadow, a cunningly contrived representation of the original. I hoped that this was not the case; I hoped that he was alive in every respect.

"I have to go," I said. "Business, you understand. But I have some news that may interest to you."

"Oh?" he said eagerly "Tell me."

"I've invested heavily in Sony, and, through negotiation, I've arranged for one of your old companies—Intertech of Hanoi—to be placed in charge of overseeing the virtual environment. I would expect you're soon going to see some changes in your particular part of Heaven."

He seemed nonplused, then a look of alarm dawned on his face. "What are you going to do?"

"Me? Not a thing." I smiled, and the act of smiling weakened my emotional restraint—a business skill I had not yet perfected—and let anger roughen my voice. "It's much more agreeable to have your dirty work handled by others, don't you think?"

▲▼▲

On occasion, Tan and I manage to rekindle an intimacy that reminds us of the days when we first were lovers, but these occasions never last for long, and our relationship is plagued by the lapses into neutrality or worse—indifference that tends to plague any two people who have spent ten years in each other's company. In our case these lapses are often accompanied by bouts of self-destructive behavior. It seems we're punishing ourselves for having experienced what we consider an undeserved happiness. Even our most honest infidelities are inclined to be of the degrading sort. I understand this. The beach at Vung Tau, once the foundation of our union, has been replaced by a night on Yen Phu Street in Binh Khoi, and no edifice built upon such imperfect stone could be other than cracked and deficient. Nonetheless, we both realize that whatever our portion of contentment in this world, we are fated to seek it together.

From time to time, I receive a communication from Vang. He does not look well, and his tone is always desperate, cajoling. I tell myself that I should relent and restore him to the afterlife for which he contracted; but I am not highly motivated in that regard. If there truly is something that dies when one ascends to Heaven, I fear it has already died in me, and I blame Vang for this.

Seven years after my talk with Vang, Tan and I attended a performance of the circus in the village of Loc Noi. There was a new James Bond Cochise, Kai and Kim had become pretty teenagers, both Tranh and Mei were thinner, but otherwise things were much the same. We sat in the main tent after the show and reminisced. The troupe—Mei in particular—were unnerved by my bodyguards, but all in all, it was a pleasant reunion.

After a while, I excused myself and went to see the major. He was huddled in his tent, visible by the weird flickerings in his eyes...though as my vision adapted to the dark, I was able make out the cowled shape of his head against the canvas backdrop. Tranh had told me he did not expect the major to live much longer, and now that I was close to him, I found that his infirmity was palpable, I could hear it in his labored breath. I asked if he knew who I was, and he replied without inflection, as he had so many years before, "Philip." I'd hoped that he would be more forthcoming, because I still felt akin to him, related through the cryptic character of our separate histories, and I thought that he might once have sensed that kinship, that he'd had some diffuse knowledge of the choices I confronted, and had designed the story of Firebase Ruby for my benefit, shaping it as a cautionary tale—one I'd failed to heed. But perhaps I'd read too much into what was sheer coincidence. I touched his hand, and his breath caught, then shuddered forth, heavy as a sob. All that remained for him were a few stories, a few hours in the light. I tried to think of something I could do to ease his last days, but I knew death was the only mercy that could mend him.

Mei invited Tan and I to spend the night in the trailer—for old times sake, she said—and we were of no mind to refuse. We both yearned for those old times, despite neither of us believing that we could recapture them. Watching Tan prepare for bed, it seemed to me that she had grown too vivid for the drab surroundings, her beauty become too cultivated and too lush. But when she slipped in beside me, when we began to make love on that creaky bunk, the years fell away and she felt like a girl in my arms, tremulous and new to such customs, and I was newly awakened to her charms. She drifted off to sleep afterward with her head on my chest, and as I lay there trying to quiet my breath so not to wake her, it came to me that future and past were joined in the darkness that enclosed us, two black rivers flowing together, and I understood that while the circus would go its own way in the morning and we would go ours, those rivers, too, were forever joined—we shared a confluence and a wandering course, and a moment proof against the world's denial, and we would always be a troupe, Kim and Kai, Mei and Tranh, Tan and I, and the major...that living ghost who, like myself was the figment of a tragic past he never knew, or—if, indeed, he knew it—with which he could never come to terms. It was a bond that could not save us, from either our enemies or ourselves, but it held out a hope of simple glory, a promise truer than Heaven. Illusory or not, all our wars would continue until their cause was long-forgotten under the banner of Radiant Green Star. —

Only Partly Here

There are legends in the pit. Phantoms and apparitions. The men who work at Ground Zero joke about them, but their laughter is nervous and wired. Bobby doesn't believe the stories, yet he's prepared to believe something weird might happen. The place feels so empty. Like even the ghosts are gone. All that sudden vacancy, who knows what might have entered in? Two nights ago on the graveyard shift, some guy claimed he saw a faceless figure wearing a black spiky headdress standing near the pit wall. The job breaks everybody down. Marriages are falling apart. People keep losing it one way or another.

Fights, freak-outs, fits of weeping. It's the smell of burning metal that seeps up from the earth, the ceremonial stillness of the workers after they uncover a body, the whispers that come when there is no wind. It's the things you find. The week before, scraping at the rubble with a hoe, like an archaeologist investigating a buried temple, Bobby spotted a woman's shoe sticking up out of the ground. A perfect shoe, so pretty and sleek and lustrous. Covered in blue silk. Then he reached for it and realized that it wasn't stuck—it was only half a shoe, with delicate scorching along the ripped edge. Now sometimes when he closes his eyes he sees the shoe. He's glad he isn't married. He doesn't think he has much to bring to a relationship.

That evening Bobby's taking his dinner break, perched on a girder at the edge of the pit along with Mazurek and Pineo, when they switch on the lights. They all hate how the pit looks in the lights. It's an outtake from *The X-Files*—the excavation of an alien ship under hot white lamps smoking from the cold; the shard left from the framework of the north tower glittering silver and strange, like the wreckage of a cosmic machine. The three men remain silent for a bit, then Mazurek goes back to bitching about Jason Giambi signing with the Yankees. You catch the interview he did with Werner Wolf? He's a moron! First time the crowd gets on him, it's gonna be like when you yell at a dog. The guy's gonna fucking crumble. Pineo disagrees, and Mazurek asks Bobby what he thinks.

"Bobby don't give a shit about baseball," says Pineo. "My boy's a Jets fan."

Mazurek, a thick-necked, fiftyish man whose face appears to be fashioned of interlocking squares of pale muscle, says, "The Jets…fuck!"

"They're play-off bound," says Bobby cheerfully.

Mazurek crumples the wax paper his sandwich was folded in. "They gonna drop dead in the first round like always."

"It's more interesting than being a Yankee fan," says Bobby. "The Yankees are too corporate to be interesting."

"'Too corporate to be interesting'?" Mazurek stares. "You really are a geek, y'know that?"

"That's me. The geek."

"Whyn't you go the fuck back to school, boy? Fuck you doing here, anyway?"

"Take it easy, Carl! Chill!" Pineo—nervous, thin, lively, curly black hair spilling from beneath his hard hat—puts a hand on Mazurek's arm, and Mazurek knocks it aside. Anger tightens his leathery skin; the creases in his neck show white. "What's it with you? You taking notes for your fucking thesis?" he asks Bobby. "Playing tourist?"

Bobby looks down at the apple in his hand—it seems too shiny to be edible. "Just cleaning up is all. You know."

Mazurek's eyes dart to the side, then he lowers his head and gives it a savage shake. "Okay," he says in a subdued voice. "Yeah…fuck. Okay."

▲▼▲

Midnight, after the shift ends, they walk over to the Blue Lady. Bobby doesn't altogether understand why the three of them continue to hang out there. Maybe because they once went to the bar after work and it felt pretty good, so they return every night in hopes of having it feel that good again. You can't head straight home; you have to decompress. Mazurek's wife gives him constant shit about the practice—she calls the bar and screams over the phone. Pineo just split with his girlfriend. The guy with whom Bobby shares an apartment grins when he sees him, but the grin is anxious—like he's afraid Bobby is bringing back some contagion from the pit. Which maybe he is. The first time he went to Ground Zero, he came home with a cough and a touch of fever, and he recalls thinking that the place was responsible. Now, though, either he's immune or else he's sick all the time and doesn't notice.

Two hookers at a table by the door check them out as they enter, then go back to reading the *Post.* Roman the barman, gray-haired and thick-waisted, orders his face into respectful lines, says, "Hey guys!" and sets them up with beers and shots. When they started coming in he treated them with almost religious deference, until Mazurek yelled at him, saying he didn't want to hear that hero crap while he was trying to unwind—he got enough of it from the fuckass jocks and movie stars who visit Ground Zero to have their pictures taken. Though angry, he was far more articulate than usual in his demand for normal treatment, and this caused Bobby to speculate that if Mazurek were transported thousands of miles from the pit and not just a few blocks, his IQ would increase exponentially.

The slim brunette in the business suit is down at the end of the bar again, sitting beneath the blue neon silhouette of a dancing woman. She's been coming in every night for about a week. Late twenties. Hair styled short, an expensive kind of punky look. Fashion-model hair. Eyebrows thick and slanted, like *accents grave.* Sharp-featured, on the brittle side of pretty, or maybe she's not that pretty, maybe she is so well-dressed, her make-up done so skillfully, that the effect is of a businesslike prettiness, of prettiness reined in by the magic of brush and multiple applicators, and beneath this artwork she is, in actuality, rather plain. Nice body, though. Trim and well-tended. She wears the same expression of stony neutrality that Bobby sees every morning on the faces of the women who charge up from under the earth, disgorged from the D train, prepared to resist Manhattan for another day. Guys will approach her, assuming she's a hooker doing a kind of Hitler office-bitch thing in order to attract men searching for a woman they can use and abuse as a surrogate for one who makes their life hell every day from nine to five, and she will say something to them and they will immediately walk away. Bobby and Pineo always try to guess what she says. That night, after a couple of shots, Bobby goes over and sits beside her. She smells expensive. Her perfume like the essence of some exotic flower or fruit he's only seen in magazine pictures.

"I've just been to a funeral," she says wearily, staring into her drink. "So, please.... Okay?"

"That what you tell everybody?" he asks. "All the guys who hit on you?"

A fretful line cuts her brow. "Please!"

"No, really. I'll go. All I want to know...that what you always say?"

She makes no response.

"It is," he says. "Isn't it?"

"It's not entirely a lie." Her eyes are spooky, the dark rims of the pale irises extraordinarily well-defined. "It's intended as a lie, but it's true in a way."

"But that's what you say, right? To everybody?"

"This is why you came over? You're not hitting on me?"

"No, I…I mean, maybe…I thought…."

"So what you're saying, you weren't intending to hit on me. You wanted to know what I say to men when they come over. But now you're not certain of your intent? Maybe you were deceiving yourself as to your motives? Or maybe now you sense I might be receptive, you'll take the opportunity to hit on me, though that wasn't your initial intent. Does that about sum it up?"

"I suppose," he says.

She gives him a cautious look. "Could you be brilliant? Could your clumsy delivery be designed to engage me?"

"I'll go away, okay? But that's what you said to them, right?"

She points to the barman, who's talking to Mazurek. "Roman tells me you work at Ground Zero."

The question unsettles Bobby, leads him to suspect that she's a disaster groupie, looking for a taste of the pit, but he says, "Yeah."

"It's really…." She does a little shivery shrug. "Strange."

"Strange. I guess that covers it."

"That's not what I wanted to say. I can't think of the right word to describe what it does to me."

"You been down in it?"

"No, I can't get any closer than here. I just can't. But…." She makes a swirling gesture with her fingers. "You can feel it here. You might not notice, because you're down there all the time. That's why I come here. Everybody's going on with their lives, but I'm not ready. I need to feel it. To understand it. You're taking it away piece by piece, but the more you take away, it's like you're uncovering something else."

"Y'know, I don't want to think about this now." He gets to his feet. "But I guess I know why you want to."

"Probably it's fucked up of me, huh?"

"Yeah, probably," says Bobby, and walks away.

"She's still looking at you, man," Pineo says as Bobby settles beside him. "What you doing back here? You could be fucking that."

"She's a freak," Bobby tells him.

"So she's a freak! Even better!" Pineo turns to the other two men. "You believe this asshole? He could be fucking that bitch over there, yet here he sits."

Affecting a superior smile, Roman says, "You don't fuck them, pal. They fuck *you*."

He nudges Mazurek's arm as though seeking confirmation from a peer, a man of experience like himself, and Mazurek, gazing at his grungy reflection in the mirror behind the bar, says distractedly, weakly, "I could use another shot."

▲▼▲

The following afternoon Bobby unearths a disk of hard black rubber from beneath some cement debris. It's four inches across, thicker at the center than at the edges, shaped like a little UFO. Try as he might, he can think of no possible purpose it might serve, and he wonders if it had something to do with the fall of the towers. Perhaps there is a black seed like this at the heart of every disaster. He shows it to Pineo, asks his opinion, and Pineo, as expected, says, "Fuck, I don't know. Part of a machine." Bobby knows Pineo is right. The disk is a widget, one of those undistinguished yet indispensable objects without which elevators will not rise or refrigerators will not cool; but there are no marks on it, no holes or grooves to indicate that it fits inside a machine. He imagines it whirling inside a cone of blue radiance, registering some inexplicable process.

He thinks about the disk all evening, assigning it various values. It is the irreducible distillate of the event, a perfectly formed residue. It is a wicked sacred object that belonged to a financier, now deceased, and its ritual function is understood by only three other men on the planet. It is a beacon left by time-traveling tourists that allows them to home in on the exact place and moment of the terrorist attack. It is the petrified eye of God. He intends to take the disk back to his apartment and put it next to the half-shoe and all the rest of the items he has collected in the pit. But that night when he enters the Blue Lady and sees the brunette at the end of the bar, on impulse he goes over and drops the disk on the counter next to her elbow.

"Brought you something," he says.

She glances at it, pokes it with a forefinger and sets it wobbling. "What is it?"

He shrugs. "Just something I found."

"At Ground Zero?"

"Uh-huh."

She pushes the disk away. "Didn't I make myself plain last night?"

Bobby says, "Yeah...sure," but isn't sure he grasps her meaning.

"I want to understand what happened...what's happening now," she says. "I want what's mine, you know. I want to understand exactly what it's done to me. I need to understand it. I'm not into souvenirs."

"Okay," Bobby says.

"'Okay.'" She says this mockingly. "God, what's wrong with you? It's like you're on medication!"

A Sinatra song, "All Or Nothing At All," flows from the jukebox—a soothing musical syrup that overwhelms the chatter of hookers and drunks and commentary from the TV mounted behind the bar, which is showing chunks of Afghanistan blowing up into clouds of brown smoke. The crawl running at the bottom of the screen testifies that the estimate of the death toll at Ground Zero has been reduced to just below five thousand; the amount of debris removed from the pit now exceeds one million tons. The numbers seem meaningless, interchangeable. A million lives, five thousand tons. A ludicrous score that measures no real result.

"I'm sorry," the brunette says. "I know it must take a toll, doing what you do. I'm impatient with everyone these days."

She stirs her drink with a plastic stick whose handle duplicates the image of the neon dancer. In all her artfully composed face, a mask of foundation and blush and liner, her eyes are the only sign of vitality, of feminine potential.

"What's your name?" he asks.

She glances up sharply. "I'm too old for you."

"How old are you? I'm twenty-three."

"It doesn't matter how old you are...how old I am. I'm much older than you in my head. Can't you tell? Can't you feel the difference? If I was twenty-three, I'd still be too old for you."

"I just want to know your name."

"Alicia." She enunciates the name with a cool overstated precision that makes him think of a saleswoman revealing a price she knows her customer cannot afford.

"Bobby," he says. "I'm in grad school at Columbia. But I'm taking a year off."

"This is ridiculous!" she says angrily. "Unbelievably ridiculous... totally ridiculous! Why are you doing this?"

"I want to understand what's going on with you."

"Why?"

"I don't know, I just do. Whatever it is you come to understand, I want to understand it, too. Who knows. Maybe us talking is part of what you need to understand."

"Good Lord!" She casts her eyes to the ceiling. "You're a romantic!"

"You still think I'm trying to hustle you?"

"If it was anyone else, I'd say yes. But you...I don't believe you have a clue."

"And you do? Sitting here every night. Telling guys you just got back from a funeral. Grieving about something you can't even say what it is."

She twitches her head away, a gesture he interprets as the avoidance of impulse, a sudden clamping-down, and he also relates it to how he sometimes reacts on the subway when a girl he's been looking at catches his eye and he pretends to be looking at something else. After a long silence she says, "We're not going to be having sex. I want you to be clear on that."

"Okay."

"That's your fall-back position, is it? 'Okay'?"

"Whatever."

"'Whatever.'" She curls her fingers around her glass, but does not drink. "Well, we've probably had enough mutual understanding for one night, don't you think?"

Bobby pockets the rubber disk, preparing to leave. "What do you do for a living?"

An exasperated sigh. "I work in a brokerage. Now can we take a break? Please?"

"I gotta go home anyway," Bobby says.

▲▼▲

The rubber disk takes its place in Bobby's top dresser drawer, resting between the blue half-shoe and a melted glob of metal that may have done duty as a cuff-link, joining a larger company of remnants—scraps of silk and worsted and striped cotton; a flattened fountain pen; a few inches of brown leather hanging from a misshapen buckle; a hinged pin once attached to a brooch. Looking at them breeds a queer vacancy in his chest, as if their few ounces of reality cancel out some equivalent portion of his own. It's the shoe, mostly, that wounds him. An object so powerful in its interrupted grace, sometimes he's afraid to touch it.

After his shower he lies down in the dark of his bedroom and thinks of Alicia. Pictures her handling packets of bills bound with paper wrappers. Even her name sounds like currency, a riffling of crisp new banknotes. He wonders what he's doing with her. She's not his type at all, but maybe she was right, maybe he's deceiving himself about his motives. He conjures up the images of the girls he's been with. Soft and sweet and ultra-feminine. Yet he finds Alicia's sharp edges and severity attractive. Could be he's looking for a little variety. Or maybe like so many people in the city, like lab rats stoned on coke and electricity, his circuits are scrambled and his brain is sending out irrational messages. He wants to talk to her, though. That much he's certain of—he wants to unburden himself. Tales of the pit. His drawer full of relics. He wants to explain that they're not souvenirs. They are the pins upon which he hangs whatever it is he has to leave behind each morning when he goes to work. They are proof of something he once thought a profound abstraction, something too elusive to frame in words, but has come to realize is no more than the fact of his survival. This fact, he tells himself, might be all that Alicia needs to understand.

Despite having urged Bobby on, Pineo taunts him about Alicia the next afternoon. His manic edginess has acquired an angry tonality. He takes to calling Alicia "Calculator Bitch." Bobby expects Mazurek to join in, but it seems he is withdrawing from their loose union, retreating into some private pit. He goes about his work with oxlike steadiness and eats in silence. When Bobby suggests that he might want to seek counseling, a comment designed to inflame, to reawaken the man's innate ferocity, Mazurek mutters something about maybe having a talk with one of the chaplains. Though they have only a few basic geographical concerns in common, the three men have sustained one another against the stresses of the job, and that afternoon, as Bobby scratches at the dirt, now turning to mud under a cold drenching rain, he feels abandoned, imperiled by the pit. It all looks unfamiliar and inimical. The silvery lattice of the framework appears to be trembling, as if receiving a transmission from beyond, and the nest of massive girders might be awaiting the return of a fabulous winged monster. Bobby tries to distract himself, but nothing he can come up with serves to brighten his sense of oppression. Toward the end of the shift, he begins to worry that they are laboring under an illusion, that the towers will suddenly snap back in from the dimension into which they have been nudged and everyone will be crushed.

The Blue Lady is nearly empty that night when they arrive. Hookers in the back, Alicia in her customary place. The juke box is off, the TV muttering—a blonde woman is interviewing a balding man with a graphic beneath his image that identifies him as an anthrax expert. They sit at the bar and stare at the TV, tossing back drinks with dutiful regularity, speaking only when it's necessary. The anthrax expert is soon replaced by a terrorism expert who holds forth on the disruptive potentials of Al Qaeda. Bobby can't relate to the discussion. The political sky with its wheeling black shapes and noble music and secret masteries is not the sky he lives and works beneath, gray and changeless, simple as a coffin lid.

"Al Qaeda," Roman says. "Didn't he useta play second base for the Mets? Puerto Rican guy?"

The joke falls flat, but Roman's in stand-up mode.

"How many Al Qaedas does it take to screw in a light bulb?" he asks. Nobody has an answer.

"Two million," says Roman. "One to hold the camel steady, one to do the work, and the rest to carry their picture through the streets in protest when they get trampled by the camel."

"You made that shit up," Pineo says. "'I know it. Cause it ain't that funny."

"Fuck you guys!" Roman glares at Pineo, then takes himself off along the counter and goes to reading a newspaper, turning the pages with an angry flourish.

Four young couples enter the bar, annoying with their laughter and bright, flushed faces and prosperous good looks. As they mill about, some wrangling two tables together, others embracing, one woman earnestly asking Roman if he has Lillet, Bobby slides away from the suddenly energized center of the place and takes a seat beside Alicia. She cuts her eyes toward him briefly, but says nothing, and Bobby, who has spent much of the day thinking about things he might tell her, is restrained from speaking by her glum demeanor. He adopts her attitude—head down, a hand on his glass—and they sit there like two people weighted down by a shared problem. She crosses her legs, and he sees that she has kicked off a shoe. The sight of her slender ankle and stockinged foot rouses in him a sly Victorian delight.

"This is so very stimulating," she says. "We'll have to do it more often."

"I didn't think you wanted to talk."

"If you're going to sit here, it feels stupid not to."

The things he considered telling her have gone out of his head. "Well, how was your day?" she asks, modulating her voice like a mom inquiring of a sweet child, and when he mumbles that it was about the same as always, she says, "It's like we're married. Like we've passed beyond the need for verbal communion. All we have to do is sit here and vibe at each other."

"It sucked, okay?" he says, angered by her mockery. "It always sucks, but today it was worse than usual."

He begins, then, to unburden himself. He tells her about him and Pineo and Mazurek. How they're like a patrol joined in a purely unofficial unity, by means of which they somehow manage to shield one another from forces they either do not understand or are afraid to acknowledge. And now that unity is dissolving. The gravity of the pit is too strong. The death smell, the horrible litter of souls, the hidden terrors. The underground garage with its smashed, unhaunted cars white with concrete dust. Fires smouldering under the earth. It's like going to work in Mordor, the shadow everywhere. Ashes and sorrow. After a while you begin to feel as if the place is turning you into a ghost. You're not real anymore, you're a relic, a fragment of life. When you say this shit to yourself, you laugh at it. It seems like bullshit. But then you stop laughing and you know it's true. Ground Zero's a killing field. Like Cambodia. Hiroshima. They're already talking about what to build there, but they're crazy. It'd make as much sense to put up a Dairy Queen at Dachau. Who'd want to eat there? People talk about doing it quickly so the terrorists will see it didn't fuck us up. But pretending it didn't fuck us up...what's that about? Hey, it fucked us up! They should wait to build. They should wait until you can walk around in it and not feel like it's hurting you to live. Because if they don't, whatever they put there is going to be filled with that feeling. That sounds absurd, maybe. To believe the ground's cursed. That there's some terrible immateriality trapped in it, something that'll seep up into the new halls and offices and cause spiritual affliction, bad karma...whatever. But when you're in the middle of that mess, it's impossible not to believe it.

Bobby doesn't look at Alicia as he tells her all this, speaking in a rushed, anxious delivery. When he's done he knocks back his drink, darts a glance at her to gauge her reaction, and says, "I had this friend in high school got into crystal meth. It fried his brain. He started having delusions. The government was fucking with his mind. They knew he was in contact with beings from a higher plane. Shit like that. He had this whole complex view of reality as conspiracy, and when he told me about it, it was like he was apologizing for telling me. He could sense his own damage, but he had to get it out because he couldn't quite believe he was crazy. That's how I feel. Like I'm missing some piece of myself."

"I know," Alicia says. "I feel that way, too. That's why I come here. To try and figure out what's missing...where I am with all this."

She looks at him inquiringly, and Bobby, unburdened now, finds he has nothing worth saying. But he wants to say something, because he wants her to talk to him, and though he's not sure why he wants this or what more he might want, he's so confused by the things he's confessed and also by the ordinary confusions that attend every consequential exchange between men and women.... Though he's not sure of anything, he wants whatever is happening to move forward.

"Are you all right?" she asks.

"Oh, yeah. Sure. This isn't terminal fucked-uppedness. 'Least I don't think it is."

She appears to be reassessing him. "Why do you put yourself through it?"

"The job? Because I'm qualified. I worked for FEMA the last coupla summers."

Two of the yuppie couples have huddled around the jukebox, and their first selection, "Smells Like Teen Spirit," begins its tense, grinding push. Pineo dances on his barstool, his torso twisting back and forth, fists tight against his chest, a parody—Bobby knows—that's aimed at the couples, meant as an insult. Brooding over his bourbon, Mazurek is a graying, thick-bodied troll turned to stone.

"I'm taking my masters in philosophy," Bobby says. "It's finally beginning to seem relevant."

He intends this as humor, but Alicia doesn't react to it as such. Her eyes are brimming. She swivels on her stool, knee pressing against his hip, and puts a hand on his wrist.

"I'm afraid," she says. "You think that's all this is? Just fear. Just an inability to cope."

He's not certain he understands her, but he says, "Maybe that's all." It feels so natural when she loops her arms about him and buries her face in the crook of his neck, he doesn't think anything of it. His hand goes to her waist. He wants to turn toward her, to deepen the embrace, but is afraid that will alarm her, and as they cling together, he becomes insecure with the contact, unclear as to what he should do with it. Her pulse hits against his palm, her breath warms his skin. The articulation of her ribs, the soft swell of a hip, the presence of a breast an inch above the tip of his thumb, all her heated specificity both daunts and tempts him. Doubt concerning their mental well-being creeps in. Is this an instance of healing or a freak scene? Are they two very different people who have connected on a level new to both of them, or are they emotional burnouts who aren't even talking about the same subject and have misapprehended mild sexual attraction for a moment of truth? Just how much difference is there between those conditions? She pulls him closer. Her legs are still crossed, and her right knee slides into his lap, her shoeless foot pushing against his waist. She whispers something, words he can't make out. An assurance, maybe. Her lips brush his cheek, then she pulls back and offers a smile he takes for an expression of regret.

"I don't get it," she says. "I have this feeling…." She shakes her head as if rejecting an errant notion.

"What?"

She holds a hand up beside her face as she speaks and waggles it, a blitheness of gesture that her expression does not reflect. "I shouldn't be saying this to someone I met in a bar, and I don't mean it the way you might think. But it's...I have a feeling you can help me. Do something for me."

"Talking helps."

"Maybe. I don't know. That doesn't seem right." Thoughtful, she stirs her drink; then a sidelong glance. "There must be something some philosopher said that's pertinent to the moment."

"Predisposition fathers all logics, even those disposed to deny it."

"Who said that?"

"I did...in a paper I wrote on Gorgias. The father of sophistry. He claimed that nothing can be known, and if anything could be known, it wasn't worth knowing."

"Well," says Alicia, "I guess that explains everything."

"I don't know about that. I only got a B on the paper."

One of the couples begins to dance, the man, who is still wearing his overcoat, flapping his elbows, making slow-motion swoops, while the woman stands rooted, her hips undulating in a fishlike rhythm. Pineo's parody was more graceful. Watching them, Bobby imagines the bar a cave, the other patrons with matted hair, dressed in skins. Headlights slice across the window with the suddenness of a meteor flashing past in the primitive night. The song ends, the couple's friends applaud them as they head for the group table. But when the opening riff of the Hendrix version of "All Along The Watchtower" blasts from the speakers, they start dancing again and the other couples join them, drinks in hand. The women toss their hair and shake their breasts; the men hump the air. A clumsy tribe on drugs.

The bar environment no longer works for Bobby. Too much unrelieved confusion. He hunches his shoulders against the noise, the happy jabber, and has a momentary conviction that this is not his true reaction, that a little scrap of black negativity perched between his shoulderblades, its claws buried in his spine, has folded its gargoyle wings, and he has reacted to the movement like a puppet. As he stands Alicia reaches out and squeezes his hand. "See you tomorrow?"

"No doubt," he says, wondering if he will—he believes she'll go home and chastise herself for permitting this partial intimacy, this unprophylactic intrusion into her stainless career-driven life. She'll stop coming to the bar and seek redemption in a night school business course designed to flesh out her résumé. One lonely Sunday afternoon a few weeks hence, he'll provide the animating fantasy for a battery-powered orgasm.

He digs in his wallet for a five, a tip for Roman, and catches Pineo looking at him with unalloyed hostility. The kind of look your great enemy might send your way right before pumping a couple of shells into his shotgun. Pineo lets his double-barreled stare linger a few beats, then turns away to a deep consideration of his beer glass, his neck turtled, his head down. It appears that he and Mazurek have been overwhelmed by identical enchantments.

▲▼▲

Bobby wakes up a few minutes before he's due at work. He calls the job, warns them he'll be late, then lies back and contemplates the large orange-and-brown water stain that has transformed the ceiling into a terrain map. This thing with Alicia...it's sick, he thinks. They're not going to fuck—that much is clear. And not just because she said so. He can't see himself going to her place, furnishings courtesy of The Sharper Image and Pottery Barn, nor can he picture her in this dump, and neither of them has displayed the urge for immediacy that would send them to a hotel. It's ridiculous, unwieldy. They're screwing around is all. Mindfucking on some perverted soul level. She's sad because she's drinking to be sad because she's afraid that what she does not feel is actually a feeling. Typical post-modern Manhattan bullshit. Grief as a form of self-involvement. And now he's part of that. What he's doing with her may be even more perverse, but he has no desire to scrutinize his motives—that would only amplify the perversity. Better simply to let it play out and be done. These are strange days in the city. Men and women seeking intricate solace for intricate guilt. Guilt over the fact that they do not embody the magnificent sadness of politicians and the brooding sympathy of anchorpersons, that their grief is a flawed posture, streaked with the banal, with thoughts of sex and football, cable bills and job security. He still has things he needs, for whatever reason, to tell her. Tonight he'll confide in her, and she will do what she must. Their mutual despondency, a wrap in four acts.

He stays forever in the shower; he's in no hurry to get to the pit, and he considers not going in at all. But duty, habit, and doggedness exert a stronger pull than his hatred and fear of the place—though it's not truly hatred and fear he feels, but a syncretic fusion of the two, an alchemical product for which a good brand name has not been coined. Before leaving, he inspects the contents of the top drawer in his dresser. The relics are the thing he most needs to explain to her. Whatever else he has determined them to be, he supposes that they are, to a degree, souvenirs, and thus a cause for shame, a morbid symptom. But when he looks at them he thinks there must be a purpose to the collection he has not yet divined, one that explaining it all to Alicia may illuminate. He selects the half-shoe. It's the only choice, really. The only object potent enough to convey the feelings he has about it. He stuffs it into his jacket pocket and goes out into the living room, where his roommate is watching The Cartoon Network, his head visible above the back of the couch.

"Slept late, huh?" says the roommate.

"Little bit," Bobby says, riveted by the bright colors and goofy voices, wishing he could stay and discover how Scooby Doo and Jackie manage to outwit the swamp beast. "See ya later."

Shortly before his shift ends, he experiences a bout of paranoia, during which he believes that if he glances up he'll find the pit walls risen to skyscraper height and all he'll be able to see of the sky is a tiny circle of glowing clouds. Even afterward, walking with Mazurek and Pineo through the chilly, smoking streets, distant car horns sounding in rhythm like an avant-garde brass section, he half-persuades himself that it could have happened. The pit might have grown deeper, he might have dwindled. Earlier that evening they began to dig beneath a freshly excavated layer of cement rubble, and he knows his paranoia and the subsequent desire to retreat into irrationality are informed by what they unearthed. But while there is a comprehensible reason for his fear, this does not rule out other possibilities. Unbelievable things can happen of an instant. They all recognize that now.

The three men are silent as they head toward the Blue Lady. It's as if their nightly ventures to the bar no longer serve as a release and have become an extension of the job, prone to its stresses. Pineo goes with hands thrust into his pockets, eyes angled away from the others, and Mazurek looks straight ahead, swinging his thermos, resembling a Trotskyite hero, a noble worker of Factory 39. Bobby walks between them. Their solidity makes him feel unstable, as if pulled at by large opposing magnets—he wants to dart ahead or drop back, but is dragged along by their attraction. He ditches them just inside the entrance and joins Alicia at the end of the bar. Her twenty-five watt smile switches on, and he thinks that though she must wear brighter, toothier smiles for co-workers and relatives, this particular smile measures the true fraction of her joy, all that is left after years of career management and bad love.

To test this theory he asks if she's got a boyfriend, and she says, "Jesus! A boyfriend. That's so quaint. You might as well ask if I have a beau."

"You got a beau?"

"I have a history of beaus," she says. "But no current need for one, thank you."

"Your eye's on the prize, huh?"

"It's not just that. Though right now, it is that. I'm"—a sardonic laugh—"I'm ascending the corporate ladder. Trying to, anyway."

She fades on him, gone to a gloomy distance beyond the bar, where the TV chatters ceaselessly of plague and misery and enduring freedom. "I wanted to have children," she says at last. "I can't stop thinking about it these days. Maybe all this sadness has a biological effect. You know. Repopulate the species."

"You've got time to have children," he says. "The career stuff may lighten up."

"Not with the men I get involved with...not a chance! I wouldn't let any of them take care of my plants."

"So you got a few war stories, do you?"

She puts up a hand, palm outward, as to if to hold a door closed. "You can't imagine!"

"I've got a few myself."

"You're a guy," she says. "What would you know?"

Telling him her stories, she's sarcastic, self-effacing, almost vivacious, as if by sharing these incidents of male duplicity, laughing at her own naïveté, she is proving an unassailable store of good cheer and resilience. But when she tells of a man who pursued her for an entire year, sending candy and flowers, cards, until finally she decided that he must really love her and spent the night with him, a good night after which he chose to ignore her completely...when she tells him this, Bobby sees past her blithe veneer into a place of abject bewilderment. He wonders how she'd look without the make-up. Softer, probably. The make-up is a painting of attitude that she daily recreates. A mask of prettified defeat and coldness to hide her fundamental confusion. Nothing has ever been as she hoped it would be—yet while she has forsworn hope, she has not banished it, and thus she is confused. He's simplifying her, he realizes. Desultory upbringing in some Midwestern oasis—he hears a flattened A redolent of Detroit or Chicago. Second-rate education leading to a second-rate career. The wreckage of mornings after. This much is plain. But the truth underlying her stories, the light she bore into the world, how it has transmuted her experience...that remains hidden. There's no point in going deeper, though, and probably no time.

The Blue Lady fills with the late crowd. Among them a couple of older middle-age who hold hands and kiss across their table; three young guys in Knicks gear; two black men attired gangsta-style accompanying an overweight blonde in a dyed fur wrap and a sequined cocktail dress (Roman damns them with a glare and makes them wait for service.) Pineo and Mazurek are silently, soddenly drunk, isolated from their surround, but the life of the bar seems to glide around Bobby and Alicia, the juke box rocks with old Santana, Kinks, and Springsteen. Alicia's more relaxed than Bobby's ever seen her. She's kicked off her right shoe again, shed her jacket, and though she nurses her drink, she seems to become increasingly intoxicated, as if disclosing her past were having the effect of a three-martini buzz.

"I don't think all men are assholes," she says. "But New York men...maybe."

"You've dated them all, huh?" he asks.

"Most of the acceptable ones, I have."

"What qualifies as acceptable in your eyes?"

Perhaps he stresses "in your eyes" a bit much, makes the question too personal, because her smile fades and she gives him a startled look. After the last strains of "Glory Days" fade, during the comparative quiet between songs, she lays a hand on his cheek, studies him, and says, less a question than a self-assurance, "You wouldn't treat me like that, would you?" And then, before Bobby can think how he should respond, taken aback by what appears an invitation to step things up, she adds, "It's too bad," and withdraws her hand.

"Why?" he asks. "I mean I kinda figured we weren't going to hook up, and I'm not arguing. I'm just curious why you felt that way."

"I don't know. Last night I wanted to. I guess I didn't want to enough."

"It's pretty unrealistic." He grins. "Given the difference in our ages."

"Bastard!" She throws a mock punch. "Actually, I found the idea of a younger man intriguing."

"Yeah, well. I'm not all that."

"Nobody's 'all that,' not until they're with somebody who thinks they are." She pretends to check him out. "You might clean up pretty nice."

"Excuse me," says a voice behind them. "Can I solicit an opinion?"

A good-looking guy in his thirties wearing a suit and a loosened tie, his face an exotic sharp-cheekboned mixture of African and Asian heritage. He's very drunk, weaving a little.

"My girlfriend...okay?" He glances back and forth between them. "I was supposed to meet her down..."

"No offense, but we're having a conversation here," Bobby says.

The guy holds his hands up as if to show he means no harm and offers apology, but then launches into a convoluted story about how he and his girlfriend missed connections and then had an argument over the phone and he started drinking and now he's broke, fucked up, puzzled by everything. It sounds like the prelude to a hustle, especially when the guy asks for a cigarette, but when they tell him they don't smoke, he does not—as might be expected—ask for money, but looks at Bobby and says, "The way they treat us, man! What are we? Chopped liver?"

"Maybe so," says Bobby.

At this the guy takes a step back and bugs his eyes. "You got any rye?" he says. "I could use some rye."

"Seriously," Bobby says to him, gesturing at Alicia. "We need to finish our talk."

"Hey," the guy says. "Thanks for listening."

Alone again, the thread of the conversation broken, they sit for a long moment without saying anything, then start to speak at the same time.

"You first," says Bobby.

"I was just thinking...." She trails off. "Never mind. It's not that important."

He knows she was on the verge of suggesting that they should get together, but that once again the urge did not rise to the level of immediacy. Or maybe there's something else, an indefinable barrier separating them, something neither one of them has tumbled to. He thinks this must be the case, because given her history, and his own, it's apparent neither of them has been discriminating in the past. But she's right, he decides—whatever's happening between them is simply not that important, and thus it's not that important to understand.

She smiles, an emblem of apology, and stares down into her drink. "Free Falling" by Tom Petty is playing on the box, and some people behind them begin wailing along with it, nearly drowning out the vocal.

"I brought something for you," Bobby says.

An uneasy look. "From your work?"

"Yeah, but this isn't the same...."

"I told you I didn't want to see that kind of thing."

"They're not just souvenirs," he says. "If I seem messed up to you... and I'm sure I do. I *feel* messed up, anyway. But if I seem messed up, the things I take from the pit, they're kind of an explanation for...." He runs a hand through his hair, frustrated by his inability to speak what's on his mind. "I don't know why I want you to see this. I guess I'm hoping it'll help you understand something."

"About what?" she says, leery.

"About me...or where I work. Or something. I haven't been able to nail that down, y'know. But I do want you to see it."

Alicia's eyes slide away from him; she fits her gaze to the mirror behind the bar, its too-perfect reflection of romance, sorrow, and drunken fun. "If that's what you want."

Bobby touches the half-shoe in his jacket pocket. The silk is cool to his fingers. He imagines that he can feel its blueness. "It's not a great thing to look at. I'm not trying to freak you out, though. I think—"

She snaps at him. "Just show it to me!"

He sets the shoe beside her glass and for a second or two it's like she doesn't notice it. Then she makes a sound in her throat. A single note, the human equivalent of an ice cube *plinking* in a glass, bright and clear, and puts a hand out as if to touch it. But she doesn't touch it, not at first, just leaves her hand hovering above the shoe. He can't read her face, except for the fact that she's fixated on the thing. Her fingers trail along the scorched margin of the silk, tracing the ragged line. "Oh, my god!" she says, all but the glottal sound buried beneath a sudden surge in the music. Her hand closes around the shoe, her head droops. It looks as if she's in a trance, channeling a feeling or some trace of memory. Her eyes glisten, and she's so still, Bobby wonders if what he's done has injured her, if she was unstable and now he's pushed her over the edge. A minute passes, and she hasn't moved. The juke box falls silent, the chatter and laughter of the other patrons rise around them.

"Alicia?"

She shakes her head, signaling either that she's been robbed of the power to speak, or is not interested in communicating.

"Are you okay?" he asks.

She says something he can't hear, but he's able to read her lips and knows the word "god" was again involved. A tear escapes the corner of her eye, runs down her cheek, and clings to her upper lip. It may be that the half-shoe impressed her, as it has him, as being the perfect symbol, the absolute explanation of what they have lost and what has survived, and this, its graphic potency, is what has distressed her.

The jukebox kicks in again, an old Stan Getz tune, and Bobby hears Pineo's voice bleating in argument, cursing bitterly; but he doesn't look to see what's wrong. He's captivated by Alicia's face. Whatever pain or loss she's feeling, it has concentrated her meager portion of beauty and suffering, she's shining, the female hound of Wall Street thing she does with her cosmetics radiated out of existence by a porcelain *Song of Bernadette* saintliness, the clean lines of her neck and jaw suddenly pure and Periclean. It's such a startling transformation, he's not sure it's really happening. Drink's to blame, or there's some other problem with his eyes. Life, according to his experience, doesn't provide this type of quintessential change. Thin, half-grown cats do not of an instant gleam and grow sleek in their exotic simplicity like tiny gray tigers. Small, tidy Cape Cod cottages do not because of any shift in weather, no matter how glorious the light, glow resplendent and ornate like minor Asiatic temples. Yet Alicia's golden change is manifest. She's beautiful. Even the red membranous corners of her eyes, irritated by tears and city grit, seem decorative, part of a subtle design, and when she turns to him, the entire new delicacy of her features flowing toward him with the uncanny force of a visage materializing from a beam of light, he feels imperiled by her nearness, uncertain of her purpose. What can she now want of him? As she pulls his face close to hers, lips parting, eyelids half-lowering, he is afraid a kiss may kill him, either overpower him, a wave washing away a tiny scuttler on the sand, or that the taste of her, a fraction of warm saliva resembling a speck of crystal with a flavor of sweet acid, will react with his own common spittle to synthesize a compound microweight of poison, a perfect solution to the predicament of his mortality. But then another transformation, one almost as drastic, and as her mouth finds his, he sees the young woman, vulnerable and soft, giving and wanting, the childlike need and openness of her.

The kiss lasts not long, but long enough to have a history, a progression from contact to immersion, exploration to a mingling of tongues and gushing breath, yet once their intimacy is completely achieved, the temperature dialed high, she breaks from it and puts her mouth to his ear and whispers fiercely, tremulously, "Thank you.... Thank you so much!" Then she's standing, gathering her purse, her briefcase, a regretful smile, and says, "I have to go."

"Wait!" He catches at her, but she fends him off.

"I'm sorry," she says. "But I have to...right now. I'm sorry."

And she goes, walking smartly toward the door, leaving him with no certainty of conclusion, with his half-grown erection and his instantly catalogued memory of the kiss surfacing to be examined and weighed, its tenderness and fragility to be considered, its sexual intensity to be marked upon a scale, its meaning surmised, and by the time he's made these judgments, waking to the truth that she has truly, unequivocally gone and deciding to run after her, she's out the door. By the time he reaches the door, shouldering it open, she's twenty-five, thirty feet down the sidewalk, stepping quickly between the parked cars and the storefronts, passing a shadowed doorway, and he's about to call out her name when she moves into the light spilling from a coffee shop window and he notices that her shoes are blue. Pale blue with a silky sheen, and of a shape that appears identical to that of the half-shoe left on the bar. If, indeed, it was left there. He can't remember now. Did she take it? The question has a strange, frightful value, born of a frightful suspicion that he cannot quite reject, and for a moment he's torn between the impulse to go after her and a desire to turn back into the bar and look for the shoe. That, in the end, is what's important. To discover if she took the shoe, and if she did, then to fathom the act, to decipher it. Was it done because she thought it a gift, or because she wanted it so badly, maybe to satisfy some freaky neurotic demand, that she felt she had to more-or-less steal it, get him confused with a kiss and bolt before he realized it was missing? Or—and this is the notion that's threatening to possess him—was the shoe hers to begin with? Feeling foolish, yet not persuaded he's a fool, he watches her step off the curb at the next corner and cross the street, dwindling and dwindling, becoming indistinct from other pedestrians. A stream of traffic blocks off his view. Still toying with the idea of chasing after her, he stands there for half a minute or so, wondering if he has misinterpreted everything about her. A cold wind coils like a scarf about his neck, and the wet pavement begins soaking into his sock through the hole in his right boot. He squints at the poorly defined distance beyond the cross-street, denies a last twinge of impulse, then yanks open the door of the Blue Lady. A gust of talk and music seems to whirl past him from within, like the ghost of a party leaving the scene, and he goes on inside, even though he knows in his heart that the shoe is gone.

Bobby's immunity to the pit has worn off. In the morning he's sick as last week's salmon plate. A fever that turns his bones to glass and rots his sinuses, a cough that sinks deep into his chest and hollows him with chills. His sweat smells sour and yellow, his spit is thick as curds. For the next forty-eight hours he can think of only two things. Medicine and Alicia. She's threaded through his fever, braided around every thought like a strand of RNA, but he can't even begin to make sense of what he thinks and feels. A couple of nights later the fever breaks. He brings blankets, a pillow, and orange juice into the living room and takes up residence on the sofa. "Feeling better, huh?" say the roommate, and Bobby says, "Yeah, little bit." After a pause the roommate hands him the remote and seeks refuge in his room, where he spends the day playing video games. *Quake*, mostly. The roars of demons and chattering chain guns issue from behind his closed door.

Bobby channel surfs, settles on CNN, which is alternating between an overhead view of Ground Zero and a studio shot of an attractive brunette sitting at an anchor desk, talking to various men and women about 9/11, the war, the recovery. After listening for almost half an hour, he concludes that if this is all people hear, this gossipy, maudlin chitchat about life and death and healing, they must know nothing. The pit looks like a dingy hole with some yellow machines moving debris—there's no sense transmitted of its profundity, of how—when you're down in it—it seems deep and everlasting, like an ancient broken well. He goes surfing again, finds an old Jack the Ripper movie starring Michael Caine, and turns the sound low, watches detectives in long dark coats hurrying through the dimly lit streets, paperboys shouting news of the latest atrocity. He begins to put together the things Alicia told him. All of them. From "I've just been to a funeral," to "Everybody's ready to go on with their lives, but I'm not ready," to "That's why I come here...to figure out what's missing," to "I have to go." Her transformation...did he really see it? The memory is so unreal, but then all memories are unreal, and at the moment it happened, he knew to his bones who and what she was, and that when she took the shoe, the object that let her understand what had been done to her, she was only reclaiming her property. Of course everything can be explained in other ways, and it's tempting to accept those other explanations, to believe she was just an uptight careerwoman taking a break from corporate sanity, and once she recognized where she was, what she was doing, who she was doing it with, she grabbed a souvenir and beat it back to the email-messaging, network-building, clickety-click world of spreadsheets and wheat futures and martinis with some cute guy from advertising who would eventually fuck her brains out and afterward tell the-bitch-was-begging-for-it stories about her at his gym. That's who she was, after all, whatever her condition. An unhappy woman committed to her unhappy path, wanting more yet unable to perceive how she had boxed herself in. But the things that came out of her on their last night at the Blue Lady, the self-revelatory character of her transformation...the temptation of the ordinary is incapable of denying those memories.

It's a full week before Bobby returns to work. He comes in late, after darkness has fallen and the lights have been switched on, halfway inclined to tell his supervisor that he's quitting. He shows his ID and goes down into the pit, looking for Pineo and Mazurek. The great yellow earthmovers are still, men are standing around in groups, and from this Bobby recognizes that a body has been recently found, a ceremony just concluded, and they're having a break before getting on with the job.

He's hesitant to join the others, and pauses next to a wall made of huge concrete slabs, shattered and resting at angles atop one another, holding pockets of shadow and worse in their depths.

He's been standing there about a minute when he feels her behind him. It's not like in a horror story. No terrible cold or prickling hairs or windy voices. It's like being with her in the bar. Her warmth, her perfumey scent, her nervous poise. But frailer, weaker, a delicate presence barely in the world. He's afraid if he turns to look at her, it will break their tenuous connection. She's probably not visible, anyway. No Stephen King commercial, no sight of her hovering a few inches off the ground, bearing the horrid wounds that killed her. She's a willed fraction of herself, less tangible than a wisp of smoke, less certain than a whisper. "Alicia," he says, and her effect intensifies. Her scent grows stronger, her warmth more insistent, and he knows why she's here. "I realize you had to go," he says, and then it's like when she embraced him, all her warmth employed to draw him close. He can almost touch her firm waist, the tiered ribs, the softness of a breast, and he wishes they could go out. Just once. Not so they could sweat and make sleepy promises and lose control and then regain control and bitterly go off in opposite directions, but because at most times people were only partly there for one another—which was how he and Alicia were in the Blue Lady, knowing only the superficial about each other, a few basic lines and a hint of detail, like two sketches in the midst of an oil painting, their minds directed elsewhere, not caring enough to know all there was to know—and the way it is between them at this moment, they would try to know everything. They would try to find the things that did not exist like smoke behind their eyes. The ancient grammars of the spirit, the truths behind their old yet newly demolished truths. In the disembodiment of desire, an absolute focus born. They would call to one another, they would forget the cities and the wars.... Then it's not her mouth he feels, but the feeling he had when they were kissing, a curious mixture of bewilderment and carnality, accented this time by a quieter emotion. Satisfaction, he thinks. At having helped her understand. At himself understanding his collection of relics and why he approached her. Fate or coincidence, it's all the same, all clear to him now.

"Yo, Bobby!"

It's Pineo. Smirking, walking toward him with a springy step and not a trace of the hostility he displayed the last time they were together. "Man, you look like shit, y'know."

"I wondered if I did," Bobby says. "I figured you'd tell me."

"It's what I'm here for." Pineo fakes throwing a left hook under Bobby's ribs.

"Where's Carl?"

"Taking a dump. He's worried about your ass."

"Yeah, I bet."

"C'mon! You know he's got that dad thing going with you." Pineo affects an Eastern European accent, makes a fist, scowls Mazurek-style. "'Bobby is like son to me.'"

"I don't think so. All he does is tell me what an asshole I am."

"That's Polish for 'son,' man. That's how those old bruisers treat their kids."

As they begin walking across the pit, Pineo says, "I don't know what you did to Calculator Bitch, man, but she never did come back to the bar. You musta messed with her mind."

Bobby wonders if his hanging out with Alicia was the cause of Pineo's hostility, if Pineo perceived him to be at fault, the one who was screwing up their threefold unity, their trinity of luck and spiritual maintenance. Things could be that simple.

"What'd you say to her?" Pineo asks.

"Nothing. I just told her about the job."

Pineo cocks his head and squints at him. "You're not being straight with me. I got the eye for bullshit, just like my mama. Something going on with you two?"

"Uh-huh. We're gonna get married."

"Don't tell me you're fucking her."

"I'm not fucking her!"

Pineo points at him. "There it is! Bullshit!"

"Sicilian ESP.... Wow. How come you people don't rule the world?"

"I can't *believe* you're fucking the Calculator Bitch!" Pineo looks up to heaven and laughs. "Man, were you even sick at all? I bet you spent the whole goddamn week sleep-testing her Certa."

Bobby just shakes his head ruefully.

"So what's it like—yuppie pussy?"

Irritated now, Bobby says, "Fuck off!"

"Seriously. I grew up in Queens, I been deprived. What's she like? She wear thigh boots and a colonel's hat? She carry a riding crop? No, that's too much like her day job. She—"

One of the earthmovers starts up, rumbling like T-Rex, vibrating the ground, and Pineo has to raise his voice to be heard.

"She was too sweet, wasn't she? All teach me tonight and sugar, sugar. Like some little girl read all the books but didn't know what she read till you come along and pulled her trigger. Yeah...and once the little girl thing gets over, she goes wild on your ass. She loses control, she be fucking liberated."

Bobby recalls the transformation, not the-glory-that-was-Alicia part, the shining forth of soul rays, but the instant before she kissed him, the dazed wonderment in her face, and realizes that Pineo—unwittingly, of course—has put his grimy, cynical, ignorant, wise-ass finger on something he, Bobby, has heretofore not fully grasped. That she did awaken, and not merely to her posthumous condition, but to him. That at the end she remembered who she wanted to be. Not "who," maybe. But how. How she wanted to feel, how she wanted to live. The vivid, less considered road she hoped her life would travel. Understanding this, he understands what the death of thousands has not taught him. The exact measure of his loss. And ours. The death of one. All men being Christ and God in His glorious fever burning, the light toward which they aspire. Love in the whirlwind.

"Yeah, she was all that," Bobby says. —

Jailwise

During my adolescence, despite being exposed to television documentaries depicting men wearing ponytails and wife-beater undershirts, their weightlifter chests and arms spangled with homemade tattoos, any mention of prison always brought to my mind a less vainglorious type of criminal, an image derived, I believe, from characters in the old black-and-white movies that prior to the advent of the infomercial tended to dominate television's early morning hours: smallish, gray-looking men in work shirts and loose-fitting trousers, miscreants who—although oppressed by screws and wardens, victimized by their fellows—managed to express, however inarticulately, a noble endurance, a working-class vitality and poetry of soul. Without understanding anything else, I seemed to understand their crippled honor, their Boy Scout cunning, their Legionnaire's willingness to suffer. I felt in them the workings of a desolate beatitude, some secret virtue of insularity whose potentials they alone had mastered.

Nothing in my experience intimated that such men now or ever had existed as other than a fiction, yet they embodied a principle of anonymity that spoke to my sense of style, and so when I entered the carceral system at the age of fifteen, my parents having concluded that a night or two spent in the county lock-up might address my aggressive tendencies, I strived to present a sturdy, unglamorous presence among the mesomorphs, the skin artists, and the flamboyantly hirsute. During my first real stretch, a deuce in minimum security for Possession With Intent, I lifted no weights and adopted no yard name. Though I wore a serpent-shaped earring, a gift from a girlfriend, I indulged in no further self-decoration. I neither swaggered nor skulked, but went from cell to dining hall to my prison job with the unhurried deliberation of an ordinary man engaged upon his daily business, and I resisted, thanks to my hostility toward every sort of authority, therapy sessions designed to turn me inward, to coerce an analysis of the family difficulties and street pressures that had nourished my criminality, with the idea of liberating me from my past. At the time I might have told you that my resistance was instinctive. Psychiatrists and therapy: these things were articles of fashion, not implements of truth, and my spirit rejected them as impure. Today, however, years down the line from those immature judgments, I suspect my reaction was partially inspired by a sense that any revelation yielded by therapy would be irrelevant to the question, and that I already knew in my bones what I now know pit to pole: I was born to this order.

While I was down in Vacaville, two years into a nickel for armed robbery, I committed the offense that got me sent to Diamond Bar. What happened was this. They had me out spraying the bean fields, dressed in protective gear so full of holes that each day when I was done, I would puke and sweat as if I had been granted a reprieve and yanked from the gas chamber with my lungs half full of death. One afternoon I was sitting by the access road, goggles around my neck, tank of poison strapped to my shoulders, waiting for the prison truck, when an old Volkswagen bus rattled up from the main gate and stopped. On the sliding panel was a detail from a still life by Caravaggio, a rotting pear lopsided on a silver tray; on the passenger door, a pair of cherubs by Titian. Other images, all elements of famous Italian paintings, adorned the roof, front, and rear. The driver peered down at me. A dried-up, sixtyish man in a work shirt, balding, with a mottled scalp, a hooked nose, and a gray beard bibbing his chest. A blue-collar Jehovah. "You sick?" he asked, and waggled a cell phone. "Should I call somebody?"

"Fuck are you?" I asked. "The Art Fairy?"

"Frank Ristelli," he said without resentment. "I teach a class in painting and sculpture every Wednesday."

"Those who can't, teach...huh?"

A patient look. "Why would you say that?"

"'Cause the perspective on your Titian's totally fucked."

"It's good enough for you to recognize. How do you know Titian?"

"I studied painting in college. Two years. People in the department thought I was going to be a hot-shit artist."

"Guess you fooled them, huh?"

He was mocking me, but I was too worn out to care. "All that college pussy," I said. "I couldn't stay focused."

"And you had places to rob, people to shoot. Right?"

That kindled my anger, but I said nothing. I wondered why he was hanging around, what he wanted of me.

"Have you kept it up? You been drawing?"

"I mess around some."

"If you'd like, I'd be glad to take a look. Why don't you bring me what you've been doing next Wednesday?"

I shrugged. "Sure, yeah. I can do that."

"I'll need your name if I'm going to hook you up with a pass."

"Tommy Penhaligon," I said.

Ristelli wrote it down on a note pad. "Okay...Tommy. Catch you Wednesday." With that, he put the van in gear and rattled off to the land of the free, his pluming exhaust obscuring my view of the detail from a Piero della Francesca painted on the rear.

Of course, I had done no drawing for years, but I sensed in Ristelli the potential for a sweet hustle. Nothing solid, but you develop a nose for these things. With this in mind, I spent the following week sketching a roach—likely it was several different roaches, but I preferred to think of it as a brother inmate with a felonious history similar to my own. I drew that roach to death, rendering him in a variety of styles ranging from realism to caricature. I ennobled him, imbued him with charisma, invoked his humble, self-abnegatory nature. I made him into an avatar among roaches, a roach with a mission. I crucified him and portrayed him distributing Oreo crumbs to the faithful. I gave him my face, the face of a guard to whom I had a particular aversion, the faces of several friends, including that of Carl Dimassio, who supplied the crank that kept me working straight through the nights. I taped the drawings on the wall and chuckled with delight, amazed by my cleverness. On the night before Ristelli's class, so wasted that I saw myself as a tragic figure, a savage with the soul of an artist, I set about creating a violent self-portrait, a hunched figure half buried in blackness, illuminated by a spill of lamplight, curled around my sketch pad like a slug about a leaf, with a harrowed face full of weakness and delirium, a construction of crude strokes and charred, glaring eyes, like the face of a murderer who has just understood the consequences of his act. It bore only a slight resemblance to me, but it impressed Ristelli.

"This is very strong," he said of the self-portrait. "The rest of them"—he gestured at the roach drawings—"they're good cartoons. But this is the truth."

Rather than affecting the heightened stoicism that convicts tend to assume when they wish to demonstrate that they have not been emotionally encouraged, I reacted as might a prisoner in one of the movies that had shaped my expectations of prison, and said with boyish wonderment, "Yeah...you think?", intending by this to ruffle the sensibilities of Ristelli's inmate assistant, a fat, ponytailed biker named Marion Truesdale, aka Pork, whose arms were inked with blue, circusy designs, the most prominent being a voluptuous naked woman with the head of a demon, and whose class work, albeit competent, tended to mirror the derivative fantasy world of his body art. In the look that passed between us then was all I needed to know about the situation: Pork was telling me that he had staked out Ristelli and I should back the fuck off. But rather than heeding the warning, I concentrated on becoming Ristelli's star pupil, the golden apple in a barrel of rotten ones. Over the next months, devoting myself to the refinement of my gift, I succeeded to such a degree that he started keeping me after class to talk, while Pork—his anger fermenting—cleaned palette knives and brushes.

Much of what I said to Ristelli during that time was designed to persuade him of the deprivation I faced, the lack of stimulation that was neutering my artistic spirit, all with an eye toward convincing him to do a little smuggling for me. Though he sympathized with my complaints, he gave no sign that he was ripe to be conned. He would often maneuver our conversation into theoretical or philosophical directions, and not merely as related to art. It seemed he considered himself my mentor and was attempting to prepare me for a vague future in which I would live if not totally free, then at least unconstrained by spiritual fetters. One day when I described myself in passing as having lived outside the law, he said, "That's simply not so. The criminal stands at the absolute heart of the law."

He was perched on a corner of an old scarred desk jammed into the rear of the art room, nearly hidden by the folded easels leaning against it, and I was sitting with my legs stretched out in a folding chair against the opposite wall, smoking one of Ristelli's Camels. Pork stood at the sink, rinsing brushes in linseed oil, shoulders hunched, radiating enmity, like a sullen child forbidden the company of his elders.

"'Cause we're inside?" I asked. "That what you're saying?"

"I'm talking about criminals, not just prisoners," Ristelli said. "The criminal is the basis for the law. Its inspiration, its justification. And ultimately, of course, its victim. At least in the view of society."

"How the hell else can you view it?"

"Some might see incarceration as an opportunity to learn criminal skills. To network. Perhaps they'd rather be elsewhere, but they're inside, so they take advantage. But they only take partial advantage. They don't understand the true nature of the opportunity."

I was about to ask for an explanation of this last statement, but Pork chose the moment to ask Ristelli if he needed any canvases stretched.

Ristelli said, "Why don't you call it a day. I'll see you next week."

Aiming a bleak look in my direction, Pork said, "Yeah…all right," and shambled out into the corridor.

"The criminal and what he emblematizes," Ristelli went on. "The beast. Madness. The unpredictable. He's the reason society exists. Thus the prison system is the central element of society. Its defining constituency. Its model." He tapped a cigarette out of his pack and made a twirling gesture with it. "Who runs this place?"

"Vacaville? Fucking warden."

"The warden!" Ristelli scoffed at the notion. "He and the guards are there to handle emergencies. To maintain order. They're like the government. Except they have much less control than the President and the Congress. No taxes, no regulations. None that matter, anyway. They don't care what you do, so long as you keep it quiet. Day to day it's cons who run the prisons. There are those who think a man's freer inside than out in the world."

"You sound like an old lifer."

Bemused, Ristelli hung the cigarette from his lower lip, lit up and let smoke flow out from his mouth and nostrils.

"Fuck you know about it, anyway?" I said. "You're a free man."

"You haven't been listening."

"I know I should be hanging on your every goddamn word. Just sometimes it gets a little deep, y'know." I pinched the coal off the tip of the Camel and pocketed the butt. "What about the death penalty, man? If we're running things, how come we let 'em do that shit?"

"Murderers and the innocent," Ristelli said. "The system tolerates neither."

It seemed I understood these words, but I could not abide the thought that Ristelli's bullshit was getting to me, and instead of pursuing the matter, I told him I had things to do and returned to my cell.

I had been working on a series of portraits in charcoal and pastel that depicted my fellow students in contemplative poses, their brutish faces transfigured by the consideration of some painterly problem, and the next week after class, when Ristelli reviewed my progress, he made mention of the fact that I had neglected to include their tattoos. Arms and necks inscribed with barbed wire bracelets, lightning bolts, swastikas, dragons, madonnas, skulls; faces etched with Old English script and dripping with black tears—in my drawings they were unadorned, the muscles cleanly rendered so as not to detract from the fraudulent saintliness I was attempting to convey. Ristelli asked what I was trying for, and I said, "It's a joke, man. I'm turning these mutts into philosopher-kings."

"Royalty have been known to wear tattoos. The kings of Samoa, for instance."

"Whatever."

"You don't like tattoos?"

"I'd sooner put a bone through my nose."

Ristelli began unbuttoning his shirt. "See what you think of this one."

"That's okay," I said, suspecting now Ristelli's interest in my talent had been prelude to a homosexual seduction; but he was already laying bare his bony chest. Just above his right nipple, a bit off-center, was a glowing valentine heart, pale rose, with a gold banner entangling its pointy base, and on the banner were words etched in dark blue: The Heart Of The Law. The colors were so soft and pure, the design so simple, it seemed—despite its contrast to Ristelli's pallid skin—a natural thing, as if chance had arranged certain inborn discolorations into a comprehensible pattern; but at the moment, I was less aware of its artistic virtues than of the message it bore, words that brought to mind what Ristelli had told me a few days before.

"The heart of the law," I said. "This mean you done crime? You're a criminal?"

"You might say I do nothing else."

"Oh, yeah! You're one of the evil masters. Where'd you get the tattoo?"

"A place called Diamond Bar."

The only Diamond Bar I'd heard of was a section of LA populated mainly by Asians, but Ristelli told me it was also the name of a prison in northern California where he had spent a number of years. He claimed to be among the few ever to leave the place.

"It's unlikely you've met anyone who's done time there," he said. "Until now, that is. Not many are aware of its existence."

"So it's a supermax? Like Pelican Bay? The hell you do to get put someplace like that?"

"I was a fool. Like you, stupidity was my crime. But I was no longer a fool when I left Diamond Bar."

There was in his voice an evangelical tremor, as if he were hearkening back to the memory of God and not a prison cell. I'd come to realize he was a strange sort, and I wondered if the reason he had been released might be due to some instability developed during his sentence. He started to button his shirt, and I studied the tattoo again.

"Doesn't look like a jailhouse tat...'least none I ever saw," I said. "Doesn't even look like ink, the colors are so clean."

"The colors come from within," Ristelli said with the pious aplomb of a preacher quoting a soothing text. "There are no jails."

▲▼▲

That conversation stayed with me. If Ristelli was not certifiably a wacko, I assumed he was well along the road; yet while he had given me no concrete information about Diamond Bar, the commingling of passion and firmness in his voice when he spoke of the place seemed evidence not of an unbalanced mind but of profound calm, as if it arose from a pivotal certainty bred in a quieter emotional climate than were most prison-bred fanaticisms. I believed everything he said was intended to produce an effect, but his motives did not concern me. The idea that he was trying to manipulate me for whatever purpose implied that he needed something from me, and this being the case, I thought it might be an opportune time to make my needs known to him.

I assumed that Pork understood how the relationship between Ristelli and me was developing. To discourage him from lashing out at me, I hired a large and scarily violent felon by the name of Rudy Wismer to watch my back in the yard, at meals, and on the block, paying for his services with a supply of the X-rated Japanese comics that were his sexual candy. I felt confident that Wismer's reputation would give Pork pause—my bodyguard's most recent victim, a bouncer in a Sacramento night club, had testified at trial wearing a mask that disguised the ongoing reconstruction of his facial features; but on the Wednesday following our discussion of tattoos, Ristelli took sick midway through class and was forced to seek medical attention, leaving Pork and me alone in the art room, the one place where Wismer could not accompany me. We went about our cleaning chores in different quarters of the room; we did not speak, but I was aware of his growing anger, and when finally, without overt warning, he assaulted me, I eluded his initial rush and made for the door, only to find it locked and two guards grinning at me through the safety glass.

Pork caught hold of my collar, but I twisted away, and for a minute or so I darted and ducked and feinted as he lumbered after me, splintering easels, scattering palettes and brushes, tromping tubes of paint, overturning file cabinets. Before long, every obstacle in the room had been flattened and, winded, I allowed myself to be cornered against the sink. Pork advanced on me, his arms outspread, swollen cheeks reddened by exertion, huffing like a hog in heat. I prepared for a last and likely ineffective resistance, certain that I was about to take a significant beating. Then, as Pork lunged, his front foot skidded in the paint oozing from a crushed tube of cadmium orange, sending him pitching forward, coming in too low; at the same time, I brought my knee up, intending to strike his groin but landing squarely on his face. I felt his teeth go and heard the cartilage in his nose snap. Moaning, he rolled onto his back. Blood bubbled from his nostrils and mouth, matted his beard. I ignored the guards, who now were shouting and fumbling for their keys, and, acting out of a cold, pragmatic fury, I stood over Pork and smashed his kneecaps with my heel, ensuring that for the remainder of his prison life he would occupy a substantially diminished rank in the food chain. When the guards burst into the room, feeling charmed, blessed by chance, immune to fate, I said, "You assholes betting on this? Did I cost you money? I fucking hope so!" Then I dropped to the floor and curled into a ball and waited for their sticks to come singing through the air.

▲▼▲

Six days later, against all regulation, Frank Ristelli visited me in the isolation block. I asked how he had managed this, and dropping into his yardbird Zen mode, he said, "I knew the way." He inquired after my health—the guards had rapped me around more than was usual—and after I assured him nothing was broken, he said, "I have good news. You're being transferred to Diamond Bar."

This hardly struck me as good news. I understood how to survive in Vacaville, and the prospect of having to learn the ropes of a new and probably harsher prison was not appealing. I said as much to Ristelli. He was standing beneath the ceiling fixture in my cell, isolated from the shadows—thanks to the metal cage in which the bulb was secured—in a cone of pale light, making it appear that he had just beamed in from a higher plane, a gray saint sent to illumine my solitary darkness.

"You've blown your chance at parole," he said. "You'll have to do the whole stretch. But this is not a setback; it's an opportunity. We need men like you at Diamond Bar. The day I met you, I knew you'd be a candidate. I recommended your transfer myself."

I could not have told you which of these statements most astonished me, which most aroused my anger. "'We?' 'A candidate?' What're you talking about?"

"Don't be upset. There's—"

"You recommended me? Fuck does that mean? Who gives a shit what you recommend?"

"It's true, my recommendation bears little weight. These judgments are made by the board. Nevertheless, I feel I'm due some credit for bringing you to their attention."

Baffled by this and by his air of zoned sanctimony, I sat down on my bunk. "You made a recommendation to the Board of Prisons?"

"No, no! A higher authority. The board of Diamond Bar. Men who have achieved an extraordinary liberty."

I leaned back against the wall, controlling my agitation. "That's all you wanted to tell me? You could have written a letter."

Ristelli sat on the opposite end of the bunk, becoming a shadow beside me. "When you reach Diamond Bar, you won't know what to do. There are no rules. No regulations of any sort. None but the rule of brotherhood, which is implicit to the place. At times the board is compelled to impose punishment, but their decisions are based not on written law, but upon a comprehension of specific acts and their effect upon the population. Your instincts have brought you this far along the path, so put your trust in them. They'll be your only guide."

"Know what my instincts are right now? To bust your goddamn head." Ristelli began to speak, but I cut him off. "No, man! You feed me this let-your-conscience-be-your-guide bullshit, and—"

"Not your conscience. Your instincts."

"You feed me this total fucking bullshit, and all I can think is, based on your recommendation, I'm being sent to walls where you say hardly anybody ever gets out of 'em." I prodded Ristelli's chest with a forefinger. "You tell me something'll do me some good up there!"

"I can't give you anything of the sort. Diamond Bar's not like Vacaville. There's no correlation between them."

"Are you psycho? That what this is? You're fucking nuts? Or you're blowing somebody lets your ass wander around in here and act like some kinda smacked-out Mother Teresa? Give me a name. Somebody can watch out for me when I get there."

"I wish I could help you more, but each man must find his own freedom." Ristelli came to his feet. "I envy you."

"Yeah? So why not come with me? Guy with your pull should be able to wangle himself a ride-along."

"That is not my fate, though I return there every day and every night in spirit." His eyes glistened. "Listen to me, Tommy. You're going to a place few will ever experience. A place removed from the world yet bound to it by a subtle connectivity. The decisions made by those in charge for the benefit of the population enter the consciousness of the general culture and come to govern the decisions made by kings and presidents and despots. By influencing the rule of law, they manipulate the shape of history and redefine cultural possibility."

"They're doing a hell of a job," I said. "World's in great goddamn shape these days."

"Diamond Bar has only recently come to primacy. The new millennium will prove the wisdom of the board. And you have an opportunity to become part of that wisdom, Tommy. You have an uncommon sensibility, one that can illustrate the process of the place, give it visual form, and this will permit those who follow in your path to have a clearer understanding of their purpose and their truth. Your work will save them from the missteps that you will surely make." Ristelli's voice trembled with emotion. "I realize you can't accept what I'm saying. Perhaps you never will. I see in you a deep skepticism that prevents you from finding peace. But accomplishment...that you can aspire to, and through accomplishment you may gain a coin of greater worth. Devote yourself to whatever you choose to do. Through devotion all avenues become open to the soul. Serve your ambition in the way a priest serves his divinity, and you will break the chains that weigh down your spirit."

▲▼▲

On my first night in jail, at the age of fifteen, a Mexican kid came over to where I was standing by myself in the day room, trying to hide behind an arrogant pose, and asked if I was jailwise. Not wanting to appear inexperienced, I said that I was, but the Mexican, obviously convinced that I was not, proceeded to enlighten me. Among other things, he advised me to hang with my own kind (i.e., race) or else when trouble occurred no one would have my back, and he explained the diplomatic niceties of the racial divide, saying that whenever another white man offered to give me five, flesh-to-flesh contact was permitted, but should a Latino, an Asian, an Arab, an Afro-American, or any darkly-hued member of the human troupe offer a similar encouragement, I was to take out my prison ID card and with it tap the other man's fingertips. In every jail and prison where I did time, I received a similar indoctrination lecture from a stranger with whom I would never interact again. It was as if the system itself urged someone forward, stimulating them by means of some improbable circuitry to volunteer the fundamentals of survival specific to the place. Ristelli's version was by far the most unhelpful I had ever heard, yet I did not doubt that his addled sermonette was an incarnation of that very lecture. And because of this; because I had so little information about the prison apart from Ristelli's prattle; because I believed it must be a new style of supermax whose powers of spiritual deprivation were so ferocious, it ate everything it swallowed except for a handful of indigestible and irretrievably damaged fragments like Ristelli; for these reasons and more I greatly feared what might happen when I was brought to Diamond Bar.

The gray van that transported me from Vacaville seemed representative of the gray strangeness that I believed awaited me, and I constructed the mental image of a secret labyrinthine vastness, a Kafkaville of brick and steel, a partially subterranean complex like the supermax in Florence, Colorado where Timothy McVeigh, Carlos Escobar, and John Gotti had been held; but as we crested a hill on a blue highway south of Mount Shasta, a road that wound through a forest of old-growth spruce and fir, I caught sight of a sprawling granite structure saddling the ridge ahead, looking ominously medieval with its guard turrets and age-blackened stone and high, rough-hewn walls, and my mental image of the prison morphed into more Gothic lines—I pictured dungeons, archaic torments, a massive warden with a bald head the size of a bucket, filed teeth, and a zero tattooed on his brow.

The road angled to the left, and I saw an annex jutting from one side of the prison, a windowless construction almost as high as the main walls, also of weathered granite, that followed the slope of the ridge downward, its nether reach hidden by the forest. We passed in among the ranked trees, over a rattling bridge and along the banks of a fast-flowing river whose waters ran a mineral green through the calm stretches, cold and clouded as poison in a trough, then foamed and seethed over thumblike boulders. Soon the entrance to the annex became visible on the opposite shore: iron doors enclosed by a granite arch and guarded by grandfather firs. The van pulled up, the rear door swung open. When it became apparent that the driver did not intend to stir himself, I climbed out and stood on the bank, gazing toward my future. The ancient stones of the annex were such a bleak corruption of the natural, they seemed to presage an imponderable darkness within, like a gate that when opened would prove the threshold of a gloomy Druid enchantment, and this, in conjunction with the solitude and the deafening rush of the river, made me feel daunted and small. The engine of the van kicked over, and the amplified voice of the driver, a mystery behind smoked windows, issued from a speaker atop the roof: "You have ten minutes to cross the river!" Then the van rolled away, gathering speed, and was gone.

At Vacaville I had been handcuffed but not shackled, not the normal procedure, and left alone now I had the urge to run; but I was certain that invisible weapons were trained on me and thought this must be a test or the initial stage in a psychological harrowing designed to reduce me to a Ristelli-like condition. Cautiously, I stepped onto a flat stone just out from the bank, the first of about forty such stones that together formed a perilous footbridge, and began the crossing. Several times, besieged by a surge of water, a damp gust of wind, I slipped and nearly fell—to this day I do not know if anyone would have come to my rescue. Teetering and wobbling, fighting for balance, to a casual observer I would have presented the image of a convict making a desperate break for freedom. Eventually, my legs trembling from the effort, I reached the shore and walked up the shingle toward the annex. The building terminated, as I've said, in an arch of pitted stone, its curve as simple as that of a sewer tunnel, and chiseled upon it was not, as might have been expected, Abandon Hope All Ye Who Enter Here or some equally dispiriting legend, but a single word that seemed in context even more threatening: WELCOME. The iron doors were dappled with orange patches of corrosion, the separate plates stitched by rows of large rivets whose heads had the shape of nine-pointed stars. There was no sign of a knocker, a bell, or any alarm I might engage in order to announce myself. Once again I gave thought to running, but before I could act on the impulse, the doors swung silently inward, and, moved less by will than by the gravity of the dimness beyond, I stepped inside.

My first impression of Diamond Bar was of a quiet so deep and impacted, I imagined that a shout, such as I was tempted to vent, would have the value of a whisper. The light had a dull golden cast and a grainy quality, as if mixed in with particles of gloom, and the smell, while it plainly was that of a cleaning agent, did not have the astringency of an industrial cleaner. The most curious thing, however, was that there were no administrative personnel, no guards, no term of processing and orientation. Rather than being kept in isolation until it was determined to which block or unit I would be assigned, on passing through the annex door I entered the population of the prison like a pilgrim into a temple hall. The corridor ran straight, broken every fifty yards or so by a short stairway, and was lined with tiers of cells, old-fashioned cribs with sliding gates and steel bars, most of them unoccupied, and in those that were occupied, men sat reading, wall-gazing, watching television. None of them displayed other than a casual interest in me, this a far cry from the gauntlet of stares and taunts I had run when I entered the population at Vacaville. Absent the customary rites of passage, undirected, I kept going forward, thinking that I would sooner or later encounter an official who would inscribe my name or open a computer file or in some other fashion notate my arrival. As I ascended the fourth stairway, I glimpsed a man wearing what looked to be a guard's cap and uniform standing at parade rest on the tier above. I stopped, expecting him to hail me, but his eyes passed over me, and without saying a word, he ambled away.

By the time I reached the sixth stairway, I estimated that I had walked approximately two-thirds the length of the annex, climbed two-thirds the height of the hill atop which the walls of the prison rested; and though I held out hope that there I might find some semblance of authority, I decided to ask for assistance and approached a lanky, pot-bellied man with a pinkish dome of a scalp that caused his head to resemble a lightly worn pencil eraser, an illusion assisted by his tiny eyes and otherwise negligible features. He was sitting in a cell to the right of the stairs, wearing—as was everyone within view—gray trousers and a shirt to match. He glanced up as I came near, scowled at me, and set down the notebook in which he had been writing. The gate to his cell was halfway open, and I took a stand well back from it, anticipating that his mood might escalate.

"Hey, brother," I said. "What's up with this place? Nobody signs you in and shit?"

The man studied me a moment, screwed the cap onto his pen. On the backs of his fingers were faint inky tracings, the ghosts of old tattoos. The precision of his movements conveyed a degree of snippishness, but when he spoke his voice was calm, free of attitude. "'Fraid I can't help you," he said.

I would have been on familiar ground if he had responded with a curse, a warning, or the fawning, fraudulent enthusiasm that would signal his perception of me as a mark, but this politely formal response met none of my expectations. "I'm not asking you to get involved, man. I just need to know where to go. I don't want to get my nuts busted for making a wrong turn."

The man's eyes fitted themselves to the wall of the cell; he seemed to be composing himself, as if I were an irritant whose presence he felt challenged to overcome. "Go wherever you want," he said. "Eventually you'll find something that suits you."

"Asshole!" I clanged my handcuffs against the bars. "Fuck you think you're talking to? I'm not some fucking fish!"

His face tightened, but he kept on staring at the wall. The interior of the cell had been painted a yellowish cream, and the wall was marred by discolorations and spots from which the paint had flaked away that altogether bore a slight resemblance to a line of trees rising from a pale ground. After a few seconds he appeared to become lost in contemplation of it. Some of the men in other cells on the ground tier had turned our way, yet none ventured to their doors, and I sensed no general animosity. I was accustomed to prisons filled with men on the lookout for breaks in the routine, any kind of action to color the monotony, and the abnormal silence and passivity of these men both intimidated and infuriated me. I took a circular stroll about the corridor, addressing the occupants of the cells with a sweeping stare, hating their mild, incurious faces, and said in a voice loud enough for all to hear, "What're you, a bunch of pussies? Where the hell I'm supposed to go!"

Some of the men resumed their quiet occupations, while others continued to watch, but no one answered, and the unanimity of their unresponsiveness, the peculiar density of the atmosphere their silence bred, played along my nerves. I thought I must have come to an asylum and not a prison, one abandoned by its keepers. I wanted to curse them further, but felt I would be slinging stones at a church steeple, so aloof and immune to judgment they seemed. Like old ladies lost in their knitting and their memory books, though not a man within sight looked any older than I. With a disrespectful, all-inclusive wave, I set out walking again, but someone behind me shouted, "Bitch!", and I turned back. The baldheaded man had emerged from his cell and was glaring at me with his dime-sized eyes. He lifted his fist and struck down at the air, a spastic gesture of frustration. "Bitch!" he repeated. "Bitch…you bitch!" He took another babyish swipe at the air and hiccupped. He was, I saw, close to tears, his chin gone quivery. He stumbled forward a step, then performed a rigid half-turn and grasped the bars of his cell, pushing his face between—it appeared that he had forgotten that his gate was open. Many of the inmates had left their cells and were standing along the tiers, intent upon him—he covered his head with his hands, as if defending himself against the pressure of their gaze, and slumped to his knees. A broken keening escaped his lips. Trembling now, he sank onto his haunches. Shame and rage contended in his face, two tides rushing together, and the instant before he collapsed onto his side, he caught the face of one and said feebly and for a last time, "Bitch!"

▲▼▲

Beyond the ninth stairway lay a deeply shadowed cellblock that had the musty, claustrophobic atmosphere of a catacomb. Walls of undressed stone set close together and mounted by iron stairs; the cells showing like cave mouths; dim white ceiling lights that had the radiant force of distant stars tucked into folds of black cloud. Fatigued and on edge, I was not up to exploring it. A cell stood open and untenanted just below the stairway, and deciding that my safest course would be to allow whoever was in charge to come to me, I entered it and sat down on the bunk. I was struck immediately by the quality of the mattress. Though it appeared to be the usual thin lumpy item, it was softer and more resilient than any prison mattress I had ever rested on. I stretched out on the bunk and found that the pillow was remarkably soft and firm. Closing my eyes, I let the quiet soothe me.

I must have been drowsing for several minutes when I heard a baritone voice say, "Penhaligon? That you, man?"

The voice had a familiar ring, and there was something familiar, too, about the lean, broad-shouldered man standing at the entrance to my cell. Framed by a heavy mass of greased-back hair, his face was narrow and long-jawed, with hollow cheeks, a bladed nose, and a full-lipped mouth. He might have been the love child of Elvis and the Wicked Witch of the West. I could not place him, but felt I should be wary.

He grunted out a laugh. "I can't look that different. Just shaved off the beard's all."

I recognized him then and sat up, alarmed.

"Don't get worked up. I'm not gonna fuck with you." He perched on the end of the bunk, angling his eyes about the cell. "You want to put up a picture or two 'fore your wall comes in, they got pretty much any kind you want in the commissary."

There were questions I might have asked concerning both the essence and the rather housewifely character of this last statement, but during my first month in minimum security, Richard Causey, then doing an eight-spot for manslaughter, had put me in the hospital for the better part of a month with injuries resulting from a beating and attempted rape; thus his comments on interior decoration sailed right past me.

"I 'spect it's been a while since anybody took the walk you did," Causey said with a trace of admiration. "Straight up from the door all the way to eight? I never saw anyone do it, that's for sure." He clasped his hands on his stomach and settled back against the wall. "Took me a year to move up here from six."

All my muscles were tensed, but he merely sat there, amiable and at ease.

"'Most everybody stops somewhere along the first few blocks," Causey went on. "They don't feel comfortable proceeding on 'til they nail down a crib."

"Is that right?"

"Yeah, they feel kinda how you felt when you got to nine. Like you best stop and give things a chance to sort themselves out. It's the same with everybody, 'cept you got a lot farther than most."

Though I may have made a neutral noise in response, I was intent upon Causey's hands, the muscles in his shoulders.

"Look here," he said. "I understand what you're feeling, but I'm not the man I used to be. You want me to leave, that's cool. I just figured you'd want to talk. I know when I came here, all I wanted was somebody to talk to."

"I'm not the man I was, either," I said, injecting menace into my voice.

"Well, that's good. Takes a different man than both of us were to do time in Diamond Bar."

I was beginning to think that, truly, Causey might have changed. No longer did he give off the hostile radiation that once he had, and his speech, formerly characterized by bursts of profanity commingled with butchered elisions, was now measured and considered by contrast. His manner was composed and the tattoo of a red spider that had centered his brow was missing. "Just wore away, I guess," he said when I asked about it. He told me what he could about Diamond Bar but cautioned that the prison was not easily explained.

"This'll piss you off...'least it did me," he said. "But can't anybody tell you how to work this place. Things come to you as you need 'em. There's a dining hall and a commissary, like everywhere else. But the food's a helluva lot better and you don't need money at the commissary. The board handles everything. Supplies, discipline, recreation. We don't have any guards. I don't—"

"I saw a guard when I was walking up."

"Everybody sees that guy, but I never heard about him whupping his stick onto anybody. Could be he does his thing so's to give people something familiar to look at."

"You saying he's an inmate?"

"Maybe. I don't know. There's a lot I haven't figured out about, but it's coming." He tapped his temple and grinned. "Best thing about the place is the plumes. You gonna love them."

"What the hell's that?"

"The queens who get you off down in Vacaville? The plumes put them away. You can't hardly tell the difference between them and a real woman."

Anxious to steer the conversation away from the sexual, I asked who I needed to watch out for and he said, "Guys down on the first three or four blocks...some of them been known to go off. They're transferred out or given punishment duty. Mostly you need to watch out for yourself. Make sure you don't screw up."

"If there's no guards, people must just walk on out of here."

Causey gave me a penetrating look. "You crossed the river, didn't you? You entered of your own free will?"

"I thought the guards were watching."

"Might have been somebody watching. I couldn't tell you. All I know is, you and me and everyone else, we chose to be here, so we're not talking about a prison full of hard-core escape artists. And Diamond Bar's not so bad. Truth is, it's the best I've had it in a while. People say it's going to be even better once they finish the new wing. Escaping crossed my mind a time or two when I was first here. But I had the feeling it wasn't such a good idea."

What Causey said made me no more certain of my estate, and after he returned to his cell I remained awake, staring at the mysterious reach of the old prison that lay beyond the ninth stair, the dim white lights and anthracitic cell mouths. Everything I knew about Diamond Bar was cornerless and unwieldy, of a shape that refused to fit the logic of prisons, and this gave me cause to wonder how much more unwieldy and ill-fitting were the things I did not know. I was accustomed to prison nights thronged with hoots, cries, whispers, complaints, screams, an uneasy consensus song like the nocturnal music of a rain forest, and the compressed silence of the place, broken intermittently by coughs and snores, inhibited thought. At length I slept fretfully, waking now and again from dreams of being chased, hunted, and accused to find the silence grown deeper, alien and horrid in its thickness. But toward dawn—one I sensed, not witnessed—I woke to an outcry that seemed to issue from beneath the old prison, such a prolonged release of breath it could only have been the product of awful torment or extreme exaltation...or else it was the cry of something not quite human, expressing a primitive emotion whose cause and color is not ours to know, a response to some new shape of fear or a tidal influence or a memory from before birth, and following this I heard a whispering, chittering noise that seemed to arise from every quarter, like the agitated, subdued congress of a crowd gathered for an event of great and solemn gravity. While that chorus lasted I was full of dread, but once it subsided, almost stricken with relief, I fell into a black sleep and did not wake again until the shadows, too, had waked and the first full day of my true incarceration had begun.

▲▼▲

During those early months at Diamond Bar I came to understand the gist of what Ristelli, Causey, and the baldheaded man had tried to tell me. Eventually one found what was suitable. Things came to you. Trust your instincts. These statements proved to be not the vague, useless pronouncements I had assumed, but cogent practicalities, the central verities of the prison. Initially I behaved as I had during my early days at Vacaville. In the dining hall, an appropriately cavernous room of cream-colored walls, with the image of a great flying bird upon the ceiling, dark and unfigured, yet cleanly rendered like an emblem on a flag…in the dining room, then, I guarded my tray with my free arm and glanced fiercely about as I ate, warning off potential food thieves. When I discovered that the commissary was, indeed, a free store, I took to hoarding cigarettes, candy, and soap. It was several days before I recognized the pointlessness of these behavioral twitches, several weeks before I grew comfortable enough to forego them. Though I was not a heavy drug user, on those occasions that I grew bored, prior to beginning my work, I had no difficulty in obtaining drugs—you only had to mention your requirements to one of several men and later that day the pills or the powder would appear in your cell. I have no idea what might have occurred if I had developed a habit, but I doubt this was a problem at the prison. It was clear that the men on my block were all either above average in intelligence or skilled in some craft or both, and that most had found a means of employing their gifts and skills that left no time for recreational excess. As to the men housed in the cellblocks below the eighth stairway and how they managed things—of them I knew little. The men of different blocks rarely mingled. But I was told that they had a less innate grasp of Diamond Bar's nature than did we. Consequently their day-to-day existence was more of a struggle to adapt. In time, if they were not transferred, they—like us—would move into the old wings of the prison.

It did not seem likely that anyone could have less firm a grasp on the subject of Diamond Bar than I did, but I adapted quickly, learned my way around, and soon became conversant with a theory espoused by the majority of the men on my block, which held that the prison was the ultimate expression of the carceral system, a mutation, an evolutionary leap forward both in terms of the system and the culture that they believed was modeled upon it. They did not claim to understand the specifics of how this mutation had been produced, but generally believed that a mystical conjunction of event (likely a systemic glitch, an alchemy of botched paperwork and inept bureaucracy), natural law, and cosmic intent had permitted the establishment and maintenance of a prison independent of the carceral system or—so said the true believers—one that acted through subtle manipulation to control both the system and the greater society whose backbone the system formed. Though this smacked of Ristelli's cant, it was not so easy to dismiss now that I saw Diamond Bar for myself. The absence of guards, of any traditional authority; the peculiar demeanor of the inmates; the comfortable beds, decent food and free commissary; the crossing of the river in lieu of ordinary official process; the man dressed as a guard whom everyone had seen and no one knew; the rapid fading of all tattoos; the disturbing dawn cry and the subsequent mutterings, a phenomenon repeated each and every morning—what could be responsible for all this if not some mystical agency? For my part, I thought the theory a fantasy and preferred another, less popular theory—that we were being subjected to an experimental form of mind control and that our keepers were hidden among us. Whenever these theories were discussed, and they were often discussed, Richard Causey, who had studied political science at Duke University prior to turning to a career of violent crime and was writing a history of the prison, would declare that though he had his own ideas, the answer to this apparently unresolvable opposition resided with the board, but that thus far their responses to his inquiries concerning the matter had been inadequate.

The board consisted of four inmates ranging in age from sixtyish to over seventy. Holmes, Ashford, Czerny, and LeGary. They met each day in the yard to, it was said, decide the important questions relating to our lives and—if you bought into the view that Diamond Bar was the purest expression of a carceral universe, the irreducible distillate of the essential human condition—the lives of everyone on the planet. To reach the yard it was necessary to pass through the old wing of the prison visible beyond the eighth stairway, and though in the beginning I did not enjoy the passage, made anxious by the gloomy nineteenth-century atmosphere of the wing's antiquated cells with their key locks and hand-forged bars, and the masses of rotting stone in which they were set, I grew accustomed to the sight and came to view the old sections of the prison as places of unguessable potential—it was there, after all, that I would someday live if I stayed at Diamond Bar. As I've noted, the prison straddled a ridge—the spine of the ridge ran straight down the middle of the yard. Most of the population would gather close to the walls or sit on the slopes, which had been worn barren by countless footsteps, but the members of the board met among the grass and shrubs that flourished atop the ridge, this narrow strip of vegetation giving the enclosed land the look of a giant's scalp pushing up from beneath the earth, one whose green hair had been trimmed into a ragged Mohawk. Rising beyond the west wall, several iron girders were visible, evidence of the new wing that was under construction. The new wing was frequently referenced in conversation as being the panacea for whatever problems existed in our relatively problem-free environment—it seemed an article of faith that prison life would therein be perfected. Again, this struck me as fiction disseminated by whoever was manipulating our fates.

Late one afternoon some four months after my arrival, myself and Causey—toward whom I had succeeded in developing a neutral attitude—and Terry Berbick, a short, thickset bank robber with a gnomish look, his curly black hair and beard shot through with gray, were sitting against the east wall in the yard, discussing the newcomer on our block, Harry Colangelo: this happened to be the baldheaded man whom I had confronted on the day I came to the prison. His furtive air and incoherent verbal outbursts had made a poor impression, and Berbick was of the opinion that Colangelo's move onto the block had been premature.

"Something confused the boy. Caught him at a crucial moment during his period of adjustment and he's never gotten squared away." Berbick glanced at me. "Might be that dust-up with you did the trick."

"It wasn't that big a deal."

"I don't know. Way he stares at you, seems like you got under his skin. It might be why he moved up to eight—so he can come back at you easier."

"I've seen it before," Causey said. "Something happens early on to fuck up a man's instincts, and next you know he goes to acting all haywire. Gets his ass transferred right out on outa here."

I was not certain that being transferred out of Diamond Bar was the bleak prospect that Causey and Berbick thought it, but saw no need to argue the point.

"There the fucker is." Causey pointed to the slope on our left, where Colangelo was moving crabwise down the ridge, his pink scalp agleam with the westering sun, eyes fixed upon us. "I think Terry nailed it. The man's all messed up behind you."

"Whatever." I turned my attention to the four old men who purportedly ruled the world. Doddering on their height, the wind flying their sparse hair up into wild frays. Behind them, the tops of the girders burned gold, like iron candles touched with holy fire. Several younger men stood near the four. When I asked who they were, Berbick said they spoke for the board.

"What?" I said. "The masters of the universe can't talk for themselves?"

Berbick rolled up to his feet, smartly dusted the seat of his trousers, acting pissed-off. "You want to find out about the board, let's go see them."

I looked at him with amusement.

"You act like you know something," he said, "but you don't know as much as we do. And we don't know dip."

"Ain't nothing," I said. "Forget it."

"Nothing bad'll happen. We'll go with you." He glanced at Causey. "Right?"

Causey shrugged. "Sure."

Berbick arched an eyebrow and said to me in a taunting voice, "It's just four old guys, Tommy. Come on!"

Colangelo, who had been sitting upslope and to the left of us, scrambled up and hurried out of our path as we climbed the ridge.

"Fucking freak!" said Berbick as we drew abreast of him.

The board members were standing in a semicircle just below the highest point of the ridge, which was tufted with two roughly globular, almost identically puny shrubs, so sparsely leaved that from a distance, seen against the backdrop of the stone wall, they looked like the models of two small planets with dark gray oceans and island continents of green. The steadfastness with which the board was contemplating them gave rise to the impression that they were considering emigration to one or the other. Drawing near, I saw that the oldest among them, Czerny, appeared to be speaking, and the others, their eyes wandering, did not appear to be listening. Holmes, a shrunken black man, bald except for puffs of cottony hair above his ears and behind his neck, was shifting his feet restlessly, and the other two, Ashford and LeGary, both grandfather-gray and gaunt, were posed in vacant attitudes. One of the younger men who shadowed them, a stocky Latino in his forties, blocked our path, politely asked what we wanted, and Berbick jerked his thumb toward me and said, "Penhaligon here wants to meet the board."

"I don't want to meet them," I said, annoyed. "I was just wondering about them."

"They're busy," the Latino said. "But I'll see."

"You trying to fuck me over?" I asked Berbick as the Latino man went to consult with the board.

He looked pleased with himself. "What could happen? It's only four old guys."

"Nothing to worry about," Causey said. "He's just giving you shit."

"I don't need you interpreting for me, okay?" I said. "You can quit acting like my fucking big sister."

"Damn!" said Berbick with surprise. "He's coming over."

With the Latino holding his elbow, Czerny was heading toward us, shuffling through the ankle-high grasses, wobbly and frail. His caved-in face was freckled with liver spots, and the tip of his tongue flicked out with lizardly insistence. He was small, no more than five feet five, but his hands were those of a much larger man, wide and thick-fingered, with prominent knuckles—they trembled now, but looked as if they had been used violently during his youth. His eyes were a watery grayish blue, the sclera laced with broken vessels, and the right one had a cloudy cast. When he reached us, he extended a hand and gave my forearm a tentative three-fingered pat, like the benediction of a senile pope who had forgotten the proper form. He mumbled something, barely a whisper. The Latino man gave ear, and when Czerny had finished, he said, "There's important work for you here, Penhaligon. You should set about it quickly."

It did not seem that Czerny had spoken long enough to convey this much information. I suspected that the Latino man and his associates were running a hustle, pretending to interpret the maunderings of four senile old men and in the process guaranteeing a soft life for themselves.

Czerny muttered something more, and the Latino said, "Come visit me in my house whenever you wish."

The old man assayed a faltering smile; the Latino steadied him as he turned and, with reverent tenderness, led him back to join the others. I framed a sarcastic comment but was stopped by Causey's astonished expression. "What's going on?" I asked.

"Man invited you to his house," Causey said with an air of disbelief.

"Yeah…so?"

"That doesn't happen too often."

"I been here almost five years, and I don't remember it ever happening," Berbick said.

I glanced back and forth between them. "Wasn't him invited me—it was his fucking handler."

Berbick made a disdainful noise, shook his head as if he couldn't fathom my stupidity, and Causey said, "Maybe when you go see him, you'll—"

"Why the fuck would I go see him? So I can get groped by some old wheeze?"

"I guess you got better things to do," Berbick said. He was acting pissed-off again, and I said, "What crawled up your ass, man?"

He started to step to me, but Causey moved between us, poked me in the chest with two fingers and said, "You little hump! You walk straight up to eight from the door.... You don't seem to appreciate what that means. Frank Czerny invites you to his house and you ridicule the man. I been trying to help you—"

"I don't want your help, faggot!"

I recognized Causey's humorless smile as the same expression he had worn many years ago prior to ramming my head into a shower wall. I moved back a pace, but the smile faded and he said calmly, "Powers that be got something in mind for you, Penhaligon. That's plain to everyone 'cept you. Seems like you forgot everything you learned about surviving in prison. You don't come to new walls with an attitude. You pay attention to how things are and behave accordingly. Doesn't matter you don't like it. You do what you hafta. I'm telling you—you don't get with the program, they gonna transfer your sorry ass."

I pretended to shudder.

"Man thinks he's a hardass," said Berbick, who was gazing up at one of the guard turrets, an untenanted cupola atop a stone tower. "He doesn't know what hard is."

"Thing you oughta ask yourself," Causey said to me, "is where you gonna get transferred to."

He and Berbick started downslope, angling toward an unpopulated section of the east wall. Alone on the height, I was possessed by the paranoid suspicion that the groups of men huddled along the wall were all talking about me, but the only evidence that supported this was Colangelo, who was standing halfway down the slope to my right, some forty feet away, almost directly beneath the spot where the board was assembled. He was watching me intently, expectantly, as if anticipating that I might come at him. With his glowing scalp, his eyes pointed with gold, he had the look of a strange pink demon dressed in prison gray, and my usual disdain for him was supplanted by nervousness. As I descended from the ridge top, he took a parallel path, maintaining the distance between us, and though under ordinary circumstances I would have been tempted to challenge him, having alienated Causey and Berbick, knowing myself isolated, I picked up my pace and did not feel secure until I was back in my cell.

▲▼▲

Over the next several days, I came to recognize that, as Causey had asserted, I had indeed forgotten the basics of survival, and that no matter how I felt about the board, about the nature of Diamond Bar, I would be well served to pay Czerny a visit. I put off doing so, however, for several days more. Though I would not have admitted it, I found the prospect of mounting the iron stair to the tier where Czerny lived intimidating—it appeared that in acknowledging the semblance of the old man's authority, I had to a degree accepted its reality. Sitting in my cell, staring up at the dim white lights beyond the ninth stair, I began to order what I knew of the prison, to seek in that newly ordered knowledge a logical underpinning that would, if not explain everything I had seen, at least provide a middle ground between the poles of faith and sophism. I repaired my relationship with Causey, a matter of simple apology, and from him I learned that the prison had been constructed in the 1850s and originally used to house men whose crimes were related in one way or another to the boomtowns of the Gold Rush. The Board of Prisons had decided to phase out Diamond Bar in the 1900s, and at this time, Causey believed, something had happened to transform a horrific place that few survived into the more genial habitation it had since become. He had unearthed from the library copies of communications between the Board of Prisons and the warden, a man named McCandless Quires, that documented the rescinding of the phase-out order and conferred autonomy upon the prison, with the idea that it should become a penal colony devoted to rehabilitation rather than punishment. During that period, every level of society had been rife with reformers, and prison reform was much discussed—in light of this, such a change as Diamond Bar had undergone did not seem extraordinary; but the fact that it had been given to Quires to oversee the change: that smacked of the bizarre, for he had been frequently reprimanded by the Board for his abuses of prisoners. Indeed, it was the atrocities perpetrated during his stewardship that had induced the Board to consider the question of reform. It was reported that men had been impaled, flayed, torn apart by the prison dogs. Quires' letters demonstrated that he had undergone a transformation. Prior to 1903, his tone in response to the Board's inquiries was defiant and blasphemous, but thereafter his letters displayed a rational, even a repentant character, and he continued to serve as warden until his retirement in 1917. There was no record of a replacement having been appointed, and Causey theorized that the board as we knew it had then come to power, though it was possible, given Quires' advanced age (88), that they had been running things for many years previously. From 1917 on, communications between Diamond Bar and the Board of Prisons steadily diminished, and in 1945, not long before VE Day, they apparently ceased altogether. It was as if the prison, for all intents and purposes, had become non-existent in the eyes of the state.

Once Causey showed me a yellowed photograph he had unearthed from the prison archives. It had been shot in the yard on a sunny day in May of 1917—the date was inscribed on the back of the photo in a crabbed script—and it depicted a group of a woman and five men, four convicts, one of them black, and the last, an elderly man with white, windblown hair and a craggy, seamed face, clad in a dark suit and tie. Causey identified the elderly man as McCandless Quires, the warden.

"And these here," he said, indicating the other four, "that's the board." He tapped each in turn. "Ashford, Czerny, LeGary, Holmes."

Judging by their faces, the men were all in their twenties. There was a rough similarity of feature between them and the old men who met each day in the yard, but the idea that they were one and the same seemed absurd.

"That's so, they'd all have to be more than a hundred," I said. "They're old, but not that old."

"Look at the shape of their heads," Causey said. "Their expressions. They all got that spacey smile. Look at Czerny's hands. See how big they are? It's them, all right."

"You need to take a breath, man. This isn't the fucking Magic Kingdom, this is prison we're talking about."

"This is Diamond Bar," he said sullenly. "And we don't know what the hell that is."

I studied the photograph more closely, concentrating on the woman. She was lovely, delicate of feature, with flowing blonde hair. Noticing my attentiveness, Causey said, "I believe that there's a plume. Quires didn't have no daughter, no wife, and she got the look of plume."

"What look is that?"

"Too perfect. Like she ain't a man or a woman, but something else entirely."

The photograph aside, what Causey told me lent a plausible historical context to the implausible reality of Diamond Bar, but the key ingredient of the spell that had worked an enchantment upon the prison was missing, and when at last I went to visit Czerny, I had retrenched somewhat and was content to lean upon my assumption that we knew nothing of our circumstance and that everything we thought we knew might well have been put forward to distract us from the truth. Climbing the stairs, passing meter after meter of stone, ash-black and broken like the walls of a mineshaft, I felt on edge. Up on the third tier, the ceiling lights shed a glow that had the quality of strong moonlight; the bars and railings were flaked with rust. Four prisoners were lounging against the railing outside Czerny's cell—the Latino who had spoken for him was not among them—and one, a long-limbed black man with processed hair, his sideburns and thin mustache giving his lean face a piratical look, separated from the rest and came toward me, frowning.

"You supposed to come a week ago and you just coming now?" he said. "That ain't how it goes, Penhaligon."

"He told me to come whenever I wanted."

"I don't care what he said. It's disrespectful."

"That kind of old school, isn't it?"

He looked perplexed.

"It's the kind of attitude you'd expect to find at Vacaville and San Q," I said. "Not at a forward-thinking joint like Diamond Bar."

The black man was about to speak, but turned back to the cell as Czerny shuffled onto the tier. I had no inclination to mock the old man. Surrounded by young men attentive as tigers, he seemed the source of their strength and not their ward. Though I did not truly credit this notion, when he beckoned, the slightest of gestures, I went to his side without hesitation. His eyes grazed mine, then wandered toward the dim vault beyond the railing. After a second, he shuffled back into the cell, indicating by another almost imperceptible gesture that I should follow.

A television set mounted on the wall was tuned to a dead channel, its speakers hissing, its screen filled with a patternless sleet of black, silver, and green. Czerny sat on his bunk, its sheets cream-colored and shiny like silk, and—since he did not invite me to sit—I took a position at the rear of the cell, resting a hand upon the wall. The surface of the wall was unusually smooth, and upon examining it I realized it was not granite but black marble worked with white veins that altogether formed a design of surpassing complexity.

During my first conversation with Causey, he had suggested I purchase some pictures from the commissary to decorate my cell "until your wall comes in." Though struck by this phrase, at the time my attention had been dominated by other concerns; but I had since discovered that once a cell was occupied, discolorations manifested on the wall facing the bunk, and these discolorations gradually produced intricate patterns reminiscent of the rock the Chinese call "picture stone," natural mineral abstractions in which an imaginative viewer could discern all manner of landscapes. The wall in my cell had begun to develop discolorations, their patterns as yet sparse and poorly defined; but Causey's wall, Berbick's, and others were fully realized. It was said these idiosyncratic designs were illustrative of the occupant's inner nature and, when reflected upon, acted to instruct the observer as to his flaws, his potentials, the character of his soul. None of them—at least none I had seen—compared to the elaborate grandeur of the one on Czerny's wall. Gazing at it, I traveled the labyrinthine streets of a fantastic city lined by buildings with spindly, spiny turrets and octagonal doorways; I explored the pathways of a white forest whose creatures were crowned with antlers that themselves formed other, even more intricate landscapes; I coursed along a black river whose banks were sublime constructions of crystal and ice, peopled by nymphs and angels with wings that dwarfed their snowy bodies like the wings of arctic butterflies. I cannot say how long I stared—quite a while, I believe, because my mouth was dry when I looked away—but from the experience I derived an impression of a convoluted, intensely spiritual intellect that warred with Czerny's drab, dysfunctional appearance. He was smiling daftly, eyes fixed on his hands, which were fidgeting in his lap, and I wondered if the audience was over, if I should leave. Then he spoke, muttering as he had out in the yard. This time I understood him perfectly, yet I am certain no intelligible word passed his lips.

"Do you see?" he asked. "Do you understand where you are now?"

I was so startled at having understood him, I could muster no reply.

He raised a hand, trailed his fingers across the bars of the gate, the sort of gesture a salesman might make to display the hang of a fabric. Assuming that he wanted me to inspect the bars, I stepped around him and bent to look at one. A bit less than halfway along its length the color and finish of the metal changed from rough and dark to a rich yellow. The join where the two colors met was seamless, and the yellow metal had an unmistakable soft luster and smoothness: gold. It was as if a luxuriant infection were spreading along the bar, along—I realized—all the bars of Czerny's cell.

I am not sure why this unsettled me more profoundly than the rest of the bizarre occurrences I'd met with at Diamond Bar. Perhaps it resonated with some gloomy fairy tale that had frightened me as a child or inflamed some even deeper wound to my imagination, for I had a sudden appreciation of Czerny as a wizardly figure, a shabby derelict who had revealed himself of an instant to be a creature of pure principle and power. I backed out of the cell, fetched up against the railing, only peripherally mindful of Czerny's attendants. The old man continued to smile, his gaze drifting here and there, centering briefly on my face, and in that broken muttering whose message I now comprehended as clearly as I might the orotund tones of a preacher ringing from a pulpit, he said, "You cannot retreat from the heart of the law, Penhaligon. You can let it illuminate you or you can fail it, but you cannot retreat. Bear this in mind."

▲▼▲

That night as I lay in my cell, immersed in the quiet of the cellblock like a live coal at the heart of a diamond, growing ever more anxious at the thought of Czerny in his cell of gold and marble, an old mad king whose madness could kill, for I believed now he was the genius of the place…that night I determined I would escape. Despite the caution implicit in Czerny's final words, I knew I could never thrive there. I needed firm ground beneath my feet, not philosophy and magic or the illusion of magic. If I were to live bounded by walls and laws—as do we all—I wanted walls manned and topped with razor wire, written regulations, enemies I could see. Yet the apparent openness of the prison, its lack of visible security, did not fool me. Power did not exist without enforcement. I would have to ferret out the traps, learn their weaknesses, and in order to do that I needed to become part of the prison and pretend to embrace its ways.

My first step in this direction was to find an occupation, a meaningful activity that would convince whoever was watching that I had turned my mind onto acceptable avenues; since my only skill was at art, I began drawing once again. But making sketches, I realized, would not generate a *bona fide* of my submersion in the life of Diamond Bar; thus I undertook the creation of a mural, using for a canvas the walls and ceiling of an empty storeroom in one of the sub-basements. I chose as a theme the journey that had led me to the prison, incorporating images of the river crossing, of Frank Ristelli, the gray van, and so forth. The overall effect was more crazy quilt than a series of unified images, although I was pleased with certain elements of the design; but for all the attention it received, it might have rivaled Piero della Francesca. Men stopped by at every hour to watch me paint, and the members of the board, along with their entourages, were frequent visitors. Czerny took particular interest in my depiction of Ristelli; he would stand in front of the image for periods up to half an hour, addressing it with his customary vacant nods. When I asked one of his attendants the reason for his interest, I was told that Ristelli was revered for a great personal sacrifice made on behalf of us all and reflecting on the origins of our common home—he had been on the verge of being made a member of the board, but had forsworn the security and comfort of the prison and returned to the world in order to seek out men suitable for Diamond Bar.

Placing Ristelli's zoned piety in context with the psychological climate of the prison, it was not difficult to understand why they perceived him to be their John the Baptist; but in the greater context of the rational, the idea was ludicrous. More than ludicrous. Insane. Recalling how laughable Ristelli's preachments had seemed back in Vacaville reinforced my belief that the population of Diamond Bar was being transformed by person or persons unknown into a brain-dead congregation of delusionaries, and fearful of joining them, I intensified my focus on escape, exploring the sub-basements, the walls, the turrets, searching for potential threats. On one of these explorative journeys, as I passed through Czerny's block, I noticed that the massive oak door leading to the new wing, heretofore always locked, was standing partway open and, curious, I stepped inside. The space in which I found myself was apparently an anteroom, one more appropriate to a modern cathedral than a jail: domed and columned, with scaffolding erected that permitted access to every inch of the roof and walls. The door on the far side of the room was locked, and there was little else to see, the walls and ceiling being white and unadorned. I was on the verge of leaving when I saw a sheet of paper taped to one of the columns. Written in pencil upon it was the following:

This place is yours to paint, Penhaligon, if you wish.

A key lay on the scaffolding beside the note—it fit the oak door. I locked the door, pocketed the key and went about my business, understanding this show of trust to signify the board's recognition that I had accepted my lot and that by taking up their charge I might earn a further degree of trust and so learn something to my benefit. To succeed in this I would have to do something that would enlist their delusion, and I immediately set about working on a design that would illustrate the essence of the delusion, The Heart of the Law. Though I began with cynical intent, as the weeks went by and my cell walls were covered with sketches, I grew obsessed with the project. I wanted the mural to be beautiful and strong to satisfy the artistic portion of my nature, my ego, and not simply to satisfy the board—in truth, I presumed they would approve of anything I did that hewed to their evangel. The dome and walls of the anteroom, the graceful volume of space they described, inspired me to think analytically about painting, something I had not done before, and I challenged myself to transcend the limits of my vision, to conceive a design that was somehow larger than my soul. I came to dwell more and more on the motive theory of Diamond Bar, that the criminal was the fundamental citizen, the archetype in whose service the whole of society had been created, and in the process I came obliquely to embrace the idea, proving, I suppose, the thesis that high art is the creation of truth from the raw materials of a lie, and the artist who wishes to be adjudged "great" must ultimately, through the use of passion and its obsessive tools, believe the lie he is intent upon illuminating. To augment my analytic capacities, I read books that might shed light on the subject—works of philosophy for the most part—and was astonished to discover in the writings of Michel Foucault a theory mirroring the less articulate theory espoused by the prison population. I wondered if it might be true, if delusion were being employed in the interests of truth, and, this being the case, whether the secret masters of Diamond Bar were contemplating a general good and the experiment of which we were a part was one that sought to evolve a generation in harmony with the grand design underlying all human culture. The books were difficult for me, but I schooled myself to understand them and became adept at knotting logic into shapes that revealed new facets of possibility—new to me, at any rate. This caused me to lose myself in abstraction and consequently diminished the urgency of my intention to escape. Like everyone who lived at Diamond Bar, I seemed to have a talent in that regard.

The design I settled upon owed more to Diego Rivera and Soviet poster art than to the muralists of the Renaissance. The walls would be thronged with figures, all reacting toward the center of the design, which was to occupy the dome and which I had not yet been able to conceptualize—I felt the image would naturally occur as a byproduct of my labors. It took three months of twelve-hour days to lay out the sketch on the walls, and I estimated that, if done properly, the painting would take a year to complete. Chances were I would be gone from Diamond Bar before then, and realizing this, when I began to paint, ensorcelled by my vision, driven by the idea of finishing in a shorter time, I worked fifteen and sixteen hours a day. Dangling in harness from the scaffolding, crouched over, forced into unnatural positions, I gained an appreciation for the physical afflictions that Michelangelo endured while painting the Sistine Chapel. Each night after work I tried to shake off the aches and pains by walking through the sub-basements of the prison, and it was during one of these walks that I encountered the plumes.

In prison, sex is an all-consuming preoccupation, a topic endlessly discussed, and from my earliest days at Diamond Bar the plumes had been recommended as a palatable alternative to self-gratification. The new wing, it was said, would house both women and men, thus ending the single unnatural constraint of prison life, and many held that the plumes would eventually become those women, evolving—as were we all—into their ideal form. Even now, Causey said, the plumes were superior to the sex available in other prisons. "It's not like fucking a guy," he said. "It feels, y'know, okay."

"Is it like fucking a woman?" I asked.

He hesitated and said, "Kinda."

"'Kinda' doesn't do it for me."

"Only reason it's different is because you're thinking about it not being a woman."

"Yeah, well. I'll pass. I don't want to think when I'm fucking."

Causey continued urging me to give the plumes a try, because—I believed—he felt that if I surrendered to temptation, I would become a complicitor in perversion, and this would somehow lessen the guilt attaching to his sexual assault on me. That he felt guilty about what had transpired between us was not in question. As our relationship progressed, he came to speak openly about the event and sought to engage me in a dialogue concerning it. Therapy, I supposed. Part of his process of self-examination. At the time, I rejected his suggestions that I visit the plumes out of hand, but they may have had some effect on me, for in retrospect I see that my initial encounter with them, though it seemed accidental, was likely an accident I contrived. I was, you see, in a heightened state of sexuality. Immersed in my work, essentially in love with it, while painting I would often become aroused not by any particular stimulus—there were no visual or tactile cues—but by the concentrated effort, itself a form of desire maintained at peak intensity for hours on end. And so on the night I strayed into the section of the prison occupied by the plumes, I was, though tired, mentally and sexually alert. I was tempting myself, testing my limits, my standards, hoping they would fail me.

Three levels down from the main walls were dozens of rooms—bedchambers, a communal kitchen, common rooms, and so forth—an area accessed by a double door painted white and bearing a carved emblem that appeared to represent a sheaf of plumes, this the source of the name given to those who dwelled within. Much of the space had the sterile decor of a franchise hotel: carpeted corridors with benches set into walls whose patterned discolorations brought to mind *art nouveau* flourishes. The common rooms were furnished with sofas and easy chairs and filled with soft music whose melodies were as unmemorable as an absent caress. No barred gates, just wooden doors. The lighting was dim, every fixture limned by a faint halation, giving the impression that the air was permeated by a fine mist. I felt giddy on entering the place, as if I had stood up too quickly. Nerves, I assumed, because I felt giddier yet when I caught sight of my first plume, a slim blonde attired in a short gray dress with spaghetti straps. She had none of the telltale signs of a transvestite or a transsexual. Her hands and feet were small, her nose and mouth delicately shaped, her figure not at all angular. After she vanished around a corner, I remembered she was a man, and that recognition bred abhorrence and self-loathing in me. I turned, intending to leave, and bumped into another plume who had been about to walk past me from behind. A willowy brunette with enormous dark eyes, dressed in the same fashion as the blonde, her mouth thinned in exasperation. Her expression softened as she stared at me. I suppose I gaped at her. The memory of how I behaved is impaired by the ardor with which I was studying her, stunned by the air of sweet intelligence generated when she smiled. Her face was almost unmarked by time—I imagined her to be in her late twenties—and reminded me of the faces of madonnas in Russian ikons: long and pale and solemn, wide at the cheekbones, with an exaggerated arch to the eyebrows and heavy-lidded eyes. Her hair fell straight and shining onto her back. There was nothing sluttish or coarse about her; on the contrary, she might have been a graduate student out for an evening on the town, a young wife preparing to meet her husband's employer, an ordinary beauty in her prime. I tried to picture her as a man but did not succeed in this, claimed instead by the moment.

"Are you trying to find someone?" she asked. "You look lost."

"No," I said. "I'm just walking...looking around."

"Would you like me to give you the tour?" She put out her right hand to be shaken. "I'm Bianca."

The way she extended her arm straight out, assertive yet graceful, hand angled down and inward a bit: it was so inimitably a female gesture, devoid of the frilliness peculiar to the gestures of men who pretend to be women, it convinced me on some core level of her femininity, and my inhibitions fell away. As we strolled, she pointed out the features of the place. A bar where the ambience of a night club was created by red and purple spotlights that swept over couples dancing together; a grotto hollowed out from the rock with a pool in which several people were splashing one another; a room where groups of men and plumes were playing cards and shooting pool. During our walk, I told Bianca my life story in brief, but when I asked about hers, she said, "I didn't exist before I came to Diamond Bar." Then, perhaps because she noticed disaffection in my face, she added, "That sounds overly dramatic, I know. But it's more or less true. I'm very different from how I used to be."

"That's true of everyone here. The thinking you do about the past, it can't help but change you."

"That's not what I mean," she said.

At length she ushered me into a living room cozily furnished in the manner of a bachelorette apartment and insisted I take a seat on the sofa, then went through a door into the next room, reappearing seconds later carrying a tray on which were glasses and a bottle of red wine. She sat beside me, and as she poured the wine I watched her breasts straining against the gray bodice, the soft definition of her arms, the precise articulation of the muscles at the corners of her mouth. The wine, though a touch bitter, put me at ease, but my sense of a heated presence so near at hand sparked conflicting feelings, and I was unable to relax completely. I told myself that I did not want intimacy, yet that was patently untrue. I had been without a woman for three years, and even had I been surrounded by women during that time, Bianca would have made a powerful impression. The more we talked, the more she revealed of herself, not the details of her past, but the particularity of her present: her quiet laugh, a symptom—it seemed—of ladylike restraint; the grave consideration she gave to things I said; the serene grace of her movements. There was an aristocratic quality to her personal style, a practiced, almost ritual caution. Only after learning that I was the one painting a mural in the new wing did she betray the least excitement, and even her excitement was colored with restraint. She leaned toward me, hands clasped in her lap, and her smile broadened, as if my achievement, such as it was, made her proud.

"I wish I could do something creative," she said wistfully at one point. "I don't think I've got it in me."

"Creativity's like skin color. Everyone's got some."

She made a sad moue. "Not me."

"I'll teach you to draw if you want. Next time I'll bring a sketch pad, some pencils."

She traced the stem of her wine glass with a forefinger. "That would be nice...if you come back."

"I will," I told her.

"I don't know." She said this distantly, then straightened, sitting primly on the edge of the sofa. "I can tell you don't think it would be natural between us."

I offered a reassurance, but she cut me off, saying, "It's all right. I understand it's strange for you. You can't accept that I'm natural." She let her eyes hold on my face for a second, then lowered her gaze to the wine glass. "Sometimes it's hard for me to accept, but I am, you know."

I thought she was saying that she was post-operative, yet because she spoke with such offhanded conviction and not the hysteria-tinged defiance of a prison bitch, I also wondered, against logic, if she might be telling the truth and was a woman in every meaning of the word. She came to her feet and stepped around the coffee table and stood facing me. "I want to show you," she said. "Will you let me show you?"

The mixture of shyness and seductiveness she exhibited in slipping out of her dress was completely natural, redolent of a woman who knew she was beautiful yet was not certain she would be beautiful enough to please a new man, and when she stood naked before me, I could not call to mind a single doubt as to her femininity, all my questions answered by high, small breasts and long legs evolving from the milky curve of her belly. She seemed the white proof of a sensual absolute, and the one thought that separated itself out from the thoughtlessness of desire was that here might be the central figure in my mural.

During the night that followed, nothing Bianca did in any way engaged my critical faculties. I had no perch upon which a portion of my mind stood and observed. It was like all good nights passed with a new lover, replete with tenderness and awkwardness and intensity. I spent every night for the next five weeks with her, teaching her to draw, talking, making love, and when I was in her company, no skepticism concerning the rightness of the relationship entered in. The skepticism that afflicted me when we were apart was ameliorated by the changes that knowing her brought to my work. I came to understand that the mural should embody a dynamic vertical progression from darkness and solidity to brightness and evanescence. The lower figures would be, as I had envisioned, heavy and stylized, but those above demanded to be rendered impressionistically, gradually growing less and less defined, until at the dome, at the heart of the law, they became creatures of light. I reshaped the design accordingly and set to work with renewed vigor, though I did not put in so many hours as before, eager each night to return to Bianca. I cannot say I neglected the analytic side of my nature—I continued to speculate on how she had become a woman. In exploring her body I had found no surgical scars, nothing to suggest such an invasive procedure as would be necessary to effect the transformation, and in her personality I perceived no masculine defect. She was, for all intents and purposes, exactly what she appeared: a young woman who, albeit experienced with men, had retained a certain innocence that I believed she was yielding up to me.

When I mentioned Bianca to Causey, he said, "See, I told ya."

"Yeah, you told me. So what's up with them?"

"The plumes? There's references to them in the archives, but they're vague."

I asked him to elaborate, and he said all he knew was that the criteria by which the plumes were judged worthy of Diamond Bar was different from that applied to the rest of the population. The process by which they entered the prison, too, was different—they referred to it as the Mystery, and there were suggestions in the archival material that it involved a magical transformation. None of the plumes would discuss the matter other than obliquely. This seemed suggestive of the pathological myths developed by prison queens to justify their femininity, but

I refused to let it taint my thoughts concerning Bianca. Our lives had intertwined so effortlessly, I began to look upon her as my companion. I recognized that if my plans for escape matured I would have to leave her, but rather than using this as an excuse to hold back, I sought to know her more deeply. Every day brought to light some new feature of her personality. She had a quiet wit that she employed with such subtlety, I sometimes did not realize until after the fact that she had been teasing me; and she possessed a stubborn streak that, in combination with her gift for logic, made her a formidable opponent in any argument. She was especially fervent in her defense of the proposition that Diamond Bar manifested the principle from which the form of the human world had been struck, emergent now, she liked to claim, for a mysterious yet ultimately beneficent reason.

In the midst of one such argument, she became frustrated and said, "It's not that you're a non-conformist, it's like you're practicing non-conformity to annoy everyone. You're being childish!"

"Am not!" I said.

"I'm serious! It's like with your attitude toward Ernst." A book of Max Ernst prints, one of many art books she had checked out of the library, was resting on the coffee table—she gave it an angry tap. "Of all the books I bring home, this is the one you like best. You leaf through it all the time. But when I tell you I think he's great, you—"

"He's a fucking poster artist."

"Then why look at his work every single night?"

"He's easy on the eyes. That doesn't mean he's worth a shit. It just means his stuff pacifies you."

She gave her head a rueful shake.

"We're not talking about Max Ernst, anyway," I said.

"It doesn't matter what we talk about. Any subject it's the same. I don't understand you. I don't understand why you're here. In prison. You say the reason you started doing crime was due to your problems with authority, but I don't see that in you. It's there, I guess, but it doesn't seem that significant. I can't imagine you did crime simply because you wanted to spit in the face of authority."

"It wasn't anything deep, okay? It's not like I had an abusive childhood or my father ran off with his secretary. None of that shit. I'm a fuck-up. Crime was my way of fucking up."

"There must be something else! What appealed to you about it?"

"The thing I liked best," I said after giving the question a spin, "was sitting around a house I broke into at three in the morning, thinking how stupid the owners were for letting a mutt like me mess with their lives."

"And here you are, in a truly strange house, thinking we're all stupid."

The topic was making me uncomfortable. "We're always analyzing my problems. Let's talk about you for a change. Why don't you confide your big secrets so we can run 'em around the track a few times?"

A wounded expression came to her face. "The reason I haven't told you about my life is because I don't think you're ready to handle it."

"Don't you trust me?"

She leaned back against the cushions and folded her arms, stared at the coffee table. "That's not it…altogether."

"So you don't trust me and there's more. Great." I made a show of petulance, only partly acting it.

"I can't tell you some things."

"What's that mean?"

"It means I can't!" Her anger didn't seem a show, but it faded quickly. "You crossed the river to come here. We have to cross our own river. It's different from yours."

"The Mystery."

She looked surprised, and I told her what I had learned from Causey.

"He's right," she said. "I won't talk about it. I can't."

"Why? It's like a vow or something?"

"Or something." She relaxed her stiff posture. "The rest of it…I'm ashamed. When I look back, I can't believe I was so disreputable. Be patient, all right? Please?"

"You, too," I said.

"I *am* patient. I just enjoy arguing too much."

I put my hand beneath her chin, trying to jolly her. "If you want, we can argue some more."

"I want to win," she said, smiling despite herself.

"Everything's like you say. Diamond Bar's heaven on fucking earth. The board's—"

"I don't want you to give in!" She pushed me onto my back and lay atop me. "I want to break you down and smash your flimsy defenses!"

Her face, poised above me, bright-eyed and soft, lips parted, seemed oddly predatory, like that of a hungry dove. "What were we arguing about?" I asked.

"Everything," she said, and kissed me. "You, me, life. Max Ernst."

▲▼▲

One day while drinking a cup of coffee in the cafeteria, taking a break from work, I entered into a casual conversation with a dour red-headed twig of a man named Phillip Stringer, an ex-arsonist who had recently moved from the eighth tier into the old wing. He mentioned that he had seen me with Bianca a few nights previously. "She's a reg'lar wild woman!" he said. "You touch her titties, you better hold on, 'cause the next thing it's like you busting out of chute number three on Mustang Sally!"

Though giving and enthusiastic in sex, Bianca's disposition toward the act impressed me as being on the demure side of "reg'lar wild woman." Nevertheless, I withheld comment.

"She was too wild for me," Stringer went on. "It's not like I don't enjoy screwing chicks with dicks. Truth is, I got a thing for 'em. But when they got a bigger dick'n I got...guess I felt a tad intimidated."

"Hell are you talking about?" I asked.

He gazed at me in bewilderment. "The plume I saw you with. Bianca."

"You're fucked up, man! She doesn't have a dick."

"You think that, you never seen a dick. Thing's damn near wide around as a Coke can!"

"You got the wrong girl," I told him, growing irritated.

Stringer glowered at me. "I may not be the sharpest knife in the drawer, but I know who the hell I'm screwing."

"Then you're a goddamn liar," I said.

If it had been another time, another prison, we would been rolling around on the floor, thumbing eyes and throwing knees, but the placid offices of Diamond Bar prevailed, and Stringer dialed back his anger, got to his feet. "I been with that bitch must be fifty times, and I'm telling you she gets hard enough to bang nails with that son-of-a-bitch. She goes to bouncing up and down, moaning, "Only for you...." All kindsa sweet shit. You close your eyes, you'd swear you's with a woman. But you grab a peek and see that horse cock waggling around, it's just more'n I can handle." He hitched up his trousers. "You better get yourself an adjustment, pal. You spending way too much time on that painting of yours."

If it were not for the phrase "only for you," I would have disregarded what Stringer said. Indeed, I did disregard most of it. But that phrase, which Bianca habitually breathed into my ear whenever she drew near her moment, seeded me with paranoia, and that night as we sat on the sofa, going over the charcoal sketches she had done of her friends, I repeated the essence of Stringer's words, posing them as a joke. Bianca displayed no reaction, continuing to study one of the sketches.

"Hear what I said?" I asked.

"Uh-huh."

"Well?"

"What do you want me to say?'

"I guess I thought you'd say something, this guy going around telling everybody you got a dick."

She set down the sketchpad and looked at me glumly. "I haven't been with Phillip for nearly two years."

It took me a moment to interpret this. "I guess it's been such a long time he mixed you up with somebody."

The vitality drained from her face. "No."

"Then what the fuck are you saying?"

"When I was with Phillip, I was different from the way I am with you."

Irritated by the obliqueness with which she was framing her responses, I said, "You telling me you had a dick when you were seeing him?"

"Yes."

Hearing this did not thrill me, but I had long since dealt with it emotionally. "So after that you had the operation?"

"No."

"No? What? You magically lost your dick?"

"I don't want to talk about it."

"Well, I do! Hell are you trying to tell me?"

"I'm not sure how it happens…it just does! Whatever the man wants, that's how I am. It's like that with all the plumes…until you find the right person. The one you can be who you really are with."

I struggled to make sense of this. "So you're claiming a guy comes along wanting you to have a dick, you grow one?"

She gave a nod of such minimal proportions, it could have been a twitch. "I'm sorry."

"Gee," I said with thick sarcasm. "It's kinda like a fairy tale, isn't it?"

"It's true!" She put a hand to her forehead, collecting herself. "When I meet someone new, I change. It's confusing. I hardly know it's happening, but I'm different afterward."

I do not know what upset me more, the implication, however improbable, that she was a shapeshifter, capable of switching her sexual characteristics to please a partner, or the idea that she believed this. Either way, I found the situation intolerable. This is not to say I had lost my feelings for her, but I could no longer ignore the perverse constituency of her personality. I pushed up from the couch and started for the door.

Bianca cried out, "Don't go!"

I glanced back to find her gazing mournfully at me. She was beautiful, but I could not relate to her beauty, only to the neurotic falsity I believed had created it.

"Don't you understand?" she said. "For you, I'm who I want to be. I'm a woman. I can prove it!"

"That's okay," I said coldly, finally. "I've had more than enough proof."

▲▼▲

Things did not go well for me after that evening. The mural went well. Though I no longer approached the work with the passion I had formerly brought to it, every brushstroke seemed a contrivance of passion, to be the product of an emotion that continued to act through me despite the fact that I had forgotten how to feel it. Otherwise, my life at Diamond Bar became fraught with unpleasantness. Harry Colangelo, who had more-or-less vanished during my relationship with Bianca, once again began to haunt me. He would appear in the doorway of the anteroom while I was painting and stare venomously until I shouted at him. Inarticulate shouts like those you might use to drive a dog away from a garbage can. I developed back problems for which I was forced to take pain medication, and this slowed the progress of my work. Yet the most painful of my problems was that I missed Bianca, and there was no medication for this ailment. I was tempted to seek her out, to apologize for my idiocy in rejecting her, but was persuaded not to do so by behavioral reflexes that, though I knew them to be outmoded, having no relation to my life at the moment, I could not help obeying. Whenever an image of our time together would flash through my mind, immediately thereafter would follow some grotesquely sexual mockery of the image that left me confused and mortified.

I retreated into my work. I slept on the scaffolding, roused by the mysterious cry that like the call of some grievous religion announced each dawn. I lived on candy bars, peanut butter, crackers, and soda that I obtained at the commissary, and I rarely left the anteroom, keeping the door locked most of the days, venturing out only for supplies. When I woke I would see the mural surrounding me on every side, men with thick arms and cold white eyes pupiled with black suns, masses of them, clad in prison gray, crowded together on iron stairs (the sole architectural component of the design), many-colored faces engraved with desperation, greed, lust, rage, longing, bitterness, fear, muscling each other out of the way so as to achieve a clearer view of the unpainted resolution that overarched their suffering and violence. At times I thought I glimpsed in the mural—or underlying it—a cohesive element I had not foreseen, something created *from* me and not by me, a truth the work was teaching me, and in my weaker moments I supposed it to be the true purpose of Diamond Bar, still fragmentary and thus inexpressible; but I did not seek to analyze or clarify—if it was there, then its completion was not dependent upon my understanding. Yet having apprehended this unknown value in my work forced me to confront the reality that I was of two minds concerning the prison. I no longer perceived our lives as necessarily being under sinister control, and I had come to accept the possibility that the board was gifted with inscrutable wisdom, the prison itself an evolutionary platform, a crucible devised in order to invest its human ore with a fresh and potent mastery, and I glided between these two poles of thought with the same rapid pendulum swing that governed my contrary attitudes toward Bianca.

From time to time the board would venture into the anteroom to inspect the mural and offer their mumbling approbation, but apart from them and occasional sightings of Causey and Colangelo, I received no other visitors. Then one afternoon about six weeks after ending the relationship, while painting high on the scaffolding, I sensed someone watching me—Bianca was standing in the doorway thirty feet below, wearing a loose gray prison uniform that hid her figure. Our stares locked for an instant, then she gestured at the walls and said, "This is beautiful." She moved deeper into the room, ducking to avoid a beam, and let her gaze drift across the closely packed images. "Your sketches weren't…." She looked up at me, brushed strands of hair from her eyes. "I didn't realize you were so accomplished."

"I'm sorry," I said, so overcome by emotion that I was unable to react to what she had said, only to what I was feeling.

She gave a brittle laugh. "Sorry that you're good? Don't be."

"You know what I mean."

"No…not really. I thought by coming here I would, but I don't." She struck a pose against the mural, standing with her back to it, her right knee drawn up, left arm extended above her head. "I suppose I'll be portrayed like this."

It was so quiet I could hear a faint humming, the engine of our tension.

"I shouldn't have come," she said.

"I'm glad you did."

"If you're so glad, why are you standing up there?"

"I'll come down."

"And yet," she said after a beat, "still you stand there."

"How've you been?"

"Do you want me to lie? The only reason I can think of for you to ask that is you want me to lie. You know how I've been. I've been heartbroken." She ran a hand along one of the beams and examined her palm as if mindful of dust or a splinter. "I won't ask the same question. I know how you've been. You've been conflicted. And now you look frightened."

I felt encased in some cold unyielding substance, like a souvenir of life preserved in lucite.

"Why don't you talk to me?" She let out a chillier laugh. "Explain yourself."

"Jesus, Bianca. I just didn't understand what was going on."

"So it was an intellectual decision you made? A reaction to existential confusion?"

"Not entirely."

"I was making a joke." She strolled along the wall and stopped to peer at one of the faces.

"I wasn't," I said. "What you told me...how can you believe it?"

"You think I'm lying?"

"I think there's drugs in the food...in the air. Or something. There has to be a mechanism involved. Some sort of reasonable explanation."

"For what? My insanity?" She backed against the wall in order to see me better. "This is so dishonest of you."

"How's it dishonest?"

"You were happier thinking I was a post-operative transsexual? It's my irrational beliefs that drove you away? Please!" She fiddled with the ends of her hair. "Suppose what I told you is true. Suppose who I am with you is who you want me to be. Who I want to be. Would that be more unpalatable than if my sex was the result of surgery?"

"But it's not true."

"Suppose it is." She folded her arms, waiting.

"I don't guess it would matter. But that's not—"

"Now suppose just when we're starting to establish something strong, you rip it apart?" A quaver crept into her voice. "What would that make you?"

"Bianca...."

"It'd make you a fool! But then of course I'm living in a drug-induced fantasy that causes you existential confusion."

"Whatever the case," I said, "I probably am a fool."

It was impossible to read her face at that distance, but I knew her expression was shifting between anger and despair.

"Are you okay?" I asked.

"God! What's wrong with you?" She stalked to the door, paused in the entrance; she stood without speaking for what seemed a very long time, looking down at the floor, then glanced sideways up at me. "I was going to prove something to you today, but I can see proving it would frighten you even more. You have to learn to accept things, Tommy, or else you won't be able to do your time. You're not deceiving anyone except yourself."

"*I'm* deceiving myself? Now that's a joke!"

She waved at the mural. "You think what you're painting is a lie. Don't deny it. You think it's a con you're running on us. But when I leave it'll be the only thing in the room that's still alive." She stepped halfway through the door, hesitated and, in a voice that was barely audible, said, "Goodbye, Tommy."

▲▼▲

I experienced a certain relief after Bianca's visit, an emotion bred by my feeling that now the relationship was irretrievably broken, and I could refocus my attention on escape; but my relief was short-lived. It was not simply that I was unable to get Bianca out of my thoughts, or even that I continued to condemn myself both for abandoning her and for having involved myself with her in the first place—it was as if I were engaged in a deeper struggle, one whose nature was beyond my power to discern, though I assumed my attitudes toward Bianca contributed to its force. Because I was unable, or perhaps unwilling, to face it, this irresolvable conflict began to take a toll. I slept poorly and turned to drink as a remedy. Many days I painted drunk, but drunkenness had no deleterious effect on the mural—if anything, it sharpened my comprehension of what I was about. I redid the faces on the lower portions of the walls, accentuating their beastliness, contrasting them with more human faces above, and I had several small technical breakthroughs that helped me create the luminous intensity I wanted for the upper walls. The nights, however, were not so good. I went to wandering again, armed against self-recrimination and the intermittent appearances of Harry Colangelo with a bottle of something, usually home brew of recent vintage. Frequently I became lost in the sub-basements and wound up passed out on the floor. During one of these wanders, I noticed I was a single corridor removed from the habitat of the plumes, and this time, not deceiving myself as to motive, I headed for the white door. I had no wish to find Bianca. I was so debased in spirit, the idea of staining my flesh to match enticed me, and when I pushed into the entryway and heard loud rock and roll and saw that the halation surrounding the light fixtures had thickened into an actual mist that caused men and plumes to look like fantastical creatures, gray demons and their gaudy, grotesque mistresses, I plunged happily into the life of the place, searching for the most degrading encounter available.

Her name was Joy, a Los Angeleno by birth, and when I saw her dancing in the club with several men under a spotlight that shined alternately purple and rose, she seemed the parody of a woman. Not that she was unfeminine, not in the least. She was Raphaelesque, like an old-fashioned Hollywood blond teetering on the cusp between beauty and slovenly middle-age, glossy curls falling past her shoulders, the milky loaves of her breasts swaying ponderously in gray silk, her motherly buttocks dimpling beneath a tight skirt, her scarlet lips reminiscent of those gelatin lips full of cherry syrup you buy at Halloween, her eyes tunnels of mascara pricked by glitters. Drunk, I saw her change as the light changed. Under the purple she whitened, grew soft as ice cream, ultimately malleable; she would melt around you. Under the rose, a she-devilish shape emerged; her touch would make you feverish, infect you with a genital heat. I moved in on her, and because I had achieved an elevated status due to my connection with the board, the men dancing with her moved aside. Her fingers locked in my hair, her swollen belly rolled against me with the sodden insistence of a sea thing pushed by a tide. Her mouth tasted of liqueur and I gagged on her perfume, a scent of candied flowers. She was in every regard overpowering, like a blond rhinoceros. "What's the party for?" I shouted above the music. She laughed and cupped both hands beneath her breasts, offering them to me, and as I squeezed, manipulating their shapes, her eyelids drooped and her hips undulated. She pulled my head close and told me what she wanted me to do, what she would do.

Whereas sex with Bianca had been nuanced, passion cored with sensitivity, with Joy it was rutting, tumultuous, a jungle act, all sweat and insanity, pounding and meaty, and when I came I felt I was deflating, every pure thing spurting out of me, leaving a sack of bones and organic stink lying between her Amazon thighs. We fucked a second time with her on top. I twisted her nipples hard, like someone spinning radio dials, and throwing back her head she spat up great yells, then braced both hands on the pillow beside my head and hammered down onto me, her mouth slack, lips glistening with saliva poised an inch above mine, grunting and gasping. Then she straightened, arched her back, her entire body quaking, and let out a hideous groan followed by a string of profane syllables. Afterward she sat in a chair at her dressing table wearing a black bra and panties, legs crossed, attaching a stocking to her garter belt, posing an image that was to my eyes grossly sexual, repellently voluptuous, obscenely desirable. As she stretched out her leg, smoothing ripples in the silk, she said, "You used to be Bianca's friend."

I did not deny it.

"She's crazy about you, y'know."

"Is she here? At the party?"

"You don't need her tonight," Joy said. "You already got everything you needed."

"Is she here?"

She shook her head. "You won't be seeing her around for a while."

I mulled over this inadequate answer and decided not to pursue it.

Joy put on her other stocking. "You're still crazy about her. I'm a magnet for guys in love with other women." She admired the look of her newly stockinged leg. "It's not so bad. Sad guys fuck like they have something to prove."

"Is that right?"

"You were trying to prove something, weren't you?"

"Probably not what you think."

She adjusted her breasts, settling them more cozily in the brassiere. "Oh, I know exactly what you were trying to prove." She turned to the mirror, went to touching up her lipstick, her speech becoming halting as she wielded the applicator. "I am...expert in these matters...like all... ladies of the evening."

"Is that how you see yourself?"

She made a kissy mouth at her reflection. "There's something else in me, I think, but I haven't found the man who can bring it out." She adopted a thoughtful expression. "I could be very domestic with the right person. Very nurturing. Once the new wing's finished...I'm sure I'll find him then."

"There'll be real women living in the new wing. Lots of competition."

"We're the real women," she said with more than a hint of irritation. "We're not there yet, but we're getting there. Some of us are there already. You should know. Bianca's living proof."

Unwilling to explore this or any facet of this consensus fantasy, I changed the subject. "So, what's your story?" I asked.

"You mean my life story? Do you care?"

"I'm just making conversation."

"We had our conversation, sweetie. We just didn't talk all that much."

"I wasn't finished."

She looked at me over her shoulder, arching an eyebrow. "My, my. You must really have something to prove." She rested an elbow on the back of the chair. "Maybe you should go hunt up Bianca."

It was a thought, but one I had grown accustomed to rejecting. I reached down beside the bed, groping for my bottle. The liquor seemed to have an immediate effect, increasing my level of drunkenness, and with it my capacity for rejection. The colors of the room were smeary, as if made from different shades of lipstick. Joy looked slug-white and bloated, a sickly exuberance of flesh strangled by black lace, the monstrous ikon of a German Expressionist wet dream.

She gave what I took for a deprecating laugh. "Sure, we can converse some more if you want." She started to unhook her brassiere.

"Leave that shit on," I said. "I'll work around it."

▲▼▲

Not long after my night with Joy, a rumor began to circulate that one of the plumes had become pregnant, and when I discovered that the plume in question was Bianca, I tried to find her. I gave the rumor little credit. Yet she had claimed she could prove something to me, and thus I could not completely discredit it. I was unsure how I would react if the rumor reflected the truth, but what chance was there of that? My intention was to debunk the rumor. I would be doing her a favor by forcing her to face reality. That, at any rate, is what I told myself. When I was unable to track her down, informed that she was sequestered, I decided the rumor must be a ploy designed to win me back, abandoned my search, and once again focused my energy upon the mural. Though a third of the walls remained unfinished, I now had a more coherent idea of the figures that would occupy the dome, and I was eager to finalize the conception. Despite this vitality of purpose, I felt bereft, dismally alone, and when Richard Causey came to visit, I greeted him effusively, offering him refreshment from my store of junk food. Unlike my other visitors, he had almost nothing to say about the mural, and as we ate on the lowest platform of the scaffolding, it became obvious that he was preoccupied. His eyes darted about; he cracked his knuckles and gave indifferent responses to everything I said. I asked what was on his mind and he told me he had stumbled upon an old tunnel beneath the lowest of the sub-basements. The door leading to it was wedged shut and would take two people to pry open. He believed there might be something significant at the end of the tunnel.

"Like what?" I asked.

"I ran across some papers in the archives. Letters, documents. They suggested the tunnel led to the heart of the law." He appeared to expect me to speak, but I was chewing. "I figured you might want to have a look," he went on. "Seeing that's what you're painting about."

I worried that Causey might want to get me alone and finish what he had started years before; but my interest was piqued, and after listening for several minutes more, I grew convinced that his interest in the tunnel was purely academic. To be on the safe side, I brought along a couple of the chisels I used to scrape the walls—they would prove useful in unwedging the door as well. Though it was nearly three in the morning, we headed down into the sub-basements, joined briefly by Colangelo, who had been sleeping in the corridor outside the anteroom. I brandished a chisel and he retreated out of sight.

The door was ancient, its darkened boards strapped with iron bands, a barred grille set at eye level. It was not merely stuck, but sealed with concrete. I shined Causey's flashlight through the grille and was able to make out moisture gleaming on brick walls. With both of us wielding chisels, it required the better part of an hour to chip away the concrete and another fifteen minutes to force the door open wide enough to allow us to pass. The tunnel angled sharply downward in a series of switchbacks, and by the time we reached the fifth switchback, with no end in view, I realized that the walk back up was going to be no fun whatsoever. The bricks were slimy to the touch, rats skittered and squeaked, and the air...dank, foul, noisome. None of these words or any combination thereof serve to convey the vileness of the stench it carried. Molecules of corruption seemed to cling to my tongue, to the insides of my nostrils, coating my skin, and I thought that if the tunnel did, indeed, lead to the heart of the law, then that heart must be rotten to the core. I tied my shirt across the lower half of my face and succeeded in filtering the reek, yet was not able to block it completely.

I lost track of the passage of time and lost track, too, of how many switchbacks we encountered, but we traveled far beneath the hill, of that much I am certain, descending to a level lower than that of the river flowing past the gate of the prison annex before we spotted a glimmer of light. Seeing it, we slowed our pace, wary of attracting the notice of whatever might occupy the depths of Diamond Bar, but the space into which we at length emerged contained nothing that would harm us—a vast egglike chamber that gave out into diffuse golden light a hundred feet above and opened below into a black pit whose bottom was not visible. Though the ovoid shape of the chamber implied artificiality, the walls were of natural greenish-white limestone, configured by rippled convexities and volutes, and filigreed with fungal growths, these arranged in roughly horizontal rows that resembled lines of text in an unknown script; the hundreds of small holes perforating the walls looked to have been placed there to simulate punctuation. A considerable ledge rimmed the pit, populated by colonies of rats, all gone still and silent at the sight of us, and as we moved out onto it, we discovered that the acoustics of the place rivaled that of a concert hall. Our footsteps resounded like the scraping of an enormous rasp, and our breath was amplified into the sighing of beasts. The terror I felt did not derive from anything I have described so much as from the figure at the center of the chamber. Dwarfed by its dimensions, suspended from hooks that pierced his flesh at nine separate points and were themselves affixed to chains that stretched to the walls, was the relic of a man. His begrimed skin had the dark granite color of the prison's outer walls, and his long white hair was matted down along his back like a moldering cape; his limbs and torso were emaciated, his ribs and hipbones protruding and his ligature ridged like cables. Dead, I presumed. Mummified by some peculiar process.

"Quires!" Causey's whisper reverberated through the chamber. "Jesus Christ! It's Quires."

The man's head drooped, his features further hidden by clots of hair. I had no evidence with which to argue Causey's claim and, indeed, not much inclination to do so. Who else, according to the history of the prison, merited the torment the man must have experienced? It did not seem possible. Quires had been in his eighties when he stepped down as warden more than eighty years before. But the existence of the chamber undermined my conception of the possible. Its silence was so liquid thick and chilling, it might have been the reservoir from which the quiet of the prison flowed. A brighter fear flickered up in me.

"Let's go back," I said. "We shouldn't be here."

At the sound of my voice, the rats offered up an uneasy chittering chorus that swirled around us like the rushing of water in a toilet. Causey was about to respond to my urging when Quires—if it was he—lifted his head and gave forth with a cry, feeble at first, but swelling in volume, a release of breath that went on and on as if issuing not from his lungs but from an opening inside him that admitted to another chamber, another voice more capable of such a prolonged expression, or perhaps to a succession of openings and voices and chambers, the infinitely modulated utterance of a scream proceeding from an unguessable source. The chittering of the rats, too, swelled in volume.

Half-deafened, hands pressed to my ears, I sank to my knees, recognizing that the cry and its accompanying chorus was pouring up through the holes that perforated the walls and into every corner of the prison, a shout torn from the heart of the law to announce the advent of a bloody dawn. Quires' body spasmed in his chains, acquiring the shape of a dark thorn against the pale limestone, and his face.... Even at a distance I could see how years of torment had compressed his features into a knot of gristle picked out by two staring white eyes. I felt those eyes on me, felt the majestic insistence of his pain and his blissful acknowledgment that this state was his by right. He was the criminal at the heart of the law, the one in whom the arcs of evil and the redemptive met, the lightning rod through which coursed the twin electricities of punishment and sacrifice, the synchronicity of choice and fate, and I understood that as such he was the embodiment of the purpose of Diamond Bar, that only from evil can true redemption spring, only from true redemption can hope be made flesh. Joyful and reluctant, willing servant and fearful slave, he was thaumaturge and penitent, the violent psychotic saint who had been condemned to this harsh durance and simultaneously sought by that service to transfigure us. Thus illuminated, in that instant I could have translated and read to you the fungal inscriptions on the walls. I knew the meaning of every projection and declivity of stone, and knew as well that the heart of the law was empty except for the exaltation of the damned and the luminous peace of the corrupted. Then Quires' cry guttered, his head drooped. The rats fell silent again, returned to their petty scuttling, and all but a residue of my understanding fled.

I staggered up, but Causey, who had also been borne to his knees by the ferocity of the cry, remained in that posture, his lips moving as though in prayer, and it occurred to me that his experience of what had happened must have been far different from mine to produce such a reverent reaction. I turned again to Quires, realizing I could not help him, that he did not want my help, yet moved to give it nonetheless, and thus I did not see Colangelo break from the tunnel behind us...nor did I see him push Causey into the pit. It was Causey's outcry, shrill and feeble in contrast to Quires', but unalloyed in its terror, that alerted me to danger. When I glanced back I saw that he had vanished into the depths, his scream trailing after him like a snapped rope, and on the spot where he had knelt, Colangelo stood glaring at me, Causey's chisel in his right hand. Had he forced a confrontation in the anteroom, anywhere in the upper levels of the prison, I would not have been so afraid, for though he was taller and heavier, I was accustomed to fighting men bigger than myself; but that dread place eroded my confidence, and I stumbled away from him, groping for my own chisel. He said nothing, made no sound apart from the stentorian gush of his breath, pinning me with his little eyes. The wan light diminished the pinkness of his skin. His lips glistened.

"The hell is your problem?" I said; then, alarmed by the reverberations of my voice, I added in a hushed tone, "I didn't do shit to you."

Colangelo let out an enervated sigh, perhaps signaling an unraveling of restraint, and rushed at me, slashing with the chisel. I caught his wrist and he caught mine. We swayed together on the edge of the pit, neither of us able to gain an advantage, equal in strength despite the difference in our sizes. The excited squeaking of the rats created a wall around us, a multiplicity of tiny cheers hardened into a shrill mosaic. At such close quarters, his anger and my fear seemed to mix and ferment a madness fueled by our breath, our spittle. I wanted to kill him. That was all I wanted. Everything else—Quires, Causey, the panic I had previously felt—dwindled to nothing.

Colangelo tried to butt me. I avoided the blow and, putting my head beneath his chin, pushed him back from the pit. He went off-balance, slipped to one knee. I wrenched my left arm free and brought my elbow hard into his temple. He slumped, still clutching my wrist, preventing me from using my chisel. I threw another elbow that landed on the hinge of his jaw, an uppercut that smacked into the side of his neck and elicited a grunt. He sagged onto his side as I continued to hit him, and when he lost consciousness I straddled his chest and lifted the chisel high, intending to drive it into his throat; but in straightening, I caught sight of Quires hanging at the center of his chains. He did not look at me, but I was certain that in some way he was watching, aware of the moment. How could he not be? He was the substance of the prison, its spirit and its fleshly essence, the male host in whom the spider of female principle had laid its eggs, and as such was witness to our every thought and action. I sensed from him a caution. Not reproval, nothing so pious. In the thin tide of thought that washed between us there was no hint of moral preachment, merely a reminder of the limit I was on the verge of transgressing. What was it Ristelli had said? "Innocents and murderers. The system tolerates neither." Madness receded, and I came to my feet. Prison logic ordained that I should push Colangelo into the pit and spare myself the inevitability of a second attack; but the logic of Diamond Bar, not Vacaville, commanded me. Numbed by the aftershocks of adrenaline and rage, I left him for the rats or whatever else fate might have in store, and with a last glance at Quires, suspended between the light of heaven and the pit, like the filament in a immense bulb, I began my ascent.

I had in mind to seek out Berbick or someone else whom Causey had befriended, to tell them what had become of him and to determine from their advice whether or not to make the events of the night and morning known to the board. Perhaps, I thought, by opening the sealed door I had violated an inviolate taboo and would suffer as a result. I might be blamed for Causey's death. But as I trudged wearily up along the switchbacks, the emotion generated by my fight with Colangelo ebbed away, and the awful chamber in which we had struggled began to dominate my thoughts. Its stench, its solitary revenant, its nightmarish centrality to the life of the prison. With each step, I grew increasingly horrified by my acceptance of the place and the changes it had worked in me. It had neutered my will, obscured my instincts, blinded me to perversity. The things I had done.... Bianca, Joy, my devotion to that ridiculous mural. What had I been thinking? Where the fuck had Tommy Penhaligon gone? I wanted to be who I was at that precise moment: someone alert to every shadow and suspicious presence; open to the influence of emotion and not governed by a pathological serenity that transformed violent men into studious, self-examining drones and, were you to believe the plumes, less violent men into women. If I returned to my cell and confided in Berbick, thereby obeying the rule of the prison, sooner or later I would be sucked back in and lose this hard-won vantage from which I could perceive its depravity and pathetic self-involvements. I had no good prospects in the world, but all I could aspire to in Diamond Bar was that one day I would go shuffling through the yard, an old man dimly persuaded that he had been gifted with the grasp of a holy principle too great for the brains of common men to hold, a principle that was no more than a distorted reflection of the instrumentality responsible for his dementia. Instead of heading to my cell, when I reached the eighth stair I kept walking down through the hill toward the annex gate, past the cells of sedate men who had grown habituated to the prison, past those of agitated new arrivals; and when I reached the gate—it was, of course, unlocked—I threw it open and stood on the threshold, gazing out upon a beautiful spring morning. Cool and bright and fresh. A lacework of sun and shadow under the dark firs. The river running green with snowmelt. I had no fear of the quick-flowing current; I had crossed it once in handcuffs, and unfettered I would cross it all the more easily. Yet I hesitated. I could not, despite my revulsion for what lay behind me, put a foot forward on the path of freedom. I felt something gathering in the woods, a presence defined by the sound of rushing water, the shifting boughs and pouring wind. A wicked immanence, not quite material, needing me to come out from the gate a step or two in order to be real. I berated myself for a coward, tried to inject my spine with iron, but second by second my apprehension grew more detailed. I had a presentiment of jaws, teeth, a ravenous will, and I backed away from the gate, not far, but far enough to slow my pulse, to think. No one walked out of prison. There must be watchers...a single watcher, perhaps. A mindless four-footed punishment for the crime of flight. I told myself this was the same illusion of threat that had driven me inside the walls many months before, but I could not disregard it. The beckoning green and gold of the day, the light rippling everywhere—these had the insubstantiality of a banner fluttered across a window, hiding a dreadful country from my sight.

Once kindled, fear caught in me and burned. The flickering of sun on water; the stirring of fallen needles; mica glinting on the face of a boulder: these were unmistakable signs of an invisible beast who slumbered by the steps of the prison. I heard a noise. It may have been someone starting a chainsaw downriver, a car engine being revved, but to my ears it was a growl sounded high in a huge throat, a warning and a bloody promise. I sprang to the gate and slammed it shut, then rested against the cold metal, weak with relief. My eyes went to the second level of the tier. Gazing down at me was a man in a guard's uniform, absently tapping the palm of his hand with a nightstick. I could hear the slap of wood on flesh, counting out the time with the regularity of a metronome, each stroke ticking off the ominous fractions of his displeasure. Finally, as if he had become sure of me, he sheathed the nightstick and walked away, the sharp report of his boot heels precisely echoing the now-steady rhythm of my heart.

▲▼▲

I spent the remainder of the day and half the night staring at the discolorations on the wall opposite my bunk—they had never come in fully, never developed into a complicated abstraction as had the walls of my fellow prisoners, possibly because the walls upon which I expended most of my energy were the ones in the anteroom of the new wing. Yet during those hours I saw in their sparse scatter intimations of the scriptlike fungus inscribed upon the walls of the chamber at the heart of the law, indecipherable to me now as Arabic or Mandarin, tantalizingly inscrutable—I suspected they were the regulations by which we lived, and contemplating them soothed me. I could not avoid recalling the chamber and the man suspended therein, but my thoughts concerning these things were speculative, funded by neither fear nor regret. If it had been Quires, one hundred-and-sixty years old and more, tortured for half that span, this lent credence to Causey's assertion that Czerny, LeGary, Ashford, and Holmes were the original board of Diamond Bar who had been photographed with the warden in 1917...and what did that say about the potentials of the prison? Time and again I returned to the truths I had sensed as Quires cried out from his chains, the dualities of punishment and sacrifice he seemed to incorporate. It was as if he were a battery through which the animating principle of the place was channeled. This was a simplistic analogy, yet when coupled with the image of a Christlike figure in torment, simplicity took on mythic potency and was difficult to deny. Now that I had proved myself unequal to traditional freedom, I was tempted to believe in the promised freedom of the new wing, in all the tenuous promise of Diamond Bar. The illusion of freedom, I realized, was the harshest of prisons, the most difficult to escape. Ristelli, Causey, Czerny, and Bianca had each in their way attempted to lead me to this knowledge, to demonstrate that only in a place like Diamond Bar, where walls kept that illusion at bay, was the road to freedom discernable. I had been a fool to disregard them.

Near midnight, a skinny, towheaded man stopped in front of my cell door and blew cigarette smoke through the bars from his shadowed mouth. I did not know him, but his arrogance and deferential attitude made me suspect he was a familiar of the board. "You're wanted at the annex gate, Penhaligon," he said, and blew another stream of smoke toward me. He looked off along the corridor, and in the half-light I saw the slant of a cheekbone, skin pitted with old acne scars.

In no mood to be disturbed, I asked, "What for?"

"Man's being transferred. Guess they need a witness."

I could not imagine why a transfer would require witnesses, and I felt the creep of paranoia; but I did not think the board would resort to trickery in the exercise of their power, and, reluctantly, I let the man escort me down through the annex.

The gate was open, and gathered by the entranceway, in partial silhouette against the moonstruck river, was a group of men, ten or twelve in all, consisting of the board and their spokesmen. Their silence unsettled me, and once again I grew paranoid, thinking that I was to be transferred; but then I spotted Colangelo off to one side, hemmed in against the wall by several men. His head twitched anxiously this way and that. The air was cool, but he was perspiring. He glanced at me, betraying no reaction—either he did not register me or else he had concluded that I was only a minor functionary of his troubles.

Czerny, along with LeGary, Ashford, and Holmes, was positioned to the left of the entrance. As I waited for whatever ritual was to occur, still uncertain why I had been invited, he came a tottering step toward me, eyes down, hands fingering his belt, and addressed me in his usual muttering cadence. I did not understand a single word, but the towheaded man, who was sticking to my elbow, said in a snide tone, "You been a bad boy, Penhaligon. That's what the man's telling you. You seen things few men have seen. Maybe you needed to see them, but you weren't prepared."

The towheaded man paused and Czerny spoke again. I could find nothing in his face to support the sternness of his previous words—he seemed to be babbling brokenly, as if speaking to a memory, giving voice to an imaginary dialogue, and thinking this, I wondered if that was what we were to him, memories and creatures of the imagination: if he had gone so far along the path to freedom that even those who lived in Diamond Bar had come to be no more than shadows in his mind.

"This is the edge of the pit," the towheaded man said when Czerny had finished. "The one you saw below is only its metaphor. Here you were closest to peril. That's why we have summoned you, so you can watch and understand."

Another spate of muttering and then the towheaded man said, "This is your final instruction, Penhaligon. There are no further lessons to be learned. From now on we will not protect you."

Czerny turned away, the audience ended, but angered by his claim that the board had protected me—I had no memory of being protected when I fought with Colangelo—and emboldened by the certainty that I was not to be transferred, I said to him, "If the pit I saw below was a metaphor, tell me where Causey is."

The old man did not turn back, but muttered something the towheaded man did not have to translate, for I heard the words clearly.

"If you are fortunate," Czerny said, "you will meet him again in the new wing."

The towheaded man nudged me forward to stand by Czerny and the rest of the board, inches away from the line demarcating the limits of the prison and the beginning of the world, a dirt path leading downward among boulders to the river flashing along its course. I have said the river was moonstruck, yet that scarcely describes the brightness of the landscape. The light was so strong even the smallest objects cast a shadow, and though the shadows beneath the boughs quivered in a fitful wind, they looked solid and deep. The dense firs and the overhang of the entrance prevented me from seeing the moon, but it must have been enormous—I pictured a blazing silvery face peering down from directly above the river, pocked by craters that sketched the liver spots and crumpled features of a demented old man. Sprays of water flying from the rocks in midstream glittered like icy sparks; the shingle on the far shore glittered as though salted with silver. Beyond it, the terrain of the opposite bank lay hidden beneath a dark green canopy, but patches of needles carpeting the margins of the forest glowed a reddish-bronze.

Who it was that shoved Colangelo out onto the path, I cannot say—I was not watching. It must have been a hard shove, for he went staggering down the slope and fell to all fours. He collected himself and glanced back toward us, not singling anyone out, it seemed, but taking us all in, as if claiming the sight for memory. He wiped dirt from his hands, and judging by his defiant posture I expected him to shout, to curse, but he turned and made for the river, going carefully over the uneven ground. When he reached the river's edge, he stopped and glanced back a second time. I could not make out his face, though he stood in the light, but judging by the sudden furtiveness of his body language, I doubted he had believed that he would get this far, and now that he had, the idea that he actually might be able to escape sprang up hot inside him, and he was prey to the anxieties of a man afflicted by hope.

Oddly enough, I hoped for him. I felt a sympathetic response to his desire for freedom. My heart raced and my brow broke a sweat, as if it were I and not that ungainly pinkish figure who was stepping from rock to rock, arms outspread for balance, groping for purchase on the slick surfaces, wobbling a bit, straining against gravity and fear. I had no apprehension of an inimical presence such as I had detected that morning, and this made me think that it had been nerves alone that had stopped me from escaping, and increased my enthusiasm for Colangelo's escape. I wanted to cheer, to urge him on, and might have done so if I had not been surrounded by the silent members of the board and their faithful intimates. That Colangelo was doing what I had not dared caused me envy and bitterness but also infected me with hope for myself. The next time I was alone at the gate, perhaps I would be equal to the moment.

The wind kicked up, outvoicing the chuckling rush of the river, sending sprays higher over the rocks, and along with the wind, the brightness of the river intensified. Every eddy, every momentary splotch of foam, every sinewy swell of water glinted and dazzled, as if it were coming to a boil beneath Colangelo. He kept going past the midpoint, steadier, more confident with each step, unhampered by the buffets of the wind. Close by the gate the boughs bent and swayed, stirring the shadows, sending them sliding forward and back over the dirt like a black film. The whole world seemed in motion, the atoms of the earth and air in a state of perturbation, and as Colangelo skipped over the last few rocks, I realized there was something unnatural about all this brilliant movement. The shapes of things were breaking down...briefly, for the merest fractions of seconds, their edges splintering, decaying into jittering bits of bright and dark, a pointillist dispersion of the real. I assumed I was imagining this, that I was emotionally overwrought, but the effect grew more pronounced. I looked to Czerny and the board. They were as always—distracted, apparently unalarmed—but what their lack of reaction meant, whether they saw what I did and were unsurprised, whether they saw something entirely different, I could not determine.

Colangelo let out a shout—of triumph, I believed. He had reached the shore and was standing with a fist upraised. The sand beneath his feet was a shoal of agitated glitter, and at his back the bank was a dark particulate dance, the forms of the trees disintegrating into a rhythm of green and black dots, the river into a stream of fiery unreality. How could he not notice? He shouted again and flipped us off. I realized that his outlines were shimmering, his prison garb blurring. Everything around him was yielding up its individuality, blending with the surround, flattening into an undifferentiated backdrop. It was nearly impossible to tell the sprays of water from sparkling currents in the air. The wind came harder, less like a wind in its roaring passage than the flux of some fundamental cosmic force, the sound of time itself withdrawing from the frame of human event, of entropy and electron death, and as Colangelo sprinted up the bank into cover of the forest, he literally merged with the setting, dissipated, the stuff of his body flowing out to be absorbed into a vibratory field in which not one distinguishable form still flourished. I thought I heard him scream. In all that roaring confusion I could not be certain, but he was gone. That much I knew. The world beyond the annex gate was gone as well, its separate forms dissolved into an electric absence of tremulous black, green, and silver motes, depthless and afire with white noise, like a television set tuned to a channel whose signal had been lost.

The board and their retainers moved away, talking softly among themselves, leaving me on the edge of the prison, of the pit, watching as—piece by piece—the forest and river and rocks reassembled, their inconstant shapes melting up from chaos, stabilizing, generating the imitation of a perfect moonlit night, the air cool and bracing, the freshness of the river sweetly palpable, all things alive with vital movement—boughs shifting, fallen needles drifting, light jumping along the surface of the water with the celerity of a charge along a translucent nerve. Even after what I had seen, I stood there a long while, tempted to run into the night, disbelieving the evidence of my senses, mistrusting the alternatives to belief, and so oppressed in spirit that I might have welcomed dissolution. A step forward, and I would be free one way or another. I stretched out a hand, testing its resistance to the dissolute power of the world beyond, and saw no hint of blurring or distortion. Yet still I stood there.

▲▼▲

The anteroom is empty of scaffolding, swept clean of plaster dust, and I am sitting in a folding chair beneath the domed ceiling, like—I imagine—a gray-clad figure escaped from the lower portions of my mural. Years down the road I may look back and judge my work harshly, but I know at this moment I have achieved my goal and created something greater than myself. The mural rises up from solidity into the diffuse, from dark specificity into layered washes of light from which less definite figures emerge…less definite, at least, from this vantage. At close quarters they are easily identifiable. Bianca is there, a golden swimmer in the air, and at her side our son, her proof made flesh, born five months after our conversation in this very room. When told of his birth I went to visit her in the newly designated maternity ward of the prison hospital. Sleeping, she looked exhausted, her color weak and cheeks sunken, yet she was beautiful nonetheless. The child slept beneath a blanket in a crib beside her bed, only the back of his head visible. My emotions seemed to be circling one another like opponents in a ring. It was so strange to think of her with a child. Now that she had established the ultimate female credential, the freak detector in my brain emitted a steady beep. It was as if I were determined to paint her with a perverse brush, to view her condition and her Mystery in terms of an aberration. At the same time, I was drawn to her as never before. All my old feelings were reinvigorated. I decided to seek a reconciliation, but when I informed her of this she told me it was not what she wanted.

"You can't hide what you feel," she said. "You're still conflicted." She gave "conflicted" a distasteful reading and closed her eyes. "I'm too tired to argue. Please go."

I sat with her a bit longer, thinking she might relent, but when she fell asleep again I left the room. We see each other on occasion. Each time we meet she searches my face but thus far has found no apparent cause for confidence there. I have little hope she will ever find me other than wanting, and the prospect of life without her grows more difficult to bear. It seems I cannot shake the skepticism that Frank Ristelli correctly attributed to me, for despite everything I have experienced at Diamond Bar, I continue to speculate that our lives are under the influence of a powerful coercive force that causes us to believe in unrealities. My chest, for instance. Some weeks ago I noticed a scatter of pale discolorations surfaced from the skin thereon, their hues and partly rendered shapes reminiscent of the tattoo on Ristelli's chest, and yet when that tattoo achieves final form, as I assume it must, I will with part of my mind seek an explanation that satisfies my cynic's soul. If the birth of a child from a woman once a man fails to persuade me of the miraculous, is there anything that will overwhelm my capacity for doubt? Only when I paint does the current of belief flow through me, and then I am uncertain whether the thing believed is intrinsic to the subject of the work or a constant of my ego, a self-aggrandizing principle I deify with my obsessive zeal.

Ristelli, too, occupies a place in the dome of the anteroom, a mangy gray ghost slipping back into the world, and Causey is there as well, tumbling toward its center where, almost buried in light, Quires hangs in his eternal torment, a promethean Christ yielding to a barbaric sacrifice. I have pored over Causey's notes and rummaged the archives in an attempt to learn more about Quires, to understand what brought him to this pass. A transcendent moment like the one that left Saul stricken on the road to Damascus, an illumination of blinding sight? Or did Quires gradually win his way to a faith strong enough to compel his redemptive act? I have discovered no clue to explain his transformation, only a record of atrocities, but I think now both answers are correct, that all our labors are directed toward the achievement of such a moment, and perhaps therein lies the root cause of my skepticism, for though an illumination of this sort would remove the barriers that keep me from my family, I fear that moment. I fear I will dissolve in light, grow addled and vague, like Czerny, or foolishly evangelical like Ristelli. The abhorrence of authority that pushed me into a criminal life resists even an authority that promises ultimate blessing. I am afflicted with a contrarian's logic and formulate unanswerable questions to validate my stance. I poison my feeble attempts at faith with the irrationalities and improbabilities of Diamond Bar.

Pleased by my celebration of their myth, the board has offered me another room to paint, and there I intend to celebrate Bianca. I have already sketched out the design. She will be the sole figure, but one repeated in miniature over and over again, emerging from flowers, aloft on floating islands, draped in shadow, dressed in dozens of guises and proximate past forms, a history of color and line flowing toward her twice lifesized image hovering like a Hindu goddess in an exotic heaven populated by her many incarnations. That I have relegated her to the subject of a painting, however contemplative of her nature, suggests that I have given up on the relationship, turned my obsession from the person to the memory of the person. This distresses me, but I cannot change the way things are. My chains still bind me, limiting my choices and contravening the will to change. In recent months, I have come to envision a future in which I am an ancient gray spider creaking across a web of scaffolding that spans a hundred rooms, leaking paintlike blood in his painful, solitary progress, creating of his life an illuminated tomb commemorating folly, mortal confusion, and lost love. Not so terrible a fate, perhaps. To die and love and dream of perfect colors, perfect forms. But like all those who strive and doubt and seek belief, I am moving rapidly in the direction of something that I fear, something whose consolations I mistrust, and am inclined to look past that inevitability, to locate a point toward which to steer. My son, whom Bianca has named Max, after—she says—her favorite painter, Max Ernst, an implied insult, a further dismissal from her life...I sometimes think my son might serve as such a point. My imagination is captivated by the potentials of a man so strangely born, and often I let myself believe he will be the wings of our liberty, the one in whom the genius of our home will fully manifest. Since he is kept apart from me, however, these thoughts have the weight of fantasy, and I am cast back onto the insubstantial ground of my own life, a gray silence in which I have rarely found a glint of promise. Tears come easily. Regrets like hawks swoop down to pluck my hopeful thoughts from midair. And yet, though I am afraid that, as with most promises of fulfillment, it will always hang beyond our grasp, an eidolon, the illusion of perfection, lately I have begun to anticipate the completion of the new wing. —

Hands Up! Who Wants to Die?

Shit happens, like they say. You know how it goes. The cops are looking at you for every nickel-and-dime robbery they can't solve, and the landlady hates your guts for no reason except she's a good Christian hater, and everything in the world is part of a clock you got to punch or else you'll be docked or fined or sentenced to listen to some ex-doper who thinks he has attained self-mastery explain your behavior as if the reasons you're a loser are a mystery that requires illumination. Otherwise it's been a kicked dog of a week. The boss man's had you stocking the refrigerator sections of the food mart, leaving you alone in the freezer while he sits and swaps Marine Corps stories with the guy supposed to be your helper, so you come off work half froze, looking for something to douse the meanness you're feeling, which could be a chore since you're a piss and a holler from being broke and New Smyrna Beach ain't exactly Vegas. Well, turns out to be your lucky night. Along about eight o'clock you wind up with a crew of rejects in a beach shack belongs to this fat old biker, snorting greasy homemade speed, swilling grape juice and vodka, with a windblown rain raising jazz beats from the tarpaper roof like brushes on cymbals. There's a woman with big brown eyes and punky peroxided hair who's a notch on the plain side of pretty, but she's got one of those black girl butts sometimes get stuck onto a white girl, and it's clear she's come down with the same feeling as you, so when the rain lets up and she says how she's got an itch to sneak onto the government property down the beach and check out what's there, when everybody tells her it ain't nothing but sand fleas and Spanish bayonet, you say, Hell I'll go with you. Ten minutes later you're helping her jump down from a hurricane fence, risking a felony bust for a better view of those white panties gleaming against the strip of tanned skin that's showing between her jeans and her tank top. She falls into you, gives you a kiss and a half, and before you can wrap her up, she scoots off into the dark and you go stumbling after.

It don't take more than that to get shit started.

—Hey, I shouted. Come on back here!

She glanced at me over her shoulder, her grin shining under a moon fresh out of hiding, then she skipped off behind some scrub palmetto. I was trying to recall her name as I ran, then a frond whacked me in the face and I slipped to a knee in the soft sand. I spotted her moving along a rise, framed by low stars. Hell you going, girl? I said, coming up beside her.

She slapped at a skeeter on her neck and said, Lookit there.

The land was all dips and rises, an old dune top gone nappy with shrubs and beach grass, but down below was a scooped-out circular area, wide and deep enough to bury a mini-mall in. Dead center of it stood a ranch house with cream-colored block walls and a composite roof and glass doors. It was a giant banana, I couldn't have been more startled.

—I heard about there was a house here, she said. But I swear I didn't believe it!

We scrambled down the slope and tromped around the house, peering in windows. Some rooms were empty, others were partly furnished, and though I wouldn't have figured on it, the sliding door at the back was unlocked. I shoved it open and she put her hands over her head and got to snapping her fingers and hip-shaked across the threshold. A big leather sofa stood by its lonesome in the middle of the room. She struck a pose beside it, skinned off her jeans and showed me what I wanted. Wasn't long before we were sweating all over each other, grunting and huffing like hogs in a hurry, our teeth clicking together when we kissed. The cushions got so slippery, we slid off onto the floor afterward and lay twisted together. The moon came pale through the flyspecked glass, but it wasn't sufficient to light the corners of the room.

—God, I could use something to drink, she said. I know there can't be nothing in the kitchen.

My carpenter's pants were puddled at the end of the couch. I undid the flap pockets and hauled out two wine coolers. What you want? I asked. Tropical Strawberry or Mango Surprise?

—I can't believe you carrying 'round wine coolers in your pocket.

—I hooked 'em off a truck when I was coming outa work.

We unscrewed the caps, clinked our bottles and drank.

—My name's Leeli, she said, sticking out her hand. I'm sorry but I forget yours.

—Maceo.

—That a family name? It's so unusual!

—It's for some guitar player my mama liked.

—Well, it's real unusual.

She seemed to be expecting me to take a turn, so I asked what a house was doing out there setting in a hole.

—Beats me. Government bought up all the land 'round here years ago. To keep people away from the Cape...'cause of the rockets, y'know? But I never knew nothing was here. My ex, his friend runs a helicopter tourist ride? I guess he saw it once.

—Maybe they opened it up for development, I said. And this here's the model home.

—Y'know, I bet you're right! She gave me a proud mama look, like my-ain't-you-smart!

I couldn't think of anything else to say, so I went to loving her up again. She started running hot and came astride me, but before she could settle herself, she let out a shriek and crawled over top the couch. I rolled my eyes back to see what had spooked her, said "Shit...Jesus!" and next thing I was hunkered behind the couch with Leeli, my heart banging in my chest.

Two men and a woman were hanging by the glass doors, nailing us with a six-eyed stare as clear in its negativity as a No Trespassing sign. The men were young, both a shade under six feet, dressed in slacks and T-shirts. A blond and a baldy. They had the look of fitness sissies, like they might have pumped some iron and run a few laps, but never put the results to any spirited use. The woman wore cut-offs and an oversized denim shirt and carried a bulky tote bag. She was fortyish and big-boned, with wavy dark hair, and her body had a sexy looseness that would still draw its share of eye traffic. Her face was full of bad days and wrong turns, the lines cutting her forehead and dragging down her mouth making it seem older than the rest of her. Way the men tucked themselves in at her shoulders, you could tell she was queen of the hive.

Leeli clutched at my arm, breathing fast. Nobody said nothing. Finally I came out from behind the couch and tossed Leeli her panties. I stepped into my pants and feeling more confident with my junk covered, I said, Have yourself a show, did ya?

—Have yourself a show? the blond man said, mocking me, and the baldy sniggered like a kid who'd seen his first dirty picture.

I pulled on my shirt. Y'know this here's government property? Y'all be in deep shit, I turn your asses in.

—You saying you the government? The woman's voice was a contralto drawl made me think of a dollop of honey hanging off the lip of a jar. You the first government man I seen got jailhouse ink on his arms. She turned to Leeli, who was tugging the tank top down over her breasts. How's about you, sweetcheeks? You in the government, too?

Leeli snatched up her jeans. You got no more right being here than we do!

The woman sniffed explosively, like a cat sneezing, and the bald man said, You can't get much more government than we are. Government's like mommy and daddy to us.

Leeli piped up, Well, whyn't you show us your ID?

The flow of feeling in the room was running high, like everyone was waiting for a direction to fly off in.

—Screw this, said the woman. We was just going for a drink. Y'all wanna come?

I was about to say we'd do our own drinking, but Leeli said, It's Margarita Night over the Dixieland! and soon everybody was saying stuff like, Looked like you was gonna fall out and God you scared the hell outa me and telling their names and their stories. Though he didn't seem up to the job, the blond man, Carl, was the woman's husband. Her name was Ava and she owned a club in Boynton Beach where the bald man, Squire, worked as a bartender. I knew a kid name of Squire back in high school who was accused of having sex with a neighbor's collie. Much as I would have enjoyed bringing this up, I kept it to myself.

We piled out through the glass doors, both Carl and Squire heading toward the water. Fuck you think you going? I asked.

—Ava got her four-by-four parked down on the beach, Squire said.

I was staring at Ava and Leeli, who were still back at the glass doors. Leeli had her head down and Ava was talking. Something didn't sit right about the way they were together.

—Government don't care what goes on at the house no more, Squire said, apparently thinking I was off onto another track. We been partying here for years.

▲▼▲

You know that kid's toy ball you can bounce and instead of coming straight back to your hand, it goes dribbling off along the floor or kicks off to the side? My expectations of the weekend had taken just that sort of wrong-angled bounce. After Leeli and I broke in the leather couch, I assumed we'd be heading over to my place, maybe coming up for air sometime Sunday. A shitkicker bar had for sure not been part of the plan.

The Dixieland was down on A1A, a concrete block eyesore with a neon sign on the roof that spelled the name in red and blue letters, except for the N was missing, which might have accounted for the gay boys who occasionally dropped in and left real quick. All the waitresses were decked out in Rebel caps and there were Confederate flags laminated on the table tops. The Friday night crowd was men in cowboy hats who had never set a horse and women with flakes of mascara clinging to their lashes and skirts so short you could see the tattooed butterflies, roses, hummingbirds and such advertising their little treasures whenever they hopped up onto a barstool. Some country & western goatboy was howling on the jukebox about the world owed him a living, while a few couples dragged around the dance floor, Ava and Leeli among them. Their relationship appeared to be deepening.

Carl fell in love with a digital beer display behind the bar that showed a bikini girl waterskiing. I was coming to understand the boy must have some empty rooms in his attic. He stood gawking at the thing like he was stoned on Jesus love. That left Squire and me alone at a table, sucking on our margaritas. Shaving his head probably hadn't done for Squire what he hoped. It made his face resemble a cream pie somebody drew a man-in-the moon face on, but he tried to sell the look as being the front door into the world of a badass individual with secrets you would want to know. It was kinda pathetic. He threw a couple of insults my way and when that didn't get a rise, he went on about how tight he was with Carl and Ava, how they'd been partying for two months solid, saying me and Leeli needed to get on board the party train, they'd sure show us a time.

—Two month vacation must get in the way of your bartending, I said and he said, Huh?, then got flustered and came back with, Oh, yeah... hell, I just work when we're there, y'know.

The juke box played the Dixie Chicks. Leeli squealed, clapped her hands, and did this slow, snaky hula, dancing like she was on stage at a titty bar and using Ava for the pole.

—We ain't hardly ever there, though. Squire said this like it was super important for me to understand. He started to spout more worthless bullshit, but I told him to hang onto the thought. I walked over to Ava and tapped her on the shoulder and said, 'Scuse me, buddy. Believe it's my turn. She flashed a condescending smile and backed off. Leeli kept her eyes closed like she didn't care what was going on, she was so lost in the music, but when I put my leg where Ava's hip had been she said, That was rude!

—Yeah she was, I said.

She punched me in the chest, but didn't leave off dry-humping my leg. Just 'cause we did the deed, don't you go waving no papers at me.

—That wasn't my intention.

She didn't hear and I said it again louder.

This ticked her off. Just what is your intention? she asked.

—I got a friend in Lauderdale lets me use his beach house. I thought we could drive down next weekend and see how it goes. But hey, you wanna fuck the old skank, do it.

—Well, maybe I will! She looped her arms about my neck and smiled me up. Or maybe I'll wait 'til after Lauderdale.

I thought the two of us were back on track, but when Ava decided to hit another bar, Leeli said in a cajoling voice, I'm having so much fun! Let's not go home yet! Wasn't until we wound up in a Daytona Beach motel on Saturday morning, sleeping in the room next to Ava's, that I realized somewhere in the middle of all those tequila shots, we'd climbed aboard the party train. I remembered telling everybody about the beach house. From that I guess the idea had developed for Ava to drive me and Leeli to Lauderdale, making frequent stops for refreshment, with Ava paying the freight. They weren't going to welcome me back at the food mart when I turned up a week late for my shift, but that world was spinning me nowhere and I thought I might take a shot at separating Ava from some of the money she'd been throwing around. I worried about her going after Leeli, though. We'd only had us the one night, but Leeli and I seemed to recognize each other's zero score in life as only folks do who're born in a neighborhood where the most you aspire to is a double-wide and sufficient loose change to afford a couple of cases on the weekend. We'd both worn out our craziness to the point where we saw we might have us a nice little run and maybe avoid killing each other at the end. Once she loosened up and that sick-of-it-all waitress hardness drained from her face, I saw a sweet seam in her no one had bothered to mine.

I left Leeli sleeping and smoked in the breezeway of the motel, watching two rat-skinny children splash and squeak in the pool, while their two hundred pound plus mama, milky breasts and thighs and belly squeezed into inner-tube shapes by a lemon-yellow bathing suit, lay on a lawn chair and simmered like a dumpling over a low flame. The drapes of Ava's room hung open a crack and I had a peek. All I saw of her was legs waving in the air and hands gripping onto a headboard. The rest was hidden underneath Squire. His pimply butt was just pumping up and down. Sitting straight in a chair beside the bed, like a schoolboy being taught a lesson, Carl was looking on with interest. Well, come get me Jesus, I said to myself. With Carl and Squire both bagging Ava, she wouldn't have much time for Leeli. I had to admire Squire's stamina, but he looked to be doing push-ups on a trampoline and if I was the boy's daddy I'd have advised him that women tend to enjoy some rhythmic variation. He finally fell off his stroke and rolled onto his back. Ava came up flushed and sweaty, hair sticking to her cheeks. She had a sip of water, spoke briefly to Carl, then straddled Squire and began more-or-less to treat him like he'd been treating her. I'd been feeling about ten cents on the dollar, but watching her work cleaned the crust off my brain. Being the gentleman I am, I decided to buy Leeli coffee and a Krispy Kreme before checking out the rest of my parts.

▲▼▲

I hated Daytona, and not just because I was born there, though every time I drove through Holly Hills, redneck purgatory, and saw those little bunkerlike concrete homes with cracked jalousie windows and chain-link fences and Big Wheels with faded colors buried in the front yard weeds, my wattles got all red and swollen. I also hated the beach, the kids who cruised it eight and nine to a convertible or rode around in ten-dollar-an-hour rent-a-buggies, the bikini girls with their inch-deep tans and MTV eyes, the boys in Hilfiger suits with an old man's dream of financial security stuck like an ax into their brains at birth. I hated the fucking piped-in circus music that played along the boardwalk, sounding like it was made of sugar beets and red dye number seven. I hated the goddamn carnival rides and the heavy-metal curses shouting from the arcades. I liked the ocean all right, liked the blue-green water inside the sandbar, the creamy ridges of foam the tide left along the margin, and the power of the combers, but I wished they rolled in to no shore. I hated the burger joints with their fried-onion stink, their white plastic tables and chairs on a concrete deck, and walk-up windows manned by high school geeks with connect-the-dot acne puzzles on their foreheads, because it was at just such a joint I committed the error in judgment that earned me a nickel in Raiford, sauntering up to the service window so wired on crank, all I could smell was the inside of my nose, pulling a fifty-dollar pistol, and before I could speak the magic words, two plain-clothes cops who were drinking milkshakes at the time snuck up behind me and said to turn around real quick, they'd like that, and later in jail, Sgt. John True, a man apparently fascinated with me, visited my cell, the first of our many nights together, and said, When I was a kid I's just like you—meaning, I suppose, he no longer considered himself a dumbass hillbilly—prior to beating me unconscious. I carried a lot of anger relating to Daytona and that afternoon while we were sitting at a white plastic table on a concrete deck, staring at baskets of onion rings and fried shrimp so heavily breaded, eating one was like eating a hush puppy with a flavorless crunchy prize inside, I let angry out for exercise.

Squire got things off to a start by going on about how easy it would be to knock over the Joyland Arcade. You gotta have balls, he said, 'cause time to do it's when it's crowded. You walk on up and let 'em see your piece and grab them bags of money! He looked to Ava like he was expecting to have his belly rubbed. She smiled and dribbled salt from a packet onto her rings.

—You got a hard-on for quarters? I asked. They don't bag nothing but the change.

—You have people with you. Three or four of 'em so you can carry more.

—You think four loads of quarters divided four ways is more'n one load divided one way? You ain't been studying your arithmetic.

—You take the bills too, Squire said. Like, of course, he knew that.

—Where am I? I asked Leeli.

Her expression begged me to shut up.

—Seriously. Did we wake up somewhere's else this morning? Some other planet where stupid rules?

Carl chuckled and I said, Fuck is your problem, man? All you do's sit around and make fun of shit. What put you so high in the roost? Far as I can tell, Squire's your intellectual superior and he ain't got the brains of a box of popcorn.

—You the one's acting superior, Ava said, and forked up some slaw.

—Fuck, I am superior! Superior to this shit. Maybe it gets you wet listening to the criminal genius here, but it don't even give me a tickle.

Squire told me to watch my mouth, I was talking to a lady, and I said, Come on, you fucking chihuahua! Step to me!

Leeli caught my arm and said, Maceo! I jerked free and swatted my shrimp basket, backhanding it across the deck. People bespotted with ketchup splatter from the basket stared at us from the adjoining tables. The assistant manager, who could have passed for fourteen, looked like he was about to cry. Leeli was yelling at me, Squire was avoiding my eyes, Ava was calmly wiping her sleeve with a napkin. Carl giggled and said, Fucking chihuahua!

One of the citizens I'd splattered, a thick-necked, Hawaiian-shirt-wearing, Chevy-Suburban-driving son of the suburbs, his belly sagging like a hundred-year-old hammock, gave his pregnant wife a comforting pat on the shoulder and heaved up from his cheeseburger, but Ava saved his ass by intercepting him on the way to our table and slipped him a twenty for his dry cleaning bill. Other folks put in their claim and once she had satisfied them, she sat back down and said to me, Temper like that, it's a wonder you still on the street.

Calmer now, I felt no call to answer. I gave her a fuck-you smile and popped one of Leeli's shrimp into my mouth. It was covered with grit that had blown up from the beach, which made it extra crunchy.

—You so smart, Ava said, whyn't you tell us how you'd handle the Joyland?

—Wouldn't nothing but a damn fool mess with it. Too many cops. Too many boyfriends might wanna play hero. You feel the need to rob something, head out on the freeway. You know the back roads along the exits, you can take down two gas stations easy and be sitting in a bar before the cops get motivated.

—I suppose it was your expertise landed you in prison.

—Oh I was a fool. No doubt about that. It don't mean I'm still a fool.

Challenged, I delivered a lecture on proper criminal procedure, most of it learned in Raiford, but salted in with personal experiences that I embellished for dramatic effect. You gotta terrorize a place, I told them. People ain't always scared, they see the gun. Sometimes they can't believe you're for real and they go to debating what to do. You don't want that, you want 'em scared. So you say something lets 'em know how scared they oughta be.

—Yeah? Squire said churlishly. Like what?

I made my hand into a gun and pointed it at his chest. Hands up! Who wants to die? You say that, it gets their attention every time.

—I like that, Carl said, grinning. Hands up who wants to die?

—Takes the punch out of it, you say it with a smile, I said. Tell 'em like you mean it.

With that, Carl jumped up and snarled, Hands up! Who wants to die?

The pregnant lady yipped and the people at the table behind me grabbed up their belongings and scooted. Ava pulled Carl down into his chair and I said to him, That'll get it done.

Leeli stood and said, Can we just go? Please!

We set off down the boardwalk toward the car and she fell into step with Ava and Carl. Irritated by this, not wanting to be stuck with Squire, I dropped off the pace, lollygagging along. That's how Leeli wanted to play it, I told myself, to hell with her. I'd find myself a sweeter can of tuna. I started eye-fucking the bikini girls strolling past and when one made a smart-ass remark, getting her friends to laughing at me, I told her once she lost that babyfat she oughta try a real dick, but right now it'd likely be too much for her.

▲▼▲

Ava drove south and then west on State Road 44 toward Orlando. She went to talking about the old days, the 60s, when there was so many

UFOs in the sky—because of the rockets at the Cape, she guessed—you could see them from out on 44 every night. Boys useta take us down here to see 'em, she said, 'cause they thought we'd let 'em get fresh while we were stargazing. Leeli, who was riding shotgun next to Carl, said, I bet they were right, huh?

—'Course they were, Ava said, and they shared a laugh.

—You ever see any UFOs? Leeli asked.

—All the time! You look up in the sky, you couldn't help seeing 'em. Pretty soon what you thought was a group of stars would get to darting around, making these really sharp turns, flying in formation.

She asked Leeli to fish around in her tote bag and find her cigarettes. Once she got a smoke going, she said, Couple times we saw one real close.

—A flying saucer?

—Uh huh. We saw this one shoot a green light from its belly. Straight down to the ground.

—Maybe it was Santa Claus you saw, I suggested. Waving his green flashlight.

Ava took a glance back toward me. You don't believe in UFOs, Maceo?

—'Bout as much as I believe in liberty and justice for all.

—Don't listen to him, Leeli said. He's a contrary sort.

I told Leeli she didn't know squat about me and then said to Ava, Whatever you saw, wasn't no flying saucer. Ain't no sense to any of that business.

—That might be, Ava said. Most things don't make sense, especially you try and understand 'em too hard.

—I suppose that's profound, but I'm just a dumb Florida Cracker. It goes right by me.

Ava flicked ash and sparks out the window. You might catch up to it one of these days, she said.

It struck me that Ava must be a lot older than I'd estimated, she was dating back in the 60s, but I didn't stay with the thought. I was a six pack along into a decent buzz and still feeling sour about Leeli, fully occupied with self-pity and scorn. When we stopped for gas I pulled Leeli aside, fed her all the I'm-sorry she could swallow and persuaded her to switch seats with Squire. I discovered a sensitive spot under her ear and before long I had her squirming pretty good, though each time my fingers traipsed near the old plantation home, she'd give them a spank. Squire began telling a lie about a beauty queen he'd gone with in high school and Ava shut him up quick, saying she needed to concentrate on the road. That clued me in she was upset about Leeli, and I felt satisfied in mind.

Scattered around the edges of Disneyworld were a number of shooting ranges where for a few dollars you could fire assault rifles. Given the encouragement this surely offered the freaks who flocked to the ranges, you had to wonder if the city fathers of Orlando didn't unconsciously long to see TV coverage of a giant blood-spattered mouse. While Carl and Squire were busy playing soldier at Buck's Guns and Sporting Gallery, me and Ava and Leeli walked to a nearby 7-11 and bought some forty-ouncers, one of which I chugged walking back to the parking lot. The girls sat talking on the hood of Ava's truck. I wasn't drunk enough to feel mean, but I felt separate from things. The cars racing along the six-lane were shiny toys with glaring headlights and dabs of meat inside. The strip malls lining the road were grimy slot-car accessories. The heat came from a neon tube inside my head and the starless orange-lit sky was a gasoline-soaked rag someone had throwed over the whole mess so's to hide it from company. What I'm saying, it wouldn't have taken much to upgrade me to mean. Ava was pitching hard at Leeli, touching her thigh, the back of her hair. I just kept working on my second forty. If I could drink fast enough, I wouldn't care what they did and I'd be able to ignore some deeper thoughts that were trying to gnaw out my brains like a squirrel with a nut meat.

When Squire and Carl returned, all hotted up from proving their marksmanship, Ava announced a surprise. She had reserved us rooms at the mouse's hotel. We'd have a few cocktails, go on some rides, and see what developed. This made Carl happy, but Squire and Leeli didn't seem to care. I sucked down a third forty on the ride over and after Ava checked us in, I told her I felt poorly and was going to my room.

—Me, too, said Leeli. I'm awful tired.

This surprised Ava as much as it did me. You sure? she said to Leeli. Space Mountain'll juice you right up.

—Naw, we'll catch y'all later. Leeli started walking so fast, she beat me to the elevator.

I had a shower while Leeli ordered room-service cheeseburgers and Cokes. The food left me placid and sleepy. I laid out on the bed in my skivvies and Leeli stood at the window, her arms folded, stern of face, like she was taking stock of a brightly lit country she'd just done conquering.

—You don't have to worry 'bout me making a move, that's what's keeping you vertical, I said. I'm through for today.

She made a noise that didn't tell me much.

I grabbed the remote from the bedside table and found a wrestling show on TV. Wrestling hasn't been the same since the prime of Hulk Hogan and the Giant and Macho Man Savage, you ask me. Back in the day your superhero had a gut just like the asshole sitting next to you in the bar and so when you smacked him with a beer bottle, you had a greater sense of accomplishment. Now there was too many pretty boys and it was more tumbling and role-playing than the honest-to-God fake it once was.

Leeli wriggled out of her jeans. Ava gave me money to buy clothes, she said. Reckon we better do it soon.

—We can get some fine clothes here. Get us some mouse shirts and mouse hats with the ears. Maybe you can get some panties with the mouse on the crotch and wear 'em inside out.

She pulled off her tank top and threw it at me in a ball. You *always* have to be a shit?

—It was a fucking joke! Jesus!

She stared at me as if she didn't believe it.

—I swear, I said.

She held the stare a second longer. Damn! she said. Why do I like you?

—You want a honest answer?

—Naw, I know why. She sat down on the bed, glum as old gravy, picked up the remote and went surfing, changing channels so fast, there was only little blurts of sound. Know what Ava told me? She says she works for the government. The FBI.

—No shit! I said. Is she a friend of Spiderman?

—She showed me her badge! Leeli bugged her eyes and stuck out her tongue.

—Give me ten bucks and I'll show you a badge. I can probably find one in the gift shop.

Leeli threw herself down on the pillow like she was trying to hurt herself. You wanna hear this or not?

—Sure. Lemme have it. I turned to lie facing her so she'd know I was listening, and rested a hand on her waist.

—She said she was an agent and Carl and Squire are in some sorta experiment. She's in charge of 'em. She says she'll pay me a ton of money to be part of it. The experiment.

—Want me to say what I'm thinking?

—I'm not an idiot! I know she likes me, and I know it could all be a story. But she's willing to pay twenty thousand dollars! For one month!

—You see the money?

Leeli gave a vigorous nod. I get five now, the rest after.

—Well, shit. I rolled onto my back. I guess this is goodbye.

—Not necessarily.

—Yeah, necessarily. I can't compete with someone throws around twenty thousand bucks.

She sat up cross-legged and muted the TV. Look, I'm not no shiny apple been sitting on the shelf like you think.

—That ain't what I think, I said, grumpy from losing out to a rich dyke.

—Then why you treating me like I don't know which end of a jar to open? I been with women. It ain't my favorite, but there's times I felt that way. And I can feel that way again. Enough to earn us twenty thousand dollars, I can.

The word *us* punched a hole in my overcast.

—I don't trust Ava, Leeli said. But with you along I don't have to trust her. So I told her you had to come with us.

—What'd she say?

—She said it'd be okay 'long as you don't get crazy 'bout I'm sleeping with the both of you.

I turned this proposition over to see if it was missing a piece. I don't know, I said. I get these mood swings.

—Oh, really! I couldn't tell. She flounced down beside me, resting her chin on my chest. Can you deal with it? 'Cause if you can't, I might not do this. But I want that money! You imagine the party we could have on twenty thousand? I bet we can get more'n twenty, you ease back and lemme treat Ava right.

I hooked my thumb under the waistband of her panties and gave the elastic a snap. You a bad woman, ain'tcha?

—Goodness me! She batted her eyelashes. I don't know what in the world more I'm gonna have to do to prove it.

▲▼▲

In the morning we had another conversation. It kicked off wrong when I said what bothered me was Ava offering twenty when she could have snagged Leeli for less. Once I got her cooled down, she said, huffily, It's not like she was comparison shopping. She's took with me. Guess you'd have trouble understanding that.

—You know that ain't it. I'm just being a realist.

—That's what a realist is? A pea-brained Florida cracker?

—Damn, Leeli! Some guy offered me twenty grand to go party with him for a month, you'd think something was screwy.

—Maybe.

—Maybe my ass!

A polite room-service knock ended this round. The waiter, a college boy with a forelock of frosted hair, rolled his cart to the table at the window, off-loaded Leeli's omelette and my breakfast steak, and stood waiting for his tip.

—I got no cash on me, I told him.

—You can add it to the bill, sir.

This was spoken like he was advising a backward child who'd stepped in shit. He had the kind of smug, fleshy face made me yearn to see it staring up from inside a roll of sheet plastic, dripping wet from a canal where he'd been swimming underwater for a week. I snatched the bill from him and wrote one billion dollars on the tip line. His eyes flicked to the amount and froze.

—I was you, hoss, I said, I'd polish up one of them special Disney smiles and waltz on outa here.

I guess he wasn't a total candy-ass. He had some size on him and I could tell he was weighing job security against the joys of bashing my face in with one of those metal domes that kept the food warm. I thought about sucker-punching him just to see how far he'd fly, but he turned on his heel and headed for the door.

—Rock on, dude, I called after him.

I sat down to eat. Leeli gave me a God-you're-hopeless look. She bit into her toast with a snap, as if somehow it might do me an injury. We ate without talking for a while, then she said, It might be true what Ava told me. 'Bout the experiment. Carl and Squire are pretty strange.

—One's a retard, other don't know he's a retard. That ain't so strange.

She diddled the fork in her eggs. I can't figure why she'd tell me that story if it wasn't true.

I had to talk around a bite of steak. To make herself look like a big deal.

—People with the money she's got, they don't hafta do that.

—If they're freaks they do. I finally got the bite chewed. Say it's true. Fuck does it matter? We still get paid.

Leeli had built a little fence of eggs around her sausage patty. Nothing this good ever works out, she said, staring at the plate like she was considering making a rock garden out of her cottage fries. What I think's gonna happen and what does happen, there's always a mile of swamp 'tween the two.

—Yeah, well, I said. There is that.

▲▼▲

With a step that was a shade perky for my tastes, Leeli ran off to tell Ava the news. For want of better occupation, I took my Disneyworld pass and went to experience America. As I waited in line the man behind me kept ramming my legs with his gray-headed mama who was sitting in a wheelchair, gripping the arms and scowling like a fury. Everywhere you turned you saw parents yelling at kids who were bawling about they didn't get this or that. Stuck in a photograph album, I supposed these same scenes would dredge up fond memories years from now. It depressed me that I wasn't able to work such a change with my own miseries. Must be I come to Disneyworld too late in life for the enchantment to do its trick.

Close by the Pirates of the Caribbean, an elderly fat man with the word Jellybean embroidered on the chest of his overalls and dozens of jellybeans stuck on his straw cowboy hat had cordoned off a section of walkway and there created portraits of celebrities from thousands of—guess what?—jellybeans. He was working on his knees, dribbling jellybeans onto a rendering of the Statue of Liberty, which except for the spiky headdress looked a whole hell of a lot like his take on the fat Elvis. People stood around saying, Isn't that amazing. He seemed so jolly in his craft, I naturally wished him ill. Odds were he was a twelve-stepper who after a lifetime of domestic abuse visited upon wife and children had gone simple enough from Jesus and caffeine to believe this shit was a suitable atonement. A four-year-old howler with the mouse on his chest and a stalk of blue cotton candy in his fist broke free of his parents and came to stand by Jellybean. Way he held the candy to his mouth and screamed, you could easily picture him at twenty-one doing the same with a microphone and getting laid by supermodels. When his mama tried to drag him off, he endeared himself to me forever by ralphing all over Miss Liberty. Jellybean offered him grandpa consolation, but I caught a glint of good old murder in his eye.

We stayed at Disneyworld four more days. Leeli spent the nights with Ava and mornings with me. The rest of the hours we traveled as a pack. At these times the air got icy. Dinners became occasions of grand formality, long bouts of chewing and swallowing broken by courteous exchanges. Please pass the butter. Would you like another dessert? Can I bring you back something? Leeli had to make sure both Ava and I got our share of flirty glances and secret smiles, and the strain of it all roughed her up some. I learned to let her relax when she came back to our room. She would take two valium from a bottle Ava had given her and sit by the window, her breath ragged, like she was pushing herself to exhale. Finally she'd smile and say, Hi or How you doing?, as if she had just noticed me.

—I can't take much more of Carl, she said one day. It's not about him watching. I'm almost grateful he's there. It kinda makes it easier to switch off my head. But the talking they do…Jesus Lord! She glanced at me for a reaction. Am I boring you?

—I was just letting you tell it.

—I know you're being sweet with me, and I appreciate it. But I'm wore out with sweetness. I could use a shot of male insensitivity. Can you handle that?

I grinned at her and said gruffly, Hell they talking about, woman?

Leeli sighed like those words had hit the spot. Ava'll stop right in the middle of things and explain what's going on. Anatomical stuff, y'know. And Carl he just sits there humming to himself.

—He don't say nothing back?

—Sometimes he asks can he go do something with Squire, and she'll say maybe later or naw it's not your time to be with Squire.

—See what I told you? He's a fucking retard.

—He's not dumb! Ava's always testing him or something. Asking him weird questions. He never gets a'one wrong. She'll ask him to do a sum and he does 'em in his head. Just snaps 'em off!

—Remember that Tom Cruise movie where his brother did all that? That guy was a retard.

—It's not just Carl. Ava, she's….

—What?

—She's a strong woman, is what it is. Sometimes I get a feeling I'm gonna drown in her, y'know. Like she's this tide rolling over me and when it goes out again, nothing's gonna be left of me. Leeli hung her chin onto her chest. I don't know I can do this for a month.

—Fine with me. Let's take the five and split.

The second hand must have galloped damn near ten times around the dial before she said, Chances this good don't come around but every so often. Let's give it a few days.

She come over to the foot of the bed and crawled up beside me and cuddled into my shoulder like she wanted to sleep. I did my best to be pillow and comforter, but the heat of her and my natural preoccupations got me all charged up. She reached her hand down and played with me awhile, then lost interest and closed her eyes. Want me take care of that for you? she asked after another bit.

—We'll have our time, I said. Whyn't you rest?

She blinked and peered at me. Wide open, those brown eyes could be like a car coming at you with its high beams on. They left me dazed and fighting for the road.

—That a real feeling I see in there? she asked.

—Whatever you see, that's what it is. You know I ain't smart enough to fake nothing.

She didn't act like she believed this. Her lights dimmed and she lay quiet. She fingered my shirt button and appeared to be studying the stubble on my chin. I asked what she was thinking.

—Lots of things.

—Say one.

—I was wondering if anybody's smart enough to know they're faking and I was wishing we already had that twenty thousand.

—Anything else?

—I was thinking you got a whole crowd of people paying rent in your skull. Different sizes, different ways of doing. But they all wearing the same face.

▲▼▲

A woman starts to get deep on you, you know it's just the coming attraction for a head movie that'll be playing six shows daily in the weeks to come. She's evaluating her prospects and unless you're a fool, you best do some evaluating your own self. Generally speaking, a commitment is being called for, but with Ava in the picture I wasn't sure how things were fitting together in Leeli's thoughts. She went to drowning in moods so wide, they'd wash over me from the next room. Sometimes she wanted me to be patient and other times she wanted me to haul her off to the monkey jungle. After playing mama's little helper at night, she needed daddy to straighten her out. I didn't have a good record when it come to treating female mental disease, but I managed it with Leeli. I gave her to know I was there for her like Oprah and Tarzan both. It surprised me that I was up to the task and when I meditated on this, I realized the feeling Leeli had spotted in me might be for real. A runty little weed sprouted from sandy soil—that was all it was. If it was going to survive, Jim Bakker and Tammy Faye would have to drop in from TV heaven and manifest a miracle. But there it waved, baking under the sky of all the shit that had ever gone wrong with me, waggling its dried-up leaves, trying like hell to grow up and learn how to whistle. Puny as it was, it stood taller than any decision I could have made to chop it down.

From Disneyworld the party train crossed the state to Ybor City, then up to Jacksonville and then back down to Silver Springs. Eleven days and we hadn't gone a mile toward Lauderdale. Often as not, whenever Leeli was with Ava and Carl, Squire would seek me out. He figured we were in the same boat, I expect. Whereas Carl had one trick, Squire was proficient in two. Like he was a grade up on Carl in Ava's pre-school. Mostly he desired to talk about how much pussy he'd been getting since a precocious early age, but it was plain he'd never gotten any that hadn't got him first. He recounted a string of fabulous conquests, each more of a joke than the last. A female jockey, a porn star, a TV actress, the girl who played center for the Dallas Sparks. They had the feel of lies he'd overheard in a bar and loved so much he'd taken them in and given them a new home. Tempted as I was to blow a hole in his picture window, I let him rave. Sooner or later he'd wind down and go to thinking about Ava. I didn't have to be a mind reader to know this. Ava thoughts stamped their brand on that boy's face. If I had thumped his head at those moments, it would've bonged like a bell.

In Silver Springs, instead of staying at the resort, we checked into a dump on a blue highway east of Ocala. A dozen frame bungalows painted beige with dark brown trim and tarpaper roofs and screen doors tucked in among palmetto and Georgia pine. From the road they looked like the backdrop for a 1940s photograph of Grandma and Grandpa on the dashboard of their Model A, off to homestead down in Stark or Sanford, right before Grandma gave birth to the next gold-star-destiny generation of Scrogginses or Culpeppers or Inglethorpes. Up close you saw them different. Tarpaper hats tipped at shady angles over chunky, sallow faces with indifferent eyes, like Chinamen with sly intentions. The screens documented tragic insect stories. Palmetto bugs the size of clothespins scuttled from crack to crack. The sheets were maps of gray and yellow countries. Facing my bed was a framed picture so dusty I could lie back and make it anything I wanted. You smelled the toilet from the steps outside. The place fucking cried out for a shotgun murder.

Of an evening the owner, Mr. Gammage, a scrawny old geezer whose bermuda shorts hung like loose sail from his hipbones, would beautify the grounds. Chop a few weeds, prune a shrub or two, cut back a climbing cactus from a palm trunk. He'd fuel his labors with glugs from a thermos that likely contained a libation stiffer than Gatorade. If he was feeling frisky he'd start his electric trimmer and hunt up stuff to trim. You could tell he loved that machine, the way he flourished it about. Watching him survey his property, hands on hips, his turkey-baster belly popped full out, it was my impression he was a happy man, though it was tough to understand why. Whenever he revved up the trimmer his wife would come to the office door and yell for him to quit making that noise. She was built short and squarish and commonly wore a dark brown housecoat. This sponsored the idea she might have given birth to the bungalows or was their spirit made flesh, or something of the sort. Her face was topped off by about a foot of forehead on which God had written a grim Commandment. I felt the air stir when she glared at me. Inside the office there was a Bible big as a microwave and I bet she would open it and pray for everything around her to disappear.

I was sitting outside my bungalow our second afternoon there, nursing a forty, when she come flying from the office and took a run at Squire. He'd fallen out on the grass near the highway, his head resting in a petunia bed. Mrs. Gammage screamed, Get outa my flowers, punching the ground with a lurching, stiff-gaited stride like an NFL guard with bad knees. Squire never moved, not even when she kicked him. She kicked him again. I wouldn't say I was spurred to action, but since I was technically supposed to be on Squire's side, I thought I should make a supportive gesture. Time I got myself on over to the petunias, she had stopped kicking and was bending to him and saying, Hey! Hey! She had a thin, bitter smell, like a bin of rutabagas. Squire's eyes were half-open, but only one iris showed.

—'Pears like you killed him, I said.

Mrs. Gammage staggered back from the petunia bed, gazing at Squire with an expression that crossed stricken with disgusted. He was already dead! I didn't do nothing coulda killed him.

—You kicked him right in the side of his chest where the heart's on. That'll do 'er every time. It's a medical fact.

I was just fucking with her, but Squire hadn't twitched and it dawned on me that he actually might be dead. His color was good, though. Only dead man I'd ever seen up close was this old boy got shot in the head outside the Surf Bar in Ormond Beach for arguing about his girlfriend should have won the wet T-shirt contest. All the color had left him straightaway. His skin had the look of gray candlewax.

Mrs. Gammage snorted and snuffled some. Maybe she was seeing herself strapped into Old Sparky over to Raiford, or maybe she hadn't yet gotten that specific with self-pity and was tearing up because she felt the victim of a vast injustice—here she'd been protecting her precious petunias and now Jesus had gone and let her down despite all everything she'd done for him. I had in mind to tell her that feeling she was having that everything had tightened up around her and no matter how hard she tried to turn with it, the world was no longer a comfortable fit, and if she made a move to pry herself loose from that terrible grip, it'd pinch her off at the neck...I would have told her after a while it got to feel natural and she likely wouldn't know what to do things didn't feel that way. Before I could advise her of this, Ava came on the run and shooed us away, babbling about how Squire was prone to these fits and she'd handle it, just to leave her alone with him because when he woke up he was scared and she could gentle him. I returned to step-sitting out front of my bungalow and Mrs. Gammage streaked toward the office to recast the deadly prayer spell she'd been fixing to hurl at the universe. Ava kneeled to Squire, hiding his upper body from sight. My forty had gone warmish, but I chugged down several swallows and wiped the spill from my chin and looked back to the petunia bed just in time to see Squire sit bolt upright. It wasn't the kind of reaction you'd expect from someone smacked down by a fit. No wooziness or flailing about. It was like Ava had shot a few thousand volts through him.

Leeli had come out of Ava's bungalow, wearing white shorts and a green halter. She wandered over to me and sat on the stoop. What you think's wrong with Squire? she asked in a hushed voice.

—Boy's so slow, maybe his brain idles out every so often.

She stared at Ava and Squire as if she was trying to figure something out. I did some staring myself, digging my eyes under that halter. The heat cooked her scent strong. I leaned closer and did a hit. She glanced up and asked, What you doing?

—I wish I was smelling breakfast, I said.

Squire and Ava scrambled up, Squire gesturing like he was wanting to explain something of importance. They made for Ava's bungalow. Leeli started to join up with them, but Ava waved her off and said she needed to tend Squire for a while. That brightened Leeli, but she watched until the door closed behind them.

—Don't none of this strike you peculiar? she asked.

—Pretty much everything strikes me peculiar. So I guess nothing does, really.

▲▼▲

If I hadn't been consumed with getting Leeli into the bungalow and the two of us shaking the walls so hard, the framed picture would shudder off its veil of dust and the palmetto bugs would prepare for the fall of creation, I might've had room for some helpful thoughts. I don't suppose it matters, though. Chances are I wouldn't have reached any conclusion. If I had, either I wouldn't have acted on it or else it would have been the same half-assed conclusion I come to without even stretching my brain. Studying on things until you couldn't tell whether what you thought was what you wanted to think and all that—it wasn't my style. I had two ways of going at the world. One, I was a furnace of a man and everything I saw was viewed in terms of how it would do for fuel. The other, I was a pitiable creature who'd been walked on for so long there was a damn dog run wore down into my skull and whenever a shadow crossed my path, my instinct was to snap my teeth. Neither of those boys gave a sugary shit about situational fucking analysis.

Ava was kept busy that night tinkering with Squire's self-esteem. 'Least that's what I believed had sucked his fire down so low, his pilot light kicked off. It was like Leeli had been busted out of jail. She wanted one of everything with me. We come close to killing each other. Toward nine we took a break, borrowed Ava's car, and brought back catfish and puppies and fries. Halfway through our greasy feast, we went at it again, smearing fish juice all over the bed. It would've took oven cleaner to scour the sheets. Long about midnight we smoked cigarettes on the steps. Fireflies bloomed in the hazy dark. The breeze hauled a smell of night-blooming cereus out from the shadows of the palms. A shine from the bulb over the office door fresh-tarred the blacktop. We had us one of those made-in-Nashville moments. Our arms around one another, heads together. Snap the photo, frame it with a heart, and stick in a word balloon with me saying something forever stupid like, Somepin' wunnerful's gonna happen to them peaches, honey. Hillbilly Hallmark. I gave Leeli a kiss that sparked a shiver and she settled in against me.

—I could stand another beer, she said.

—Want me to fetch it?

—Naw, it's too much trouble.

Skeeters whined. A night bird said its name about three hundred times in a row. The TV inside the office flickered a wicked green, an evil blue, a blast of white, as if Mrs. Gammage was receiving communication from an unholy sphere. I wouldn't have much cared if the rest of everything was just this hot and black and quiet.

▲▼▲

Squire seemed fine to me, especially for someone who looked to be a goner, but Ava was still acting mothery the next morning. Around noon she herded us into the car and drove to Silver Springs for, I guess, a give-Squire-love day. At a stall near the gift shop she bought a T-shirt with his face airbrushed on it by a genuine T-shirt artist. Squire had the good sense not to wear the thing. Wanna go see the tropical fish? she asked of Carl and Squire both. Squire said he didn't know, whatever, and Carl repeated the word fish until he figured out how to spray spittle when saying it. We crammed into a glass-bottomed boat with a mob of lumpy fiftyish women in baggy slacks and floral blouses. I assumed they were a church group, because they appeared to be the cut-rate harem belonging to this balding, gray-haired individual with a banker's belly and a sagging, doleful face, dressed like a Wal-mart dummy in slacks with an elastic waistband and a sweated-through sports shirt. A pretty blonde in a captain's hat steered the boat and as we glided across the springs, her voice blatted from the speakers, identifying whatever portion of nature's living rainbow we were then passing over. The man stood the whole trip, clutching a pole for balance, providing his own commentary and sneaking glances at Leeli, who was wearing short-shorts. He was trying to make some general point relating to the fish. It had a charry Unitarian flavor, a serving of God and fried turnip slices. All the ladies nodded and favored him with doting gazes. Squashed between two of them was a chubby kid about fourteen who had the miserable air of a hostage. One of the women whispered urgently at him, probably telling him to pay attention or sit up straight. He stared cross-eyed into nowhere, dreaming of columbining the bunch of us. I winked at him, wanting him to know that some of us so-called adults could be dangerous haters, too, when forced to ooh and aah over a glittery mess of edible sea bugs. This only got him hating me extra special. If somebody had slipped him a piece, they would've found me with my splattered head resting on a cellulite-riddled thigh.

After the boat ride we headed for a Howard Johnson's restaurant down the road from the resort. The reverend and his flock had beaten us there and were crammed into a circular booth across from ours. The ladies chattered away, the kid stared at his fries like they were a heap of golden brown logs on which he was roasting his mom in miniature. Part of my problem was I've been cursed with this inept paranoia that sees danger everywhere except where danger lies. Though I'd done nothing criminal recently, the reverend's presence made me feel criminally guilty. I fiddled with the suspicion that his turning up at the restaurant was police-related. That he'd recognized me for the perpetrator of a crime I'd committed and forgot. Now and then his fruity voice cut through the chatter. He was still going on about the damn fish.

—Did you notice, he asked, how the entire school turned as one? Indeed, all the actions of the underwater world seemed in concert, as though directed by a single mind. Is it such a leap to conceive that our actions are so directed?

Hell yes! would've been my answer, but Carl thought this was about the best thing he'd ever heard. He jumped around in his seat, repeating portions of the reverend's lesson and said to Ava, You see? See what I mean?, like these phrases connected with an argument they'd been having.

—I know, she said, and patted his hand to calm him.

—A single mind directed! he said loudly.

Several of the ladies were shooting pissy looks his way. Anna shushed him and said they'd talk about it later. But Carl wanted to talk about it right then and there. I'd never seen him so heated up. Whenever the reverend's voice carried to us, Carl would go to chuckling, spitting back the reverend's words, saying, Yes! Yes!, and sputtering other foolishness, giving this weird sort of affirmation, like he was a shouter in a retard church.

Eventually, urged on by his outraged ladies, the reverend scooted out of the booth and ambled over. He clasped his hands at his belly, delivered us a patient look, and asked Carl if he wouldn't mind toning it down.

Carl beamed at him and said, Yes! A single mind!

Leeli said, Can't you see the man ain't right! Ava offered an apology and I said, You best take your fat ass on back to the hen house, or they gonna need another rooster.

The reverend armored his face with a smile and looked down on me from a peak of blessed understanding. Young man, he said. Actually he said a good bit more, but the words young man were all I heeded. When I was five Reverend Nichols from the First Baptist told my mama having such a sweet little fellow as me by his side would be an asset when he was doing fund-raising, and since this gave her more time for drinking, she loaned me out to him on a regular basis. Young man, he'd say once we were alone, wanna sit on my lap while I drive? Young man, I'm gonna open you to God's greatest gift. I didn't much appreciate anybody calling me young man, and I sure as hell didn't want it from a preacher. I caught him by the collar and yanked him down so he was gawking into the leavings of my chicken-fried steak. The only thing I recall saying was, Cocksucking holy Joe motherfucker, but I know I expanded on that considerable. People were tugging at me, women were screaming, something struck the side of my head, but I was serene in the midst of it, talking to the reverend, showing him the ketchup-smeared edge of my steak knife.

Rougher hands grabbed me and the reverend broke free. Two guys wearing aprons wrangled me into the aisle, where we did some wrestling and grunting and swearing. A swung purse the size of a satchel knocked one guy off me. I clocked the other with a gut punch that cured him of upright and put him on his knees kissing the carpet like a devout Arab. Shouting people choked the aisle, a few wanting to get at me, the rest trying to get away. I heard Leeli cry, Maceo!, but I couldn't find her in the crowd, so I beelined for the exit, shoving aside Christian and heathen alike. The manager loomed ahead of me. A porky fellow in a maroon shirt and a black tie, his skin that spoiled pumpkin color comes either from a tanning booth or somewheres in India. A wedge of old ladies blocked him off to the left, clearing a path, and I went toward the door. That's when Carl shouted the magic words.

—Hands up! he said with sincere ferocity. Who wants to die?

The manager had retreated behind the cash register and Carl, beaming like a lottery winner, was pointing a blue steel automatic in his general direction, swinging the muzzle to cover the counter and a portion of window. People started hitting the ground, hiding in the booths, and wasn't more than a couple of seconds before the only ones standing were the five in our party and the manager. You could hear whispering and sobbing and the wheedle of some old pop song turned into a symphony, but it was stone quiet compared to how it had been. Ava slapped at her tote bag, gave it a squeeze, and that told me where Carl had got his shiny new toy.

—Give it to me, Carl, I said, easing toward him a step.

—Okay. He kept on swinging the gun back and forth kind of aimlessly, like it had a momentum that was carrying his arms through an arc.

—Give me the gun, Ava said. You don't need that gun now.

Squire was at her shoulder, nodding as if he firmly supported this idea, and Leeli, smart girl, was halfway out the door.

The manager made a move for something under the register. Ava and I both shouted a warning to Carl. I said, Watch it, man!, and Ava spoke what sounded like a word in a foreign language—I couldn't tell for sure because our shouts mixed together. Carl whipped the gun around and fired just before the manager fired, the explosions overlapping. Carl's head jerked, blood sprayed. His bullet kicked the manager into a buffet cart. He fell behind the counter. A few screams speared the quiet. Smoke lazied in the air. Somebody's lunch treat sizzled and blackened on the griddle. I stepped forward and snatched the gun from Carl. There was blood all over his face, but he was still smiling. Ava wrapped him in a hug and hustled him to the door. I had a quick look back of the counter. The manager was staring off into someplace I never want to see. Frightened eyes were locked on me from every direction, like forest animals peeping at a mangy tiger that had interrupted their play. I fired a shot into the ceiling and told them not to twitch forever and ran like hell.

▲▼▲

In the truck everybody talked at once, except for Squire. He was gazing out the passenger-side window, having himself a fine vacation. Ava and Leeli fussed over Carl in the back seat, and I drove fast toward Ocala. I hadn't put a face on the wrongness of what happened, but it nibbled at the edges of a fucked-up angry fear that raised a red shadow in my brain and jammed spikes into my bone-holes, making all my limbs want to stiffen and wiggle like a bug with a pin through its guts. Leeli urged me to drive faster and Ava said, Take us back to the motel! This all stirred in with Oh Gods and Carl repeating over and over in a sunny voice, Hands up who wants to die, shaping a child's song of the line. I told them to shut the fuck up, then I yelled it. For half a minute it was quiet. A big shopping mall come floating up on our left. I slowed and swung the car into it. Ava screeched, What're you doing? as I swerved into a parking slot away from the buildings, hidden by other cars from the highway. I switched off the engine. She clawed at my shoulder, cursing and giving orders.

I turned to her and saw that the manager's bullet had dug a furrow along Carl's jawline. The wound was oozing blood, yet he didn't seem to mind. I'm gonna find us another car, I said. But we ain't going back to no motel.

Ava objected to this and I said, Here's your keys. Go where the fuck you want. I'm getting the hell gone.

I climbed out and told Leeli to come along with me.

Ava caught Leeli's arm. I need her here!

—Well, I need a look-out, so fuck what you need!

—Take Squire, she said.

—Yeah, that'll help. Come on, Leeli.

Leeli hesitated.

A cop car whipped past on the highway, howling like a devil with a hotfoot.

—Goddamn it! Now! I said. You wanna wait around 'til he comes back for us?

Leeli hopped out and glanced uncertainly between me and Ava. She blinked and shivered as if the sun was killing her.

For the first time ever I saw a distinct lack of confidence in Ava's face. You better not leave us here! she said. I swear to God!

—I wasn't thinking on it, I said.

▲▼▲

There was some sort of promotion going on within the mall. The lot was more crowded than you'd expect. Jolly old farts wearing gaudy sport coats and blue Shriner-type hats were holding bunches of balloons on strings, handing them out to children and mommies, collecting money to cure some great evil that would never die, and two lanes of parking were used up by a carnival with a little Ferris wheel, kiddie rides, game and snack stalls. Some high school girls strolled in a small pod, twelve tits in a row, those belonging to a hefty redhead nosing out a close race. They were eyed by a pack of high school boys whose thoughts of rape had likely gotten sly and civilized during hygiene class. Senior citizens dressed in peppy colors gazed soberly at the wheel. I reckon they were recalling greater wheels from the big glorious world that had died out from under them. Treacly music played—the same, it seemed, that played everywhere I traveled.

Ava's gun was stuck in my belt, under my shirt. Its weight made me walk taller than I should have felt. I held hands with Leeli, hoping to persuade folks we were a young couple hot for some corn dogs or whatever hell meat they were pushing at the carnival. We skirted the more populated area of the lot. I spotted a newish Ford van with smoked windows. We snuck up on it from the rear. Just as I was ready to pounce, Leeli warned me off. Standing a few cars over was a huddle of men in blue hats. These old fellows had ridded themselves of balloons. They were laughing, the nudge-nudge laughing men do when they hear a real good smutty joke. The fattest of them had a two-handed grip on his belly, like he was about to lift up a slab of fat and show them something even funnier. Of a sudden the men rested hands on each other's shoulders, forming a circle, and bowed their heads, praying, I supposed, for more balloons or for Jesus to cover the point spread against Satan or that one of the high school girls would lose her mind and fuck them.

Out front of the Home Depot was an old Chevy panel van. I busted the driver's window with the gun butt and hotwired it. The engine shook like the mounts were loose and made a tired, trebly noise until I got it idling. Leeli brushed glass off her seat and jumped in. I headed the van toward the nearest exit and she dug her fingers into my thigh and asked where I was going.

—South fucking America if we can get that far, I said.

A pinch of time zipped by. Turn it around, she said.

—That's not gonna happen.

—I mean it! You turn this thing right around!

—Fuck you going on about?

—I'm serious! She reached out with her left foot and stomped on the brake, nearly swerving me into a parked Camry. I'm not running out on my friends.

She kind of hiccuped over the word friends, but kept her gaze firm and determined.

—Your friends? You talking about the Munsters back there?

Her eyes flicked away.

—Oh, okay. You're talking about those twenty thousand friends. This ain't about twenty thousand dollars no more, Leeli. This here's about twenty-to-life.

—I don't care!

—You'll care when those lifer bitches with the tattooed mustaches start wanting to get cozy.

She opened the door, planted one foot on the asphalt. I'm not staying 'less you go back for Ava and them.

—Those motherfuckers gonna get us killed! They almost *got* us killed!

—Way I see it, you didn't act such a fool with that preacher, Carl wouldn't never done nothing!

I put my eyes out the windshield. A lost balloon was sailing off into the blue—it vanished as it crossed the sun. Damn it, Leeli! Get your ass back in here!

She slid down from the seat and stood in the glare, defiant as a dog off its chain.

I gunned the engine. I'm leaving!

She slammed the door shut.

—Something wrong with those people, I said. Man's shot in the face and it don't even phase him? Fuck is that? This ain't nothing we should be messing with.

She took off walking. Her round little butt looked real tasty in those shorts.

—Aw, Leeli! Come on back here, girl!

▲▼▲

I'm not a complete fool. I understand it's all about pussy, but pussy must be a sickness with me, otherwise I cannot explain why I let myself get pulled back into a situation I knew was a dead loser. A psychiatrist might say I was hunting for just such a situation, but if Leeli had been one of the reverend's old gals, I wouldn't have wasted a second before putting her in the rear view. I admit self-destruction is the way of my life. The way of every life, maybe. But the style Leeli brought to her walk-off scene, switching her hips and arching her back and giving a sad, pouty look over her shoulder, psychology wasn't that huge a factor.

I told her to drive and funneled Ava, Carl, and Squire into the rear of the van, then climbed in behind the passenger seat so I could keep an eye on everybody. Squire was by the doors, legs kicked out, his head wobbling like he was listening to private music. Ava was next to the wheel hub, comforting Carl, who rested his good cheek on her shoulder.

—Get east, I said to Leeli. Use the interstate and keep it under the limit.

Ava asked, Where we going? It was loud in the van and she had to shout it.

—Friend of mine's place in South Daytona!

She thought about this and nodded gloomily.

—Wanna tell me what's going on? I pointed to Squire and then Carl.

She shook her head. Not now! She shifted to accommodate Carl's weight and said, I'd like my gun back!

—I like maple sugar on my oatmeal, I told her. But sometimes I gotta do without!

The sun was bouncing along just above the palm tops like a dragged bait, and the light was growing orangey, and a brown shadow gathered in the rear of the van. It was all calming somehow, the shadow and the rattling, droning speed. I felt submerged in it, a man sitting at the bottom of a swimming pool, unmindful of trouble in the air, and I worked the ride into a movie, not a big spectacular with sinister terrorist plots or world-shattering disasters, but a movie from back when stars used to play in crummy little stories about nobodies on their way to damnation. Creedence and Lynard Skynard for the soundtrack. My daddy's kind of songs, but I liked them all the same. I found one cigarette left in my crumpled pack and lit up. It didn't taste a thing like movie smoke must taste, clean and savory, a working man's reward, but my exhales hazed the air so it looked old-fashioned and yellowy brown, 1970s air, air with some character, and I sat fingering the gun, trying to put my mind onto a future different from the sort promised by the movie I was in, but thinking mainly about the manager, what a strange thing it was for a man to come halfway around the world from a place where they had monkeys and elephants and shit to go with their nuclear bombs just to catch a bullet in a HoJos and die staring up at track lighting and Styrofoam ceiling tile.

Rickey Wirgman, who I'd called my friend, was more of a brother fuck-up and former criminal associate, like a cousin you don't have much use for but deal with on occasion. His grandfather had left him some property on the edge of the marshlands near South Daytona, a collection of weathered frame buildings alongside a stretch of open water that grandpa, if not for a crack habit and some harsh words spoken to a fellow inmate in the Volusia County Jail that caused his history to take a sudden tragic turn, might have developed into a full-blown financial disaster. A fishing camp had been his thought. In the years since he'd inherited, Rickey had run a contest to see what would fall apart the fastest, himself or the roof he slept under. He sold off pieces of the land to survive and recreated with the finest dope and the nastiest hookers. The sheds and cabins were rotting away, but the marsh was pretty in the twilight. Black watercourses meandering through tall green grasses, here and there a tiny humped island thick with palms going to silhouettes in the soft gray light, and pelicans crossing in black flapping strings against a streak of rose along the horizon, like a caption in a cool language. Exotic-looking. A Discovery Channel place. The grass was tamped down around the relics of the fishing camp. Seemed like some huge, heavy thing had made an emergency landing, maybe a big jetliner bellying in, and the survivors had squatted where they'd been spilled until death had swallowed them too, and now their shelters were decaying. Scattered around in the higher grass behind the cabins were beat-up refrigerators and washing machines and stoves. They got you thinking it wasn't a plane had crashed, but one of those bird dinosaurs, and its teeth had busted from its mouth or it had laid a number of curious square white eggs before passing.

We hid the van behind a shed and straggled toward the main lodge. Lodge was a hundred-dollar name for a structure that was the house equivalent of a crooked old beekeeper who had stroked out in his sleep while wearing his hat and veil. Window shadows for eyes and a gnawed-off nose opening into a screen porch and boards the color of cigarette ash and a slumped partial second story with tattery shingle tiles drooping off the roof edge. There were no lights. Frogs bleeped out in the marsh, like electric raindrops, and skeeters would cover your arm unless you kept swiping them off.

—Nobody's home, Leeli said in an exhausted tone.

—Maybe. It don't matter. The porch stair creaked and bowed to my step. The billowed-out screens were rusted through in patches, torn loose from the railing. Just pick out some rooms, I said. I'll see if anybody's here.

I left the others to creep around and scare the spiders and explored some. You couldn't find a grayer place, you searched in a cemetery. Every square inch and object had run out of time and stopped being what it once was. Phantom things that resembled tables and chairs and rugs and pictures on the walls and the walls themselves were just ghosts made of dust and habit and a gray smothery smell. The kitchen sink was gray and so were the stains on it. Peels of linoleum curled up from the floor like eucalyptus bark. The only bit of color I noticed was three custom car magazines poking from beneath an empty bookcase. Rickey's version of the redneck dream.

From down the hall came a gentle muttering. Around the corner I caught sight of a pale flickery glow escaping through a half-closed door. I pushed it open. A lounge chair faced a pint-sized color TV set on an orange crate. The chair was an island throne rising from an ocean of beer cans, pizza boxes, take-out cartons, grocery sacks, empty tins, condom packets, shrinkwrapped cookies, crumpled tissues, video cases, batteries. You name it, it was there. Stretched in the chair, wearing bib overalls, lording it over this his solitary realm, was the fucking vulture god of decay. He was thinner than the last I saw him, his beard about six inches longer, but he still had the worst comb-over in Central Florida. The dirt on his ankles made an argyle pattern. His right arm dangled off the chair arm, his fingers almost touching a settlement of pill bottles on the floor. He was watching football. The Gators and somebody. I asked who was winning and he tipped back his head, trying to find me, but not in an awful hurry about it.

—Shit! The word leaked out of him like a last gasp. He gave a blitzed laugh, two grunts and a hiccup. That you, man?

I picked a straight chair from beside a sheetless mattress in the corner and sat so he could watch me and the TV both.

—Maceo. He made a fumbly gesture, patting an invisible dog by his knee. Crazy motherfucker. Where you been?

—Raiford. New Smyrna for a while after.

—Oh, yeah…right. Rickey's face was gaunt, greasy with sweat, ready to crack and sag. The bridge of his nose was swollen and had a ragged cut across it that wasn't healing too good.

I asked what he was up to and he said, Dilaudid. Crystal meth. Mostly dilaudid lately. You want some? I got a shitload.

—There's people with me. We need to hide out here a couple or three days.

He blinked rapidly. It was like part of his brain was attempting to semaphore another part that trouble was at hand, but the message didn't come through. Yeah...okay, he said feebly. Wherever you want, y'know. There's rooms. His eyes, charcoal smudges, returned to the TV. A faint cheer mounted as a tiny guy in blue-and-orange scampered down the sideline. The Gators were kicking ass. Rickey made a grinding, choking noise in the back of his throat. I knew that paved-over feeling in the esophagus, the warm dry space that kept him safe from the guttering of his own life, the valueless thoughts featherdusting the inside of his skull. Like a perfect fever.

—I'll take a few of them Dilaudid, you don't mind, I said.

—I told you go ahead. His fingernail ticked one of the bottle caps. I got a whole shitload.

I kneeled by the chair, palmed one of the bottles and shook four white tabs out of another.

—You get settled, come on back you wanna talk. Rickey wriggled his ass around as if he had an itch.

—Yeah, maybe. We're kinda wore down.

—Hey, Maceo!

I could see him looking for a way to hold me there. I guess I'd reminded him he was lonely.

—'Member that little honey you's fucking, one with the blue streak in her hair?

—Twila, I said.

—Yeah, her. She got the virus. He said this with the sort of cheerful expectancy you might use to announce the birth of twins. 'Spect some of them NASCAR boys better get theyselves checked, he went on. Last I heard, she was passing out blowjobs at Mac's Famous Bar like they was dollar kisses.

—She musta knew what she was doing. Twila didn't give a shit. My feet crunched the litter ocean as I stepped toward the door.

—Maceo?

—What?

—You wanna bring me something from the 'frigerator? I got pizza in there and I'm too fucked-up to walk.

—I'll do 'er in a while.

The corridor had gone dark. I stood a moment, getting my bearings, and heard Rickey quietly say, Oh, God...God! Maybe he was hurting, maybe the veil of the future had lifted and he saw a shadow stealing toward him. Or maybe it was the Gators done something stupid.

▲▼▲

Leeli had spread sheets on the bed in a room off the kitchen, and sealed a hole in the window screen with a stuffed rag, and secured a lamp for the bedside table. She was sitting on the bed, her knees tucked to her chin, tanned legs agleam in the tallowy light.

—What we gonna do? she asked.

—I told you what I wanted to do back in Ocala.

She hid her face, resting her forehead on her knees. It's not back in Ocala now. We gotta figure something to do.

—Don't know about you, but I'm getting high. I showed her the pills.

—What is it?

—Dilaudid.

—Is it something good?

—It's evil. You gonna fucking adore it.

I powdered a handful of pills in the bottom of a teacup and let Leeli feed her nose from the tip of a knife blade.

—Oooh, she said, sliding down in the bed, closing her eyes.

—What I tell ya?

I did more than Leeli, enough so the world fitted around me like a warm liquid glove and there were little sparkles at the corners of my sight and when I moved my hand I felt the exact curve of my shoulder and the muscles playing sweetly in my arm. I lay back next to Leeli. The ceiling was bare gray boards and beams with black grainy patterns and sparkles pricking the gaps that were probably stars. It looked distant and enormous, part of some ancient building that was proud of itself, a church where saints and great soldiers were buried, and terrible instruction was regularly given to the faithful, lots of Go-thous and Verily-thee-must-hastens that resulted in dungeons filled with bones and chained apes with blood on their teeth and crestfallen martyrs, but it didn't have no message for me. My eyelids were trying to droop and my mind drooped too, blissfully trivial, noticing stuff about the high, the tremor in my leg, a pincushion sensation in my left foot, a nerve jigging in my chest. Something landed softly on my stomach, its warmth spreading like a melting pat of butter. Leeli's palm. Feel up to having some fun? she asked. Her hand slipped lower and she flicked my zipper.

—I ain't never gonna say no, but I'm pretty damn wasted.

—Me, too. I don't really need to or nothing. I just want to see what it's like...when I'm like this, y'know. Okay?

We fucked like space babies in no gravity, coming together at goofy angles, forgetting for long moments what we were doing, our minds scatting on some loopy riff, reawakened by the touch of lips, a breast, something that got us all juicy and eager for a time, speeding it up and lapsing again into slow motion, into stillness. It took Leeli damn near an hour to come and once she started it took her almost the same to stop. She curled up into me after like a dazed, sleek bug that had eaten too much of a leaf and said, Sweet Jesus. That was amazing! I was too gassed to respond. If we'd been a pair of spiders, she could have gnawed off my legs and laid eggs in my belly and I wouldn't have argued the matter.

Leeli had some trouble sleeping due to the itching that goes with the Dilaudid wearing off, but finally her breathing grew even and deep. I did a few more hits, pulled on my pants and went onto the porch. A wind had sprung up, driving away the skeeters and quieting the frogs. Clouds edged with milky light were racing the moon, parting around it, and the grasses gave forth with an approving chorus, like the sound Leeli made when the Dilaudid rushed upon her, only louder by a million throats, seeming to appreciate the architecture of dust and reflected fire in the sky, the hosanna clouds, the lacquered moon-colored water, the grasses tipped in silver, the black cut-outs of the palm islands like left-over pieces of Africa. I had that feeling of small nobility and pure solitude the world wants you to feel when it reveals this side of itself, so you'll believe nature was this awesome beautiful peaceful rock concert deal before man come along and doggy-fucked it full of disease, and not the bloody, biting, eat-your-meat-while-it's-alive horror show it truly is. That night I was okay about feeling this way and I walked along the shore, sucking in the odors of fish and frogs and the millions of unrecorded deaths that had accompanied the HoJo manager's as if they were the latest Paris perfumes.

I thought I was out there on my lonesome, just me and a scrap of wilderness and Dilaudid, but when I climbed a hummock to avoid wading through the marsh, I spied Ava, Carl, and Squire standing at the tip of a grassy point about sixty feet farther along. Ava was gesturing at the sky like she was naming stars or teaching about the weather or something. Squire and Carl, whose jaw was bandaged, were gazing upward. I was too fogged to jam their nature walk in with all the other nothing junk I knew concerning them and make any sense of it, but when they strolled off still farther from the lodge, I realized this was my opportunity to take a peek at Ava's personals and maybe scoop up some cash. I hustled back as fast I could, which was not real fast, and located the room where she was bunking. Her tote bag was stuffed under a pillow. I found no money, but among the keys and Kleenex and cosmetics and all was a badge holder holding a photo ID. Official evidence that Ava was affiliated with the FBI. A fake, I thought, but then remembered where I'd met up with her and wasn't so sure. At the bottom of the bag was a leatherette photo album. The first picture was an overexposed black and white shot of Ava and Carl leaning against a vintage Chevy Impala. The 'sixty-two convertible. She appeared to be around seventeen, eighteen, and wore white socks and buckle shoes and a print dress with a belling skirt that covered her legs to the mid-calves. Carl had on jeans and a sport shirt with its tail hanging out. He looked no younger than he did now. Another guy sat behind the wheel of the Impala. His face was a blur of sunlight, but going by his round head, I guessed this to be Squire. Both Ava and Carl were grinning and pointing at a shield-shaped sign on the shoulder of the road. The sign was also blurred, but readable: State Road 44.

Several of the remaining pictures were shots of Carl, some of Ava and Carl. A few recent ones showed them with Squire. None of these said much to me, not like the first. Seeing that Ava had aged, though not so much as she should have, and Carl hadn't aged a day, this gave rise to *Star Trek* movies in my head. Space aliens, UFOs, abductions, secret government projects, intelligent robots, all kinds of happy horseshit. A couple of times I thought I'd figured out who they must be, but if they were aliens or whatever on the run from the government, what the hell were they doing on government property? If they were working with the government, why were they hanging out with the likes of Leeli and me? And what was that house doing in the dunes near the Cape? A trap for lowlifes such as myself, I decided. That was it. Damn straight. Alien creatures from beyond the stars were studying the pork rind set. Government super-clones were learning how to mimic the scum of the earth so they would be in place to assassinate the redneck Jesus, who'd be coming to a womb in Kissimmee any day now. Or could be robot killers who did the evil bidding of the Bush administration were given vacations during which they hung out with real folks and fucked them up every whichaway. Or Squire and Carl were aliens who'd suffered brain damage in the Roswell crash and Ava was their rehab nurse, training them in the ways of society, and their vibrations were keeping her young. I got somewhat insane behind all this, creating tabloid headlines, picturing me and Leeli on the talk shows, discussing her alien lesbian lover with Jerry and Jay and David and the rest, going out to Hollywood to attend the premiere of the movie about our life story. Gradually I calmed down. There was bound to be a logical explanation for the photo and Carl's recuperative powers and everything else. I told myself I'd get to the bottom of it eventually.

▲▼▲

I woke the following morning with a pistol barrel poking my nose and Rickey's hand on my throat and his burnt-out eyes giving me a close-up of the dark sour-smelling rathole they opened into. It was like the little room he lived in was inside him, too. Straggles of hair curtained off his face, but did nothing to filter his rotten breath.

—Motherfucker, you stole my dope! he said.

Leeli gave a squeak and rolled off the bed, covering herself with the sheet.

—Where the fuck is it? Rickey asked.

—I took four goddamn tabs! I said. You want 'em back, you gonna have to scrape out my nose!

—Don't think I won't! He screwed the barrel down hard against my cheek. I'm missing a bottle.

—He didn't take nothing! Leeli said. I promise!

—You check around by your chair? I asked. Jesus, you could hide a Volkswagen under all the crap you got on your floor.

His face lost some intensity.

—I guess you were so clearheaded last night, you couldn't have set it down somewheres and forgot, I said. You would know if you give it a kick accidental when you got up to piss or something.

Thought confused his expression. He backed away from the bed, the pistol angled toward the side.

—Jesus Christ! I sat up and swung my legs onto the floor. Fuck you so crazy about, anyway? You said you had a good goddamn supply.

—It's gotta last the weekend, he said sullenly.

—You run out, I know you'll get you some more. I pulled on my undershorts. What's wrong with you, man? Busting in here like that. I ever cheat you before? I ever treat you anything but righteous?

Rickey puzzled over that. The words came slow from his mouth, like slobber off a bull's lip. I can't recall.

—Well, you'd remember if I did, wouldn't you?

—I s'pose so. Yeah. He lowered the pistol and let out a soggy, rueful snort of laughter. Fuck, man. Y'know, I...just people been fucking me around a lot lately.

—If you can't find it, don't come back in here busting on me about it. You know you gonna find it sooner or later in that mess. Someday you run out, you gonna be stumbling around and it'll turn up under your big toe. Be like finding a diamond in a cornfield.

This fairly brightened Rickey—he nodded energetically, seeing a vision of that glorious day. I noticed Leeli cowering in the corner, looking extra fine with her breasts gathered above her arm and her ass sticking out from the sheet.

—Hey, Leeli. Get your tail over here, I said. This here's my ol' pal Rickey.

I tried to move Rickey on out of there before he could get paranoid again, but his eyes were leaving tracks all over Leeli, even after she covered everything up, and he kept hanging around. He began asking why we needed to hide and such. I told him some lies and when that didn't stop his questions, I said I wanted to borrow his car so we could buy food and stuff. The best way to derail Rickey's suspicions always was to beg a favor. If he could deny you something, he'd start feeling masterful and forget whatever was bothering him. I argued and pleaded, but he was resolute. Nobody drives my car but me, he said. Like everyone in the world was dying to park their behinds in his funky-smelling shitbox so they could race off to Monaco and display this automotive jewel before graceful society. It ended with Rickey agreeing to bring us food himself and stalking off to search for his missing Dilaudid with head held high.

—That was sly, way you managed that, Leeli said, giving me a smooch. You're pretty smart for white trash.

—Guess what that makes me in the real world, I said.

▲▼▲

Rain and guns. I think it must've been raining when the first gun was drawn hot from its tempering fire, because when it comes rain, I get a itch to handle a gun if I've got one. Which is a roundabout way of saying it rained and Rickey went for food, Leeli hunkered beside me on the bed fixing her nails, while I sat turning Ava's Colt in my hands, picking at the plaque on the grip, rubbing a little raised, rough patch alongside the chamber, thinking gun thoughts, testing its heft and balance, knowing that if I was really pretty smart I would walk down to the water's edge and toss it on in. Having a gun was not in my best interests. Without one, if I was at a beach party, let's say, and some worthless drunken individual tipped over my beer and said diddley dog about it, the worst could happen was busted knuckles and a hospital trip—but I had a gun, God knows, that beer might seem like the very selfsame beer for which the Founding Fathers sacrificed their lives, and I'd be called upon to uphold its sacred honor.

It was an uncommon hard and lasting rain. A drizzle started about ten o'clock and five minutes later it was like a billion hailstones were bouncing off the roof, filling the house with a roar. A weird slivery darkness ensued. The cloud bellies passing over us were black as Satan's boot soles and the wind flattened the marsh grasses with a constant rush. The rain slacked off many times during the day, a couple of times it stopped altogether and the land yielded up a sodden, animal smell; but it kept returning in strength. Rickey drove off to buy food. Carl and Squire sat on the porch playing a hand-held game of some kind. Leeli got a little closer to her new best friend, Mr. Dilaudid, and fell asleep. I wedged the Colt in my waist and paid a visit to Ava.

Her door was open a foot and I stuck my head in without knocking. She was standing at the window, stark naked, arms folded beneath her breasts and hair loose about her shoulders, gazing out at the rain. She must have felt me there, because she turned her head and delivered me a flat, unsurprised stare. What do you want? she asked.

—A few words would be good.

—I guess it's inevitable.

—I'll wait out here while you throw something on.

—No need. We're like family now.

Ava went back to watching the weather and I let my eyes out for a run. Though her face was hagging out, her body belonged to a woman in her prime. She wanted to give me a show, it didn't bother me none. The door proved to be stuck open. I eased in and perched on a straight chair set next to a dresser with its drawers stove-in. Her room was shabbier than ours. Rat turds speckled the boards along the molding and spiderwebs spanned the corners. The bed was so swaybacked, some of the springs were flush to the floor.

—I sneaked a look at your photograph album last night, I said.

—Oh? What did you think?

—I think you're damn sexy for a woman's gotta be in her fifties.

—Sixty-one, she said. I'm sixty-one.

—Okay. A woman in her sixties. And Carl, how old is he?

—Carl. Her smile had a fond quality. Carl's ageless.

—Squire, too. He ageless?

—In a way.

She crossed to the bed with a three-step stroll and laid herself out, back against the headboard, arms spread on the pillows. Her pubic hair was trimmed to a neat strip and she had a long waist to go with her trophy chest. She reminded me of this naked woman in a painting one of my high school teachers had prattled on about, some rich horny bitch from another century lying on a couch and looking at you with a similar scornful, seductive attitude.

—If you want to come over here with me, it's all right, she said.

—I'm fine where I am.

—Leeli won't mind, that's what's worrying you.

—You don't know nothing about that, believe me.

She shrugged, smiled.

—Why would you even want me to come over there? I asked. We ain't got nothing going on.

—I like sex.

—So do I, but....

—Oh I see! You have to like the girl first. You require an emotional attachment.

I didn't care for her mocking me and I was tempted to fuck her knock-kneed, but that would have been playing with her deck. I don't have to like her all that much, I said. Helps if I like her some, though.

Her smile cut itself a wider curve. You don't like me a tiny bit?

—I ain't even sure what the fuck you are. Whyn't you clear that up for me?

The rain came harder, spitting through the window screen, drops darkening a wedge of floor beneath it. Some giant's stomach grumbled and the light dimmed.

—You gonna shoot me if I don't tell you?

—That wasn't my intention.

—No? Yet you come in here with my gun on display.

—Just making a point.

—The point being, you might be prepared to shoot me.

—You want me to shoot you? You keep pissing me off, maybe I will. Don't seem like it would affect you that much, anyway. Or is it just the boys who's good at taking bullets?

This was the first real conversation I'd had with Ava. I'd seen that on the outside she was a cool, collected sort. Now I was coming to think coolness ran deep in her, that instead of a heart, a little refrigeration unit was humming in her chest, pumping out frosty air. She seemed like a lotta women I'd known who'd survived bar fights that passed for marriages. Women who felt you couldn't do nothing more to them than had been done already. Yet I didn't accept that picture of her. She was too steady, too unconcerned. I had a notion that her steadiness came from a perception of my weaknesses. Like she was X-raying me, reading all my flaws.

—You'd like me to tell you a story, she said. Is that it?

—A true story. I don't want no fairy tales.

—All right.

She proceeded to whip one off about how she and Carl had been dating back in the 60s while she was in high school and he was in college, and they had gone down to State Road 44 to look at the flying saucers and have sex, and a saucer had abducted them, worked some weird change on them both, and set them back on earth for God knows what purpose, maybe just as test subjects, and they were prodded this way and that by alien agencies—powerful ones that penetrated every layer of society, even the FBI—and they were always being put in strange situations, and this was why they had been at the house in the dunes when Leeli and I showed up.

I was about to ask if Squire was an alien agent, one who was doing the prodding, when she launched into a second story, saying Carl and Squire had been hybrid clone babies, grown from human eggs and alien juice extracted from a dead UFO pilot, and she'd been in charge of them when the government decided the experiment wasn't producing any valuable result and decided to kill the two boys, so Ava, with the help of highly placed friends, had run off with them, and they'd been pursued for a time, but then the government changed their minds and thought the thing to do was let the boys run, acquire life experiences, and see if they developed into a crop worth harvesting. They lived in constant fear of judgment, she said. Never knowing if the government would change their minds again. She was worried that Carl shooting the HoJo's manager might be the last straw and the government would send their killers.

I wondered if she could've tapped into my thoughts of the night before and devised these stories to suit my tabloid fantasies. Why'd you tell two stories? I asked. You told me just the one, I might've believed it.

—You're not a believer, Ava said. You're a doubter. Don't matter what I say, you're gonna pick at it.

The rain had ceased and you could hear everything dripping. A bluejay began jattering and a dog started going crazy at the sound. Four-legged somethings, probably squirrels, skittered across the roof. All those noises, it was like the world was surfacing to snatch a breath before the rain went to drowning it again.

—Carl's my son, Ava said. He's the spitting image of his daddy. He's dead...Carl Senior. He was killed in a car wreck right before we was about to marry. I was already pregnant. Carl was born retarded and he's got lotta other problems. There's this disease makes his nerves not work right. He can't hardly feel a thing. It's killing him. I don't know how much longer he's got. Not long, I expect. Squire, he's just this fella I met in a bar over in Boynton Beach. He keeps me happy and he's simple enough to relate to Carl. Carl Senior's daddy worked for NASA. One of the directors. Even though I never married his son, he was kind to us. When he died he left a trust for me and Carl. The house where you met us? He had it built for us. Pulled some strings so we could have access. The government don't care about the land no more and his friends make sure people leave us be when we're there. Ava crossed her legs and clasped her hands behind her head. That fly any higher for you?

—You're a piece of fucking work, I'll give you that, I said.

Ava grinned. You'll never know 'til you cut you a slice.

—What the hell you hanging around with us for, you got all this money?

—I like Leeli. I like you, too. Different, though. I was enjoying myself with y'all until yesterday.

—The thing gets me, I said after studying on things a patch, is how come you don't seem so worried about your son or your old boyfriend or your experimental subject, whichever he is...about him committing murder.

—Oh we'll be all right. I got confidence in you.

—Now that's a lie.

—You got us outa Ocala, didn't you? With your experience in these matters and my money, we're gonna do fine. I was thinking about Mexico.

—Mexico?

—Uh-huh. I was thinking I'd charter a plane and we'd lay low for a few and then jump on over. After Leeli finishes her time with me, the two of you can skedaddle. Twenty thousand'll go a long way in Mexico.

—Whyn't you just call your bigwig friends to haul your ass outa this?

—Maybe I will, things don't go well. But you know how it is, Maceo. You got a favor in the bank, you want to hold back from using it long as you can.

My thoughts skipped back and forth from story to story. I didn't believe any of them, but I kind of believed them all. I suspected there was a spoonful of truth in each, or that each was a stand-in double for a truth she hadn't spoken.

—It don't matter who I am, who Carl and Squire are, she said. We still hafta deal with the problem.

Trying to decide what to believe and what to do about it tied knots in my thought strings. Ava lay grinning at me, looking from the neck down like a dessert tray. I gave myself a nudge toward the bed, pretending to buy the proposition that if I tore one off with her, I'd have a better feel for the situation. Old hayseed philosophers gathered in the boiler room of my brain, swapped round a bottle, and spewed dipshit wisdoms: You can't say how a peach tastes 'til the juice runs down your chin. Staring at the groceries don't tell you who the cook is. Video footage of a naked, sucked-dry corpse, its mouth wrenched open in a final agony, was playing in the den, with graphics reading ALIEN EMBRACE KILLS REDNECK LOVER. I stayed where I was, speculating pro and con upon what I might be missing.

The door shrieked as someone shoved against it. Squire squeezed on in, followed by Carl. Squire glared at Ava, at me, and Carl beamed. His bandage was soaking wet, smudged with dirty finger marks.

—Hi, honey, Ava said.

—That man went for food's coming down the drive, Squire said.

—That's nice. Soon we can have us a feast! She patted the bed, an invitation, and Squire, good dog that he was, laid down beside her. Carl gazed at the chair I was on for a second, then plunked himself down on the floor next to the bed. Squire began toying with Ava's nipples, kissing her neck. The rain swept back in. I heard a clattering from the front of the lodge, a door slamming, but I didn't turn from watching Squire and Ava. The rainy noise seemed to be tightening the space around us, compressing and heating the air. I told myself the minute Squire started taking off his clothes, I was gone, but there was something mesmerizing about Ava, about the lush, lazy strain of her belly, the slow surges of her hips, and the way her eyes would graze me every so often. I felt the cold pull of her. The sexy warmth of her surface was a dream and beneath lay an undertow that sucked all the swimmers who'd strayed out past the bar into whatever deep lightless place her story really sprung from. I had a glimmering of how it would be to go with the flow, to stroke hard and arrow down into her dark, to reach the great secret at the bottom, whether toothy maw or golden kingdom, it wasn't much important, because you were bound to be part of it, and as Squire's fingers traipsed between her thighs and her hips lifted, I thought what I was feeling now was closer to the truth than anything she'd said, and knew that she was willful and careless and irresistibly strong. The instant I understood this, however, I declared bullshit on it. I was watching a dirty movie, I told myself, and not falling down no rabbit hole.

—Fuck y'all doing? Rickey had popped his head in and was gawking at the bed, where Squire and Ava hadn't missed a beat.

—Notice how the entire school turns as one, Carl said happily.

—Hallelujah! I said. The single mind's directing.

Rickey slid himself in past the stuck door. I could see he was hoping to get in on the act, but was all puffed up and ready to be outraged in case he couldn't. Goddamn it! he said, and stepped over to the window, getting a side angle on the center ring. I don't want no weird shit going on in my house!

—God, no! I said. There's never been no weird shit like people fucking and people watching going on out here. Not in this holy temple.

Rickey might have said something back, but his mouth stopped working, because right then Ava opened her legs and Squire started wrestling off his jeans.

—That's Ava there showing her rosy, I said to Rickey. Squire, he's the boy 'bout to have some fun. Down there in the front row, that's Carl.

—In concert, said Carl. In simple harmony and balance.

—Carl's got this kinda religious thing going, I told Rickey.

This inspired Carl to point at me and say, Hands up! Who wants to die?

Rickey pricked up his ears at that, but again gave no response. Squire had climbed on board the Ava train and was making tracks for the station, giving out with chuffing noises. The springs backed him up with a jangly, crunchy rhythm and the rain kept drumming and Ava sang a lyric with a single breathy word. Carl nodded, smiled. Rickey's eyes cut toward me—I expect he was wanting a sign it would be okay for him to mix in.

The floorboards creaked. Leeli had crept in and was nailing me with a .45 caliber stare. She said, You asshole!, and ducked back out. Catching a last glimpse of Ava's heels and Squire's pimply backside, I wheeled up from the chair and after her. I checked the porch and saw Leeli standing with her arms folded out in the rain. I didn't think she was crying or nothing, just had a mad on. Rickey came up at my shoulder and said, Hey, man! Is that Ava, she doing everybody?

—Don't be shy, boy. Ask her.

—You serious?

—She ain't gonna screech and hold her knees together if you do. She'll just tell you yes or no.

—Cool.

—You might wanna wait to ask 'til Squire's finished, I said as he turned away.

—Oh...yeah. Okay.

—But you better go back on in now. You wanna be there so you can get next.

He set off again and I called to him, asked where the food was.

—Kitchen, he said and slipped into Ava's room.

Eight Burger King take-out sacks were resting on the kitchen table. I found one full of double cheeseburgers and carried it onto the porch.

Leeli! I shouted, and waggled the sack out through the hole in the screen door. I got burgers!

Her head twitched, but she didn't turn. I sat on the porch steps under the porch overhang and unwrapped a cheeseburger and had a bite. Soaked through, Leeli's yellowy white hair had the look of the down on a baby chick. She glared at me similar to how this drunk Seminole boy I'd met in the Panama Beach lock-up one fine morning had glared: sideways, his shoulders rolled forward, with his close eye wide and the other narrowed. I figured Leeli and that Seminole had about the same ambition toward me.

I finished the burger and Leeli stomped over, snatched the bag and switched past me into the lodge. Don't you come after me! she said. I'm not talking to you.

—I hear you, sugar, I said. I'll be right in.

▲▼▲

With her belly full, Leeli's mood improved. She was near to purring, curled up on the bed and looking out at the rain, but still it took me a few tries to drag her into a conversation. I was just sitting there, I said, when they started going at it. What you expect me to do?

—Leave, she said. I know how Ava and Squire get. You had plenty of warning.

—That mean you watched 'em?

—She wants me to!

—Then why go beating on me about it?

She clammed up, so I worked another angle, and when that didn't satisfy her, I said, 'Member what you told me 'bout how you felt sometimes Ava was drowning you? I think I got a taste of what you were talking about.

A little something tweaked behind Leeli's face, but she didn't let it out.

—Yeah, it was strange, I said. It was like she was pulling on me. Maybe that's why I kept setting there.

—She's a witch, Leeli said. I swear she is.

—I don't know 'bout that.

—That's right! You don't know fuck all! I'm telling you she's got this power...it just eats away at you 'til you're nothing. 'Til you're like Carl or Squire.

I spun this around and then said, That's how come you think Carl and Squire are slow?

—Sometimes I think that. Leeli picked at a fray on the pillowcase. Sometimes I think she just wore 'em away.

The witchy woman had tried to draw me close and drown me in her power. This seemed crazier than what Ava had told me, but only a little. Thinking about Ava as someone who left you hollow inside but still walking around wasn't that tough a chore. I'd known regular folks who could do the same sort of job on you and I said as much to Leeli.

—Naw, un-uh, it's more'n that. It's what you were saying. She pulls at you, but she's not playing you. It's who she is, know what I mean? It's like that's all she is...this force.

A lightning crack ran violet down the eastern sky, like we were inside a gray egg that was cracking open in the middle of hell. The thunder came a few seconds later.

—You pull at me, too, I said. Know that? You been pulling at me since New Smyrna.

Leeli's face went little-girl serious and big-eyed.

I eased down beside her, laid a hand on her hip.

—I'm scared, she said. Ava wants to go to Mexico. I can't think what to do.

—Let's leave tonight. Let's just go.

—Where? Where can we go?

—This old boy I got to know in Raiford runs with some bikers got land over 'round Palatka. Cops never come near their place. We could stay 'long as we want.

—Maybe you'd be comfortable with a buncha bikers, but I wouldn't. She snuggled in closer. Maybe we should go with Ava and the second we get to Mexico, that's it. Money or not.

—I don't like the idea of traveling more miles with her.

—It's the safest way. Won't be no security to pass through with a charter. Leeli picked up my hand from her hip and moved it around so I was holding her. 'Less you got something better'n bikers.

I considered Lauderdale, but Lauderdale was a hell of a drive and we couldn't stay for long at my friend's house.

—Ain't you scared? Leeli asked. I can't tell if you are or not.

—I'm past scared, I'm on into survive. That's why I say get shut of 'em now.

We left it hanging that way and closed the door and got foolish on the bed. Desperate straits and the desire to forget them lit up our nerves and made us better lovers. Leeli like to have died in my arms and my heart was sprained and limping in my chest, I worked it so long and furious. I left her drowsing and went into the kitchen and had another burger and a purple milk shake that tasted like nothing purple and puddled like melted plastic in my stomach. The TV was playing in Rickey's room. I figured Ava must have kicked him to the curb.

I returned to the bedroom and drifted beside Leeli. My flesh felt light and insubstantial and everything had the sharpness of an important memory, how you feel the thing remembered before you see and smell and taste it. It was like the world itself was forming a memory that used me how a pearl uses a sore spot, sealing me in so I could be dug out at some later date to be admired. The rain blew slanty, then straightened out, then it blew sideways and the lightning moved closer. The air darkened to an ashy color. Things bumped and clanked against some section of the lodge. You'd have thought the rain had turned to chains. The marsh grass rippled with pantherish fury, twisting and flowing in every direction. The storm smell was ozone and dank trouble.

Sleep wouldn't take me. I got dressed and padded down the hall to visit Rickey. He was in his chair, scratching himself, watching the local news with the sound low. He gave a disinterested, Hey, and paid me no mind as I drew up a chair.

—You get laid? I asked.

—Damn! Did I! That woman's got some evil fucking ways!

Rickey didn't look much different for the experience and I thought the last shriveled-up scrap of soul must have been sucked out before Ava got to him.

He craned his neck to see me. How long y'all staying?

—Day or two. Why, you wanna go again with her?

—She promises not to kill me.

—Better ask for the pony ride next time.

Rickey coughed out a laugh and spat into the garbage alongside his chair. He spaced out on the TV and I couldn't think of anything more to say. Rickey wasn't much of a talker but he enjoyed people with him when he watched his programs. I knew if I didn't hang out a while, he'd feel he wasn't being respected, so I sat there dead-headed, peering at his mess. Must have been every kind of candy wrapper in the world scattered around that floor. It was like investigating a cave where some sick animal had puked up a month of bad meals. The next time I glanced toward the TV, I saw a blonde woman in a pants suit with her microphone stuck in the face of the gray-haired reverend I'd manhandled back in Ocala. I told Rickey to hit the volume, and when he was slow to act, I grabbed the remote and did it myself. The reverend shook his head mournfully and said, There was so much confusion, I don't know which one actually fired. It was the skinny one I saw holding the gun, but that's after the shooting. All I can tell you for certain is I heard somebody shout, Hands up! Who wants to die? And then I heard the shots.

—Hands up! Who wants to die? The blonde reporter acquired a serious look as the camera went to a close-up on her. Vikay Choudhoury responded to that challenge with a hero's answer and now he lies dead. She paused for effect and said, This is Gloria Renard. Channel Twelve—

I thumbed the mute button. There was a cold spread of panic inside me, like I was standing on the edge of a cliff and had just lost my balance.

—You get on outa here, Maceo! Rickey stared at me through the straggles of his hair. I mean right fucking now!

—I didn't kill nobody, I said.

—I don't care you did or you didn't. Every damn cop in Volusia knows who it is says that dumb fucking hands-up-who-wants-to-die bullshit. You think they won't be snooping 'round here? Wonder is, they ain't here already.

—We can't leave now. They be on us 'fore we get clear the driveway.

Rickey reached down beside his hip and produced his pistol. I'll shoot you my own self, you don't get on out.

Anger was a cold snake snapping out of me. I ripped the gun from his hand, then I stood and began punching him. He tried to block the first couple with his forearms, but each one was a lesson I'd been taught to deliver, a preachment of old pain. The blows drove him lower in the chair until his butt was hanging half off the seat and his head was jammed into the join of the cushions and there was blood in his eyes. I couldn't have said why, but the sight of him unconscious jabbed another red-hot stick into my brain. I smashed the pistol against the wall again and again. The trigger guard fell off and the cylinder popped out from the housing and I threw the rest to the floor. I knew Rickey was right about the cops. Maybe that was what set me off. That and recognizing how good a look at my face I'd given everybody in the HoJos. When God invented the notion of crazy trumping common sense, He must've had me in mind for the standard model. Everything considered, it was a goddamn miracle I'd come this far in life.

▲▼▲

The storm lived around us. Seemed the lodge was a battery discharging thunder cracks and splintered lightning that made stretches of churning marsh grass bloom for unholy seconds against the dark gulf of land and sky. I told Leeli about Rickey and the reverend and the cops and tried once again to persuade her to leave with me. She wouldn't budge. Mexico, she kept saying, was the way to go. I didn't put up all that much of an argument, having no better choice to offer. We brought Ava and Carl into the conversation, leaving Squire asleep, and stood on the porch in the flickering light and hashed things out. The storm appeared to frighten Carl. He sat in one of the rotted porch chairs, his hands to his ears, rocking his upper body.

Leeli said she knew of a little rural airport west of New Smyrna where we could charter a plane, no questions, and Ava said she and Carl and Leeli would use Rickey's car and take care of it right away.

—Like hell! I said. We'll go together.

—You crazy? You know how it is when there's a big storm, Ava said. Accidents and drownings. Cops'll be all over the highway. There'll be roadblocks. They see you, we're finished.

—That's right! Leeli said. They gonna be too busy to worry 'bout looking for us now.

—I'll be damned I'm gonna let you run off without me, I said.

—We can't run off! Won't nothing be flying 'til the storm blows out. But we set things up, we can fly soon as it does.

—Just you go then, I said to Ava.

—I can't leave Carl. You see how he is. And I need Leeli to point the way.

A pitchfork of lightning ripped away the dark and the thunder had a metallic sound, like somebody was pounding out a dent in the sky. Wind shivered the lodge and slammed loose boards.

—Naw, I said. Leeli can give you directions.

—What if I get 'em wrong? You got Squire here. Ain't that enough of a guarantee?

I couldn't see Ava's face in that moment, but I thought I felt slyness steaming off of her. Tell her the directions, Leeli, I said.

—All those country roads. Leeli put a hand to her brow like a mentalist trying to make contact. I can show her, but I don't know I can tell her.

Rain drove in through the screen and we all moved back from it except for Carl, who just sat there rocking.

—I don't trust you no more'n you trust me, I said to Ava. We gonna have to work something else out.

Another lightning flash brought leached colors to the porch and fitted a long shadow beneath every object. Things looked to be tilted, as if the wind had knocked the lodge askew.

—Hang on, Ava said, and went off toward her bedroom.

Leeli caught my hand and said something I didn't catch, but had the sound of an assurance, and then Ava came back out onto the porch and handed me a thick envelope.

—Fuck's this? I asked.

—The rest of the money I promised Leeli. You can hold it while we're gone.

Leeli's eyes got stuck on the envelope as I inspected the contents. Hundred dollar bills and plenty of them.

—That guarantee enough for ya? Ava asked. 'Tween Squire and the money, it's 'bout the best I can do.

I stuffed the envelope into my hip pocket. Leeli unstuck her eyes. I could see it was a strain for her and that she didn't love the idea of leaving the envelope behind. All right, I said. I started to deliver a warning, to pose consequences, but there didn't seem much point to it. We all knew the lay of the land.

—All right, I repeated. Let's get it rolling.

▲▼▲

You know how it goes. Sometimes you're so deep in the world, so mired in its trouble, you forget that you were born, you forget you were raised to be a dead man, you think you got where you're standing all on your own and that you're holding destiny in your hands, and when somebody passes you a golden ticket that's stamped Freedom or Foreverafter, you don't check to see if the ink's dry or if there's printing on the back, because you're walking the road your daddy cut for you and stepping along in clothes your mama sewed, because it's the tendency of your kind to believe the lottery can be won, great prizes are within your grasp, and though the only winning ticket ever came your parents' way was an error in their favor made by a bartender or a grocery clerk, though you understand you're their homemade fool, you just can't accept that the rules of their life apply to you. That golden ticket is a guarantee all right, a twenty-four karat guaranteed loser. You know this in your heart, but you hang onto the bitch like it was a pass through the Gates of Glory or a voucher for an all-expenses-paid weekend at Casino World on the Redneck Riviera, whichever premium you prefer.

Thoughts such as these slammed my head as I dug through Rickey's pockets, hunting for his keys. He was still unconscious, his face swollen from the beating I'd supplied him. Looked like he'd pissed off a swarm of bees. The keys were in the bib pocket of his overalls. I stood jingling them in my hand, holding a last debate over the wisdom of giving them to Ava. An old movie was playing on the TV. Japanese men in moonsuits were gazing awestruck at a fleet of flying saucers that soon began incinerating them with fiery beams. Watching them turn into bright wavering silhouettes and vanish somehow made my decision for me.

Things moved right smartly after that. Ava and Carl went for the car, Leeli gave me a pert little kiss and said, Be back soon, and ran off after them. I patted my hip pocket to make certain the money was still there. A minute later I was standing on the porch steps, watching a pair of red taillights, one patched with duct tape, jouncing along over the uneven ground toward the highway, shining up tracers of rain. I had a moment of dissatisfaction with my decision and I pulled Ava's gun from the waist of my jeans with half a thought of shooting out a tire. The car stopped at the end of the drive. There wasn't any traffic I could see and I wondered what was going on. A creep of paranoia stirred me from the steps and out in the rain. I imagined Ava and Leeli arguing over whether or not to betray me. Thunder mauled the sky. The car swung out onto the highway. I felt like six kinds of fool, with the rain running down my neck, alone as ever was, the gun cold and weighty in my hand.

The night grew wilder yet, the thunder continuous. A ring of fiery stick men a thousand feet tall jabbed and flashed on the horizons, penning me into their magic circle. There was such a confusion of light and sound, it rooted me to the spot. Behind the lodge a clump of palms bulked up solid, taking the shape of a black frowning Buddha in my mind, scrunched up and angry from having me in his sight. It seemed I could feel the wickedness of that place and time, the mortal separation from the flow of life that wickedness enforces. I was flying, stranded on a scrap of soggy marsh that had been chewed off from the planet and set to spinning loose in the void. The rain needled my cheeks and brow, spitting alternately dark and silver. The lodge looked to be changing shape, crouching like a beast one second, the next blurring into an emblem of negativity, a symbol on a rippling banner, then collapsing back into the ruinous thing it pretended to be. I had the idea this was my night, my big moment, that I was being showed a reflection of everything I'd said and thought and done, the chaos of my life given larger, windier form, and this was the only celebration of my useless days I'd likely get, this storm too small to have a name but big enough to damage the unprepared, the tore-down spaces, the vacant properties of the world. Then I glanced south to where Ava and Carl and Leeli had gone and saw a flash of green. Not a dazzling seam and not the dull flicker of heat lightning, but a dynamic burst of bright neon color like an enormous bug zapper taking a hit. The color hung in the air, draping its afterimages around the palm crowns, and I recalled Ava's story about the green light coming from the UFO. I tried to think of something else it could have been. I expect there must have been a hundred possibilities, but I couldn't come up with one. The rain slowed to a drizzle and as if the green flash had been a cue, the storm began to fade, flaring up now and again with a grumble and a distant snip of fire, then fading even more, its battery running low. Drips and plops succeeded the fury of the wind. Through scudding clouds you could glimpse a freckling of stars, and soon a slice of moon surfaced from the horizon. I knew Carl and Ava and Leeli were gone. It wasn't the flash that told me so. Too many thoughts were flapping around in my attic for me to work that part of it out. The alignment of the world, the wrecked lodge and foundered cabins, the swaying grasses and the dark water slurping at the mucky bank, the stars and all the rest—it was like a sign saying Gone had been struck through every layer of creation.

Naturally I didn't entirely believe this sign. Despite Ava's anything-goes attitude toward screwing, I figured Squire must do something special for her, and I just knew Leeli wasn't about to leave that money on the table. I patted my hip pocket again and this time I found nothing. No bulge, no envelope sticking out. I patted my other pockets and looked on the ground close by. Since I'd come out from the porch to watch them drive away, I hadn't hardly moved a step, but there was no sign of the envelope. I told myself the wind must have took it. I searched along the edge of the water, near the porch, and as I was poking around in the grass, kicking scrap wood and fallen shingles aside, growing more desperate every second, because with or without Leeli I needed that money to get clear of Volusia County, it occurred to me there might never have been an envelope. Maybe Ava was that much of a witch. Maybe she'd handed me a parlor trick, an illusion, and made Leeli and me see what she wanted. Maybe Leeli had been in on the hustle and just pretended to be worried about the money. It was her, wasn't it, led me to Ava in the first place? The missing envelope and the green flash and the stories Ava told, they all washed together into a stew of possibilities. I couldn't separate out anything from it that sounded more than half true.

I stopped my searching and stood by the water. The clouds had slid off to the north, except for a wedge that was convoying the rising moon. The stars were thick. It was as if there had been no storm, just a gentle rain that smeared the vegetable smells around into a sickly green sweetness. I told myself I must be wrong about everything. Before long they'd be pulling into the driveway, talking about our plane ride. But fool though I was, I wasn't that big of a fool. I could mumble all the pretty wishes I wanted to, but gone was still the impression I got.

I felt like a baby trapped under a bear rug, unable to crawl, too smothered to cry, and I must've stood by the water damn near an hour, trying to poke holes in the weighty thing that held me down. I was flummoxed by a question I wasn't even sure had been asked, stumped and dumb, unable to work out a plan or think of a direction to travel in. I didn't know what to do. Hitchhike out of there? Drive away in a van every cop in Central Florida was probably on the look-out for? Heading into the marsh and living off mullet and gator tail was about my only option. The skeeters began to trouble me. Mostly I let them have my blood, but I spanked a few dead. Seemed like I'd been living with my brain switched off and now a recognition stole over me not just of how fucked I was at the moment, but how fucked the normal weather was in Maceo's world. Everything was returning to normal. The frogs squelched up their bleepy cries. Cicadas established a drone. A fish jumping for a bug out in the marsh made a squishy plop and I could have sworn it was my own heart's sound. Squire came out onto the porch steps, rubbing his stubbly scalp, sleepy as a tick full of juice, and asked, Where they all at?

—Went to charter a plane.

He gaped at me. They gone? Ava and everybody?

—Yeah.

—We gotta go find 'em! He tripped on the bottom step and reeled out sideways into the yard, catching a furl of the rusted screen to right himself. He was wearing jeans that still had creases in the legs and that stupid T-shirt with his face spraypainted on it Ava had bought him in Silver Springs. Move it! he said. We gotta find 'em now!

He got to scooting around the yard, little dashes this way and that, like a dog with the runs in a hurry to locate a good place to do his business. Which way they go? he asked.

—I told you. They went to charter a plane somewheres 'round New Smyrna.

—They ain't gone to New Smyrna! Dumb motherfucker! They ain't going nowhere near New Smyrna!

Usually somebody calls me a dumb motherfucker, I don't have much of an argument. It's not much different from saying that the grass is pretty green or the water looks wet. But Squire irked me with his agitated movement and his two round faces, the one on his chest smiling, the other scowling, both of them staring at me.

—Leave me be! I walked off a few paces and gazed out into the marsh. With the passage of the storm, heat was coming back into the world. A drop of sweat trickled down my side. The air was slow and thick and humid. Something with curved black wings scythed across the low-hanging moon. A dullness swept over my thoughts, an oppressive, clammy feeling like the first sign of a fever.

—You just gonna stand there? Squire grabbed onto my shoulder and spun me about. We gotta get us a move on!

—Don't put your hands on me, I said.

—Aw, Jesus! He wheeled away from me and looked to the sky. Thank you for sticking me with this ignorant fucking hillbilly!

I refitted my eyes to the marsh, the stirring grasses and the moon-licked water to the east.

—Goddamn it! Squire said. You'n me, we need to work together. I can find 'em!

It struck me that he was speaking with more authority than he'd previously displayed, but I didn't concern myself with this. Wasn't that it didn't tweak my interest, just I was more interested in the way my head was emptying out, like a car engine giving little ticks as it cools.

Squire went to hammering at me, trying to rouse me to action, and finally I said, What you want me to do, asshole? Drive you around in a stolen van 'til we get popped?

—We don't hafta go far. Won't be on the road more'n a few minutes.

—They been gone an hour...maybe more. You think they just circling out there?

—Trust me, man. I know what I'm talking about.

—Trust you? I said. Fuck you! Now I told you, leave me be.

I stepped away along the shore and stopped at the very edge of the water, my shoes sinking into the muck, wanting to restore the glum yet comforting acceptance into which my thoughts had been sinking. Squire followed me, giving orders, pleading, working every angle. Didn't matter what he said, it was all the same to my ears, a yammering that bored holes in my skull and poured itself in hot and heavy like lead into a mold. I told him to shut up. He kept at it. I told him again to shut up and it didn't even put a hitch in his delivery. I was acting like I had shit for brains, he said. Behaving like a child. Didn't matter what he said. Every word hardened into a white-hot ingot, stacks of them crowding the space between my ears. I tried to see past him, past the heat growing inside me, looking to cool my eyes in the lavender cave of sky among the last clouds where the moon floated. It wasn't a help.

—What do I gotta do, spell it out for your sorry ass? Squire said. What the fuck's it gonna take to get through?

He punched at my shoulder with the heel of his hand.

—Don't be doing that, I said.

—It don't bother you, you set there and watched Ava and them roll off into the fucking sunset, but this here—he punched at me again—that bothers you?

A thready strip of cloud spooled out across the moon, a golden bridge unraveling.

—You are hillbilly shit piled high, y'know that? Squire said. I heard him kick at the ground and then his voice came from a distance away: Guess you must like the idea of ol' Ava licking your girlfriend's pussy.

I turned on him, seeing only those two ugly round faces, one atop the other mutant-style, and I lifted my right hand. I was kind of surprised to see the gun—guess I'd forgotten I was holding it—and maybe it was surprise twitched my trigger finger, or maybe another flickering snake tongue of anger. Or maybe I just wanted to kill him, though I had the notion somewhere in the back of my mind that he was not a man, he'd eat the bullet, lie there a while, then sit up all of a sudden the way he'd done back in Ocala. The shot punched out the left eye of his lower face. He gave a melancholy grunt, like a hog disappointed by its supper, and went spinning to the ground. Heart's blood came from his chest in such a hurry, it might've had somewhere more important to go. Speckles of wet dirt clung to his cheek. His one true eye was open blind and the other was pressed into the earth. I thought I heard a voice of wind and rustling grass say my name in welcome.

▲▼▲

You might not understand, but then again you might, how when you reach the end of the road and still find yourself breathing, the unraveled threads that tied you to your life resemble a puzzle you could easily have solved if you'd been one ounce smarter or one inch less crazy, and you think now that you've gained a perspective, you can probably develop some sort of reasonable explanation for all the crap you hadn't understood, but when you gather those threads up they hang limp from your fist and don't none of the frayed ends match, and you realize they weren't really connected, they had no more connection to each other than stalks of dead grass floating on marsh water, and everything you depended on being true was just a tricky kind of emptiness that looked like something real, and so when I tried to fit Squire cooling out at my feet and the bossy way he'd acted in with Ava's stories, it only made a deeper puzzle, one I knew I'd never get straight.

I kept the gun aimed at him, hoping he'd sit up, halfway hoping he would just so I could shoot his ass again. Anger seeped out of my skin, leaving me shaky. The painted eye on Squire's chest smoldered. I had an urge to throw the gun into the marsh, but I didn't have enough fire in me to follow through and I dropped it on the ground. Thing to do, I realized, was to gather food and whatever else I could use from the lodge and hightail it into the marsh. I'd need the gun. My chest felt scraped hollow and filled with cold gas. It cost me some effort to reach for the gun. I bent over halfway, put my hands on my knees, and stalled there. A black rope was being pulled through my head, scouring out the positive thoughts.

—Stand up straight, motherfucker!

Rickey was leaning against the side of the porch, holding a sawed-off 12-gauge with a taped grip. Didn't appear he could see out of one eye, but the other was working good and pinned on me.

—Come thisaway! he said.

I walked a few steps toward him. He gestured with the sawed-off and told me to sit.

—You a cocksure son-of-a-bitch, leaving me alive. Rickey spat a dark wad of blood and saliva.

The wet soaked through the seat of my pants. Rickey started toward me, weaving a little, then thought better of it and leaned back against the porch. His face was all lumped and discolored, like an atomic war radiation victim.

—I saw you kill that boy, he said. Kill him how you'd do a sick dog. You didn't useta be that cold, man. Something happen in Raiford make you that way?

I didn't have no answers for him.

—You liked to kill me, but I don't kill so easy. Rickey fumbled in his pocket and fetched out a cell phone. One fine morning a few years from now, they be strapping you down and fixing to kill you. You remember me on that day, Maceo.

He thumbed three numbers, gave a show of doing it so I'd know he was calling 911. I drew up my knees and rested my head on my arms. Rickey talked for a minute, too low for me to hear.

—Hey, Maceo!

He'd moved to the steps and was sitting on the bottom one, the sawed-off angled across his knees.

—Hands up! Who wants to die? he said. How you like them apples, huh?

A queer little road of moonlight slithered off along the water into the east. I wished I could follow it. I wished there was a tree with hundred dollar bills for leaves growing out behind the lodge, and that Rickey was too weak and sore to pull off both barrels before I could reach him, and that the end of this world was the beginning of the next, and I wished I'd had more time with Leeli.

—I feel them police dogs panting, Rickey said, stretching out his legs and getting comfortable. I feel that heat humming out along the road.

It come to seem all like a painting, then. One you'd see in a museum with a brass plate on a frame enclosing a night on the marshlands south of South Daytona, a night wild with stars and a wicked moon hanging like a bone grin among the remains of the running clouds, a gray tumbledown lodge with a stove-in roof and a lumpy, bloody man sitting on the steps, aiming a chest-buster at another man sitting in the grass, and a corpse lying near the water's edge, gone pale and strange. It would look awful pretty and have the feeling of something going on behind the scenes. Like silver nooses were hanging from the stars and important shapes were hiding back of the clouds, big ones with the heads of beasts, showing a shade darker than the blue darkness of the sky. It was that rich, dark blue give the picture a soul. The rest of it was up to you. You could study it and arrive at all sorts of erroneous conclusions.

—Damn if I don't believe I can smell 'em, Rickey said. Y'know the smell I'm talking about? That oiled-up leather and aftershave smell them state pigs have? He spat again. You shouldn't go fucking over your friends, man. It just don't seem to never work out.

I took another stab at explaining things to myself. Witches and spacemen and scum of the earth. Somewhere in all that slop of life was a true thing. I knew in my gut it was an amazing thing, unlike any you'd expect to meet up with on your way through hell, and I believed if I was to chew on it a time, jot down a list of what I saw and what I thought, I might understand who Ava and Carl and Squire were. But I'd always been bound for this patch of chilly ground. It wasn't worth pursuing how I got there, whether it was some old dog of a reason bit my ass or fate jumped the curb and knocked me down an unknown road.

A thought of Leeli twinged my heart. Appeared I'd cared about that old girl somewhat deeper than I knew.

The air-horn of an eighteen-wheeler bawled out on the highway, something huge going crazy, and trailing behind it, almost lost in the roar of tires and engine, a siren corkscrewed through the night.

Rickey spat up more blood.

Like they say, shit happens.

I figure that about tells it.

Dead Money

I knew slim-with-sideburns was dead money before Geneva introduced him to the game. Dead money doesn't need an introduction; dead money declares himself by grinning too wide and playing it too cool, pretending to be relaxed while his shoulders are racked with tension, and proceeds to lose all his chips in hurry. Slim-with-sideburns-and-sharp-features-and-a-gimpy-walk showed us the entire menu, plus he was wearing a pair of wraparound shades. Now there are a number of professional poker players who wear sunglasses so as not to give away their tells, but you would mistake none of them for dead money and they would never venture into a major casino looking like some kind of country-and-western spaceman.

"Gentlemen," Geneva said, shaking back her big blonde hair. "This here's Josey Pellerin over from Lafayette."

A couple of the guys said, Hey, and a couple of others introduced themselves, but Mike Morrissey, Mad Mike, who was in the seat next to mine, said, "Not *the* Josie? Of Josie and the Pussycats?"

The table had a laugh at that, but Pellerin didn't crack a smile. He took a chair across from Mike, lowering himself into it carefully, his arms shaking, and started stacking his chips. Muscular dystrophy, I thought. Some wasting disease. I pegged him for about my age, late thirties, and figured he would overplay his first good hand and soon be gone.

Mike, who likes to get under players' skins, said, "Didn't I see you the other night hanging out with 'A Boy Named Sue?' "

In a raspy, southern-fried voice, Pellerin said, "I've watched you on TV, Mister Morrissey. You're not as entertaining as you think, and you don't have that much game."

Mike pretended to shudder and that brought another laugh. "Let's see what you got, pal," he said. "Then we can talk about my game."

Geneva, a good-looking woman even if she is mostly silicon and Botox, washed a fresh deck, spreading the cards across the table, and shuffled them up.

The game was cash only, no-limit Texas Hold 'Em. It was held in a side room of Harrah's New Orleans with a table ringed by nine barrel-backed chairs upholstered in red velvet and fake French Colonial stuff—fancy swords, paintings with gilt frames, and such—hanging on walls the color of cocktail sauce. Geneva, who was a friend, let me sit in once in a while to help me maintain the widely held view that I was someone important, whereas I was, in actuality, a typical figment of the Quarter, a man with a few meaningful connections and three really good suits.

It wasn't unusual to have a couple of pros in the game, but the following week Harrah's was sponsoring a tournament with a million dollar first prize and a few big hitters were already filtering into town. Aside from Mad Mike, Avery Holt was at the table, Sammy Jawanda, Deng Ky (aka Denghis Khan), and Annie Marcus. The amateurs in the game were Pellerin, Jeremy LeGros, an investment banker with deep pockets, and myself, Jack Lamb.

Texas Hold 'Em is easy to learn, but it will cost you to catch on to the finer points. To begin with, you're dealt two down cards, then you bet; then comes the flop, three up cards in the center of the table that belong to everyone. You bet some more. Then an up card that's called the turn and another round of betting. Then a final up card, the river, and more betting...unless everyone has folded to the winner. I expected Pellerin to play tight, but five minutes hadn't passed before he came out firing and pushed in three thousand in chips. LeGros and Mike went with him to the flop. King of hearts, trey of clubs, heart jack. Pellerin bet six thousand. LeGros folded and Mike peeked at his down cards.

"They didn't change on you, did they?" asked Pellerin.

Mike raised him four thousand. That told me Pellerin had gotten into his head. The smart play would have been either to call or to get super aggressive. A middling raise like four thousand suggested a lack of confidence. Of course with Mad Mike, you never knew when he was setting a trap. Pellerin pushed it again, raising ten K, not enough to make Mike bag the hand automatically. Mike called. The card on the turn was a three of hearts, pairing the board. Pellerin checked and Mike bet twenty.

"You must have yourself a hand," said Pellerin. "But your two pair's not going to cut it. I'm all in."

He had about sixty thousand stacked in front of him and Mike could have covered the bet, but it wasn't a percentage play—losing would have left him with the short chip stack and it was too early in the evening to take the risk. He tried staring a hole through Pellerin, fussed with his chips, and eventually mucked his hand.

"You're not the dumbest son-of-a-bitch who ever stole a pot from me," he said.

"Don't suppose I am," said Pellerin.

As I watched—and that is what I mainly did, push in antes and watch—it occurred to me that once he sat down, Pellerin had stopped acting like dead money, as if all his anxiety had been cured by the touch of green felt and plastic aces. He was one hell of a hold 'em player. He never lost much and it seemed that he took down almost every big pot. Whenever he went head-to-head against somebody, he did about average...except when he went up against Mad Mike. Him, he gutted. It was evident that he had gotten a good read on Mike. In less than two hours he had ninety percent of the man's money. He had also developed a palsy in his left hand and was paler than he had been when he entered.

The door opened, the babble of the casino flowed in and a security man ushered a doe-eyed, long-legged brunette wearing a black cocktail dress into the room. She had some age on her—in her mid-thirties, I estimated—and her smile was low wattage, a depressive's smile. Nonetheless, she was an exceptionally beautiful woman with a pale olive complexion and a classically sculpted face, her hair arranged so that it fell all to one side. A shade too much make-up was her only flaw. She came up behind Pellerin, bent down, absently caressing the nape of his neck, and whispered something. He said, "You going to have to excuse me, gentleman. My nurse here's a real hardass. But I'll be glad to take your money again tomorrow night."

He scooted back his chair; the brunette caught his arm and helped him to stand.

Mike, who had taken worse beats in his career, overcame his bad mood and asked, "Where you been keeping yourself, man?"

"Around," said Pellerin. "But I've been inactive 'til recently."

▲▼▲

I smelled something wrong about Pellerin. Wrong rose off him like stink off the Ninth Ward. World-class poker players don't just show up, they don't materialize out of nowhere and take a hundred large off Mad Mike Morrissey, without acquiring some reputation in card rooms and small casinos. And his success wasn't due to luck. What Pellerin had done to Mike was as clean a gutting as I had ever witnessed. The next two nights, I stayed out of the game and observed. Pellerin won close to half a million, though the longest he played at a single sitting was four hours. The casino offered him a spot in the tournament, but he declined on the grounds of poor health—he was recovering from an injury, he said, and was unable to endure the long hours and stress of tournament play. My sources informed me that, according to the county records, nobody named Josey Pellerin lived in or near Lafayette. That didn't surprise me. I knew a great number of people who had found it useful to adopt another name and place of residence. I did, however, manage to dredge up some interesting background on the brunette.

Jocundra Verret, age forty-two, single, had been employed by Tulane University nearly twenty years before, working for the late Dr. Hideki Ezawa, who had received funding during the 1980s to investigate the possible scientific basis of certain voodoo remedies. She had left the project, as they say, under a cloud. That was as much as I could gather from the redacted document that fell into my hands. After Tulane, she had worked as a private nurse until a year ago; since that time, her paychecks had been signed by the Darden Corporation, an outfit whose primary holdings were in the fields of bioengineering and medical technology. She, Pellerin and another man, Dr. Samuel Crain, had booked a suite at Harrah's on a corporate card, the same card that paid for an adjoining suite occupied by two other men, one of whom had signed the register as D. Vader. They were bulky, efficient sorts, obviously doing duty as bodyguards.

I had no pressing reason to look any deeper, but the mention of voodoo piqued my interest. While I was not myself a devotee, my parents had both been occasional practitioners and those childhood associations of white candles burning in storefront temples played a part in my motivation. That night, when Pellerin sat down at the table, I went searching for Ms. Verret and found her in a bar just off the casino floor, drinking a sparkling water. She had on gray slacks and a cream-colored blouse, and looked quite fetching. The bodyguards were nowhere in sight, but I knew they must be in the vicinity. I dropped onto the stool beside her and introduced myself.

"I'm not in the mood," she said.

"Neither am I, chère. The doctor tells me it's permanent, but when I saw you I felt a flicker of hope."

She ducked her head, hiding a smile. "You really need to go. I'm expecting someone."

"Under different circumstances, I'd be delighted to stick around and let you break my heart. But sad to say, this is a business call. I was wondering how come a bunch like the Darden Corporation is bankrolling a poker player."

Startled, she darted her eyes toward me, but quickly recovered her poise. "The people I work for are going to ask why you were talking to me," she said evenly. "I can tell them you were hitting on me, but if you don't leave in short order, I won't be able to get away with that explanation."

"I assume you're referring in the specific to the two large gentlemen who've got the suite next to yours. Don't you worry. They won't do anything to me."

"It's not what they might do to *you* that's got me worried," she said.

"I see. Okay." I got to my feet. "That being the case, perhaps it'd be best if we talked at a more opportune time. Say tomorrow morning? Around ten in the coffee shop?"

"Please stay away from me," she said. "I'm not going to talk to you."

As I left the bar, I saw the bodyguards playing the dollar slots near the entrance—one glanced at me incuriously, but kept on playing. I walked down the casino steps, exiting onto Canal Street, and had a smoke. It was muggy, the stars dim. High in the west, a sickle moon was encased in an envelope of mist. I looked at the neon signs, the traffic, listened to the chatter and laughter of passersby with drinks in their hands. Post-Katrina New Orleans pretending that it was the Big Easy, teetering on the edge of boom or bust. Though Verret had smiled at me, I could think of no easy way to hustle her, and I decided to give Billy Pitch a call and see whether he thought the matter was worth pursuing.

I had to go through three flunkies before I got to Billy. "What you want?" he said. "You know this is *Survivor* night."

"I forgot, Billy. Want me to call back? I can call back."

"This is the two-hour finale, then the reunion show. Won't be over 'til eleven and I'm shutting it down after that. Now you got something for me or don't you?"

I could hear laughter in the background and I hesitated, picturing him hunched over the phone in his den, a skinny, balding white man whom you might mistake for an insurance salesman or a CPA, no doubt clad in one of his neon-colored smoking jackets.

"Jack, you better have something good," Billy said. "Hair's starting to sprout from my palms."

"I'm not sure how good it is, but—"

"I'm missing the immunity challenge. The penultimate moment of the entire season. And I got people over, you hear?"

Billy was the only person I knew who could pronounce vowels with a hiss. I gave him the gist of it, trying not to omit any significant details, but speeding it along as best I could.

"Interesting," he said. "Tell me again what she said when you spoke to her."

I repeated the conversation.

"It would seem that Miz Verret's agenda is somewhat different from that of the Darden Corporation," Billy said. "Otherwise, she'd have no compunction about reporting your conversation."

"That was my take."

"Voodoo business," he said musingly.

"I can't be sure it's got anything to do with voodoo."

"Naw, this here is voodoo business. It has a certain taint." Billy made a clicking noise. "I'll get back to you in the morning."

"I was just trying to do you a favor, Billy. I don't need to be involved."

"Honey, I know how it's supposed to work, but you're involved. I got too many eggs in my basket to be dealing with anything else right now. This pans out, I'm putting you in charge."

The last thing I had wanted was to be in business with Billy Pitch. It wasn't that you couldn't make a ton of money with Billy, but he was a supremely dangerous and unpleasant human being, and he tended to be hard on his associates. Often he acted precipitately and there were more than a few widows who had received a boatload of flowers and a card containing Billy's apologies and a fat check designed to compensate for their loss and his lamentable error in judgment. In most cases, this unexpected death benefit served to expunge the ladies' grief, but Alice Delvecchio, the common-law wife of Danny "Little Man" Prideau, accused Billy of killing her man and, shortly after the police investigation hit a dead end, she and her children disappeared. It was rumored that Billy had raised her two sons himself and that, with his guidance, hormone treatments, and the appropriate surgery, they had blossomed into lovely teenage girls, both of whom earned their keep in a brothel catering to oil workers.

Much to my relief, no call came the following morning. I thought that Billy must have checked out Pellerin and Verret, found nothing to benefit him, and hadn't bothered getting back to me. But around ten o'clock that evening, I fielded a call from Huey Rafael, one of Billy's people. He said that Billy wanted me to run on out to an address in Abundance Square and take charge of a situation.

"What's up?" I asked.

"Billy says for you to get your butt over here."

Abundance Square was in the Ninth Ward, a few blocks from the levee, and was, as far as I knew, utterly abandoned. That made me nervous.

"I'm coming," I said. "But I'd like to know something about the situation. So I can prepare for it, you understand."

"You ain't need nothing to prepare you for this." Huey's laugh was a baritone hiccup. "Got some people want watching over. Billy say you the man for the job."

"Who are these people?" I asked, but Huey had ended the call.

I was angry. In the past, Billy had kept a close eye on every strand of his web, but nowadays he tended to delegate authority and spent much of his time indulging his passion for reality TV. He knew more about *The Amazing Race* and *The Runway Project* than he did about his business. Sooner or later, I thought, this practice was going to jump up and bite him in the ass. But as I drove toward the Ninth Ward, my natural paranoia kicked in and I began to question the wisdom of traipsing off into the middle of nowhere to hook up with a violent criminal.

Prior to Katrina, Abundance Square had been a housing project of old-style New Orleans town homes, with courtyards and balconies all painted in pastel shades. It had been completed not long before the hurricane struck. Now it was a waste of boarded-up homes and streets lined with people's possessions. Cars, beds, lamps, bureaus, TV sets, pianos, toys, and so on, every inch of them caked with dried mud. Though I was accustomed to such sights, that night it didn't look real. My headlights threw up bizarre images that made it appear I was driving through a post-apocalyptic version of Claymation Country. I found the address, parked a couple of blocks away, and walked back to the house. A drowned stink clotted my nostrils. In the distance, I heard sirens and industrial noise, but close at hand, it was so quiet you could hear a bug jump.

Huey answered my knock. He was a tall drink of water. Six-five, six-six, with a bluish polish to his black skin, a lean frame, pointy sideburns, and a modish goatee. He wore charcoal slacks and a high-collared camp shirt. Standing in the door, a nickel-plated .45 in hand, he might have been a bouncer at the Devil's strip club. He preceded me toward the rear of the house, to a room lit by a kerosene lantern. At its center, one of Pellerin's bodyguards was tied to a wooden chair. His head was slumped onto his chest, his face and shirt bloody. The air seemed to grow hotter.

I balked at entering and Huey said, "What you scared of, man? Lord Vader there ain't going to harm you. Truth is, he gave it up quick for being a Jedi."

"Where's the other guy?" I asked.

"Man insisted on staying behind," Huey said.

I had a sinking feeling, a vision of the Red House at Angola, guards strapping me down for the injection. "Jesus Christ," I said. "You tell Billy I'm not going down for murder."

Huey caught me by the shoulder as I turned to leave and slammed me up against the wall. He bridged his forearm under my jaw, giving me the full benefit of his lavishly applied cologne, and said, "I didn't say a goddamn thing about murder, now did I?" When I remained silent, he asked me again and I squeezed out a no.

"I got things to take care of," he said, stepping back. "Probably take me two, three hours. Here go." He handed me the .45 and some keys. "You get on upstairs."

"Who's up there?"

"The card player and his woman. Some other guy. A doctor, he say."

"Are they...." I searched for a word that would not excite Huey. "Uninjured?"

"Yeah, they fine."

"And I'm supposed to keep watch, right? That's all?"

"Billy say for you to ask some questions."

"What about?"

"About what they up to."

"Well, what did he tell you?" I pointed at the bodyguard. "I need something to go on."

"Lord Vader wasn't too clear on the subject," said Huey. "Guess I worked him a little hard. But he did say the card player ain't a natural man."

▲▼▲

Some rooms on the second floor of the townhouse were filled with stacked cots, folding tables and chairs, and with bottled water, canned food, toilet paper, and other supplies. It seemed that Billy was planning for the end times. In a room furnished with a second-hand sofa and easy chairs, I found Verret, Pellerin, and a man in his fifties with mussed gray hair and a hangdog look about the eyes. I assumed him to be Doctor Crain. He was gagged and bound to a chair. Verret and Pellerin were leg-shackled to the sofa. On seeing me, Crain arched his eyebrows and tried to speak. Pellerin glanced up from his hand of solitaire and Verret, dressed in freshly ironed jeans and a white T-shirt, gave me a sorrowful look, as if to suggest she had expected more of me.

"It's the night shift," Pellerin said and went back to turning over cards.

"Can you help us?" asked Verret.

"What's up with him?" I pointed at Crain with the gun.

"He annoyed our previous keeper." Pellerin flipped over an ace and made a satisfied noise. "He's an annoying fellow. You're catching him at his best."

"Can you help us?" Verret asked again, with emphasis.

"Probably not." I pulled a chair around and sat opposite the two of them. "But if you tell me what's going on with you, what's the relationship between the Darden Corporation and Tulane, the Ezawa project... I'll try to help."

Pellerin kept dealing, Verret gave no response, and Crain struggled with his bonds.

"Do you know where you are?" I asked. "Let me you clue you in."

I told them who had ordered their kidnapping, mentioning the Alice Delvecchio incident along with a couple of others, then reiterated that I could probably be of no help to them—I was an unwilling participant in the process. I was sorry things had reached this pass, but if I was going to be any help at all, they ought to tell me what was up; otherwise, I couldn't advise them on how to survive Billy Pitch.

Verret looked to Pellerin, who said, "He ain't that damn sorry. Except where his own sorry ass is concerned."

"Is he telling the truth?" she asked.

"More-or-less."

Crain redoubled his efforts to escape, forcing muted shouts through his gag.

"I guess that's why you're so expert at the tables," I said to Pellerin. "You're good at reading people."

"You have no idea, Small Time," he said.

I wiggled the gun. "You're not in a position to be giving me attitude."

"You going to shoot me?" He gave a sneering laugh. "I don't think so. You're about ready to piss yourself just hanging onto that thing."

"Josey!" Verret started to stand, then remembered the shackles. "I'll tell you," she said to me. "But I'd rather do it in private."

Crain threw a conniption fit, heaving himself about in his chair, attempting to spit out his gag.

"You see," she said. "He's going to act like that every time I tell you something. I have to use the restroom, anyway."

I undid the shackles, then I locked Crain and Pellerin in and escorted her down the hall, lagging behind a step so I could check out her butt. When she had finished in the john, we went into one of the storerooms. I set up a couple of folding chairs and we sat facing one another.

"May I have some water," she asked.

"Help yourself."

She had a drink of water, then sat primly with the plastic bottle resting on one knee. I knew I had to watch myself with her—I'd always been a sucker for tall brunettes who had that lady thing going. She must have had a sense of this, because she worked it overtime.

"Here's what I know," I said. "The Ezawa project was investigating voodoo remedies. And Josey Pellerin, according to your bodyguard, is not a natural man. That suggests...well, I'm not sure. Why don't you just tell me everything?"

"Everything? That'll take a long time." She screwed the bottle cap on and off. "The project wasn't considered important at the outset. The only reason Ezawa got funding was because he was a golfing buddy of one of the trustees. And he *was* brilliant, so they were willing to give him some leeway. He isolated a bacterium present in the dirt of old slave graveyards. He used dirt from the graveyard at the Myrtles—that old house over in Saint Francisville? The bodies were buried in biodegradable coffins, or no coffins at all, and the micro-organisms in the dirt had interacted with the decomposing tissues."

She left room for me to ask a question, but I had none.

"A DNA extract from datura and other herbs was introduced into the growth medium," she said. "Then the bacteria were induced to take up DNA and chromosomes from the extract, and Ezawa injected the recombinant strain into the cerebellum and temporal lobes of a freshly dead corpse. The bacteria began processing the corpse's genetic complement and eventually the body was revivified."

"Whoa! Revivified?" I said. "You mean, it came back to life?"

She nodded.

"How long were these people dead?" I asked.

"On the average, a little under an hour. The longest was about an hour and a half. The process required a certain amount of time, so the bodies had to be secured quickly."

"Makes you wonder, doesn't it? Getting the paperwork done for releasing a body generally takes more than an hour."

"I don't know," she said.

"Jesus. Ezawa was basically making zombies. High-tech zombies."

She started, I presumed, to object, but I headed her off.

"Don't bullshit me," I said. "I grew up voodoo. Datura's one of the classic ingredients in the old recipe books. I bet he tried goat's rue, too...and Angel's trumpet. The man was making zombies."

She frowned. "What I was going to say, the term was appropriate for most of the patients. They were weak. Helpless. They rarely survived longer than a day. But there were a few who lived longer. For months, some of them. We called them 'slow-burners.' We moved them out to a plantation house in bayou country and brought in a clinical psychologist to assess their new personalities. You see, the patients developed personalities markedly different from the ones they originally had. The psychologist, Doctor Edman, he believed these personalities manifested a kind of wish-fulfillment. His theory was that the process changed a portion of the RNA and made it dominant. 'The bioform of their deepest wish,' that's how he put it. The patients manufactured memories. They recalled having different names, different histories. In effect, they were telling us—and themselves—a new life story, one in which they achieved their heart's desire. The amazing thing was, they had abilities commensurate with these stories."

I could have used some of Pellerin's ability to read people. What she had told me had a ring of authenticity, but if I were to accept it as true, I would have to rearrange my notion of what was possible. I started to speak, but I was on shaky ground and wasn't certain which questions to ask.

"It's hard to believe," she said. "But it's the truth." She let some seconds slip past and then, when I remained mute, as if she were trying to keep the conversation going, she went on: "I disagreed with Edman about a great many things. He demanded that we allow the patients to find their own way. He believed we should let their stories come out naturally. But I thought if we prompted them some, if we reminded them of their original identities...I don't mean give them every detail, you understand. Just their names and a little background. That would have afforded them a stronger foundation and perhaps we wouldn't have had so many breakdowns among the slow-burners. These people were re-inventing themselves out of whole cloth. They were bound to be unstable. I was hoping Crain would agree with me, but...." She made a contemptuous gesture, then seemed to remember where she was. "Do you want to know anything else?"

I still was at a loss for words, but I managed to say, "So I'm guessing Pellerin's a slow-burner."

"Yes. He was born Theodore Rankin. He's forty-three. He believes he's the world's best poker player. And he may well be."

"What was he before?"

"A bartender. He was killed during a robbery. I don't know how the corporation got hold of the body."

"The corporation. I assume they took the project over after it went in the toilet at Tulane."

"That's right. But there was a gap of ten years or so."

"Why're they so interested in a poker player?"

"It's not the poker playing per se that's of interest, it's the patients' underlying abilities. Their potentials go far beyond the life story they construct for themselves. We don't understand what they can do. None of them lived long enough. But with the advances in microbiology made during the last two decades, Doctor Crain thinks Josey may live for years. He's developing more rapidly than the others, too. That may be a result of improvements in the delivery system. We used a heart pump at Tulane, but now they—"

"I don't have to know the gearhead stuff." I mulled over what she had told me. "You were fired from the original project. Why would Darden hire you? Where do you fit in?"

Verret toyed with the bottle cap. "I helped a patient escape. I couldn't go along with what they were doing to him anymore. He developed some astonishing abilities while he was on the run. I'm the only person who's dealt with someone that advanced."

"What sort of abilities we talking about?"

"Perceptual, for the most part. Changes in visual capacity and such."

She said this off-handedly, but I doubted she was being straight with me. I decided not to push it, and I asked what they had been doing at Harrah's.

"At Tulane we kept the patients confined," she said. "But Crain thought Josey would develop more rapidly if we exposed him to an unstructured environment under controlled conditions." She gave a rueful laugh. "Turns out we didn't have much control."

"How much does Pellerin know?"

"He knows he was brought back to life. But he doesn't know about the new personality...though he suspects something's wrong there. It's up to me to determine when he's ready to hear the truth. Things go better if we tell them than if we let them piece it together on their own."

"I still don't understand your function. What exactly is it you do?"

"Patients need to bond with someone in order to create a complex personality. They have to be controlled, carefully manipulated. We were trained to instill that bond, to draw out their capabilities."

She folded her arms, compressed her lips. I had the thought that, though none of what she had told me was comedy club material, talking about her role in things distressed her more than the rest.

"If the other therapists are good-looking as you," I said, "I bet that instilling thing goes pretty easily."

That seemed to distress her further.

"Come on, chère," I said. "You going to be just fine. Y'all can be a significant asset for Billy, and that works to your advantage."

She leaned forward, putting a hand on my knee; the touch surprised me. "Mister Lamb," she said, and I said, without intending to, "Jack. You can call me Jack."

"I want to be able to count on you, Jack. Can I count on you?"

"I told you I don't have any control over the situation."

"But can you be a friend? That's all I'm asking. Can we count on you to be a friend?"

Those big brown eyes were doing a job on me, but I resisted them. "I haven't ever been much good as a friend. It's a character flaw, I'm afraid."

"I don't believe that." She sat back, adjusting her T-shirt so it fit more snugly. "You can call me Jo."

▲▼▲

I contacted Billy Pitch, though not during prime time, fearing I might interrupt *The Surreal Life* or *Wife Swap*, and I told him what I had learned, omitting any mention of the "remarkable powers" that might soon be Pellerin's, stressing instead his developing visual capacity. I wasn't sure why I did this—perhaps because I thought that Billy, already powerful, needed no further inducement to use his strength intemperately. He professed amazement at what I had to say, then slipped into business mode.

"I got an idea, but it needs to simmer, so I'm going to stash you away for a while," he said. "Get everybody ready to travel tonight."

"By 'everybody,'" I said, "you don't mean me, right? I got deals cooking. I have to—"

"I'll handle them for you."

"Billy, some of what I got going requires the personal touch."

"Are you suggesting I can't handle whatever piddly business it is you got?"

"No, that's not it. But there's—"

"You're not going to thwart me in this, are you, Jack?"

"No," I said helplessly.

"Good! Call my secretary and tell her what needs doing. I'll see it gets done."

That night we were flown by private jet to an airstrip in South Florida, and then transported by cigarette boat to Billy's estate in the Keys. Absent from our party was Dr. Crain. I never got to know the man. Each time I walked him to the john or gave him food, he railed at me, saying that I didn't know who I was dealing with, I didn't understand what was involved, causing such a ruckus that I found it easier to keep him bound and gagged in a separate room. I warned him that he was doing himself no good acting this way, yet all he did was tell me again I didn't know who I was dealing with and threaten me with corporate reprisals. When it was time to leave, I started to untie him, but Huey dropped a hand onto my shoulder and said, "Billy say to let him be."

"He's a doctor," I said. "He's the only one know's what's going on. What if Pellerin gets sick or something?"

"Billy say let him be."

I tried to call Billy, but was met with a series of rebuffs from men as constricted by the literal limits of their orders as Huey. Their basic message was, "Billy can't be disturbed." Crain's eyes were wide, fixed on me; his nostrils flared above the gag when he tried to speak. I made to remove it, but Huey once again stayed my hand.

"Let him talk," I said. "He might—"

"What he going to say, Jack?" Huey's glum, wicked face gazed down at me. "You know there ain't nothing to say?"

He steered me into the corridor, closed the door behind us and leaned against it. "Get a move on," he said. "Ain't nothing you can do, so you might as well not think about it."

Yet I did think about it as I descended the stair and walked along the corridor and out into the drizzly New Orleans night. I thought about Crain waiting in that stuffy little room, about whether or not he knew what was coming, and I thought that if I didn't change the way things were headed, I might soon be enduring a similar wait myself.

▲▼▲

Some weeks later I watched a videotape that captured Jo's interaction with one of the short-lived zombies whose passage from death to life and back again she had overseen at Tulane. By then, I had become thoroughly acquainted with Pellerin and the zombie on the tape didn't interest me nearly as much as Jo's performance. She tempted and teased his story out of him with the gestures and movements of a sexier-than-average ballerina, exaggerated so as to make an impression on the man's dim vision, and I came to realize that all of her movements possessed an element of this same controlled grace. Whether she was doing this by design, I had no clue; by that time I had tumbled to the fact that she was a woman who hid much from herself, and I doubted that she would be able to shed light on the matter.

Over the space of a month, Pellerin grew from a man whom I had mistaken for dead money into a formidable presence. He was stronger, more vital in every way, and he began to generate what I can only describe as a certain magnetism—I felt the back of my neck prickle whenever he came near, though the effect diminished over the days and weeks that followed. And then there were his eyes. On the same day I interrogated Jo, I was escorting him to the john when he said, "Hey, check this out! Small Time." He snatched off his sunglasses and brought his eyes close to mine. I was about to make a sarcastic remark, when I noticed a green flickering in his irises.

"What the fuck!" I said.

Pellerin grinned. "Looks like a little ol' storm back in there, doesn't it?"

I asked him what it was and he told me the flickers, etched in an electric green, signaled the bacteria impinging on the optic nerve.

"They're bioluminescent," he said. "Weird, huh? Jocundra says it's going to get worse before it gets better. People are going to think I'm the goddamn Green Lantern."

Though he had changed considerably since that day, his attitudes toward almost everyone around him remained consistently negative—he was blunt, condescending, an arrogant smart-ass. Yet toward Jo, his basic stance did change. He grew less submissive and often would challenge her authority. She adapted by becoming more compliant, but I could see that she wasn't happy, that his contentiousness was getting to her. She still was able to control him by means of subtle and not-so-subtle manipulation, but how long that control would last was a matter for conjecture.

The island where we were kept was Billy's private preserve. It was shaped roughly like a T, having two thin strips of land extending out in opposite directions from the west end. Billy's compound took up most of the available space. Within a high white brick wall topped by razor wire were a pool, outbuildings (including a gym and eight bungalows), a helicopter pad, and a sprawling Florida-style ranch house that might have been designed by an architect with a Lego fetish—wings diverged off the central structure and off each other at angles such as a child might employ, and I guessed that from the air it must resemble half a crossword puzzle. There were flat screen TVs in every room, even the johns, and all the rooms were decorated in a fashion that I labeled *haute mafia*. The dining room table was fashioned from a fourteenth-century monastery door lifted from some European ruin. The rugs were a motley assortment of modern and antique. Some of the windows were stained-glass relics, while others were jalousies; but since heavy drapes were drawn across them, whatever effect had been intended was lost. Every room was home to a variety of antiquities: Egyptian statuary, Greek amphorae, Venetian glassware, German tapestries, and so on. In my bathroom, the toilet was carved from a single block of marble, and mounted on the wall facing it, a section of a Persian bas-relief, was yet another flat screen. It was as if someone with the sensibility of a magpie had looted the world's museums in order to furnish the place, and yet the decor was so uniformly haphazard, I had the impression that Billy was making an anti-fashion statement, sneering at the concept of taste. Elvis would have approved. In fact, had he seen the entirety of Billy's house, he would have returned home to Graceland and redecorated.

Beyond the wall was jungly growth that hid the house completely. The beach was a crescent of tawny sand fringed by palms and hibiscus shrubs and Spanish bayonet, protected by an underwater fence. A bunkerlike guard house stood at the foot of the concrete pier to which the cigarette boat was moored, and a multicultural force (Cuban, white, African-American) patrolled within and without the walls. The guards, along with gardeners and maids, were housed in the bungalows, but they entered the house frequently to check on us. If we stepped outside they would dog us, their weapons shouldered, keeping a distance, alert to our every movement. It was easier to find privacy inside the house. Relative privacy, at any rate. Knowing Billy, I was certain that the rooms were bugged, and I had given up on the idea that I could keep anything from him. Whenever Pellerin and Jo were closeted in their rooms, I would walk along corridors populated by suits of armor and ninja costumes fitted to basketwork men and gilt French chairs that, with their curved legs and positioned between such martial figures, looked poised for an attack. I would poke into rooms, examine their collection of *objets d'art*, uniformly mismatched, yet priceless. Sometimes I would wonder if I dared slip one or two small items into my pocket, but most of my thoughts were less concerned with gain than with my forlorn prospects for survival.

Occasionally in the course of these forays, I would encounter a maid, but never anyone else, and thus I was surprised one afternoon when, upon entering a room in the northernmost wing with a four-poster bed and a fortune in gee-gaws littering the tables and bureaus, I saw Jo standing by the entrance to a walk-in closet, inspecting the dresses within. She gave a start when I spoke her name, then offered a wan smile and said, "Hello."

"What are you doing here?" I said.

"Browsing." She touched the bodice of a green silk dress. "These clothes must have cost hundreds of thousands of dollars. They're all designer originals."

"No, I meant aren't you supposed to be with Pellerin."

"I need breaks from Josey," she said. "His intensity gets to me after a while. And he's getting more independent, he wants time to himself. So...." She shrugged. "I like to come here and look at the clothes."

She stepped into the closet and I moved into the room so I could keep her in view.

"He must bring a lot of women here," she said. "He's got every imaginable size."

"It's hard for me to think of Billy as a sexual being."

"Why's that?"

"You'd have to know him. I've never seen him with a woman on his arm, but I suppose he has his moments."

She went deeper into the closet, toyed with the hem of a dress that bore a pattern like a moth's wing, all soft grays and greens, a touch of brown.

I perched on the edge of the bed. "Why don't you try it on?"

"Do you think he'd mind?" she asked.

"Go for it."

She hesitated, then said, "I'll just be a second," and closed the closet door.

The idea that she was getting naked behind the door inspired a salacious thought or two—I was already more than a little smitten. When she came out, she was barefoot. She did a pirouette and struck a fashion magazine pose. I was dumbstruck. The dress was nearly diaphanous, made of some feathery stuff that clung to her hips and flat stomach and breasts, the flared skirt reaching to mid-thigh.

"You like?" she asked. "It's a little short on me."

"I didn't notice."

She laughed delightedly and went for another spin. "I could never afford this. Not that I care all that much about clothes. But if I had a couple of million, I'd probably indulge."

Shortly thereafter she went back inside the closet, re-emerging wearing her jeans and a nondescript top. It seemed that she had exchanged personalities as well as clothes, for she was once again somber and downcast. "I've got to get back," she said.

"So soon?"

She stopped by the door. "I come here most days about this time," she said. "A little earlier, actually." Then, after a pause, she added, "It's nice having someone to wear clothes for."

We started meeting every day in that room. It was plain that she was flirting with me, and I imagine it was equally plain that I was interested, but it went on for over a month and neither one of us made a move. For my part, the fear of rejection didn't enter in. I was used to the man-woman thing being a simple negotiation—you either did the deed or you took a pass—but I thought if I did make a move, I might frighten her off, that she needed to feel in control. If I had been free of constraint, my own agent, I might have given up on her…or maybe I wouldn't have. She was the kind of woman who required a period of courtship, who enjoyed the dance as much as the feast, and she caused you to enjoy it as well. Basically an unhappy soul, she gave the impression of being someone who had been toughened by trouble in her life; but whenever she was happy, there was something so frail and girlish about the mood, I believed the least disturbance could shatter it. I grew more entranced by her and more frustrated day-by-day, but I told myself that not getting involved was for the best—I needed to keep clear of emotional entanglements and concentrate on how to stay alive once Billy came back into the picture. That didn't prevent me, however, from exploring certain of her fantasies.

I knew that she had been married when she was a teenager and one morning while we sat on the bed, her cross-legged at the head and me sort of side-saddle at the foot, I asked her about it. She ran a finger along a newel post, tracing the pattern carved into it, and said, "It was just…foolishness. We thought it would be romantic to get married."

"I take it, it wasn't."

She gave a wan laugh. "No."

"Would you ever do it again?"

"Marry? I don't know. Maybe." She smiled. "Why? Are you asking?"

"Maybe. Tell me what type of man it is you'd marry. Let's see if I fit the bill."

She lay down on her side, her legs drawn up, and considered the question.

"Yeah?" I said.

"You're serious? You want me to do this?"

"Let's hear it, chère. Your ideal man."

"Well…." She sat up, fluffed the pillow, and lay down again. "I'd want him to have lots of money, so maybe a financier. Not a banker or anything boring like that. A corporate tiger. Someone who would take over a failing company and reshape it into something vital."

"Money's the most important qualification?"

"Not really, but you asked for my ideal and money makes things easier."

She had on a blouse with a high collar and, as often happened when thinking, she tucked in her chin and nibbled the edge of the collar. I found the habit sexy and, whenever she did it, I wanted to touch her face.

"He'd be a philanthropist," she said. "And not just as a tax dodge. He'd have to be devoted to it. And he'd have an introspective side. I'd want him to know himself. To understand himself."

"A corporate raider with soul. Isn't that a contradiction?"

"It can happen. Wallace Stevens was an insurance executive and a great poet."

"I like to think of myself as an entrepreneur when I'm feeling spunky. That's like a financier, but I'm getting that we're talking about two different animals."

"You've got possibilities," she said, and smiled. "You just need molding."

"How about in the looks department?" I asked. "Something George Clooney-ish? Or Brad Pitt?"

She wrinkled her nose. "Movie stars are too short. Looks aren't important, anyway."

"Women all say that, but it's bullshit."

"It's true! Women have the same kind of daydreams as men, but when it comes to choosing a man they often base their choices on different criteria."

"Like money."

"No! Like how someone makes you feel. It's not quantifiable. I would never have thought I could...."

She broke off, thinning her lips.

"You would never have thought what?"

"This is silly," she said. "I should check on Josey."

"You never would have thought you could be attracted to someone you met at gunpoint?"

She sat up, swung her legs off the side of the bed, but said nothing.

"You might as well confess, chère," I said. "You won't be giving away any secrets."

She stiffened, as if she were going to lash out at me, but the tension drained from her body. "It's the Stockholm Syndrome," she said.

"You reckon that's it? We are for sure stuck on this damn island, and there's not a whole lot to distract us. And technically I am an accomplice in your kidnapping. But there's more to it than that."

"You're probably right," she said, coming to her feet. "If we'd met on our own in New Orleans, I'd probably have been attracted to you. But that's neither here nor there."

"Why not? Because Pellerin's your priority?"

She shrugged as if to say, yes.

"Duty won't keep you warm at night," I said.

"Keeping warm has never been my biggest goal in life," she said with brittle precision. "But should that change, I'll be sure to let you know."

▲▼▲

I didn't go outside much. The guards made me nervous. When I did it was usually to have a swim, but some nights I went along the shore through a fringe of shrubs and palms to the west end, the crosspiece of the T, a place from which, if the weather was clear, I could make out the lights on a nearby Key. And on one such night, emerging from dense undergrowth onto a shingle of crushed coral and sand, littered with vegetable debris, I spotted a shadow kneeling on the beach. Wavelets slapping against the shingle covered the sound of my approach and I saw it was Pellerin. I hadn't realized he could walk this far without help. He was holding a hand out above the water, flexing his fingers. It looked as if he were about to snatch something up. Beneath his hand the water seethed and little waves rolled away from shore. It was such a mediocre miracle, I scarcely registered it at first; but then I realized that he must be causing this phenomenon, generating a force that pushed the waves in a contrary direction. He turned his head toward me. The green flickers in his eyes stood out sharply in the darkness. A tendril of fear uncoiled in my backbrain.

"What's shaking, Small Time?" he said.

"Don't call me that. I'm sick of it."

He made a soft, coughing noise that I took for a laugh. "Want me to do like Jocundra and call you Jackie boy?"

"Just don't call me Small Time."

"But it suits you so well."

"You been through a rough time," I said. "And I can appreciate that. But that doesn't give you the right to act like an asshole."

"It doesn't? I could have sworn it did."

He came to his feet, lost his balance. I caught him by the shirtfront and hauled him erect. He tried to break my grip, but he was still weak and I held firm. He had a soapy smell. I wondered if Jo had to help him bathe.

"Let me go," he said.

"I don't believe I will."

"Give me another month or two, I promise I'll tear you down to your shoelaces, boy."

"I'll be waiting."

"Let me go!"

He pawed at my hand and I let loose of the shirt. That electric green danced in his eyes again.

"'Pears you growing a pair. Love must be making you bold." He hitched up his belt. "Yeah, I been catching you looking at Jocundra. She looks at you the same. If I wasn't around, the two of you be going at it like. But I *am* around."

"Maybe not for too long," I said.

"I might surprise you, boy. But whatever. As long as I'm here, Jocundra not going to stray. She's just dying for me to tell her about every new thing I see. She finds it fascinating."

"What do you see?"

"I'm not telling you, pal. I'm saving all of my secrets for sweet cheeks." He took a faltering step toward the house. "How's about we make a little side bet? Bet I nail her before you."

I gave him a shove and he went over onto his back, crying out in shock. A guard stepped from the shadow of the trees—I told him to be cool, I had things covered. I reached down and seized hold of Pellerin's arm, but he wrenched free.

"You want to lie there, fine by me," I said, and started back along the shore.

He called to me, but I kept walking.

"Know what I see in your future, Small Time?" he shouted as I passed into the trees. "I see lilies and a cardboard casket. I see a black dog taking a piss on your grave."

What he said didn't trouble me, but I was troubled nonetheless. When I had reached for his arm, I had brushed the fingers of his right hand, the same hand that he'd been holding above the water. I wouldn't have sworn to it, but it seemed that his fingertips had been hot. Not just warm. Burning hot. As if they'd been dipped into a bowl of fire.

▲▼▲

If pressed to do so, I might have acknowledged Jo's right to value her duties, but I was unreasonably angry at her. Angry and petulant. I kept to my room for a day and a half after that night on the beach, lying around in my boxers and doing some serious drinking, contemplating the notion that I was involved in a romantic triangle with a member of the undead. On the morning of the second day, I realized that I was only hurting myself and had a shower, changed my shorts. Still a little drunk, I was debating whether or not to see what was up in the rest of the house, when someone knocked on my door. Without thinking, I said, "Yeah, come in," and Jo walked into the room. I thought about making a grab for my trousers, but I was unsteady on my feet and feared that I'd stumble and fall on my ass; so I sat on the edge of the bed and tried to act nonchalant.

"How are you feeling," she asked.

"Peachy," I said.

She hesitated, then shut the door and took a seat in a carved wooden chair that likely had been some dead king's throne. "You don't look peachy," she said.

I'd cracked the drapes to check on the weather and light fell directly on her—she was the only bright thing in a room full of shadow. "I had a few drinks," I told her. "Drowning my sorrows. But I'm pulling it together."

She nodded, familiar with the condition.

"How come you didn't tell me your boy could do tricks?" I asked.

"Josey? What are you talking about?"

I told her what Pellerin had been doing with the ocean water and she said she hadn't realized he had reached that stage. She hopped up from the chair, saying she had to talk to him.

"Stay," I said. "Come on. You got all day to do with him. Just stay a while, okay?"

Reluctantly, she sat back down.

"So," I said. "You want to tell me what that is he was doing."

"My previous patient developed the ability to manipulate electromagnetic fields. He did some remarkable things. It sounds as if Josey's doing the same."

"You keep saying that. Remarkable how? Give me an example."

"He cured the sick, for one."

"Did he, now?"

"I swear, it's the truth. There was a man with terminal cancer. He cured him. It took him three days and cost him a lot of effort, but afterward the man was cancer-free."

"He cured a guy of cancer by...what? Working his electromagnetic fields?"

"I think so. I don't know for sure. Whatever he did, it produced a lot of heat." She crossed her legs, yielding up a sigh. "I wish it had stopped with that."

I asked what had happened.

"It's too long a story to tell, but the upshot was, he built a *veve*.... Do you know what a *veve* is?"

"The things they draw on the floors of voodoo temples? Little patterns?"

"That's them. They relate to the voodoo gods, the *loas*." She flicked a speck of something off her knee. "Donnell...my patient. He built the *veve* of Ogoun Badagris out of copper. Several tons of copper. It was immense. He said it enabled him to focus energy. He used to walk around on top of it and...one day there was an explosion." She made a helpless gesture. "I don't understand what happened."

Neither did I understand. I couldn't wrap my brain around the idea that Pellerin might be some kind of green-eyed Jesus; yet I didn't believe she was lying.

"What do think was going on with him?" I asked. "With Pellerin. I mean, what's your theory? You must have a theory."

"You want to hear? I've been told it's pretty out there."

"Yeah, and nothing about this is out there, so your theory's got to be way off base."

She laughed. "Okay. The bacteria we injected into Josey was the same strain we used at Tulane. All the slow-burners have reproduced those designs in one way or another. It's as if they're expressing the various aspects of Ogoun. Doctor Crain's theory was that because the bacteria eventually infested the entire brain, the patients used more of their brains than normal people—this resulted in what seemed to be miraculous powers. And since the bacterial strain was the same, it prevailed upon the host brain to acquire similar characteristics. That makes a certain amount of sense as far as it goes, but Crain was trying to explain voodoo in terms of science, and some of it can't be explained except in voodoo terms."

She paused, as if to gather her thoughts. "Someday we may discover a biochemical factor that makes the patients prone to seeing the *veve* patterns. But we'll never be able to explain away all the mystery surrounding Ezawa's work. I think he discovered the microbiological analogue of possession. In a voodoo ceremony, a possession occurs quickly. The god takes over your body while you're dancing or having a drink. You jerk around as the god acclimates to the flesh, and then you begin acting like that god. With the bacteria, it takes longer and the transition's smoother. You notice a growing awareness in the patients that they're different. Not just because they've come back from the dead. The real difference lies in the things they see and feel. They sense there's something qualitatively different about themselves. They recognize that they have their own agendas. They grow beyond their life stories the way Jesus and Buddha outgrew the parameters of their lives. Things Donnell said...they led me to believe that the bacteria allowed them to access their *gro bon ange*. Do you know the term? The immortal portion of the soul? According to voodoo, anyway. And that in turn opened them to the divine. As the bacterial infestation increased, they became more open. The slow-burners all demonstrated behavioral arcs that fit the theory. I guess it sounds crazy, but no one's come up with anything better."

She seemed to be waiting for me to speak.

"You're right," I said. "That's out there."

"Donnell was seeing these peculiar shadows before he died. I think he was seeing peoples' souls. I can't come close to proving it, of course, but there were things he told me...." She sighed in exasperation. "I begged Crain to let me work with Josey my way. I thought if I started from a position of intimacy, we could forge a bond strong enough to endure until the end. We'd see the maturation of the new personality. If my theory's right, we'd have a captive god fully integrated with a human personality. Whatever a god is. That might be something we could determine. Who knows what's possible?" The energy drained from her voice and her tone softened. "As things stand I doubt we'll ever get any further than I got with Donnell. He should have been given the space to evolve, but all they did was harass him."

"I'm getting you liked this Donnell," I said.

Her face sharpened. "Yes."

"How about Pellerin?"

"He's not very likeable. Part of it is, he's afraid of everything. Confused. He doesn't know yet who or what he is. He may never know. So he tends to be angry at everyone. That said, he's coarse, he's truculent and difficult to be around." She made a sad face and pushed up from her throne. "I wish I didn't have to go, but I should get back to him."

"Jo?"

"Uh-huh?"

"Remember when you asked if you could count on me as a friend? For what it's worth...."

"I know," she said, coming toward me.

"We've been forced onto the same side, but...."

She embraced me, pulling my head down onto her shoulder. I breathed in her warm, clean smell, and kissed her neck. She tensed, but I nuzzled her neck, her throat, and she let her head fall back. When I kissed her on the mouth, she kissed me back, fully complicit, and, before long, we were rolling around on the bed. I worked her T-shirt up around her neck and had disengaged the catch of her bra, a hook located under a flare of white lace between the cups, when I realized that, although she was not resisting, neither was she helping out as she had a moment earlier. I slid my hand under the bra, but she remained motionless, reactionless, and I asked what was the matter.

"I can't cope with this. You're the first man I've been attracted to in a long time. A very long time." She adopted an injured expression, like the one a child might display on running up against a rule that denied it a treat. "I want to make love with you, but I can't."

My hand was still on her breast and desire crowded all coherent thought from my head.

"Say something." She shifted, turning on her side, and my hand was no longer happy.

"Does this have anything to do with Pellerin?"

"Partly."

"You're sleeping with him?"

"No, but I might have to. It may be the only way to control him."

"Is that how you controlled Donnell?"

"It wasn't like that! I was in love with him."

"You loved him."

"I know it sounds strange, but I was…."

I experienced a flash of anger. "It sounds twisted."

She froze.

"You ever think," I said, "you might have a kink for dead guys?"

She held my eyes for a second, then sat up, rehooked her bra and tugged down her T-shirt.

"Maybe I do," she said. "Maybe I find them a vast improvement."

"I'm sorry," I said. "I didn't mean that. I was just…."

"What did you mean?"

"It was frustration talking."

"Don't you think I'm frustrated, too? I could probably find an insult to toss at you if I wanted."

I could have pointed out that she was the cause of her own frustration, but I'd already dug myself a hole and saw no good reason to pull the dirt down on top of me.

"I'm sorry," I said. "I truly am."

"It's not important," she said icily. "I've heard it before."

She flung herself off the bed.

"Jo," I said despairingly.

"Oh," she said, stopping in the doorway. "I nearly forgot. Your employer has a message for you. He'll be arriving in three days. Maybe you'll find his company less perverse than mine."

▲▼▲

I wasn't accustomed to viewing myself as an employee, and it took me a hiccup to translate the term "your employer" into the name Billy Pitch. I'd been anticipating his arrival, but the news was a shock nonetheless. My dalliance with Jo, brief and unsatisfying as it was, had placed our time on the island in the context of a courtship, and I needed to reorder my priorities. I knew I had to tell Billy everything—he had likely already heard it and our first conversation would be a test of my loyalty—and I would have to put some distance between Jo and me. You might have thought this would be an easy chore, given the state of the relationship, yet I was down the rabbit hole with her, past the point where longing and desire could be disciplined. Even my most self-involved thoughts were tinged with her colors.

Like advance men for Pharaoh, Billy Pitch's retinue arrived before him. Security people, chef, barber, bed fluffer, and various other functionaries filtered into the compound over the next day and a half. A seaplane brought in Billy the following morning and, after freshening up, accompanied by an enormous bodyguard with the coarse features of an acromegalic giant, he swept into the foyer of the main wing, the most grotesquely decorated room of all, dominated by a fountain transplanted from nineteenth-century Italy, with floors covered by pink and purple linoleum and vinyl furniture to match. It had been over a year since I had seen Billy in the flesh, but I had known him for almost a decade and he had always seemed ageless in a measly, unprepossessing way—I was thus pleased to note a pair of bifocals hanging about his neck and that his fringe of hair was turning gray. He wore a garish cabana set that left his bony knees and skinny forearms bare. The outfit looked ridiculous, but amplified his air of insectile menace. He directed a cursory glance toward Pellerin, sitting on a plum-colored sofa, but his gaze lingered on Jo, who stood behind him.

"My, my! Aren't you the sweet thing?" Billy wagged a forefinger at her. "Who's she remind me of, Clayton?"

The bodyguard, a mighty android in a blue silk T-shirt and white linen jacket, rumbled that he couldn't say, but she did look familiar.

"It'll come to me." He tipped his head pertly to one side and said to me, "Let's talk."

He led me into a room containing a functional modern desk and chairs and one of the ubiquitous flat screens, where I delivered my report. When I had done, he said, "Good job. Very good job." He drummed his fingers on the desk. "Do you believe her? You think that boy is a miracle worker? Or you think maybe that girl in there's gone crazy."

"It sounds crazy," I said. "But everything I've seen so far backs her up."

He nodded like he wasn't so much agreeing with me, but rather was mulling something over. "Let me show you a piece of tape I landed. Part of the Ezawa project at Tulane. The sound's no good, but the picture speaks volumes."

He switched on the TV and the tape began to play. The original of the tape had been a piece of film. It had an old-fashioned countdown—10, 9, 8, etc.—and then the tape went white, flickered, and settled into a grainy color shot of an orderly removing electrodes from the chest of a man wearing a hospital gown. He appeared to be semi-conscious and was sitting in a wheelchair. Rail-thin, with scraggly dark hair and rawboned hillbilly face. A woman in a nurse's uniform came into view, her back to the camera, and there was a blurt of sound. The legend "Tucker Mayhew" was briefly superimposed over the picture. Another blurt of sound, the woman speaking to the orderly, who left the room. Then the woman moved behind the wheelchair and I saw it was a younger, less buxom Jo, her make-up so liberally applied as to seem almost grotesque.

Billy asked why the heavy make-up and I replied, "She said they don't see very well at first. Must be to help with that."

Jo began to touch the man's shoulders and neck. Initially he was unresponsive, but soon the touches came to act like shocks on him, though he was still out of it. He twitched and stiffened as if being jabbed with needles. His eyelids fluttered open and his eyes showed green flashes, already brighter than Pellerin's.

"The part where she's touching him went on longer," Billy said. "I had it edited down."

The man's eyes opened. Jo left off touching him and moved away. He gaped, glanced around, his face a parody of loss. Jo spoke to him and he located her again. The change in his expression, from woebegone to gratified, was so abrupt as to be laughable. The sound came and went in spurts, and what I could hear was garbled, but I caught enough to know she was teasing out his life story, one he was inventing in order to please her, one that fit the absence in his mind. His eyes tracked her as she performed movements that in their grace and ritual elegance reminded me of Balinese dancers, yet had something as well of the blatant sexuality of bartop strippers you see in clubs on the edge of the Quarter. She passed behind the wheelchair and again touched him on the back of the neck.

Billy paused the tape. "There. Look at that."

The man had his head back and mouth open, searching for Jo, and she was about to touch him again, her long fingers extended toward the nape of his neck. Her smile was, I thought, unreadable, yet the longer I stared at it, the more self-satisfied it seemed. The image trembled slightly.

"Anybody doing that job is going to look bad from time to time," I said.

"But that's the job she does, honey," Billy said. "You can't get around that." He unpaused the tape and muted the sound. "Know what it puts me in mind of? Those women who marry men on death row. It's all about being in control for them. They control the visits, letters...everything. They don't have to have sex, yet they have all the emotional content of a real relationship and none of the fuss. And it's got a built-in expiration date. It's a hell of a deal, really. Of course our Miz Verret, she took it farther than most."

A jump in the film, another edit. The man's eyes blazed a fiery green that appeared to overflow his sockets. His coordination had improved, he made coherent gestures and talked non-stop. He struggled to stand and nearly succeeded, and then, after making an obviously impassioned statement, he fell back, dead for the second time. Jo stood beside the body for almost a minute before closing his eyes. A faint radiance shone through the lids. An orderly removed the body as Jo made notes on a clipboard. The screen whited out and another countdown started. Billy switched off the TV.

"Forty-seven minutes," he said. "Scratch one zombie. You got to be careful around that girl."

"Billy, I was—"

"I know. You were trying to get a little. But I'd hate to see you screw this up over a piece of ass." His voice acquired a pinched nastiness. "Especially since the bitch is such a freak!" He peered at me over top of his glasses, as if assessing the impact of his words. He sighed. "Let's go have a chat with them, shall we?"

We went back into the living room. Clayton and the other bodyguard stood at ease. Billy took a chair opposite the sofa where Pellerin was sitting and I hovered at his shoulder. Behind Pellerin, Jo tried to make eye contact with me, but I pretended not to notice.

"Mister Pellerin," said Billy. "I have a question for you."

Pellerin looked at me and said, "This dab of cream cheese is the badass you warned us about?"

"Clayton?" said Billy. "Would you mind?"

Two strides carried Clayton to the sofa. He backhanded Pellerin viciously, knocking his sunglasses off. Jo shrieked and Clayton stood poised to deliver another blow.

"In the stomach," Billy said.

Clayton drove his fist into Pellerin's belly, and Billy signaled him to step back. Jo hurried around the couch to minister to Pellerin, who was trying to breathe, bleeding from a cut on his cheek.

"I'm not a very good businessman," said Billy sadly. "I let things get personal. I miss out on a lot of opportunities that way, but I've learned if you can't have fun with an enterprise, it's best to cut your losses. Do you need a moment, Mister Pellerin?"

"You could have killed him!" Jo said, glancing up from Pellerin.

"Precisely." Billy church-and-steepled his fingers. "Your boy there's a valuable commodity, yet because of my intemperate nature I might have done the unthinkable. Do we understand each other? Mister Pellerin?"

Pellerin made a stressed yet affirmative noise.

"Good. Now...my question. Is your ability such that you can control the play of seven or eight good card players so as to achieve a specific result?"

With considerable effort, holding his belly, Pellerin sat up. "How specific?"

"I'd like you to arrange it so that you and a certain gentleman outlast all the rest, and that he has a distinct advantage in chips at that point. Let's say a four to one advantage. Then I'd like you to beat him silly. Take all his chips as quickly as you can."

"That's risky," said Pellerin. "The guy could get a run of great cards. It's hard playing heads-up from that far down. You can't bluff effectively. Why do you want me to do it that way? If you let me play my game, I can guarantee a win."

"Because he'll want the game to continue if he thinks you lucked out. He'll offer you a check, but you tell him it's cash or nothing."

"What if he—" Pellerin began, and Billy cut him off: "No what-ifs. Yours not to wonder why, yours but to do or die." He looked to Clayton. "Is that Byron?"

"Tennyson," said Clayton. "'The Charge of the Light Brigade.'"

"Yes, of course!" He gave himself a pretend-slap for having forgotten. "Well. Can you do the job, Mister Pellerin?"

"I'll need a little luck, but...yeah. I guess I can do it."

"We all need a little luck." Billy popped out of the chair. "You'll be leaving for Fort Lauderdale day after tomorrow. The Seminole Paradise

Casino. I'll have my people watching, so don't worry about anything untoward. You will be closely watched. I'll give Jack the details. He can tell you all about it."

He walked away briskly, but then he turned and pointed at Jo. "I got it! *Big Brother All-Stars.* The seventh season. You remember, Clayton?"

Clayton said, maybe, he wasn't sure.

"Come on, man! Erica. The tall bitch with the big rack. She played the game real sneaky."

"Oh, yeah," said Clayton. "Yeah, I can see it."

▲▼▲

The Seminole Paradise Hard Rock Hotel and Casino was a hell of a mouthful for what amounted to your basic two-hundred-dollar-per-room Florida hotel complete with fountain display and an assortment of clubs and bars notable for the indifferent quality of their cuisine and the bad taste evident in their decor. Particularly annoying was Pangaea, a club decorated with "authentic tribal artifacts" that likely had been purchased from a prop supply company. The entire complex was a surfeit of fakes. Fake breasts, fake smiles, fake youth, fake people. Why anyone would choose such a place to put a dent in their credit cards, I'll never know—maybe it offered them the illusion that they were losing fake money.

We went down to the casino early the same afternoon we checked in, and Pellerin nabbed a chair at one of the poker tables. I watched for a while to ascertain whether he was winning—he was—and went for a stroll. I wanted to see how far my leash would stretch. There were several men hanging about who might be Billy's people and I was interested to learn if any of them would follow me. I also wanted to get clear of the situation and gain some perspective on things. Once I reached the entrance to the grounds, I turned right and walked along the edge of the highway, working up a sweat in the hot sun, until I came to a strip mall with about twenty-five or thirty shops, the majority of them closed. It was Sunday in the real world.

A Baskin-Robbins caught my eye. The featured flavors were banana daiquiri and sangria. Sangria, for fuck's sake! I bought two scoops of vanilla by way of protesting the lapsed integrity of ice cream flavors and ate it sitting on the curb. I tried to problem-solve, but all I did was churn up mud from the bottom of my brain. The assignment that had been forced upon us—upon Pellerin—was to attract the interest of a wealthy developer named Frank Ruddle, an excellent poker player who frequented the Seminole Paradise. Pellerin's job was to play sloppy over the course of a couple of weeks. That way he would set himself up as a mark and Ruddle would invite him to the big cash game held each month at his Lauderdale home. According to Billy's scenario, once Ruddle went bust, he would feel compelled to open his vault in order to obtain more cash. At this point Billy's people would move in on the game. He wanted something from that vault. I thought it might be more of a trophy than anything of actual value, and that his real goal was purely personal. The plan was paper-thin and smacked of Billy at his most profligate. There were a dozen holes in it, a hundred ways it could go wrong, but Billy was willing to spend our lives for the chance to gain a petty victory. Had the aim of the exercise been to secure the item at any cost, it could have been far more easily achieved. That he was willing to squander an asset with (if Jo were to be believed) unlimited potential was classic late-period Billy Pitch. If we failed, it was no skin off his butt. He'd wait for his next opportunity and while away the hours throwing Tanqueray parties for his fellow reality-show addicts. And if we succeeded, he might decide that his victory would not be secure so long as we were alive. I saw a couple of outs, but the odds of them working were not good.

Across from the mall lay a vacant lot overgrown with weeds, sprinkled with scrub palmetto, and adjoining it was another, larger lot that had been cleared for construction, the future site of LuRay Condominiums—so read a sign picturing a peppy senior citizen couple who seemed pleased as all get out that they would soon be living next door to a casino where they could blow their retirement in a single evening. Farther along was a cluster of tiny redneck dwellings set among diseased-looking palms. Squatty frame houses with shingle roofs and window-unit air conditioners and front yards littered with sun-bleached Big Wheels and swing sets. They looked deserted, but each of them harbored, I imagined, a vast corpulent entity with dyed hair and swollen ankles, who survived on a diet of game shows and carbohydrates, and went outside once a day to check the sky for signs of the Rapture. Now and then a car zipped past and, less frequently, one pulled into the mall and disgorged a porky Florida Cracker family desirous of some Burger King or a couple of bare-midriffed Britney Spears clones in search of emergency eye liner.

This dose of reality caused the mud to settle, the sediment to wash from my thoughts, but clarity did not improve my prospects. I tossed my trash into a bin. Zombie hold 'em players and doe-eyed ladies who were a little damaged...I wanted that crap out of my head, I wanted things back the way they had been. Small Time. That was me. Yet I was content with my small-time life. I was adept at it, I was pleased with my general lack of ambition. Tentatively, I gave the trash bin a kick. It quivered in fear, and that inspired me to unload on it. The bin rolled out into the parking lot and I kept on kicking it. I crushed its plastic ribs, I flattened it and squeezed out its soggy paper-and-crumpled-plastic guts. Inside the Baskin-Robbins, people stared but didn't appear terribly alarmed. They were accustomed to such displays. Heat drove men insane in these parts. The manager took a stand by the door, ready to defend his tubs of flavored goo, but the moment passed when I might have stormed his glassed-in fortress and engendered the headline "Five Dead In Baskin-Robbins Spree Killing—Louisiana Native Charged In Crime." I strode out to the highway, fueled by a thin, poisonous anger, and was nearly struck by a speeding Corvette that veered onto the shoulder. Dizzy with adrenaline, I gazed off along the road. Despite the vegetation, I felt I was on the edge of a desert. Weeds stirred in a fitful breeze. One day the Great Sky Monkey, sated with banana daiquiri ice cream, would drop down from the Heavenly Banyan Tree to use the place for toilet paper. I tried to calm myself, but everywhere I cast my eye I saw omens and portents and outright promises of doom. I saw a wine bottle shattered into a spray of diamonds on the asphalt, I saw a gray-haired man poking his cane feebly at a dead palm frond, I saw a sweaty twelve-year-old girl with a mean, sexy face pedaling her bicycle full tilt toward me, and I saw a black car with smoked windows idling beside a Dumpster under the killing white glare of the sun.

▲▼▲

Frank Ruddle looked like an empty leather gym bag. He had recently lost a great deal of weight, something he proclaimed loudly and often, and his skin had not tightened sufficiently to compensate. Forty-something; with thinning blond hair and a store-bought orange tan and a salesman's jaunty manner; these attributes—if attributes they were—had been counterbalanced by dewlaps, jowls and an overall lack of muscle tone. His outfits always included some cranberry article of clothing. A tie, a pair of slacks, a shirt. I assumed this was his lucky color, for it was not a flattering one, serving to accent his unhealthiness. At the tables, prior to making a bold play, he was in the habit of kissing a large diamond signet ring. He appeared to have taken a shine to Pellerin, perhaps in part because Pellerin was an even unhealthier specimen than he, and, when sitting at the same table, he would applaud Pellerin's victories, including those won at his expense, with enthusiasm.

"Damn!" he would say, and give an admiring shake of the head. "I didn't see that coming."

Pellerin, in heads-up play, let Ruddle win the lion's share of the pots and took his losses with poor grace. Watching him hustle Ruddle was like watching a wolf toy with a house pet, and I might have felt sorry for the man if I had been in a position to be sympathetic.

We had been at Seminole Paradise ten days before Ruddle baited his hook. As Pellerin and I were entering the casino in the early afternoon, he intercepted us and invited us for lunch at the hotel's fake Irish pub, McSorely's, a place with sawdust on the floor, something of an anomaly, as I understood it, among fake Irish pubs. Pellerin was in a foul mood, but when he saw the waiter approaching, a freckly, red-headed college-age kid costumed as a leprechaun, he busted out laughing and thereafter made sport of him throughout the meal. The delight he took from baiting the kid perplexed Ruddle, but he didn't let it stand in the way of his agenda. He buttered Pellerin up and down both sides, telling him what a marvelous player he was, revisiting a hand he had won the night before, remarking on its brilliant disposition. Then he said, "You know, I'm having some people over this weekend for a game. I'd be proud if you could join us."

Pellerin knocked back the dregs of his third margarita. "We're going to head on to Miami, I think. See what I can shake loose from the casinos down there."

Ruddle looked annoyed by this rebuff, but he pressed on. "I sure wish you'd change your mind. There'll be a ton of dead money in the game."

"Yeah?" Pellerin winked at me. "Some of it yours, no doubt."

Ruddle laughed politely. "I'll try not to disappoint you," he said.

"How much money we talking here?"

"There's a five hundred thousand dollar buy-in."

Pellerin sucked on a tooth. "You trying to hustle me, Frank? I mean, you seen me play. You know I'm good, but you must think you're better."

"I'm confident I can play with you," Ruddle said.

Pellerin guffawed.

"I beg your pardon?" said Ruddle.

"I once knew a rooster thought it could run for president 'til it met up with a hatchet."

Ruddle's smile quivered at the corners.

"Shit, Frank! I'm just joshing you." Pellerin lifted his empty glass to summon the leprechaun. "This is a cash game, right?"

"Of course."

"What sort of security you got? I'm not about to bring a wad of cash to a game doesn't have adequate security."

"I can assure you my security's more than adequate," said Ruddle tensely.

"Yeah, well. Going by how security's run at the Seminole, your idea of adequate might be a piggybank with a busted lock. I'll send Jack over to check things out. If he says it's cool, we'll gamble."

I sent Ruddle a silent message that said, See what I have to put up with, but he didn't respond and dug into his steak viciously, as if it were the liver of his ancient enemy.

Somehow we made it through lunch. I pushed the small talk. Movies, the weather.... Ruddle offered curt responses and Pellerin sucked down margaritas, stared out the window and doodled on a napkin. After Ruddle had paid the check, I steered Pellerin outside and, to punish him, dragged him on a brisk walk about the pool. He complained that his legs were hurting and I said, "We need to get you in shape. That game could go all night."

I walked him until he had sweated out his liquid lunch, then allowed him to collapse at a poolside table not far from the lifeguard's chair. They must have treated the water earlier that day, because the chlorine reek was strong. In the pool, a huge sun-dazzled aquamarine with a waterfall slide at its nether end, packs of kids cavorted under their parents' less-than-watchful eyes, bikini girls and speedo boys preened for one another. Close at hand, an elderly woman in a one-piece glumly paddled along the edge, her upper body supported by a flotation device in the form of a polka-dotted snail. The atmosphere was of amiable chatter, shrieks, and splashings. A honey-blonde waitress in shorts and an overstrained tank top ambled over from the service bar, but I brushed her off.

"You got a plan?" Pellerin asked out of the blue.

"A plan? Sure," I said. "First Poland, then the world."

"If you don't, we need to start thinking about one."

I cocked an eye toward him, then looked away.

"That's why I played Ruddle like I did," Pellerin said. "So you could get a line on his security."

"We do what Billy tells us," I said. "That's our safest bet."

Three boys ran past, one trying to snap the others with a towel; the lifeguard whistled them down.

"I did have a thought," I said. "I thought we could tell Ruddle what Billy's up to and hope he can protect us. But that's a short-term solution at best. Billy's still going to be a problem."

"I like it. It buys us time."

"If Ruddle goes for it. He might not. I'm not sure how well he knows Billy. He might be tight with him, and he might decide to give him a call."

A plump, pale, middle-aged man wearing a fishing hat and bathing trunks, holding a parasol drink, negotiated the stairs at the shallow end of the pool, stood and sipped in thigh-deep water.

"I'll check out Ruddle's security. It may give me an idea." I put my hands flat on the table and prepared to stand. "We should look in on Jo before you start playing."

Pellerin's lips thinned. "To hell with her."

"You two got a problem?"

"She lied to me."

"Everyone fibs now and again."

"She lied about something pretty crucial."

I suspected that Jo had told him he hadn't always been Josey Pellerin. "Mind if I ask what?"

"Yeah," he said. "I mind."

I watched him out of the corner of my eye. His features relaxed from their belligerent expression and he appeared to be tracking the progress of something through the air. I asked what he was looking at, half-expecting him to claim that he had discovered a microscopic planet with an erratic orbit, but he said, "A gnat." Then he laughed. "A gnat with a fucking aura."

"You see that shit all the time?"

"Auras? Yeah. Weirder stuff than that."

"Like what?"

"Shadows." He fumbled in his pocket and fished out a wad of bills, napkins, gum wrappers—there must have been thirty or forty hundreds in with the debris; he selected a twenty, tossed the rest on the table and hailed the blonde waitress. "Margarita rocks," he told her. "Salt."

"Better slow down," I said. "If you're going to play poker, that is."

"You kidding me? I need a handicap to play with those old ladies."

I let my thoughts wander, vaguely mindful of the activity in the pool, speculating on the rate of skin cancers among the patrons of the Seminole Paradise, reflecting on the fact that I had not seen a single Seminole during our stay, if one omitted the grotesque statue of Osceola in the lobby, fashioned from a shiny yellowish brown material—petrified Cheese Whiz was my best guess. The waitress set Pellerin's margarita down on the table; her eyes snagged on the cash strewn across it. She offered Pellerin his change and he told her to keep it. He tilted his head, squinted at her name tag, and said, "Is waitressing your regular job, Tammy, or just something you do on the side?"

Tammy didn't know how to take this. She flashed her teeth, struck a pose that accentuated her breasts and said, "I'm sorry?"

"Reason I ask," said Pellerin, "I wonder if you ever done any hostessing? I'm throwing a party up in my suite tonight. Around ten o'clock. And I was hoping to get a couple of girls to help me host it. You know the drill. Take care of the guests. See that everyone's got a drink. You'd be doing me a huge favor." He reached into his other pocket, peeled what looked to be about a grand off his roll and held it out to her. "That's a down payment."

A light switched on in Tammy's brain and she re-evaluated Pellerin. "So how many guests are we talking about?" she asked.

"I'm the only one you'd have to worry about." Pellerin gave a lizardly smile. "But I can be a real chore."

"Why, I think we can probably handle it." Tammy accepted the bills, folded them, stashed them next to her heart. "Around ten, you say?"

"I'm in the Everglades Suite," said Pellerin. "Wear something negligible. And one more thing, darling. It'd be nice if your friend was a Latina. Maybe a Cuban girl. On the slender side. Maybe her name could be...Thomasina?"

"Why, isn't that a coincidence! That's my best friend's name!" Tammy turned and twitched her cute butt. "See ya tonight."

As she sashayed off, Pellerin slurped down half his margarita and sighed. "Ain't freedom grand?"

"What was that bullshit?" I said. "You're in the Everglades Suite?"

"Three nights from now, we could be lying in a landfill," he said. "I booked myself a suite and I'm going to have me a party."

"This isn't wise," I said. "Suppose she gets a look at your eyes?"

"Did you get a load of the brain on that girl? I could tell her I was down in the Amazon and got stung by electric bees, she'd be fine with it."

I wasn't too sure about that, but then I was distracted from worry by thinking about Jo all alone in Room 1138.

"Yeah, boy!" said Pellerin, and grinned—he'd been watching me. "What they say is true. Every cloud has a silver lining."

I made no response.

"Hell, if Jocundra don't do it for you," he said, "I'm sure Tammy and Thomasina wouldn't mind accommodating another guest."

"That's all right."

"On second thought, I believe you're the kind of guy who needs that old emotion lotion to really get off."

"Shut your hole, okay?"

Pellerin finished his margarita, signaled Tammy for another. I was through cautioning him about his drinking. Maybe he'd drop dead. That would let us off the hook. More people had jumped into the pool—it looked like a sparkling blue bowl of human head soup. There came a loud screech that resolved into "The Pina Colada Song" piped in over speakers attached to the surrounding palms. I was half-angry, though I couldn't have told you at what, and that damn song exacerbated my mood. Tammy brought the margarita and engaged in playful banter with Pellerin.

"Does your friend want a friend?" she asked. "Because I bet I could fix him up."

"Naw, he's got a friend," said Pellerin. "The trouble is, she ain't treating him all that friendly."

"Aw! Well, if he needs a friendly-ier friend, you let me know, hear?"

I shut my eyes and squeezed the arms of my chair, exerting myself in an attempt to suppress a shout. Eventually I relaxed and my mind snapped back into on-duty mode. "What kind of shadows?" I asked Pellerin.

He gazed at me blankly. "Huh?"

"You said you were seeing shadows. What kind?"

"You're starting to sound like Jocundra, man."

"What, is it a big secret?"

He licked salt off the rim of his glass. "I don't guess they're shadows, really. They're these black shapes, like a man, but they don't have any faces. Sometimes they have lights inside them. Shifting lights. They kind of flow together."

I laughed. "Sounds like a lava lamp?"

"Everybody's got one," he said. "But it's not an aura. It's more substantial. I see patterns, too. Like...." He poked around in the pile of money and trash on the table and plucked out a napkin bearing the McSorely's logo. "Like this here. The whole thing creeps me out."

On the napkin were several sketches of what appeared to be ironwork designs: *veves*. I asked why it creeped him out.

"When we were on the island," Pellerin went on, "I found these books on voodoo. And while I was leafing through them, I saw that same design. It's used in the practice of voodoo. Called a *veve*. That there's the *veve* of Ogoun Badagris, the voodoo god of war. And this...." He pointed to a second sketch. "This one's Ogoun in his aspect as the god of fire. I get that one a lot." He paused and then said, "You know anything about it?"

I had no doubt that he could read me if I lied and, although it was my instinct to lie, I didn't see any reason to hide things from him anymore; yet I didn't want to freak him out, either.

"Jo told me she had another patient who saw this same sort of pattern," I said.

"What else she tell you?"

"She said he did some great things before—"

"Before he died, right?"

"Yeah."

There ensued a silence, during which I noticed that the song playing over the speakers was now "Margaritaville".

"She told me he got to where he could cure the sick," I said.

He stared at me. "Fuck."

"Let's get through the weekend, then you can worry about it," I said.

"Easy for you to say."

"It's a lot to process, I give you that. But you can't—"

"I knew she was holding back, but...man!" He picked up his drink, put it back down. "You know, I don't much fucking care if we get through the weekend."

"I care," I said, but he appeared not to hear me, gazing out across the pool toward the hedge of palms and shrubbery that hid the concrete block wall that separated Seminole Paradise from a Circuit City store.

"You ever have the feeling you're on the verge of understanding everything?" he said. "That if you could see things a tad clearer, you'd have the big picture in view? I mean the *Big Picture*. How it all fits together. That's where I'm at. But I'm also getting this feeling I don't fucking want to see the big picture, that it's about ten shades darker than the picture I already got." He chewed on that a second, then heaved up to his feet. "I'm going to the casino."

"Wait a second!" I said as he walked away.

I busied myself plucking the hundreds out of the mess we'd made on the table, and I pressed the clutter of bills into his hands. He seemed startled by the money, as if it were an unexpected bonus, but then he stepped to the edge of the glittering pool and said in a loud voice, "Hey! Here you go, you lucky people!" and tossed the money into the air.

There couldn't have been more than four or five thousand dollars, but for the furore it caused, it might have been a million. As the bills fluttered down, people surged through the water after them; others sprawled on the tiles in their mad scramble to dive into the pool. Children were elbowed aside, the elderly were at risk. A buff young lad surfaced with a joyous expression, clutching a fistful of bills, and was immediately hauled under by a bikini girl and her boyfriend, their faces aglow with greed. The water was lashed into a froth as by sharks in a feeding frenzy. Terrified screams replaced the prettier shrieks that had attended rough-housing and dunkings. One man dragged a woman from the mêlée and sought to give her mouth-to-mouth, whereupon she kicked him in the groin. The lifeguard's umbrella toppled into the water. He shouted incoherent orders over his mike. This served to increase the chaos. He began blowing his whistle over and over, an irate clown with his cheeks puffed and a nose covered in sun block.

Pellerin was laughing as I pulled him away from the pool, and he was still laughing when I shoved him through the double glass doors of the hotel. I adopted a threatening pose, intending to lecture him, and he made an effort to stifle his laughter; but then I started laughing, too, and his mirth redoubled. We stood wheezing and giggling in the lobby, giddy as teenage girls, drawing hostile stares from the guests waiting in line at Reception, enduring the drudgery of check-in. At the time I assumed that we were laughing at two different things, or at different aspects of the same thing, but now I'm not so sure.

▲▼▲

That picture of Pellerin laughing by the side of the pool, bills fluttering out above the water…it emerges from the smoke of memory like a painted dream, like one of those images that come just before a commercial break in a television drama, when the action freezes and the colors are altered by a laboratory process. Though it seems unreal, the rest—by comparison—seems in retrospect less than unreal, a dusting of atoms, whispers, and suggestions of hue that we must arrange into a story in order to lend body to this central moment. Yet the stories we create are invariably inaccurate and the central moments we choose to remember change us as much or more as we change them, and so, in truth, my memories are no more "real" than Josey Pellerin's, although they have, as Jo would put it, more foundation…. But I was saying, that picture of Pellerin beside the pool stayed with me because, I believe, it was the first time I had acknowledged him as a man and not a freak. And when I went to see him late the next morning, it was motivated more by curiosity over how he'd made out with Tammy and Thomasina than by caretaker concerns.

The door to the suite had been left ajar. I sneaked a look inside and, seeing no one around, eased into the foyer. The living room was empty, an air-conditioned vacancy of earth tones and overstuffed furniture, with potted palms and a photomural of the Everglades attempting a naturalistic touch. Everything was very neat. Magazines centered on the coffee table; no empty glasses or bottles. On the sideboard, a welcome basket of fruit, wine, and cheese was still clenched in shrinkwrap.

I proceeded down the hall and came to an open door. Wearing a terrycloth bathrobe and sunglasses, Pellerin sat beside the rumpled bed, his feet propped on a table covered with a linen cloth and laden with dishes and metal dish covers, drinking champagne out of a bottle and eating a slice of pizza, looking out the window at the overcast. In the bed, partly covered by the sheets, a brown-skinned girl lay on her belly, black hair fanned across her face. Thomasina. There was nary a sign of Tammy, though the bed was king-sized and she might well have been buried beneath the covers. I knocked and he beckoned me to come on in. A big scorch mark on the wall behind his head, about the size of a serving tray, caught my notice. I asked what had happened and he told me that Tammy had shot an aerosol spray through a lit cigarette lighter, producing a flamethrower effect.

"You know those sons-of-bitches wouldn't let me order in a pizza last night," he said. "Is that bullshit or what? I had to bribe the bellboy." He pointed to a Domino's box on the floor—it held two slices fettered with strings of congealed cheese—and told me to help myself.

I declined, sat opposite him, and he asked what time it was.

"Around eleven." I picked up a plastic pill bottle from the table. The label read:

R. Saloman
Viagra 50 mg.
1 tablet as needed.

"Who's R. Saloman?" I asked.

"Beats me. Friend of the bellboy, maybe. The kid's a walking pharmacy." Pellerin scratched his chest. "Want some room service?"
"I'm okay."

"How about some coffee? Sure, you want some coffee."

He reached for the phone, ordered coffee and sweet rolls. Thomasina stirred but did not wake.

"Where's Tammy?" I asked.

"In the head? Or she might have gone home. We were doing shots last night and she got sick."

"You trying to kill yourself, man? Maybe you haven't noticed, but you're not in the best of shape."

Pellerin had a swig of champagne. "You my fairy godmother now?"

"I'm just being solicitous of your health."

"Because that was Jocundra's job, and I shit-canned her."

"Look, don't get the idea you're in charge here. You're not in charge."

"Oh, I'm far from having that idea. We all know who's in charge."

Jocundra's voice called from the living room. "Josey!"

"In here, darling!" He gave me a wink. "This ought to be good."

Seconds later, Jocundra materialized in the doorway, dressed in jeans and a man's pinstriped dress shirt with the sleeves neatly rolled up. Her eyes stuck on Thomasina, then went to me and Pellerin. "I need to talk to you. I'll come back."

"Don't be that way," said Pellerin. "We're all pals. Sit with us. We got coffee coming."

She had another glance at Thomasina, then came to the table and took the chair between me and Pellerin.

"I spoke to management," she said. "They're not going to kick us out, but you're banned from the pool area."

"Damn!" said Pellerin. "And here I was dying for a swim."

Jocundra started to speak, likely to reprimand him, but thought better of it. An edgy quiet closed in around us.

"You know they got a couple of live gators in that pond in the courtyard? That's why there's a fence around it." Pellerin shook his head in mock amazement. "They don't never show themselves. Can't say as I blame them."

Another stretch of quiet.

"I'm going over to Ruddle's house later to see what I can see," I said. "It's right on the water. That might be good for us. It's a potential avenue of escape if things go south."

There would probably have been another interval of silence, if not for Tammy who, wearing a towel turbaned around her hair and nothing else, entered the room, said, "Oops!", and tippy-toed to the bed, slipping in under the covers next to Thomasina. She sat up, shook out her hair, and said to me, "Is this your friend? She's so pretty!"

"Hey, babe!" Pellegrin said. "I thought you went home."

"I was making myself sweet for you," said Tammy in a little-girl voice.

"I'll be in my room," said Jocundra.

"Why you acting this way?" Pellerin caught her wrist. "Like you been wronged or something. If anyone's been wronged, it's me. Sit down and be polite. There's no reason we can't act like friends."

Tammy, baffled, gestured at me and said to Pellerin, "I thought she was *his* friend."

Jocundra twisted free and walked out. I caught up to her in the living room. "Hey, slow down," I said, blocking the door to the suite.

She folded her arms and lowered her head, shielding her eyes with one hand, as if close to tears. "Let me by!"

"All right." I moved aside, inviting her to leave. "You're not helping him by behaving like this. You're not helping me, you're not helping yourself. But go ahead. Take a break. I'll handle things. Just try and pull yourself together by Saturday night."

She stood a moment, then walked over to a sofa, stood another moment and sat down.

"Why're you getting so bent out of shape?" I dropped into a chair. "I thought you didn't have a strong connection with this guy."

"I don't!"

"Then why—"

"Because I *couldn't* make a connection with him. It's my fault he's alone."

"He's not exactly alone," I reminded her.

"You know it's not the same. He needs someone with him who understands what he's going through."

With two people breathing in it, the room seemed almost airless, like a room in a Motel 6 with bolted-shut plastic windows. I thought about yanking back the drapes and opening the glass door onto the balcony, but I couldn't muster the energy.

"He's not exercising," Jocundra said. "He's not taking his meds."

"Maybe you should have slept with him."

"I tried once, but...I couldn't. And that's your fault."

I was about to ask her why it was my fault—I knew why, but I wanted to hear her say it—when Pellerin limped into the room.

"I've been taking my meds. And I'm not a fool." He lowered himself into a chair, smirking at us. "You crazy kids! Why don't you run away and get hitched?"

Jo's startled expression waned; she folded her hands in her lap and bowed her head, like Anne Boleyn awaiting the inevitable.

"It's no big thing," said Pellerin. "Really. So how about we ditch the soap opera and move on?"

"I'm worried about you," Jo said.

"Fine. Worry about me," said Pellerin. "But don't get all fucked up behind it."

The doorbell bonged and a man's voice called out, "Room service."

"I'll get it," I said.

I prevented the room service guy from entering, but he peered over my shoulder as I signed for the coffee and rolls. After I had poured coffee for me and Jo, Pellerin asked if I'd see whether the girls wanted anything, so I walked back to the bedroom to check and found Tammy and Thomasina engaged in activity that would have made the White

Goddess blush. I returned to the living room and, in response to Pellerin's inquiring look, said, "They're good."

"We were thinking," Jo said, "that we should have a Plan B."

I joined her on the sofa, tore open a package of Sweet 'n Low and dumped the contents into my coffee. "I didn't realize we had a Plan A."

"Confessing to Ruddle," said Pellerin.

"That's our plan? Okay." I stirred the coffee. "Maybe we could create a disturbance. Get away in the confusion. I don't know."

Pellerin said, "You're not exactly an expert criminal, are you?"

"I'm not a criminal at all. I arrange things, I put people together. It's a gray area."

"He's an entrepreneur." Jo smiled at me as if to cut the sting of what she'd said.

A shift in alignment seemed to have occurred—judging by that remark, she had repositioned herself closer to Pellerin than to me. I wondered if she were aware of this. A cruel comment came to mind, but I chose not to make it.

"We could cause a major earthquake, and I doubt it would help," I said. "Josey can walk pretty good, but I expect running's going to be called for and he's not up to that."

Even the coffee sucked at Seminole Paradise—I set my cup down. Pellerin fiddled with the sash of his robe and Jo clinked a spoon against her cup, tapping out a nervous rhythm.

"What about the stuff I saw you doing on the island?" I asked Pellerin. "The night we had that dust-up on the beach, you were doing things with the water. Pushing waves around."

A hunted expression flashed across his face, and I had the thought that he might be hiding something. "I can do a few parlor tricks," he said.

"What's your best one?" I asked. "Give us a demonstration."

"All right." He leaned over the table and put a napkin in an ashtray. "Sometimes I can do it, but other times...not so much."

He concentrated on the napkin, wiggled his fingers like a guitar player lightly fingering the strings. After about twenty, thirty seconds, smoke began to trickle up from the napkin, followed by a tiny flame. He snuffed it out with a spoon. Jo made a speech-like noise, but didn't follow up.

"That's my biggie," he said, leaning back. "If we had another month, I might could do something more impressive. But...." He shrugged, then said to Jo, "If we come through this, I want you to tell me about Ogoun Badagris. How that relates to me."

She nodded.

"You know, that might have possibilities," I said. "If you could start an electrical fire, we—"

"I don't want to talk about this anymore," he said. "After you get back from Ruddle's, we'll talk then."

"I'll tell you now if you want," Jo said. "About Ogoun. It won't take too long."

Pellerin suddenly appeared tired, pale and hollow-cheeked, slumping in his chair, but he said, "Yeah, why don't you?"

I was tired, too. Tired of talking, tired of the Seminole Paradise, tired of whatever game Jo was playing, tired of listening to my own thoughts. I told them I was off to Ruddle's place and would return later that afternoon. On my way out, I heard a hissing from down the hallway. Tammy, wearing bra and panties, waved to me and retreated toward the bedroom, stopping near the door.

"Is your friend going to stay?" she asked in a stage whisper.

"For a while."

She frowned. "Well, I don't know."

"You don't know what?"

"We didn't bargain on a four-way, especially with another woman."

"You got something against women? It didn't look like you did."

Tammy didn't catch my drift and I told her what I had witnessed.

"That's different," she said primly.

"Would more money help?"

She perked up. "Money always helps."

"I'm going out now, but I'll take care of you. I promise?"

"Okay!" She stood on tip-toe and kissed my cheek.

"One more thing," I said. "Jo's kind of shy, but once you start her up, she's a tigress."

"I bet." Tammy shivered with delight. "Those long legs!"

"So in a few minutes why don't you...maybe the both of you. Why don't you go out there and warm her up? She really loves intimate touching. You know what I mean? She likes to be fondled. She may object at first, but stay with it and she'll melt. I'll get you your money. Deal?"

"Deal! Don't worry. We'll get her going."

"I'm sure you will," I said.

▲▼▲

The one salient thing I learned at Ruddle's was that a pier extended out about a hundred feet into the water from a strip of beach, and at the end of the pier was moored a sleek white Chris Craft that had been set up for sports fishing—the keys to the boat, the *Mystery Girl*, were kept in a small room off the kitchen that also contained the controls to the security system. The house itself was a postcard. Big and white and ultra-modern, it looked like the Chris Craft's birth mother. An Olympic-sized pool fronted the beach, tennis courts were off to the side. The grounds were a small nation of landscaped palms and airbrushed lawn, its borders defined by a decorous electric fence topped with razor wire and guarded by a pink gatehouse with a uniform on duty. There was a plaque on the gate announcing that the whole shebang was called *The Sea Ranch*, but it would have been more apt if it had been named *The Sea What I Got*.

Ruddle's son showed me around—a blond super-preppie with a Cracker accent that had acquired a New Englander gloss. During our brief time together he said both "y'all" and "wicked haahd," as if he hadn't decided which act suited him best. He was impatient to get back to his tanned, perfect girlfriend, an aspiring young coke whore clearly high on more than life. She sat by the pool, listening to reggae, painting faces on her toenails, and flashed me an addled smile that gave me a contact high. I made sure to ask the kid a slew of inane questions ("Is that door sealed with a double gromit?" "What kind of infrared package does that sensor use?"), delaying and stalling in order to annoy him until, growing desperate, he gave me the run of the house and scurried back to her side.

The card room could be isolated from the remainder of the house. It had no windows and soundproofed walls, a bar, and, against the rear wall, three trophy cases celebrating Ruddle's skill at poker. The place of honor was held by a ring won at a World Series of Poker circuit tournament in Tunica, Mississippi. It was flanked by several photographs of Ruddle with poker notables, Phil Ivey and Chris "Jesus" Ferguson and the like, who were apparently among those he had defeated. I was inspecting the table, an elegance of teak and emerald felt lit by a hanging lamp, when a lean, long-haired, thirtyish man in cut-offs walked in, holding an apple, and asked in a Eurotrash accent what I was doing. I told him I was casing the joint.

"No, no!" He wagged a finger at me. "This is not good...the drugs."

I explained that "casing the joint" meant I was looking the house over, seeing whether it would be possible to burglarize it.

He took a bite of his apple and, after chewing, said, "I am Torsten. And you are?"

I thought he had misunderstood me again, but when I had introduced myself, he said, "You have chosen a bad time. There will be many here this weekend. Many guards, many guests."

"How many guards?" I asked.

"Perhaps five...six." He fingered the edge of the table. "This is excellent work."

"Are you a friend of the family?"

"Yes, of course. Torsten is everyone's friend." He strolled around the table, trailing a hand across the felt, and said, "Now I must go. I wish you will have success with your crime."

Later that afternoon as I was preparing to leave, sitting in my rental car and making some notes, I spotted him outside the house. He was carrying a Weed Whacker, yelling at an older man who was pruning bushes, speaking without a trace of an accent, cussing in purest American. There might be, I thought, a lesson to be drawn from this incident, but I decided that puzzling it out wasn't worth the effort. While driving back to the hotel, I noticed that a motorcyclist in a helmet with a tinted faceplate was traveling at a sedate rate of speed and keeping behind me. Whenever I slowed, he dropped back or switched lanes, and when I parked in the hotel lot, he placed a call on his cell phone. Aggravated and wanting to convey that feeling, I walked toward him, but he kicked over the engine and sped off before I could get near.

A Do Not Disturb card was affixed to the doorknob of the Everglades Suite, so I went down to 1138. Jo, who had been napping, let me in and went into the bathroom to wash her face. I sat at her table and put my feet up. She came back out and lay down on the bed, turned to face me. After I'd briefed her on what I had learned, she said softly, "I'm glad you're back."

"I'm glad you're glad," I said glibly, wondering at the intimacy implied by her tone.

She shut her eyes and I thought for a moment she had drifted off. "I'm afraid," she said.

"Yeah. Me, too."

"You don't act afraid."

"If I let myself think about Saturday, I get to shaking in my boots." I leaned toward her, resting my elbows on my knees. "We got to tough it out."

"I'm not feeling very tough."

I said something neutral and she reached out her hand, inviting me to take it. She caressed my wrist with her fingertip. Holding her hand while sitting on the edge of the chair grew awkward, and I moved to the bed. She curled up against me. I stroked her hair, murmured an assurance, but that seemed insufficient, so I kicked off my shoes and lay down, wrapping my arms around her from behind.

"I'm sorry," she said.

"For what?"

"For how I behaved on the island. For this morning. You must think I'm a terrible tease. But when I see Josey like that, I feel I should comfort him, even though...."

"What?"

She shook her head. "Nothing."

"Say."

Her eyes teared; she pressed my hand against her breast. "It's not him I want to comfort. You know that."

I told her not to cry.

She drew a deep breath, steadying herself. "That's how I was brought up," she said. "I was taught to deny what I wanted, that I had to let it come second to what everyone else wanted."

"It's okay."

"No! It's not! I watched my mother wither away taking care of my daddy, his brothers, of every stray that wandered by. She could scarcely let a second pass without doing something for him. I swore I wouldn't be like her. But I'm exactly like her."

I came to realize that we were less having a conversation than engaging in a litany: she, the priestess, delivering the oration, and I, the acolyte, offering appropriate responses. And as we continued this ritual of confession and assurance, the words served to focus me on the hollow of her throat, the pale skin below her collarbone, the lace trim of a brassiere peeking out between the buttons of her shirt, until the only things in the world were the sound of her voice and the particulars of her body. For all it mattered, she could have been reciting a butcher's list or reading from a manual on automotive maintenance.

"Feeling that way screwed up almost every relationship I ever had," she said. "Because I *didn't* feel that way. Not at heart...not really. It was just a rule I couldn't break. I resented men for making me obey the rule, but they didn't enforce it. I did. I couldn't simply be with them, I couldn't enjoy them. And now I don't care about rules, I finally don't care, and it's too late."

I told her it wasn't too late, we'd pull through somehow.

Dominus vobiscum,

Et cum spiritus tuo.

Tears slipped along the almost imperceptible lines beside her eyes. I propped myself up on an elbow, intending to invoke some further optimistic cliché, wanting to make certain that she had taken it to heart. Lying half-beneath me, searching my face, her expression grew strangely grave, and then her tongue flicked out to taste my mouth, her hips arched against mine. The solicitude, the tenderness I felt...all that was peeled away to reveal a more urgent affinity, and I tore at her clothing, fumbling with buttons, buckle, snaps, rough with her in my hurry. She cried out in abandon, as if suffering the pain of her broken principles. Cities of thought crumbled, my awareness of our circumstance dissolved, and a last snatch of bleak self-commentary captioned my desire—I saw in my mind's eye the image of a red burning thing in a fiery sky, not a true sun but a great shear of light in which was embedded an indistinct shape, like that of a bird flying sideways or a woman's genital smile, and beneath it a low, smoldering wreckage that stretched from horizon to horizon, in which the shadows of men crouched and scuttered and fled with hands clamped to their ears so as to muffle the echoes of an apocalyptic pronouncement.

▲▼▲

We spent that night and most of the next day in 1138. Every so often I would run up and check on Pellerin, but my concern was perfunctory. We stayed in bed through the afternoon and, late in the day, as Jo drowsed beside me, I analyzed what had happened and how we had ended up like this, who had said what and who had done what. Our mutual approach seemed to have been thoroughly crude and awkward, but I thought that, if examined closely, all the axiomatic beams that supported us, the scheme and structure of every being, could be perceived as equally crude and awkward...yet those scraps of physical and emotional poetry of which we were capable could transform the rest into an architecture of Doric elegance and simplicity. The romantic character of the idea cut against my grain, but I couldn't deny it. One touch of her skin could make sense out of stupidity and put the world in right order.

About seven o'clock, simply because we felt we should do something else with the day, we walked down to the strip mall, to the Baskin-Robbins, and sat by the window in the frosty air conditioning. I had two scoops of vanilla; she had a butterscotch sundae. We ate while the high school girls back of the counter listened to the same Fiona Apple song again and again, arguing over the content of the lyrics as if they espoused an abstruse dialectic. Jo and I talked, or rather I talked and she questioned me about my childhood. I told her my father had been a saxophone player in New Orleans and that my mother had run off when I was seven, leaving me in his care. Jo remarked that this must have been hard on me, and I said, "He wasn't much of a dad. I spent a lot of time running the streets. He was primarily concerned with dope and women, but when he was in the mood, he could be fun. He taught me to play sax and guitar, and made up songs for me and got me to learn them. I could have done worse."

"Do you remember the songs?"

"Bits and pieces."

"Let's hear one!"

After considerable persuasion, I tapped out a rhythm on the tabletop and sang in a whispery voice:

> *"I said, Hey, hey! Devil get away!*
> *Get a move on, boy...*
> *I'll lay the saint's ray on ya.*
> *Shake a calabash skull,*
> *Make the sign of the jay...*
> *Don't you give me no trouble,*
> *or as sure as you're born,*
> *I'll make you jump now, Satan,*
> *'cause I got your shinbone."*

"They most of them were like that one," I said. "The old man was a bear for religion. He'd haul me down to the temple once or twice a week and have me anointed with some remedy or another."

"I can picture you singing that when you were a little boy," she said. "You must have been cute."

In the darkened parking lot, I saw the black car I had noticed a few days earlier, the occupants invisible behind smoked glass. The sight banished my nostalgia. I asked Jo what she had told Pellerin the previous day when she talked to him about Ogoun Badagris.

"I told him about Donnell," she said.

"About the big copper *veve* and all?"

"Yes." She licked the bottom of her spoon.

"How about your theory? About the Ezawa process being an analogue of possession. You tell him about that?"

"I couldn't lie to him anymore."

"What'd he say?"

"He was depressed. I told him if we got out of this situation, he'd live a long time. Long enough to understand everything that was happening to him. That depressed him even more. He said that didn't motivate him to want to live that long. I tried to cheer him up, but...." She pinned me with a stern look. "Did you sic those girls on me?"

"What girls?" I asked innocently.

"You know which ones."

"I was pissed at you. I'm over it now, but I was seriously pissed."

"Then you would have been delighted by my reaction." She dabbed at her lips with a napkin. "Once they came in, that was it for the conversation."

"So y'all had some fun, did you?"

"Maybe," she said, drawing out the first syllable of the word, giving it a playful reading. "I thought the dark-haired girl was very attractive. You never know, do you, when love will strike?"

"Is that right?"

"Mm-hmm. Think I should have gotten her number?"

"We could invite her on the honeymoon, if you want."

"Is that what we're having? A honeymoon?"

"It might have to do for one," I said.

Not long afterward, we left the Baskin-Robbins and, as we crossed the lot, I noticed a motorcyclist, the same one, judging by his bike, who had tailed me the day before. He was parked about ten slots down from the black car. I thought Billy must be getting paranoid, now that he was close to his goal, and had doubled up on security. We walked along the shoulder through the warm black night. Moths whirled under the arc lamps like scraps of pale ash. Jo's shampoo overbore the bitter scents of the roadside weeds. She slipped a hand into mine and by that simple gesture charged me with confidence. Despite the broken paths we had traveled to reach this night, this sorry patch of earth, I believed we had arrived at our appointed place.

▲▼▲

There was some talk that we should approach Ruddle prior to the game, but I convinced Pellerin and Jo that the wisest course was to wait until we had a better idea of the connection between Ruddle and Billy Pitch. We held a strategy session before the limo picked us up, but since our strategy was basically to throw ourselves on Ruddle's mercy, the meeting was more-or-less a pep rally. Pellerin, however, was beyond pepping up. As Jo and I led the cheers, he glumly flipped through channels on the TV and, instead of his usual pre-game ritual of slamming drinks, sipped bottled water.

During the drive, Pellerin sat with a suitcase full of cash between his legs, flipping the handle back and forth, creating a repetitive clicking noise that I found irritating. I rested my eyes on Jo. She had on the black cocktail dress that she wore the first time I saw her. Whenever she caught me looking, her smile flickered on, but would quickly dissolve and she would return to gazing out the window. I managed to sustain my confidence by rehearsing what I intended to say to Ruddle. But as we pulled past the gatehouse and the lights of that enormous house floated up against the dark, like a spaceship waiting to take on abductees, I felt a tightness in my throat and, the second we stepped through the door, I realized that Plan A was out the window and, probably, Plan B as well. Standing with a group of middle-aged-to-elderly men at the entrance to the living room, wearing what looked to be powder blue lounging pajamas, was Billy Pitch. Clayton was not in evidence, but close by Billy's shoulder stood a lanky individual with a prominent Adam's apple and close-cropped gray hair and a cold, angular hillbilly face. I recognized him from New Orleans—Alan Goess, a contract killer. Clayton, I assumed, was too showy an item for Billy to take on a trip. Seven or eight young men in private security uniforms waited off to one side, watching their elders with neutral expressions, but contempt was evident in their body language.

Ruddle steered Pellerin away and introduced him to the other players, who were dressed in clothes that appeared to have been bought from the same Palm Beach catalog. Clad in burgundy, olive, nectarine, coral, aqua, and plum, they bore a passing resemblance to migratory birds from different flocks gathered around a feeder. He introduced Billy as an old friend, not a player.

"Not a *poker* player, anyway," said Billy, giving Pellerin's hand a three-fingered shake.

Goess's eyes licked Jo head to toe. She didn't seem as anxious as I would have thought, or else she kept her anxiety contained. With Goess in the picture, my best guess was that Billy planned to humiliate Ruddle, then kill him. Whatever his plans, the odds against our surviving the evening had lengthened. I tried to think of an out, but nothing came to me. Ruddle shepherded us across the living room, a considerable acreage with a high ceiling, carpeted in a swirly blue pattern that was interrupted now and again by a sofa grouping or a stainless steel abstract sculpture—it reminded me of the showroom of an upscale car dealer, minus the cars. I wanted to cut Pellerin out of the herd and tell him about Goess, but the opportunity did not arise.

A dealer had been brought in for the occasion, a motherly brunette carrying some extra pounds, dressed in a tuxedo shirt and slacks; a thin, sleek Cubano was behind the bar, dispensing drinks with minimal comment. Some of the men seemed to have a prior relationship with the dealer; they cracked jokes at her expense, addressing her as Kim. Goess and Billy took chairs on opposite sides of the central trophy case, separating themselves from each other, and from Jo and I, who sat in the corner, with Pellerin facing us at the table. Once everyone was settled and a few last pleasantries observed, Kim said, "The game is Texas Hold 'Em, gentlemen. No Limit. The buy-in is five hundred thousand. Play will run until eight AM, unless an extension is agreed upon. If you go bust, you can make a second buy-in, but not a third."

The buy-ins commenced, cash being traded for chips. The cash was placed in a lockbox and then wheeled off on a luggage cart by two of Ruddle's employees. This done, Kim dealt the first hand.

For the better part of an hour, some chips passed back and forth, but no serious damage was done and the men bantered amiably between hands, telling dumb stories about one another and chortling, huh huh huh, like apes at a grunt festival. As best I could judge, there were two dangerous players apart from Ruddle and Pellerin—a portly man with heavy bags under his eyes by the name of Carl, who rarely spoke other than to raise or check or call, and an ex-jock type with an Alabama accent, his muscles running to fat, whom everybody called Buster and treated with great deference, laughing loudly and long at his anecdotes, though they were none too funny. The remaining four were dead money, working their cards without discernable stratagem or skill.

"We can gossip and trade antes all night," said Ruddle, "but I call that a ladies' bridge tournament, not a poker game."

"I didn't notice you stepping up, Frank," said Pellerin. "You been betting like you playing with your mama's pin money."

The table shared a chuckle.

Ruddle took it good-naturedly, but there was an edge to his smile and I knew he couldn't wait to hurt Pellerin.

Truthfully, my mind was not on the game, but on Billy and Goess. The transfer of the lockbox to the vault made it clear that Billy's true interest did not lie in that direction. My uneasiness intensified and it must have showed, because Jo gave my hand a squeeze. The play remained less than aggressive until, several hands later, Pellerin check-raised Ruddle's bet after the flop by twenty thousand.

"I bid five clubs," he said, causing another outburst of laughter.

Having watched him play every day at the Seminole Paradise, I knew this was a move he had been setting up ever since he arrived in Florida. He'd backed off a lot of players with it in the casino and it usually signified a bluff, something of which Ruddle would be aware. Now, I thought, he might have a hand. The flop was the four of spades, the seven of spades, and the seven of clubs. Pellerin bet another twenty thousand. From the way Ruddle had bet before the flop, I figured him to be holding a second pair, probably queens or better. If Pellerin wasn't bluffing, he might have a third seven. Ruddle, after thinking it over, called the raise. Everyone else got out of the way. The turn card was the queen of hearts. Pellerin pushed out thirty thousand in chips.

"You got the nuts?" Ruddle asked him.

"There's one way to find out," said Pellerin.

Ruddle riffled a stack of chips and finally called. "Now we're playing poker," he said.

The river card was the eight of spades. With four spades face up, both men had the possibility of a flush draw.

"I hate to do this to our gracious host, but I'm all in," Pellerin said.

"Call," said Ruddle. He didn't wait for Pellerin to show his hand—he slapped his hole cards down on the table. Ace of diamonds and ace of spades. He had made an ace-high flush.

"You got the high flush, all right." Pellerin turned over his cards. "But mine's all in a row."

His hole cards were the five and six of spades, filling an eight-high straight flush.

The other players responded with shocked "Damns!" and "Holy craps!" Having lost close to half a million on the turn of a card, when there were only a couple of hands that could have beaten him, four sevens or a gutshot straight flush, Ruddle was speechless. Pellerin had been lucky, but he had played the hand so that if the cards were friendly, he was in position to take advantage.

"If you'd re-raised on the turn, I would have folded. Shit, all I had was a draw." Pellerin began to stack his winnings. "Who was it said Hold 'Em's a science, but No Limit is an art? I must be one hell of an artist." He waved at the bartender. "Jack Black on the rocks. A double."

I expected Billy to be angry that Pellerin had moved on Ruddle so early in the evening, and I scrunched down so I could see him through the glass of the trophy case. He was sitting placidly, as if watching an episode of *The Amazing Race*, but I detected a little steam in the way his neck was bowed. Jo caught my eye and we exchanged a disconcerted vibe.

"Yes sir," Pellerin said expansively. "You might have whupped a bunch of Leroys and Jim Bobs down in Tunica, but this here's a different world, Frank."

Ruddle stood and, walking stiffly, left the room. Some of the other gamblers followed him, doubtless to commiserate over the bad beat.

Kim called for a short break, and Billy stepped over to me and whispered, "What's he doing?"

"I'll find out," I said.

Billy's nose was an inch from my face—I could smell his breath mints. "I want the bastard to suffer! You tell him that!"

He went to join the commiserators. I pulled Pellerin aside and told him Billy was upset.

"He'll get his pound of flesh," said Pellerin. "This'll make it easier to manage the game. Ruddle will play tight for a while, and that gives me time to clear out the garbage."

"Don't do anything stupid," I whispered. "The guy in the camel blazer's a hired killer. I know him from New Orleans. Alan Goess."

"Is he? No lie?" His eyes flicked toward Goess and he smiled. "Hey, guy!" he said to Goess. "How they hanging?"

For a split-second, the real Alan Goess came out from behind his rattlesnake deadboy guise, and I got a hint of his underlying madness; then the curtain closed and he said, "I'm doing well. So are you, from the looks of things."

"Looks can be deceiving," said Pellerin. "Yea, I am a troubled soul, but a firm believer in the Light and the Resurrection. How about yourself?"

"'Fraid not," said Goess. "I've never yet seen anyone come back."

"You just think you haven't," Pellerin said, and would have said more, but I hustled him out of the room and told him not to screw around with Goess.

"I got it under control, boss," he said. "I know exactly what I'm doing."

In the living room, Billy was having a chat with Carl, and Buster had cornered Jo. The other players were huddled up around Ruddle, patting him on the back, saying that Pellerin had been lucky, encouraging him to get back in the game. I gazed out the window toward the *Mystery Girl*, floating serene and white under the dock lights, impossibly distant.

Ruddle had had more chips than Pellerin, so the beat hadn't wiped him out; but he didn't have enough left to compete and he made a second buy-in of a quarter-million. The game resumed, albeit with a less convivial atmosphere. The room, small already, seemed to have shrunk and the men sat hunched and quietly tense under the hanging lamp. Conversation was at a minimum...except for Pellerin. He drank heavily and whenever he won a pot he'd offer up a disparaging comment, engaging the ire of one and all. After taking forty grand off Buster, he said, "Where'd you learn poker, old son? From some guy named Puddin' in the jock dorm?"

Buster said, "Why don't you shut up and play cards?"

This notion was seconded by some of the others.

"In case you didn't notice, I'm playing cards," said Pellerin. "Damned if I can figure out what you're playing."

When Buster won a pot at his expense, he said, "Jesus must love a hillbilly fool."

I had to admire Pellerin. Though he had a distinct advantage in the game, it took great skill to manipulate the fortunes of six other poker players. Ruddle gradually built his stack, winning back the majority of the chips he had lost. His mood grew sunnier and he began to joke around with the table, but when involved in a hand with Pellerin, he was barely civil, speaking brusquely if at all. By one o'clock, two lesser players had been driven out and another was teetering on the brink, down a quarter of a million, pushing in antes and mucking his cards hand-after-hand. At three-thirty, Buster decided to cut his losses and withdrew.

"Thanks for the contribution, Busted...I mean, Buster," said Pellerin, grinning hugely. "We going to miss you, sure enough."

Kim called for another break and everyone made for a buffet that had been set up in the living room. Billy gave me a thumbs-up before heading over to the food. Standing apart from the rest, I told Jo about Goess and said that we had better do something soon or else I didn't like our chances.

"I thought we were going to wait until the last minute," she said.

"Far as I can see, this is the last minute."

She seemed amazingly calm. "I have go to the restroom. Just wait, okay? Don't do anything."

I watched her cross the living room, her long legs working the dress, hips rolling under the silky fabric, and then went back into the card room, where Pellerin was playing with his chips.

"If you've got something in mind," I said, "now might be the time to try it."

"Right now?"

"Whenever you see an opening."

He nodded. "All right. Y'all be ready. I'll give you a warning beforehand." He picked up a stack of chips and let them dribble through his fingers. "Life ain't never as sweet as it appears," he said.

"What that supposed to mean?"

"Just my personal philosophy."

"Fuck a bunch of personal philosophy. Get your mind right! Okay? When it comes time, I'll handle Goess."

"You take care of Billy. Leave Goess to me."

"You think you up to it?"

"It's a done deal," he said.

"What are you going to do?"

He spread the deck of cards face-up on the table and started nudging out the painted cards with the tip of his forefinger.

"Tell me!" I said.

"I believe I may have to violate his personal space," said Pellerin.

I would have inquired of him further, but people began to wander back into the card room, carrying plates of food. Ruddle, Kim and Carl took their places at the table. Jo patted my arm and gave me a steady look that said everything's okay, but it was not okay and she knew it...unless she had slipped gears and gone to Jesus. Billy, Goess, and a straggler came in. I sought to make eye contact with Billy, but he stared straight ahead. The game resumed three-handed, with Carl winning a decent pot. Pellerin made his bets blind, not bothering to check his cards, tossing in chips until after the flop, and then folding. As Kim was about to deal a second hand, he stood up and said, "Gentlemen. And ladies. Before we begin what promises to be an exhilarating conclusion to the evening, I'd like to propose a toast."

He lifted his glass. With his left hand, I noticed. His right hand was afflicted with a palsy, the fingers making movements that, though they were spasmodic, at the same time seemed strangely deft.

"Frank," Pellerin went on. "You have my deepest gratitude for hosting this lovely occasion. I'd love to stick around and pluck your feathers, but...duty calls. I want to thank you all for being so patient with my abusive personality. Which, I should say, is not entirely my own. It comes to you courtesy of the folks at Darden, where your good health is our good business."

"Are you through?" Ruddle asked.

"In a minute." Pellerin's voice acquired a sarcastic veneer. "To Miz Jocundra Verret. For her ceaseless and unyielding devotion. You'll always be my precious sunflower. And to Jack Lamb, who—sad to say—is probably the closest thing to a friend I have in this world. What are friends for if not to fuck over each other? Huh, Jack?"

"Sit your ass down," said Carl. "You're drunk."

"True enough." Pellerin gestured with his glass, sloshing liquor across the table. "But I'm not done yet."

Billy gave a squawk and leaped from his chair, backing away from Goess. I leaned forward and had a look. Goess's eyes bulged, his hands gripped the arms of the chair, his face was red, glistening with sweat, and his neck was corded. He began to shake, as if in the grip of a convulsion.

"To Mister Alan Goess, who's about to burst into flames!" Pellerin raised his glass high. "And let's not forget Billy Pitch, at whose behest I came here tonight. I hear you like those reality shows, Billy. Are you digging on this one?"

The Cuban bartender had seen enough—he ran from the room. Buster started toward Goess, perhaps thinking he could render assistance, and Pellerin said, "Y'all keep back, now. Combustion's liable to be sudden. Truth is, I suspect he's already dead."

"It's a trick," said Carl. "The guy's faking it."

Pellerin whipped off his sunglasses. "What you think, Tubby? Am I faking this, too?"

Green flashes were plainly visible in his eyes.

Ruddle threw himself back from the table. "Jesus!"

"Not hardly." Pellerin laughed. "You folks familiar with voodoo? No? Better prepare yourself, then. Because voodoo is most definitely in the house."

Everyone in the room was frozen for a long moment, their attention divided between Goess and Pellerin. Goess's skin blistered, the blisters bursting, leaking a clear serum, and then there came a soft *whumpf*, a big pillowy sound, and he began to burn. Pale yellow flames wreathed his body, licking up and releasing an oily smoke. I smelled him cooking. Kim screamed, and people were shouting, crowding together in the doorway, seeking to escape. Billy dipped a hand into his voluminous hip pocket. I grabbed his shoulder, spun him about, and drove my fist into his prunish face, knocking him into a trophy case, shattering the glass. His mouth was bleeding, his scalp was lacerated, but he was still conscious, still trying to extricate something from his pocket. I kicked him in the gut, again in the head, and bent over his inert body, fumbled in the pocket and removed a switchblade and a platinum-and-diamond money clip that pinched a thick fold of bills. The clip was probably worth more than the bills. With millions resting in Ruddle's vault, I felt stupid mugging him for chump change. Jo's hands fluttered about my face. She said something about listening to reason, about waiting, but I was too adrenalized to listen and too anxious to wait. I gave Billy a couple of more kicks that wedged him under the wreckage of the trophy case, and then, shoving Jo ahead of me, glancing back at Goess, who sat sedately now, blackening in the midst of his pyre, I went out into the living room.

Ruddle's security was nowhere to be seen, but Ruddle, Kim, and the rest were bunched together against the picture window, their egress blocked by tracks of waist-high flame that crisscrossed the blue carpet, dividing the room into dozens of neat diamond-shaped sections. It was designer arson, the fire laid out in such a precise pattern, it could have been the work of a performance artist with a gift for pyrotechnics. Beside a burning sofa from which smoke billowed, Pellerin appeared to be orchestrating the flames, conducting their swift, uncanny progress with clever movements of his fingers, sending trains of fire scooting across the floor, adding to his design. I recalled the scorch mark on his bedroom wall. Along with everyone else in this lunatic circumstance, Pellerin had been holding something back. I thought if you could see the entirety of the pattern he was creating, it would be identical to one of the *veves* he had sketched on the napkin that day by the pool. I maneuvered as close to him as I dared and shouted his name. He ignored me, continuing to paint his masterpiece. The fire crackled, snacking on the rug, gnawing on the furniture, yet the noise wasn't sufficiently loud to drown out the cries of Ruddle and his guests. Some were egging on Buster and another guy, who were preparing to pick up a sofa and ram it against the window. I shouted again—again Pellerin ignored me. Bursts of small arms fire, like popcorn popping, sounded from the front of the house.

Billy's people, I told myself.

"Did you hear that?" Jo clutched my arm.

I bellowed at Pellerin. He looked at me from, I'd estimate, twenty-five feet away, and it was not a human look. His features were strained, his lips drawn back, stretched in a delirious expression, part leer and part delighted grin. That's how it seemed, that he had been made happy beyond human measure, transported by the perception of some unnatural pleasure, as if the fire were for him a form of release. I was frightened of him, yet I felt a connection, some emotional tether, and I was afraid *for* him as well. I urged him to come with us, to make a try for the boat. He stared as if he didn't recognize me, and then his smile lost its inhuman wideness.

"Come on, man!" I said. "Let's go!"

He shook his head. "No way."

"What the hell are you doing? You're going to die here!"

His smile dimmed and I thought his resolve was weakening, that he would break through the fences of flame separating us and join us in flight; but all he did was stand there. Behind me, I heard an explosive crash as the window gave way; the gunfire grew louder.

"Listen!" I said. "That's Billy's men out there! You want them to catch you?"

"That ain't Billy! Don't you believe it!" He pointed at Jo. "Ask her!"

Despite the high ceiling, smoke was beginning to fill the room, drifting down around us, and Jo was bent over, coughing.

"This shit isn't working for me." Pellerin seemed to be talking mostly to himself. "It's just not acceptable."

I understood what he meant, but I entreated him once more to come with us. He shook his head again, an emphatic no. Turning his attention to the fire, he performed a series of complex gestures. The latticework of flames surrounding us appeared to bend away from his fingers and a path opened, leading toward the kitchen. The heat was growing intolerable—I had no choice but to abandon him. My arm around Jo's waist, I started along the path, but she panicked, fighting against me, scratching my face and slapping the side of my head. I hit her on the point of the jaw, picked her up in a fireman's carry as she sagged, and broke into a stumbling run.

The sky was graying as I emerged from the house and staggered across the lawn; the *Mystery Girl* lurched in my vision with each step, appearing to recede at first, as though I were on a treadmill that kept carrying me backwards. The small arms fire had intensified—at least a dozen weapons were involved. I had no idea what was happening, and not much of an idea where I was going. If the boat had gas, I thought I would head north and search for the entrance to the intercoastal waterway, try and make it to Tampa where I had friends. But if Billy had survived, Tampa would not be safe and I didn't know where to go. Not New Orleans, that was for sure. I could have kicked myself for not shooting the scummy little weasel when I had the chance.

The planks resounded to my footsteps as I pounded along the dock, and the smells of creosote and brine hit me like smelling salts. When I reached the *Mystery Girl,* I laid Jo in the stern. She moaned, but didn't wake. I climbed the ladder to the pilot deck, keyed the ignition, and was exultant when the engine turned over. The needle on the fuel gauge swung up to register an almost-full tank. I pulled away from the dock and opened up the throttle. There was a light chop on the water close to shore, but farther out, beyond the sandbar, the surface was smooth and glassy, with gentle swells. Crumbling banks of fog blanketed the sea ahead. Once inside them we'd be safe for a while. I wondered what had gotten into Pellerin, whether it was Ogoun Badagris or simply a madness attaching to having been brought back to life by bacteria that infested your brain and let you use more of it. Maybe there wasn't any difference between the two conditions. Jo's first slow-burner had gone out in much the same way, in the midst of a huge *veve*, so you were led to conclude that some pathology was involved...and yet it might be the pathology of a god trapped in a human body. I remembered how he'd smiled, leering at his fiery work, and how that smile had planed seamlessly down into a human expression, as if the man he was had merely been the god diminished by the limitations of the flesh.

I cleared my mind of ontological speculation and focused on practical matters, but when I tried to think what we were going to do once we reached Tampa, it was like trying to walk on black ice and I wound up staring at the flat gray sea, listening to the pitch of the engine. I zoned out and began to think about Pellerin again. Formless thoughts, the kind you have when you're puzzled by something to the point that you can't even come up with a question to ask and are reduced to searching the database, hoping that some fact will provoke one.

I had all but forgotten about Jo and when she called out to me, I turned toward the sound of her voice, full of concern. She came scrambling up the ladder and, once she had solid footing, she told me to cut the engines, having to shout to make herself heard. The wind lashed her hair about, and she held it in place with one hand.

"Are you crazy?" I gestured at the fog bank. "Once we're into the fog, we'll be okay."

"We'll never get away! If I thought we could, I'd go with you. You know that, don't you?"

"You are going with me," I said. "What's the problem?"

She didn't answer, and I glanced over at her. She had moved away from me and was standing with her legs apart, aiming a small automatic with a silver finish. A .28 caliber Barretta. With that black cocktail dress on, she might have stepped out of a Bond movie. She had to be wearing a thigh holster. The unreality of it all tickled me and I couldn't repress a laugh.

"Where'd you get that thing?" I asked her. "Out of a cereal box?" She fired, and a bullet dug a furrow in the control console an inch from my hand.

I recoiled from the console. "Christ!"

"I'm sorry," she said.

She looked sorry. Her make-up was mussed. The heat of the fire had caused her to sweat, and sweat had dragged a mascara shadow from the corner of her eye, simulating a tear. She told me again to cut the engines, and this time I complied. The boat lifted on a light swell. I heard the faint cries of seagulls—they sounded like the baying of tiny, trebly hounds. I heard another noise, then. Two dark blue helicopters were approaching from the south.

"Who the hell is that?" I shouted.

"Calm down. Please! This is...." The wind drifted hair across her face; she brushed it aside and said weakly, "It's the only way. They're relentless, they keep coming after you."

"You did this? You told them where we were?"

"They always knew! They never went away! Don't you get it?"

"You knew the whole time? Why didn't you tell me?"

"I didn't know. Not for sure, not at first. And what good would it have done? You didn't listen to Doctor Crain."

"I would have listened to you," I said.

One of the helicopters positioned itself off the port side of the *Mystery Girl*; the side door had been slid back and someone in harness sat in the opening. I couldn't see what he was doing. The other helicopter hovered above the boat. A gilt script D was painted on the nacelle.

"I love you, Jack," Jo said.

"Yeah, uh-huh."

"I do! Back at the hotel...they contacted me. They were going to step in, but I convinced them to keep the experiment going."

"The experiment. This was an experiment?"

"I told them we might learn more about Josey if he went through with the game. Maybe that was wrong of me, but I wanted some time with you."

I was unable to line up all the trash she'd told me about her mother, how it had warped her, with her capacity for betrayal. Yet what she had said smacked of a childish willfulness and a clinical dispatch that, I realized, functioned as a tag-team in her personality. Until that moment, I had not understood how dangerous these qualities made her.

"I can lose them in the fog," I said.

"You can't. You don't know them."

"I'm damn well going to try. You think they'll let me go after what I've seen? They just wiped out twenty people!"

"I'm sure they didn't kill them all."

"Oh...well. Fuck! That's all right, then."

I punched in the ignition; the engine sputtered and caught, rumbling smoothly.

"Don't, Jack! Please!"

"I'm fucking dead if they catch me. Do you understand? I am dead!"

The barrel of the automatic wavered.

"You're not going to shoot me," I said.

I pushed the throttle forward. Jo said again, "Don't," and I felt a blow to my back, a wash of pain. I was out of it for a while, and when I was able to gather my senses, I found myself lying on the deck, with my head jammed up against the base of the control console. I knew I'd been shot, but it felt like the bullet had come from something larger than a .28. The guy in the harness, maybe. I was hurting some, but a numb feeling was setting in. It was a chore to concentrate. My thoughts kept slipping away. Jo knelt beside me. I locked on to her face. Looking at her steadied me. "Did you..." I said. "Did you shoot...?"

"Don't talk," she said.

Silhouetted against the gray sky, a man was being lowered from the helicopter overhead, along with a metal case that dangled from a hook beside him. It seemed as big as a coffin. The sight confused me visually, and in other ways as well. I closed my eyes against it.

Jo laid a hand on my cheek. The touch cooled the embers of my anger, my disappointment with her, and I was overwhelmed with sentiment. Bits of memory surfaced, whirled, dissolved. She lay down on the deck beside me. She became my sky. Her face hanging above me blotted out the chopper and the man descending.

"I'll take care of you, I promise," she said.

Her brown eyes were all that was holding me. A gurgling came from inside my chest. She started raving, then. Getting angry, swearing vengeance, weeping. It was like she thought I'd passed out, like I wasn't there. Half of it, I didn't understand. She said they would regret what they'd made her do, she'd make certain I remembered everything, and I would help her make them pay. I didn't recognize her, she was so possessed by pain and fury. She laid her head on my chest. I wanted to tell her the weight was oppressive, but I couldn't form the words. The lengths of her hair were drowning me. Her voice, the helicopter rotors, and the fading light merged into a gray tumult, an incoherence.

"Jack..."

▲▼▲

...Jack...

A jolt, as of electricity, to the back of my neck.

Jack...Jack Lamb...

My eyelids fluttered open.

A gray ocean surrounded me, picked out by vague shapes.

Jack Lamb...Jack...

Another jolt, more intense than the first. I tried to move, but I was very weak and I succeeded only in turning my head. Someone passed across my field of vision, accompanied by a perfumey scent. Wanting to catch their notice, I made a scratchy noise in my throat. The effort caused me to pass out.

Jack...

"Jack? Are you awake?" A woman's voice.

"Yeah," I said, my tongue thick, throat raw.

Something was inserted between my lips and a cool liquid soothed the rawness. My chest hurt. My whole body hurt.

"How's that? Better?" The voice had a familiar ring.

"I can't see," I said. "Everything's a blur."

"The doctor says you'll be seeing fine in a few days."

I asked for more water and, after I had drunk, I said, "I know you... don't I?"

"Of course. Jocundra...Jo." A pause. "Your partner. We live together. Don't you remember?"

"I think. Yeah."

"You've been through a terrible ordeal. Your memory will be hazy for a while."

"What happened to me?"

"You were shot. The important thing is, you're going to be fine."

"Who shot me? Why...what happened?"

"I'll tell you soon. I promise. You don't need the stress now."

"I want to know who shot me!"

"You have to trust me," she said, placing a hand on my chest. "There's psychological damage as well as physical. We have to go cautiously. I'll tell you when you're strong enough. Won't you trust me 'til then?"

I asked her to come closer.

Something swam toward me through the gray. I made out a crimson mouth and enormous brown eyes. Gradually, the separate features resolved into a face that, though blurred, was indisputably open and lovely.

"You're beautiful," I said.

"Thank you." A pause. "It's been a while since you told me that."

Her face withdrew. I couldn't find her in the murk. Anxious, I called out. "I'm here," she said. "I'm just getting something."

"What?"

"Cream to rub on your chest and shoulders. It'll make you feel better."

She sat on the bed—I felt the mattress indent—and she began massaging me. Each caress gave me a shock, albeit gentler than the ones I had felt initially. Soft hands spread the cream across my chest and I began to relax, to feel repentant that I had neglected her. I offered apology for doing so, saying that I must have been preoccupied.

Her lips brushed my forehead. "It's okay. Actually, I'm hopeful...."

"Hopeful? About what?"

"It's nothing."

"No, tell me."

"I'm hoping some good will come of all this," she said. "We've been having our problems lately. And I hope this time we spend together, while you recuperate, it'll make you remember how much I love you."

I groped for her hand, found it. We stayed like that a while, our fingers mixing together. A white shape melted up from the grayness. I strained to identify it and realized it was her breast sheathed in white cloth.

"I'm up here," she said, laughter in her voice, and leaned closer so I could see her face again. "Do you feel up to answering a few questions? The doctor said I should test your memory. So we can learn if there's been any significant loss."

"Yeah, okay. I'm feeling more together now."

I heard papers rustling and asked what she was doing.

"They gave me some questions to ask. I can't find them." More rustling. "Here they are. The first one's a gimmee. Do you recall your name?"

"Jack," I said confidently. "Jack Lamb."

"And what do you do? Your profession?"

I opened my mouth, ready to spit out the answer. When nothing came to me, I panicked. I probed around in the gray nothing that seemed to have settled over my brain, beginning to get desperate. She touched the inside of my wrist, a touch that left a trail of sparkling sensation on my skin, and told me not to force it. And then I saw the answer, saw it as clearly as I might see a shining coin stuck in silt at the bottom of a well, the first of a horde of memories waiting to be unearthed, a treasure of anecdote and event.

Firmly, and with a degree of pride as befitted my station, I said, "I'm a financier." —

Stars Seen Through Stone

I was smoking a joint on the steps of the public library when a cold wind blew in from no cardinal point, but from the top of the night sky, a force of pure perpendicularity that bent the sparsely leaved boughs of the old alder shadowing the steps straight down toward the earth, as if a gigantic someone above were pursing his lips and aiming a long breath directly at the ground. For the duration of that gust, fifteen or twenty seconds, my hair did not flutter but was pressed flat to the crown of my head and the leaves and grass and weeds on the lawn also lay flat. The phenomenon had a distinct border—leaves drifted along the sidewalk, testifying that a less forceful, more fitful wind presided beyond the perimeter of the lawn. No one else appeared to notice. The library, a blunt nineteenth-century relic of undressed stone, was not a popular point of assembly at any time of day, and the sole potential witness apart from myself was an elderly gentleman who was hurrying toward McGuigan's Tavern at a pace that implied a severe alcohol dependency. This happened seven months prior to the events central to this story, but I offer it to suggest that a good deal of strangeness goes unmarked by the world (at least by the populace of Black William, Pennsylvania), and, when taken in sum, such occurrences may be evidence that strangeness is visited upon us with some regularity and we only notice its extremes.

Ten years ago, following my wife's graduation from Princeton Law, we set forth in our decrepit Volvo, heading for northern California, where we hoped to establish a community of sorts with friends who had moved to that region the previous year. We chose to drive on blue highways for their scenic value and decided on a route that ran through Pennsylvania's Bittersmith Hills, knuckled chunks of coal and granite, forested with leafless oaks and butternut, ash and elder, that—under heavy snow and threatening skies—composed an ominous prelude to the smoking red-brick town nestled in their heart. As we approached Black William, the Volvo began to rattle, the engine died, and we coasted to a stop on a curve overlooking a forbidding vista: row houses the color of dried blood huddled together along the wend of a sluggish, dark river (the Polozny), visible through a pall of gray smoke that settled from the chimneys of a sprawling prisonlike edifice—also of brick—on the opposite shore. The Volvo proved to be a total loss. Since our funds were limited, we had no recourse other than to find temporary housing and take jobs so as to pay for a new car in which to continue our trip. Andrea, whose specialty was labor law, caught on with a firm involved in fighting for the rights of embattled steelworkers. I hired on at the mill, where I encountered three part-time musicians lacking a singer. This led to that, that to this, Andrea and I grew apart in our obsessions, had affairs, divorced, and, before we realized it, the better part of a decade had rolled past. Though initially I felt trapped in an ugly, dying town, over the years I had developed an honest affection for Black William and its citizens, among whom I came to number myself.

After a brief and perhaps illusory flirtation with fame and fortune, my band broke up, but I managed to build a home recording studio during its existence and this became the foundation of a career. I landed a small business grant and began to record local bands on my own label, Soul Kiss Records. Most of the CDs I released did poorly, but in my third year of operation, one of my projects, a metal group calling themselves Meanderthal, achieved a regional celebrity and I sold management rights and the masters for their first two albums to a major label. This success gave me a degree of visibility and my post office box was flooded with demos from bands all over the country. Over the next six years I released a string of minor successes and acquired an industry-wide reputation of having an eye for talent. It had been my immersion in the music business that triggered the events leading to my divorce and, while Andrea was happy for me, I think it galled her that I had exceeded her low expectations. After a cooling-off period, we had become contentious friends and whenever we met for drinks or lunch, she would offer deprecating comments about the social value of my enterprise, and about my girlfriend, Mia, who was nine years younger than I, heavily tattooed, and—in Andrea's words—dressed "like a color-blind dominatrix."

"You've got some work to do, Vernon," she said once. "You know, on the taste thing? It's like you traded me in for a Pinto with flames painted on the hood."

I stopped myself from replying that it wasn't me who had done the trading in. I understood her comments arose from the fact that she had regrets and that she was angry at herself: Andrea was an altruist and the notion that her renewed interest in me might be partially inspired by envy or venality caused her to doubt her moral legitimacy. She was attractive, witty, slender, with auburn hair and patrician features and a forthright poise that caused men in bars, watching her pass, to describe her as "classy." Older and wiser, able by virtue of the self-confidence I had gained, to cope with her sharp tongue, I had my own regrets; but I thought we had moved past the point at which a reconciliation was possible and refrained from giving them voice.

In late summer of the year when the wind blew straight down, I listened to a demo sent me by one Joseph Stanky of Mckeesport, Pennsylvania. Stanky billed himself as Local Profitt Jr. and his music, post-modern deconstructed blues sung in a gravelly, powerful baritone, struck me as having cult potential. I called his house that afternoon and was told by his mother that "Joey's sleeping." That night, around 3 AM, Stanky returned my call. Being accustomed to the tactless ways of musicians, I set aside my annoyance and said I was interested in recording him. In the course of our conversation, Stanky told me he was twenty-six, virtually penniless, and lived in his mother's basement, maintaining throughout a churlish tone that dimmed my enthusiasm. Nevertheless, I offered to pay his bus fare to Black William and to put him up during the recording process. Two days later, when he stepped off a bus at the Trailways station, my enthusiasm dimmed further. A more unprepossessing human would be difficult to imagine. He was short, pudgy, with skin the color of a new potato and so slump-shouldered that for a moment I thought he might be deformed. Stringy brown hair provided an unsightly frame for a doughy face with a bulging forehead and a wispy soul patch. His white T-shirt was spattered with food stains, a Jackson Pollack work-in-progress; the collar of his windbreaker was stiff with grime. Baggy chinos and a trucker wallet completed his ensemble. I knew this gnomish figure must be Stanky, but didn't approach until I saw him claim two guitar cases from the luggage compartment. When I introduced myself, instead of expressing gratitude or pleasure, he put on a pitiful expression and said in a wheedling manner, "Can you spot me some bucks for cigarettes, man? I ran out during the ride."

I advanced him another hundred, with which he purchased two cartons of Camel Lights and a twelve-pack of Coca-Cola Classic (these, I learned, were basic components of his nutrition and, along with Quaker Instant Grits, formed the bulk of his diet), and took a roundabout way home, thinking I'd give him a tour of the town where he would spend the next few weeks. Stanky displayed no interest whatsoever in the mill, the Revolutionary-era Lutheran Church, or Garnant House (home of the town's founding father), but reacted more positively to the ziggurat at the rear of Garnant House, a corkscrew of black marble erected in eccentric tribute to the founding father's wife, Ethelyn Garnant, who had died in childbirth; and when we reached the small central park where stands the statue of her son, Stanky said, "Hey, that's decent, man!" and asked me to stop the car.

The statue of William Garnant had been labeled an eyesore by the Heritage Committee, a group of women devoted to preserving our trivial past, yet they were forced to include it in their purview because it was the town's most recognizable symbol—gift shops sold replica statuettes and the image was emblazoned on coffee mugs, postcards, paperweights, on every conceivable type of souvenir. Created in the early 1800s by Gunter Hahn, the statue presented Black William in age-darkened bronze astride a rearing stallion, wearing a loose-fitting shirt and tight trousers, gripping the reins with one hand, pointing toward the library with the other, his body twisted and head turned in the opposite direction, his mouth open in—judging by his corded neck—a cry of alarm, as if he were warning the populace against the dangers of literacy. Hahn did not take his cues from the rather sedentary monuments of his day, but, improbably, appeared to have been influenced by the work of heroic comic book artists such as Jim Steranko and Neal Adams, and thus the statue had a more fluid dynamic than was customary...or perhaps he was influenced by Black William himself, for it was he who had commissioned the sculpture and overseen its construction. This might explain the figure's most controversial feature, that which had inspired generations of high school students to highlight it when they painted the statue after significant football victories: thanks to an elevated position in the saddle, Black William's crotch is visible, and, whether intended or an inadvertency, an error in the casting process that produced an unwanted rumple in the bronze, it seems that he possessed quite a substantial package. It always gladdened my heart to see the ladies of the Heritage Committee, embarked upon their annual spring clean-up, scrubbing away with soap and rags at Black William's genital pride.

I filled Stanky in on Black William's biography, telling him that he had fought with great valor in the Revolutionary War, but had not been accorded the status of hero, this due to his penchant for executing prisoners summarily, even those who had surrendered under a white flag. Following the war, he returned home in time to watch his father, Alan Garnant, die slowly and in agony. It was widely held that William had poisoned the old man. Alan resented the son for his part in Ethelyn's death and had left him to be raised by his slaves, in particular by an immense African man to whom he had given the name Nero. Little is known of Nero; if more were known, we might have a fuller understanding of young William, who—from the war's end until his death in 1808—established a reputation for savagery, his specialities being murder and rape (both heterosexual and homosexual). By all accounts, he ruled the town and its environs with the brutal excess of a feudal duke. He had a coterie of friends, who served as his loyal protectors, a group of men whose natures he had perverted, several of whom failed to survive his friendship. Accompanied by Nero, they rode roughshod through the countryside, terrorizing and defiling, killing anyone who sought to impede their progress. Other than that, his legacy consisted of the statue, the ziggurat, and a stubby tower of granite block on the bluff overlooking the town, long since crumbled into ruin.

Stanky's interest dwindled as I related these facts, his responses limited to the occasional "Cool," a word he pronounced as if it had two syllables; but before we went on our way he asked, "If the guy was such a bastard, how come they named the town after him?"

"It was a PR move," I explained. "The town was incorporated as Garnantsburgh. They changed it after World War Two. The city council wanted to attract business to the area and they hoped the name Black William would be more memorable. Church groups and the old lady vote, pretty much all the good Christians, they disapproved of the change, but the millworkers got behind it. The association with a bad guy appealed to their self-image."

"Looks like the business thing didn't work out. This place is deader than Mckeesport." Stanky raised up in the seat to scratch his ass. "Let's go, okay? I couldn't sleep on the bus. I need to catch up on my Zs."

▲▼▲

My house was one of the row houses facing the mill, the same Andrea and I had rented when we first arrived. I had since bought the place. The ground floor I used for office space, the second floor for the studio, and I lived on the third. I had fixed up the basement, formerly Andrea's office, into a musician-friendly apartment—refrigerator, stove, TV, et al—and that is where I installed Stanky. The bus ride must have taken a severe toll. He slept for twenty hours.

After three weeks I recognized that Stanky was uncommonly gifted and it was going to take longer to record him than I had presumed—he kept revealing new facets of his talent and I wanted to make sure I understood its full dimension before getting too deep into the process. I also concluded that although musicians do not, in general, adhere to an exacting moral standard, he was, talent aside, the most worthless human being I had ever met. Like many of his profession, he was lazy, irresponsible, untrustworthy, arrogant, slovenly, and his intellectual life consisted of comic books and TV. To this traditional menu of character flaws, I would add "deviant." The first inkling I had of his deviancy was when Sabela, the Dominican woman who cleaned for me twice a week, complained about the state of the basement apartment. Since Sabela never complained, I had a look downstairs. In less than a week, he had trashed the place. The garbage was overflowing and the sink piled high with scummy dishes and pots half-full of congealed grits; the floors covered in places by a slurry of cigarette ash and grease, littered with candy wrappers and crumpled Coke cans. A smell compounded of spoilage, bad hygiene and sex seemed to rise from every surface. The plastic tip of a vibrator peeked out from beneath his grungy sheets. I assured Sabela I'd manage the situation, whereupon she burst into tears. I asked what else was troubling her and she said, "Mister Vernon, I no want him."

My Spanish was poor, Sabela's English almost non-existent, but after a few minutes I divined that Stanky had been hitting on her, going so far as to grab at her breasts. This surprised me—Sabela was in her forties and on the portly side. I told her to finish with the upstairs and then she could go home. Stanky returned from a run to the 7-11 and scuttled down to the basement, roachlike in his avoidance of scrutiny. I found him watching *Star Trek* in the dark, remote in one hand, *TV Guide* (he called it "The Guide") resting on his lap, gnawing on a Butterfingers. Seeing him so at home in his filthy nest turned up the flame under my anger.

"Sabela refuses to clean down here," I said. "I don't blame her."

"I don't care if she cleans," he said with a truculent air.

"Well, I do. You've turned this place into a shithole. I had a metal band down here for a month, it never got this bad. I want you to keep it presentable. No stacks of dirty dishes. No crud on the floor. And put your damn sex toys in a drawer. Understand?"

He glowered at me.

"And don't mess with Sabela," I went on. "When she wants to clean down here, you clear out. Go up to the studio. I hear about you groping her again, you can hump your way back to Mckeesport. I need her one hell of a lot more than I need you."

He muttered something about "another producer."

"You want another producer? Go for it! No doubt major labels are beating down my door this very minute, lusting after your sorry ass."

Stanky fiddled with the remote and lowered his eyes, offering me a look at his infant bald spot. Authority having been established, I thought I'd tell him what I had in mind for the next weeks, knowing that his objections—given the temper of the moment—would be minimal; yet there was something so repellent about him, I still wanted to give him the boot. I had the idea that one of Hell's lesser creatures, a grotesque, impotent toad, banished by the Powers of Darkness, had landed with a foul stink on my sofa. But I've always been a sucker for talent and I felt sorry for him. His past was plain. Branded as a nerd early on and bullied throughout high school, he had retreated into a life of flipping burgers and getting off on a 4-track in his mother's basement. Now he had gravitated to another basement, albeit one with a more hopeful prospect and a better recording system.

"Why did you get into music?" I asked, sitting beside him. "Women, right? It's always women. Hell, I was married to a good-looking woman, smart, sexy, and that was my reason."

He allowed that this had been his reason as well.

"So how's that working out? They're not exactly crawling all over you, huh?"

He cut his eyes toward me and it was as if his furnace door had slid open a crack, a blast of heat and resentment shooting out. "Not great," he said.

"Here's what I'm going to do." I tapped out a cigarette from his pack, rolled it between my fingers. "Next week, I'm bringing in a drummer and a bass player to work with you. I own a part-interest in the Crucible, the alternative club in town. As soon as you get it together, we'll put you in there for a set and showcase you for some people."

Stanky started to speak, but I beat him to the punch. "You follow my lead, you do what I know you can..." I said, leaving a significant pause. "I guarantee you won't be going home alone."

He waited to hear more, he wanted to bask in my vision of his future, but I knew I had to use rat psychology; now that I had supplied a hit of his favorite drug, I needed to buzz him with a jolt of electricity.

"First off," I said, "we're going to have to get you into shape. Work off some of those man-tits."

"I'm not much for exercise."

"That doesn't come as a shock," I said. "Don't worry. I'm not going to make a new man out of you, I just want to make you a better act. Eat what I eat for a month or so, do a little cardio. You'll drop ten or fifteen pounds." Falsely convivial, I clapped him on the shoulder and felt a twinge of disgust, as if I had touched a hypo-allergenic cat. "The other thing," I said. "That Local Profitt Junior name won't fly. It sounds too much like a country band."

"I like it," he said defiantly.

"If you want the name back later, that's up to you. For now, I'm billing you as Joe Stanky."

I laid the unlit cigarette on the coffee table and asked what he was watching, thinking that, for the sake of harmony, I'd bond with him a while.

"*Trek* marathon," he said.

We sat silently, staring at the flickering black-and-white picture. My mind sang a song of commitments, duties, other places I could be. Stanky laughed, a cross between a wheeze and a hiccup.

"What's up?" I asked.

"John Colicos sucks, man!"

He pointed to the screen, where a swarthy man with Groucho Marx eyebrows, pointy sideburns, and a holstered ray gun seemed to be undergoing an agonizing inner crisis. "Michael Ansara's the only real Klingon," Stanky looked at me as if seeking validation. "At least," he said, anxious lest he offend, "on the original *Trek*."

Absently, I agreed with him. My mind rejoined its song. "Okay," I said, and stood. "I got things to do. We straight about Sabela? About keeping the place...you know? Keeping the damage down to normal levels?"

He nodded.

"Okay. Catch you later."

I started for the door, but he called to me, employing that wheedling tone with which I had become all too familiar. "Hey, Vernon?" he said. "Can you get me a trumpet?" This asked with an imploring expression, screwing up his face like a child, as if he were begging me to grant a wish.

"You play the trumpet?"

"Uh-huh."

"If you promise to take care of it. Yeah, I can get hold of one."

Stanky rocked forward on the couch and gave a tight little fist-pump. "Decent!"

I don't know when Stanky and I got married, but it must have been sometime between the incident with Sabela and the night Mia went home to her mother. Certainly my reaction to the latter was more restrained than was my reaction to the former, and I attribute this in part to our union having been joined. It was a typical rock and roll marriage: talent and money making beautiful music together and doomed from the start, on occasion producing episodes in which the relationship seemed to be crystallized, allowing you to see (if you wanted to) the messy bed you had made for yourself.

Late one evening, or maybe it wasn't so late—it was starting to get dark early—Mia came downstairs and stepped into my office and set a smallish suitcase on my desk. She had on a jacket with a fake fur collar and hood, tight jeans, and her nice boots. She'd put a fresh raspberry streak in her black hair and her make-up did a sort of Nefertiti-meets-Liza thing. All I said was, "What did I do this time?"

Mia's lips pursed in a moue—it was her favorite expression and she used it at every opportunity, whether appropriate or not. She would become infuriated when I caught her practicing it in the bathroom mirror.

"It's not what you did," she said. "It's that clammy little troll in the basement."

"Stanky?"

"Do you have another troll? Stanky! God, that's the perfect name for him." Another moue. "I'm sick of him rubbing up against me."

Mia had, as she was fond of saying, "been through some stuff," and, if Stanky had done anything truly objectionable, she would have dealt with him. I figured she needed a break or else there was someone in town with whom she wanted to sleep.

"I take it this wasn't consensual rubbing," I said.

"You think you're so funny! He comes up behind me in tight places. Like in the kitchen. And he pretends he has to squeeze past."

"He's in our kitchen?"

"You send him up to use the treadmill, don't you?"

"Oh…right."

"And he has to get water from the fridge, doesn't he?"

I leaned back in the chair and clasped my hands behind my head. "You want me to flog him? Cut off a hand?"

"Would that stop it? Give me a call when he's gone, okay?"

"You know I will. Say hi to mom."

A final moue, a moue that conveyed a *soupçon* of regret, but—more pertinently—made plain how much I would miss her spoonful of sugar in my coffee.

After she had gone, I sat thinking non-specific thoughts, vague appreciations of her many virtues, then I handicapped the odds that her intricate make-up signaled an affair and decided just how pissed-off to be at Stanky. I shouted downstairs for him to come join me and dragged him out for a walk into town.

A mile and a quarter along the Polozny, then up a steep hill, would bring you to the park, a triangular section of greenery (orange-and-brownery at that time of year) bordered on the east by the library, on the west by a row of brick buildings containing gentrified shops, and, facing the point of the triangle, by McGuigan's. For me alone, it was a brisk half-hour walk; with Stanky in tow, it took an extra twenty minutes. He was not one to hide his discomfort or displeasure. He panted, he sagged, he limped, he sighed. His breathing grew labored. The next step would be his last. Wasn't it enough I forced him to walk three blocks to the 7-11? If his heart failed, drop his bones in a bucket of molten steel and ship his guitars home to Mckeesport, where his mother would display them, necks crossed, behind the urn on the mantle.

These comments went unvoiced, but they were eloquently stated by his body language. He acted out every nuance of emotion, like a child showing off a new skill. Send him on an errand he considered important and he would give you his best White Rabbit, head down, hustling along on a matter of urgency to the Queen. Chastise him and he would play the penitent altar boy. When ill, he went with a hand clutching his stomach or cheek or lower back, grimacing and listless. His posturing was so pitifully false, it was disturbing to look at him. I had learned to ignore these symptoms, but I recognized the pathology that bred them—I had seen him, thinking himself unwatched, slumped on the couch, clicking the remote, the Guide spread across his lap, mired in the quicksand of depression, yet more arrogant than depressed, a crummy king forsaken by his court, desperate for admirers.

On reaching the library, I sat on a middle step and fingered out a fatty from my jacket pocket. Stanky collapsed beside me, exhausted by the Polozny Death March he had somehow survived. He flapped a hand toward McGuigan's and said, hopefully, "You want to get a beer?"

"Maybe later."

I fired up the joint.

"Hey!" Stanky said. "We passed a cop car on the hill, man."

"I smoke here all the time. As long as you don't flaunt it, nobody cares."

I handed him the joint. He cupped the fire in his palm, smoking furtively. It occurred to me that I wouldn't drink from the same glass as him—his gums were rotting, his teeth horribly decayed—but sharing a joint? What the hell. The air was nippy and the moon was hidden behind the alder's thick leaves, which had turned but not yet fallen. Under an arc lamp, the statue of Black William gleamed as if fashioned of obsidian.

"Looks like he's pointing right at us, huh?" said Stanky.

When I was good and stoned, once the park had crystallized into a Victorian fantasy of dark green lawns amid crisp shadows and fountaining shrubs, the storefronts beyond hiding their secrets behind black glass, and McGuigan's ornate sign with its ruby coat of arms appearing to occupy an unreal corner in the dimension next door, I said, "Mia went back to her mom's tonight. She's going to be there for a while."

"Bummer." He had squirreled away a can of Coke in his coat pocket, which he now opened.

"It's normal for us. Chances are she'll screw around on me a little and spend most of the time curled up on her mom's sofa, eating Cocoa Puffs out of the box and watching soaps. She'll be back eventually."

He had a swig of Coke and nodded.

"What bothers me," I said, "is the reason she left. Not the real reason, but the excuse she gave. She claims you've been touching her. Rubbing against her and making like it was an accident."

This elicited a flurry of protests and I-swear-to-Gods. I let him run down before I said, "It's not a big deal."

"She's lying, man! I—"

"Whatever. Mia can handle herself. You cross the line with her, you'll be picking your balls up off the floor."

I could almost hear the gears grinding as he wondered how close he had come to being deballed.

"I want you to listen," I went on. "No interruptions. Even if you think I'm wrong about something. Deal?"

"Sure...yeah."

"Most of what I put out is garbage music. Meanderthal, Big Sissy, The Swimming Holes, Junk Brothers—"

"I love the Junk Brothers, man! They're why I sent you my demo." I gazed at him sternly—he ducked his head and winced by way of apology.

"So rock and roll is garbage," I said. "It's disposable music. But once in a great while, somebody does something perfect. Something that makes the music seem indispensable. I think you can make something perfect. You may not ever get rock star money. I doubt you can be mainstreamed. The best you can hope for, probably, is Tom Waits money. That's plenty, believe me. I think you'll be huge in Europe. You'll be celebrated there. You've got a false bass that reminds me of Blind Willie Johnson. You write tremendous lyrics. That fractured guitar style of yours is unique. It's out there, but it's funky and people are going to love it. You have a natural appeal to punks and art rockers. To rock geeks like me. But there's one thing can stop you—that's your problem with women."

Not even this reference to his difficulties with Sabela and Mia could disrupt his rapt attentiveness.

"You can screw this up very easily," I told him. "You let that inappropriate touching thing of yours get out of hand, you *will* screw it up. You have to learn to let things come. To do that, you have to believe in yourself. I know you've had a shitty life so far, and your self-esteem is low. But you have to break the habit of thinking that you're getting over on people. You don't need to get over on them. You've got something they want. You've got talent. People will cut you a ton of slack because of that talent, but you keep messing up with women, their patience is going to run out. Now I don't know where all that music comes from, but it doesn't sound like it came from a basement. It's a gift. You have to start treating it like one."

I asked him for a cigarette and lit up. Though I'd given variations of the speech dozens of times, I bought into it this time and I was excited.

"Ten days from now you'll be playing for a live audience," I said. "If you put in the work, if you can believe in yourself, you'll get all you want of everything. And that's how you do it, man. By putting in the work and playing a kick-ass set. I'll help any way I can. I'm going to do publicity, T-shirts…and I'm going to give them away if I have to. I'm going to get the word out that Joe Stanky is something special. And you know what? Industry people will listen, because I have a track record." I blew a smoke ring and watched it disperse. "These are things I won't usually do for a band until they're farther along, but I believe in you. I believe in your music. But you have to believe in yourself and you have to put in the work."

I'm not sure how much of my speech, which lasted several minutes more, stuck to him. He acted inspired, but I couldn't tell how much of the act was real; I knew on some level he was still running a con. We cut across the park, detouring so he could inspect the statue again. I glanced back at the library and saw two white lights shaped like fuzzy asterisks. At first I thought they were moving across the face of the building, that some people were playing with flashlights; but their brightness was too sharp and erratic, and they appeared to be coming from behind the library, shining through the stone, heading toward us. After ten or fifteen seconds, they faded from sight. Spooked, I noticed that Stanky was staring at the building and I asked if he had seen the lights.

"That was weird, man!" he said. "What was it?"

"Swamp gas. UFOs. Who knows?"

I started walking toward McGuigan's and Stanky fell in alongside me. His limp had returned.

"After we have those beers, you know?" he said.

"Yeah?"

"Can we catch a cab home?" His limp became exaggerated. "I think I really hurt my leg."

▲▼▲

Part of the speech must have taken, because I didn't have to roust Stanky out of bed the next morning. He woke before me, ate his grits (I allowed him a single bowl each day), knocked back a couple of Diet Cokes (my idea), and sequestered himself in the studio, playing adagio trumpet runs and writing on the Casio. Later, I heard the band thumping away. After practice, I caught Geno, the drummer, on his way out the door, brought him into the office and asked how the music was sounding.

"It doesn't blow," he said.

I asked to him to clarify.

"The guy writes some hard drum parts, but they're tasty, you know. Tight."

Geno appeared to want to tell me more, but spaced and ran a beringed hand through his shoulder-length black hair. He was a handsome kid, if you could look past the ink, the brands, and the multiple piercings. An excellent drummer and reliable. I had learned to be patient with him.

"Overall," I said, "how do you think the band's shaping up?"

He looked puzzled. "You heard us."

"Yes. I know what I think. I'm interested in what you think."

"Oh...okay." He scratched the side of his neck, the habitat of a red and black Chinese tiger. "It's very cool. Strong. I never heard nothing like it. I mean, it's got jazz elements, but not enough to where it doesn't rock. The guy sings great. We might go somewhere if he can control his weirdness."

I didn't want to ask how Stanky was being weird, but I did.

"He and Jerry got a conflict," Geno said. "Jerry can't get this one part down, and Stanky's on him about it. I keep telling Stanky to quit ragging him. Leave Jerry alone and he'll stay on it until he can play it backwards. But Stanky, he's relentless and Jerry's getting pissed. He don't love the guy, anyway. Like today, Stanky cracks about we should call the band Stanky and Our Gang."

"No," I said.

"Yeah, right. But it was cute, you know. Kind of funny. Jerry took it personal, though. He like to got into it with Stanky."

"I'll talk to them. Anything else?"

"Naw. Stanky's a geek, but you know me. The music's right and I'm there."

The following day I had lunch scheduled with Andrea. It was also the day that my secretary, Kiwanda, a petite Afro-American woman in her late twenties, came back to work after a leave during which she had been taking care of her grandmother. I needed an afternoon off—I thought I'd visit friends, have a few drinks—so I gave over Stanky into her charge, warning her that he was prone to getting handsy with the ladies.

"I'll keep that in mind," she said, sorting through some new orders. "You go have fun."

Andrea had staked out one of the high-backed booths at the rear of McGuigan's and was drinking a martini. She usually ran late, liked sitting at the front, and drank red wine. She had hung her jacket on the hook at the side of the booth and looked fetching in a cream-colored blouse. I nudged the martini glass and asked what was up with the booze.

"Bad day in court. I had to ask for a continuance. So...." She hoisted the martini. "I'm boozing it up."

"Is this that pollution thing?"

"No, it's a pro bono case."

"Thought you weren't going to do any pro bono work for a while."

She shrugged, drank. "What can I say?"

"All that class guilt. It must be tough." I signaled a waitress, pointed to Andrea's martini and held up two fingers. "I suppose I should be grateful. If you weren't carrying around that guilt, you would have married Snuffy Huffington the Third or somebody."

"Let's not banter," Andrea said. "We always banter. Let's just talk. Tell me what's going on with you."

I was good at reading Andrea, but it was strange how well I read her at that moment. Stress showed in her face. Nervousness. Both predictable components. But mainly I saw a profound loneliness and that startled me. I'd never thought of her as being lonely. I told her about Stanky, the good parts, his writing, his musicianship.

"The guy plays everything," I said. "Guitar, flute, sax, trumpet. Little piano, little drums. He's like some kind of mutant they produced in a secret high school band lab. And his voice. It's the Jim Nabors effect. You know, the guy who played Gomer Pyle? Nobody expected a guy looked that goofy could sing, so when he did, they thought he was great, even though he sounded like he had sinus trouble. It's the same with Stanky, except his voice really is great."

"You're always picking up these curious strays," she said. "Remember the high school kid who played bass, the one who fainted every time he was under pressure? Brian Something. You'd come upstairs and say, 'You should see what Brian did,' and tell me he laid a bass on its side and played Mozart riffs on it. And I'd go—"

"Bach," I said.

"And I'd go, 'Yeah, but he faints!' " She laughed. "You always think you can fix them."

"You're coming dangerously close to banter," I said.

"You owe me one." She wiggled her forefinger and grinned. "I'm right, aren't I? There's a downside to this guy."

I told her about Stanky's downside and, when I reached the part about Mia leaving, Andrea said, "The circus must be in town."

"Now you owe me one."

"You can't expect me to be reasonable about Mia." She half-sang the name, did a little shimmy, made a moue.

"That's two you owe me," I said.

"Sorry." She straightened her smile. "You know she'll come back. She always does."

I liked that she was acting flirty and, though I had no resolution in mind, I didn't want her to stop.

"You don't have to worry about me," she said. "Honest."

"Huh?"

"So how talented is this Stanky? Give me an example."

"What do you mean, I don't have to worry about you?"

"Never mind. Now come on! Give me some Stanky."

"You want me to sing?"

"You were a singer, weren't you? A pretty good one, as I recall."

"Yeah, but I can't do what he does."

She sat expectantly, hands folded on the tabletop.

"All right," I said.

I did a verse of "Devil's Blues," beginning with the lines:

"There's a grapevine in heaven,
There's a peavine in hell,
One don't grow grapes,
The other don't grow peas as well..."

I sailed on through to the chorus, getting into the vocal:

"Devil's Blues!
God owes him..."

A bald guy popped his head over the top of an adjacent booth and looked at me, then ducked back down. I heard laughter.

"That's enough," I said to Andrea.

"Interesting," she said. "Not my cup of tea, but I wouldn't mind hearing him."

"He's playing the Crucible next weekend."

"Is that an invitation?"

"Sure. If you'll come."

"I have to see how things develop at the office. Is a tentative yes okay?"

"Way better than a firm no," I said.

We ordered from the grille and, after we had eaten, Andrea called her office and told them she was taking the rest of the day. We switched from martinis to red wine, and we talked, we laughed, we got silly, we got drunk. The sounds of the bar folded around us and I started to remember how it felt to be in love with her. We wobbled out of McGuigan's around four o'clock. The sun was lowering behind the Bittersmiths, but shed a rich golden light; it was still warm enough for people to be sitting in sweaters and shirts on park benches under the orange leaves.

Andrea lived around the corner from the bar, so I walked her home. She was weaving a little and kept bumping into me. "You better take a cab home," she said, and I said, "I'm not the one who's walking funny," which earned me a punch in the arm. When we came to her door, she turned to me, gripping her briefcase with both hands and said, "I'll see you next weekend, maybe."

"That'd be great."

She hovered there a second longer and then she kissed me. Flung her arms about my neck, clocking me with the briefcase, and gave me a one-hundred percent all-Andrea kiss that, if I were a cartoon character, would have rolled my socks up and down and levitated my hat. She buried her face in my neck and said, "Sorry. I'm sorry." I was going to say, For what?, but she pulled away in a hurry, appearing panicked, and fled up the stairs.

I nearly hit a parked car on the drive home, not because I was drunk, but because thinking about the kiss and her reaction afterward impaired my concentration. What was she sorry about? The kiss? Flirting? The divorce? I couldn't work it out, and I couldn't work out, either, what I was feeling. Lust, certainly. Having her body pressed against mine had fully engaged my senses. But there was more. Considerably more. I decided it stood a chance of becoming a mental health issue and did my best to put it from mind.

Kiwanda was busy in the office. She had the computers networking and was going through prehistoric paper files on the floor. I asked what was up and she told me she had devised a more efficient filing system. She had never been much of an innovator, so this unnerved me, but I let it pass and asked if she'd had any problems with my boy Stanky.

"Not so you'd notice," she said tersely.

From this, I deduced that there *had* been a problem, but I let that pass as well and went upstairs to the apartment. Walls papered with flyers and band photographs; a grouping of newish, ultra-functional Swedish furniture—I realized I had liked the apartment better when Andrea did the decorating, this despite the fact that interior design had been one of our bones of contention. The walls, in particular, annoyed me. I was being stared at by young men with shaved heads and flowing locks in arrogant poses, stupid with tattoos, by five or six bands that had tried to stiff me, by a few hundred bad-to-indifferent memories and a dozen good ones. Maybe a dozen. I sat on a leather and chrome couch (it was a showy piece, but uncomfortable) and watched the early news. George Bush, Iraq, the price of gasoline…fuck! Restless, I went down to the basement.

Stanky was watching the Comedy Channel. *Mad TV.* Another of his passions. He was slumped on the couch, remote in hand, and had a Coke and a cigarette working, an ice pack clamped to his cheek. I had the idea the ice pack was for my benefit, so I didn't ask about it, but knew it must be connected to Kiwanda's attitude. He barely acknowledged my presence, just sat there and pouted. I took a chair and watched with him. At last he said, "I need a rhythm guitar player."

"I'm not going to hire another musician this late in the game."

He set down the ice pack. His cheek was red, but that might have been from the ice pack itself…although I thought I detected a slight puffiness. "I seriously need him," he said.

"Don't push me on this."

"It's important, man! For this one song, anyway."

"What song?"

"A new one."

I waited and then said, "That's all you're going to tell me?"

"It needs a rhythm guitar."

This tubby little madman recumbent on my couch was making demands—it felt good to reject him, but he persisted.

"It's just one song, man," he said in full-on wheedle. "Please! It's a surprise."

"I don't like surprises."

"Come on! You'll like this one, I promise."

I told him I'd see what I could do, had a talk with him about Jerry, and the atmosphere lightened. He sat up straight, chortling at *Mad TV*, now and then saying, "Decent!", his ultimate accolade. The skits were funny and I laughed, too.

"I did my horoscope today," he said as the show went to commercial.

"Let me guess," I said. "You're a Cancer."

He didn't like that, but maintained an upbeat air. "I don't mean astrology, man. I use The Guide." He slid the *TV Guide* across the coffee table, pointing out an entry with a grimy finger, a black-rimmed nail. I snatched it up and read:

> *"King Creole: *** Based on a Harold Robbins novel. A young man (Elvis Presley) with a gang background rises from the streets to become a rock and roll star. Vic Morrow. 1:30."*

"Decent, huh!" said Stanky. "You try it. Close your eyes and stick your finger in on a random page and see what you get. I use the movie section in back, but some people use the whole programming section."

"Other people do this? Not just you?"

"Go ahead."

I did as instructed and landed on another movie:

> *"A Man and a Woman: **** A widow and a widower meet on holiday and are attracted to one another, but the woman backs off because memories of her dead husband are still too strong. Marcello Mastroiani, Anouk Aimee. 1:40."*

Half-believing, I tried to understand what the entry portended for me and Andrea.

"What did you get?" asked Stanky.

I tossed the *Guide* back to him and said, "It didn't work for me."

▲▼▲

I thought about calling Andrea, but business got in the way—I suppose I allowed it to get in the way, due to certain anxieties relating to our divorce. There was publicity to do, Kiwanda's new filing system to master (she kept on tweaking it), recording (we laid down two tracks for

Stanky's first EP), and a variety of other duties. And so the days went quickly. Stanky began going to the library after every practice, walking without a limp; he said he was doing research. He didn't have enough money to get into trouble and I had too much else on my plate to stress over it. The night before he played the Crucible, I was in the office, going over everything in my mind, wondering what I had overlooked, thinking I had accomplished an impossible amount of work that week, when the doorbell rang. I opened the door and there on the stoop was Andrea, dressed in jeans and a bulky sweater, cheeks rosy from the night air. An overnight bag rested at her feet. "Hi," she said, and gave a chipper smile, like a tired girl scout determined to keep pimping her cookies.

Taken aback, I said, "Hi," and ushered her in.

She went into the office and sat in the wooden chair beside my desk. I followed her in, hesitated, and took a seat in my swivel chair.

"You look...rattled," she said.

"That about covers it. Good rattled. But rattled, nonetheless."

"I am, too. Sorta." She glanced around the office, as if noticing the changes. I could hear every ticking clock, every digital hum, all the discrete noises of the house.

She drew in a breath, exhaled, clasped her hands in her lap. "I thought we could try," she said quietly. "We could do a trial period or something. Some days, a week. See how that goes." She paused. "The last few times I've seen you, I've wanted to be with you. And I think you've wanted to be with me. So...." She made a flippy gesture, as if she were trying to shade things toward the casual. "This seemed like an opportunity."

You would have thought, even given the passage of time, after all the recriminations and ugliness of divorce, some measure of negativity would have cropped up in my thoughts; but it did not and I said, "I think you're right."

"Whew!" Andrea pretended to wipe sweat from her brow and grinned.

An awkward silence; the grin flickered and died.

"Could I maybe go upstairs," she asked.

"Oh! Sure. I'm sorry." I had the urge to run up before her and rip down the crapfest on the wall, chuck all the furniture out the window, except for a mattress and candles.

"You're still rattled," she said. "Maybe we should have a drink before anything." She stretched out a hand to me. "Let's get good and drunk."

As it happened, we barely got the drinks poured before we found our groove and got busy. It was like old times, cozy and familiar, and yet it was like we were doing it for the first time, too. Every touch, every sensation, carried that odd *frisson*. We woke late, with the frost almost melted from the panes, golden light chuting through the high east windows, leaving the bed in a bluish shadow. We lay there, too sleepy to make love, playing a little, talking, her telling me how she had plotted her approach, me telling her how I was oblivious until that day at lunch when I noticed her loneliness, and what an idiot I had been not to see what was happening.... Trivial matters, but they stained a few brain cells, committing those moments to memory and marking them as Important, a red pin on life's map. And then we did make love, as gently as that violence can be made. Afterward, we showered and fixed breakfast. Watching her move about the kitchen in sweats and a T-shirt, I couldn't stop thinking how great this was, and I wanted to stop, to quit footnoting every second. I mentioned this as we ate and she said, "I guess that means you're happy."

"Yeah! Of course."

"Me, too." She stabbed a piece of egg with her fork, tipped her head to the side as if to get a better angle on me. "I don't know when it was I started to be able to read you so well. Not that you were that hard to read to begin with. It just seems there's nothing hidden in your face anymore."

"Maybe it's a case of heightened senses."

"No, really. At times it's like I know what you're about to say."

"You mean I don't have to speak?"

She adopted the manner of a legal professional. "Unfortunately, no. You have to speak. Otherwise, it would be difficult to catch you in a lie."

"Maybe we should test this," I said. "You ask my name, and I'll say, Helmut or Torin."

She shook her head. "I'm an organic machine, not a lie detector. We have different ways. Different needs."

"Organic. So that would make you...softer than your basic machine? Possibly more compliant?"

"Very much so," she said.

"You know, I think I may be reading you pretty well myself." I leaned across the table, grabbed a sloppy kiss, and, as I sat back down, I remembered something. "Damn!" I said, and rapped my forehead with my knuckles.

"What is it?"

"I forgot to take Stanky for his haircut."

"Can't he take care of it himself?"

"Probably not. You want to go with us? You might as well meet him. Get it over with."

She popped egg into her mouth and chewed. "Do we have to do it now?"

"No, he won't even be up for a couple of hours."

"Good," she said.

▲▼▲

The Crucible, a concrete block structure on the edge of Black William, off beyond the row houses, had once been a dress outlet store. We had put a cafeteria in the front, where we served breakfast and lunch—we did a brisk business because of the mill. Separate from the cafeteria, the back half of the building was given over to a bar with a few ratty booths, rickety chairs and tables. We had turned a high-school artist loose on the walls and she had painted murals that resembled scenes from J.R.R. Tolkien's lost labor-union novel. An immense crucible adorned the wall behind the stage; it appeared, thanks to the artist's inept use of perspective, to be spilling a flood of molten steel down upon an army of orc-like workers.

There was a full house that night, attracted by local legends, The Swimming Holes, a girl band who had migrated to Pittsburgh, achieving a degree of national renown, and I had packed the audience with Friends of Vernon whom I had enjoined to applaud and shout wildly for Stanky. A haze of smoke fogged the stage lights and milling about were fake punks, the odd goth, hippies from Garnant College in Waterford, fifteen miles away: the desperate wanna-be counter-culture of the western Pennsylvania barrens. I went into the dressing rooms, gave each Swimming Hole a welcome-home hug, and checked in on Stanky. Jerry, a skinny guy with buzzcut red hair, was plunking on his bass, and Geno was playing fills on the back of a chair; Ian, the rhythm guitarist, was making a cell call in the head. Stanky was on the couch, smoking a Camel, drinking a Coke, and watching the Sci-Fi Channel. I asked if he felt all right. He said he could use a beer. He seemed calm, supremely confident, which I would not have predicted and did not trust. But it was too late for concern and I left him to God.

I joined Andrea at the bar. She had on an old long-sleeved Ramones shirt, the same that she had worn to gigs back when my band was happening. Despite the shirt, she looked out of place in the Crucible, a swan floating on a cesspool. I ordered a beer to be carried to Stanky, a shot of tequila for myself. Andrea put her mouth to my ear and shouted over the recorded music, "Don't get drunk!", and then something else that was lost in the din. I threw down the shot and led her into the cafeteria, which was serving coffee and soda to a handful of kids, some of whom appeared to be trying to straighten out. I closed the door to the bar, cutting the volume by half.

"What were you saying?" I asked.

"I said not to get drunk, I might have use for you later." She sat at the counter, patted the stool beside her, encouraging me to sit.

"They're about to start," I said, joining her. "I've only got a minute."

"How do you think it'll go?"

"With Stanky? I'm praying it won't be a disaster."

"You know, he didn't seem so bad this afternoon. Not like you described, anyway."

"You just like him because he said you were a babe."

I took a loose cigarette from my shirt pocket, rolled it between my thumb and forefinger, and she asked if I was smoking again.

"Once in a while. Mainly I do this," I said, demonstrating my rolling technique. "Anyway…Stanky. You caught him on his best behavior."

"He seemed sad to me." She lifted a pepper shaker as she might a chess piece and set it closer to the salt. "Stunted. He has some adult mannerisms, adult information, but it's like he's still fourteen or fifteen."

"There you go," I said. "Now ask yourself how it would be, being around a twenty-six year old fourteen-year-old on a daily basis."

One of the kids, boys, men…there should be, I think, a specific word for someone old enough to die for his country, yet can't grow a proper mustache and is having difficulty focusing because he recently ate some cheap acid cut with crank. One of the guys at the end of the counter, then, came trippingly toward us, wearing an army field jacket decorated with a braid of puke on the breast pocket, like a soggy service ribbon. He stopped to leer at Andrea, gave me the high sign, said something unintelligible, possibly profane, and staggered on into the club.

It had been Andrea's stance, when we were married, that episodes such as this were indicative of the sewer in which she claimed I was deliquescing, AKA the music business. Though I had no grounds to argue the point, I argued nonetheless, angry because I hated the idea that she was smarter than I was—I compensated by telling myself I had more soul. There had been other, less defined reasons for anger, and the basic argument between us had gotten vicious. In this instance, however, she ignored the kid and returned to our conversation, which forced me to consider anew the question of my milieu and the degradation thereof, and to wonder if she had, by ignoring the kid, manipulated me into thinking that she had changed, whereas I had not, and it might be that the music business was to blame, that it had delimited me, warped and stunted my soul. I knew she was still the smart one.

The music cut off mid-song and I heard Rudy Bowen, my friend and partner in the Crucible, on the mike, welcoming people and making announcements. On our way back into the club, Andrea stopped me at the door and said, "I love you, Vernon." She laid a finger on my lips and told me to think about it before responding, leaving me mightily perplexed.

Stanky walked out onto the stage of the Crucible in a baggy white T-shirt, baggy chinos and his trucker wallet. He would have been semi-presentable had he not also been wearing a battered top hat. Somebody hooted derisively, and that did not surprise me. The hat made him look clownish. I wanted to throw a bottle and knock it off his head. He began whispering into the mike. Another hoot, a piercing whistle. Not good. But the whisper evolved into a chant, bits of Latin, Spanish, rock and roll clichés, and nonsense syllables. Half-spoken, half-sung, with an incantatory vibe, scatted in a jump-blues rhythm that the band, coming in underneath the vocal, built into a solid groove, and then Stanky, hitting his mark like a ski jumper getting a lift off a big hill, began to sing:

> *"I heard the Holy Ghost moan…*
> *Stars seen through stone…"*

Basically, the song consisted of those two lines repeated, but sung differently—made into a gospel plaint, a rock and roll howl, a smooth Motown styling, a jazzy lilt, and so on. There was a break with more lyrics, but the two lines were what mattered. The first time he sang them, in that heavy false bass, a shock ripped through the audience. People looked up, they turned toward the stage, they stopped drinking, their heads twitched, their legs did impromptu dance steps. Stanky held the word "moan" out for three bars, working it like a soul singer, then he picked up the trumpet and broke into a solo that was angry like Miles, but kept a spooky edge. When he set the trumpet down, he went to singing the lyric double time, beating the top hat against his thigh, mangling it. The crowd surged forward, everyone wanting to get next to the stage, dancing in place, this strange, shuffling dance, voodoo zombies from hell, and Stanky strapped on his guitar. I missed much of what happened next, because Andrea dragged me onto the dance floor and started making slinky moves, and I lost my distance from the event. But Stanky's guitar work sent the zombies into a convulsive fever.

We bumped into a punk who was jerking like his strings were being yanked; we did a threesome with a college girl whose feet were planted, yet was shaking it like a tribal dancer in a *National Geographic* Special; we were corralled briefly by two millworkers who were dancing with a goth girl, watching her spasm, her breasts flipping every whichaway. At the end of the song, Jerry and Geno started speaking the lyric into their mikes, adding a counterpoint to Stanky's vocal, cooling things off, bringing it down to the creepy chant again; then the band dropped out of the music and Stanky went a capella for a final repetition of his two lines.

Applause erupted, and it was as idiosyncratic as the dancing had been. This one guy was baying like a hound; a blonde girl bounced up and down, clapping gleefully like a six-year-old. I didn't catch much of the set, other than to note the audience's positive response, in particular to the songs "Average Joe" and "Can I Get A Waitress?" and "The Sunset Side of You"—I was working the room, gathering opinions, trying to learn if any of the industry people I'd invited had come, and it wasn't until twenty minutes after the encore that I saw Stanky at the bar, talking to a girl, surrounded by a group of drunken admirers. I heard another girl say how cute he was and that gave me pause to wonder at the terrible power of music. The hooker I had hired to guarantee my guarantee, a long-legged brunette named Carol, dish-faced, but with a spectacular body, was biding her time, waiting for the crowd around Stanky to disperse. He was in competent hands. I felt relief, mental fatigue, the desire to be alone with Andrea. There was no pressing reason to stay. I said a couple of good-byes, accepted congratulations, and we drove home, Andrea and I, along the Polozny.

"He's amazing," she said. "I have to admit, you may be right about him."

"Yep," I said proudly.

"Watch yourself, Sparky. You know how you get when these things start to go south."

"What are you talking about?"

"When one of your problem children runs off the tracks, you take it hard. That's all I'm saying." Andrea rubbed my shoulder. "You may want to think about speeding things up with Stanky. Walk him a shorter distance and let someone else deal with him. It might save you some wear and tear."

We drove in silence; the river widened, slowed its race, flowing in under the concrete lees of the mill; the first row house came up on the right. I was tempted to respond as usually I did to her advice, to say it's all good, I've got it under control, but for some reason I listened that night and thought about everything that could go wrong.

▲▼▲

Carol was waiting for me in the office when I came downstairs at eight o'clock the following morning. She was sitting in my swivel chair, going through my Rolodex. She looked weary, her hair mussed, and displeased. "That guy's a freak," she said flatly. "I want two hundred more. And in the future, I want to meet the guys you set me up with before I commit."

"What'd he do?" I asked.

"Do you really want to know?"

"I'm kind of curious…yeah."

She began to recite a list of Stanky-esque perversions, and I cut her off.

"Okay," I said, and reached for my checkbook. "He didn't get rough, did he?"

"Au contraire." She crossed her legs. "He wanted me to—"

"Please," I said. "Enough."

"I don't do that sort of work," she said primly.

I told her I'd written the check for three hundred and she was somewhat mollified. I apologized for Stanky and told her I hadn't realized he was so twisted.

"We're okay," she said. "I've had…hi, sweetie!"

She directed this greeting to a point above my shoulder as Andrea, sleepily scratching her head, wearing her sweats, entered the office. "Hi, Carol," she said, bewildered.

Carol hugged her, then turned to me and waved good-bye with my check. "Call me."

"Pretty early for hookers," Andrea said, perching on the edge of the desk.

"Let me guess. You defended her."

"Nope. One of her clients died and left her a little money. I helped her invest. But that begs the question, what was she doing here?"

"I got her for Stanky."

"A reward?"

"Something like that."

She nodded and idly kicked the back of her heel against the side of the desk. "How come you never were interested in the men I dated after we broke up?"

I was used to her sudden conversational U-turns, but I had expected her to interrogate me about Carol and this caught me off-guard. "I don't know. I suppose I didn't want to think about who you were sleeping with."

"Must be a guy thing. I always checked out your girlfriends. Even the ones you had when I was mad at you." She slipped off the desk and padded toward the door. "See you upstairs."

I spent the next two days between the phone and the studio, recording a good take of "The Sunset Side Of You"—it was the closest thing Stanky had to a ballad, and I thought, with its easy, Dr. John-ish feel, it might get some play on college radio:

"I'm gonna crack open my Venetian blind
and let that last bit of old orange glory shine,
so I can catch an eyeful
of my favorite trifle,
my absolutely perfect point of view...
That's an eastbound look,
six inches from the crook
of my little finger,
at the sunset side of you..."

Stanky wasn't happy with me—he was writing a song a day, sometimes two songs, and didn't want to disrupt his creative process by doing something that might actually make money, but I gamed him into cutting the track.

Wednesday morning, I visited Rudy Bowen in his office. Rudy was an architect who yearned to be a cartoonist, but who had never met with much success in the latter pursuit, and the resonance of our creative failures, I believe, helped to cement our friendship. He was also the only person I knew who had caught a fish in the Polozny downstream from the mill. It occupied a place of honor in his office, a hideous thing mounted on a plaque, some sort of mutant trout nourished upon pollution. Whenever I saw it, I would speculate on what else might lurk beneath the surface of the cold, deep pools east of town, imagining telepathic monstrosities plated with armor like fish of the Mesozoic and frail tentacled creatures, their skins having the rainbow sheen of an oil slick, to whom mankind were sacred figures in their dream of life.

Rudy's secretary, a matronly woman named Gwen, told me he had gone out for a latte, and let me wait in his private office. I stepped over to his drafting table, curious about what he was working on. Held in place on the table was a clean sheet of paper, but in a folder beside the table was a batch of new cartoons, a series featuring shadowy figures in a mineshaft who conversed about current events, celebrities, et al, while excavating a vein of pork that twisted through a mountain.... This gave rise to the title of the strip: *Meat Mountain Stories*. They were silhouettes, really. Given identity by their shapes, eccentric hairstyles, and speech signatures. The strip was contemporary and hilarious. Everything Rudy's usual work was not. In some frames, a cluster of tiny white objects appeared to be floating. Moths, I thought. Lights of some kind. They, too, carried on conversations, but in pictographs. I was still going through them when Rudy came in, a big, blond man with the beginnings of a gut and thick glasses that lent him a baffled look. Every time I saw him, he looked more depressed, more middle-aged.

"These are great, man!" I said. "They're new, right?"

He crossed the room and stood beside me. "I been working on them all week. You like 'em, huh?"

"I love them. You did all this this week? You must not be sleeping." I pointed to the white things. "What're these?"

"Stars. I got the idea from that song Stanky did. 'Stars Seen Through Stone.' "

"So they're seeing them, the people in the mine?"

"Yeah. They don't pay much attention to them, but they're going to start interacting soon."

"It must be going around." I told him about Stanky's burst of writing, Kiwanda's adventures in office management.

"That's odd, you know." He sipped his latte. "It seems like there's been a real rash of creativity in town. Last week, some grunt at the mill came up with an improvement in the cold forming process that everybody says is a huge deal. Jimmy Galvin, that guy who does handyman work? He invented a new gardening tool. Bucky Bucklin's paying his patent fees. He says they're going to make millions. Beth started writing a novel. She never said anything to me about wanting to write, but she's hardly had time for the kids, she's been so busy ripping off the pages. It's not bad."

"Well, I wish I'd catch it," I said. "With me, it's same old same old. Drudgeree, drudgeroo. Except for Andrea's back."

"Andrea? You mean you guys are dating?"

"I mean back as in back in my house. Living with me."

"Damn!" he said. "That's incredible!"

We sat in two chairs like two inverted tents on steel frames, as uncomfortable as my upstairs couch, and I told him about it.

"So it's going okay?" he asked.

"Terrific, I think. But what do I know? She said it was a trial period, so I could get home tonight and she might be gone. I've never been able to figure her out."

"Andrea. Damn! I saw her at the club, but I didn't realize she was with you. I just had time to wave." He leaned across the space between us and high-fived me. "Now maybe you'll stop going around like someone stole your puppy."

"It wasn't like that," I said.

He chuckled. "Naw. Which is why the people of Black William, when asked the date, often reply, 'Six years, a month, and twelve days since the advent of Vernon's Gloom.'"

We moved on to other topics, among them the club, business, and, as I made to leave, I gestured at Rudy's grotesque trophy and said, "While those creative juices are flowing, you ought to design a fishing lure, so I can watch you hook into the Loch Polozny Monster."

Rudy laughed and said, "Maybe if I have a couple of minutes. I'm going to keep working on the comic. Whatever this shit is, it's bound to go away."

▲▼▲

I was fooling around in the studio one evening, ostensibly cleaning up the tape we'd rolled the previous weekend at the Crucible, hoping to get a live rendition of "Stars Seen Through Stone" clean enough for the EP, but I was, instead, going over a tape I'd made, trying to find some ounce of true inspiration in it, finding none, wondering why this wave of creativity—if it, indeed, existed—had blessed Rudy's house and not mine. It was after seven, Stanky was likely on his way home from the library, and I was thinking about seeing if Andrea wanted to go out, when she leaned in the doorway and asked if she was interrupting. I told her, no, not at all, and she came into the booth and sat next to me at the board, looking out at the drum kit, the instruments, the serpents' nest of power cords.

"When we were married, I didn't get what you saw in this," she said. "All I saw was the damage, the depravity, the greed. Now I've been practicing, I realize there's more-or-less the same degree of damage and greed and depravity in every enterprise. You can't see it as clearly as you do in the music business, but it's there."

"Tell me what I see that's good."

"The music, the people."

"None of that lasts," I said. "All I am's a yo-yo tester. I test a thousand busted yo-yos, and occasionally I run across one that lights up and squeals when it spins."

"What I do is too depressing to talk about. It's rare when anyone I represent has a good outcome, even if they win. Corporations delay and delay."

"So it's disillusionment that's brought us together again."

"No." She looked at me steadily. "Do you love me?"

"Yeah, I love you. You know I do. I never stopped. There was a gap—"

"A big gap!"

"The gap made it more painful, but that's all it did."

She played with dials on the sound board, frowning as if they were refusing to obey her fingers.

"You're messing up my settings," I said.

"Oh...sorry."

"What's wrong?"

"Nothing. It's just you don't lie to me anymore. You used to lie all the time, even about trivial things. I'm having trouble adjusting."

I started to deny it, but recognized that I couldn't. "I was angry at you. I can't remember why, exactly. Lying was probably part of it."

"I was angry at you, too." She put her hands back on the board, but twisted no dials. "But I didn't lie to you."

"You stopped telling me the truth," I said. "Same difference."

The phone rang; in reflex, I picked up and said, "Soul Kiss."

It was Stanky. He started babbling, telling me to come downtown quick.

"Whoa!" I said. "If this is about me giving you a ride—"

"No, I swear! You gotta see this, man! The stars are back!"

"The stars."

"Like the one we saw at the library. The lights. You better come quick. I'm not sure how long it'll last."

"I'm kind of busy," I said.

"Dude, you have got to see this! I'm not kidding!"

I covered the phone and spoke to Andrea. "Want to ride uptown? Stanky says there's something we should see."

"Maybe afterward we could stop by my place and I could pick up a few things?"

I got back on the phone. "Where are you?"

Five minutes later we were cutting across the park toward the statue of Black William, beside which Stanky and several people were standing in an island of yellow light—I had no time to check them out, other than to observe that one was a woman, because Stanky caught my arm and directed me to look at the library and what I saw made me unmindful of any other sight. The building had been rendered insubstantial, a ghost of itself, and I was staring across a dark plain ranged by a dozen fuzzy white lights, some large, some small, moving toward us at a slow rate of speed, and yet perhaps it was not slow—the perspective seemed infinite, as if I were gazing into a depth by comparison to which, all previously glimpsed perspectives were so limited as to be irrelevant. As the lights approached, they appeared to vanish, passing out of frame, as if the viewing angle we had been afforded was too narrow to encompass the scope of the phenomenon. Within seconds, it began to fade, the library to regain its ordinary solidity, and I thought I heard a distant gabbling, the sound of many voices speaking at once, an army of voices (though I may have manufactured this impression from the wind gusting through the boughs); and then, as that ghostly image winked out of existence, a groaning noise that, in my opinion, issued from no fleshly throat, but may have been produced by some cosmic stress, a rip in the continuum sealing itself or something akin.

Andrea had, at some point, latched onto my arm, and we stood gaping at the library; Stanky and the rest began talking excitedly. There were three boys, teenagers, two of them carrying skateboards. The third was a pale, skinny, haughty kid, bespotted with acne, wearing a black turtleneck sweater, black jeans, black overcoat. They displayed a worshipful attitude toward Stanky, hanging on his every word. The woman might have been the one with whom Stanky had been speaking at the Crucible before Carol made her move. She was tiny, barely five feet tall, Italian-looking, with black hair and olive skin, in her twenties, and betrayed a compete lack of animation until Stanky slipped an arm around her; then she smiled, an expression that revealed her to be moderately attractive.

The skateboarders sped off to, they said, "tell everybody," and this spurred me to take out my cell phone, but I could not think who to call. Rudy, maybe. But no one in authority. The cops would laugh at the report. Stanky introduced us to Liz (the woman lowered her eyes) and Pin (the goth kid looked away and nodded). I asked how long the phenomenon had been going on before we arrived and Stanky said, "Maybe fifteen minutes."

"Have you seen it before?"

"Just that time with you."

I glanced up at Black William and thought that maybe he *had* intended the statue as a warning...though it struck me now that he was turning his head back toward the town and laughing.

Andrea hugged herself. "I could use something hot to drink."

McGuigan's was handy, but that would have disincluded Pin, who obviously was underage. I loaded him, Stanky, and Liz into the back of the van and drove to Szechuan Palace, a restaurant on the edge of the business district, which sported a five-foot-tall gilt fiberglass Buddha in the foyer that over the years had come to resemble an ogre with a skin condition, the fiberglass weave showing through in patches, and whose dining room (empty but for a bored wait-staff) was lit like a Macao brothel in lurid shades of red, green, and purple. On the way to the restaurant, I replayed the incident in my head, attempting to understand what I had witnessed not in rational terms, but in terms that would make sense to an ordinary American fool raised on science fiction and horror movies. Nothing seemed to fit. At the restaurant, Andrea and Pin ordered tea, Liz and Stanky gobbled moo shu pork and lemon chicken, and I picked at an egg roll. Pin started talking to Andrea in an adenoidal voice, lecturing her on some matter regarding Black William, and, annoyed because he was treating her like an idiot, I said, "What does Black William have to do with this?"

"Not a thing," Pin said, turning on me a look of disdain that aspired to be the kind of look Truman Capote once fixed upon a reporter from the *Lincoln Journal-Star* who had asked if he was a homosexual. "Not unless you count the fact that he saw something similar two hundred years ago and it probably killed him."

"Pin's an expert on Black William," Stanky said, wiping a shred of pork from his chin.

"What little there is to know," said Pin grandly, "I know."

It figured that a goth townie would have developed a crush on the local bogeyman. I asked him to enlighten me.

"Well," Pin said, "when Joey told me he'd seen a star floating in front of the library, I knew it *had* to be one of BW's stars. Where the library stands today used to be the edge of Stockton Wood, which had an evil reputation. As did many woods in those days, of course. Stockton Wood is where he saw the stars."

"What did he say about them?"

"He didn't say a thing. Nothing that he committed to paper, anyway. It's his younger cousin, Samuel Garnant, we can thank for the story. He wrote a memoir about BW's escapades under the *nom de plume* Jonathan Venture. According to Samuel, BW was in the habit of riding in the woods at twilight. 'Tempting the Devil,' he called it. His first sight of the stars was a few mysterious lights—like with you and Joey. He rode out into the wood the next night and many nights thereafter. Samuel's a bit vague on how long it was before BW saw the stars again. I'm guessing a couple of weeks, going by clues in the narrative. But eventually he did see them, and what he saw was a lot like what we just saw." Pin put his hands together, fingertips touching, like a priest preparing to address the Ladies' Auxiliary. "In those days, people feared God and the Devil. When they saw something amazing, they didn't stand around like a bunch of doofuses saying, 'All right!' and taking pictures. BW was terrified. He said he'd seen the Star Wormwood and heard the Holy Ghost moan. He set about changing his life."

Stanky shot me one of his wincing, cutesy, embarrassed smiles—he had told me the song was completely original.

"For almost a year," Pin went on, "BW tried to be a good Christian. He performed charitable works, attended church regularly, but his heart wasn't in it. He lapsed back into his old ways and before long he took to riding in Stockton Woods again, with his manservant Nero walking at his side. He thought that he had missed an opportunity and told Samuel if he was fortunate enough to see the stars again, he would ride straight for them. He'd embrace their evil purpose."

"What you said about standing around like doofuses, taking pictures," Andrea said. "I don't suppose anyone got a picture?"

Pin produced a cell phone and punched up a photograph of the library and the stars. Andrea and I leaned in to see.

"Can you email that to me?" I asked.

Pin said he could and I wrote my address on a napkin.

"So," Pin said. "The next time BW saw the stars was in eighteen-oh-eight. He saw them twice, exactly like the first time. A single star, then an interval of a week or two and a more complex sighting. A month after that, he disappeared while riding with Nero in Stockton Wood and they were never seen again."

Stanky hailed our waitress and asked for more pancakes for his moo shu.

"So you think the stars appeared three times?" said Andrea. "And Black William missed the third appearance on the first go-round, but not on the second?"

"That's what Samuel thought," said Pin.

Stanky fed Liz a bite of lemon chicken.

"You're assuming Black William was killed by the stars, but that doesn't make sense," said Andrea. "For instance, why would there be a longer interval between the second and third sightings? If there *was* a third sighting. It's more likely someone who knew the story killed him and blamed it on the stars."

"Maybe Nero capped him," said Stanky. "So he could gain his freedom."

Pin shrugged. "I only know what I read."

"It might be a wavefront," I said.

On another napkin, I drew a straight line with a small bump in it, then an interval in which the line flattened out, then a bigger bump, then a longer interval and an even bigger bump.

"Like that, maybe," I said. "Some kind of wavefront passing through Black William from God knows where. It's always passing through town, but we get this series of bumps that make it accessible every two hundred years. Or less. Maybe the stars appeared at other times."

"There's no record of it," said Pin. "And I've searched."

The waitress brought Stanky's pancakes and asked if we needed more napkins.

Andrea studied the napkin I'd drawn on. "But what about the first series of sightings? When were they?"

"Seventeen-eighty-nine," said Pin.

"It could be an erratic cycle," I said. "Or could be the cycle consists of two sequences close together, then a lapse of two hundred years. Don't expect a deeper explanation. I cut class a bunch in high school physics."

"The Holy Ghost doesn't obey physical principles," said Stanky pompously.

"I doubt Black William really heard the Holy Ghost," Andrea said. "If he heard what we heard tonight. It sounded more like a door closing to me."

"Whatever," he said. "It'll be cool to see what happens a month from now. Maybe Black William will return from the grave."

"Yeah." I crumpled the napkin and tossed it to the center of the table. "Maybe he'll bring Doctor Doom and the Lone Ranger with him."

Pin affected a shudder and said, "I think I'm busy that day."

▲▼▲

Pin sent me the picture and I emailed it to a gearhead friend, Crazy Ed, who lived in Wilkes-Barre, to see what he could make of it. Though I didn't forget about the stars, I got slammed with business and my consideration of them and the late William Garnant had to be put on the backburner, along with Stanky's career. Against all expectations, Liz had not fled screaming from his bed, crying Pervert, but stayed with him most nights. Except for his time in the studio, I rarely saw him, and then only when his high school fans drove by to pick up him and Liz. An apocryphal story reached my ear, insinuating that she had taken on a carload of teenage boys while Stanky watched. That, if true, explained the relationship in Stanky-esque terms, terms I could understand. I didn't care what they did as long as he fulfilled his band duties and kept out of my hair. I landed him a gig at the Pick and Shovel in Waterford, filling in for a band that had been forced to cancel, and it went well enough that I scored him another gig at Garnant College. After a mere two performances, his reputation was building and I adjusted my timetable accordingly—I would make the college job an EP release party, push out an album soon thereafter and try to sell him to a major label. It was not the way I typically grew my acts, not commercially wise, but Stanky was not a typical act and, despite his prodigious talent, I wanted to have done with this sour-smelling chapter in my life.

Andrea, for all intents and purposes, had moved in, along with a high-energy, seven-month-old Irish Setter named Timber, and was in process of subletting her apartment. We were, doubtless, a disgusting item to everyone who had gotten to know us during our adversarial phase, always hanging on one another, kissing and touching. I had lunch with her every day—they held the back booth for us at McGuigan's—and one afternoon as we were settling in, Mia materialized beside the booth. "Hello," she said and stuck out a hand to Andrea.

Startled, Andrea shook her hand and I, too, was startled—until that moment, Mia had been unrelentingly hostile in her attitude toward my ex, referring to her as "that uppity skank" and in terms less polite. I noticed that she was dressed conservatively and not made up as an odalisque. Instead of being whipped into a punky abstraction, her hair was pulled back into a ponytail. The raspberry streak was gone. She was, in fact, for the first time since I had known her, streakless.

"May I join you?" Mia asked. "I won't take up much of your time."

Andrea scooted closer to the wall and Mia sat next to her.

"I heard you guys were back together," said Mia. "I'm glad."

Thunderstruck, I was incapable of fielding that one. "Thanks," said Andrea, looking to me for guidance.

Mia squared up in the booth, addressing me with a clear eye and a firm voice. "I'm moving to Pittsburgh. I've got a job lined up and I'll be taking night classes at Pitt, then going full-time starting next summer."

Hearing this issue from Mia's mouth was like hearing a cat begin speaking in Spanish while lighting a cheroot. I managed to say, "Yeah, that's.... Yeah. Good."

"I'm sorry I didn't tell you sooner. I'm leaving tomorrow. But I heard you and Andrea were together, so..." She glanced back and forth between Andrea and myself, as if expecting a response.

"No, that's fine," I said. "You know."

"It was a destructive relationship," she said with great sincerity. "We had some fun, but it was bad for both of us. You were holding me back intellectually and I was limiting you emotionally."

"You're right," I said. "Absolutely."

Mia seemed surprised by how smoothly things were going, but she had, apparently, a pre-arranged speech and she by-God intended to give it.

"I understand this is sudden. It must come as a shock..."

"Oh, yeah."

"...but I have to do this. I think it's best for me. I hope we can stay friends. You've been an important part of my growth."

"I hope so, too."

There ensued a short and—on my end, anyway—baffled silence.

"Okay. Well, I...I guess that's about it." She got to her feet and stood by the booth, hovering; then—with a sudden movement—she bent and kissed my cheek. "Bye."

Andrea put a hand to her mouth. "Oh my God! Was that Mia?"

"I'm not too sure," I said, watching Mia walk away, noting that there had been a complete absence of moues.

"An important part of her growth? She talks like a Doctor Phil soundbyte. What did you do to her?"

"I'm not responsible, I don't think." I pushed around a notion that had occurred to me before, but that I had not had the impetus to consider more fully. "Do you know anyone who's exhibited a sudden burst of intelligence in the past few weeks? I mean someone who's been going along at the same pace for a while and suddenly they're Einstein. Relatively speaking."

She mulled it over. "As a matter of fact, I do. I know two or three people. Why?"

"Tell me."

"Well, there's Jimmy Galvin. Did you hear about him?"

"The gardening tool. Yeah. Who else?"

"This guy in my office. A paralegal. He's a hard worker, but basically a drone. Lately, whenever we ask him to dig up a file or find a reference, he's attached some ideas about the case we're working on. Good ideas. Some of them are great. Case-makers. He's the talk of the office. We've been joking that maybe we should get him to take a drug test. He's going back to law school and we're going to miss...." She broke off. "What's this have to do with the new Mia?"

I told her about Rudy's cartoons, Beth's novel, Kiwanda's newfound efficiency, the millworker, Stanky's increased productivity.

"I can't help wondering," I said, "if it's somehow related to the stars. I know it's a harebrained idea. There's probably a better explanation. Stanky...he never worked with a band before and that may be what's revving his engines. But that night at the Crucible, he was so polished. It just didn't synch with how I thought he'd react. I thought he'd get through it, but it's like he was an old hand."

Andrea looked distressed.

"And not everybody's affected," I said. "I'm not, for sure. You don't seem to be. It's probably bullshit."

"I know of another instance," she said. "But if I tell you, you have to promise to keep it a secret."

"I can do that."

"Do you know Wanda Lingrove?"

"Wasn't she a friend of yours? A cop? Tall woman? About five years older than us?"

"She's a detective now."

The waitress brought our food. I dug in; Andrea nudged her salad to the side.

"Did you hear about those college girls dying over in Waterford?" she asked.

"No, I haven't been keeping up."

"Two college girls died a few days apart. One in a fire and one in a drowning accident. Wanda asked for a look at the case files. The Waterford police had written them off as accidents, but Wanda had a friend on the force and he slipped her the files and showed her the girls' apartments. They both lived off-campus. It's not that Wanda's any great shakes. She has an undistinguished record. But she had the idea from reading the papers—and they were skimpy articles—a serial killer was involved. Her friend pooh-poohed the idea. There wasn't any signature. But it turned out, Wanda was right. There was a signature, very subtle and very complicated, demonstrating that the killer was highly evolved. Not only did she figure that out, she caught him after two days on the case."

"Aren't serial killers tough to catch?"

"Yes. All that stuff you see about profiling on TV, it's crap. They wouldn't have come close to getting a line on this kid with profiling. He would have had to announce himself, but Wanda doesn't think he would have. She thinks he would have gone on killing, that putting one over on the world was enough for him."

"He was a kid?"

"Fourteen years old. A kid from Black William. What's more, he'd given no sign of being a sociopath. Yet in the space of three weeks, he went from zero to sixty. From playing JV football to being a highly organized serialist. That doesn't happen in the real world."

"So how come Wanda's not famous?"

"The college is trying to keep it quiet. The kid's been bundled off to an institution and the cops have the lid screwed tight." Andrea picked at her salad. "What I'm suggesting, maybe everyone *is* being affected, but not in ways that conform to your model. Wanda catching the kid, that conforms. But the kid himself, the fact that a pathology was brought out in him...that suggests that some people may be affected in ways we don't notice. Maybe they just love each other more."

I laid down my fork. "Like with us?"

A doleful nod.

"That's crazy," I said. "You said you'd been plotting for months to make a move."

"Yes, but it was a fantasy!"

"And you don't think you would have acted on it?"

"I don't know. One thing for certain, I never expected anything like this." She cut her volume to a stage whisper. "I want you all the time. It's like when we were nineteen. I'm addicted to you."

"Yeah," I said. "Same here."

"I worry that it'll stop, then I worry that it won't—it's wreaking havoc with my work. I can't stop thinking about you. On a rational level, I know I'm an animal. But there's a place in me that wants to believe love is more than evolutionary biology. And now this thing with the stars. To think that what I'm feeling could be produced by something as random as a wavefront or a supernatural event, or whatever...it makes me feel like an experimental animal. Like a rabbit that's been drugged. It scares me."

"Look," I said. "We're probably talking about something that isn't real."

"No, it's real."

"How can you be sure? I only just brought the subject up. We can't have been discussing it more than five minutes."

"You convinced me. Everything you said rings true. I know it here." Andrea touched a hand to her breast. "And you know it, too. Something's happening to us. Something's happening to this town."

▲▼▲

We stepped back from that conversation. It was, I suppose, a form of denial, the avoidance of a subject neither of us wished to confront, because it was proof against confrontation, against logic and reason, and so we trivialized it and fell back on our faith, on our mutuality. Sometimes, lying with Andrea, considering the join of her neck and shoulder, the slight convexity of her belly, the compliant curve of a breast compressed into a pouty shape by the weight of her arm, the thousand turns and angles that each seemed the expression of a white simplicity within, I would have the urge to wake her, to drive away from Black William, and thus protect her, protect us, from this infestation of stars; but then I would think that such an action might destroy the thing I hoped to protect, that once away from the stars we might feel differently about one another. And then I'd think how irrational these thoughts were, how ridiculous it was to contemplate uprooting our lives over so flimsy a fear. And, finally, having made these brief rounds of my human potential, I would lapse again into a Praxitelean scrutiny, a sculptor in love with his stone, content to drift in and out of a dream in which love, though it had been proved false (like Andrea said, an animal function and nothing more), proved to be eternally false, forever and a day of illusion, of two souls burning brighter and brighter until they appeared to make a single glow, a blazing unity concealed behind robes of aging flesh.

The world beat against our door. Pin's photograph was printed on the third page of the *Black William Gazette,* along with the news that the University of Pittsburgh would be sending a team of observers to measure the phenomenon, should it occur again, as was predicted (by whom, the *Gazette* did not say). There was a sidebar recounting Black William's sordid history and Jonathan Venture's version of BW's involvement with the stars. The body of the article...well, it was as if the reporter had been privy to our conversation at the Szechuan Palace. I suspected that he had, if only at second-hand, since my wavefront theory was reproduced in full, attributed to "a local pundit." As a result of this publicity, groups of people, often more than a hundred, mostly the young and the elderly, came to gather in front of the library between the hours of five and nine, thus depriving me of the customary destination of my evening walks.

Stanky, his ego swollen to improbable proportions by two successful performances, by the adulation of his high school fans ("Someone ought to be writing everything Joey says down," said one dreamy-eyed fool), became increasingly temperamental, lashing out at his bandmates, at me, browbeating Liz at every opportunity, and prowling about the house in a sulk, ever with a Coke and cigarette, glaring at all who fell to his gaze, not bothering to speak. In the mornings, he was difficult to wake, keeping Geno and Jerry waiting, wasting valuable time, and one particular morning, my frustration with him peaked and I let Timber into his bedroom and closed the door, listening while the happy pup gamboled across the mattress, licking and drooling, eliciting squeals and curses from the sleepy couple, an action that provoked a confrontation that I won by dint of physical threat and financial dominance, but that firmly established our unspoken enmity and made me anxious about whether I would be able to maneuver him to the point where I could rid myself of him and show a profit.

A gray morning, spitting snow, and I answered the doorbell to find a lugubrious, long-nosed gentleman with a raw, bony face, toting a briefcase and wearing a Sy Sperling wig and a cheap brown suit. A police cruiser was parked at the curb; two uniformed officers stood smoking beside it, casting an indifferent eye toward the Polozny, which rolled on blackly in—as a local DJ was prone to characterize it—"its eternal search for the sea." Since we were only a couple of days from the EP release, I experienced a sinking feeling, one that was borne out when the man produced a card identifying him as Martin Kiggins of Mckeesport, a Friend of the Court. He said he would like to have a word with me about Joseph Stanky.

"How well do you know Joseph?" he asked me once we had settled in the office.

Kiwanda, at her desk in the next room, made a choking noise. I replied that while I had, I thought, an adequate understanding of Joseph as a musician, I was unfamiliar with the details of his life.

"Did you know he has a wife?" Kiggins was too lanky to fit the chair and, throughout our talk, kept scrunching around in it. "And he's got a little boy. Almost two years old, he is."

"No, I didn't know that."

"Poor little guy nearly didn't make it that far. Been sick his whole life." Kiggins' gaze acquired a morose intensity. "Meningitis."

I couldn't get a handle on Kiggins; he acted as if he was trying to sell me something, yet he had arrived on my doorstep with an armed force and the authority of the law.

"I thought meningitis was fatal," I said.

"Not a hundred percent," said Kiggins cheerlessly. "His mother doesn't have insurance, so he didn't get the best of care."

"That's tough."

"She's on welfare. Things aren't likely to improve for the kid or for her. She's not what you'd call an attractive woman."

"Why are we talking about this?" I asked. "It's a sad story, but I'm not involved."

"Not directly, no."

"Not any damn way. I don't understand what you're looking for."

Kiggins seemed disappointed in me. "I'm looking for Joseph. Is he here?"

"I don't know."

"You don't know. Okay." He put his hands on his knees and stood, making a show of peering out the window at his cop buddies.

"I really don't know if he's here," I said. "I've been working, I haven't been downstairs this morning."

"Mind if I take a look down there?"

"You're goddamn right, I mind! What's this about? You've been doing a dance ever since you came in. Why don't you spit it out?"

Kiggins gave me a measuring look, then glanced around the office—I think he was hoping to locate another chair. Failing this, he sat back down.

"You appear to be a responsible guy, Vernon," he said. "Is it okay I call you Vernon?"

"Sure thing, Marty. I don't give a shit what you call me as long as you get to the point."

"You own your home, a business. Pay your taxes...far as I can tell without an audit. You're a pretty solid citizen."

The implicit threat of an audit ticked me off, but I let him continue. I began to realize where this might be going.

"I've got the authority to take Joseph back to Mckeesport and throw his butt in jail," said Kiggins. "He's in arrears with his child and spousal support. Now I know Joseph doesn't have any money to speak of, but seeing how you've got an investment in him, I'm hoping we can work out some arrangement."

"Where'd you hear that?" I asked. "About my investment."

"Joseph still has friends in Mckeesport. High school kids, mainly. Truth be told, we think he was supplying them with drugs, but I'm not here about that. They've been spreading it around that you're about to make him a star."

I snorted. "He's a *long* way from being a star. Believe me."

"I believe you. Do you believe me when I tell you I'm here to take him back? Just say the word, I'll give a whistle to those boys out front."

Kiggins shifted the chair sideways, so he could stretch out one leg. "I know how you make your money, Vernon. You build a band up, then you sell their contracts. Now you've put in some work with Joseph. Some serious time and money. I should think you'd want to protect your investment."

"Okay." I reached for a cigarette, recalled that I had quit. "What's he owe?"

"Upwards of eleven thousand."

"He's all yours," I said. "Take the stairs in back. Follow the corridor to the front of the house. First door on your right."

"I said I wanted to make an arrangement. I'm not after the entire amount."

And so began our negotiation.

If we had finished the album, I would have handed Stanky over and given Kiggins my blessing, but as things stood, I needed him. Kiggins, on the other hand, wouldn't stand a chance of collecting any money with Stanky in the slam—he likely had a pre-determined figure beneath which he would not move. It infuriated me to haggle with him. Stanky's wife and kid wouldn't see a nickel. They would dock her welfare by whatever amount he extracted from me, deduct administrative and clerical fees, and she would end up worse off than before. Yet I had no choice other than to submit to legal blackmail.

Kiggins wouldn't go below five thousand. That, he said, was his bottom line. He put on a dour poker face and waited for me to decide.

"He's not worth it," I said.

Sadly, Kiggins made for the door; when I did not relent, he turned back and we resumed negotiations, settling on a figure of three thousand and my promise to attach a rider to Stanky's contract stating that a percentage of his earnings would be sent to the court. After he had gone, my check tucked in his briefcase, Kiwanda came to stand by my desk with folded arms.

"I'd give it a minute before you go down," she said. "You got that I'm-gonna-break-his-face look."

"Do you fucking believe this?" I brought my fist down on the desk. "I want to smack that little bitch!"

"Take a breath, Vernon. You don't want to lose any more today than just walked out of here."

I waited, I grew calm, but as I approached the stairs, the image of a wizened toddler and a moping, double-chinned wife cropped up in my brain. With each step I grew angrier and, when I reached Stanky's bedroom, I pushed in without knocking. He and Liz were having sex. I caught a fetid odor and an unwanted glimpse of Liz's sallow hindquarters as she scrambled beneath the covers. I shut the door partway and shouted at Stanky to haul his ass out here. Seconds later, he burst from the room in a T-shirt and pajama bottoms, and stumped into the kitchen with his head down, arms tightly held, like an enraged penguin. He fished a Coke from the refrigerator and made as if to say something; but I let him have it. I briefed him on Kiggins and said, "It's not a question of morality. I already knew you were a piece of crap. But this is a business, man. It's my livelihood, not a playground for degenerates. And when you bring the cops to my door, you put that in jeopardy."

He hung his head, picking at the Coke's pop top. "You don't understand."

"I don't want to understand! Get it? I have absolutely no desire to understand. That's between you and your wife. Between you and whatever scrap of meat loaf shaped like the Virgin Mary you pretend to worship. I don't care. One more screw-up, I'm calling Kiggins and telling him to come get you."

Liz had entered the kitchen, clutching a bathrobe about her; when she heard "wife," she retreated.

I railed at Stanky, telling him he would pay back every penny of the three thousand, telling him further to clean his room of every pot seed and pill, to get his act in order and finish the album; and I kept on railing at him until his body language conveyed that I could expect two or three days of penitence and sucking up. Then I allowed him to slink by me and into the bedroom. When I passed his door, cracked an inch open, I heard him whining to Liz, saying, "She's not *really* my wife."

I took the afternoon off and persuaded Rudy to go fishing. We bundled up against the cold, bought a twelve-pack of Iron City and dropped our lines in Kempton's Pond, a lopsided period stamped into the half-frozen ground a couple of miles east of town, punctuating a mixed stand of birch and hazel—it looked as if a giant with a peg leg had left this impression in the rock, creating a hole thirty feet wide. The clouds had lowered and darkened, their swollen bellies appearing to tatter on the leafless treetops as they slid past; but the snow had quit falling. There was some light accumulation on the banks, which stood eight or nine feet above the black water and gave the pond the look of an old cistern. The water circulated like heavy oil and swallowed our sinkers with barely a splash. This bred the expectation that if we hooked anything, it would be a megalodon or an ichthyosaur, a creature such as would have been trapped in a tar pit. But we had no such expectation.

It takes a certain cast of mind to enjoy fishing with no hope of a catch, or with the faint hope of catching some inedible fishlike thing every few years or so. That kind of fishing is my favorite sport, though I admit I follow the Steelers closely, as do many in Black William. Knowing that nothing will rise from the deep, unless it is something that will astound your eye or pebble your skin with gooseflesh, makes for a rare feeling. Sharing this with Rudy, who had been my friend for ten years, since he was fresh out of grad school at Penn State, enhanced that feeling. In the summer we sat and watched our lines, we chatted, we chased our depressions with beer and cursed the flies; in winter, the best season for our sport, there were no flies. The cold was like ozone to my nostrils, the silence complete, and the denuded woods posed an abstract of slants and perpendiculars, silver and dark, nature as Chinese puzzle. Through frays in the clouds we glimpsed the fat, lordly crests of the Bittersmiths.

I was reaching for another Iron City when I felt a tug on the line. I kept still and felt another tug, then—though I waited the better part of a minute—nothing.

"Something's down in there," I said, peering at the impenetrable surface.

"You get a hit?" Rudy asked.

"Uh-huh."

"How much line you got out?"

"Twenty, twenty-five feet."

"Must have been a current."

"It happened twice."

"Probably a current."

I pictured an enormous grouper-like face with blind milky-blue globes for eyes, moon lanterns, and a pair of weak, underdeveloped hands groping at my line. The Polozny plunges deep underground east of the bridge, welling up into these holes punched through the Pennsylvania rock, sometimes flooding the woods in the spring, and a current was the likely explanation; but I preferred to think that those subterranean chambers were the uppermost tiers of a secret world and that now and again some piscine Columbus, fleeing the fabulous madness of his civilization, palaces illumined by schools of electric eels controlled by the thoughts of freshwater octopi, limestone streets patrolled by gangs of river crocs, grand avenues crowded with giant-snail busses and pedestrian trout, sought to breach the final barrier and find in the world above a more peaceful prospect.

"You have no imagination," I said.

Rudy grunted. "Fishing doesn't require an imagination. That's what makes it fun."

Motionless, he was a bearish figure muffled in a down parka and a wool cap, his face reddened by the cold, breath steaming. He seemed down at the mouth and, thinking it might cheer him up, I asked how he was coming with the comic strip.

"I quit working on it," he said.

"Why the hell'd you do that? It was your best thing ever."

"It was giving me nightmares."

I absorbed this, gave it due consideration. "Didn't strike me as nightmare material. It's kind of bleak. Black comedy. But nothing to freak over."

"It changed." He flicked his wrist, flicking his line sideways. "The veins of pork…you remember them?"

"Yeah, sure."

"They started growing, twisting all through the mountain. The mineworkers were happy. Delirious. They were going to be rich, and they threw a big party to celebrate. A pork festival. Actually, that part was pretty funny. I'll show it to you. They made this enormous pork sculpture and were all wearing porkpie hats. They had a beauty contest to name Miss Pork. The winner…I used Mia for a model."

"You're a sick bastard, you know that?"

Again, Rudy grunted, this time in amusement. "Then the stars began eating the pork. The mineworkers would open a new vein and the stars would pour in and choff it down. They were ravenous. Nothing could stop them. The mineworkers were starving. That's when I started having nightmares. There was something gruesome about the way I had them eating. I tried to change it, but I couldn't make it work any other way."

I said it still didn't sound like the stuff of nightmares, and Rudy said, "You had to be there."

We fell to talking about other things. The Steelers, could they repeat? Stanky. I asked Rudy if he was coming to the EP release and he said he wouldn't miss it. "He's a genius guitar player," he said. "Too bad he's such a creep."

"Goes with the territory," I said. "Like with Robert Frost beating his wife. Stanky's a creep, he's a perv. A moral dwarf. But he is for sure talented. And you know me. I'll put up with perversity if someone's talented." I clapped Rudy on the shoulder. "That's why I put up with you. You better finish that strip or I'll dump your ass and start hanging with a better class of people."

"Forget the strip," he said glumly. "I'm too busy designing equipment sheds and stables."

We got into a discussion about Celebrity Wifebeaters, enumerating the most recent additions to the list, and this led us—by loose association only—to the subject of Andrea. I told him about our conversation at McGuigan's and what she had said about the outbreak of creativity, about love.

"Maybe she's got a point," Rudy said. "You two have always carried a torch, but you burned each other so badly in the divorce, I never would have thought you'd get back together." He cracked open a beer, handed it to me, and opened one for himself. "You hear about Colvin Jacobs?"

"You mean something besides he's a sleazeball?"

"He's come up with a plan to reduce the county's tax burden by half. Everybody says it's the real quill."

"I'm surprised he found the time, what with all those congressional junkets."

"And Judy Trickle, you hear about her?"

"Now you're scaring me."

"I know. Ol' Juggs 'R Us Judy."

"She should have been your model for Miss Pork, not Mia. What'd she do? Design a newfangled bra?"

"Lifts *and* separates."

"You mean that's it?"

"You nailed it."

"No way!"

"She's been wearing a prototype on the show the last few days. There's a noticeable change." He did a whispery voiceover voice. "The curves are softer, more natural."

"Bullshit!"

"I'm serious. Check her out."

"I got better things to do than watch *AM Waterford.*"

"I remember the time when you were a devoted fan."

"That was post-Andrea...and pre-Andrea." I chuckled. "Remember the show when she demonstrated the rowing machine? Leotards aren't built to handle that sort of stress."

"I knew the guy who produced her back then. He said they gave her stuff like that to do, because they were hoping for a Wardrobe Incident. They weren't prepared for the reaction."

"Janet Jackson's no Judy Trickle. It was like a dam bursting. Like... help me out here, man."

"Like the birth of twin zeppelins."

"Like the embodiment of the yang, like the Aquarian dawn."

Rudy jiggled his line. "This is beginning to border on the absurd."

"You're the one brought her up."

"I'm not talking about Judy, I'm talking about the whole thing. The outbreak."

"Oh, okay. Yeah, we're way past absurd if Miz Trickle's involved. We're heading toward surreal."

"I've heard of five or six more people who've had...breakthroughs, I suppose you'd call them."

"How come I don't hear about these people except from you? Do you sit in your office all day, collecting odd facts about Black William?"

"I get more traffic than you do, and people are talking about it now."

"What are they saying?"

"What you'd expect. Isn't it weird? It must be the water, the pollution. I've even heard civic pride expressed. Someone coined the phrase, 'Black William, Pennsylvania's Brain Capital.'"

"That's taking it a bit far." I had a slug of Iron City. "So nobody's panicking? Saying head for the hills?"

"Who said that?"

"Andrea. She was a little disturbed. She didn't exactly say it, but she seemed to think this thing might not be all good."

He tightened his lips and produced a series of squeaking noises. "I think Andrea's right. Not about head for the hills. I don't know about that. But I think whatever this is, it's affecting people in different ways. Some of them emotionally."

"Why's that?"

"I...." He tipped back his head, stared at the clouds. "I don't want to talk anymore, man. Okay? Let's just fish."

It began to snow again, tiny flakes, the kind that presage a big fall, but we kept fishing, jiggling our lines in the dead water, drinking Iron City. Something was troubling Rudy, but I didn't press him. I thought about Andrea. She planned to get off early and we were going to dinner in Waterford and maybe catch a movie. I was anticipating kissing her, touching her in the dark, while the new James Bond blew stuff up or (this was more likely) Kenneth Branagh destroyed *As You Like It*, when a tremor ran across the surface of the pond. Both Rudy and I sat up straight and peered. "T-Rex is coming," I said. An instant later, the pond was lashed into a turbulence that sent waves slopping in all directions, as if a large swimmer had drawn near the surface, then made a sudden turn, propelling itself down toward its customary haunts with a flick of its tail. Yet we saw nothing. Nary a fin nor scale nor section of plated armor. We waited, breathless, for the beast to return.

"Definitely not a current," said Rudy.

▲▼▲

Except for the fact that Rudy didn't show, the EP release went well. The music was great, the audience responsive, we sold lots of CDs and souvenirs, including Average Joe dogtags and a Joe Stanky's Army khaki T-shirt, with the pear-shaped (less so after diets and death marches) one's silhouette in white beneath the arc of the lettering. This despite Stanky's obvious displeasure with everyone involved. He was angry at me because I had stolen his top hat and refused to push back the time of the performance to 10 o'clock so he could join the crowd in front of the library waiting for the return of Black William (their number had swelled to more than three hundred since the arrival of the science team from Pitt, led by a youngish professor who, with his rugged build and mustache and plaid wool shirts, might have stepped out of an ad for trail mix). He was angry at Geno and Jerry for the usual reasons—they were incompetent clowns, they didn't understand the music, and they had spurned the opportunity to watch TV with him and Liz. Throughout the hour and a quarter show, he sulked and spoke not a word to the audience, and then grew angry at them when a group of frat boys initiated a chant of "Skanky, Skanky, Skanky...." Yet the vast majority were blown away and my night was made when I spotted an A&R man from Atlantic sneaking around.

I was in my office the next morning, reading the *Gazette*, which had come late to the party (as usual) and was running a light-hearted feature on "Pennsylvania's Brain Capital," heavy on Colvin Mason quotes, when I received a call from Crazy Ed in Wilkes-Barre, saying that he'd emailed me a couple of enhancements of Pin's photograph. I opened the emails and the attachments, then asked what I was looking at.

"Beats me," said Ed. "The first is up close on one of those white dealies. You can get an idea of the shape. Sort of like a sea urchin. A globe with spines...except there's so many spines, you can't make out the globe. You see it?"

"Yeah. You can't tell me what it is?"

"I don't have a clue." Ed made a buzzing noise, something he did whenever he was stumped. "I assumed the image was fake, that the kid had run two images together, because there's a shift in perspective between the library and the white dealies. They look like they're coming from a long way off. But then I realized the perspective was totally fucked up. It's like part of the photo was taken though a depth of water, or something that's shifting like water. Different sections appear to be at different distances all through the image. Did you notice a rippling effect...or anything like that?"

"I only saw it for a couple of seconds. I didn't have time to get much more than a glimpse."

"Okay." Ed made the buzzing noise again. "Have you opened the second attachment?"

"Yep."

"Once I figured out I couldn't determine distances, I started looking at the black stuff, the field or whatever. I didn't get anywhere with that. It's just black. Undifferentiated. Then I took a look at the horizon line. That's how it appeared to you, right? A black field stretching to a horizon? Well, if that was the case, you'd think you'd see something at the front edge, but the only thing I picked up was those bumps on the horizon."

I studied the bumps.

"Kinda look like the tops of heads, don't they?" said Ed.

The bumps could have been heads; they could also have been bushes, animals, or a hundred other things; but his suggestion gave me an uneasy feeling. He said he would fool around with the picture some more and get back to me. I listened to demos. Food of the Gods (King Crimson redux). Corpus Christy (a transsexual front man who couldn't sing, but the name grew on me). The Land Mines (middling roots rock). Gopher Lad (a heroin band from Minnesota). A band called Topless Coroner intrigued me, but I passed after realizing all their songs were about car parts. Around eleven-thirty I took a call from a secretary at Dreamworks who asked if I would hold for William Wine. I couldn't place the name, but said that I would hold and leafed through the Rolodex, trying to find him.

"Vernon!" said an enthusiastic voice from the other side of creation. "Bill Wine. I'm calling for David Geffen. I believe you had drinks with him at the Plug Awards last year. You made quite an impression on David."

The Plugs were the Oscars of the indie business—Geffen had an ongoing interest in indie rock and had put in an appearance. I recalled being in a group gathered around him at the bar, but I did not recall making an impression.

"He made a heck of an impression on me," I said.

Pleasant laughter, so perfect it sounded canned. "David sends his regards," said Wine. "He's sorry he couldn't contact you personally, but he's going to be tied up all day."

"What can I do for you?"

"David listened to that new artist of yours. Joe Stanky? In all the years I've known him, I've never heard him react like he did this morning."

"He liked it?"

"He didn't like it...." Wine paused for dramatic effect. "He was knocked out."

I wondered how Geffen had gotten hold of the EP. Mine not to reason why, I figured.

Wine told me that Geffen wanted to hear more. Did I have any other recorded material?

"I've got nine songs on tape," I said. "But some of them are raw."

"David likes raw. Can we get a dupe?"

"You know...I usually prefer to push out an album or two before I look for a deal."

"Listen, Vernon. We're not going to let you go to the poorhouse on this."

"That's a relief."

"In fact, David wanted me to sound you out about our bringing you in under the Dreamworks umbrella."

Stunned, I said, "In what capacity?"

"I'll let David tell you about that. He'll call you in a day or two. He's had his eye on you for some time."

I envisioned Sauron spying from his dark tower. I had a dim view of corporate life and I wasn't as overwhelmed by this news as Wine had likely presumed I would be. After the call ended, however, I felt as if I had modeled for Michelangelo's Sistine Chapel mural, the man about to be touched by God's billionaire-ish finger. My impulse was to tell Stanky, but I didn't want his ego to grow more swollen. I called Andrea and learned she would be in court until mid-afternoon. I started to call Rudy, then thought it would be too easy for him to refuse me over the phone. Better to yank him out of his cave and buy him lunch. I wanted to bust his chops about missing the EP release and I needed to talk with someone face-to-face, to analyze this thing that was happening around Stanky. Had the buzz I'd generated about him taken wings on a magical current? The idea that David Geffen was planning to call seemed preposterous. Was Stanky that good? Was I? What, if anything, did Geffen have in mind? Rudy, who enjoyed playing Yoda to my Luke, would help place these questions in coherent perspective.

When I reached Rudy's office, I found Gwen on the phone. Her make-up, usually perfect, was in need of repair; it appeared that she had been crying. "I don't know," she said with strain in her voice. "You'll have to...no. I really don't know."

I pointed to the inner office and mouthed, Is he in?

She signaled me to wait.

"I've got someone here," she said into the phone. "I'll have to...yes. Yes, I will let you know. All right. Yes. Goodbye." She hung up and, her chin quivering, tried several times to speak, finally blurting out, "I'm so sorry. He's dead. Rudy's dead."

I think I may have laughed—I made some sort of noise, some expression of denial, yet I knew it was true. My face flooded with heat and I went back a step, as if the words had thrown me off-balance.

Gwen said that Rudy had committed suicide early that morning. He had—according to his wife—worked in the office until after midnight, then driven home and taken some pills. The phone rang again. I left Gwen to deal with it and stepped into the inner office to call Beth. I sat at Rudy's desk, but that felt wrong, so I walked around with the phone for a while. Rudy had been a depressed guy, but hell everyone in Black William was depressed about something. I thought that I had been way more depressed than Rudy. He seemed to have it together. Nice wife, healthy income, kids. Sure, he was a for-shit architect in a for-shit town, and not doing the work he wanted, but that was no reason to kill yourself.

Standing by the drafting table, I saw his wastebasket was crammed with torn paper. A crawly sensation rippled the skin between my shoulder blades. I dumped the shreds onto the table. Rudy had done a compulsive job of tearing them up, but I could tell they were pieces of his comic strip. Painstakingly, I sorted through them and managed to reassemble most of a frame. In it, a pair of black hands (presumably belonging to a mineworker) were holding a gobbet of pork, as though in offering; above it floated a spiky white ball. The ball had extruded a longish spike to penetrate the pork and the image gave the impression that the ball was sucking meat through a straw. I stared at the frame, trying to interpret it, to tie the image in with everything that had happened, but I felt a vibration pass through my body, like the heavy, impersonal signal of Rudy's death, and I imagined him on the bathroom floor, foam on his mouth, and I had to sit back down.

Beth, when I called her, didn't feel like talking. I asked if there was anything I could do, and she said if I could find out when the police were going to release the body, she would appreciate it. She said she would let me know about the funeral, sounding—as had Gwen—like someone who was barely holding it together. Hearing that in her voice caused me to leak a few tears and, when she heard me start to cry, she quickly got off the phone, as if she didn't want my lesser grief to pollute her own, as if Rudy dying had broken whatever bond there was between us. I thought this might be true.

I called the police and, after speaking to a functionary, reached a detective whom I knew, Ross Peloblanco, who asked my connection to the deceased.

"Friend of the family," I said. "I'm calling for his wife."

"Huh," said Peloblanco, his attention distracted by something in his office.

"So when are you going to release him?"

"I think they already done the autopsy. There's been a bunch of suicides lately and the ME put a rush on this one."

"How many's a bunch?"

"Oops! Did I say that? Don't worry about it. The ME's a whack job. He's batshit about conspiracy theories."

"So...can I tell the funeral home to come now?"

Peloblanco sneezed, said, "Shit!", and then went on: "Bowen did some work for my mom. She said he was a real gentleman. You never know what's going on with people, do ya?" He blew his nose. "I guess you can come pick him up whenever."

The waters of the Polozny never freeze. No matter how cold it gets or how long the cold lasts, they are kept warm by a cocktail of pollutants and, though the river may flow more sluggishly in winter, it continues on its course, black and gelid. There is something statutory about its poisonous constancy. It seems less river than regulation, a divine remark rendered daily into law, engraving itself upon the world year after year until its long meander has eaten a crack that runs the length and breadth of creation, and its acids and oxides drain into the void.

Between the viewing and the funeral, in among the various consoling talks and offerings of condolence, I spent a great deal of time gazing at the Polozny, sitting on the stoop and smoking, enduring the cold wind, brooding over half-baked profundities. The muted roaring of the mill surrounded me, as did dull thuds and clunks and distant car horns that seemed to issue from the gray sky, the sounds of business as usual, the muffled engine of commerce. Black William must be, I thought, situated on the ass-end of Purgatory, the place where all those overlooked by God were kept. The dead river dividing a dying landscape, a dingy accumulation of snow melting into slush on its banks; the mill, a Hell of red brick with its chimney smoke of souls; the scatters of crows winging away from leafless trees; old Mrs. Gables two doors down, tottering out to the sidewalk, peering along the street for the mail, for a glimpse of her son's maroon Honda Civic, for some hopeful thing, then, her hopes dashed, laboriously climbing her stairs and going inside to sit alone and count the ticks of her clock: these were evidences of God's fabulous absence, His careless abandonment of a destiny-less town to its several griefs. I scoffed at those who professed to understand grief, who deemed it a simple matter, a painful yet comprehensible transition, and partitioned the process into stages (my trivial imagination made them into gaudy stagecoaches painted different colors) in order to enable its victims to adapt more readily to the house rules. After the initial shock of Rudy's suicide had waned, grief overran me like a virus, it swarmed, breeding pockets of weakness and fever, eventually receding at its own pace, on its own terms, and though it may have been subject to an easy compartmentalization—Anger, Denial, et al—that kind of analysis did not address its nuances and could not remedy the thousand small bitternesses that grief inflames and encysts. On the morning of the funeral, when I voiced one such bitterness, complaining about how Beth had treated me since Rudy died, mentioning the phone call, pointing out other incidences of her intolerance, her rudeness in pushing me away, Andrea—who had joined me on the stoop—set me straight.

"She's not angry at you," Andrea said. "She's jealous. You and Rudy... that was a part of him she never shared, and when she sees you, she doesn't know how to handle it."

"You think?"

"I used to feel that way."

"About me and Rudy?"

She nodded. "And about the business. I don't feel that way now. I guess I'm older. I understand you and Rudy had a guy thing and I didn't need to know everything about it. But Beth's dealing with a lot right now. She's oversensitive and she feels...jilted. She feels that Rudy abandoned her for you. A little, anyway. So she's jilting you. She'll get over it, or she won't. People are funny like that. Sometimes resentments are all that hold them together. You shouldn't take it personally."

I refitted my gaze to the Polozny, more-or-less satisfied by what she had said. "We live on the banks of the River Styx," I said after a while. "At least it has a Styx-ian gravitas."

"Stygian," she said.

I turned to her, inquiring.

"That's the word you wanted. Stygian."

"Oh...right."

A silence marked by the passing of a mail truck, its tire chains grinding the asphalt and spitting slush; the driver waved.

"I think I know why Rudy did it," I said, and told her what I had found in the office wastebasket. "More than anything he wanted to do creative work. When he finally did, it gave him nightmares. It messed with his head. He must have built it into this huge thing and...." I tapped out a cigarette, stuck it in my mouth. "It doesn't sound like much of a reason, but I can relate. That's why it bites my ass to see guys like Stanky who do something creative every time they take a piss. *I* want to write those songs. *I* want to have the acclaim. It gets me thinking, someday I might wind up like Rudy."

"That's not you. You said it yourself—you get pissed off. You find someplace else to put your energy." She rumpled my hair. "Buck up, Sparky. You're going to live a long time and have lots worse problems."

It crossed my mind to suggest that the stars might have played some mysterious part in Rudy's death, and to mention the rash of suicides (five, I had learned); but all that seemed unimportant, dwarfed by the death itself.

At one juncture during that weekend, Stanky ventured forth from TV-land to offer his sympathies. He may have been sincere, but I didn't trust his sincerity—it had an obsequious quality and I believed he was currying favor, paving the way so he might hit me up for another advance. Pale and shivering, hunched against the cold; the greasy collar of his jacket turned up; holding a Camel in two nicotine-stained fingers; his doughy features cinched in an expression of exaggerated dolor: I hated him at that moment and told him I was taking some days off, that he could work on the album or go play with his high school sycophants. "It's up to you," I said. "Just don't bother me about it." He made no reply, but the front door slamming informed me that he had not taken it well.

On Wednesday, Patty Prole (nee Patricia Hand), the leader of the Swimming Holes, a mutual friend of mine and Rudy's who had come down from Pittsburgh for the funeral, joined me and Andrea for dinner at McGuigan's, and, as we strolled past the park, I recalled that more than a month—thirty-four days, to be exact—had elapsed since I had last seen the stars. The crowd had dwindled to about a hundred-and-fifty (Stanky and Liz among them). They stood in clumps around the statue, clinging to the hope that Black William would appear; though judging by their general listlessness, the edge of their anticipation had been blunted and they were gathered there because they had nothing better to do. The van belonging to the science people from Pitt remained parked at the southeast corner of the library, but I had heard they were going to pull up stakes if nothing happened in the next day or two.

McGuigan's was a bubble of heat and light and happy conversation. A Joe Henry song played in the background; Pitt basketball was on every TV. I had not thought the whole town dressed in mourning, but the jolly, bustling atmosphere came as something of a shock. They had saved the back booth for us and, after drinking for a half-hour or so, I found myself enjoying the evening. Patty was a slight, pretty, blue-eyed blonde in her late twenties, dressed in a black leather jacket and jeans. To accommodate the sober purpose of this trip home, she had removed her visible piercings. With the majority of her tattoos covered by the jacket, she looked like an ordinary girl from western Pennsylvania and nothing like the exotic, pantherine creature she became on stage. When talk turned to Rudy, Andrea and I embraced the subject, offering humorous anecdotes and fond reminiscence, but Patty, though she laughed, was subdued. She toyed with her fork, idly stabbing holes in the label on her beer bottle, and at length revealed the reason for her moodiness.

"Did Rudy ever tell you we had a thing?" she asked.

"He alluded to it," I said. "But well after the fact. Years."

"I bet you guys talked all about it when you're up at Kempton's Pond. He said you used to talk about the local talent when you're up there sometimes."

Andrea elbowed me, not too sharply, in mock reproof.

"As I remember, the conversation went like this," I said. "We were talking about bands, the Swimming Holes came up, and he mentioned he'd had an affair with you. And I said, 'Oh, yeah?'. And Rudy said, 'Yeah.' Then after a minute he said, "Patty's a great girl.' "

"That's what he said? We had an affair? That's the word he used?"

"I believe so."

"He didn't say he was banging me or like that?"

"No."

"And that's all he said?" Patty stared at me sidelong, as if trying to penetrate layers of deception.

"That's all I remember."

"I bet you tried to get more out of him. I know you. You were hungering for details."

"I can't promise I wasn't," I said. "I just don't remember. You know Rudy. He was a private guy. You could beat on him with a shovel and not get a thing out of him. I'm surprised he told me that much."

She held my gaze a moment longer. "Shit! I can't tell if you're lying."

"He's not," said Andrea.

"You got him scoped, huh? He's dead to rights." Patty grinned and leaned against the wall, putting one fashionably booted foot up on the bench. "Rudy and me...it was a couple weeks right before the band left town. It was probably stupid. Sometimes I regret it, but sometimes I don't."

Andrea asked how it happened, and Patty, who obviously wanted to talk about it, said, "You know. Like always. We started hanging out, talking. Finally I asked him straight out, 'Where's this going, Rudy?' Because we only had a couple of weeks and I wanted to know if it was all in my head. He got this peculiar look on his face and kissed me. Like I said, it didn't last long, but it was deep, you know. That's why I'm glad Rudy didn't tell everyone how it was in the sack. It's a dumb thing to worry about, but...." Her voice had developed a tremor. "I guess that's what I'm down to."

"You loved him," said Andrea.

"Yeah. I did." Patty shook off the blues and sat up. "There wasn't anywhere for it to go. He'd never leave his kids and I was going off to Pittsburgh. I hated his wife for a while. I didn't feel guilty about it. But now I look at her.... She was never part of our scene. With Vernon and Rudy and the bands. She lived off to the side of it all. It wasn't like that with you, Andrea. You had your law thing going, but when you were around, you were into it. You were one of the girls. But Beth was so totally not into it. She still can't stand us. And now it feels like I stole something from her. That really sucks."

Platitudes occurred to me, but I kept quiet. Andrea stirred at my side.

"Sometimes it pays to be stupid," Patty said gloomily.

I had a moment when the light and happy babble of the bar were thrust aside by the gonging thought that my friend was dead, and I didn't entirely understand what she meant, but I knew she was right.

Patty snagged a passing waitress. "Can I get a couple of eggs over?" she asked. "I know you're not serving breakfast, but that's all I eat is breakfast." She winked broadly at the waitress. "Most important meal of the day, so I make every meal breakfast."

The waitress began to explain why eggs were impossible, but Patty cut in, saying, "You don't want me to starve, do ya? You must have a couple of eggs back there. Some fries and bacon. Toast. We're huge tippers, I swear."

Exasperated, the waitress said she'd see if the cook would do it.

"I know you can work him, honey," Patty said. "Tell him to make the eggs dippy, okay?"

▲▼▲

We left McGuigan's shortly after eight, heading for Corky's, a workingman's bar where we could do some serious drinking, but as we came abreast of the statue, Patty said, "Hey, let's go talk to Stanky." Stanky and Liz were sitting on the base of the statue; Pin and the other boys were cross-legged at their feet, like students attending their master. The crowd had thinned and was down, I'd guess, to about a hundred and twenty; a third of that number were clustered around the science van and the head scientist, who was hunched over a piece of equipment set up on the edge of the library lawn. I lagged behind as we walked over and noticed Liz stiffen at the sight of Patty. The boys gazed adoringly at her. Stanky cast me a spiteful glance.

"I heard your EP, man," Patty said. "Very cool."

Stanky muttered, "Yeah, thanks," and stared at her breasts.

Like me, Patty was a sucker for talent, used to the ways of musicians, and she ignored this ungracious response. She tried to draw him out about the music, but Stanky had a bug up his ass about something and wouldn't give her much. The statue loomed above, throwing a shadow across us; the horse's head, with its rolling eyes and mouth jerked open by the reins, had been rendered more faithfully than had Black William's face...or else he was a man whose inner crudeness had coarsened and simplified his features. In either case, he was one ugly mother, his shoulder-length hair framing a maniacal mask. Seeing him anew, I would not have described his expression as laughing or alarmed, but might have said it possessed a ferocious exultancy.

Patty began talking to the boys about the Swimming Holes' upcoming tour, and Andrea was speaking with Pin. Stanky oozed over to me, Liz at his shoulder, and said, "We laid down a new song this afternoon."

"Oh, yeah?" I said.

"It's decent. 'Misery Loves Company.' "

In context, it wasn't clear, until Stanky explained it, that this was a title.

"A guy from Dreamworks called," he said. "William Wine."

"Yeah, a few days back. Did Kiwanda tell you about it?"

"No, he called today. Kiwanda was on her break and I talked to him."

"What'd he say?"

"He said they loved the tape and David Geffen's going to call." He squinched up his face, as if summoning a mighty effort. "How come you didn't tell me about the tape? About him calling before?"

This, I understood, was the thing that had been bothering him. "Because it's business," I said. "I'm not going to tell you about every tickle we get. Every phone call."

He squinted at me meanly. "Why not?"

"Do you realize how much of this just goes away? These people are like flies. They buzz around, but they hardly ever land. Now the guy's called twice, that makes it a little more interesting. I'll give it a day or two, and call him back."

Ordinarily, Stanky would have retreated from confrontation, but with Liz bearing witness (I inferred by her determined look that she was his partner in this, that she had egged him on), his macho was at stake. "I ought to know everything that's going on," he said.

"Nothing's going on. When something happens, I'll tell you."

"It's my career," he said in a tone that conveyed petulance, defiance, and the notion that he had been wronged. "I want to be in on it, you know."

"Your career." I felt suddenly liberated from all restraint. "Your career consists of my efforts on your behalf and three hours on-stage in Nowhere, Pennsylvania. I've fed you, I've given you shelter, money, a band. And now you want me to cater to your stupid whims? To run downstairs and give you an update on every little piece of Stanky gossip because it'll gratify your ego? So you can tell your minions here how great you are? Fuck you! You don't like how I'm handling things, clear the hell out of my house!"

I walked off several paces and stood on the curb, facing the library. That rough cube of Pennsylvania granite accurately reflected my mood. Patches of snow dappled the lawn. There was a minor hubbub near the science truck, but I was enraged and paid it no mind. Andrea came up next to me and took my arm. "Easy, big fella," she said.

"That asshole's been under my roof for what? Two months? It feels like two years. His stink permeates every corner of my life. It's like living with a goat!"

"I know," she said. "But it's business."

I wondered if she was hammering home an old point, but her face gave no sign of any such intent; in fact, her neutral expression dissolved into one of befuddlement. She was staring at the library, and when I turned in that direction, I saw the library had vanished. An immense rectangle—a window with uneven edges—had been chopped out of the wall of the world, out of the night, its limits demarked by trees, lawn, and sky, and through it poured a flood of blackness, thicker and more sluggish than the Polozny. Thick like molasses or hot tar. It seemed to splash down, to crest in a wave, and hold in that shape. Along the top of the crest, I could see lesser, half-defined shapes, vaguely human, and I had the thought that the wave was extruding an army from its substance, producing a host of creatures who appeared to be men. The temperature had dropped sharply. There was a chill, chemical odor and, close above our heads (five feet, I'd estimate), the stars were coasting. That was how they moved. They glided as though following an unseen track, then were shunted sideways or diagonally or backward. Their altitude never changed, and I suspect now that they were prevented from changing it by some physical limitation. They did not resemble stars as much as they did Crazy Ed's enhancement: ten or twelve globes studded with longish white spines, the largest some eight feet in diameter, glowing brightly enough to illumine the faces of the people beneath them. I could not determine if they were made of flesh or metal or something less knowable. They gave forth high-frequency squeaks that reminded me, in their static quality, of the pictographs in Rudy's cartoons, the language of the stars.

I'm not sure how long we stood there, but it could not have been more than seconds before I realized that the wave crest was not holding, it was inching toward us across the lawn. I caught Andrea's hand and tried to run. She screamed (a yelp, really), and others screamed and tried to run. But the wave flowed around us, moving now like black quicksilver, in an instant transforming the center of town into a flood plain, marooning people on islands of solid ground bounded by a waist-high flood that was coursing swiftly past. As Andrea and I clung together, I saw Stanky and Liz, Pin and Patty, the rest of the kids, isolated beside the statue—there were dozens of such groupings throughout the park. It seemed a black net of an extremely coarse weave had been thrown over us all and we were standing up among its strands. We stared at each other, uncertain of our danger; some called for help. Then something rose from the blackness directly in front of me and Andrea. A man, I think, and fully seven feet tall. An African negro by the scarifications on his face. His image not quite real—it appeared to be both embedded in the tarry stuff and shifting over its surface, as if he had been rotoscoped. At the same time, a star came to hover over us, so that my terror was divided. I had from it an impression of eagerness—the feeling washed down upon me; I was drenched in it—and then, abruptly, of disinterest, as if it found Andrea and me unworthy of its attention. With the onset of that disinterest, the black man melted away into the tar and the star passed on to another group of stranded souls.

The largest groups were those two clustered about the science van. Figures began to sprout from the tar around them, and not all of these were men. Some were spindly as eels, others squat and malformed, but they were too far away for me to assign them a more particular identity. Stars hovered above the two groups, and the black figures lifted people one by one, kicking and screaming (screams now issued from every corner of the park), and held them up to the stars. These did not, as in Rudy's cartoons, suck in the meat through one of their spikes; they never touched their victims. A livid arc, fiery black in color, leaped between star and human, visible for a split-second, and then the figure that had lifted the man or woman, dropped him or her carelessly to the ground and melted back into the flood, and the star moved on. Andrea buried her face in my shoulder, but I could not turn away, transfixed by the scene. And as I watched these actions repeated again and again—the figure melting up, lifting someone to a star, and then discarding him, the victim still alive, rolling over, clutching an injured knee or back, apparently not much the worse for wear—I realized the stars were grazing, that this was their harvest, a reaping of seed sown. They were harvesting our genius, a genius they had stimulated, and they were attracted to a specific yield that manifested in an arc of fiery black. The juice of the poet, the canniness of the inventor, the guile of a villain. They failed to harvest the entire crop, only that gathered in the park. The remainder of those affected would go on to create more garden tools and foundation garments and tax plans, and the stars would continue on their way, a path that now and again led them through the center of Black William. I must confess that, amid the sense of relief accompanying this revelation, I felt an odd twinge of envy when I realized that the genius of love was not to their taste.

How did I know these things? I think when the star hovered above us, it initiated some preliminary process, one incidental to the feelings of eagerness and disinterest it projected, and, as it prepared to take its nutrient, its treasure (I haven't a clue as to why they harvested us, whether we were for them a commodity or sustenance or something else entire), we shared a brief communion. As proof, I can only say that Andrea holds this same view and there is a similar consensus, albeit with slight variances, among all those who stood beneath the stars that night. But at the moment the question was not paramount. I turned toward the statue. The storefronts beyond were obscured by a black rectangle, like the one that had eclipsed the library, and this gave me to believe that the flood was pouring off into an unguessable dimension, though it still ran deep around us. Stanky and Liz had climbed onto the statue and were clinging to Black William's leg and saddlehorn respectively. Patty was leaning against the base, appearing dazed. Pin stood beside her, taking photographs with his cell phone. One of the kids was crying, and his friends were busy consoling him. I called out, asking if everyone was all right. Stanky waved and then the statue's double reared from the flood—it rose up slowly, the image of a horse and a rider with flowing hair, blacker than the age-darkened bronze of its likeness. They were so equal in size and posture and stillness, it was as if I were looking at the statue and its living shadow. Its back was to me, and I cannot say if it was laughing. And then the shadow extended an arm and snatched Stanky from his perch. Plucked him by the collar and held him high, so that a star could extract its due, a flash of black energy. And when that was done, it did not let him fall, but began to sink back into the flood, Stanky still in its grasp. I thought it would take him under the tar, that they would both be swallowed and Stanky's future was to be that of a dread figure rising blackly to terrify the indigenes in another sector of the plenum. But Black William—or the agency that controlled him—must have had a change of heart and, at the last second, just as Stanky's feet were about to merge with that tarry surface, dropped him clear of the flood, leaving him inert upon the pavement.

The harvest continued several minutes more (the event lasted twenty-seven minutes in all) and then the flood receded, again with quicksilver speed, to form itself into a wave that was poised to splash down somewhere on the far side of that black window. And when the window winked out, when the storefronts snapped back into view, the groaning that ensued was much louder and more articulated than that we'd heard a month previously. Not a sound of holy woe, but of systemic stress, as if the atoms that composed the park and its surround were complaining about the insult they had incurred. All across the park, people ran to tend the injured. Andrea went to Liz, who had fallen from the statue and tearfully declared her ankle broken. Patty said she was dizzy and had a headache, and asked to be left alone. I knelt beside Stanky and asked if he was okay. He lay propped on his elbows, gazing at the sky.

"I wanted to see," he said vacantly. "They said..."

"They?" I said. "You mean the stars?"

He blinked, put a hand to his brow. As ever, his emotions were writ large, yet I don't believe the look of shame that washed over his face was an attempt to curry favor or promote any agenda. I believe his shame was informed by a rejection such as Andrea and I experienced, but of a deeper kind, more explicit and relating to an opportunity lost.

I made to help him up, intending to question him further; but he shook me off. He had remembered who he was, or at least who he had been pretending to be. Stanky the Great. A man of delicate sensibilities whom I had offended by my casual usage and gross maltreatment. His face hardened, becoming toadlike as he summoned every ounce of his

Lilliputian rage. He rolled up to his knees, then got to his feet. Without another word to me, he arranged his features into a look of abiding concern and hurried to give comfort to his Liz.

▲▼▲

In the wider world, Black William has come to be known as "that town full of whackos" or "the place where they had that hallucination," for as with all inexplicable things, the stars and our interaction with them have been dismissed by the reasonable and responsible among us, relegated to the status of an aberration, irrelevant to the big picture, to the roar of practical matters with which we are daily assailed. I myself, to an extent, have dismissed it, yet my big picture has been enlarged somewhat. Of an evening, I will sit upon the library steps and cast my mind out along the path of the stars and wonder if they were metaphoric or literal presences, nomads or machines, farmers or a guerilla force, and I will question what use that black flash had for them, and I will ponder whether they were themselves evil or recruited evil men to assist them in their purpose simply because they were suited to the task. I subscribe to the latter view; otherwise, I doubt Stanky would have wanted to go with them...unless they offered a pleasurable reward, unless they embodied for him the promise of a sublime perversion in exchange for his service, an eternal tour of duty with his brothers-in-arms, dreaming in that tarry flood. And what of their rejection of him? Was it because he was insufficiently evil? Too petty in his cruelty? Or could it have been he lacked the necessary store of some brain chemical? The universe is all whys and maybes. All meanings coincide, all answers are condensed to one or none. Nothing yields to logic.

Since the coming of the stars, Black William has undergone a great renewal. Although in the immediate aftermath there was a hue and cry about fleeing the town, shutting it down, calmer voices prevailed, pointing to the fact that there had been no fatalities, unless one counted the suicides, and but a single disappearance (Colvin Jacobs, who was strolling through the park that fateful night), and it could be better understood, some maintained, in light of certain impending charges against him (embezzlement, fraud, solicitation). Stay calm, said the voices. A few scrapes and bruises, a smattering of nervous breakdowns—that's no reason to fling up your hands. Let's think this over. Colvin's a canny sort, not one to let an opportunity pass. At this very moment he may be developing a skin cancer on Varadero Beach or Ipanema (though it is my belief that he may be sojourning in a more unlikely place). And while the town thought it over, the tourists began to arrive by the busload. Drawn by Pin's photographs, which had been published around the world, and later by his best-selling book (co-authored by the editor of the *Gazette*), they came from Japan, from Europe, from Punxsutawney and Tuckhannock, from every quarter of the globe, a flood of tourists that resolved into a steady flow and demanded to be housed, fed, T-shirted, souvenired, and swindled. They needed theories upon which to hang their faith, so theory-making became a cottage industry and theories abounded, both supernatural and quasi-scientific, each having their own battery of proponents and debunkers. A proposal was floated in the city council that a second statue be erected to commemorate Black William's visitation, but the ladies of the Heritage Committee fought tooth and nail to preserve the integrity of the original, and now can be seen twice a year lavishing upon him a vigorous scrubbing.

Businesses thrived, mine included—this due to the minor celebrity I achieved and the sale of Stanky and his album to Warner Brothers (David Geffen never called). The album did well and the single, "Misery Loves Company," climbed to No. 44 on the Billboard charts. I have no direct contact with Stanky, but learned from Liz, who came to the house six months later to pick up her clothes (those abandoned when Stanky fled my house in a huff), that he was writing incidental music for the movies, a job that requires no genius. She carried tales, too, of their nasty breakup, of Stanky's increasing vileness, his masturbatory displays of ego. He has not written a single song since he left Black William—the stars may have drained more from him than that which they bred, and perhaps the fact that he was almost taken has something to do with his creative slump. Whatever his story, I think he has found his true medium and is becoming a minor obscenity slithering among the larger obscenities that serve a different kind of star, anonymous beneath the black flood of the Hollywood sewer.

The following March, I went fishing with Andrea at Kempton Pond. She was reluctant to join me, assuming that I intended to make her a stand-in for Rudy, but I assured her this was not the case and told her she might enjoy an afternoon out of the office, some quiet time together. It was a clear day, and cold. Pockets of snow lay in the folds and crinkles of the Bittersmiths, but the crests were bare, and there was a deeper accumulation on the banks than when Rudy and I had fished the pond in November. We had to clear ourselves a spot on which to sit. The sun gilded the birch trunks, but the waters of the pond were as Stygian and mysterious as ever.

We cast out our lines and chatted about doings in her office, my latest projects—Lesion (black metal) and a post-rock band I had convinced to call themselves Same Difference. I told her about some loser tapes that had come my way, notably a gay Christian rap outfit with a song entitled "Cruisin' For Christ (While Searching For The Heavenly City)." Then we fell silent. Staring into the pond, at the dark rock walls and oily water, I did not populate the depths with fantasies, but thought instead of Rudy. They were memorial thoughts untainted by grief, memories of things said and done. I had such a profound sense of him, I imagined if I turned quickly enough, I would have a glimpse of a bulky figure in a parka, wool cap jammed low on his brow, red-cheeked and puffing steam; yet when I did turn, the figure in the parka and wool cap was more clearly defined, ivory pale and slender, her face a living cameo. I brushed a loose curl from her eyes. Touching her cheek warmed my fingertip. "This is kind of nice," she said, and smiled. "It's so quiet."

"Told you you'd like it," I said.

"I do."

She jiggled her line.

"You'll never catch anything that way." I demonstrated proper technique. "Twitch the line side-to-side."

Amused, she said, "I really doubt I'm going to catch anything. What were you and Rudy batting? One for a thousand?"

"Yeah, but you never know."

"I don't think I want to catch anything if it resembles that thing he had mounted."

"You should let out more line, too."

She glanced at me wryly, but did as I suggested.

A cloud darkened the bank and I pictured how the two of us would appear to God, if God were in His office, playing with His Gameboy: tiny animated fisher folk hunched over their lines, shoulder-to-shoulder, waiting for a tiny monster to breach, unmindful of any menace from above. Another cloud shadowed us. A ripple moved across the pond, passing so slowly, it made me think that the waters of the Polozny, when upthrust into these holes, were squeezed into a sludgy distillate. Bare twigs clattered in a gust of wind.

"All these years," Andrea said. "All the years and now five months…."

"Yeah?"

"Everyday, there'll be two or three times when I see you, like just now, when I look up and see you, and it's like a blow…a physical blow that leaves me all ga-ga. I want to drop everything and curl up with you."

"Me, too," I said.

She hesitated. "It just worries me."

"We've had this conversation," I said. "I don't mind having it again, but we're not going to resolve anything. We'll never figure it out."

"I know." She jiggled her line, forgetting to twitch it. "I keep thinking I'll find a new angle, but all I come up with is more stupidity. I was thinking the other day, it was like a fairy tale. How falling back in love protected us, like a charm." She heel-kicked the bank. "It's frustrating when everything you think seems absurd and true all at once."

"It's a mystery."

"Right."

"I go there myself sometimes," I said. "I worry about whether we'll fall out of love...if what we feel is unnatural. Then I worry if worrying about it's unnatural. Because, you know, it's such a weird thing to be worried about. Then I think, hey, it's perfectly natural to worry over something you care about, whether it's weird or not. Round and round. We might as well go with the flow. No doubt we'll still be worrying about it when we're too old to screw."

"That's pretty old."

"Yep," I said. "Ancient."

"Maybe it's good we worry." Then after a pause, she said, "Maybe we didn't worry enough the first time."

A second ripple edged the surface, like a miniature slow tsunami. The light faded and dimmed. A degree of tension seemed to leave Andrea's body.

"You want to go to Russia?" she asked. "I've got this conference in late May. I have to give a paper and be on some panels. It's only four days, but I could take some vacation."

I thought about it. "Kiwanda's pretty much in control of things. Would we have to stay in Russia?"

"Don't you want to go clubbing in Moscow? Meet new people? I'll wear a slutty dress and act friendly with strangers. You can save me from the white slavers—I'm sure I'll attract white slavers."

"I'll do my best," I said. "But some of those slavers are tough."

"You can take 'em!" She rubbed the side of her nose. "Why? Where do you want to go?"

"Bucharest."

"Why there?"

"Lots of reasons. Potential for vampires. Cheap. But reason number one—nobody goes there."

"Good point. We get enough of crowds around here."

We fell silent again. The eastern slopes of the Bittersmiths were drowning in shadow, acquiring a simplified look, as of worn black teeth that still bore traces of enamel. But the light had richened, the tree trunks appeared to have been dipped in old gold. Andrea straightened and peered down into the hole.

"I had a nibble," she said excitedly.

I watched the surface. The water remained undisturbed, lifeless and listless, but I felt a presence lurking beneath, a wise and deliberate fish, a grotesque, yet beautiful in the fact of its survival, and more than a murky promise—it would rise to us this day or some other. Perhaps it would speak a single word, perhaps merely die. Andrea leaned against me, eager to hook it, and asked what she should do.

"It's probably just a current," I said, but advised her to let out more line. —